D0428783

BUMS

To: My Good friend
and Brooklyn Dodger
fan, John,
From: An old N.Y. Giant
fan, Bill

BY THE SAME AUTHOR:

DYNASTY: When Rooting for the Yankees
Was Like Rooting for U.S. Steel

THE BRONX ZOO (with Sparky Lyle)

GUIDRY (with Ron Guidry)

NUMBER 1 (with Billy Martin)

BALLS (with Graig Nettles)

BUMS

AN ORAL HISTORY OF THE BROOKLYN DODGERS

Peter Golenbock

G. P. PUTNAM'S SONS / NEW YORK

Copyright © 1984 by Peter Golenbock
All rights reserved. This book, or parts thereof, may not be reproduced in any form without permission in writing from the publisher. Published on the same day in Canada by General Publishing Co. Limited, Toronto.

The author gratefully acknowledges permission from the following sources to reprint material in their control:

The *Daily News* for the untitled poem by Dan Parker, published in 1945, copyright © 1945 by The Daily News.

John Holway for material from *Voices from the Great Black Baseball Leagues* by John Holway, copyright © 1975 by John Holway. Published by Dodd, Mead & Company, Inc.

Roger Kahn and Harper & Row, Inc. for material from *The Boys of Summer* by Roger Kahn, copyright © 1971, 1972 by Roger Kahn.

The *New York Post* for columns from the *New York Post* by Jimmy Cannon (February, 1949, copyright © 1949 by The New York Post) and Milton Gross (October, 1956, copyright © 1956 by The New York Post).

The New York Times for the headlines "Shotton Upholds Stock," from an article published October 2, 1950, copyright © 1950 by The New York Times Company.

Harold Parrott and Holt, Rinehart and Winston Publishers for material from *The Lords of Baseball* by Harold Parrott, copyright © 1976 by Harold Parrott.

Viking Penguin Inc. for the poem "Hometown Piece for Messrs. Alston and Reese" by Marianne Moore in *The Complete Poems of Marianne Moore*, copyright © 1959 by Marianne Moore.

Viking Penguin Inc. and Frank Graham, Jr. for material from *A Farewell to Heroes* by Frank Graham, Jr., copyright © 1981 by Frank Graham, Jr.

Designed by Richard Oriolo

Library of Congress Cataloging in Publication Data

Golenbock, Peter, date.
Bums—an oral history of the Brooklyn Dodgers.

Includes index.
1. Brooklyn Dodgers (Baseball team)—History. I. Title.
GV875.B7G65 1984 796.357'64'0974723 84-2167
ISBN 0-399-12846-8
ISBN 0-399-13060-8 Limited Edition
Printed in the United States of America

This book is dedicated to each and every one of those Brooklyn Dodger fans who lost so much, so soon, for so little reason. It is dedicated to Jackie, Mr. Rickey, Burt, Chuck, Gil, Junior, Billy, and the other Brooklyn Dodgers who have gone to their heavenly reward. It is also dedicated to Joe Flaherty, who though not a Bum at heart, will always be one in spirit. And to my Uncle Justin, who took me to the 1956 World Series and introduced me to Jackie Robinson. I shall miss you both.

IN MEMORIAM

Jackie Robinson
Branch Rickey
Gil Hodges
Burt Shotton
Bruce Edwards
Pete Reiser
Hugh Casey
Dixie Walker
Bud Podbielan
Erv Palica
Dan Bankhead
Billy Cox
Charley Dressen
Junior Gilliam
Karl Spooner
Red Smith
Connie Desmond
Lillian Golenbock
Aunts Shirley, Gert, and Gladys
Ray Sklarin
Glenn Anders
Justin Golenbock

CONTENTS

"Hitting a ball and scoring a run are in a way what all of us try to do all our lives. Baseball becomes a symbol, win or lose, and the romance never really ends."

—BRANCH RICKEY

"Baseball, like some other sports, poses as a sacred institution dedicated to the public good, but it is actually a big, selfish business with a ruthlessness that many big businesses would never think of displaying."

—JACKIE ROBINSON

"The Dodger fans have paramount rights in the Brooklyn club. They are more important than the stockholders, the officials, the players, or anybody else."

—WALTER O'MALLEY

Murgatroyd Darcy, the belle of Canarsie
Went 'round with a fellow named Rodge.
At dancing the rhumba or jitterbug number,
You couldn't beat Rodge at this dodge.
Throughout the cold weather, the pair danced together,
But when the trees bloomed again,
Miss Murgatroyd Darcy, the belle of Canarsie
To Rodgers would sing this refrain:

Leave us go root for the Dodgers, Rodgers,
That's the team for me.
Leave us make noise for the boistrous boys
On the B.M.T.
Summer or winter or any season,
Flatbush fanatics don't need no reason.
Leave us go root for the Dodgers, Rodgers,
That's the team for me.

—DAN PARKER

THE PARK WITH NOBODY IN IT

By Bob Cooke

(Parodied from Joyce Kilmer's poem,
The House with Nobody in It)

Whenever I go to Flatbush, on the subway BMT
I pass by a poor old ball park, where the turnstiles rust by degree.
I know I've passed it a hundred times but I always stop for a
minute.
And look at the park, the tragic park, the park with nobody in it.

And this park on the way to Flatbush needs thirty thousand pairs
of eyes
And somebody ought to cheer it up, by coming out there under
the skies
It needs new life and laughter and the seats should be occupied
'Cause what it needs the most of all are some people sitting inside.

Now if I had a lot of money and all my debts were paid
I'd put a gang of men to work with brush and saw and spade
I'd buy that park and fill it up the way it used to be
With fellows like Snider and Hodges and a great guy named Pee
Wee.

They say the park isn't haunted, but I hear there are such things
That hold the talk of Dodgers, their mirth and sorrowings,
I know this park isn't haunted but I wish it were I do
'Cause it wouldn't be so lonely if it had a ghost or two.

A park that has done what a park should do, a park that has
sheltered life
That has put its loving concrete arms around a Dodger fan and his
wife
A park that has echoed a baseball song, held up a rookie's
stumbling feet
Is the saddest sight when it's left alone that ever your eyes could
meet.

So whenever I go to Flatbush with the help of the BMT
I never walk by the empty park without pausing in hopes I won't see
A park standing there, empty and barren, with some seats falling apart
'Cause I can't help thinking the poor old park is a park with a broken heart.

1

Charley Ebbets

A coldhearted scalawag by the name of Ned Hanlon was determined to do in 1902 what a ruthless, money-hungry scalawag by the name of Walter O'Malley ended up doing fifty-five years later: Hanlon wanted to transfer the borough's beloved baseball team out of Brooklyn. And Hanlon might well have gotten his way, except for one steadfastly loyal Dodger employee who not only loved Brooklyn passionately but had a deep and unwavering faith that there was something very special about playing there. Brooklyn was his life, and it was his home. Charley Ebbets was the employee's name, Brooklyn's first recorded saint.

Since its founding in 1883, Ebbets had labored for the team, called the Dodgers because the ballpark was situated at a confluence of trolley tracks, and one took one's life in one's own hands dodging the trolley cars to get to the game. He began as a program and ticket hawker, and as the owners came to recognize his industriousness and loyalty, he was elevated to business manager. Majority stockholder Harry von der Horst rewarded Ebbets, making him an owner by selling him several of his shares. von der Horst was impressed with Ebbets and figured he would work even harder if he were a part owner. When in 1902, Harry Von der Horst became ill, he put his stock interest up for sale. It was then that Hanlon, the Dodger manager, announced his intention to buy the stock, take over the team, and move it to Baltimore, where he had previously managed.

Ebbets had no money, but he swore that he would find a way to keep the Dodgers in Brooklyn. He summoned all of his friends, and after pleading the merits of baseball in Brooklyn, he found one man of means, a furniture dealer—Henry Medicus—who had enough faith in Ebbets that he lent him the funds to buy Von der Horst's stock. And so it was that Ebbets, not Hanlon, became the new owner of the Dodgers. And as a result, the Dodgers stayed.

From the first, Ebbets showed he was an uncommon team owner—he believed that his first loyalty should be to the fans. Ebbets was operating dangerously in debt. He didn't have money for new players, and the team rarely finished in the top half of the standings, but when in 1906 the rival New York Giants, led by another former Baltimore star, John McGraw, offered him a fabulous sum of $30,000 for two of his best players, Ebbets

The Bettmann Archive

CHARLES EBBETS

refused to give in to the sweet allure of the money. He told a friend, "The Brooklyn fans deserve the best team I can give them."

And for his fans, Ebbets dreamed of a modern park that would seat more than 25,000. Brooklyn wasn't much more than a series of cow pastures then, and to his associates that park Ebbets wanted to build seemed to be folly.

The Dodgers played in a wooden stadium called Washington Park, so named because it stood on a site where George Washington fought one of a string of losing battles against the British during the Revolutionary War. Ebbets would take walks through the borough in search of a site for the stadium he was determined to erect. While walking through Flatbush, searching, he wandered through a malodorous four-and-a-half-acre slum in the notorious Pigtown section. It was a wild, craggy piece of land, with shanties scattered over it, and in the middle of this nest of poverty was a large, gaping pit into which the shanty dwellers threw their fetid, steaming garbage. Farmers from the area brought their pigs there to feed. Hence Pigtown.

When he checked the deeds to see who owned the land, Ebbets discovered forty claims of ownership, either by deed or squatters rights. He formed a corporation and, disguising his true purpose, bought the first parcel in 1908. Midway through the three years it took him to secure the other parcels, word leaked out as to his objective, and several of the plot owners hiked their prices sharply. By the end of 1911, he had been able to acquire the entire area except for one parcel—he had been unable to locate the owner. Private dicks traced the man first to California, then to Berlin, then to Paris. Ultimately he was found—in Montclair, New Jersey.

Ebbets sent a purchasing agent to ask how much the owner wanted. The agent had no way of knowing whether the man had learned of the true purpose of the purchase, but when he told the owner that he was interested in the land, the owner laughed. He had forgotten that he had owned it. "Why would anyone be interested in land in Pigtown?" he asked, adding, "Would $500 be all right?"

Ebbets now had the land, and even though he was up to his handlebar mustache in debt, his bank lent him enough money to begin construction. The squatters were driven out, the shanties torn down, the garbage pit filled, and the area leveled, and on March 4, 1912, Ebbets, wearing a black bowler and an elegant overcoat, stomped a shovel into the ground to begin the excavation.

At the ceremony a reporter asked Ebbets what he was going to name the new park. "Washington Park, the same as the old park, I suppose," Ebbets said.

The newspaperman replied, "Why don't you call it Ebbets Field? It was your idea and nobody else's, and you've put yourself in hock to build it. It's going to be your monument, whether you like to think about it that way or not."

Ebbets thoughtfully considered what the reporter had said. "All right," said Ebbets, "that's what we'll call it. Ebbets Field."

The Magic of Ebbets Field

Under the ownership of Charley Ebbets, the Brooklyn Dodgers won two pennants in 1916 and 1920. They lost both Series; the former to pitcher Babe Ruth and the Boston Red Sox, the latter to the Cleveland Indians when Dodger pitcher Burleigh Grimes gave up the first grand slam home run in Series history, and when a Dodger batter, Clarence Mitchell, hit into the first and only unassisted triple play.

Ebbets in 1913 had hired as manager the portly Wilbert Robinson, and it was Robinson who led the team from 1914 until 1931. So long as Ebbets ran things, the Dodgers were respectable, but Ebbets died in 1925, and none of the other club officials knew anything about running a baseball team. They chose the manager, loveable Uncle Robbie, as Dodger president.

Obese, friendly, something of a clown, Robbie sat at the front-office controls, his hands up in the air as the tiller went its own way. The team, known as the Robins in his honor, was for the boids, as it finished sixth the last four years of the 1920s. Many of the veteran players, unable to take Robinson seriously, decided to take fuller advantage of the ancillary joys of playing major league baseball. For such night prowlers, the road became much more fun. The players formed the 0 for 4 Club. They could play around all they wanted, but if Robinson caught them, they would be expelled from the club.

Robinson didn't know about the 0 for 4 Club—he didn't know much of what was going on—but because the players were making so many mental errors, he announced that he was forming a club of his own, the Bonehead Club. Every time a player made a mistake, the player had to put $10 into a fund. That afternoon Robinson screwed up the batting order that he presented to the umpires before the game, and when the Pirate manager caught it, the mistake cost the Dodgers the game. Wrote *New York Sun* reporter Eddie Murphy, "The manager of the Dodgers formed a Bonehead Club before yesterday's game and promptly elected himself a charter member."

During Robinson's last few years, the team became known as the "Daffiness Boys." On the field the Dodgers were capable of just about anything imaginable. Floyd Caves "Babe" Herman joined the Dodgers and immediately became a crowd favorite. He had a lifetime batting average of .324 and in two successive years hit .381 and .393, but his fielding and base running lapses forged his legend. Herman once doubled into a double play during an exercise in comedy in which three runners ended up all sliding, diving, or striving to reach third base. On another occasion, a fly ball almost hit Herman in the head.

One time Herman was on the bench with a minor injury, and as he sat in the dugout, the opposing team was staging a rally. The batter hit the ball down the left-field line, and Robinson stood up, trying to see whether the ball was fair or foul. Unsure, he asked Herman, who was sitting next to him.

"What happened out there, Babe?"

The Babe looked up from the newspaper he was reading. "I don't know, Robbie," he said. "I was reading the paper."

The Bettmann Archive

WILBERT ROBINSON

BABE HERMAN

Because of the nature of the team, Herman was revered for his bumbling rather than blamed for his failings. The fans adored him, in large part because he was one of the best hitters in the game. Reporters made him out to be a clown, though in fact he was an intelligent, serious man. But there was no getting around his eccentricities.

One day Herman, upset with what the reporters were saying about him, cornered Joe Gordon of the *New York American* and asked him to go easy on him. "You make me look like a clown all the time," said Herman. Replied Gordon, "I don't make you look like a clown. I only write about you looking like a clown."

Herman was genuinely upset. "I'm serious," he said. "I know you write real funny stuff about me. I even have to laugh at it myself sometimes. But give me a break, will you? Look, I'm a ballplayer. I make a living playing ball, like you make yours writing, and I got a wife and kid to support. If you keep on making fun of me, it's going to hurt me. People will think of me as a joke ballplayer, and it will hurt my reputation with the ballclub. Do you see what I mean?"

Gordon said he understood. "I never thought of it that way, Babe. From now on, I promise you, I will stop poking fun at you."

Herman thanked him. He fumbled in his pockets and pulled out the butt of a cigar and stuck it in his mouth. Gordon reached for matches. Herman puffed a couple of times, and smoke began to rise from the end of the cigar. "Never mind," said Herman, "it's lit."

Gordon couldn't believe Herman had been carrying around a lighted cigar in his pocket. "It's all off," Gordon screamed. "Nobody who carries around lighted cigars in his pocket can tell me he isn't a clown!"

Wilbert Robinson hung on through 1931, when Ebbets's remaining partner, Steve McKeever, forced him out, but the Dodgers in the 1930s nevertheless continued to be colorful, though inept. Casey Stengel, who once went to bat with a small bird under his baseball cap and who then tipped his cap, allowing the bird to fly free, was named manager in 1934. Casey provided some laughs for the baseball writers, but the Dodgers continued their lease on the lower half of the standings, and he was let go in 1937. The march of characters onto the field continued. A fellow would get traded to Brooklyn, and the fans would never know whether it would result in buffoonery or an ecclesiastical blessing. There was pitcher Clyde "Pea Ridge" Day, who was a hog caller from, where else, Pea Ridge, Arkansas. Pea Ridge would stand on the mound when he struck someone out and call, "Sooooooeeeeey, pig. Sooooooeeeey." Another pitcher was a flake with the handle of Cletus Elwood "Boots" Poffenberger. Called the Baron, Poffenberger was on a train traveling west when in the middle of the night he decided he was going to sneak off. He was walking tiptoe, his shoes in his hands,when one of the other players stopped him. If he hadn't, the Baron would have been a goner when he hit the ground.

Two other pitchers with equally wondrous nicknames, Walter "Boom-Boom" Beck and Luke "Hot Potato" Hamlin, also pitched for the team. Beck's nickname was onomatopoetic. The first "boom" was the ball hitting the bat, and the second "boom" was the ball hitting the outfield wall. His best year with the Dodgers was 1933 when he was 12-20. The other pitcher, Hamlin, was a mediocre pitcher with one great failing. He would try to throw fastballs past fastball hitters, and the balls would leave Ebbets Field faster than they left Hamlin's hand. A ballgame would be close, and then Hamlin would throw up a juicy serving, and there would go another home run, along with the game. Everyone would moan, "Hot Potato did it again." Hamlin, though not quite a .500 pitcher, had one great year. In 1939 Hot Potato was 20-13 and gave Dodger fans something to crow about. After two more seasons, he was gone.

In the seventeen years between 1922 and 1938, the Dodgers finished sixth eleven times and seventh once. The closest they had come to a pennant was in 1924 when they were edged out by John McGraw's Giants. And yet, though attendance had dropped as the Depression descended full force on the country, in no other city were the fans as loyal and devoted as were the Dodger fans.

Though the Depression made life even tougher on Brooklyn's ethnic Americans, it was mostly the best of times. Money was hard to come by, and a full-time job was a prayer's answer, but it was an era when the people next door were neighbors and not strangers, when the neighborhoods reverberated with the sounds of youngsters playing games in the street, when hitting a pinky three sewers was a feat, when stoops held a special place in the hearts of boys growing up.

To the fans the Dodgers were an extension of their family, representatives of their borough, and an important part of their lives, and they were proud of the Dodgers no matter how poorly they played, much as parents might still love a child with a D-plus average in school. Dodger fans were always able to rejoice in the small victories, a well-pitched game or a rare home run that won a game.

The Dodger players during the dark days of the Depression were blue-collar workers who had to scrap and scuffle every day on very little money, just like their fans had to, and the attempt was enough. No matter how poorly the team was doing, the residents of Brooklyn loved their Dodgers with a lifetime, all-encompassing passion never seen before or since.

BILL REDDY: "My father was a longshoreman, and there weren't always ships to unload, and there were days when we didn't have much to go around, but no matter how bad the day was or how dismal the prospects were, there was always the Dodgers and Ebbets Field. A friend would ask, 'Do you want to go to the game?' Most times I'd say, 'Sure, let's find some bottles.' We'd try to find empty milk of magnesia bottles. They were ten cents. Soda bottles were a nickel. We'd go through empty lots, go into hallways of apartment houses. The best thing was to go down to Ocean Parkway, where the apartments were, and we'd get in through the basements and go into the halls and cadge any bottles that were lying outside the apartment doors. Or we'd ring the doorbell in the lobby, and when a lady in the apartment answered, we'd say we were from the store and tell her to put the empties on the dumbwaiter. 'We'll take them back and give you credit,' we'd say. Some of these women would put them on, drop the dumbwaiter down, and we'd take the bottles and run.

"Then, we'd go to the A&P or to Daniel Reaves and cash them in. Many a time a clerk would say to me, 'How come you got so many bottles? Your mother don't buy here.' They knew, but someway or other, you'd cadge fifty-five cents and go to Ebbets Field."

Ebbets Field itself had something to do with the love affair. It was a tiny, comfortable park seating only 32,000, not one of the massive ballyards, such as the Polo Grounds or Yankee Stadium. Ebbets Field was personal and familiar, and the fans responded to that. It was a suitable place for falling in love with the game.

Bobby McCarthy: "Ebbets Field was small, and everything was close. It was a homey park. It was built right so you could feel you were behind third base almost when you were out in the bleachers. I think it was the only stadium where the bleacher seats, which had curved backs and were covered, were the same as the rest of the seats.

"My Dad and I would go to Ebbets Field, and we'd bring a big bag of sandwiches, five or six packs of Yankee Doodles, and you bought a soda for a nickel, and my father would get cold beer, and you had a whole day's entertainment.

"Gladys Gooding played the organ, and there was the Dodger Symphony—they were lively and they could play. And I remember when Old Golds was one of the sponsors, every time one of the Dodgers hit a home run, they'd slide a carton of Old Golds down the screen. Behind the catcher they had a big screen to prevent people from getting hit by foul balls, and the announcers sat high up behind that, and as the carton would slide down the screen, everyone would go, 'Woooooooooo.' And one time Tommy Brown hit a home run, but because he was only eighteen, they wouldn't give Brown his carton.

"They had a sign out in the outfield, it said, 'Hit this sign. Win a suit.' Abe Stark was the borough president of Brooklyn, and he owned a clothing store, and it was his sign, but in order to win the suit you had to hit the sign on the fly. But the sign was near the ground. And the right fielder was stationed right in front of it. The batter had to hit a 400-foot-long and three-foot-high line drive to hit it.

"Ebbets Field had so much going for it. Players would hit home runs over the forty-foot-high screen in right field into Bedford Avenue, and many times I would stand out there to catch a ball, but I never caught one. I was too slow. The closest I got, the ball was bouncing around loose, and I went for it, and seventeen guys jumped on top of me and almost broke my arm."

Bill Reddy: "You'd walk into Ebbets Field on the center-field gate side of the field, and you started up this ramp, and you walked up like there was no end to it, and finally, you came through an opening and into where the seats were, and you looked down, and there was the diamond. And it *was* a diamond. It glistened. The grass was green. I've been to Ireland, and they have the greenest grass I've ever seen since, and still it wasn't as green as the grass at Ebbets Field. The grass was beautiful, and the field was manicured so beautifully—the base paths cut out with brown dirt, the foul lines on either side—and when you took one look at it, your heart beat faster. You sat on boards, planks in the bleachers, and you sat in the summer heat and sweated. Sitting there was a dream come true.

"You sat down and watched batting and fielding practice—the best part of the day. In those days the Dodger fans were mostly cabdrivers, insurance men who didn't have to work in the afternoon, night workers, kids who played hooky from school, and teachers who played hooky from school—though some days there were more sportswriters writing up the game than people who paid to come in. But you would go out to the bleachers and sit in the same place every day and see and listen to the same people every day, and what you'd do literally would be to pick apart every Dodger that was down on the field.

"But once the game started, let no voice be raised against the Dodgers. Now the enemy was out there, and believe me, when the other team took the field for fielding practice, they used to get a Brooklyn greeting that was out of this world.

"I remember Tex Rickart, the PA announcer at Ebbets Field. I knew Tex, because when I was working in a hardware store on Prospect Avenue, he was one of our customers. Tex had a film distributing business, his main livelihood. I can remember Tex walking about the field with a megaphone, but when they got the PA system, that's when Tex came into his own. You never heard anyone say it like Tex. 'A little boy has been found lost.' 'Will the fans along the outfield railing please remove their clothes.' He would intone, 'The tickets for the forthcoming games will be sold in the marble rotunda.' My God, the marble rotunda!

"The marble rotunda was the main entrance to Ebbets Field, and on a busy ballday was like getting into a merry-go-round. The ticket sellers stood behind gilded cages like circus boxes. People would be pushing and shoving, trying to figure out which gate to go through, which ticket seller had the best seats left.

"My father was a great baseball buff, a purist. I used to say to him, 'Let's go to Ebbets Field.' He'd look at me in amazement. 'Ebbets Field? What do you want to go to Ebbets Field for? If you want to see real baseball, we should go to Yankee Stadium.' I'd say, 'But Pop, I want to go see the Dodgers.' He'd say, 'Are you kidding? What do you want to watch those clowns for?' I'd get so mad I wanted to hit him.

"We'd go to Ebbets Field, and my Dad would say to me, 'Call those guys outfielders? You should have seen the old Red Sox outfield of Tris Speaker, Harry Hooper, and Duffy Lewis. Greatest outfield there ever was.' Of course, every time he told the story, Tris Speaker was playing closer and closer to second base until I got to where I believed Speaker used to practically stand on the shortstop's shoulders and then run back into deep center field to make a catch.

N.Y. Daily News Photo

"Or he'd name the entire 1907 Detroit Tiger outfield, Ty Cobb, Sam Crawford, and Davy Jones. And he'd have me crazy, because how can you come back at him? With Frenchy Bordagaray? Frenchy may have been good, but he was no Ty Cobb. But what did I care? Hell, Frenchy was a Dodger, and that was good enough for me.

"But then, after so many years of mediocrity, the Dodgers finally started to change. A wild man by the name of Larry MacPhail came in in 1937. The first thing he did was to paint the park over and made it clean and give you a toilet that you could visit without your feeling like a horse going to a horse trough. That was a big thing for the fans.

"The second thing he did was get himself a corps of ushers and deck them out in bright uniforms and have them stand out on the field after a game. Things were starting to change. You could go to the bathroom to take a leak and not have to worry about worms crawling up the walls and biting you. And you could buy a program or a beer from a guy who didn't look like a fugitive from a chain gang. And the ushers were there to help you find your seat.

"And then in 1938, in Burleigh Grimes's last year as manager, MacPhail got Leo Durocher from St. Louis to play shortstop and made him manager the next year, and he brought Dolph Camilli in to play first base, and then he started bringing in pitchers: Larry French, Vito Tamulis, who had a tantalizing slow pitch, Kirby Higbe, and Whitlow Wyatt, oh God, a master, and Fat Freddie Fitzsimmons. When the Dodgers were playing Pittsburgh or Philadelphia, all Fat Freddie had to do was walk out on the field and throw his glove down, and they gave up. In 1939 you could see it coming. Third place. Then second place in 1940, and you knew that in 1941 that they were finally going to do it. 'Nothing is going to stop us now.' My God! All this because of MacPhail. Who the hell was this guy anyway?"

Larry and Leo

The phones had been silent in the Dodger offices in 1938. New York Bell had discontinued service because the bill hadn't been paid. For the Dodger employees actively searching for jobs that paid better and more promptly, this was especially inconvenient. In the outer chamber of the office, process servers and bill collectors milled around, demanding or begging to be paid. The Dodgers were more than $1 million in debt, and they owed the Brooklyn Trust Company alone more than $500,000. Brooklyn, the shakiest franchise in baseball, was on the verge of going out of business.

Desperate in the face of foreclosure by the bank, the quarreling heirs of original owners Charley Ebbets and Steve McKeever, who heretofore had been unable to agree on anything, went to National League President Ford Frick to get his opinion as to what they should do to keep from going under. Frick advised that they hire a strong general manager with baseball experience, one who would not be fleeced by other teams and who could make the Dodgers respectable. When they asked Frick to suggest someone, Frick, in turn, sought the counsel of Branch Rickey, the most successful fleecer in the National League, the brains behind the always powerful St. Louis Cardinals. The Dodgers were desperate. A name, Branch, a name. Rickey proposed a longtime friend and business associate, Leland Stanford MacPhail.

Rickey and MacPhail had been classmates at the Unversity of Michigan law school in 1910 despite the fact that Rickey was seven or eight years older than MacPhail, because Rickey had played major league baseball with the Browns and the Yankees from 1905 through 1907 before entering Ohio Wesleyan University and then enrolling at Michigan Law.

MacPhail was a rich kid, a playboy, a reprobate from Grand Rapids, Michigan, whose father once had run a general store and had been a shylock on the side. When the boy was ten, the father sold the store and began to set up, one by one, a chain of twenty-one banks in small towns in Michigan. The father lived in several different towns during young Larry's childhood, establishing a quixotic and nomadic pattern that would be a constant throughout his entire life—Larry MacPhail never stayed in one place very long. After skipping from town to town as a child, MacPhail enrolled in Staunton Military Academy in Virginia. He sought and gained an appointment to Annapolis, but once he was accepted, he decided he didn't want to go and instead went to Beloit College in Wisconsin. Then in 1910 he spent the one year at the University of Michigan Law School, where he met Rickey. Larry was greatly interested in sports, erroneously viewed himself as a great athlete, and admired Rickey, who had once been a major leaguer. Rickey was, of course, also interested in sports, and he admired MacPhail for having so much money. And they became friends.

After the one year in law school, MacPhail continued his unpredictable journey. He went on to George Washington University, where he could be near the government's inner circle. He had hoped to be appointed a consul, but when he was offered a consulship in France, he turned it down. Instead he moved to Chicago and joined a big law firm. While working there he helped reorganize a bankrupt tool firm, and he did such a good job that the tool firm hired him away from the law firm, and shortly after joining the tool firm, he quit and moved to Nashville to run a clothing store. In 1917 Larry quit the clothing business and joined the 114th Field Artillery, a unit of volunteers organized by Colonel Luke Lea, the owner of a Nashville paper, a U.S. Senator, and a drinking buddy of MacPhail's.

When MacPhail returned from the war, he settled in Columbus, Ohio, practiced law, officiated Big Ten football games, and sold real estate and used cars. He also rekindled his friendship with Branch Rickey, who now was working for the St. Louis Cardinals and who had a business proposition for his well-heeled classmate.

Rickey had established a way of acquiring players cheaply by setting up farm teams, stating his mining theory: "If you dig up enough rocks, a small percentage of them will become gems."

He now asked MacPhail if he would be interested in investing some money and running the Columbus team. MacPhail had had no previous experience in baseball, but he had something every businessman needs: access to money.

N.Y. Daily News Photo

LARRY MACPHAIL

MacPhail went to his father, and it became a case of, "My son, Larry, has he got a deal for you." And so after MacPhail's father invested about $100,000, MacPhail, through Rickey, got his start in baseball in 1930 at Columbus, where he rebuilt his first franchise.

MacPhail had his own way of doing things. He was a heavy drinker and had great difficulty keeping his temper when under the influence. He was a loudmouth. He was a boor. But he had a genius for running a baseball team. His primary tenet was that one had to spend money to make money, and he proved his theory by rebuilding Columbus to where it was the most solid team in the Cardinal chain, but because the extravagant MacPhail tended to go overboard spending other people's money, he made Cardinal owner Sam Breadon nervous, and Breadon canned him.

Nevertheless MacPhail had made money running Columbus, and more important, he firmly established himself as a doer, a whirlwind who knew how to rebuild a franchise, and so when Cincinnati Reds owner Sid Weil, an undertaker by trade, found himself in deep financial trouble, Rickey, who was by then was considered to be the most astute man in the game, again suggested that MacPhail take over.

MacPhail induced another Cincinnati businessman, Powell Crosley, to buy the team from Weil and put him in charge. MacPhail spent freely, got rid of old players, began night baseball, hired radio announcer Red Barber, and built a winning team, but by 1937 he quit after getting drunk and punching out Crosley.

Consequently, although he insisted he was on the verge of a nervous breakdown, he was free in late 1937 when at Rickey's suggestion he was first asked to take on the Dodgers. Having learned from past experience. MacPhail refused, saying, "I'll take the job if you lay the kind of money I want on the line for me, give me a free hand, and fix it up with the bank so when I want some real money for operating purposes, I can walk in there and get it." How much money did he want? When he told them, they couldn't believe it. And how much for operating expenses? He mentioned a figure, and they began talking among themselves. After listening to the babble for a short period, MacPhail looked at his watch, looked at them, and said, "If I can't do business here, I know where I can." He slapped the top of the desk with his palm. "Well, what about it?"

Close to bankruptcy and not having much choice, they hired him. He ordered them to prepare a contract and barked that he would be back in a couple of days to sign it. And as he looked around the dingy offices, he asked, "Is this all there is?" It was, he was told. "When I'm in charge here," he bellowed, "we'll have to have more space. We'll start by knocking down those walls . . ." He pointed, and then he turned and left. MacPhail hadn't an inkling as to who owned the offices on the other side of the walls. He didn't much care, either.

After MacPhail took the job, he returned to Cincinnati where he told his former traveling secretary, John McDonald, "John, I am going to be president of the Daffiness Boys. I'm going to turn Brooklyn inside out, upside down, and win pennants every year."

Dodgers
Billy Herman

When MacPhail returned as boss, he kept his word to the directors that he would be spending large sums of money. He borrowed $200,000 to fix up Ebbets Field, and then he borrowed another $50,000 to buy first baseman Dolph Camilli, during a period when a box seat sold for $2.50. When MacPhail told the directors about the $50,000 for Camilli, one of them thought he heard wrong. "You mean the $50,000 is for a whole team, don't you?" he asked. MacPhail then announced the advent of night baseball in Brooklyn and charged $72,000 worth of lights from General Electric. He hired Red Barber from Cincinnati, signed fifteen scouts and sent them after prospects, hired Babe Ruth as a coach, made Leo Durocher manager, bought six minor league teams and signed working agreements with six others, hired Branch Rickey's son, Branch, Jr., to run the farm system, and then started spending money for players, more than $1 million by 1941.

MacPhail became the embodiment of Brooklyn. He was much like the fans. He was loud. Whenever he walked into a room, his voice was heard over all others. He was ornery. He wanted things done his way, and he wanted his orders carried out quickly without question. He was often angry. Employees who didn't follow orders or who made mistakes got a withering blast from his sharp tongue. And if he was unhappy with one of his players, he let the players know it in the newspapers. He hated the Giants. He hated the Yankees. He hated anyone standing in the way of success for his team.

He promised Brooklyn a winner, regardless of cost, and with his acumen for collecting talent, he built a respectable team almost entirely from the castoffs of other teams. In 1939 he claimed pitcher Hugh Casey from the roster of the Memphis minor league team, bought Whitlow Wyatt from minor league Milwaukee, traded for patched-up outfielder Dixie Walker, and paid an unheard of $75,000 for Louisville shortstop Pee Wee Reese. In 1940 he signed Cardinal prospect Pete Reiser for $100 after Baseball Commissioner Kenesaw Mountain Landis freed him from the Cardinal chain, and he signed slugger Joe Medwick to play left field. While sitting in the box seats during the 1940 World Series in Detroit, where the Tigers and Reds were playing, he made two deals on the same day, acquiring fastball pitcher Kirby Higbe from the Phillies for $100,000 and catcher Mickey Owen from Rickey and the Cardinals for $60,000. If Rickey had known MacPhail was getting Higbe, he never would have sold Owen to MacPhail. Moreover, Giant owner Horace Stoneham was under the impression that he was about to acquire Higbe, only to see to his horror that MacPhail had stolen him away for more money. By keeping both deals secret, MacPhail got both men. Thanks to the resources of the Brooklyn Trust Company.

MacPhail continued to work tirelessly and to spend money. He paid $90,000 and sent two minor leaguers to the Chicago Cubs for all-star second baseman Billy Herman. Herman remembers his surprise over the trade.

BILLY HERMAN: "I had been with the Cubs for ten years. The Cubs had a young second baseman they'd brought up from the Coast League, a kid named Lou Stringer. He'd had a great spring training, they felt he was going to be a fine ballplayer, and they wanted to give him an opportunity to play. So they figured I was expendable.

"We were in the New York at the time, at the Commodore Hotel. I remember Larry MacPhail called me on the telephone at about two in the morning.

" 'I've just made a deal for you.' he said.

" 'At two in the morning?' I asked.

" 'What's the difference?' he said."

Despite the exorbitant cost, MacPhail felt with Herman the Dodgers would finally be pennant contenders.

Of all his decisions, perhaps the one that put his stamp of bellicosity on the Dodgers of the 1940s was the replacement of Burleigh Grimes as manager after the 1938 season with one of his players, a gambler and street hustler who combined ferocity with guile to outwit, outmaneuver, and outrage the opposition. The player's name was Leo Durocher.

Leo Durocher grew up in a seedy tenement in West Springfield, Massachusetts, a close friend of a boy named Gerald Chapman, who in 1926 was hanged in Connecticut for killing a prison guard. As a teenager, Durocher worked in a battery factory in Springfield, and to supplement his income, he hustled pool at Smith's Billiard Academy. He became the house player, and he rarely lost. He also developed an unsavory reputation, hanging out with low-level mob guys, card sharks, hustlers, and gamblers.

When Durocher signed with Hartford in 1925, Paddy O'Connor was the manager. O'Connor warned Durocher about the friends he hung out with, but Durocher refused to give them up, and in fact he kept his old pool hall buddies throughout most of his baseball career. In those days players hung their clothes on nails, and soon after Durocher arrived to play for the team, the other players began finding money missing from their wallets. O'Connor suspected Durocher, and to catch him, he marked a $5 bill, put it in his wallet, left the wallet in his pants pocket in his locker, and waited to see who swiped it. When the bill disappeared, O'Connor trailed Durocher to the Heublein Hotel, where Durocher sat down for supper. After eating, Durocher paid the bill—with the marked money. He had been caught red-handed.

The other players wanted Durocher suspended from the team immediately. They wanted him blackballed from baseball, and if they had gotten their way, it is possible Durocher's baseball career would have ended right then. But O'Connor, who saw an opportunity to win a pennant with Durocher at shortstop, told the players, "We have a chance to win. I promise you that if you let him stay, I'll get rid of him at the end of the season." Hartford did win a pennant, and true to his word, O'Connor sold Durocher—to the New York Yankees.

Durocher played two games for the Yankees in 1925, and though a poor hitter, was a quick, agile shortstop, and he made the Yankees to stay in 1928. Nevertheless he irritated the Yankee veterans by wearing flashy clothes and strutting around in them. Some of the other players began calling him "Fifth

Avenue," because of his penchant for plaids, stripes, and various combinations of garish clothing. At night he would leave his apartment at the Picadilly, go out in dinner clothes, eat a fancy meal, and go to a show.

Once, while in spring training, manager Miller Huggins was sitting outside the Princess Martha Hotel in St. Petersburg when he noticed Durocher all dressed up in a tuxedo sneaking out the back way. Huggins, along with coaches Art Fletcher and Charley O'Leary, stared as Leo got into a chauffeured limo.

The next day Huggins called him in. "Did you come down here to play baseball or to wear evening clothes?" the manager asked.

"No sir, Mr. Huggins." Then Durocher tried to explain: "I came to play baseball, but this was a very fine affair and I had an invitation, and you had to have evening clothes."

"And you had them right with you," said Huggins.

"Yes, sir," said Durocher as though it was only natural.

Huggins said, "Let me give you a little tip, son. Put them right back in the trunk and don't you ever let me see you with those on again. That's the end of evening clothes. Do you understand me?" Durocher nodded, and he never took them out again, except when he was in New York and no one was keeping an eye on him.

There was also a ruthless streak in him that made the other players distrust him. They felt if Durocher wanted something, he would find a way to get it, regardless of the morality or the feelings of others. Whatever he was doing, he had to win or succeed, which was the same thing as winning. He displayed this heavyhandedness in his relationships with women. When he was living in California, he dated several of the most famous and glamorous movie stars. While married to movie star Laraine Day, Leo was not shy about admitting to a writer friend of his that he was romancing another blond Hollywood bombshell. The writer, unabashedly and understandably jealous, said to Durocher, "How do you do it? You're bald, and you're not that young. How?"

"Kid," said Durocher, placing a hand on the writer's shoulder. "When you pick one of them up at 7:00, you've got to make your first move fast. You make sure you put your hand on their snatch at 7:05. Seven oh five! Now, one of two things can happen. Sure, they can knock your hand off. All right. It's 7:05. No go? Tough, but it's still early yet. Plenty of time to call another broad. But suppose she don't knock your hand off. Well, then hello dear. You know you're in, an you ain't gonna waste the evening.

"Kid. You'd be surprised. Some damn famous broads don't knock your hand off."

On the field he showed the same singularity of purpose and the same disregard for public opinion. Vince Lombardi never said, "Winning isn't everything. It's the only thing." What Lombardi really said was, "Trying to win isn't everything. It's the only thing." Lombardi was a humanist. He wasn't the ruthless winning über alles fanatic he was cracked up to be. But Durocher was. The only thing that mattered to him was victory. And it was this fanatic drive combined with his insufferable arrogance that the Yankee vets felt was unbecoming in a teammate.

In one of his very first game as a Yankee, the opposition was the Detroit

Tigers, and playing the outfield for Detroit was Robert "Fatty" Fothergill, a short, fat fireplug with a .326 lifetime batting average. It was the ninth inning, the bases loaded, the winning runs on base, and Fothergill at the plate when Durocher threw his arms up and called time. He ran in toward home plate, and began screaming at the umpire, "What's going on here? You can't have two men standing in the batter's box at the same time." The umpire at first couldn't figure out what Durocher was talking about. Then he looked at the rotund Fothergill. Furious at the nerve of the rookie loudmouth, Fothergill began swearing at Durocher. His concentration lost, he struck out, ending the game.

In an era when a rookie was seen and rarely heard, Durocher showed deference to no one, including the game's greatest stars. In one game against the Detroit Tigers, Ty Cobb rounded second, and as he stood poised waiting to make his next move, Durocher gave him a hip. Cobb, who may have been the fiercest, toughest competitor ever to play the game, threatened that he would "get" Durocher. Durocher opened his mouth wide, indicating he would shove the baseball down Cobb's throat. Durocher then screamed, "You're an old man. The game has passed you by. You ought to get out."

On other teams Leo would have been respected for his fierceness, but on the staid, conservative Yankees, Leo was seen as a thug. Even Babe Ruth, who liked almost everyone, hated Durocher. Once, when Ruth lost his wrist-watch, he accused Durocher of stealing it, though he never had any real proof that Durocher had taken it. For years opposing players would stand in the dugout during a game swinging a watch back and forth, taunting Durocher for stealing the Babe's watch. Ruth was the superstar of his era, but Durocher showed little respect for the great home run hitter, calling the Babe "that baboon," often deriding his intelligence, and making remarks inferring that Ruth, who had a dark complexion, was really a negro.

While with the Yankees Durocher spent many of his off hours hanging out in pool halls up and down Broadway, in joints such as Crenshaw's, where he would hustle anyone foolish enough to take him on. He became close friends with two young punks named George Raft and Billy Rose. Other nights he visited such establishments as Jimmy Durante's Club Durant, hangout for such men as Al Capone, Waxey Gordon, and Lucky Luciano; the Partridge Club, the classiest gambling house anywhere in the world; and Larry Fay's El Fey Club, where society's cream such as the Vanderbilts, the Astors, and the Whitneys dined alongside such men as Arnold Rothstein, Dutch Schultz, and Louis Lepke.

Durocher also frequented the swanky night clubs—the Stork Club, the Cotton Club, which was run by Connie Immerman and where Cab Calloway and Bill "Bojangles" Robinson performed, and the Tavern, which was run by Toots Shor.

Making no more than $5,000, Durocher lived way above his meager salary, and his reputation as a deadbeat grew when he began writing bad checks to several shopkeepers near Yankee Stadium. One even put a Durocher rubber check in his store's front window. Durocher was counting on a big check from playing in the 1929 World Series to bail him out. Unfortunately for him the Yankees finished sixteen games behind Philadelphia.

Durocher's sole ally on the Yankees was the manager, Miller Huggins, who had also had trouble with his Yankee stars. One time Ruth and left fielder Bob Meusal got roaring drunk, and as their train was racing along, they grabbed Huggins, and standing on the platform of the last car, Ruth held the manager's left leg and Meusal held his right leg, and they dangled his head inches from the trackbed. On the Yankees, sometimes it was hard to tell the good guys from the bad guys. But it was Huggins who recognized Durocher's all-encompassing passion for winning and who encouraged his combativeness, his shrewdness, and his willingness to take chances. Huggins loved when Durocher taunted the opposing players. "That's the way I want you to play, son," Huggins would tell him, and Durocher would stick his chest out even farther.

Huggins, however, was a sick man. By the end of the 1929 season, he was coughing frequently, a low, rasping wheeze, and he turned the club over to Art Fletcher for the final two weeks. When, in late September, Huggins died, whatever chances Durocher had of staying on with the Yankees died with him. Durocher, moreover, didn't help himself when during contract negotiations he told general manager Ed Barrow to "go and fuck yourself."

Although Durocher was arguably the best-fielding shortstop in the league, the new manager, pitcher Bob Shawkey, put him on waivers. And not one of the other American League teams picked him up. He went to Cincinnati.

When he arrived in the Queen City, Reds manager Big Dan Howley told Durocher, "If you start popping off around here and getting yourself into jams, I'll hit you in the head first with the bat and then I will put 'Peoria' across the front of your shirt and make it stick. You've got a chance to become a great ballplayer—or to wind up in the minors in a hurry. Take your choice."

Durocher didn't change his habits. He continued to postdate checks and neglect to make them good. He was even called on the carpet before Commissioner Landis. He also got in trouble when he dated a young girl who became pregnant and forced him to marry her. A couple months later she recanted, said it was not his baby, and the marriage was annulled.

But management in Cincinnati loved him. A baseball player can get away with anything, including murder, if he is excelling on the field, and Durocher played superb shortstop for Cincinnati for three years and part of a fourth, until St. Louis Cardinal shortstop Charley Gelbert shot off a piece of his foot in a hunting accident. At that time Cincinnati was desperate for a starting pitcher, and so Cincinnati sent Durocher to the Cardinals in exchange for the Cardinals' star pitcher, Paul Derringer.

Durocher arrived in St. Louis deep in debt. The president of the Cardinals, Branch Rickey, made Durocher a personal project.

BRANCH RICKEY: "When he came to St. Louis, Leo was in trouble. No fewer than thirty-two creditors were breathing down his neck, suing or threatening to sue. An impossible situation. I proposed that I go to his creditors and arrange for weekly payments on his debts. This meant a modest allowance of spending money for Leo himself. But Leo agreed.

"There were other matters to be straightened out. Leo's associates at the time were hardly desirable ones. But he was not the kind of man to take kindly to criticism of his friends. I thought a lot about Leo's associations, but I didn't see what I could do about them."

But Rickey was nevertheless innovative in his attempt to build Durocher's self-confidence. He got him a job coaching the baseball team of the U.S. Naval Academy in the off-season, a job Durocher enjoyed and from which he derived great satisfaction. Rickey also encouraged Durocher to get married. Durocher had just gone through the annulment proceedings, and he had fallen in love with Grace Dozier, a fashionable and prosperous dress designer from St. Louis and a social acquaintance of Rickey's, and though Leo kept asking her to marry him, she was reluctant to do so in the middle of the baseball season. Leo told Rickey, and Rickey told her he saw no reason why the wedding could not take place, and with five games left in the 1934 season, Durocher and Grace Dozier were married.

That fall, with Durocher at shortstop, the Cardinals won the pennant. Durocher put his stamp on the team with his aggressiveness and drive, and in fact, it was he who labeled the team the Gas House Gang.

Durocher and pitcher Dizzy Dean had been sitting in the dugout talking about the pennant race, and Dean, who was contemptuous of the American League, said, "I don't know whether we can win in this league, but if I wuz in that other league, we sure would win."

Durocher replied, "They wouldn't let us in the other league. They would say that we are a lot of gas house ballplayers."

Reporter Frank Graham, who was eavesdropping in the dugout, quoted Durocher in his column, and so the Gas House Gang was born.

By the end of the 1937 season, Leo had decided he could manage the Cardinals better than player/manager Frankie Frisch, and he said it loud and often enough that Frisch, who was as abrasive and strong-willed as Durocher, told Branch Rickey there wasn't room on the team for both of them. Frustrated over Durocher's continued irresponsibility, Rickey traded Durocher for four players to his friend MacPhail in Brooklyn.

Around the same time MacPhail brought in Durocher, he also hired Babe Ruth to be first-base coach. MacPhail had planned to replace Burleigh Grimes with Ruth, whose fondest desire was to become a manager, and he might have gotten it if Durocher hadn't stood in his way. The first day Durocher was in uniform, Ruth told his former Yankee teammate, "Kid, stick with me, 'cause I'm gonna be taking over Grimes's job." Durocher felt pity for the Babe. He knew he had been hired only as a freak, to hit home runs during batting practice to draw fans. Durocher told Ruth, "You've got a lot of gall plotting to take this man's job. After all, he's been good enough to take you on here. And let me tell you something. You are insulting me. You are insulting me, Babe, by assuming I'm going to help you undermine him."

B
Leo Durocher
Brookly

As time passed his harassment of the Bambino increased. Late in the 1938 season, a young baseball writer reported in a story that during the game Ruth, coaching at first, had flashed the hit-and-run sign to the batter.

After hearing about the article, Durocher in a loud voice so everyone in the clubhouse could hear, said, "How could that big baboon have flashed the hit-and-run sign when he didn't even know what it was?" Ruth, flashing anger, was sitting nearby on a three-legged stool in front of his narrow locker, and just as Ruth made a move to get up from his seat to go for Durocher, Durocher gave the Babe a violent shove, propelling the famous man backward into the locker. Pouncing, Durocher began slapping the Babe's face. Manager Grimes and several of the Dodger players rushed over to break it up.

Durocher once again had played the percentages and won. Leo knew that if the Babe got to him first, he would have been a goner. Durocher also knew that fights get broken up fast. By shoving him into his locker, Leo figured he could get his shots in, and before the Babe could come back at him, the fight would be over.

After tempers had cooled, Grimes told Durocher, "The next time you do that, I'll fine you. He belongs to me." Durocher knew then that Grimes had heard the Babe had been after his job.

Grimes didn't tell MacPhail about the fight, but MacPhail found out—word of the fight was all over the league—and the Dodger president decided against making Ruth his next manager. When MacPhail let Grimes go after the '38 season, Leo Durocher got his fondest wish. And with Durocher as the new manager, Babe Ruth's career in baseball had come to an end.

Burleigh Grimes asserts that it was he who first suggested Durocher to MacPhail. Grimes had been a tough competitor in his nineteen-year career as a pitcher, and he saw the same qualities in Durocher that Yankee manager Miller Huggins had seen. The Dodgers were mired in sixth place late in the 1938 season when Grimes learned he was not going to be rehired as manager the next year.

BURLEIGH GRIMES: "Not too long before the end of the 1938 season, MacPhail called me in and told me he was going to make a change.

" 'I expected that,' I said.

" 'It isn't really your fault,' he said.

"Then he asked me if I had any suggestions as to who might replace me.

" 'Yes,' I said, 'I do. You've got a guy on the club who's smart, got guts, and ought to make a damned good manager.'

" 'Who would that be?' he asked.

" 'Durocher,' I said.

" 'Do you really think so?'

" 'I certainly do,' I said. 'I certainly do.' "

He was not the only one who did. Dodger traveling secretary John McDonald also thought Durocher was the best choice.

JOHN MCDONALD: "MacPhail wanted Billy Herman, the Cub second baseman, to replace Grimes. Another candidate was Frankie Frisch. I had suggested

Durocher, but MacPhail was vehement. 'Never,' he said. 'The guy can't even manage himself. Look at all the bouncing checks, the unpaid alimony.'

"But a month later, while riding with him in a cab, MacPhail said to me, 'Hey John, I just got a great idea. A manager who can also play star ball for us will save us a big salary.'

" 'Who do you have in mind?' I asked.

" 'Durocher,' he said.

" 'That's a great idea,' I said. 'How'd you happen to think of Leo?' "

The Lip

From the spring training of his very first season, Durocher and MacPhail fought bitterly and in public. There were like two lovers who alternately adore and hate one another. Similar in temperament, they were fiery, profane, given to outbursts, hot-headed, and supremely egomaniacal. One was an addicted gambler. The other was an alcoholic. One was reckless. The other was impetuous. And so long as MacPhail kept sober, Durocher was free of his outbursts. Unfortunately for Leo there was a saying about MacPhail: "With no drinks he was brilliant, with one he was a genius. With two he was insane. And rarely did he stop at one." Former Baseball Commissioner Happy Chandler once said about him, "When he was sober, he was one of the best baseball men I ever saw. When he drank too much whiskey, he'd push little ducks in the pond and hit little girls."

And fire his manager, as many as sixty times over four seasons. After MacPhail slept it off, he would act as though nothing had happened, ignoring any "firing," but through all those firings, Durocher never *really* knew, until the next morning, whether he was out or not.

Durocher's conduct didn't calm things any. Durocher often would commit an outrageous act, as though he were daring MacPhail to act. Running his first spring training at Hot Springs, Arkansas, in 1939, Durocher went to the Belvedere Country Club for dinner with coaches Charley Dressen and Andy High, and a couple of others, and for $2, each of them bought a bingo card. Durocher bought five cards, and when the caller announced I-17, Durocher screamed "That's me," and he was brought the jackpot of $660. Durocher had gone to bed around four in the morning, and at eight, the phone rang. It was MacPhail. "You're fired."

"For what?"

"You're a gambler," MacPhail told him.

"What the hell are you talking about, Larry?"

"I just saw it in this morning's papers. You won the big bingo prize."

"That's right. My coaches were there. I bought some bingo cards, and I won. What's wrong with that?"

"That's gambling. You're fired. Turn the club over to Andy High."

Durocher said, "To High? It's all right if you want to fire me, but how the fuck can you give it to High? Give it to Dressen. You got to make Dressen the manager."

MacPhail screamed, "Don't tell me who to make the manager."

Durocher screamed, "Go fuck yourself," and he slammed down the phone. And went right on managing.

The very next day Durocher was playing golf, and when his caddy moved while he was putting, Durocher dressed him down, swearing angrily. When the caddy responded, Durocher slugged him. This, too, made the papers, and though he hadn't had the team for two weeks, MacPhail again wanted to dump him as manager and fired him over the telephone. Leo pleaded, "If I lose this job, my wife will divorce me." Leo promised to reform. MacPhail, however, was adamant. Leo was fired.

The next morning Durocher was packing his clothes to return home when the phone rang. "Hi, Leo, I'd like your opinion about . . ." and he asked Durocher about a player he was thinking of acquiring. MacPhail didn't mention the firing. It was as though the incident never happened. Durocher unpacked, and he learned something about alcoholics in general and MacPhail in particular. High drama was what counted. The play was the thing.

Durocher was one of those people who insisted on getting his way, no matter what the cost. During that spring training, Durocher was looking over the Dodgers' minor leaguers when he noticed the superior speed of one of the young infielders. Durocher watched the hard line drives off the kid's bat, saw that he was a switch hitter, and immediately decided that the unknown minor leaguer should start for the Dodgers. He had the boy transferred to the Dodger camp and put him in a Dodger uniform. It was around 100 degrees in St. Pete, and Durocher, who was looking for a position to play the boy, inserted him in his spot at shortstop. He had never played the position before. Playing in two games for the Dodgers, the boy went 7 for 7 and got on base eleven straight times. Durocher started bragging that the boy was the greatest prospect he had ever seen, and he predicted that the kid would lead the Dodgers into the World Series. "What have I got here? What have I stumbled upon?" Durocher asked himself. "This is a dream. I never saw anything like this."

The minor leaguer's name was Pete Reiser, and reporters started calling him "Pistol Pete." But when stories began appearing in the New York papers about Reiser, MacPhail inexplicably sent Durocher a telegram: DO NOT PLAY REISER AGAIN.

What Durocher didn't know was that his publicizing Reiser could have gotten MacPhail in serious trouble. Only the devious MacPhail was in no position to tell Durocher that. In 1938 Baseball Commissioner Kenesaw Mountain Landis had declared more than 100 of St. Louis Cardinal President Branch Rickey's fine young minor leaguers as free agents, ruling that Rickey had held them down in the minors illegally. Of the 100, there was only one Rickey badly wanted to retain, Reiser. Rickey had personally discovered him on the sandlots of St. Louis, and he had used the boy to chauffeur him around before sending him to Class-D ball. Then, to Rickey's dismay, Landis ruled that Reiser was a free agent.

Rickey immediately called MacPhail, who more than anyone else in baseball was beholden to Rickey, and as a personal favor, Rickey asked his disciple to sign Reiser and hide him in the Dodger chain for a couple of years. The plan, as Rickey designed it, was that at the end of two years, MacPhail would sell or trade the youngster back to St. Louis. For all Rickey had done for MacPhail, this wasn't asking all that much. Rickey was convinced his boy would be the greatest player in the game. He was the fastest runner in baseball, could throw with both hands, and was fearless. In two years, Rickey would have him back. At the same time he instructed Reiser to sign for whatever the Dodgers offered him. MacPhail offered a piddling $100, and Reiser signed with the Dodgers.

It was a highly unethical and illegal deal, one that would have gotten both the pious Rickey and the conniving MacPhail in deep trouble with Landis. And because Durocher was not the type of guy anyone could trust, they couldn't tell Leo, whose eye for talent had drawn him immediately to the nineteen-year-old prospect.

As he did with Willie Mays more than ten years later, Leo adopted Reiser as his own. Leo made him the starting shortstop during spring training and had him tabbed as the starter for the season opener.

Seeing the articles in the papers, Rickey called MacPhail on the phone and accused him of a doublecross. MacPhail, appalled, sent the telegram to Durocher ordering him to ship Reiser to the minors. Durocher ignored the order.

Durocher, who was bragging that the kid was going to lead the Dodgers to the 1940 pennant, contended that it was he who determined who played and who didn't, and he announced his determination to play the best nine players the Dodgers had. Including Reiser.

MacPhail flew in to confront Durocher and ordered a press release announcing Durocher's dismissal. This time it was coach Bill Killefer who was to take his place.

At the meeting MacPhail began the discussion by calling Durocher "stupid" and "sonofabitch" and "shmuck." Durocher said calmly, "If you don't want me to manage your ballclub, that's all right. You're the boss. I'm not mad, so don't you be mad. But stop calling me those names. Don't . . . call . . . me . . . those . . . names."

MacPhail wouldn't stop, and Durocher responded by flattening MacPhail with one punch. MacPhail responded by getting up, going over to Durocher, hugging him, and bursting into tears. They walked out the door together and went off to the ballpark.

The next day the mercurial MacPhail paid Durocher a friendly visit at the ballpark. "I'm glad we had our little talk yesterday," said MacPhail. "I really feel we understand each other better now." Leo still didn't understand why MacPhail was being so stubborn about Reiser, but he saw how determined MacPhail was, and he stood by as MacPhail shipped the boy to Elmira.

This pattern of what Durocher saw as MacPhail's meddling continued throughout MacPhail's tenure. In 1940 Durocher took himself out and installed rookie Pee Wee Reese as shortstop, against MacPhail's express wishes. One time MacPhail shouted at Durocher, "I'm paying you to see some of that sparkling infield play I've been reading about in the papers. You don't think I'm paying you just to manage, do you? With the players I've dug up for you," MacPhail bragged, "I could manage this club myself and do a damned sight better job than you have."

Durocher replied, "You manage the ballclub? Don't make me laugh."

MacPhail: "You're fired."

Durocher: "Get somebody else to manage your lousy ballclub."

There were days when the MacPhail/Durocher soap opera turned comical—almost.

HAROLD ROSENTHAL: "One time Larry was drunk, and he went up to see his traveling secretary, John McDonald, to tell him to prepare a press release that he was firing the son of a bitch, Durocher. McDonald, figuring MacPhail would cool off, stalled for time, fiddling around with the typewriter, taking his sweet time. With MacPhail standing over him, McDonald kept taking breaks, and MacPhail kept saying, 'Come on. Let's go,' and McDonald kept stalling until MacPhail finally shouted, 'Goddamn it, you're fired too. Because you can't type. Put that in the release, but make sure Durocher's name comes first.' "

Both stayed, of course.

COOKIE LAVAGETTO: "MacPhail and Leo caused a lot of confusion. Christ, they were always fighting. Leo getting fired, quitting. I didn't pay any attention to it. I just went out and played ball and did the best I could. I just let it roll right over my head."

As did the rest of the players. The MacPhail-Durocher pas de deux served only to enhance the image of the Dodgers as a hard-drinking, scrappy, rough-hewn, brawling bunch, an image richly deserved. In baseball the type of manager often is reflective of the personality of the owner. Corporate men hire corporate managers. Eccentric men hire eccentric managers. And on the Dodgers, the eccentric boss not only hired the fiery hooligan Durocher but purchased and traded for like-minded players as well.

The prototypical Dodgers during the MacPhail-Durocher era were starting pitcher Kirby Higbe and relief pitcher Hugh Casey. Both players had the worst habits of their bosses. Like MacPhail, Higbe and Casey loved to drink, and like Durocher, they loved to gamble and romance good-looking women, and when they walked out onto the field, they were as mean as catshit.

Higbe was a good old boy from Columbia, South Carolina, a southerner, as were so many major leaguers. Of the Dodgers, Casey was from Atlanta, Georgia, Dixie Walker from Pascagoula, Mississippi, Pee Wee Reese from Louisville, Kentucky, Mickey Owen from Nixa, Missouri, and Whitlow Wyatt from Kensington, Georgia. Kirby Higbe could have been a character in one of Ring Lardner's novels. Or from the pen of William Faulkner.

SPIDER JORGENSEN: "Hig and I roomed together one year. Hig would never take anything on the road with him, just his clothes. We'd get into town, go to the hotel, and in those days they had concession stands with a drug counter right there in the lobby, and he'd look around and then go up to his room and pick up the phone and call up the bell captain. He'd say, 'This is Kirby Fucking Higbe, and I'm in room two fucking fourteen, and send me up a tube of tooth fucking paste, one of those bristle fucking tooth fucking brushes, and a carton of Lucky fucking Strikes.' Hig called me Skinhead, and he'd say, 'Hey Skin, you want anything?' I'd say, 'I'll get a couple of Cokes.' He said, 'And send up a half a dozen CocafuckingColas.' Then he'd hang up the phone, pick up the paper, and go on into the crapper.

"There was a knock on the door. I said, 'Hig, your stuff is here.' He said, 'Skin, take care of it. I'll get you later.' But of course he didn't. So the first time I got stuck, but not after that."

HOWIE SCHULTZ: "Kirby Higbe was my first roommate. Kirby would see me at breakfast and always asked me if he snored. I'd say, 'You'd better ask someone else,' because, you see, I didn't see much of Old Hig.

"He would get into a new town, and he'd get on the phone and order two bacon, lettuce, and tomato sandwiches with Durkee's dressing. And two shots of Southern Comfort. That was his arrival snack all the time.

"The one real tragic situation that Hig went through was at the end of the '43 season. The last series we played was in Cincinnati, and we got our paychecks. He went down to the hotel and cashed his, and he had thirteen $100 bills, and he went across the river into Covington, Kentucky, and the next morning he had to borrow tip money from me.

"That was a lesson in finance for me, boy."

REX BARNEY: "Kirby was something else. He was always running around, and his wife, Ann, must have been a saint to put up with it. Kirby went into the service and got sent to the Pacific, and when he was about ready to come home, he sent Ann a wire. It read: 'ARRIVING APRIL 1. MEET ME ON THE DOCK IF YOU WISH TO BE THE FIRST. KIRBY.' She was on the dock.

"After he was home about two weeks, a letter came to his home, perfumed and all. His wife opened it, a passionate letter from Manila. It's from a nurse Kirby had been living with off and on in the Philippines, and it talked about how much she had missed him. Kirby came home from a road trip, and Ann confronted him with the letter. You know what he said? Are you ready for this? Kirby said, 'It must be another Kirby Higbe'!

"Another time she caught him in bed with a girl. He jumped up, threw his clothes on, ran down the stairs as Ann is yelling and screaming at him, and when he gets down to the bottom of the stairs, he points up to the top and says, 'It wasn't me.' "

SPIDER JORGENSEN: "When Hig and I were together on the Giants later on, ole Hig went through his Billy Graham period. Before he was Kirby Fucking Higbe, and now he was into Christ. Leo had told me that. He said, 'Hig doesn't drink any more. He isn't Kirby Fucking Higbe anymore.' Hig had even converted a couple of the players to go to church with him on Sunday.

Kirby Higbe

Anyway it was during spring training, and we were in Louisville, and we were in the clubhouse because it was raining. And from that clubhouse you can look out a window and see the people in the lobby. And I knew Hig had a girl with him, because he always had me go along with them, and I could never figure out why. This was while he was on this religious kick, but I didn't say anything. And one of our teammates, Joe Lafata, who had been going to church because of Hig, was looking out the window, and he saw this girl, and suddenly he realized that though Hig had been telling everyone she was my girl, she was really his! Joe looks at Hig and he says, 'Higbe, you dirty rotten son of a bitch. Higbe, you're no fucking good.' Higbe says, 'Now wait a minute, Joe. Think of the Bible. Think of the Lord. Joe, you're swearing.' Lafata says, 'No, Higbe. No. I knew you when you were Kirby Fucking Higbe. I see that gal out there. That's your gal. And you're still Kirby Fucking Higbe.' And that was about the end of Higbe's religious kick."

Higbe's soul mate was reliever Hugh Casey. Unlike Higbe, who was talkative, friendly, and gregarious, Casey was a loner. His only close friend on the Dodgers, in fact, was Hig. Casey threw a hard slider, and he had great control, and he had another attribute that brought him great success on the mound: He was a tough, mean competitor. Encouraged by Durocher, Casey, like Higbe, enjoyed throwing dusters. Unlike Higbe, Casey had a terrible temper.

One time Casey got into an argument with plate umpire George Magerkurth, who had called a balk on him. When play resumed Casey was so angered that he instructed his catcher, Bruce Edwards, to stay low and not move. Casey threw a high fastball right at Magerkurth's mask. A surprised Magerkurth just did jerk his head as the ball whistled past his left ear.

CARL FURILLO: "Casey was basically a nice guy, but sometimes he could be real mean and sarcastic. He was southern, moody. Sarcastic and moody. He'd be friends with you one time, and even if you went out with him the night before, went out to dinner with him or did him a favor, the following day, if things didn't go right on the field, he'd chew you out like you were a piece of dirt.

"And he was one guy who liked to drink. Hell, yeah. We would go to Boston, and he would have a little handbag, and a normal guy would have a little handbag and a toothbrush or maybe a shirt or something. Not him. He'd have two quarts of whiskey in it. If he needed a shirt, he'd buy one up there. Oh, he went through money like water. He always had a pocketful of money. And he used to hang around with the racket boys. I know, 'cause one time I was invited to go to Staten Island for a dinner with the racket boys. Only I didn't know it at the time. They had asked him to bring some ballplayers along, and so he asked me and Bob Ramazzotti and maybe Dick Whitman. So I'm sitting there, and who is sitting next to me but the guy in charge of nickelodeons. A racketeer. Casey was like brothers with them."

* * *

Bill Reddy: "Casey could drink, let me tell you. Casey could drink till it was coming out of his ears, and then he'd bottle it and drink it again.

"One time Hugh was mad. Someone was passing bad checks, forging his name. So me and a friend of mine who knew Hugh went over to Hugh Casey's place and met Casey. He said, 'Let's have a few drinks. Some bum is going around cashing checks, and we'll hit a few places and see if we can catch him.' I said, 'What are you going to do if you do catch him?' Hugh said, 'We'll break his arms or something.' Okay, fine. We started over by Ebbets Field and started visiting bars to see if we could catch the guy. We went down Seventh Avenue and stopped at the Old Reliable. Then we went down Flatbush Avenue to Deron's. As we worked our way downtown, we had a drink or two at each bar. We were coming along Seventh Avenue when I was forced to drop out. I was getting a headache, and I just couldn't go on. I left the two of them.

"Hugh and my friend wound up in a brawl in the Flatlands somewhere. Before the fight ended, Hugh had thrown someone through a plate-glass window of a saloon. But the police didn't arrest him, because he was Hugh Casey.

"The next day was Saturday, and I went out to Ebbets Field. Casey was warming up. I said, 'Hi, Hughie, how'd you make out last night?' He said, 'What the hell is that your business? Who are you?' He didn't even remember me, the bum."

Kirby Higbe: "Hugh was kind of a loner. Outside of me, he didn't care too much about messin' around with other ballplayers, not that he didn't like them. He was just that type of fella. He would go up to his room after a ballgame and read a western magazine or western book and smoke them big cigars. That's about all Hugh would do. And drink. He'd have a few drinks, as most people did back in them days.

"I remember Hugh and I, when we were in spring training in Cuba, we'd go down to the Nacional casino and shoot dice with Ernest Hemingway."

Billy Herman: "Hemingway would come out to the ballpark every day. He liked to hang around with ballplayers, and we got to talking, and he found out Casey liked to hunt and Higbe liked to hunt and I liked to hunt and so did Larry French and Augie Galan, a bunch of us, so one day he invited us out to this gun club to shoot skeet. In Havana you shot at live pigeons, which was unusual. They had a man in a trap underneath the ground, and the man would grab the pigeon and throw it up through the hole in the ground, and it would take off, and to score you had to shoot the pigeon before it got outside a ring drawn on the ground about thirty feet in diameter.

"Ernest wouldn't miss very often. He was a good shot. He belonged to skeet clubs all over the world. Hemingway took a lot of pride in the macho activities, drinking and fighting and shooting. He was a crack shot. Closest one to him among the players was me. I wasn't quite as good a shot as he was. I could give him a fight, but I couldn't beat him.

"We were at the gun club until dark, at which point Hemingway invited us all up to his house. It was up in the hills, overlooking Havana. When we arrived, he excused himself, and then he came back with an enormous silver tray, and on it were bottles, mixers, glasses, ice—everything we needed. He set it up on a little bookstand in the middle of the floor. And we started drinking.

"This was March 1942. Pearl Harbor had been in December, three months before. He had been a war correspondent, and we were questioning him about how bad the war was going to get, and he was pretty accurate in his predictions. He said just about what would happen, which was that Japan would keep moving and moving and moving. And he was a big game hunter, and he was talking about his experiences in Africa, and he also talked about his experiences during the Spanish Civil War.

"We had had quite a bit to drink. He brought out some food. After we ate, we had a few more drinks. It was getting pretty late, and Mrs. Hemingway excused herself and went to bed. By then Hemingway was really loaded.

"Before you knew it, Hemingway was looking over at Hugh Casey, kind of sizing him up. Hemingway had a funny little grin on his face. He said to Hugh, 'You and I are about the same size. I think you and I would make a good match.'

"Hugh Casey was a very quiet man, and he wasn't saying much. Hugh never said much. Casey just grinned.

" 'Come on,' Hemingway said. 'I've got some boxing gloves. Let's just spar. Fool around a bit.'

"Hugh didn't want to, but Ernest kept insisting. Casey grinned and shrugged his shoulders. Hemingway went and got the boxing gloves. He came back and slipped on a pair of gloves and handed Casey the other pair. As Hugh was pulling his gloves on, Hemingway suddenly hauled off and belted him. He knocked Casey into that bookstand, and the tray with all the booze and glasses and ice smashed on the hard marble floor. Hemingway's wife came running out.

" 'What happened?' she asked.

" 'Oh, it's all right, honey,' he said. 'Hughie and I are just having a little fun. You go on back to bed.'

"She looked at him, looked at Hugh, looked at the mess on the floor, and then went back into the bedroom.

"Casey didn't say a thing about the sneak punch. He just got up and finished putting on the gloves. Then they started sparring. Hemingway hadn't bothered to clean up, and as they moved back and forth across the floor, you could hear the broken glass crunching on the marble floor.

"Without saying a single word, Casey started hitting him. Really belting him. Casey knocked him down. Then Casey belted him across some furniture, and there was another crash as Hemingway took a lamp and table down with him. His wife came running out again. Hemingway told her it was all right, to go back to bed, that it was all in fun.

"Hemingway was getting angry. He'd no sooner get up than Hugh would knock him down again. Finally he got up this one time, made a feint with his left hand, and kicked Casey in the balls.

"That's when we figured it had gone far enough. We made them take the gloves off.

" 'Let's have another drink,' Hemingway said.

"We figured it was time for us to leave. We told him we had to be back at the hotel at twelve o'clock.

" 'Well,' he said. 'I'm too drunk to drive you back to Havana. I'll have my chauffeur drive you.'

"Ole Ernest was the type of man who didn't want anyone to get the best of him doing anything, so as we were getting ready to leave for the drive back to the hotel, he pulled Casey aside, and he said, 'Hey look, spend the night with me. You got the best of me. You beat the hell out of me. I was real drunk, but tomorrow morning we'll both be sober, and we'll duel.' He said, 'You pick it. Knives. Guns. Swords. Anything you want. You pick the weapon.' He was dead serious about it. Ernest wanted to kill him.

"We grabbed Casey, ran him out of there, and took him home.

"The next day Ernest came back to the ballpark. His wife made him come. After he slept off his drunkenness, he was a very embarrassed person. He was apologizing all over the place, almost in tears. He said, 'I don't know what got into me.'

"I knew exactly what got into him. About a quart, that's what."

Kirby Higbe: "Ernest was at the ballpark all the time. He was a tough son of a gun. You know when all them bridges were blown up in *For Whom the Bells Tolled*? He said he done it hisself. He said he was writing about hisself blowing up the bridges, not some other guy. I never did read that book. Course he was in that Spanish revolution too. He was just tough. A tough old son of a gun. A big fellow, and quite a writer too. I wish he had been living when I wrote my book, *The High, Hard One*. He could have helped me out. That Ernest, he was some writer.

"And ole Ernest and Casey just hit it off. Those were two of a kind really. Ole Ernest killed hisself. Shot himself in the mouth with a shotgun, just like ole Casey did. I hope I don't do the same thing. You know, ole Ernest and Gary Cooper were great friends, and when Gary died, Ernest killed hisself not long afterward. Always wondered if that had anything to do with it. But Ernest told me and Casey one time that he had seen and done everything in the world. Ole Ernest, I never will forget him. And I never will forget ole Casey. The two of them, they were something."

Al Gionfriddo: "It was such a shame what happened to Hugh. A girl accused him of getting her pregnant. She was a young girl, maybe nineteen or twenty years old. She wasn't a bad-looking girl, but crazy for ballplayers. Shit, she screwed just about every ballplayer in the country. Every time you went into a hotel, whether it was New York or other towns, she was standing in the lobby, waiting for the ballplayers. I remember when I was with Pittsburgh, and we came to New York, the first one you saw was her. And when I was with Montreal, she was there, waiting for the Triple-A players. She loved ballplayers. And at the time Hugh was having problems with his wife. She had left him. They had separated. She didn't want to live in Brooklyn. She wanted to stay in Georgia. But she had come up, and they were having some family problems, and then this girl slapped Hugh with a paternity suit, and his wife found out about it, and that was it for their marriage. Hugh loved Kay so, and it just ate him up inside. And to me it was a tragedy. Because it could have been anybody's baby. At the time he still had his bar and his money, and I guess she figured he was a ripe target. And it was a shame. He was good old country folk. I can still see that big smile and his chaw of tobacco. Hugh was a great guy, he was."

KIRBY HIGBE: "I was playing in the South Atlantic League, 1951, when Hugh died. We wuz in Jacksonville, and a sportswriter from Atlanta called me and said, 'Hig, what do you think?' I said, 'About what?' He said, 'Casey killed hisself in a hotel room in Atlanta.' I said, 'That's hard for me to believe.' But they tell me he killed hisself over his wife, that he was talking to her on the phone when he took a shotgun, put it to his mouth, and throwed his brains right up to the ceiling.

"He wuz always crazy about Kay, but they wuz always fighting, and they were separated, and he asked her if she was coming back, and she just laughed, and he pulled the trigger.

"Casey and I wuz good friends. I was always crazy about ole Casey."

With tough, veteran pitchers like Higbe, Casey, and Fred Fitzsimmons to do Durocher's dirty work, the Dodgers were often involved in beanball wars, and fights on the field were not uncommon. After all, Durocher hadn't a scruple in his body. As a player, he brought whatever tricks he knew, dirty or otherwise, with him. As a manager, he made a science out of dirty play, and his most effective weapon was the beanball. It was Durocher's style of play, what Leo expected of his men. His pitchers would throw at your head and keep throwing at your head until you either became intimidated or you threw back at his batters and forced him to stop. In 1942 six of the other seven National League teams complained to Commissioner Landis that the Dodger pitchers were headhunters. Leo was warned, but the beanballs continued.

In other ways Durocher would take advantage when he could get away with it. He would razz you until you were ready to charge into the Dodger dugout and hit him with a bat. He never actually uttered the lines, "Nice guys finish last," but it became part of his legend and certainly was his credo. Leo was not a nice guy, and he wasn't shy about admitting it. Meanwhile, around the league, everyone hated Durocher and the Dodgers. The veterans on the team loved playing for him.

KIRBY HIGBE: "Leo was a typical Dodger, and one of the best managers I've ever seen. If his mother was playing shortstop and he was going down to break up the double play, he says he'd cut her legs off, and I believe him. He wanted to win that bad, and that's the only way to play. I know when I was on the Phils, we'd get our brains beat out and then go over and congratulate somebody that whipped you bad, and I never believed in that. Leo didn't either. He'd say, 'Don't fraternize on the field. If you all are going out for a steak after the game, okay, take 'em, but not during the ballgame. During the game, don't talk to them.' And he was right, of course. Leo wouldn't tell us to throw at batters, but what he'd say was, 'Don't let them take the bread and butter out of your mouth.' You knew what he meant."

In one game Dodger pitcher Les Webber hit every batter in the Cardinal lineup. In retaliation to Durocher's antagonistic approach, opposing pitchers threw beanballs that struck down both Pee Wee Reese and Pete Reiser in 1940, Mickey Owen in 1941, and Dolph Camilli twice in 1942.

Durocher would sit in the dugout, poised for a fight. Before one game, during batting practice, the Dodgers' Dixie Walker and the Cubs' shortstop, Lennie Merullo, exchanged words and then started punching, and Leo stepped on the top step of the Dodger dugout and yelled, "Charge," as the entire Dodger team raced onto the field to engage in a brawl before maybe 600 early birds. There was no umpire to break it up, no league officials. Just two teams in a mass brawl.

At the slightest hint of a faulty decision by an umpire, Durocher would streak onto the field to antagonize the men in blue. He also persisted as a master bench jockey.

One time in Chicago, Durocher began riding the Cubs' starting pitcher, Claude Passeau, a large, mean man. Passeau couldn't figure out who was doing the razzing, and he was becoming unglued, and after yet another blast from Durocher, he threw down his glove and began walking toward the dugout. Passeau shouted, "The guy who made the last crack doesn't have the guts to come out and back it up." When he heard this, Durocher said to outfielder Joe Gallagher, "Joe, get out there and hit." Gallagher went over to the bat rack, picked up a bat and walked out of the dugout just as Passeau was coming by. Passeau swung at him, and of course, Gallagher had no idea why. Both got thrown out of the game, much to the Dodgers' advantage.

On the Cubs' next trip into Brooklyn, Passeau finally learned that it was Durocher who had been riding him. Warming up on the mound before the start of the game, Passeau wound up and from the mound fired a fastball into the Dodger dugout inches from Durocher's head.

Sometimes Durocher would antagonize his own players. An outspoken critic, he would give his critique of a particular player on the bench in front of everyone. The following was directed to a Dodger runner on first base after Durocher had given him the steal sign:

> Go on, run. My God, what are you standing there for? Run, or lay down and die. Why, he's paralyzed. That man's paralyzed. No, he's going backward. Well, finally. Whoa, whoa, whoa, WHOA. Get back on that bag, you ignorant dummy. Of all the bonehead—wait a minute. What in hell are they trying to pull out there? Out? The hell he was out.

He turned to a coach. "Hold this paper," he said. And with that out of the dugout he raced to argue another call.

* * *

His own players often hated Durocher. Ironically, when the Dodgers lost, Durocher would be cordial and pleasant. But after the Dodgers won a game, he could be very bad to be around. He was apt to pick out a particular play he didn't like and strike out at the offending player.

During one victory pitcher Bobo Newsom threw a spitter, surprising catcher Bobby Bragan, who allowed a passed ball on the pitch. In the clubhouse after the game, with writer Tim Cohane standing there, Durocher cornered Newsom, accused him of trying to show up Bragan, who was a favorite of Durocher's, and suspended him. Cohane wrote this in an article, and when the other players read it, they mutinied. The next day veteran Arky Vaughan threw his uniform at Durocher's feet and yelled, "If that's the way you're running this ballclub, you can have my uniform." Dixie Walker offered his too. The other players glared at Leo from their lockers. Durocher, in his defense, scurried to find a scapegoat and placed the blame directly on the shoulders of the writer, Cohane, who he shamelessly told the players was "a liar."

In a face to face meeting in front of all the players, Cohane backed Durocher down and got him to admit that the story was true. Newsom turned to Leo and said, "Yesterday you told the players you didn't say it."

Durocher replied lamely, "You know how you talk to a ballplayer." Then as a salve he told Newsom, "I said I was going to suspend you for the season, but you only got three days, didn't you?"

Newsom turned and walked away disgusted.

BILLY HERMAN: "I didn't like Leo. He didn't treat all the players the same. He played favorites. He wasn't trustworthy; too often he didn't tell you the truth, and he would do everything he could to protect himself, no matter what it did to you.

"One day we were playing the Giants in Brooklyn. This was 1943. Some of our better players had gone into the service, and I had become the fourth-place hitter. It was the sixth inning or so, and we loaded the bases with one out, trailing by a run or two. I came up. The count went to two and nothing, and when I looked down at Charley Dressen, the third-base coach, he was giving me the take sign! I don't know what was going through his mind, because you don't order a take in a situation like that. But the sign was there, and I had to take. It was a strike. The next pitch was outside, and now it was three and one. I looked down at Dressen, and again he was flashing a take sign. By this time I was boiling. I was hitting around .330, and he'd got me batting fourth, and he's taking the bat out of my hands. So I took again, and it was a strike. Full count. The next pitch came in, and with both runners running, I hit a line shot right at the third baseman for a double play. The inning's over, and we didn't score, and now I'm really mad. I'm furious.

"I went out to my position, and Camilli was rolling the ball around the infield to us. He threw it to me, and I picked it up, and before making the throw, in the dugout I could see Durocher sitting on the bench with his chin in his hand, looking down. I don't know what possessed me—I was tempo-

Dodgers

rarily mad—but instead of throwing to Camilli, I fired it toward the dugout as hard as I could. I had a good, accurate arm. It skipped off the grass in front of the dugout and hit Durocher square in the forehead. Down he went, headfirst, onto the floor of the dugout. I tell you, I made one hell of a throw!

"Albie Glossop, who was playing shortstop, yelled over to me, 'Goddamn, you hit Durocher. Right between the eyes.'

"I said, 'That's exactly what I was trying to do.'

"I figured I was in for a healthy fine, but Leo never said a word.

"At the end of that season I went into the service, and I didn't return for almost three years. It was spring training of '46, and Leo was fooling around with Herman Franks. They were always buddy buddy. Herman said to Leo, 'Do you remember the time you were sitting on the bench and someone threw the ball and hit you between the eyes?'

"All Durocher said was, 'Yeah, that goddamned Herman.' Other than that he never said a word. How do you figure a guy like that?"

The Fans

Under MacPhail and Durocher, the Dodgers finally became a team deserving of its loyal and worshipful fans, many of whom had been waiting since the early 1920s for the Dodgers to once again become competitive. Charley Ebbets had always thought first of the fans, but when he died in 1925, though the fans stuck by their team through thin and thin, management hadn't reciprocated. The players, however, recognized that the Brooklyn fans were special, and often they went out of their way to show their appreciation.

It was before the days of television, before the players became celebrities. Their feats were legendary, but their faces were not familiar except to those who saw them on the field in the park, and so they could venture into the public without being afraid. There was an informal, nonprofessional quality to Ebbets Field and the Dodgers. It was very personal. The fans loved the players. The players loved the fans. All a player had to do was walk out onto the field, and the fans would begin waving at him and hollering to be waved back at, and they would throw down little vials of holy water and religious medals, and when a ballplayer had a birthday, there would always be one or two homemade cakes in the clubhouse for him.

In Ebbets Field there might be 5,000 fans in the park, but it would sound like ten times as many. Five fanatical fans that made up the Dodger Symphony would play and dance on top of the dugout and walk through the stands playing their ragtime music, and when the umps came out before the game, they would play "Three Blind Mice," until the year when the National League added a fourth umpire to the crew, lousing up their little joke. If an opposing pitcher was knocked out, the symphony would razz him by playing, "The Worms Crawl In, the Worms Crawl Out," and they would wait for an opposing batter who made out to return to the dugout and sit down, and just as that player's backside would touch the bench, the cymbal from the symphony would crash, and the Dodger fans would applaud and chuckle at the player's embarrassment.

It was all so spontaneous. These were not people sent by P.R. agents to dress in chicken costumes to manufacture support. These were fans who bought their tickets and went to the games for the sheer love of rooting. Never had there been such involvement. Today, some clubs have Camera Day. On that day you can have your picture taken with your favorite player. But how often can a fan actually go down and shake a player's hand? At Ebbets Field before each game, the fans would line up along the railing, and the players would walk along and shake hands with everybody and sign autographs and chat about that afternoon's game. For many of the fans, the Dodgers became part of their family. And every once in a while, the Dodgers made a fan part of theirs.

IRVING RUDD: "I remember when I was a kid, I used to major in hooky. I would run off to the ballpark at the drop of a hat. And one day, when I was twelve years old, I was standing outside the ballpark, and a Dodger pitcher by the name of Clise Dudley came by, and he recognized me, because I was always hanging around the park. He said, 'How ya'll doin', son?' I said, 'Fine, Clise.' He said, 'Ya'll goin' to the game today?' I said, 'I'm trying to get a job on the turnstile. If you work four innings, they let you in to watch the game.' 'Come with me,' Dudley said, and he walked me right into the ballpark.

"Another day I was hanging around outside the ballpark, holding my scrapbook under my arm, when Al Lopez came out of the clubhouse. He was a kid catcher, about twenty years old, and he's got with him a guy by the name of Hollis Thurston, who had been a good pitcher with the White Sox, and a guy by the name of Louis "Buck" Newsom, who was Bobo later, Jake Flowers, and Clise. I'm standing there in my knickers, and Lopez says to me, 'Hey kid, how 'bout going to dinner with us?' I said, 'Gee, I have to ask my mother.' He said, 'Give her a call.' Who had a phone in those days? A phone in Brownsville? I told him we didn't have a phone. They asked me where I lived, and I told them, 'Powell Street in Brownsville,' and Lopez said, 'We'll drop you off on the way home. You ask your mother.' And he added, 'Wash your face, too, and put another pair of pants on.' I was a sloppy kid in those days.

"So we got into the car, and I sat on Newsom's lap, and they drove me to Brownsville.

"I went upstairs, and my mother came down to say hello. 'Take care of my son,' she says. They say, 'Sure, Mom, don't worry about it.' And they took me to a Spanish restaurant near the St. George Hotel. Lopez knew about this joint. I had *arroz con pollo*. And after they fed me, they brought me back to the hotel, and we sat around till midnight bullshitting about baseball. And then they brought me home.

"It was so different then. I remember going up to Dazzy Vance when he was leaving the ballpark. I said, 'Hey Daz, that pitch you threw in the ninth inning . . .' He said, 'Kid, let me tell you about it. Now, you got a guy like

Hack Wilson playing against you . . .' and as we walked, we talked about the game. And that's the way it was then."

If the young fans were polite and mannerly, the players were not reluctant to take the time to talk baseball with them.

LARRY KING: "My friends and I weren't among the autograph hounds. We were questioners. We would wait around after the game for the players to come out, and as they walked to the subway or to their cars, we would run along the streets with them and question them about the game. We were intensely curious. 'Hey Dixie, what was it like to end the ninth inning?' Dumb questions, I suppose, but in general the players were responsive.

"I once ran along the street with Pee Wee Reese for four blocks. I wanted to ask him about bunting, because he bunted differently from the rest of the guys. He had a quick bunt, didn't square as much, and I asked him about that, and he told me it was the way he had learned it from the guy who taught him in high school. I asked him if he really got his name Pee Wee because he was a marble player. 'Is the marble story true?' I asked him. 'Yeah,' he said. 'It's true. I was the marble champion of Louisville, and Pee Wee was my shooter. I didn't use an immie. I used a Pee Wee.'

"That was fascinating to me."

The Brooklyn fans weren't nearly as considerate of the opposing players as they were of their beloved Dodgers, and the opposing players didn't always appreciate the fanaticism of the Dodger rooters.

BOBBY MCCARTHY: "I remember a game with the Boston Braves. They had an outfielder by the name of Jim Russell, a good ballplayer, kind of a mediocre hitter. It was 4–4, top of the ninth, bases loaded, the Braves are up, and they pinch hit Russell. I'm in the bleachers in Ebbets Field with my sandwiches and my Yankee Doodles, and it's the ninth inning, so the food's gone by now, and Russell gets up and hits a grand slammer.

"I'm ten years old, and I was a terrible sore loser. So I get up to leave, and I run out of the ballpark, and I guess Russell, being a pinch hitter, they let him go home early, so here I am walking out the ballpark, and out of the side door comes a ballplayer. So I run up to him, and I hand him my scorecard and I say, 'Are you a ballplayer?' He says, 'Yeah.' I say, 'Would you sign your autograph?' and so he signs it. And you know the way players are. I couldn't read it. I looked at it, and I said, 'Who are you?' He said, 'I'm Jim Russell.' And I yelled, 'Here, take it back.' And I threw it at him.

"You should have seen the look on Jim Russell's face."

JOHN BELSON: "The native Brooklyn kids were incredible with the ballplayers coming out of the park. 'Hey, mister, gimme your autograph. Gimme your autograph. Gimme your autograph.' And the players would sign for a while, and as soon as they stopped, the kid they stopped with would lay on the most vituperative, 'Ya no fucking good. Ya did it for him, ya won't do it for me.'

"Phil Cavarretta came out of the park on a day when he went something like 6 for 8 in a doubleheader, and the Cubs had managed to lose both games in the ninth inning. Lost both games. And Cavarretta did not feature losing. And these kids came at him. Several Cub players were walking virtually in a convoy, and he was at the head of it, and he kept saying, 'Nothing, nothing, nothing.' He had on a black hat, black shirt, white tie. And the face on him—in his youth he had his jaw set in a line and his eyes fierced up—he looked like a hit man. And he reached the top of the stairs of the subway on his way down, and with these Oliver Twist, Faganish kids hanging around him, one of them called him a 'Guinea fuck,' and *badoom,* he pushed the kid right down the subway stairs. *Zoom.* It looked like Richard Widmark with the lady in the wheelchair. Cavarretta screamed after him, 'Go suck your mother's tit, you little whoremaster.' But those kids were like wire. It didn't make any difference. You couldn't hurt them."

The Dodger fans were part of the show, part of the sights and sounds that made Ebbets Field so special. Some of those fans became almost as renowned as the players they came to watch. The other Dodger fans may not have known their names, but they could count on them being there and adding to the noise and craziness.

Among the regulars was a man by the name of Eddie Battan. Eddie was known for his tin whistle. Wherever Eddie sat, throughout the stadium, you could hear a "peep, peep, peep, peep," and it would be Eddie. All through the game, you could hear that peculiar tinny sound of "peep, peep, peep, peep, peep."

Another of the Dodger regulars was a man known for screaming, "Coooookie, Cooooookie, Coooookie," in adulation of his hero, third baseman Cookie Lavagetto. Few knew that his name was Jack Pierce, and at every game Pierce would buy three seats, one for himself, one for a friend, and one for his balloons, which were his trademark.

COOKIE LAVAGETTO: "Jack Pierce was part owner of Lottie and Jack's restaurant close by where I lived, right there by the St. George Hotel. Jack was Jack of Lottie and Jack. I lived in a small hotel about a block away, and I ate at his restaurant practically every day.

"Jack Pierce used to bring the balloons with my name on them into his box along with his bartender. At first he blew up the balloons himself, but then he started bringing a blower, usually the bartender, and then finally he found out about gas.

"The balloons he filled up himself would fly around inside the ballpark, and there were complaints about that. But when he got his gas, the balloons would go straight up.

"Besides the balloons, he put out cards, 'Cookie for President. Always good in the clutch.' He also put out a newspaper. Christ, he spent a fortune out there every day."

The most famous of the Dodger fans—perhaps the most famous fan in baseball history—was named Hilda Chester, a plump, pink-faced woman with a mop of stringy gray hair. Hilda began her thirty-year love affair with the Dodgers in the 1920s. She had been a softball star as a kid, or so she said, and she once told a reporter that her dream was to play in the big leagues or to start a softball league for women. Thwarted as an athlete, she turned to rooting. As a teenager she would stand outside the offices of the *Brooklyn Chronicle* every day, waiting to hear the Dodger score. After a while she became known to the sportswriters, who sometimes gave her passes to the games. In her twenties Hilda worked as a peanut sacker for the Stevens Brothers, Harry, George, and Frank, who owned most of the concession stands across the country. In those days peanuts came in fifty-pound sacks, and it was her job to put the peanuts into the individual bags before the ballgame. She enjoyed most sports, including horse racing, and in her capacity as peanut sacker she was able to work and attend the Dodger games. By the 1930s she was attending games regularly, screaming lustily, one of hundreds of Ebbets Field regulars.

Shortly after suffering a heart attack, she began her rise to fame. Her physician forbade her from yelling, and when she was sufficiently recovered, she returned to Ebbets Field with a frying pan and an iron ladle. Banging away on the frying pan from her seat in the bleachers, she made so much noise that everyone, including the players, noticed her. It was the Dodger players in the late 1930s who presented Hilda Chester with the first of her now-famous brass cowbells.

In 1941 Hilda suffered a second heart attack, and when she entered the hospital this time, she was an important enough personality that Durocher and several of the players went to visit her. As a result Durocher became Hilda's special hero, and by the mid-1940s she was almost the team mascot. Sometimes during short road trips, Hilda even went with the team. Hilda loved Leo, and when Durocher struck a Dodger fan with brass knuckles and was sued, Hilda perjured herself in court, trying to trump up a reasonable explanation for Leo's barbarity. "This man called me a cocksucker," she lied to the judge, "and Leo came to my defense."

During the games Hilda lived in the bleacher seats with her bell. Durocher had given her a lifetime pass to the grandstand, but she preferred sitting in the bleachers with her entourage of fellow rowdies. With her fish peddler voice, she'd say, "You know me. Hilda wit da bell. Ain't it trillin'? Home wuz never like dis, mac." When disturbed her favorite line was, "Eacha heart out, ya bum."

One night in Philadelphia, where she had faithfully followed the Dodgers, a local fan began criticizing Dixie Walker, calling him a has-been. "You're all through!" the Philly fan shouted.

"Oh yeah?" Hilda yelled at him, pointing to Walker in right field. "Look where he is, and look where you are."

Hilda had a voice that could be heard all over the park. It stood out above all the other voices, and the players could hear her raspy call followed by the clanging of her cowbell all through a game. At least once Hilda even was involved in a game's outcome.

PETE REISER: "I remember one time, it was in either '41 or '42, we were in the seventh inning of a game. I was going to take my position in center field, and I hear that voice: 'Hey, Reiser!' It was Hilda. There could be 30,000 people there yelling at once, but Hilda was the one you'd hear. I look up, and she's dropping something onto the grass. 'Give this note to Leo,' she yells. So I pick it up and put it in my pocket. At the end of the inning I start heading in.

"Now MacPhail used to sit in a box right next to the dugout, and for some reason he waved to me as I came in, and I said, 'Hi, Larry,' as I went into the dugout. I gave Hilda's note to Leo and sat down. Next thing I know he's getting somebody hot in the bullpen; I think it was Casey. Meanwhile, Wyatt's pitching a hell of a ballgame for us. In the next inning, the first guy hits the ball pretty good and goes out. The next guy gets a base hit. Here comes Leo. He takes Wyatt out and brings in Casey. Casey got rocked a few times, and we just did win the game, just did win it.

"Leo had this rule that after a game you didn't take off your uniform until he said so. Usually he didn't invoke it unless we'd lost a tough one. But this day, he goes into his office and slams the door without a word. We're all sitting there waiting for him to come out. Finally the door opens and out he comes. He points to me.

" 'Don't you ever give me another note from MacPhail as long as you play for me.'

"I said, 'I didn't give you any note from MacPhail.'

" 'Don't tell me!' he yells. 'You handed me a note in the seventh inning.'

" 'That was from Hilda,' I said.

" 'From Hilda?' he screams. I thought he was going to turn purple. 'You mean to say that wasn't from MacPhail?'

"I hadn't even looked at the note, just handed it to him. Leo had heard me say something to MacPhail when I came in and figured the note was from Larry. It seems what the note said was: 'Get Casey hot. Wyatt's losing it.' So what you had was somebody named Hilda Chester sitting in the center-field bleachers changing pitchers for you."

The Gold Dust Twins

It is certainly true that the Dodgers had their share of bad luck over their history, but they twice caught lightning in a bottle.

In 1941 the Dodgers' two leading everyday players were two kids who made the team only because lady luck had been shining on Brooklyn: shortstop Pee Wee Reese, who the Red Sox never should have let get away, and outfielder Pete Reiser, who would have been a Cardinal but for the controversial ruling by Commissioner Landis.

Reese had been a spectacular minor league infielder, both fast and quick, with great range, poise, and maturity. He had been only a fair hitter, but his fielding was so outstanding that there was little question that he would be an instant sensation in the big leagues. Playing for Louisville, Reese should have been the anchor of the Boston Red Sox infield for years to come. Fortunately for Brooklyn, events combined to send Reese to the Dodgers.

PEE WEE REESE: "I was born on a farm between two small towns called Bradingberg and Ekron, about fifty miles from Louisville. I've always said I was born in Ekron, but I wasn't really. I'm not sure what town it was. But I moved off the farm at age seven. It was 1925, and at the time farming was difficult. We grew tobacco, some corn, just something to survive on. We were very poor, five children, trying to make a living on not too good of a farm.

"When we moved to Louisville, my dad did odd jobs. Worked for the Ford Motor Company. Course, my dad had no education. Of the children, I was the only one graduated from high school. There was not a lot of education in my family. It was the early '30s, the Depression years, and he took any kind of job he could get. We all worked. I worked selling box lunches, and I delivered papers. My sisters, who were younger than I was, they worked. You could work then at any age, and they worked for the telephone company, and we all lived together and threw the money into the pot.

"When I got out of high school in 1936, jobs were tough to get, and I worked in a furniture company and Mengel Box Company, making twenty-five cents an hour, and you worked ten hours a day, which added up to $2.50. And then I went to work for the telephone company, and I got a big raise to $18 a week. I was an apprentice cable splicer.

"When I finally decided to go and play ball in 1938, the man who got me the job at the telephone company said to me, 'Pee Wee, I think you're making a big mistake by quitting your job and going away to play baseball.' I said, 'Mr. Lane, I'm young. I may as well give it a shot.' And thank heavens I did.

"I had only played five games my senior year in high school. I was not large enough. Hell, when I graduated, I was about five foot four and weighed 120 pounds. I played ball for my church team, the New Covenant Presbyterian Church, and we won the city championship in 1937, and we won a trip to the 1937 World Series. A man by the name of Captain Neal, who was the general manager of the Louisville Colonels, which was a Double-A ball team, evidently noticed me, and he asked me if I wanted to play professional ball.

"And I was fortunate it wasn't a good club. It was independently owned, so consequently we didn't have too many good players, so I got to stay with the team and play. So sometimes it helps to be in the right place at the right time.

"I played for this 1938 club, and the next year the team was purchased by Donie Bush and Frank McKinney, and we had a working agreement with the Boston Red Sox. In '39 they brought up players from the Red Sox, so we ended up that year with a pretty good ballclub. In fact we ended up winning the Little World Series.

"And at this point I thought I was going directly to the Red Sox. No question. Bobby Doerr, the Red Sox second baseman, told me he was looking forward to it. Joe Cronin was the manager and the shortstop and getting older, and Bobby figured I would be there.

"Supposedly Bush and McKinney bought the Colonels just so they could acquire my contract, and having a working agreement with the Red Sox, Boston had first choice if they wanted me. But evidently Mr. Cronin thought he could play a few more years, and he talked them out of buying me, and Bush and McKinney sold me to the Brooklyn Dodgers in 1939 for $75,000.

"I was very disappointed. It was July, and I was going to an all-star game in Kansas City, the American Association all-stars against the Kansas City Royals, who were leading the league at that point, and I was on the train, and one of the Louisville writers told me that I had been sold to Brooklyn. I said something like, 'Gee Christmas, that's the last place in the world I'd want to go to. All you ever read about is guys getting hit in the head by fly balls, three guys ending up on one base.' I told them, 'I don't want to go there.' Which was kind of a stupid thing for me to say. It didn't go over too well in Brooklyn.

"I didn't go with the Dodgers until spring training of 1940. We were training in Clearwater, and I weighed all of 155 pounds soaking wet. Looking like I was sixteen, I guess. When I got there, I didn't know any of the fellas on the team, and I was scared to death. But within a few days, Dolph Camilli, Harry Lavagetto, and Pete Coscarart, which was the whole infield, made me feel at home. Wherever they went, they took me with them. Why did they do it? Beats the hell out of me. I was just a scared kid from Kentucky, and these guys had been up in the majors for a while. I guess it was because I was just such a helluva nice kid—if you'll accept that.

"When I got there, Leo at this time was thirty-five or so, and he was managing, and he probably wanted somebody to take his place. But I got hit in the head by Jake Mooty of the Cubs, and I was in the hospital for eighteen days.

"In those days people used to sit in the bleachers in center field, and it was a warm, summer July day, a lot of white shirts out there, and the place was packed. Mooty released the ball, and I never saw it. I never thought anyone could hit me in the head, but he did.

"And then after I came back, in August I slid into second base and broke a bone in my ankle, so I was out for the rest of the year. So I only played eighty-four games my first year.

"When I opened the 1941 season with a brace on my ankle, it got me to wondering, because it was a tough year. We won the pennant, and I guess I contributed something, but I didn't have too good a year. I was having problems at bat and in the field, and it got to where I didn't feel too easy in the games. But naturally, I would never ask out of the lineup, though Larry MacPhail was pressuring Leo to take me out, and he did for one game. But Leo hadn't played for a while, and it was tough on him. Leo had a little trouble with a fly ball, going back over his head, and he decided he better put me back in the lineup. In spite of me, we won the pennant."

"Pee Wee" Reese

BILL REDDY: "There wasn't much that Durocher could teach Pee Wee. I remember a story I heard in a gin mill. A guy had been talking to Durocher about Reese, and Durocher started laughing. He said that Pee Wee had come over to him to ask for advice. Leo figured to himself, 'Finally the kid was coming over to the old master to ask him about playing shortstop.' Leo said, 'Sure Pee Wee, what do you want to know?' Reese said, 'Skip, where do you buy your clothes?'

"They talk about the great shortstops. There was Honus Wagner and Marty Marion, Phil Rizzuto and Luke Appling, but Reese is right up there with them, and nobody gives Pee Wee the credit they should. He was a great shortstop and a forceful leader on the diamond. He was the best at turning his back to the plate and going out into short left field for a fly ball. And Reese could make the plays look so easy.

"Durocher would hit infield practice, third to first, short to first, second to first, and with an eye toward the crowd, Durocher would always end the infield practice by stationing Reese in the hole and then hitting a grass-cutter over second base. Reese would run from near third base, his glove hand down on the ground, and he'd grab the damn ball and pick it up and flip it over to first base. He was a joy to watch."

The Dodgers' second joy to watch, twenty-two-year-old Pete Reiser, had by 1941 become the magnificent performer that first Rickey and then Durocher had predicted. He ran the bases with abandon, led the league in hitting at .343, covered the outfield like a blanket, and created tremendous excitement with his daring play.

During the 1940 season, MacPhail had still been trying to cover Reiser up in Elmira so he could return him to St. Louis at the end of the year. But by June of 1940, Reiser was hitting .378, stealing bases, creating excitement with his hell-bent, daredevil style of play. His manager, Bill Killefer, could not understand what the boy was doing in the minors. Like Durocher, Killefer knew talent, and he knew that Reiser belonged in the big leagues. Like Durocher, Killefer had befriended the immensely talented Reiser, who had languished in the minors while he was with the Cardinals. Landis had freed him just for that reason.

Killefer threatened MacPhail that if he didn't bring Reiser to the Dodgers, he would personally sell Reiser to a major league team, even if MacPhail forbade him from doing so. Against the wall, MacPhail was forced to call Rickey and tell him he could no longer protect the boy. Rickey and MacPhail had already worked out the deal that would return Reiser to St. Louis. Reiser and three minor leaguers would be sent to Rickey in exchange for all-star outfielder Joe Medwick. Yet MacPhail knew there was no way he could trade Reiser without serious repercussions in Brooklyn and elsewhere. "They'd lynch me here if I traded Reiser away even up for Medwick right now," MacPhail told Rickey. "Durocher has talked too much, and the reporters have written every word. The fans here are so excited about the kid that there would be a scandal. I just can't give him back to you."

And Rickey was forced to agree. Neither executive could afford scrutiny

Pete Reiser

of their clandestine dealings. But Rickey was not going to give Reiser away. He wanted big money. And so MacPhail kept Reiser and shipped the three minor leaguers plus outfielder Ernie Koy to St. Louis for Medwick and pitcher Curt Davis. And as payment for keeping Reiser, MacPhail threw in an astronomical $250,000. It was an expenditure the press and, more important, the Dodger board members could not understand. And of course MacPhail could not reveal to them the real reason why he was doing it.

When Reiser came up to the Dodgers in 1940, Durocher intended him to be an infielder. When Pee Wee Reese broke an ankle, Durocher moved him to short. Then when Cookie Lavagetto's appendix burst, he moved him to third, where he might well have been the best third baseman in the league. In fifty-eight games, Reiser hit .293 and scored thirty-four times, and at age twenty-one, looked to be a star for many years to come.

Then in 1941, in a touch of inspiration, Durocher moved the multifaceted Reiser onto the pastures of center field.

With Reese and Reiser in the field and Higbe and Casey on the mound, the Dodgers seemed headed for their first pennant since 1920. Their rivals were the St. Louis Cardinals, the remnants of the Gas House Gang of the '30s. Led by Stan Musial, Enos Slaughter, Marty Marion, and some excellent pitchers, the Dodgers and Cardinals fought for pennants all through the 1940s.

KIRBY HIGBE: "I think during the 1940s, us and the Cardinals wuz a bigger rivalry than the Giants wuz. We used to fight the Cardinals all the time. One time we got in a free-for-all with the Cardinals. I ran out there, got hit from behind, and I didn't know who the hell hit me. Old Mort Cooper was a pretty good pitcher. So was Ernie White. And Howie Pollet was a good one. And of course, they had Musial and Slaughter, and Terry Moore was the best center fielder I ever seen. He played right behind second base, and he'd go back and git 'em off the wall.

"I tell ya, we had some pretty good battles."

With time running out in the '41 season, the Dodgers and the Cardinals battled into the final day.

LEO DUROCHER: "We played a doubleheader in Philly the Sunday before the final game, and we won the first game easy and I was all set to let Curt Davis go in the second one, when MacPhail came in the clubhouse and asked: 'Who yuh workin' this game . . . Luke Hamlin?' I said, 'No, Davis,' and he didn't say nothin' and walked out.

"Well, I got thinkin' about Davis and Hamlin and whipsawin' myself and finally wound up with Hamlin, and Litwhiler hit a homer off him with the bags loaded in the first inning, and we blew it. I was afraid to shave that night because I couldn't stop shakin' and finally I went to a barber and I thought of Casey Stengel as I got in the chair; the time he dropped two in one afternoon, walked into a shop, sat down and told the barber:

" 'Once over and never mind cutting my throat. I may do that myself later in the evening.'

"That just shows you how things were going when we got to Boston for the final two games. We won the first, thanks to Dixie Walker's three-run triple in the eighth, and that only made things worse. I didn't close an eye all night. Pee Wee Reese had booted one to give Boston the lead, and I lay awake wondering if maybe I hadn't better take him out the next day and play myself. I got up outta bed four times . . . the last time at a quarter after 5 . . . and made out different lineups. Finally, I just stayed up.

"Oh, how the morning dragged. Every time I picked up a paper I read where if we won and the Cards lost, we were 'in' and then I'd have more coffee. It was a helluva relief to get into the uniforms; just putting it on seemed to quiet me a little, and I'd keep telling myself, 'What you worryin' for? Whitlow Wyatt's pitching, and he's been beating these mugs five straight times. He'll handcuff 'em.' I remember as we were walkin' out on the field, ole Whitlow came by and maybe he figured the skipper could stand some cheering up, and he put his hand on my shoulder and said: 'Get me one run today. They won't score.' That's all.

"We got him the run right off the bat. Walker singled, went to third on two infield outs and then Medwick topped a ball toward third. I saw it might be a hard play for Tom Earley, the Boston pitcher, and hollered to Joe: 'Run for your life.' I thought afterward that must have sounded funny as hell, because what else would he do, but anyway, he beat the play by a step and Walker came home. In the next inning Owen was on second with two out and took third as Dixie singled again, too short for Mickey to score. But Walker got himself trapped off first and maneuvered around long enough to let Owen score before he was caught.

"I was feeling a little better by then, and so help me if that Rowell, at second, didn't make three straight errors in the third and give us another run. You'd a thought those guys were winning the pennant. They were so damn anxious to beat us, like everyone else in the league, and they blew up. He kicked Camilli's grounder, just an easy roller, and then threw it away, and he fell all over Medwick's ball and Dolph scored from second. About the time Reiser hit a homer in the seventh to make the score 5 to 0, the guys in the press box were hollerin' down that the Cards were losing 3 to 1, and somebody on our bench let out a yip, and I shut him up. It was too soon to shake hands with ourselves.

"In the eighth Rowell got the fourth hit off Wyatt, and they sent up Frank Demaree to pinch hit. He was ready, and he hit one. I can close my eyes now and see Billy Herman going for that ball.

"He made the goddamnest stop I've seen in many a day. He just dove, almost full length, after it and still kept his feet. That was the end. We were home. I started to laugh, like a kid who knows Santa Claus is coming that night. Wyatt went through the motions in the ninth, and we carried him into the clubhouse. It's funny to see big, swearing men cry, but they did. Everybody was tired and worn and happy!"

But the day wasn't over for Durocher. One more time, he incurred MacPhail's wrath, and once again he was "fired."

Whitlow Wyatt

LEO DUROCHER: "That ride to New York was something! We had a special train. We drank up $1,400 worth of beer, Scotch, and champagne on the trip. Tony Martin, the movie guy, got up to make a speech, and somebody hit him smack in the face with a hot steak. The gang yelled, 'Sit down, ya bum, this isn't your party,' and from then on it was a riot.

"At New Haven the conductor got a wire from MacPhail telling him he'd board the train at 125th Street in New York. I didn't know anything about a wire, but the conductor came to me and asked if we wanted to stop there. I told him no. We knew there'd be a mob in Grand Central Station and some of the fellows wanted to get off at 125th and slip home, but I vetoed that. I told them: 'I don't care if they tear your clothes off. We belong to those fans. They've been waiting twenty-one years for this chance to celebrate, and we've gotta go through with it. There'll be no stop.'

"We went right on through. MacPhail was standing on the platform with Sam Breadon and Branch Rickey. They were on their way to see Rochester in the playoffs. We passed 'em up, just like that, went roaring right on, and I got a glimpse of MacPhail, and I said to myself, 'Oh, oh, there'll be hell to pay about this.' There was. I met him in a Hotel New Yorker elevator. He never said a word. Didn't congratulate me or the team or a thing; just looked at me. We got off at the same floor, walked into the same suite together, never talked.

"People began to come in and he called me into another room. Still didn't say anything about the pennant. 'Why didn't you have the train stopped at 125th?' he shot at me. I told him I didn't know he'd sent a wire. I told him why we decided to go on through, so the players wouldn't get off. He was plenty mad. Told me I might have called him up and asked and a lot of junk and finally I said I was runnin' the team, not the fucking train, and he barked back, 'Well, you're not even runnin' the team any longer. You're fired!'

"So I said, 'All right,' and walked out and went up to my own room. Somebody sent up word the newsreel men were waiting below, and I refused to come down. I never did, either. They had to use Joe Medwick, and I never saw the pictures afterward. Maybe they didn't use 'em. I stayed where I was and finally went to bed. I was so tired I coulda slept standin' up. About 3 o'clock in the morning, the phone rang. It was MacPhail.

" 'You comin' by the office in the morning?' he asked.

"Twice as mad now, because I'd been asleep, I yelled into the phone, 'What for, to get my money?' and hung up. In about two minutes it rang again.

" 'No,' he said, 'I want to talk over some things about the Series with you.' I said, 'Okay,' and went back to sleep."

The 1941 World Series began rather routinely, with Dodger pitcher Curt Davis losing to the Yankee's Red Ruffing 3–2 in the first game, and then Wyatt beating Spud Chandler 3–2 in the second. In Game Three Durocher sent forty-year-old Fred Fitzsimmons against Yankee pitcher Marius Russo. It was to be the first of two consecutive dark and gloomy days for the Dodgers and their fans. The fates were churning a conspiracy against the Dodgers.

B
Fred Fitzsimmons
Dodgers

BILLY HERMAN: "We were taking batting practice before the third game in Brooklyn. I was practicing hitting the ball to right field, and on my last cut I took a lousy swing at a pitch and tore a rib-cage muscle. I was trying to hit it to right field, and the ball was way inside, and I was a little off-balance, and I went ahead and swung, and when I did, the pain just rushed into me. I could hardly breathe. I went into the clubhouse, and they taped me up, but I was in a lot of pain. I went ahead and tried to play. The last thing you want is to sit out the World Series. I came up to bat in the bottom of the first inning, took one swing and hit the ball hard, but I almost collapsed from the pain. I had to leave the game, and I didn't play again until the last inning of the last game. Leo used a pinch hitter for Coscarart, our second baseman, and he asked me if I could go in and play defensively for half an inning. I said, 'Yeah, I can,' but I couldn't. It hurt so bad I couldn't turn over in bed for a month."

Herman's misfortune preceded an even worse piece of ill luck.

BILL REDDY: "Fat Freddie had the Yankees dead. He had them chained. They couldn't do a thing with him. And I was sitting out in the bleachers going crazy. Joe DiMaggio was right below us by the famous Ebbets Field gate. It was the seventh inning of a scoreless game, and Russo got up and hit the ball back through the box and hit Freddie squarely in the leg. How the ball hit Fitzsimmons is something I'll never understand because Freddie was famed as a fielder. He used to take infield practice with the second infield, even playing second or short. But Russo hit him, and his kneecap was broken, and Freddie was out, and Hugh Casey came in, the Yankees scored two runs, and we lost the ballgame. I went home sick. I remember riding on the trolley car that ran from Ebbets Field along Parkside Avenue and throwing up out the window."

If that game made Reddy and the other Dodger fans sick, the next one was even worse, one of the darkest moments in Dodger history. It would leave an open wound that would fester for almost a decade and a half.

The day began in anger. Kirby Higbe, who had won twenty-two games to lead the Dodgers and was scheduled to start the game, stormed into Durocher's office before the game in a rage and told him off.

KIRBY HIGBE: "I had a real good record, and we won the pennant, and that's the one time I got mad at Durocher. I'm 22–9, the winningest pitcher he has, and he didn't start me until the fourth game of the Series. The first two wuz okay, but when he come to start Fitzsimmons in the third game, that's when I got mad. And when it came my turn to pitch in that fourth game, I just wasn't in shape to pitch. Really. I hadn't throwed a ball, and I reckon I lasted about two and two-thirds innings."

After Higbe was knocked out with the Dodgers losing 3–0, Brooklyn rallied for four runs. Larry French, Johnny Allen, and Hugh Casey had pitched shutout ball in relief.

Mickey Owen
Dodgers

With the Dodgers leading 4–3 in the top of the ninth, Hugh Casey got John Sturm to ground out to Pete Coscarart at second, and then Red Rolfe tapped back to Casey, who threw him out at first. Tommy Henrich was the next batter, and with two out, Casey ran the count to two strikes, and on the next pitch threw a breaking ball that the Yankee batter swung at and missed for strike three and the ball game. The game was over! Until a gasp from the crowd reflected the realization that Dodger catcher Mickey Owen had been unable to catch the pitch. The ball passed his glove and rolled all the way back to the wall behind home plate. An alert Henrich saw the ball get past Owen and raced to first base safely. In a game that should have ended with the Dodgers victorious by 4 to 3, the Yankees were handed a second chance.

Now Casey could have just as easily retired the next batter, and Brooklyn never would have suffered as it did, but it didn't work out that way. Casey was rattled, and he rushed, and DiMaggio singled to left and Keller doubled to right, scoring Henrich and DiMaggio both. Then Dickey walked and Joe Gordon doubled, and the Yankees had four runs and the ballgame, leaving all of the deeply pious Brooklyn to wonder whether God was indeed dead.

JOEL OPPENHEIMER: "For many Dodger fans, it all began in October 1941. I grew up in Yonkers, just outside New York City, and I was walking with my cousin through the Yonkers streets. I was eleven. It was a pleasant day, and as we walked we could hear the radio broadcasting the Series as we passed house after house. We were walking to Uncle Morris and Aunt Gus's, and we were able to follow the game as we walked, and we were very happy the Dodgers were winning.

"It was the bottom of the ninth, and the Dodgers were only one out away from winning the game, and I motioned for my cousin to stop, and in front of one of the homes on a hilly street in Yonkers I listened for the third out to end the game.

"There were two strikes, and the pitcher threw, and the announcer shouted, 'Strike three,' and then he was shouting that the Dodger catcher had let the ball get past him, enabling the runner to get to first base. My heart leapt. I shouted, 'More Yankee perfidy.' And at that moment, I knew the Dodgers were going to lose. It's a feeling a poker player has when he feels lucky, a tangible feeling people with ESP know they have until it ebbs away. I knew the magic was gone and that nothing could stop the inevitable. Which, of course, is exactly what happened. Several base hits later, the Dodgers had lost the game.

"I thought, 'Why God, why?' Why had God done it to us and given it to them? Why?"

Actually despite denials by all involved—Hugh Casey swore it was a curveball—the probability was that Hugh Casey threw Owen a spitter. "It was a little wet slider," according to Pee Wee Reese, "and the ball kind of broke real sharply to the right and kinda got by his glove. We had it in our pocket, and I'm saying, 'It sure looks like we're gonna get our ass beat.' And we sure did."

It was sound baseball strategy really for Casey to throw a spitball on that pitch. The rule was that if the umpire caught a pitcher throwing a spitball, the pitcher would be thrown out of the game. But if Casey were to throw a spitter with two outs and two strikes in the bottom of the ninth and if Henrich were to miss, then how could the umpire throw him out? The game would be over.

After a 3–1 loss to the Yankees in the finale, MacPhail went into a deep depression and began a drinking bout that conceivably could have culminated in his trading the entire Brooklyn Dodger team!

PETE REISER: "I believe that this is a true story. I can't prove it, but knowing Larry MacPhail, I would bet it's true. After we lost the 1941 Series, MacPhail was so mad at us that he made a deal with the St. Louis Browns to trade the entire Dodger team to St. Louis for $3 or $4 million and all the Browns players.

"I was living in St. Louis during the off-season, and I kept hearing rumors that the owner of the Browns, Don Barnes, was running around St. Louis trying to raise the $3 million. The banks wanted to know what he wanted the money for. He told them, 'I'm buying the Dodger ballclub for St. Louis.' They all thought he was out of his mind.

"I don't know if MacPhail really would have gone through with it, but can you imagine what would have happened in Brooklyn if the St. Louis Brown players all had turned up there one day wearing Dodger uniforms?"

A Lost Pennant; MacPhail Resigns

World War II changed the face of baseball everywhere, and in Brooklyn it was no different. The war was on, and anticipation of a string of Dodger pennants ended when the Japanese attacked Pearl Harbor and the draft-eligible players left for boot camp to prepare for war.

Cookie Lavagetto was the first Dodger to go. He enlisted in the navy in February. Reese and Reiser, both twenty-one, would surely go. Both married the same day, March 29, during spring training. When they told MacPhail, instead of congratulations, his critical response was, "Well, there goes the pennant." Reiser eventually did cost the Dodgers the pennant, but it was not because of his sex life.

In 1942 the Dodgers again trained in Havana. All through the spring, Durocher and some of the other Dodgers had played "low ball" poker, in which the worst hand wins the pot, and the stakes were high. At the airport on the way out of Cuba, the players pulled out the cards, and when a policeman approached, Kirby Higbe, Augie Galan, and Johnny Rizzo told him to "get lost." The cop arrested them. Playing cards for money in public places was illegal in Cuba, and if it hadn't been for a Cuban official assigned to protect the celebrated visitors, the players would have been tossed in jail.

"This is the gamblingest club I ever saw," said pitcher Larry French. "Give any one of several players the right odds, and he will bet you that your ear falls off next Thursday."

This was not lost on MacPhail.

Having been denied a World Series victory, MacPhail bore down as hard as ever on Durocher. At Cincinnati MacPhail's unstable nature had led him to the brink of a nervous breakdown. Unable to control his drinking, furious at having lost the 1941 World Series in so improbable a way, MacPhail was back on the edge. His bouts with Durocher were becoming more emotional, less rational.

During the spring of 1942, MacPhail innocently asked Durocher, "Have the boys been behaving?"

LEO: "Never better."

MACPHAIL: "Has Johnny Allen behaved?"

LEO: "He made curfew every night."

MacPhail then produced a report from a private detective proving that Allen and several other players had many nights stayed out long after curfew, some nights not even bothering to come home.

MACPHAIL: "Allen's through, and so are you."

LEO: "You can't fire me. I won the only pennant for Brooklyn in twenty years. And Allen can pitch nine innings every time out."

MACPHAIL: "But not for me. You're fired."

MacPhail began swearing at Durocher, and as Durocher went to swing at him, reporters came between them. When order was restored, the two men were shamed into shaking hands, and as their hands met, they both burst into tears and passionately hugged each other.

Despite the continued fighting between the drunk and disorderly MacPhail, and the intense and excitable Durocher, the Dodgers raced out in front and seemed destined for a second pennant. It was late in July, the team thirteen games in front, Reiser was batting .383, causing Dodger fans to anticipate the wording on his Hall of Fame plaque.

But in July, with Reiser patrolling center field as usual, Enos Slaughter hit a high and deep drive over Reiser's head. Reiser, who was totally without fear, raced at top speed, his back to the plate, running dead out toward straight center field in the direction of the Ebbets Field's exit gate, and as he neared the wall, he grazed the flag pole, still sure he would make the catch, and continued his pursuit. His teammates watched in horror as he ran out of room. Reiser actually caught the ball before he hit, but as it fell into his glove, his head struck the concrete wall. "It felt like a hand grenade went off inside my head," Reiser would say later. He lost consciousness, and the ball fell out of his glove, and Slaughter completed an inside-the-park home run. Durocher raced out to administer to his young star, and he was relieved that Reiser was able to walk into the clubhouse. But there he collapsed.

In the hospital the next day, Reiser was told by the Cardinal physician, Dr. Robert Hyland, that he was through for the season. Dr. Hyland diagnosed his injuries as a fractured skull and a severe concussion.

The unstable and paranoid MacPhail, however, refused to accept the di-

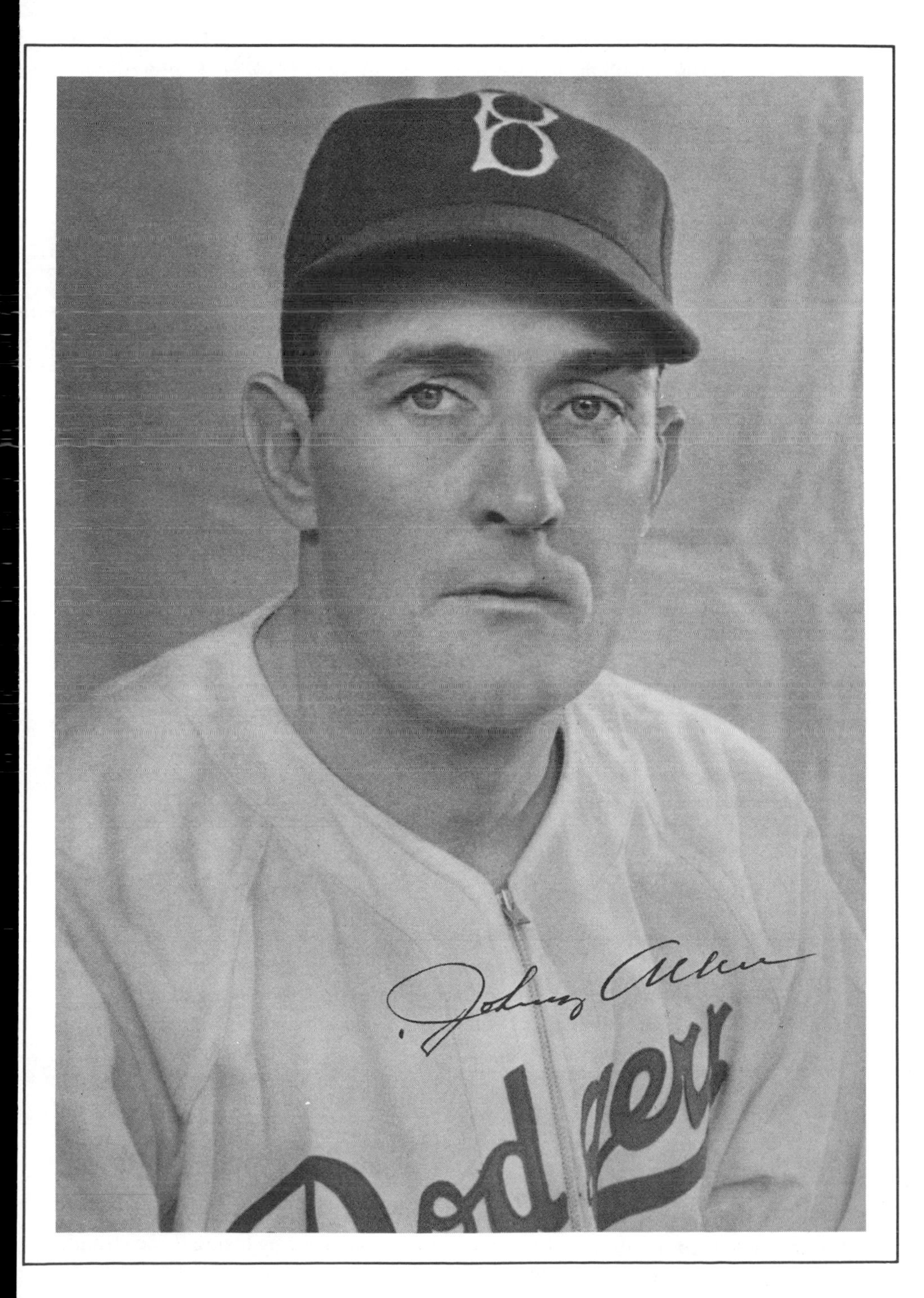

agnosis. He was convinced this was a plot by Rickey and his doctor to keep Reiser out of the lineup so the Cardinals could take away his pennant.

It isn't clear why the Dodger physician didn't prevent Reiser from playing, except that MacPhail ran things. Once MacPhail decided Reiser could play, there was no overruling him.

Just three days after the accident, though he was seeing double and experiencing searing head pains, Reiser was back in uniform and sitting on the Dodger bench.

Durocher had promised the doctor he wouldn't play him. He swore Reiser would be on the bench only to give moral support, but it was the thirteenth inning of a tie game, men were on base, the Dodgers needed a base hit, and Reiser was the league's best hitter. Durocher asked Reiser if he was up to it, and Reiser, a fierce competitor who would never refuse an opportunity to contribute, eagerly accepted. Reiser singled to win the game, but rounding thc base lost his equilibrium and fell. In Brooklyn the Dodger physicians strongly advised MacPhail to keep Reiser out for the rest of the season.

But the Dodgers were beginning to lose their lead, and MacPhail wouldn't let Reiser stay out, and neither would Durocher. The team needed him, MacPhail and Durocher wanted him, and the youngster was willing to try.

Despite continuing double vision, Reiser played, though he hit below .200 during the final two months of the season. From his .383 high, his year-end average was but .310. He rarely got a key hit, and in the field he was shaky. In no small part because Durocher played him before he was ready, the Dodgers lost their pennant, and Reiser lost his chance at the Hall of Fame. Reiser, who would have been compared to Joe DiMaggio, Ted Williams, or Stan Musial, played at his superior skill level for exactly a half a season before he was struck down. Rickey, who loved the boy, agonized over what he perceived to be MacPhail's role in damaging his prodigy. Said Rickey about MacPhail, "That character should never have been entrusted with anything that fine."

Reiser, however, never blamed Durocher.

PETE REISER: "I have never, ever blamed Leo for keeping me in there. I blame myself. He wanted to win so badly it hurt, and I wanted to win so bad it hurt. I've heard a lot of guys knock Leo for all sorts of things, but I've always said this about him: If you don't know him, you hate his guts, but if you do know him, you love him. He was the best. He was aggressive, and he always fought for you. Always."

With five weeks to go in 1942, the Dodgers were seven and a half games in front of the Cardinals. From Pennsylvania Station the Dodgers headed west for a final road trip on board a train dubbed the Victory Special. Their optimism was premature, as they began their road tour by losing three straight to the Cardinals, the first game a 2–1 loss in fourteen innings, the second a 1–0 loss in ten. Though Curt Davis won the fourth game to preserve some sanity, Durocher was screaming for pitching help. MacPhail spent $25,000 for devil-may-care Bobo Newsom, a flaky and well-traveled veteran who played for twenty years and rarely spent more than two years in a row on any one team. When the rotund Newsom walked into the clubhouse, he told his new teammates, "I'll take care of you boys. You got nothing to worry about. Ole Bobo's here." But even with the addition of Newsom, MacPhail had premonitions that the Dodgers were not going to win.

KIRBY HIGBE: "I never will forget, we were ten games out in front of the Cardinals in 1942, and we beat Philadelphia 1–0. Larry MacPhail called us over after the game, and he said, 'I'm telling you boys, the Cardinals are going to beat you out if you're not careful. You guys are getting lackadaisical, you think you have it clinched, and before you know it, they are going to beat you out.' And in '42, damn if they didn't."

Even before the season was out, the Dodger stockholders, led by George V. McLaughlin, representing the Brooklyn Trust Company, decided that MacPhail was no longer stable enough to run the team. They had forbade him from spending the cash to acquire Newsom, MacPhail's "pennant insurance," and Newsom's 2–2 record did not help the Dodgers to a pennant as promised. This was one of the excuses they lamely cited for getting rid of the man who had saved the franchise. In truth the Age of the Bottom Line was slowly eating away at the business of baseball. Stockholders were the ones calling the shots, and the bottom line in Brooklyn was that, because of MacPhail's extravagant spending, they were not getting big enough dividend checks. Winning was no longer enough. Now they wanted someone who would lead them to victory as well as to a fat check at the end of the year.

Ironically, if MacPhail had allowed a substitute for the ailing Reiser, the Dodgers might have won the pennant, and MacPhail might have had a better chance at keeping his job. Instead, taking the gracious way out, on September 24, 1942, MacPhail resigned. The next year Rickey took over in Brooklyn, but he was too late to save his prodigy. Reiser would never regain his top form, and the relationship between Rickey and MacPhail would never be the same.

At his final press conference, MacPhail expressed contempt for the other directors. He told reporters, "It is true I spent a lot of money around here. I have spent about a million for ballplayers, and this year alone, I spent $250,000 on repairs to the ball park. But I leave the Brooklyn club with $300,000 in the bank and in a position to pay off the mortgage. We have paid off $600,000 we owed the Brooklyn Trust Company and have reduced the mortgage another $600,000, to $320,000. I have sold the radio rights for 1943 for $150,000. We have drawn a paid attendance of more than a million at home in each of the last four years, and whether we win the pennant or not, and it doesn't look as if we will, since we're two games behind with only three to play, the future of the club is bright, even under wartime conditions."

And so the colorful and always tempestuous MacPhail withdrew from the New York baseball scene—for a while. In a few years he would be back in baseball, running the New York Yankees—and causing grief for the Dodgers.

During September the Dodgers won 20 and lost 5, but the Cards were 21 and 5 and won the pennant by two games. The Dodgers had won 104 games, a team record.

At the end of the season, MacPhail accepted a commission as colonel in the U.S. Army. Our country would be made safe for democracy once more.

2

The Neighborhood

In the afternoons after school and on weekends, the youngsters made the neighborhoods in Brooklyn reverberate with the sounds of playing varied ball games in the streets, stickball, stoopball, or Catch a Fly and You're Up, games adapted to city living by inventive, sports-loving children. The streets had not yet been taken over by the automobile, because in Brooklyn there was a speedy and safe subway system that for five cents could take an explorer anywhere he wished to go in the borough and beyond. It was a time when the radio was a Godsend for everyone, especially for the poor. Once you got past the initial purchase price, you didn't have to spend money on entertainment. The radio was all you needed, and into your home would come Bing Crosby, Kate Smith, Burns and Allen, Groucho Marx, and the Shadow, who knew what lurked in the hearts of men.

It was a time when crime was infrequent and rarely violent and when property, traditions, and parents were all respected. Girls were all virgins, the institution of marriage was inviolate, and best of all, a bleacher seat at Ebbets Field was only fifty-five cents.

It was a time when enclaves of ethnic groups lived harmoniously alongside each other. A typical Brooklyn neighborhood of the 1930s was that of Windsor Terrace, a small Irish enclave to the south and west of Ebbets Field. It is a neighborhood that exists today only in the mind, but to those lucky enough to have grown up in Brooklyn, it is as real now as it was then.

JOE FLAHERTY: "When I think of my boyhood growing up in Brooklyn, I think of the magic of the streets. Whenever my saintly mother gets mad at me, she says, 'Joseph, you were nothing but a street kid anyway.' But hell, we all were. At that time the street was the center of neighborhood culture. The streets thrived. They weren't dangerous. Strangers couldn't walk onto your block and muck around, because so many people were playing in the streets at all hours. The only time anyone got hurt was when someone got hit with a stickball bat or fell out of a tree.

"When you walked out of your house, you would walk right into a stickball game, and if you didn't have enough players for stickball, you played Catch a Fly and You're Up, which was one guy at bat, the rest of you down the street, and if you caught a fly off his bat, you got to hit. On ground balls,

NYT Pictures

you had to roll the ball in and hit the bat in such a way that the ball would hit the bat and jump away before the batter could catch it. And if you only had two people, you would draw a batter's box against a wall, and you pitched to the other guy. And on the wall behind the pitcher, there were marks going up indicating single, double, triple, home run.

"I remember, in the neighborhood where we lived, every house had a cement stoop, which was six or seven steps, off of which we played a game called Single, Double, Triple, Home Run. You put two guys in the outfield, playing across a gutter in the street. You would wind up and throw the ball against the stoop and try to hit the point of a step. If you could do that, the ball would really go, on a line drive. If the ball bounced once before you caught it, it was a single. Two bounces, a double, three bounces a triple, and four bounces or more, a home run.

"And guys could play the wall as well as Dixie Walker. We even knew the bounces off the fire escapes. The ball would be dangling up in the fire escape, and the outfielder would be running to the spot where he figured the ball would come down, and while we were playing, the older men in the neighborhood would sit out with their growlers of beer and watch the games, and these games would be echoing all over the streets. Cheers would be coming out from the different stoops. And the men would spend their evenings sitting on their stoops in their strapped undershirts, and women would be together on a different stoop, gabbing, and the radio would be blaring Red Barber and the Dodger game, and when it got dark, the kids began playing ring-a-levio or Kick the Can, or Three Feet to Germany, all the exotic games which disappeared with the emergence of the automobile.

"I remember mothers constantly yelling out windows for their kids to come in, and the kids would never come. Whenever a mother called, the other kids would tell her that her son was on the opposite team playing ring-a-levio and was hiding and that as soon as we found him and captured him, he'd come. We'd tell her, 'It isn't his fault he's late for supper. He's been hiding for a half an hour.' So we always had an edge. The mothers didn't particularly believe it, but they couldn't beat their kids with a clear conscience, so usually they didn't.

"And what was so wonderful was that in our world of street games, no one was excluded. Even if you were the worst shlub in the world, nobody said, 'You can't play.' There was no Little League mentality. There was always a spot in right field where nobody hit the ball, or if someone did hit it there, it would be an event like the sinking of the Titanic, but at least you were in the game, and you got your lick up at bat. Maybe you were the last one picked, but by God, you got picked.

"Back in those days, the Italians and Irish people didn't refer to their neighborhood by name but by which church you went to. Today the neighborhood is called Park Slope by the nouveau riche. In those days, when someone asked where you came from, you said, 'Holy Name,' or 'Immaculate Heart of Mary,' which in Brooklyn was always known as 'Our Lady of Perpetual Help.' And you never went to Manhattan. Manhattan was always referred to as 'The City,' and it was always said with a certain dread. Manhattan was where in the bars they served you bottled beer, where you never knew the price, and you always thought you were getting bilked.

"Prospect Avenue was the main thoroughfare, where the bars and markets were, and all the shopkeepers were Dodger fans. It was impossible to go into a store with the *Daily News* under your arm without talking baseball. People just constantly talked baseball, arguing. They lived and breathed with the Dodgers.

"And the idea of walking through Prospect Park to see a rare night game at Ebbets Field—you felt like F. Scott Fitzgerald first seeing the ivory towers of New York. You would walk around the lake on a balmy summer's evening, and fathers and sons, hundreds of kids, would be chattering, talking, walking along, and then you would get to within perhaps 200 yards of the ballpark, and from the horizon the rim of lights of Ebbets Field would become visible, and you'd keep walking, and all of a sudden the sky would be lit up. My God, it was like the Emerald City, and as you got closer, you'd pick up your pace, and you'd give your tickets and go charging inside."

The Coming of Mr. Rickey

With MacPhail ousted, the Dodger directors sought a more stable and less controversial replacement. The last time he was consulted, Ford Frick had asked Branch Rickey to recommend a strong hand to run the Dodgers. This time, when Frick was consulted and turned to Rickey, Rickey offered up himself. He and St. Louis Cardinal owner Sam Breadon were on the outs, and Rickey was looking to make a move. Frick told Dodger stockholder Jim Mulvey, "Branch will be the one to restore quiet. He will be a restraining influence on Durocher, and he will put an end to another situation on your ballclub. You know what I mean by that, Jim."

Mulvey did. Frick was referring to the gambling hall atmosphere. Durocher's clubhouse was open to all his hanger-on, showbiz, and fast-lane friends, including notorious bookmakers and other assorted wise guys. They hung around the clubhouse, as Durocher and a number of his players bet horses and played cards. When Rickey had Durocher in St. Louis, Rickey had taken him under his wing and tried to make a better citizen out of him. Mulvey and the board hoped that Rickey would try to do it again.

In September of 1942, a triumvirate of Rickey, Brooklyn chemical manufacturer John L. Smith, and an attorney who worked for the Brooklyn Trust Company and had been on the Dodgers since 1933, Walter O'Malley, each bought twenty-five percent of the Dodgers stock. Dearie Mulvey, daughter of former Dodger owner Steve McKeever, and her husband, Jim, held the remaining twenty-five percent. The total cost of their seventy-five percent was $1,046,000. Each new owner paid $82,000 down. The remaining $800,000 was financed by $75,000 paid by Smith, $75,000 that O'Malley had to pay from his share of future club profits, and the balance was lent by the Brooklyn Trust Company. Rickey was installed as president and given a five-year contract to run the team.

Rickey was pleased with the presence in the deal of John Smith, who, like Rickey, was a fervent Christian and a self-made man. Smith, whose Pfizer Company marketed and distributed the wonder drug penicillin, admired Rickey's business acumen, his clean living, and his baseball knowledge. Rickey was optimistic and expected that Brooklyn would be his final stop in his long and highly respected career.

The third partner, Walter O'Malley, was graduated from Fordham Law School in 1920. Wealthy to begin with—his father had given him a cabin cruiser that slept eight when he graduated from the University of Pennsylvania engineering school—the astute and calculating O'Malley built up a thriving law practice during the Depression by representing bankrupt companies. While some of his bankrupt colleagues were plunging out of windows, the shrewd and opportunistic O'Malley was getting richer. He wisely invested his money in a building-materials firm, in the Long Island Railroad, in the Brooklyn Borough Gas Company, the New York Subways Advertising Company, a couple of hotels, and a beer firm. And as his influence grew, he began to be noticed by the big shots running Brooklyn's Democratic machine, among them Judge Henry Ughetta and the president of the Brooklyn Trust Company, George V. McLaughlin.

O'Malley was hired by banker McLaughlin and given the job of instituting and carrying out mortgage foreclosures against failing businesses. Later McLaughlin asked him to handle the legal affairs for the Dodgers. From the beginning of their relationship, the politically sensitive O'Malley courted the powerful McLaughlin, and in addition to acting as McLaughlin's legal representative, O'Malley at times was his bodyguard, valet, chauffeur, adopted son, confidant, and right-hand man. And when McLaughlin put together the Dodger deal, he included O'Malley as a reward for faithful service. At the press conference at which the three men were introduced, Smith told reporters that he would leave the running of the team to Mr. Rickey. O'Malley said nothing. Reporters wondered how O'Malley fit into the picture. Many assumed that he was merely a stand-in for McLaughlin. O'Malley was ignored—and underestimated.

Just as MacPhail had taken center stage when running the Dodgers, so did Rickey, whose rumpled mien belied his shrewdness and intelligence. Stout, with Benjamin Franklin glasses, Rickey had a somewhat comical look, with big, strong, and gnarled hands and a slovenly appearance. As he talked and ate, he would gesture, and he would spill food all over himself, which prompted one of his employees to observe, "Everything the boss eats looks good on him."

Money was always very important to Rickey. His father had built the Free-Will Baptist Church in his Duck Run, Ohio, hometown, and though Rickey had followed in his father's Godly footsteps, Rickey once told a reporter that "for all their moral substance, my parents hadn't harvested much of a worldly reward."

Rickey was often ribbed about his love of money. To finance his education, he played pro baseball, where he was seen as something of an oddball because he refused to perform on Sundays, as it was against his religious beliefs. He was a catcher with the Browns and the Yankees, and in one game he allowed thirteen stolen bases. Remarked a former Dodger employee of his: "Nobody has stolen anything on him since."

Since his college days, Rickey had been an astute judge of baseball talent. Though he had become a pro player, he was objective and farsighted enough in assessing his own ability to decide that his limited physical talent would never allow him to make big money. In order to do that, he decided, he would have to find another route to financial independence.

To help pay his way through law school, he took a part-time job coaching the university baseball team, and his star player, George Sisler, had the talent to become a Hall of Fame first baseman who twice hit over .400 and who finished with a fifteen-year career batting average of .340. After completing his law studies, Rickey was felled by tuberculosis, and after a prolonged recuperation, he had a brief fling at the law.

BRANCH RICKEY: "I had gone to Boise, Idaho, from Saranac, New York, to try to gain back my strength. I got an office and hung out a shingle and waited for clients. None came. Finally, I went to court one day, and the judge appointed me attorney for a man who was being held on a charge the newspapers used to describe as white slavery.

"I was apprehensive, but at last I summoned enough courage to go over to the jail and see the client. Oh, he was a horrible creature. I can see him now, walking slowly up to the bars and looking me up and down with contempt. He terrified me. I began to shake like a leaf. After a minute he said, 'Who the hell are you?'

"I tried to draw myself up a little, and then I said, 'Sir, my name is Branch Rickey. The court has appointed me your attorney, and I would like to talk to you.' He looked me up and down and then spat at my feet. Then he delivered what turned out to be the final words of our association. He said, 'Get the hell out of here.'

"I not only got out of there, I got out of the state of Idaho. I went to St. Louis and took a job with the Browns."

Rickey took himself very seriously and was most comfortable when he was pontificating. It was the day of India's Mahatma Gandhi, who preached in parables much as Rickey did, and the sportswriters began calling Rickey "The Mahatma." One day he told *New York Tribune* sportswriter Harold Rosenthal how highly he thought of baseball writers, saying that whenever he wanted to hire someone for the Dodger front office, he would inevitably turn to a writer because writers were so reliable. What he really meant was that he turned to baseball writers because the writers always seemed to be hanging breathlessly and obsequiously on every word he uttered.

Rickey had hired Harold Parrott, a reporter from the *Brooklyn Eagle,* to be the Dodger road secretary, just for this reason.

N.Y. *Daily News* Photo

LEO DUROCHER AND BRANCH RICKEY

* * *

HAROLD ROSENTHAL: "Rickey told me, 'Parrott impressed me right from the start. They sent him out to do a column on me, and I started to talk, and before I could get a word out, Parrott had his pencil and pad out and was writing everything down.'

"To Rickey, because Harold was writing down every word he said, that made him a good reporter. And a good bet to be a loyal employee."

Rickey came straight from the chautauqua circuit. He was a spellbinder and philosopher who often would make a point by telling a story. During spring training, for instance, he would gather his minor league managers around him, and among other advice, he would inform them that part of what he expected them to do was to become an active part of their respective communities. "All it takes," he would say, "is the right kind of effort."

And then came his story:

BRANCH RICKEY: "There used to be an old boy who'd sit in the railroad station and wait for the trains to come in. Once in a while a man would get off, put his bags down, and say to the old boy, 'What kind of town is this?' Invariably, the old boy would say, 'What kind of town do you come from?' 'Oh,' the man might say, 'everyone's cutthroat—hooray for me, the hell with you.' The old boy would say, 'That's the kind of town this is.'

"A few days later another train would stop, and another man would get off. He'd see the old boy sitting there and ask him the same question, 'What kind of town is this?' The old boy would give him the same answer. 'What kind of town do you come from?' 'Oh,' the man might say, 'very cooperative. Everybody helping one another.' 'That's the kind of town this is,' the old boy would say."

Rickey was invited once to Brooklyn Technical School to give the graduation address. An impressionable youngster who had been in the audience remembers what to him was the highlight of the speech:

ROGER KAHN: "He was tremendously charismatic, and I never forgot the show he put on. During his lecture Mr. Rickey picked up a big jar that was filled with raisins and nuts. And I don't know how he did it, but he shook up the jar, and the nuts and raisins separated. He said, 'You're going out in the great game of life, and let me show you something.' He held up the jar. 'What I always want you to notice is what happens in life occurs right here in this jar. The nuts come out on top.' "

It genuinely bothered Rickey, moreover, that "the nuts come out on top." He believed in God, Jesus, and the Bible, and except in the case of player salaries, was an advocate of fairness, decency, and fair play.

MacPhail had been partial to the hard-drinking, double-fisted, old-fashioned type of player. Rickey preferred players with exemplary family backgrounds, and when he took over the Dodgers, he instructed his scouts to include a background check in the scouting report.

REX BARNEY: "Mr. Rickey never put up with characters. The Brooklyn Dodgers and Ebbets Field had always been known for their characters, but that stopped when Mr.Rickey took over. If we had a guy who was the least bit troublemaker, that guy was gone. Mr. Rickey didn't care how good he was. He didn't care."

Rickey didn't purge the wild bunch already on the club, but of the hundreds of players the Dodgers signed after his arrival, very, very few were gamblers, skirt chasers, or boozers. Under Rickey there would be a different breed of player: gentlemen, family men, solid citizens. With the coming of Branch Rickey, the Daffiness Days were at an end. And some of the old timers left with them.

To Rickey over-the-hill players were called "anesthetics," by which Rickey meant a player who had lost a step or two in the field or on the bases. Rickey knew that most managers, Durocher included, preferred the veterans with long experience who would never disgrace you with a bad play. Yet he also knew that such players weakened a team, because by not giving the young prospects a chance, at some point the team would suddenly get old, and the team would be in deep trouble. Also, by not moving up young players, the eager kids in the farm system became discouraged, and some would drop out prematurely.

When Rickey arrived in Brooklyn, the team was laden with veterans. Almost immediately Joe Medwick, Johnny Allen, Whitlow Wyatt, Dolph Camilli, Paul Waner, and Fred Fitzsimmons were traded or released.

Because it was wartime and most of his prospects were fighting in the war, the fruits of his talent scouting would not ripen for several years. Just as the fans were scrounging for scrap metal to bring to the park to help the war effort to earn free tickets to Dodger games, so Rickey had to scrounge for bodies for the Dodger team.

In 1943 Larry French, Hugh Casey, Pee Wee Reese, Pete Reiser, Johnny Rizzo, Billy Herman, and Higbe all went into the armed services. With little talent in the minors available to replace them, in 1943 the Dodgers finished third.

KIRBY HIGBE: "Ya know, buddy, we had a real good ballclub, and if it hadn't been for the war, we would have won a lot more pennants. The Cardinals won in 1942, '43, '44, and again in 1946. They didn't lose the men to the service the Dodgers did. They sure didn't. We had pretty nearly an all-star team. The best infield in baseball. Until the war."

With so many of their stars missing to action, it was no wonder the Dodgers finished seventh in 1944, despite 4-F outfielder Dixie Walker leading the league with a .357 batting average. And it was surprising a patchwork Dodger team did as well as third in 1945, with the presence on the team of such players as Eddie Basinski, a concert violinist with only marginal skills as a second baseman, and a sixteen-year-old shortstop, Tommy Brown.

HOWIE SCHULTZ: "No one remembers Eddie Basinski. Eddie could really play the violin. As a kid he had played in the Buffalo Symphony, and after he left the Dodgers, he ended up playing for the Seattle Symphony.

"I remember Leo had been needling Basinski about his violin playing. He would bring the violin and practice in his room. Leo told him, 'I'll give you a suit if you'll play the violin for us.' So one day Eddie brought his violin into the clubhouse, and he was a virtuoso. So Leo said, 'Well, I guess I owe you a suit. What kind of suit do you want?' Eddie's response was, 'Where did you get yours?' Leo's suit was probably five times more expensive than what Ed ever paid for a suit."

LARRY KING: "Tommy Brown was the youngest player before Joe Nuxhall made it to the majors at age fifteen. He was a wartime Dodger shortstop who was lucky if he hit three home runs a year, but in batting practice he would hit tremendous home runs, and Dick Young would keep count, and in August Young announced that Brown had hit his sixtieth home run to break Ruth's record during batting practice.

"Brown once fielded a ground ball and threw it past Howie Schultz into the upper deck. One time somebody hit a ground ball to Brown, and the ball went through his legs, but Brown continued the motions as though he had fielded it, and he made a phantom throw to first, and Howie Schultz stretched as though he was going to catch it, and Augie Galan, who was in left field, was fooled watching the play, and when the ball rolled by him, Brown was charged with a four-base error. Galan said, 'I kinda thought it might have gone through him, but when Schultz stretched and Brown followed through, I figured he had thrown the ball.' "

In his search for wartime bodies, Mr. Rickey instructed his scouts to scour the college campuses for prospects, and from across America, Rickey and his scouts signed peach-faced youngsters such as Ralph Branca, a broad-shoulder fastball pitcher from NYU, Howie Schultz, a six-foot-seven first baseman from Hamline University in Saint Paul, and Clyde King, a brainy pitcher off the campus of the University of North Carolina.

RALPH BRANCA: "I grew up in Mount Vernon, New York, and I was a Giant fan. In high school, my brother, who was a year and a half older than I was, and I pitched for Davis High School and won twenty-six games in a row. I finally lost 1–0 when a guy hit a single to center, and it went through the center fielder's legs for a three-base error.

"It was 1942, I was sixteen, and my brother and I went for tryouts with the Giants first, naturally, but it rained, and when we came back the next day I never did get to pitch. I can see why. I was six feet two, 135, and they looked at me and saw this skinny, scrawny blade. When we went to the stadium, the Yankees liked me, but they wrote on my card, 'Too young. Get in touch with him next year,' but they never did. Our third trip was the longest, a subway ride on the IRT. We went from 241st Street in the Bronx all the way to Sheepshead Bay in Brooklyn for a tryout with the Dodgers. We left at seven in the morning, took our sandwiches and uniforms and went out. I threw, and the Dodgers liked me, and the next year they had me come back and pitch batting practice, and that certainly made an impression on a seventeen-year-old kid.

"The Dodgers were on top of things. They were on the ball, and they got me to sign in June of 1943, right out of high school. I got a new glove and a supporter with a cup in it, and I didn't know what the hell to do with it, and that's the truth. I got $90 a month to go to Olean in the Pony League.

"I played there June and July, and when I came home, NYU offered me a basketball scholarship. I told my friend, 'I can't play for them. I played pro ball.' He said, 'They don't know. Just go.' And I went and played a year at NYU. And that year I started to mature. I weighed 178 for basketball and weighed 205 by the time baseball season was over. And I could throw ninety-five miles an hour. NYU played thirteen games, and I started twelve of them, and I lost a couple. I lost to Army 2–1 when the center fielder made an error on the ball, and it went through his legs for the winning run.

"And in 1944, right out of NYU, age eighteen, I was pitching for the Dodgers."

Clyde King had tried to get into Navy ROTC at the University of North Carolina but had flunked the vision test. He had impressed the Dodger scouts and later so impressed Mr. Rickey with his skills, poise, and control that the normally parsimonious Rickey allowed King to name his signing price.

Clyde King: "I started with the Dodgers in 1944. I was nineteen. I was a sophomore at the University of North Carolina at Chapel Hill, where I was a starting guard on the basketball team and a starting pitcher in baseball. Howie Haak was a lieutenant commander at the pre-flight school at Chapel Hill, and he used to umpire our games when I pitched. I guess Howie Haak saw something he liked, because he was continually asking me to consider a tryout with the Dodgers.

"He said, 'If you don't like it, you can always come back.' I left Raleigh on the train and went to Penn Station. I took a cab over to 215 Montague Street, and Mr. Rickey was waiting for me. We talked for about an hour, and he said, 'What kind of bonus do you want?' I picked what I thought was a ridiculous figure out of the hat. I said, 'Five thousand.' Without flinching, he said, 'That's fine.' And he yelled at Jane Ann Jones, his secretary, to bring a contract. And for many years, I was known as Rickey's boy. Many years later I asked him, 'If I had asked for more, would I have gotten it?' In a kidding sort of way, he said, 'You'll never know, will you?'

"I remember the first game I pitched in. It was 1944. Mickey Owen was the catcher. We must have been seven runs behind, and it was late in the game. The bases were loaded, and no one was out, and Owen came out to the mound. He had never seen me pitch before. He said, 'Don't pay any attention to the fingers I'm putting down. Just throw fastballs.' I was primarily a curveball pitcher, but I guess he figured, 'Here's a young college kid, nineteen, he's probably wild, and the game's out of reach.' And so I got the first two hitters out, and the next guy hit a double and knocked in all three runs.

"The next morning I got a note from Mr. Rickey asking me to be in his office at ten o'clock. He said, 'What kind of pitches do you have?' I said, 'I have a fastball, a curveball, and a change-up.' He said, 'How many curves did you throw last night?' I said, 'I didn't throw any.' He said, 'How many fastballs?' I said, 'I threw twelve.' He asked why I didn't throw any curves or change-ups. I said, 'Because Mickey Owen told me not to.' He said, 'That's your first lesson. You're the boss out there. The catcher only suggests, and you have to approve it. If you don't like it, change it.' And that was my first lesson from Mr. Rickey.

"Not long after that we were playing the Giants in Ebbets Field, and somebody hit a high foul ball right by home plate, and the catcher threw his mask off, and I went and ran in and picked the mask up, and the catcher caught the ball. I didn't know it, but that night the writers were talking to Mr. Rickey, and he told them that was the smartest play he'd seen in years, that Mickey Owen had actually stepped where the mask was and that if I hadn't picked it up, he wouldn't have caught the ball. He said, 'This young man is a bright young man. His head is two years ahead of his arm.' My close friends say my arm never did catch up.

"But I was always so proud, because I liked the way he thought, and he liked the way I was always thinking about baseball. I remember the first time I saw Mel Ott get a base hit, he rounded first and went way toward the bag at second and then came back, so I told Dixie Walker, who played right field, I said, 'If he gets a hit off me to right, I'm going to run to the first base foul line, come up the line behind him, and you pick up the ball and fire it in to first base.' And sure enough, Howie Schultz went over to field the ground ball, and the ball went through to right field, and now Howie was all the way over toward second, and I went down the foul line behind Ott, and Walker, who was a veteran about finished, he got the biggest thrill when he fired the ball back to me, and we trapped Ott off first. He said, 'I've been playing right field in Ebbets Field all these years, and nobody ever suggested that.' Here I was, nineteen years old. Gee, it was fun."

For manager Leo Durocher this was a new challenge. Durocher had been one of those managers who preferred the veteran player. Now he had to relate to a group of untried youngsters. He and his coaches taught the kids sound baseball, and he could be generous and paternalistic, but sometimes the brash way he taught them offended the young players. Veterans used to him would take the blustery and profane Durocher less seriously. The young players too often took his criticism to heart, and their feelings were hurt by his sharp tongue.

HOWIE SCHULTZ: "Leo was kind of a split personality. He was a warm, generous person and treated us like members of his own family. I remember when Rex Barney and I first came to the team. Leo had apparently seen our luggage on the train station platform, because he told us our luggage was not big league. Leo piled us into his cab and took us down to his luggage place, and he saw that we got the right kind of luggage, like a father would do.

"I didn't agree with all the things he did and said, especially his treatment of us on the ballfield, and I don't suppose anyone else did either, but I don't think anyone ran a ballgame, once that first pitch was thrown, any better than Leo did. Still he was impatient with the limitations that rookies and young ballplayers have, and Rickey was bringing them in by the carload starting in '43.

"I can remember one game, Brooklyn was playing the Giants, and it was 0–0 into the twelfth or thirteenth inning. Clyde King was pitching, and from about the seventh inning on he had pitched shutout ball. Ace Adams was pitching for the Giants, and he had been setting us down. We got the bases loaded with two outs, and we're in the last of the thirteenth, and I was the next batter. I was getting up from the on-deck circle, and Leo called my name, and I figured he was going to put in a left-handed pinch hitter. I came back to the bench, and he called me over to him, and here I am leaning way down, and he was leaning back looking at me, and he said, 'I'll give you $100 if you can get hit in the ass.'

"And I didn't know whether to collapse, laugh, or hit him with the bat. So I went up there, and as luck would have it, I got a base hit, and we won the ballgame. And I don't know how Leo did it, but by the time I got to the clubhouse door, Leo was standing there with ten $10 bills, and he gave me the 100 bucks. I said to him, 'If I'm worth $100, Clyde must be worth at least that much,' and Leo went and gave Clyde some money. I don't know how much, but I'll bet Clyde would remember.

Clyde King: "Sure I do. After the game was over, he gave Howie $100. I went and took a shower, and I was in my locker putting on my clothes, and Leo came up to me and handed me a little package. I kept it for years. It was a package with a money wrapper around it, with ten $10 bills. Brand new. And he gave it to me! For no reason at all! I said, 'What's this for?' He said, 'That's for saving the game. That's for giving us a chance to win.'

"Once I pitched for him in Chicago four days in a row in relief, and he appreciated it so much that when we got back to Ebbets Field, the clubhouse boy, John Griffith, called me and he said, 'Leo's got a coat for you. He wants you to come in and try it on.' I went into his office in the clubhouse, and Leo said, 'Here's a coat that I ordered for myself, but it is too big for me. I want you to try it on and see if it fits.' So I did, and it fit perfectly. I'll never forget. It was blue and white plaid. In fact it was almost the colors of the University of North Carolina, and I was tickled to death.

"I didn't think much about it, but three days later, Ben Dillon, who at that time was doing tailormade clothes for all of the guys—he would come in and measure us and make jackets and suits—came into the clubhouse. I said to Ben, 'One of these days I'm gonna want you to make me a sport coat like the one that Leo gave me that was too big for him.' He said, 'What do you mean?' And I told him how Leo called me in and gave me the coat. I said, 'In fact, it's right here.' He said, 'Yeah, I know about it.' I said, 'How?' He said, 'Leo called me from Chicago and asked me if I knew your size. I told him I did, and he said, 'Make Clyde a nice-looking sports coat.'

"You see, Leo didn't want me to think he was doing it for what I had done for him. He told me he had ordered it for himself and that it was too big. And the more I thought about it, the more I realized that Durocher would never make a mistake like that."

Scratching for a Tie

At the beginning of the 1946 season, Rickey brought up to the Dodgers a crop of rookies including a trio of unknowns named Carl Furillo, Dick Whitman, and Gene Hermanski, who patrolled the outfield opening day. In the infield Howie Schultz was at first base. There was a rookie named Bob Ramazzotti at third and a rookie catcher named Bruce Edwards. Dodger fans sort of grasped for familiar names. Pee Wee Reese continued to star at shortstop, and Billy Herman was still at second. But Dixie Walker was on the bench. And Pete Reiser, arguably the best Dodger, was injured.

It was a season perfect for giving Durocher a forum to show off his genius. Though his players were raw, they had talent. It was merely a question of finding the right men for the right positions at the right times, and Durocher juggled, shuttling in and out over the course of the season four first basemen, four second basemen, two shortstops, eight third basemen, nine outfielders, and four catchers. On the final day, only Reese and Furillo were still on the field from his opening day lineup. It was surely the shrewdest handling of men since John McGraw, despite the fact that a number of his youngsters resented Leo's gruff ways and his egotistical manner. Furillo, a young, idealistic straight arrow who believed in honesty, the Ten Commandments, and giving a dollar's work for a dollar's pay, from the start intensely hated the win-at-all-costs Durocher. Theirs would be feud that would endure.

Carl Furillo: "I was a rookie in 1946. I had just spent thirty-eight months in the service, and I can remember it was January 22 when I went by train to Sanford, Florida, where the Dodgers had what they called advance training for all ballplayers that was in the service. Mr. Rickey was there and young Rickey, his son, and all the scouts, George Sisler, Sr., was there. And Durocher had the best coaches there, I'll say that much for him. And then Durocher came down a little later on. He was down there with his wife—he had quite a few. And I found out later, young Branch told the scouts, I found out about it later, he said, 'I want you to leave Furillo alone for at least thirty days cause I want him to get in shape. Don't heckle him.' Young Rickey told me later. He says, 'I didn't want them to bother you. I wanted you to feel at home and get in shape gradually,' and after thirty days they sent in a report on me, and the report was in my favor. I was signed to a minor league contract, and they wanted to sign me to a Brooklyn contract, but they didn't want to give me any money.

"I played all the way until I got up to Brooklyn, and it was time for us to go to Boston to start the season, and I went to see Leo, and he showed me a contract for $3,750. I said, 'I can't survive on that.' He said to me, 'Take it or leave it.' I hated Durocher's guts from that day on. I said to myself, 'Here I just come out of the service, I didn't have no job, nothing at the time. I needed a few dollars extra to get me along and all, and then he offered me that contract and said, 'Take it or leave it.'

"Montreal used to come down to play us during spring training, and they were a nice bunch of guys. But I had a manager at Montreal who was a no-good so-and-so because he pegged me as a drinker. Clay Hopper was his name, and at that time he was bucking like hell for Durocher's job, and he did everything in the book to try and get it. In fact he even took pictures of some of the boys at the beach at Daytona. The boys were sitting there having a few beers, and he even had one of the girls take pictures of them so he could give them to Mr. Rickey so he could say, 'Durocher can't handle his men.'

"So I was in Daytona, at the hotel where Montreal was, and some of the waiters—I got along good with the waiters—brought in a tray of beer, and there must have been four or five of us there, and if I had one beer, I'm lucky, 'cause at the time I didn't care for beer. I used to be a soda man. So one of the kids went out and told the waiter to bring us more beer, and they brought another tray of beer, and who the hell walks in behind him but Clay Hopper. He says, 'Well, I see, Furillo, you really fouled yourself up.' I said, 'What are you talking about?' I hadn't even finished one beer. He said, 'What's all the beer and garbage?' I said, 'I didn't drink them.' See, there was only me and Bob Ramazzotti there. The rest disappeared. I said, 'I don't care what you do, but I didn't drink this.'

"So Brooklyn finally called me up, and I was playing ball, and do you know that Rickey had me followed? One day I was going from Chicago to St. Louis, it was always a beautiful run, I used to love that run. You could sit in the coach and see farm country and wide open spaces. So young Rickey sat down next to me, and he says, 'Carl, I have to apologize to you.' I said, 'About what?' He said, 'That rumpus they had down in Florida about you being a drinker.' I says, 'What do you mean?' He says, 'We found out the hard way that you don't even associate with it.' I said, 'I could have told you that and saved you a lot of money. I don't like alcohol. I prefer sodas. But one thing I can say about Clay Hopper. He wants Durocher's job in the worst way.'

"But see, what got me mad about Durocher again, we were coming north, and I went to him and told the truth. I told him what happened. And he said to me, 'Don't worry about it.' So then this picture came out about these guys drinking over in Daytona Beach, and he walked up to me and said, 'Why the hell did you lie to me?' I said, 'What are you talking about? I told you the truth.' He said, 'You're a Goddamn liar.' See, he thought I had told him a lie about my drinking at the party, but then when Clay Hopper said I was drinking, that made him look bad because I was ready to go to Brooklyn, and it looked like he couldn't handle his men. I said, 'Leo, I told you the truth.' He said, 'You're a liar.' I said, 'You can go to hell.' And I didn't like him from that day on.

"As far as I was concerned, Durocher had a lot to learn about the young ballplayer. He knew his onions, but he was not good for young ballplayers. Durocher was not a good manager because he thought everybody had to be top-notch, top-notch, top-notch, and instead of trying to be nice and putting good words to the guys, say what the guys like to hear, soft-soaping them. Not him. He was strictly all for Leo. Durocher had tried to do everything possible for publicity, everything he could think of. He knew his baseball, and that's about all. He didn't know how to handle young players. He wanted to be in the front all the time. He wanted the publicity. He wanted the limelight. He loved that. Believe me, he was no ballplayer's manager."

The one thing that gave the 1946 season structure was the revival of the prewar Dodger–Cardinal rivalry. In early August the Dodgers led by two games over the Cards, but despite Durocher's brilliant shifting of pitchers, his shuffling lineups, pinch hitting, scrapping, bunting, hit and running, stealing bases, despite a 42–16 record at Ebbets Field, the Dodgers could not keep up with the Cardinals, who took a two-game lead going into September. And as soon as the Cards took the lead, the press decided who to blame: Branch Rickey. The press had never liked or trusted the old parsimonious Bible-thumper. Reporters often felt they were being manipulated by Rickey, who they found to be sanctimonious and stuffy. In general most reporters are wary of demagogues, especially those wrapped in religious garb, and when Rickey spoke to them in parables, the reaction was "what a bullshit artist he is."

Rickey, furthermore, came just as the war was heating up, and a plummeting in the fortunes of the Dodgers seemed to coincide with his arrival. Reporters had liked MacPhail because he was great copy. Blunt and forthright, MacPhail spoke his piece and never cared about the consequences. MacPhail also treated them to as much booze as they could ever drink, and some of them drank rivers.

Rickey also had a glaring flaw that hurt his reputation badly. He was greedy for money. The writers knew that Rickey paid among the lowest salaries in baseball. They also knew he was one of the highest-paid executives.

Many saw him as a hypocrite. He refused to attend games on Sunday because of a promise he had made to his dear mother. But he always called in to learn the attendance figure. When a plane would fly overhead during a Sunday game, the players would point and say, "There goes Mr. Rickey, counting the crowd." Reporters had a saying about Rickey: "The more he talks, the more we count the spoons."

Since his arrival in 1943, Rickey had been selling washed-up veterans, such as Medwick, Camilli, Wyatt, and Fitzsimmons, clearing out the vets for the kids from his farm system, which was the finest in the business. At its peak Rickey had 700 players in the farm system, and the ones he didn't keep for the Dodgers, he traded to other teams for cash. And his eye never failed him. Not one of the players he let go turned out to be as good as any of the ones he kept.

Whether the reporters didn't understand Rickey's system or didn't care to understand isn't clear, but writers such as *Daily News* columnist Jimmy Powers emphasized the money Rickey was making from selling off the castoffs, and his criticism of Rickey's selling of these players became part of his campaign to humiliate and degrade Rickey and to drive him out of Brooklyn.

Ever since he had started in baseball, Rickey had had the philosophy that a hungry player was a better player, and following through on that, he paid his players substandard wages. Also he felt that as general manager, it was his job to get the players as cheaply as possible, and it was their job to fight him. If they weren't up to it, he felt, that was their problem. The flaw in that logic was that he held all the cards.

At St. Louis, where Rickey got to keep twenty percent of the profits he made on player sales, he made $88,000 in 1941 and about the same amount in 1942, on a base salary of $50,000. When he took over the Dodger presidency in 1943, his base salary was $65,000. On top of that, he continued to get his twenty percent of the profits on player sales. At this time, the average ballplayer was making between $5,000 and $6,000, and some were making as little as $3,300 for a season.

Rickey could be an out and out con man about it. Here is a conversation Frank Graham recorded of Rickey negotiating on the phone with a holdout for the 1943 season:

RICKEY: "Do you know you should be here?"
HOLDOUT: "I ain't moving until I get the money I want."
RICKEY: "Money! Money! Is that all you think about? Have you no pride in the Brooklyn club? Wait! Don't answer. Have you no regard for your fellow players? Do you realize they are here every day, toiling hard to get in shape, their minds and hearts set on winning the pennant?"
HOLDOUT: "Yeah, I know all about that."
RICKEY: "But do you know they look for you every day?"
HOLDOUT: "No."
RICKEY: "That they ask for you? That they know they need you if they are going to win this pennant on which they have their hearts set?"
HOLDOUT: "They do?"
RICKEY: "Yes! And do you know that I have given them my promise you will be here? And moreover, that I have promised the newspapermen that you will come, and that nine photographers were here today looking for you?"
HOLDOUT: "They were? Nine photographers looking for me?"
RICKEY: "Yes. Now will you come?"
HOLDOUT: "I'm starting tomorrow, boss."
RICKEY: "That's a good boy. And when you get here, we will look over your contract again."

According to Graham, Rickey hung up and turned to his secretary. "See if you can round up nine photographers from somewhere—anywhere—to come up here for a few days. I have an idea I might need them."

When catcher Mickey Owen and hard-hitting outfielder Luis Olmo jumped the Dodgers to play in the outlaw Mexican League in the spring of 1946, reporters blamed the Dodger boss. Jimmy Powers wrote that if Rickey hadn't been so cheap the two players never would have defected.

Powers's vituperation increased in June, when Rickey traded away the popular second baseman, Billy Herman. Powers, who had hung the label "El Cheapo" on Rickey, suggested that Rickey had released Herman because he no longer wanted to pay his $20,000 salary. In July Powers derisively wrote:

> One reader suggests that all fans get together and each donate a $20 bill upon entrance to the park. A grocery store chain has kindly consented to donate twenty empty barrels.
>
> If the fans will help fill these barrels with $20 bills, perhaps Rickey's desire for milking money out of the franchise will be satisfied, and he will pack his carpetbags and go away to another town and run his coolie payroll there.

Powers was right that money was at issue, of course. But Herman wasn't sent packing because Rickey didn't want to pay his salary. Rickey had negotiated with Herman and beaten him soundly. Herman knew he wasn't making the money a star of his caliber should have been making, and he staged a rebellion of sorts, and when Rickey learned what had happened, he let Herman go. But because Rickey didn't want to hurt Herman's image, he never revealed why he let him go.

Harold Parrott: "The truth was that I had probably been the one to 'fire' Herman. The manager of the hotel where he stayed during a spring training weekend in Miami soaked me for damage to one of his rooms. Herman had obviously staged a wild party. Augie Galan, Herman's roommate, would gladly have chipped in with his share, but Billy, who had been a great star, got stubborn because he wanted to stick Rickey with the bill. He didn't think the Old Man was paying him enough.

"I gave Herman a chance to pay for the damages quietly, but he refused. Once on the books of the Brooklyn club, the brawl, and the damages, soon came to light. Incidentally, it must have been a pretty good party; they had to get a plasterer to dislodge the whiskey glasses that were imbedded in the ceiling.

"When he learned of Herman's caper, Rickey acted fast. He had a young Dodger team and didn't want any night crawlers around to teach his kids bad habits. Within a week, Billy Herman was on his way to the Boston Braves. If indeed a pennant did turn on that deal—and it was unlikely, because Eddie Stanky was doing a great job at second base for us—it was because of a measly $30 bill for damages!"

* * *

BILLY HERMAN: "I got the blame for it, but I didn't do it. I wasn't even in my room that night. It was my room all right, but I had traded rooms with another player. I won't tell you his name. But I switched rooms with him so he and his buddy, my roommate, could party. I just went up to the other room and slept, and I didn't know anything about it until I checked out the next morning. I wasn't even there.

"Still, it might well have been the reason Rickey traded me, because Rickey was an idiot about those kinds of things anyway. It was also true that I was making too much money for Rickey to pay. He was a tight, cheap, old bastard. It was all right that he traded me. I didn't care. I got more money with Boston. I just wasn't going to complain and get someone else in trouble."

Also, if Herman had been the skillful star he had once been, it is doubtful Rickey would have let him go. But Herman was thirty-seven, slowing down, and with Stanky waiting to step in, expendable.

COOKIE LAVAGETTO: "When we get old, we get old. We don't move as much. They wanted to play Eddie Stanky at second instead of Herman because he could manipulate better, move around better. You gotta cover ground if you're going to play. You just can't stand there waving at those balls."

The criticism of Rickey was not limited to the columnists. The Dodgers' young pitcher, Ralph Branca, was one of Rickey's new breed, a college boy, and because he was fairly sophisticated, he saw how Rickey kept everybody's salary down, and he tried to fight the system.

Branca believed that he had pitched very effectively in 1945. As a nineteen-year-old rookie, he had been 5–6 and with a most respectable 3.03 era, and when over the winter, Rickey sent him a contract calling for a salary of a measly $3,300, the same money he had made the year before, Branca had the temerity to send Rickey the contract back unsigned. Worse, he had the balls to tell the *Daily News* about it.

In 1946 as punishment, Branca sat on the bench almost all season long. It wasn't until mid-September that Branca got to pitch, and when he finally was unleashed, Durocher started him in the first game of the playoffs against the Cardinals. In '46, the Dodgers finished the season tied with the Cardinals. Branca's benching surely cost the Dodgers the pennant. Why didn't he get to pitch? Branca feels he knows:

RALPH BRANCA: "When I returned the contract unsigned, I didn't send a letter, didn't send nothing. I didn't know protocol. I called my brother at home, and I told him, 'Send it back,' and he did. And that rubbed Rickey wrong, and he didn't talk to me, didn't communicate with me from the end of January until I went back down to Daytona Beach to talk to him about it. I guess it was his way of punishing me by letting me sit home and come mealymouth crawling back to him. I asked him for $6,000, and he lied to me. He said, 'No young guy in your age bracket is making that kind of money.' Well, I knew for a fact that another of the young pitchers was making $6,500, and to call a spade a spade, he couldn't shine my shoes as a prospect or a pitcher, but he was one of Rickey's favorites so he was making more money than I did. And I ended up signing for $5,000.

"And basically, in '46, they blew the pennant because Rickey was ticked off at me because of what Jimmy Powers wrote in the *Daily News*. I had done an interview with one of Jimmy's cohorts, and I told him I hadn't made any money and that I had been looking to make a few dollars from baseball. It was after I told him about our salary negotiations that Powers wrote the article in which he branded Rickey, 'El Cheapo.' And listen, I wasn't the lowest paid guy! But Rickey must have read what I said in the Powers column and held it against me. I didn't start a single game until the middle of September!

"I remember I reported something like March 17, and I pitched about three innings the first week, and then went five innings against the University of Miami, and then seven innings. And by the time the Dodgers started the regular season, I was one of the starting pitchers. Well, the very first game I pitched I got hit in the back of my elbow by a line drive. It was a knuckleball hit by, of all guys, Whitey Wietleman, who couldn't hit a ball hard, but when I went to catch it, it dipped under my glove and hit me in the arm. And so I didn't start for a couple of starts, and then they forgot about me. Two weeks went by, three weeks, and one day coach Charley Dressen said to me, 'I want you to pitch batting practice.' I said, 'You can't make any money pitching batting practice, Charley.' And Charley got ticked off at me, and I was in his doghouse. And they didn't use me until the end of June. They used me in mop-up relief, and I got everybody out, and now I've pitched maybe five times, pitched about eighteen innings, and they have three hits off me and no runs. So now I'm no longer mop-up relief, I go to difficult relief, and in September they finally start me in a game.

"We were playing a doubleheader against the Cardinals, and before the second game, Dressen said to me, 'We're going to start you, but Vic Lombardi is going to warm up, and you're going to pitch to one batter, and then we're going to bring him in.' I was angry. I remember saying to myself, 'Ah, the sacrificial lamb. My ass!' Being angry, I guess it pumped me up, the adrenaline got to flowing, 'cause in the first inning I got them out on five pitches. I walked in, and Durocher said, 'Keep throwing like that, kid. We're going to keep you in.'

"I ended up pitching a three-hit shutout, and that was really the game that made me a pitcher, because after that, I believed in myself, that I could pitch and win a crucial game. We won and went into first place by a couple of percentage points. I beat the Cardinals, 5–0, and that made me, that was the tempering of Ralph Branca. I became a believer in myself that year.

"And I came right back, and I pitched another shutout, and during the regular season in '46 my record was 3–0, and I was the one Durocher picked to pitch the first game of the playoffs.

"And there never should have been a playoff. The three of them, Rickey, Dressen, and Durocher, blew the pennant, 'cause I had pitched very effectively in '45, but I had held out, and they didn't pitch me in '46. If they had pitched me, you know we would have won at least one more game than we did."

With the right breaks, the Dodgers still might have won. But with two games left in the season and the Dodgers in a good position to win the pennant, Pete Reiser broke his ankle. And once again, Durocher was responsible.

PETE REISER: "It was like old times as we fought the Cardinals down to the wire for the pennant. There were two days to go, and I was playing with a very bad hamstring pull. Before the game I told Leo, 'I can play, but I can't run.' In the first inning I reached first on a walk, and then the next thing I knew, he had flashed the steal sign. I got off to take my lead, and the pitcher made a routine throw over, and I tried to slide back in. My spike caught, and I could hear my ankle crack. Leo came running out. 'Get up,' he was screaming, 'you're all right.'

"But the pain was terrible. I said, 'Not this time, Skip. It's broke.' The bone was sticking out through the skin."

Durocher's immediate and typical reaction was to look for someone to blame. He lashed out at the Ebbets Field groundskeeper. "The rocklike ground grabbed his spikes," said Durocher with Shakespearean imagery.

Never did Leo admit that Reiser told him he was in no shape to play.

On the final day, September 29, the Dodgers were shut out by Mort Cooper of the Braves, and then all the players remained in the clubhouse to listen to the broadcast of the Cardinals–Cubs game. When the Cardinals lost, the Dodgers had backed into a tie, and they would have to play a best-two-out-of-three playoff with the Cardinals for the pennant.

The First Playoff

When the Cards lost on the final day of the regular season, the Dodgers found themselves involved in the first playoff in National League history. Starting the first game for the Dodgers was Ralph Branca, who had control problems and didn't get through the third inning.

RALPH BRANCA: "I'm twenty years old, and I start the first playoff game in National League history. And I got beat. They didn't really hit the ball hard. It was just a bunch of nub hits, and I don't say that because I'm prejudiced. It's the truth. Joe Garagiola hit one off the end of the bat over Lavagetto's head at third. Lavagetto was playing in, and it went over his head and spun in the dirt and didn't even get to the outfield. Harry Walker hit a chop over my head. Not exactly wore me out. I was just a twenty-year-old kid starting in the first playoff game, and I got beat."

The only runs scored by the Dodgers in that first game were driven in by six foot seven inch first baseman Howie Schultz. Reporters called him Stretch because he had a physical resemblance to Stretch Kelly, who had starred at first base for the Giants, and they called him Steeple because he was religious and also because of his height. He was the tallest player in the big leagues. One time Willard Mullin drew a cartoon of Schultz in the *Sporting News* and titled it the Leaning Tower of Flatbush.

HOWIE SCHULTZ: "I could handle the glove pretty well. An excellent target. The infielders loved me. I had one problem. I just didn't stay strong through the season. Because when I felt good, I felt I could hit almost anybody, but I just seemed to get tired too quickly. In 1944 I was leading the league in both home runs and runs batted in around the 4th of July. Then I just dissolved the latter part of the season. When I started to feel weak, I would press. You try too hard. You're not swinging the bat any more. You're pulling it around. Those big bouncers to shortstop get to be pretty common."

In the second and final game of the playoffs Schultz will always be remembered for striking out in the ninth inning with the bases loaded to end the Dodger season.

HOWIE SCHULTZ: "Those playoff games were really monumental. The first one was in St. Louis against Howie Pollet, and at that time Eddie Stevens was playing first against right-handers, and I was playing against left-handers, and so I played against Pollet and hit a home run, and I drove in the two runs we scored.

"There was nobody on base, and he threw me a change of pace and got it high, and I just did hit it into the left-field seats, nothing fancy. He made a mistake, and I don't know if it was blind luck or not, but I hit it out.

"In the ninth, with runners on first and third, I hit a line drive to right center, a base hit, and Enos Slaughter cut across from right field, got it on the second hop, and Bruce Edwards, who was on first, tried to go to third, and Slaughter made a strong throw and threw him out by twenty-five feet, which was the key play in the ballgame, because I ended up on second base, and had he been safe, we would have had men on second and third and only one out. The score ended up 4 to 2, so those would have been two big base runners. But Edwards became the second out, and the next out ended the game.

"Red Munger, a right-hander, pitched the second game for the Cards, so I sat. They got a big lead quick, and when we got into the last inning, we were losing 8–1. In the ninth we scored three runs to make it 8–4, and then we loaded the bases. The tying run was up. Dick Whitman was our next batter. He was a left-handed batter, and they brought Harry Brecheen in to pitch, and so Leo sent me up to pinch hit against Brecheen. I went up there, the tying run.

"I remember hitting the first pitch down the left-field line, and it hit just outside the chalk mark, and after that, the count went to 3 and 2. The bases were loaded, the fans were going crazy, and Brecheen threw me a letup screwball, and I almost fell down swinging at it. Missing.

George Brace Photo

HOWIE SCHULTZ

"And so that's how you go from hero to goat in one day. So before God and 30,000 fans, I struck out with the bases loaded to end the Dodgers' playoff bid in 1946."

After the game, Cardinal manager Eddie Dyer told reporters: "There is something I want you all to know. It was Branch Rickey who assembled this team. He got these ballplayers while he was still running this ballclub before the war. And he is responsible for what I know about this game."

There were rumors that swirled around the Dodger clubhouse that in 1947 Durocher would leave the Dodgers to manage the Yankees for his old boss MacPhail. Durocher told reporters, "MacPhail gave me my first chance to manage. He was a great boss here and supplied me with anything a manager could ask. But since 1930 the man I work for here, Branch Rickey, has been like a father to me. So I'll probably be here till I die, if he's still here."

But events were conspiring against both Durocher and Rickey. When the Dodgers lost the playoff, there was an outcry in the press that Rickey really hadn't wanted to win the pennant, that he was happier finishing second because by doing that, he maintained fan interest without having to pay higher salaries. It was a charge that had been leveled against him with the Cardinals, but one that was not only unfounded and untrue but utterly ridiculous. Rickey loved to win as badly as Leo—the big reason certainly why he kept Leo.

Rickey's position was further eroded because John L. Smith, who was dying of cancer, no longer was a Rickey supporter. Smith's loyalties had been wooed and won by the third man in the triumvirate, Walter O'Malley, who was plotting Rickey's—and Durocher's—ouster.

When O'Malley was with his political friends, one of his main sports was making fun of Rickey. It went so far that one time at a political meeting in Brooklyn's Bossert Hotel, O'Malley taped a portrait of Rickey on the wall, and he and his high-rolling buddies played pin the tail on the donkey. O'Malley had begun a subtle but effective campaign to undermine Rickey in any way he could. O'Malley derided Rickey's slovenly appearance, bad-mouthed his handling of players, and complained continually about Rickey's exorbitant salary. He called him a "psalm-singing fake" and enjoyed using Jimmy Powers's sobriquet of "El Cheapo." At the worst of Powers's smear campaign against him, Rickey had gone to O'Malley, the Dodger attorney, and asked O'Malley's advice as to whether he should sue. O'Malley told him not to. "Every newspaperman would hate you," O'Malley told him. And so Powers's campaign continued unabated, and the fans picked up his chant, until it became so uncomfortable for Rickey's wife and family to attend games that they stopped going.

And yet at the end of the 1946 season, when Rickey, trying to get out from under that label, gave each of his players a new Studebaker as a token of his gratitude for their trying so hard, it was O'Malley who went to the press complaining that Rickey was giving away money that rightfully should have gone to the Dodger stockholders—himself included, of course.

At the end of the '46 season, all the directors got financial statements indicating that the Dodgers had made a net profit of $451,000. Rickey had sold surplus players of questionable talent to the suckers running the other major league teams left short of talent by the war, adding $239,000 to the Dodger coffers.

And yet O'Malley was still complaining that Rickey was making too much money. In 1947 Rickey would be entering the final year of a five-year contract. The ambitious and conniving O'Malley didn't want the contract renewed. He wanted the Dodgers all to himself. And Rickey would come to know what many others learned over the next few decades: Whatever O'Malley wanted, O'Malley got.

3

Leo Gets in Dutch

When Branch Rickey accepted the post of top Dodger in February 1943, Baseball Commissioner Kenesaw Mountain Landis issued Rickey an order: "You must break up that nest of horseplayers and card sharks."

Upon Rickey's arrival in Brooklyn, he was informed that Durocher had once again surrounded himself with gamblers, bookmakers, racing handicappers, ticket scalpers, and "fast friends," just as he had when he played in St. Louis. All enjoyed access to Leo's clubhouse and even the dugout. Three bookmakers had sued Durocher for uncollected horse-racing debts, and Rickey was deeply concerned that Durocher's bad habits might one day get him in serious trouble.

The first thing Rickey did was make Durocher crawl to get his job back. Rickey pretended that he didn't want Leo because of his unsavory attitudes and shady friends, and Rickey followed this with a public discussion of the evils of gambling. He denounced Leo and the players who gambled, and only then did he re-sign him as manager. Because of the pressure to act on the gambling situation, Rickey used coach Charley Dressen as a scapegoat. Rather than get rid of Durocher, he got rid of Dressen, who also loved gambling, especially the nags. Dressen was often seen in the company of professional handicapper Memphis Engleberg, to whom Dressen owed money. Yet before the season was over, when the heat was off, Rickey quietly hired him back.

Howie Schultz: "The gambling on the Dodgers wasn't going on as heavily as before I was there, because Rickey had put a stop to it already. Gambling was not that much a factor when I was there. But the scuttlebutt was that Leo was into Higbe's paycheck every two weeks, and one of the other player's as well. They'd sit around and play gin in the clubhouse.

"Leo was a professional card player. You name the game, and he could play it better than all of us. Hig and the others thought they could beat him, but they did not have the mentality to go with it. He just fleeced them."

Kirby Higbe: "Leo and I played together quite a bit. He would play me gin rummy, and he would win, but he never took a dime from me. He'd beat me and always say, 'If you win the next time you pitch, we'll call all this even.' And nine times out of ten, I'd win. Well, it made me bear down a little harder. It was good for me and him both. Durocher, pardner, was the best manager I ever played for. By far.

"Me and Jimmy Wasdell played gin rummy, and sometimes we'd be partners with a couple of others. Sometimes we'd play Hollywood. Depended on how we felt. We'd play pretty good stakes though. A quarter a point, two dollars a box, and ten dollars a game. Them's pretty good stakes.

"But let me tell you something. Leo and Billy Herman and Johnny Rizzo were the ones who used to do the big card playin'. They played for the big money. They played pinochle. I never did know how to play pinochle. They played a hell of a lot, and they played for pretty good money. We never knew exactly how Leo done, all we had wuz hearsay, whether he won or didn't."

And yet Rickey, who during his entire career was maligned for being conservative and Puritanical, despite his religious and moral convictions against everything Durocher stood for, never once stopped supporting Durocher, even when Durocher's life-style continued to get him into trouble.

Toward the end of the 1944 season, Rickey had asked Leo to meet him at Kingston, New York, where the Dodgers were to play an exhibition game, so the two could look over prospects. Leo never showed up. He went to the race track instead. The next morning, when Rickey found out, he phoned coach Charley Dressen. Rickey told him, "Durocher is through. You are the new manager." Dressen immediately called Durocher and advised him to rush to Rickey and plead with him for his job. Durocher did, and he kept the job. Out of his loyalty to Leo, Dressen kept the story quiet.

Afterward, a friend told Rickey: "I knew you wouldn't fire him."

"How did you know?"

"Because he's your favorite reclamation project."

"You're right," said Rickey, "and I would hate to admit that I was defeated."

Leo had an inability to keep out of trouble. On June 8, 1945, Durocher was arrested, charged, and indicted for assault of a fan. The complainant was twenty-one, a 200-pound loudmouthed Brooklyn kid just out of the army.

HOWIE SCHULTZ: "I was there when Leo and the fan got into it. I was playing first base that day, and Curt Davis was pitching. And there was a leatherlung fan behind the third base dugout up in the upper deck, and he was just unmerciful to Davis. Those of us in the infield and in the dugout could hear him. He was saying stuff like, 'You're over the hill. Don't fall down on the mound, old man.' That kind of stuff. And Curt was about forty at the time. [According to reports, the fan also called Durocher a crook and a bum, and a motherfucker.]

"Because I was on the field, I wasn't aware of what happened, but apparently Leo called one of the ushers—we had what you would call a security officer, a huge guy around 270 pounds, and Leo told him to go up in the stands and get this guy. And he did. The security officer brought the fan down to the area behind the dugout underneath the stands, and Leo confronted him."

* * *

The security guard's name was Joe Moore. Among the young Dodger rooters who often tried to sneak into the park, Moore was notorious. He would bellow, "If I catchya, you're gonna get a kick right in the ass," but fortunately for the kids, his gross weight slowed him down, and he didn't catch the kids—often.

As per Durocher's wishes, Moore brought the kid to him under the stands. With Moore holding the kid, Durocher said, "You've got a mother. How would you like it if someone called her names?"

According to the kid, he never got a chance to answer. Moore swung his beefy right arm and smashed his right fist into the fan's face, using brass knuckles. The kid slumped to the floor, and when he got to his feet again, Durocher, who had taken the brass knuckles from Moore, brutally gave the fan another smash to the face. Bleeding and terrified, the kid somehow managed to get up and flee down the corridor, pursued by Moore and Durocher. Getting away, he went directly to the Empire Boulevard Police Station and swore out warrants of arrest for Durocher and Moore. He then went to the hospital, where an exam showed his jaw to be broken.

The next morning Durocher and Moore were arrested and released on $1,000 bond. Durocher was facing a felony conviction, and after the grand jury returned an indictment, his baseball career was in serious jeopardy.

HOWIE SCHULTZ: "Leo wound up in court, hit with both criminal and civil lawsuits. But the judge's name was Rabinowitz [Leibowitz actually] or something similar to that, and he was a real good Dodger fan, and the criminal suit was dismissed."

In the end it didn't end up costing Leo a nickel out of his own pocket. The fan agreed to a settlement of $6,750, and Leo's insurance company footed the bill.

In the spring of 1945, while the Dodgers were training in Bear Mountain, actor George Raft, Durocher's closest friend, was staying in Durocher's midtown New York City apartment, and during the course of a crap game, a mark accused Raft of taking him for $12,500 by using loaded dice to make thirteen straight passes.

What's curious is that the mark didn't complain to D.A. Frank Hogan until seven months after the incident, and what's even more curious is that in October 1946 columnist Westbrook Pegler, who rarely attacked entertainers or athletes—usually saving his barbs for politicians, especially Franklin and Eleanor Roosevelt—wrote three highly inflammatory columns directed against Raft and Durocher.

In one of the columns Pegler wrote about the alleged crooked dice game:

> Martin Shurin, the chump of the evening, a young man with illusions about celebrities, particularly movie actors, is disenchanted now. He lost $12,500 to Raft in a few minutes, and, in the ensuing notoriety, shot off his mouth, perhaps untruthfully, about his earnings as a subcontractor

in the war business of supplying parts. He may have exaggerated. . . .

Shurin recalls that in the scramble for position at the crap table, he found himself alongside Raft. He would have preferred a place where he could retrieve the dice and count the spots as Raft ran up his thirteen passes, all fours and tens, most of them the hard way. . . .

However, a spot next to the great man was a place of honor, so he did not scuffle and began to lay the conventional price against fours and tens. He says he gave Raft $1,500 in currency and a check for $1,000 that night and sent him ten $1,000 bills a few days later. . . .

Durocher's choice of companions has been a matter of deep concern to Branch Rickey, the business manager of the Dodgers. The old practice of "whispering out" players and even managers "for the good of the game" could be revived. . . .

If the moving picture business knows that one of its stars prefers the underworld and doesn't care, that is one matter. Nobody would bet on the outcome of a picture, but a few killings on fixed ball games would degrade something that the public, perhaps without realizing as much, has come to regard as an American ideal or treasure.

According to Raft, Shurin's story and Pegler's telling of it was a total fabrication. Raft didn't make thirteen passes in a row, and he didn't collect much of what he won, he said. Later Shurin was arrested by police for passing bad checks. But the publicity had hurt Durocher, more even than Raft, who openly hung out with mobsters, including his best friend, Las Vegas entrepreneur Bugsy Siegel.

When Rickey read Pegler's columns, he phoned Durocher and made him promise that Raft would never again use his apartment.

These, however, were not the last of the charges against Durocher. Apparently someone high up in the Dodger organization had leaked information to Pegler that Durocher's telephone had been tapped and that Leo was heard talking with gangster Joe Adonis. Moreover, the unnamed Dodger official told Pegler that Leo's signature had appeared on checks in the notorious $800,000 Morganthaler swindle.

Fortunately for Durocher, Rickey was a stout defender. After thoroughly checking out the information, Rickey discovered that there was far less to Durocher's wrongdoing than met the eye. Adonis had not called Durocher, but rather it had been one of his henchmen to remind Leo of a promise to send some bats and balls to a church in New Jersey. And the signature on the check in the swindle was among thousands impounded from a check-cashing firm.

Rickey suspected that there was someone in his organization out to get Durocher. By making Durocher look bad, the perpetrator was also tainting Rickey. Rickey felt he was sure he knew who it was, though he was powerless to do anything about it. As a protective move, Rickey called Commissioner Happy Chandler and asked Chandler to help him to convince Durocher to keep out of further trouble. Rickey had just signed Durocher to a $50,000-

a-year contract for 1947, and he didn't want to take the chance that his high-rolling manager might be suspended.

In November of 1946 Chandler and Durocher met secretly on the fairway of the Claremont Country Club in Berkeley, California. During the conversation Chandler asked Durocher, "Do you know a man by the name of Bugsy Siegel?" Durocher said he had a nodding acquaintance with him. "Don't nod to him any more," said Chandler. Chandler asked him if he knew Joe Adonis. A nodding acquaintance, said Durocher. "Don't nod to him any more either," said Chandler.

Chandler also ordered Durocher to move out of Raft's Coldwater Canyon, California, home, where Leo was living. Chandler threatened that if Durocher continued to see Raft, Siegel, or Adonis he would be suspended from baseball.

From the day Durocher packed up and left Raft, his relationship with Raft was never the same. Though he realized Durocher had to stay away in order to keep his job, Raft to his death denied fleecing Shurin, denied all the allegations in Pegler's article, and felt bitter that Durocher had bent under Chandler's pressure to move out.

Durocher kept his nose clean—as far as his hanging out with unsavory characters. But then he did something that put him in dutch with the Catholic Church. He fell in love with his neighbor's wife. In December of 1946 Ray Hendricks, the husband of actress Laraine Day, publicly accused Durocher of being a "love pirate." He charged that "Durocher clandestinely pursued the love" of Miss Day while "posing as a family friend."

Durocher had been accused of outrageous acts before, including being a kleptomaniac, a deadbeat, a liar, a card cheat, and a brawler, but the public outcry against what it viewed as his adultery was the most violent. Making things worse was Leo's decision to ignore the California judge, who ruled that Leo and Miss Day had to live apart for one year before they could marry. Before the judge's decree had time to dry, Miss Day flew to Juarez, Mexico, for a divorce, and Leo flew to El Paso, Texas, where the two were married.

In February of 1947 the Catholic Youth Organization condemned Durocher for "undermining the moral training of Brooklyn's Roman Catholic youth by his conduct both on and off the baseball diamond."

The CYO had a membership of over 50,000 youngsters, of whom a third belonged to the Dodger Knothole Club, and the threat was that if Durocher remained manager, these youngsters would defect to the Giants or the Yankees.

Rickey, a thoughtful, religious man, was deeply hurt by Durocher's public spanking by the Catholic Church. During several long meetings with the Reverend Vincent Powell, who had made the announcement against Durocher, Rickey kept asking whether Catholics still believed in mercy and forgiveness. Wouldn't it be better, Rickey asked the Reverend Powell, to use Durocher's appeal to youngsters in a positive way rather than blacken the man's character? "Can we ignore a tremendous force like this and surrender it to Satan?" Rickey asked. "Don't you see what a terrific force we can make Leo for good, and against evil?"

But the prelate was unmoved.

Rickey had reason to wonder who had put the churchmen up to this. Brooklyn's Catholics had never attacked Hitler or Mussolini the way they were going after Leo.

HAROLD PARROTT: "O'Malley, the original smiling Irishman when it came to blarney, carried a large prayerbook in the Catholic Church. He was respected by the clergy and could easily have stopped all the anti-Durocher nonsense had he wanted to. His best pal was Judge Henry Ughetta, head of the Sons of Italy and a Knight of St. Gregory, which meant his connections went all the way to Rome. One word from them both, and the Reverend Powell, as well as Monsignor Edward Lodge Curran, another anti-Leo scold, would have piped down, and so would their Catholic Youth Organization.

"But O'Malley never gave the word. Obviously, O'Malley enjoyed seeing Durocher on the red-hot rotisserie, because Leo was Branch Rickey's favorite reclamation project, and that meant the Old Man would collect some of the critics' heat."

Adding to the pressure on Durocher, the press proceeded to dredge up every scandal involving the manager since his days with the Yankees when he was accused of stealing Babe Ruth's watch. There was the divorce suit filed in 1934 by his first wife, Ruby Hartley Durocher. In it she charged that one night when she came home at two A.M. after playing bridge with friends, Leo punched her in the jaw and tied her up in a bedsheet. The papers again detailed the assault charges by the former GI and the dice games in Leo's apartment.

And then early in 1947, events continued to hurt Leo. In January, minor league czar Judge W. G. Bramham suspended the manager of the Houma, Louisiana, team and four of his players and suspended a player on the Abbeville team, all for listening to "propositions" from gamblers and not reporting them. All denied the charges, but none ever played baseball again. The Evangeline League fix scandal, as it was called, made headlines across the nation.

Two days later boxing's golden boy, Rocky Graziano, told Manhattan DA Frank Hogan that in December he had been offered $100,000 to throw a Madison Square Garden fight against a stiff named Cowboy Reuben Shank. Graziano pulled out of the fight, using a sore back as a convenient excuse. Graziano insisted he did not know the name of the man who made the offer.

In March the headline in the *Daily News* read: "GRID STARS GOT $1,000, SAYS PARIS. FIXER NAMES FILCHOCK, HAPES." On page three gambler Alvin Paris testified in court that Merle Hapes and Frank Filchock, the two brightest stars on the New York football Giants, had each accepted $500 in cash from winnings on bets that Paris had made for them on a game against the Washington Redskins. It was part of the testimony that a gambler by the name of Harvey Stemmer, convicted of bribing Brooklyn College basketball players, had tried to fix the Giants–Bears championship game. According to Paris, Hapes was desperate for the money and was willing to go along, but that Filchock refused, killing the plot.

Five days later, on March 10, there was another *News* headline: "GAMBLERS YANKEE GUESTS: LIP."

Perhaps it was because Larry MacPhail, now a Yankee owner, had stolen away his right-hand man, Charley Dressen. Perhaps it was because MacPhail and Leo were feuding over Leo's refusal to join MacPhail as Yankee manager. Perhaps it was because Durocher was still stung at having to give up his friend Raft. Perhaps it was just because Leo was incapable of controlling his temper. But when he spotted two of his gambling cronies sitting in one of MacPhail's boxes at a spring training game against the Dodgers in Havana, Durocher exploded. Only a few months earlier, Chandler had warned Durocher to stay away from gamblers, and here was MacPhail doing just what Durocher had been forbidden to do. Where was the justice?

Before the game, Durocher stalked up and down the dugout, pointing across the field into the stands at the gamblers and muttering to reporters, "Look over there." One of the men standing nearby was a newcomer, reporter Dick Young of the *Daily News*.

DICK YOUNG: "Leo was pointing at MacPhail, who had Memphis Engleberg and Connie Immerman as his guests. Memphis Engleberg was a well-known bookmaker, a gambler, and a very nice guy, as a lot of those guys are. Immerman ran the casino in Havana. And Leo was holding court in the dugout, saying, 'Look over there. He has gamblers as his guest. If I did that, I'd get kicked out of baseball.'

"Leo was bringing this thing to a boil, and I can remember that Milt Gross and myself went down during the game to MacPhail's box, and I said, 'Is this man your guest?' and MacPhail got surly and said, 'He's not in my box. He's across the aisle.' But he was just pulling a technicality, and so we said, 'But is he your guest?' We pushed it, and he said, 'What are you, a district attorney? I don't have to answer your questions.' We said, 'We just wanted to get your side.' And we went back and wrote it, and that kind of threw fuel on the fire. The next thing you knew, Durocher was out on his ass."

The next day, the two gamblers were again seated in MacPhail's private box. This time, Durocher himself made their presence public in his weekly column for the *Brooklyn Eagle*.

If ever Durocher opened an embarrassing can of worms, this was it, especially in light of the football probe. The last thing baseball needed was a hint of scandal involving gamblers. The problem with Leo, moreover, was that in his own mind, he had never done anything improper in his life. He always denied having shady characters as friends. He denied hitting the kid with brass knuckles. He denied having done anything wrong in marrying Laraine Day. And to this day, he says that his accusing MacPhail of having gamblers in his box was just needling between baseball buddies. It was a favorite plaint of Leo's: "What did I do? What did I do?"

But to outside observers, Leo didn't seem so blameless. Some felt he was digging his own grave, especially during a time when people were questioning the honesty of pro sports. The next day *News* columnist Jimmy Powers wrote:

"With each outburst, the Lip is rapidly washing himself up. We still believe the day is not too far when it will be manager Dixie Walker." Two days later Commissioner Happy Chandler announced that he would hold a hearing into whether Leo's conduct was detrimental to baseball.

Said Chandler: "I am a patient man, but I do eventually break down. Maybe it is time Durocher decided whether he is a baseball manager or a columnist."

On March 16 MacPhail filed formal charges against Durocher and Rickey, saying the Dodger executives had slandered both himself and Dressen. In his statement MacPhail said, "I know Memphis Engleberg, and to my knowledge he never bets on baseball games. He wasn't my guest, but I wouldn't bar him from Yankee Stadium. I go to the races and do not forbid my players from going. Incidentally, Memphis often visits the Dodger clubhouse as a personal friend of Durocher's."

There it was. Despite all the warnings, Durocher was still keeping company with known gamblers.

Leo Gets Nailed

Branch Rickey wasn't worried. Or at least he said he wasn't worried. All he had to do was identify the guests in MacPhail's box as known gamblers and submit proof that they had been given the tickets by the Yankees, and Leo would be in the clear. Reporter Herb Goren of the *New York Sun* was prepared to file an affidavit saying that Memphis Engleberg had told him that he had gotten the tickets from MacPhail.

But Rickey and most of the writers failed to gauge the direction of the wind. Commissioner Happy Chandler knew it was his job to protect the reputation of professional baseball, and he was fed up with Durocher. He was tired of his antisocial behavior and the subsequent headlines and of having to warn him without seeing any perceptible improvement in his actions.

On March 24 Commissioner Chandler conducted a hearing. MacPhail, at Chandler's request, quoted the accusations about the two gamblers in his box from the article that Durocher and his ghost, Harold Parrott, had written in the *Brooklyn Eagle.* After MacPhail had finished, Durocher looked at MacPhail and said, "As far as I'm concerned, it's all baseball jargon. I didn't mean anything derogatory in that article about you. I have no ax to grind with you, Larry. I'm not mad at you. I wasn't insinuating anything about you. I needled you, but it was purely baseball and nothing personal." And Durocher apologized to his old boss. With that, MacPhail tore up the article, put his arm around Durocher and said, "You've always been a great guy with me and always will be a great guy. Forget it. It's over."

But it wasn't over with Chandler. The hearing was really a charade. Chandler had decided that Leo had gotten into trouble once too often. He suspended Durocher for the rest of the season.

* * *

Happy Chandler: "I had met Leo when he was playing with Cincinnati. Leo was just a bad boy, pardner. And I think I almost made a good boy out of him, but that was right difficult to do. He'd been in trouble so much. When Leo was a player in Cincinnati, Leo would get all spiffed up, dressed to kill, spending all his money, while his mother was working at the Netherlands Plaza Hotel scrubbing floors. Son, he would hold the lamp while his mother was cutting wood.

"Babe Ruth once told me, 'Leo stole my watch.' That's why they now have trunks in the clubhouse, to keep an eye on everyone's valuables.

"I started as commissioner in 1945, and he started right away. He hit a fellow in Brooklyn. Once he broke a fellow's jaw with brass knucks that he borrowed from a Brooklyn policeman. This fellow had been razzing him, and then he said the fellow had slipped on a water trough. That was not true. So they got together at the trial and paid this fellow off, you understand. I don't want to argue justice in the courts of Brooklyn, but I kept up with the trial of the case, and when they finished, the prosecution complimented the defense, and the defense complimented the prosecution for their feeble efforts to prosecute, and they settled the thing. If ever there was a miscarriage of justice in which both sides applauded themselves, this was it. They didn't fool me at all, of course. I knew how crazy they were in Brooklyn about their ball team. I was not unaware of that.

"And then there was the gambling. Durocher and the actor George Raft were gambling with baseball players, taking the players for more than they could afford to lose. And they were going to the races, and I have no particular objection to them, except they don't let the people at the bank who put their hands in the till go to the races, and there is a line there that you ought to draw, and my line was, 'Association with known and notorious gamblers.' I told Leo, 'That's apt to get you in trouble, and you ought not to do it.' That was long before the suspension.

"I warned him. I did everything I could. Of course, I knew Durocher and Charley Dressen and George Raft associated with each other. Leo and George was closer than a dead heat. Leo wasn't about to forsake George.

"Raft came to me after I suspended Leo and said, 'I want to see you, commissioner. I've been given a bum rap.'

"I said, 'I didn't give it to you, George.' I said, 'Do you have a baseball contract?' He said, 'No, sir.' I said, 'Take your business someplace else, because I don't have to be bothering with you. I do have to be bothered with Durocher.'

"I can't tell you exactly when, but it was sometime before I suspended Durocher that I turned Leo over to Rickey. I said, 'Rickey, you ought to be responsible for this fellow, and you've been good to him, and you ought to show him the error of his ways. You ought to straighten him out.' I did everything I could, and I've never pled this in my own defense, but I did everything I could to see that Durocher mended his ways, and I had hopes that Rickey would be the one to get him to do it. I thought it was Rickey's main responsibility. But ultimately, Rickey had to come to me to convince Leo to sever his relationships with those people.

"My suspension of Durocher was not precipitous, you understand. MacPhail's complaint was almost irrelevant. I had him out at hole number seventeen at the Claremont Country Club in Berkeley. I was playing, and I asked him to come, and he met me out there. Again I was going out of my way to keep him from suffering what he later suffered. I again warned him about the gamblers. I think I did everything I was required to do to try to save this fellow before I suspended him.

"And then there was the Laraine Day thing. We stood there on the green a while, and he told me the story of his being in this man's house with this man's wife, arguing who was going to take her. Leo and Laraine Day's husband were actually in the husband's house out in California, arguing with her husband who she was going to stay with, Durocher or her husband! I told Leo, 'If you come down to my part of the country and do that, I won't have to be bothered with you, because they'll kill you.' He thought about it soberly. I was trying to convince him that that was something you just didn't do. I said, 'You're in this man's house with his wife? She's his wife, not yours.' I was trying to get him to put his relationship with the woman on a basis where he wouldn't get killed or get in trouble. Hell, I didn't know what kind of fellow he was dealing with.

"But Leo kept doing things. Finally I said to Rickey, 'I don't believe you are going to take care of this fellow, so why don't you turn him back over to me. I'll take care of him.' And I know I almost made a good boy out of him. I know it helped him. How much? I don't know.

"The final straw was this gambler's mess with this fellow in Havana, where Leo accused MacPhail of associating with gamblers. That was not a big deal on MacPhail's part. That was Rickey and MacPhail complaining about each other. They had been close once. Rickey had raised MacPhail in the baseball business, but later they didn't speak to each other. They really had quite an enmity. All it did was bring all this out into the open. I had known about it all the time, but it brought notoriety and publicity.

"It was just an accumulation of instances, and after each one I had sought to git him on the straight path, and Rickey couldn't do it, and Rickey understood it was beyond his control, that Leo was a bad boy and undisciplined. Leo went into a place, not like he owned it, but like he didn't give a damn who owned it. And when he went in, he went in without thinking how he was going to git out. The fella was not well-educated, and the only thing he could do was play baseball and manage. He was a fair player, and he was a pretty good manager, with the exception that he didn't know how to handle young players.

"I wasn't anxious to make any bad publicity for Durocher. But he just kept making trouble for me, and I just didn't want to have any more of it. It was instance after instance. And that's the reason I said 'numerous instances' when I suspended him. And I said it that way because I didn't want to give him adverse publicity. Why would I want to do that?

"I'll tell you something else you'd be interested in. Mr. Justice Murphy was governor of Michigan before he was appointed to the United States Supreme Court by Franklin Roosevelt, and he and I were close friends. While the Durocher controversy was going on, Justice Murphy wrote me a letter. It said, 'Commissioner, you are a man of honor and a man of character, and I know you don't intend to put up with his conduct. If you let Durocher manage Brooklyn this year, we will have the Catholic Youth Organization desert the ballgames. They won't take part in baseball in Brooklyn.'

"Because of Leo's conduct, the Catholic youth were not going to take part in the baseball program in Brooklyn! Well, those kids were entitled to people they can respect. That's too great an opportunity for a fellow to stay on that baseball field and conduct himself that way. With that situation, I felt I had to take some drastic action.

"Murphy was a big Catholic, you understand, and he was one of my very good friends, and he said, 'I know you're going to take some action about it.'

"I had exhausted my patience with him. Hey, do you think I became commissioner to punish ballplayers? And I can say this now, because the time is long since passed, but every time a ballplayer got his tit in the wringer, I tried to help him. I thought that was one of my main jobs. And there were fellows who were amenable to admonitions and suggestions, but I never had to punish anyone like I did him. He was the only one who got any serious punishment.

"I told Rickey, 'You take charge of him, and if you don't, I'm going to.' And he couldn't. So I stood him aside for a year. That was necessary, and believe me, that was a mild penalty. I felt that if I made an error in this case, it was on the side of mercy. I let the Dodgers pay him. I knew they paid him. I didn't say anything, because I don't know what he would have done without the money.

"They said Leo wasn't going to do it. I said, 'If I live, he'll do it.' And Leo never appealed the decision. He never protested. He just took it."

At the meeting at which he eventually announced the penalties, Chandler excused MacPhail and asked Rickey, "How much would it hurt you folks to have your fellow out of baseball?" Rickey emitted a gasp. Tears began to roll down his cheeks. In a half-sobbing voice he said, "Happy, what on earth is the matter with you? Why, that boy has more character than the fellow you just sent out of the room."

Rickey fully blamed MacPhail, and they didn't cross paths again until the 1947 World Series, when they ran into each other leaving Yankee Stadium. MacPhail's Yankees had defeated Rickey's Dodgers in the Series. Larry went over to shake Rickey's hand. But Rickey refused and told MacPhail never to speak to him again.

The relationship between Durocher and Rickey was never the same again either. Laraine Day had constantly been telling Leo about Rickey, "This man is not your friend," and her judgment was a contributing factor in Durocher's suspicion that Rickey was somehow responsible for the suspension, despite the fact that Rickey had done everything he could to save him. Just before Durocher was suspended, Rickey had called his staff together and told them:

"Leo is down. But we are going to stick by Leo. We are going to stick by Leo until hell freezes over!"

But Leo, who had a need to place blame, turned on Rickey. The next year, when Dodger pitcher Kirby Higbe was traded to Pittsburgh, Durocher called Higbe from California and said, "Kirby, he sold you down the river just like he did me."

Dodger fans blamed Chandler. Some have never forgiven him for Durocher's suspension.

BILL REDDY: "In my opinion, Chandler suspended Durocher to justify his job. They said Durocher was hanging out with fellows who were a bad influence on baseball. I say it's a lot of baloney. Chandler was one of the weakest baseball commissioners we ever had. He was a nothing. Chandler and nothing would be the same thing in my estimation. He had to justify his job. He had to make an example of someone. And he did it with Durocher."

But there was another man as responsible as anyone for Durocher's fall from grace, only at the time nobody was aware of his backstage maneuvering. Soft-spoken, gentle, smiling Walter O'Malley was not at all upset by the recent events. In just a few more years, Rickey would be out too.

4

The Legacy of Happy Chandler

One might wonder why it was that Durocher was suspended for a year while MacPhail got off with only a $2,000 fine and why Chandler made a finding that the gamblers had not been guests of MacPhail's when all evidence—including a photograph of them sitting together—pointed to the fact that they had.

Part of the reason was that in baseball there has always been a double standard, one set of strict rules of conduct for the hired hands and another set for the owners. A hired hand couldn't bet the horses, but it was all right for an owner to own them. Or even a track.

Another reason MacPhail got off so easy may have had something to do with the fact that MacPhail was the prime mover behind Chandler's landing the commissioner's job. It had been a brilliant coup on MacPhail's part. Here's how he did it:

After Commissioner Landis died in November of 1944, a meeting was held in Cleveland on April 24, 1945, ostensibly to discuss the four men who might succeed him. All sixteen clubs were represented. J. Edgar Hoover was one of the candidates, as was Robert Hannegan of the Democratic National Committee. Chandler's name was not even under consideration. The owners had no intention of electing anyone that day. They just wanted to feel each other out.

During the meeting MacPhail made a seemingly innocent suggestion that the owners hold a mock election to see who they would like as commissioner. When the ballots were counted, the tally revealed that Albert B. "Happy" Chandler, the senator from Kentucky, had received eleven first-place votes, two second-place votes, and three thirds. Considering that Chandler had not been one of the four men under consideration, it was certainly more than coincidence that his name should come up on every single one of the ballots!

MacPhail, visibly pleased with the results of the mock election, said to the others, "Baseball needs a new commissioner in a hurry. If that's the way we feel, what are we waiting for?" Cardinal owner Sam Breadon, agreeing with MacPhail, quickly made a motion for them to vote for real. To be elected, Chandler needed twelve votes. He got eleven on the first ballot, twelve on the second, and on a third ballot, to put up a front of unity, he was elected unanimously.

When the meeting ended, MacPhail stoutly denied to reporters that he had lobbied for Chandler prior to the meeting. Chandler himself was telling the truth when he assured reporters that he had had no idea that he was going to be the new commissioner "until two days ago when MacPhail told me about it at dinner."

MacPhail undoubtedly figured that Chandler, who had been both governor of and a senator from Kentucky and had a reputation for doing favors for friends, would be grateful to him and support not only MacPhail and his Yankees, but the other baseball owners as well. It was one of the few times in his life when MacPhail totally misjudged another man. Shortly after Chandler was elected, he declared that he would place himself squarely on the side of the players because the owners could take care of themselves and the players needed someone to stand up for them. MacPhail immediately wired Chandler to keep his big mouth shut, but the commissioner ignored his former supporter.

Chandler also surprised MacPhail on the issue of baseball's integration, again taking the side of the underdog.

Baseball hadn't always been segregated. Right after the Civil War, during baseball's infancy, blacks played alongside whites. Two brothers, Moses Fleetwood "Fleet" Walker and Welday Wilberforce Walker, both played for Toledo in the American Association, and Fleet Walker and black pitching star George Stovey played for Newark in the 1880s when more than twenty blacks held positions in various leagues around the country.

The first recorded move to exclude "the colored" in professional baseball occurred in 1882 when Adrian "Cap" Anson—an Iowan, not a southerner—came to Toledo with his Chicago White Stockings and ordered Toledo's Fleet Walker off the field. "Get that nigger off the field," he said, "or I will not allow my team to take the field." To its credit the Toledo management told Anson to buzz off, and despite Walker's presence Anson's team played.

Five years later Anson brought his team to Newark, where he again demanded that a black, Stovey, not be allowed to play. This time the Newark management caved in, and Stovey, not wishing to cause embarrassment to his employers, voluntarily left the field. Later when Anson learned that John Montgomery Ward was going to buy Stovey for the New York Giants, Anson successfully moved to bar black-skinned players from "organized baseball."

The Tri-State League adopted such a rule in 1888. It was repealed shortly afterwards, but to appease the southern teams, the northern owners joined in a gentleman's agreement not to hire black players on the ground that they were keeping their southern brethren from being embarrassed, lest they suffer the humiliation of having to play with inferior black men.

The one manager with the guts to try to buck the barrier was New York Giant manager John McGraw. McGraw, who began managing the Giants in 1902, had scouted a black star of the Columbia Giants by the name of Charley Grant, and after he signed him to a Giant contract, McGraw tried to fool reporters and everyone else by contending that Grant was not a Negro but rather a full-blooded American Indian. But when the Giants played an exhibition in Baltimore, Grant's black followers packed the ballpark, and McGraw's deception was uncovered. Sometime later McGraw tried to sign a shortstop named Haley and get him through by saying he was Cuban. Again it didn't work. Not even the powerful McGraw could break baseball's immovable color bar.

Branch Rickey believed that the color bar was outdated. World War II had accelerated integration, and he realized that the day would come when the blacks would have purchasing power to become a significant percentage of baseball's audience.

Rickey knew that the color bar was not going to be broken until the death of Baseball Commissioner Kenesaw Mountain Landis, a Tennessean who postured as a liberal but who had done everything in his power—and he was a powerful man—to keep blacks from playing major league baseball since being installed as baseball commissioner in 1920.

The first rumblings against the status quo began in the '40s, when black activist Paul Robeson confronted Landis, demanding to know why black men, who were dying for their country, were not permitted to play professional baseball. Robeson, who had been an All-American football player at Rutgers, told Landis that blacks played in football, track, and even professional croquet. Why not baseball?

With great solemnity, Judge Landis told Robeson that there was no rule on the books prohibiting a black man from joining a major league team. It was up to the owners to hire whom they pleased. Landis could get away with such a cavalier statement because he knew that the owners weren't about to give a Negro the opportunity. Chicago White Sox manager Jimmy Dykes had held a tryout for shortstop Jackie Robinson and pitcher Nate Moreland, but owner Charley Comiskey refused to sign them. Later, the Red Sox tried out Jackie Robinson, Marvin Williams, and Sam Jethroe. Coach Hugh Duffy wanted to sign all three of them, but owner Tom Yawkey refused to approve. For years Yawkey avoided signing Negro players, saying that he was waiting for a "great one." Having passed up a dozen or so Hall of Fame players, he became the last owner in either league to sign a black.

Then in the mid-1940s William Benswanger, owner of the Pittsburgh Pirates, tried to sign Josh Gibson, the Negro League's equivalent to Babe Ruth. Faced with an actual challenge, Commissioner Landis turned down the request, intoning, "The colored ballplayers have their own league. Let them stay in their own league."

In 1944 Landis also prevented Bill Veeck from purchasing the cellar-dwelling Philadelphia Phillies and reviving them by hiring the best players from Negro League baseball. As soon as Landis heard the plan, he arranged for the Philadelphia owner, Gerry Nugent, to turn the team back to the National League so that Veeck would have to deal with National League President Ford Frick. Frick then allowed lumber dealer William Cox to buy the team for about half of what Veeck had offered. According to Veeck, Frick was bragging all over the baseball world that he had stopped Veeck from "contaminating the league."

But it was Landis who was the instigating force. Once, before 30,000 fans,

Negro pitching stars Satchel Paige and Hilton Smith defeated a major league all-star team in Chicago's Wrigley Field, and afterward, the Communist newspaper, *The Daily Worker,* ran an editorial demanding that Landis open baseball to blacks. In the article Leo Durocher was quoted as saying he'd leap at the chance to hire a black player if he could. "Hell," Durocher was quoted as saying, "I've seen a million good ones."

Landis immediately called Durocher into his office, and when Durocher came out, he sheepishly told the press he had been misquoted. Landis then made a statement that there was no rule barring blacks.

Shortly before Landis died on November 25, 1944, reporter Wendell Smith of the *Pittsburgh Courier,* a black weekly, discussed the issue with Landis. Landis's parting words to him were, "There is nothing further to discuss."

But with Landis's death, the prime barrier against integrating the major leagues was gone. Under Happy Chandler, things would be different.

HAPPY CHANDLER: "For twenty-four years Judge Landis wouldn't let a black man play. I had his records, and I read them, and for twenty-four years Landis consistently blocked any attempts to put blacks and whites together on a big league field. He even refused to let them play exhibition games. Now, see, I had known Josh Gibson and Buck Leonard and Satchel Paige, and, of course, Josh died without having his chance, and I lamented that, because he was one of the greatest players I ever saw, a great catcher and a great hitter, and I thought that was an injustice.

"For twenty-four years the record will show that my predecessor said, 'If you're black, you can't play.' Why? Because that's what the owners wanted him to do. Landis has a reputation as an independent commissioner that he doesn't deserve.

"I was named the commissioner in April 1945, and just as soon as I was elected commissioner, two black writers from the *Pittsburgh Courier,* Wendell Smith and Rick Roberts, came down to Washington to see me. They asked me where I stood, and I shook their hands and said, 'I'm for the Four Freedoms, and if a black boy can make it at Okinawa and go to Guadalcanal, he can make it in baseball.'

"My quote was printed in the *Pittsburgh Courier,* and when Rickey saw that, he began making plans."

From the time Chandler made his Four Freedoms statement in April 1945, Branch Rickey took just four months to select the man with the qualifications to break baseball's color barrier. Rickey, however, had been "making plans" long before then. Rickey had opposed discrimination since the turn of the century when he was the twenty-one-year-old baseball coach of Ohio Wesleyan University. His star catcher, Charles "Tommy" Thomas, had been prevented from registering at a South Bend, Indiana, hotel with the rest of the team the night before a game with Notre Dame.

BRANCH RICKEY: "He was a splendid young man. He was a Negro from Upper Michigan, and his family was the only Negro family in that area. When he

Geo1ge Brace Photo

HAPPY CHANDLER AND WIFE

came to Ohio Wesleyan he was, by and large, unaware that he was a Negro in a white world. He had had no unpleasant experiences.

"When the room clerk pulled back the register and said, 'We do not take Negroes here,' I was stunned, and the boy didn't know what hit him. I explained to the room clerk that this was the catcher for the Ohio Wesleyan team, and that the Ohio Wesleyan had complete reservations, that we were guests of Notre Dame.

"The room clerk was blunt and rude and vocally firm. He said they did not register Negroes, and that they were not going to register this one, and he didn't care if it was the Ohio Wesleyan baseball team or football team or what.

"Quite a crowd had gathered around by now listening and watching. I said to the room clerk, 'Well, now. We have to have some way out of this. He has to have a place to sleep. Would you object if he slept in the extra bed in my room, as long as you don't have to register him?' And the clerk said, 'All right. You can do that.'

"When I finished registering the rest of the team, I went up to the room, pushed open the door, and went inside. And there was this fine young man, sitting on the edge of his chair, crying. He was crying as though his heart would break. His whole body was wracked with sobs. He was pulling frantically at his hands, pulling at his hands. He looked at me and he said, 'It's my skin. If I could just tear it off, I'd be like everyone else. It's my skin. It's my skin, Mr. Rickey.' "

It was a scene Rickey never forgot. Rickey hated the system, and racism in baseball embarrassed him, but he too knew that as long as Judge Kenesaw Mountain Landis, from Kenesaw Mountain, Georgia, was commissioner, there was no way he would be able to change anything, and so he kept his thinking to himself as he waited for the day when Landis would step down.

Rickey knew he would someday sign black players. It was just a question of when. In 1940 Rickey drove into the parking lot adjacent to the Polo Grounds, where he was accosted by a twelve-year-old Negro boy named Arthur George Rust, Jr. Rust was the son of a prosperous real estate owner. He had grown up in an affluent section of Sugar Hill in Harlem, and though he dearly loved the game of baseball, he was aware enough to recognize that all of his favorite major leaguers were white. As Rust would say years later, "The toughest thing for me was rooting for a bunch of cracker ballplayers."

When the youngster saw Rickey and his wife getting out of the car, he walked over to them and introduced himself. "Mr. Rickey, I'm Arthur Rust," and he asked for an autograph. Rickey signed and introduced the boy to his wife. Then Rust said, "By the way, do you think Negroes will ever play major league baseball?" Rickey put his arm around the boy and began walking with him up Eighth Avenue. Rickey told Rust, "Young man, one of these days you are going to live to see it happen."

And so it had been on Rickey's mind for a long time. He knew there would be opposition when he acted, because no one—not even his family—was for it. When Rickey finally decided to go ahead with his bold plan to integrate major league baseball, the first person Rickey confided in was Jane Rickey, his wife of many years, whom he called Ma.

Jane Rickey pleaded with him: "Why should you be the one to do it? Haven't you done enough for baseball? Can't someone else do something for a change?"

His son, Branch, Jr., who was in charge of the Dodger farm system, told him, "It means we'll be out of scouting in the South."

"For a while," said Branch, Sr., "not forever."

Nothing would sway him. In August of 1945 Rickey sent scout Clyde Sukeforth to watch the Negro League's Kansas City Monarchs and to learn something about the team's shortstop, Jackie Robinson.

CLYDE SUKEFORTH: "They had a colored club in Brooklyn, the Brown Bombers, and Rickey had us believing that we were scouting for them. He didn't give anybody an idea that he was looking for a fella that could break the color line. He just wanted a list of all the colored ballplayers in the Negro National League. We found some pretty outstanding players down there: Robinson and Johnny Wright and Roy Campanella and Don Newcombe.

"Josh Gibson was in the league, but he was quite old, and his habits were not especially good. He had the reputation of being a drinker. Satchel Paige, everyone figured, was too old. We might have missed something there.

"One day in August 1945, Mr. Rickey called me in and he said, 'The Kansas City Monarchs are playing the Lincoln Giants at Comiskey Park in Chicago Friday night. I want you to see that game, go up to that fellow Robinson, and introduce yourself,' which is something we never did. Usually when we wanted information we got it through Oscar Charleston, the old Negro League first baseman. He knew all those people. Oscar worked for the Pennsylvania Railroad in the North Philadelphia station. He had a pretty good job there, and he could get off most anytime he wanted. He knew all the people in the colored league, and if we got interested in somebody, why, we'd call Oscar, and we could find out all about a boy, about his habits, how much he'd been to school, what sort of boy he was. For Jackie we didn't need Oscar, though. His record was pretty well-known. He was a UCLA college boy, and he was better known than most of the colored boys.

"So I went to Chicago, and I identified myself when Robinson came on the field, talked to him, and he couldn't understand why I was there. I told him who had sent me and that Mr. Rickey told me to talk to him and to pay particular attention to his arm. Mr. Rickey said, 'I want to know if that fellow has a shortstop's arm. Ask him to have somebody hit a ball in the hole to him during practice.' I went through all that with Robinson, and he said, 'I'll be glad to show you my arm, but I'm not playing. I fell on my shoulder last night, and I won't be able to play for several days.' Well, he took batting practice.

"Mr. Rickey had told me, 'If you like his arm, bring him in, and if his schedule won't permit it, make an appointment for me, and I'll go out and see him.' Well, that's when I really became suspicious. That's when I knew it wasn't the Brown Bombers, that this was the real thing. I knew the reports on him were good, and in any event, there are other positions besides shortstop if the fella's good enough. And knowing well how Mr. Rickey liked to talk to people and study them and look right through them, I thought to myself, 'This fella's going to be out of the game for several days, why not take him to Brooklyn and let Mr. Rickey talk to the guy?'

"I had two berths on the train, he had one and I had one opposite, and before we retired we talked a little bit about race relations. Also, he kept asking me, 'Why does Mr. Rickey want to see me?' and I'd tell him, 'I wish I could answer that, but I can't.' In my own mind I knew why, but I couldn't say.

"In the morning I got up and said, 'Let's go back to the dining car and get some coffee,' and he said, 'I don't eat much breakfast. I'll wait and eat with the boys.' I said, 'Why I think it would be perfectly all right if you went back.' He said, 'I'll wait,' and so he waited and ate breakfast with the porters.

"So I brought Jackie in for a conference, and I introduced him to Mr. Rickey, and I said, 'Mr. Rickey, I haven't seen this fellow throw,' but he evidently didn't hear me because when he wrote his book a few years later, he called me in and asked me where it was that I saw Robinson play. I never saw Robinson play! All I did was bring him in for a conference.

"I was in the room when Mr. Rickey talked to the fella. His first question was: 'You got a girl?' Jackie told him about Rachel, his fiancée. Mr. Rickey said, 'When we get through today you may want to call her up, because there are times when a man needs a woman by his side.' Then Mr. Rickey said, 'Jack, I've been looking for a great colored ballplayer, but I need more than a great player. I need a man who will accept insults, take abuse, in a word, carry the flag for his race.' He told him, 'I want a man who has the courage not to fight, not to fight back. If a guy slides into you at second base and calls you a black son of a bitch, I wouldn't blame you if you came up swinging. You'd be right. You'd be justified. But,' he said, 'you'd set the cause back twenty years. I want a man with courage enough not to fight back. Can you do that?'

"Well, Jackie sold himself right quick. He thought about it for perhaps three minutes before he answered, and finally he said, 'If you want to take this gamble, I promise you there'll be no incidents.' If he had said it right off quick without giving it thought, then it wouldn't have carried as much weight. But he thought it out, and he was a long time in answering.

"Afterward Rickey told me that there may have been other boys that could do it, but Robinson had the college background, and he was pretty active with the NAACP. Mr. Rickey felt that he would work hard not only for himself, but the cause, that he had all the qualifications, on and off the field."

The First

Jackie Robinson had spent most of his early life fighting for something, a dangerous practice considering that in America in the 1940s a black man could

Clyde Sukeforth

be hung for daring to act uppity. He had been born January 31, 1919, in Cairo, Georgia, the grandson of a plantation slave and the last of five children born to a sharecropper and his wife. The sharecropper, Jerry Robinson, was working the land under an oppressive system that left him and millions of other Negro sharecroppers financially not much better off than slaves.

Six months after Jackie was born, Jerry Robinson informed his wife Mallie that he was going to visit a brother somewhere in Texas. He had been complaining about farming life, and when he told her that he was going, Mallie had a dark feeling that her man was not coming back. She later learned that Jerry had run to Texas all right, but with the wife of a neighboring sharecropper.

When he didn't return, Mallie decided to work the land herself, but when she complained to the plantation owner that she wasn't getting fair pay, he ordered her and her family off his property. Worried for her safety, she went to Pasadena, California, where she had a brother. Jackie was one year old. His older brother Mack was six when the family made the journey. Mack's most vivid memory of the trip while riding the train west through Texas in a car reserved for blacks is hearing the thud of rocks thrown at the Jim Crow car by white youths.

Mallie Robinson moved her family in with her brother, and she began taking in washing and ironing and doing domestic work for the white families of Pasadena. After six months Mallie Robinson and her family rented a home of their own—in a predominantly white neighborhood. Mack remembers that the whites enjoyed throwing rocks at the young black and Mexican kids. Then one afternoon the older brothers of the black kids got together, and they retaliated. "Some of the white kids got hurt, and that was the end of that," Mack said. After that, there was just the usual taunt of "nigger."

A few years later Mallie moved again, across town—into another white neighborhood, where she continued working to raise her kids.

RACHEL ROBINSON: Jack's mother bought a house on a corner in a white neighborhood. She had it when I first met Jack. You see, Pasadena was not integrated. There were no black neighborhoods.

"She chose Pasadena because she wanted to be near her brother. And she worked hard just to put food on the table for the five children. Jackie's older sister, Willa Mae, had to take over and became a second mother. In fact Mallie never had baby sitters, and she did not keep her other children home to take care of Jackie. She would send him off to school with Willa Mae, and when the school objected, she just told them that she had to work and that she wasn't going on welfare and that Willa Mae had to take care of him. So Willa Mae would keep him in a sandbox outside, and she'd run in and out and manage him. That's how they got him through until he got to kindergarten when he was two and a half."

When the Robinsons moved into their new home, there was quite a bit of unrest. As more blacks and Mexicans moved in, the hostility increased, but there was no violence.

Yoshi Hasegawa grew up in Pasadena with Jackie. Yoshi was in the eighth grade, Jackie in the tenth, when they met. Yoshi too felt the barriers that separated people in a segregated society and felt the discrimination, but for the Japanese it wasn't nearly as bad as for the blacks.

YOSHI HASEGAWA: "There weren't a lot of blacks. There were six or seven in a class and sometimes less. When we ate lunch, the blacks sat on one side of the table, and the Japanese sat on the other side, and we monopolized a whole area. We were friendly, but we each knew our place. My best girl friend was a black girl. But my mother just would not accept this idea. But to me, she was just a friend. I used to tell my mother, 'We're not getting married. We're just friends.' But she never came to my house, and I never went to hers. Her mother always used to ask me to come, but I just never did. It was one of those unwritten laws. You just didn't.

"Jackie had some Japanese friends that lived on the same street that he did. Many times going home, he would be walking, and he would tease the girls and give everybody a hard time. He was such a happy-go-lucky person. A lot of fun. Real naughty. He always had tricks up his sleeve to worry the girls. He would chase us down the street, and if he caught you, he'd give you a squeeze. Most of the time he was teasing. He was just teasing all the time. But I never associated with him. It's one of those things. We just didn't. It was two separate kinds of lives. We didn't intermingle. He hung out with all blacks. My friends were Japanese. At that time, that's the way it was. I never went to his house, and he never came to mine. People knew their place.

"Discrimination against the blacks and Japanese was obvious, though a subtle statement. And there was nothing you could do about it. You felt it from the teachers. But the Negro kids had a harder time of it because scholastically many of them didn't keep up. It was harder for them.

"When Jackie was in junior high school, the coach didn't like Negroes. They weren't blacks at the time. They were Negroes. He was the physical education coach, and he did his best to keep Jackie out, but Jackie was so good he had to relent. Jackie had an uphill struggle all the way. He had to pave the way. And Pasadena Junior College was also not too receptive, but they just knuckled under because he was so good.

"At first the coaches didn't give him good positions and ignored him and tried to put the white kids in. But it got so the white kids put pressure on the coach. Because I remember that though the white kids were really good, he was outstanding. He used to make ninety-nine-yard touchdown runs. I haven't seen a touchdown like that ever. The way the guy used to run! There isn't anything like it! He'd go zigzagging all the way down, and nobody could catch him. He had those crazy legs."

Jackie became a star athlete in football, basketball, and baseball, first at Pasadena Junior College and then at UCLA, where he and Kenny Washington led his football team to within one yard of a Rose Bowl appearance. In basketball he was All-American honorable mention, and in track he broke a national record for the long jump previously set by his brother Mack, who had finished second to Jesse Owens in the 200-meter run in the 1936 Olympics in Berlin. Jackie was also a dominant baseball player. Whatever sport Robinson played, he was hard to beat. He excelled in tennis, golf, Ping-Pong, bowling, and in track he could have run in the 1940 Olympics had there been one. Robinson gained recognition as the nation's most versatile athlete, and some say that had he been white and from the East, he would have been rated as a better all-around athlete than the legendary Jim Thorpe.

RACHEL ROBINSON: "When I met Jackie, he had already established somewhat of a reputation. He was a letterman in four sports. He was very famous on campus and in the area because UCLA had good teams in those days. He was known as a football star and a basketball star. He was not known in baseball at all, and he held a broad jump record. And he won some local tennis tournaments. The only thing he didn't do was swim.

"Jackie never concentrated on track. He probably could have gone to the Olympics. He was really concentrating on football and basketball. When he left school, he didn't want to be a professional football player for any length of time because he already had some permanent injuries as a result of it. He had bone chips in his ankle, which couldn't be removed, so he didn't think he wanted to be a professional football player.

"After going to PJC for two years, he played sports two years at UCLA and then he lost interest in school once he had used up his athletic eligibility and couldn't play. The university encouraged him to stay on and finish and get his degree, but he was concerned that his mother had worked long enough and hard enough, and his brothers were in college, and they felt they needed to get out and start helping her.

"So he quit school and took a job with a National Youth Administration work camp, working with youngsters. When the war broke out, the government closed the camp, and when he was laid off from that he made some money with the Honolulu Bears in football. One of the attractions of playing for the Bears was that they gave you a job working at Hickam Field. Jackie was on his way home from Honolulu to Los Angeles the day Pearl Harbor was bombed. They blacked out the ship.

"After Pearl Harbor, Jackie went into the service for thirty-six months."

Jackie had applied for officer candidate school, and in January of 1943 he became a second lieutenant in the army, where he was a constant thorn in the side of his superiors. At Fort Riley, in Kansas, there were only a half-dozen seats for blacks in the PX, and so blacks would have to wait in line to eat while white-only tables remained unused. Robinson teamed up with Joe Louis, who was also based there, and they badgered the brass and finally got more seats for blacks.

Jackie had been asked to play on the Fort Riley football team, and he came out for practice, but before the first scrimmage against the University of Missouri, Robinson was virtually ordered to accept a pass to visit his folks back home. The real reason, he knew, was that the brass didn't want a Negro

Jackie Robinson
Dodgers

playing on the team. When Robinson came out for the baseball team, again he was denied the right to play.

PETE REISER: "I was based at Fort Riley, Kansas, where we had a terrific baseball team. We had Rex Barney, Harry Walker, Joe Garagiola, Lonny Frey, Creepy Crespi, Al Brazle, Murry Dickson, and Ken Heintzelman, among others.

"One day we were out at the field practicing when a Negro lieutenant came out for the team. An officer told him, 'You have to play with the colored team.' That was a joke. There was no colored team. The black lieutenant didn't speak. He stood there for a while, watched us work out, and then he turned and walked away. I didn't know his name then, but that was the first time I saw Jackie Robinson. I can still see him slowly walking away."

Some things Robinson couldn't fight. Other things he could.

RACHEL ROBINSON: "They made him morale officer to give him an official role. This is pure speculation, but I believe they made him morale officer because the other way he would have been such a troublemaker. They finally shifted him out of Fort Riley because they didn't like his activities. Also, because of his ankle they put him on limited service, and when his unit went overseas, they wouldn't take him, and they sent him to Fort Breckinridge in Kentucky, where he was finally court martialled about a trumped up bus incident. He had refused to sit in the back of a post bus. The bus driver called the MPs, accusing him of sitting in front with a white woman. Very trumped up. He had good counsel, and he won that.

"Jackie was so effective because of the way he presented himself. He went in as an officer and became lieutenant right off the bat, and he had the ability to mobilize others. Though he didn't call press conferences, he knew those tools were always available to him, and he would not have been reluctant to use them if he couldn't get what he wanted in other ways."

In November of 1944, anxious to rid itself of the uppity nigger, the army gave Robinson an honorary discharge. In April of 1945, Robinson joined the Kansas City Monarchs of the Negro American League for $400 a month.

Robinson loved playing baseball, but off the field he was living an extremely unhappy life. Rachel was in nursing school, so he had to be alone. On the road the bus rides seemed endless, they couldn't stay in white hotels, and in some towns the beds in the Jim Crow hotel had so many bedbugs that the players had to lay newspaper down between the mattress and the sheets. Sometimes there was no place where they could get something to eat, not even in the black hotels, which often did not have eating facilities. Greasy spoons even refused to serve them. At best they were allowed to order a sodden hamburger and a cup of coffee to carry out. And in this fashion, they traveled from town to town, logging up to 30,000 miles during the summer as they played game after game barnstorming around the country.

For Robinson, this was no life, even though he was making pretty good money—for a Negro. Every day he would write Rachel letters proclaiming his love, and she would write back. Making life easier for him was the knowledge that she was working hard getting her degree in nursing and that his being away gave her the time to complete her studies with top grades. Jackie had asked her to marry him while he was at UCLA, and she said she would not do so until she got her degree. Otherwise she was afraid she would never finish. He knew that the time was drawing near when they would marry, and it helped keep him going.

RACHEL ROBINSON: "Out of the five years we were engaged—we got engaged my second year in college—we once figured that we hadn't been together for even a year, 'cause he was always off someplace, either in the army for three years, and then with the Monarchs. He would write every day and send candy once a month. When he was with the Monarchs, he told me very little about what was happening. The letters were personal. 'I love you. I love you. I love you.' It was more that kind of letter writing. Nevertheless I knew Jackie was very unhappy with the life he was leading with the Monarchs. He didn't see it as fun or funny, the one-night stands, living on a bus, eating out of back windows.

"The Monarchs, for Jackie, were never talked about as something permanent. He always talked about it as making extra money until he could settle down into something, till we got married and knew what we were going to do. So I doubt very much whether he would have put up with that for very long. It just wasn't his style. It was terrible for a person like him, because a lot of their games were played in the South, and it was a constant holding back, controlling yourself under those circumstances. But in those days, there was absolutely no choice. But because he played for the Monarchs that year, he eventually got his chance with the Dodgers. There's something about destiny in that somewhere, I think.

"I remember when he had the meeting with Rickey, Jack called me. He said it was very secret and he couldn't tell me a lot over the telephone. He really didn't appreciate the magnitude of it at that point. He just saw it as an opportunity, as something exciting, and that he would have a chance. When he called, he told me he would be going to Montreal, and that's about it.

"Mr. Rickey was the one very concerned about the preparation. He really thought the preparation was extremely important to the success of the venture. So he laid out the groundwork in Brooklyn. He fixed us up with a family in Bed-Stuy. He saw them as a family we could turn to for things. Very community-minded people and very warm, generous, and loving people, and they became our second family. He made the first contact for us long before we even came to Brooklyn."

When it was announced that the Brooklyn Dodgers had chosen Robinson as the first Negro to play in "organized baseball," his Kansas City teammates couldn't believe it. In forty-one games playing in the Negro American League, Robinson hit .345, hit ten doubles, four triples, and five home runs, and was the West's shortstop in the East–West all-star game, but most of them hadn't liked Robinson. He was not a southerner. He was a California boy, a hothead who didn't know his place. He was college-educated, and they thought he felt superior to them. Also, he was a rookie, and his teammates felt that the first should have been a Negro League veteran such as Josh Gibson, Satchel Paige, Buck Leonard, or Monte Irvin, who later proved his worth with the New York Giants.

OTHELLO "GANGSTER" RENFROE: "He had a different baseball background from most of us in the Negro American League, because he played under white coaches. We never had any doubt about Jackie's ability, but we wondered whether or not he could take the stuff that he took in the majors. We never thought he could take it. A couple times we would pull up to service stations in Mississippi where drinking fountains said 'white' and 'black,' and we'd have to leave without our change, Jackie'd get so mad. If Mr. Rickey had known about Jackie's temperament, I don't think he would have signed him.

"We had a lot of ballplayers we thought were better players. We always thought Ted Strong was about the most ideal ballplayer. He had all the tools, a switch hitter who could play just about anywhere—first base, shortstop, outfield. But they picked Jackie for his intelligence."

HILTON SMITH: "Actually Jackie didn't look that good. He was a little old to be a major league rookie—twenty-seven—but there weren't any good young ballplayers then. Willie Wells was better than Jackie at that position, but the Dodgers picked him on account of he played college baseball; he'd played with white boys before."

The day after Robinson signed with Rickey to play for Montreal, Jackie left with an all-star Negro team for Caracas, Venezuela.

BUCK LEONARD: "When we got down there, Robinson didn't look too good because he hadn't been playing as long as some of us. He was a hustler, but other than that he wasn't a top shortstop. We said, 'We don't see how he can make it.'

"And even when the Dodgers took Robinson, I said, 'If he doesn't make it, they're going to be through with us for the next five or ten years. And if he does make it, maybe they are going to keep him in the minors for a long time.' But we were wrong."

What these Negro League ballplayers also didn't understand was that Robinson's signing would ultimately mean the demise of the Negro Leagues. Most of the Negro ballplayers thought that Robinson would be an isolated case. But it took only a couple of years for the full impact of Robinson's signing on the Negro Leagues to sink in.

In 1947, because of Robinson, attendance was down alarmingly for Negro League games. Nearly all Negro League teams lost money. Nineteen forty-eight was a disaster. The fans no longer showed up for games at all, and by 1949 the Negro League teams began trying to sell their players wholesale to keep from going under. In 1950 the New York Giants paid $15,000 to the Birmingham Black Barons for nineteen-year-old Willie Mays. In 1952 Milwaukee bought eighteen-year-old Henry Aaron from the Indianapolis Clowns, and in 1953 the Cubs bought twenty-two-year-old Ernie Banks from the Kansas City Monarchs.

When the major league teams began buying youngsters, the Negro Leagues were doomed. The Negro Leagues could stand the loss of a Robinson, or maybe even a Satchel Paige. But when all of a sudden the kids were going to the majors, the Negro Leagues didn't have any talent coming up, and that's what killed them. Two-and-a-half years after Mays came up in 1951, the Negro Leagues folded.

Montreal

On October 23, 1945, it was announced that Jackie Robinson had signed a contract to play for the Montreal Royals for the 1946 season. In the North there was only a ripple of reaction, but for the masses of disillusioned Negroes in the South, Jackie Robinson's entry into baseball meant so much more. Because not only was Robinson going to play baseball, but he was going to play it *with whites*. He was going to get the opportunity to prove to the white community that he could be just as good as they were. And so, when Jackie Robinson arrived in Ed Charles's hometown of Daytona Beach to begin spring training with the Royals, Robinson's arrival was heralded in the Negro community as an event of major significance.

Ed Charles: "I was thirteen years old when Jackie Robinson signed to play with Montreal. I was not aware that Jackie was going to be based in Daytona Beach with the Montreal club, but as soon as we found out, as soon as the media released the news, we got all excited, and it was like, 'Hey, we can't hardly wait.' I was like a little boy waiting for Christmas and Santa Claus to see what kind of toys he was going to bring us. We were waiting on Jackie, because this was the first time we were going to have any kind of socialization of the races in the deep South, and if he succeeded he was going to open the door to Christ Almighty, to blacks as well as other minorities in baseball.

"That Jackie Robinson had signed and was coming down here, I looked at that and said, 'Okay, maybe now we're going to begin to start living the American dream like the rest of the citizens, maybe now we're going to make some headway to right what I had seen to be these types of wrongs, the inhuman treatment of our people, the hardships on blacks. And it gave me a little hope that perhaps at last we were on the right track as far as living the type of American dream, this freedom of opportunity we were supposed to have in this country.

"Jackie coming down to Daytona made a definite impact on the lives of the blacks in my community. I was just a kid, and I was awed by it all, and

I prayed for him. I would say, 'Please God, let him show the whites what we can do and that we can excel like they can.' "

Jackie Robinson reported to the Daytona Beach camp of the Montreal Royals in late February 1946. Because Robinson could not stay with the team under the Jim Crow laws, Branch Rickey had arranged that he and his new bride, Rachel, would stay in the home of black political organizer Joe Harris. The problems started, however, even before the Robinsons arrived in Florida. During their journey from Los Angeles to Daytona Beach, Jackie and Rachel got their first taste of life together in the deep South.

RACHEL ROBINSON: "Jackie and I had gotten married just before spring training in February, and we left Los Angeles on a flight for Florida two weeks later. We got as far as New Orleans, when as we were coming in, we were paged, and we were asked to get off the plane. With no real explanation of why we were the only couple taken off, we were told we would be put on another plane later. We didn't know we had been bumped because in the South, a white couple waiting for seats took priority over a black couple that already had seats. It was my first experience in the South—I had never seen the blacks–whites signs for drinking fountains and ladies rooms. And I refused to do anything that I was directed to do in that airport. And nothing happened. Everybody was just astounded. That was the feeling of rebellion in us right off the bat.

"We hadn't known what we were going to meet before we got down there, and we had discussed together that we would not eat under the circumstances that they wanted us to eat—we couldn't eat in the dining room, even in the airport, and so we bought apples and candy, and we ate that all the way to Daytona Beach. We did not eat one meal.

"They left us in the New Orleans airport all day long. Finally, we were told that we might as well go to a hotel because we weren't going to get out that day. They said they promised to call us. They didn't. So we went back to the airport the next day, and we finally got on another plane, and an hour later, we got bumped in Pensacola, Florida. When we landed, I sat on the plane, and Jack told me to wait there while he got off. A stewardess told me that I better go, and when I got off, there was Jack arguing with the dispatcher. The story they gave us was that they had to lighten the plane because they were expecting bad weather, that they were putting on more fuel. But we saw a white couple getting on in our place, and Jack was just furious, and he talked and talked and talked, but in the meantime, the plane took off without us. Then we insisted they help us, because we didn't know what to do, and so they sent us into town with a car and driver, and apparently they had told the driver to go to a hotel, where they asked the black staff if any of them would take us in. They finally took us to the home of a woman who didn't have room for us. Her kids were sleeping in the living room. And so we thanked them, and we decided to take a bus the rest of the way 'cause Jack was very anxious to get there on time. He certainly didn't want to show up late the first day.

"We got on the bus, and it was empty, and we sat up toward the front. We knew better. As whites got on, the driver came back, and Jackie was asleep, and he tapped me and said, 'Move back,' and I told Jack we'd better move back. It was a very distressing trip, because it was our first encounter with helplessness. Any other time we would have been able to do something about it. But in this situation we had nothing to do but comply. We went and moved back, and we traveled through a lot of farm country and as more and more blacks got on, our back seats became very crowded, and we worked out a whole system so that nobody failed to get a seat at some point. We would sit forward or sit back, making room for everyone, and we got closer to our own people. And it was a very positive experience. Nobody knew who Jack was. Nobody knew anything about it. I had my little fur piece of jacket given me as a wedding present. I was all dressed up, and some of the others were in farm clothes, and we looked different, but no one could identify him. And we would go into a grocery store and get whatever we needed to eat until we got to Jacksonville, and by this time we had wired Mr. Rickey, and he had a car meet us in Jacksonville, and it took us the rest of the way. But that whole trip and our entry into the South was good in the sense that it sharpened for us the drama of what we were about to go into. We got a lot tougher thereafter."

The Montreal players, meanwhile, were awaiting Robinson's arrival. Spider Jorgensen, who played the 1946 season with Robinson at Montreal, remembers the day Robinson first appeared in camp.

SPIDER JORGENSEN: "Branch Rickey had assembled a camp of all his players, including everyone who was returning from the war. There were about 600 players down there. And that was when Rickey brought the blacks in. He brought Robinson and John Wright, a pitcher. They had signed Robinson over the winter, and there had been talk among the players, and I remember the first day they brought him in. They brought him in right about noon, because we had already been out on the field, and we were eating lunch. Robinson came walking in with John Wright, a black pitcher, and Wendell Smith, a black reporter from the *Pittsburgh Courier*.

"After lunch we started warming up, and he started warming up with all the rest of us. I never thought too much about it, because in California I had played with blacks in our winter leagues, and even on the junior college team, we had them on our club. I roomed with a southerner named Marv Rackley. He really wasn't that concerned either. You didn't go up and hug them or kiss them or anything like that; you just observed them, talked to them, played catch. Hell, I didn't think anything about it. But some of the southern boys were a little concerned. I didn't have time to worry any about him. I was worried enough about myself."

After lunch, Montreal Royals manager Clay Hopper scheduled a chalk talk, and it was during that meeting that Robinson walked through the clubhouse door and joined his new teammates. The door opened, everyone turned

around, and Jackie came in. When Hopper, who was born and bred in Mississippi, saw Robinson, he commented aloud, "Well, when Mr. Rickey picked one, he sure picked a black one."

Hopper initially had begged Rickey, "Please don't do this to me. I'm white, and I've lived in Mississippi all my life. If you do this, you're going to force me to move my family and my home out of Mississippi."

But Rickey was not sympathetic. He told Hopper, "You can manage correctly, or you can be unemployed." As a further warning, Rickey threatened, "You manage this fellow the way I want him managed, and you'd better figure out how I want him managed."

Hopper's obsequious answer was, "Yes, Mr. Rickey," but Hopper made it clear he was not happy about it, despite Robinson's heroics that began in the first game when he homered for Montreal over the left-field fence in Jersey City to win the game. Early in the season, Rickey and Hopper were standing together, and when Robinson made a diving play to get an out, Rickey commented that he thought Robinson was "superhuman." Hopper replied, "Do you really think a nigger's a human being?"

Controversy swirled around Robinson almost immediately. After two days of practice at Sanford, Florida, Robinson was forced to return to Daytona Beach, where the Montreal Royals were training. Sanford civic groups explained: "We don't want no Nigras mixing with no whites here."

During one exhibition game in De Land, Florida, Robinson slid across home plate in the first inning of the game, but a policeman walked onto the diamond and ordered Robinson off the field. "No niggers don't play with no white boys," he told him. "Get off the field right now, or you're going to jail."

As Robinson faced the policeman, the crowd rose to its feet. The Indianapolis players, standing out in the field, stood and watched. Robinson turned and headed for the dugout as Clay Hopper came out to talk to the policeman.

"What's wrong?" Hopper asked.

"We ain't havin' Nigras mix with white boys in this town," he said. "You can't change our way of living. Nigras and white, they can't sit together and they can't play together and you know damn well they can't get married together."

Hopper didn't answer.

"Tell that Nigra I said to git," the policeman said.

Through Robinson's ordeal, his teammates were never more than mere spectators. They expressed neither opinions nor feelings about what Robinson was going through. They made no overtures of support for him. To his teammates, he was an object of curiosity there for them to scrutinize.

From the first day, Robinson faced a difficult situation, in large part because he was black but also because he was vying for the job at second base against a popular French Canadian infielder, making Robinson the outsider competing against the hometown boy. Some of his teammates, as well as the fans, were rooting against him. Adding to the pressure was the fact that during spring training Robinson wasn't hitting.

* * *

RACHEL ROBINSON: "We had come through a difficult spring. He had been in a slump, and Jackie was terrified that he really wasn't going to make it. He had not hit at all down in Daytona Beach. And yet the worry was not that he didn't have the capacity, the worries were over whether they would give him enough time to settle in and be able to do it. So early on in the year, the pressure was really on."

SPIDER JORGENSEN: "Most of the older fellas, especially the pitchers, never thought he would hit, because he was a lunger. They'd throw him fastballs inside, and he'd fight them off and hit them on the fist, foul them back, but he could always hit the breaking ball, and he was one of those guys who was a better hitter with two strikes.

"The older guys didn't think he'd hit for average, but he had so much damn speed that you might hit him on the fist, but he'd hit a blooper over the infield for a base hit, and he'd get one hit bunting, and then he'd cream a couple of curveballs. And he did hit for average. He had a slow start, but right from the start we figured he was going to be part of our ballclub, and he was. As it turned out, he fit right in."

Robinson had two other factors working in his favor, both thanks to Rickey. He had a manager who knew better than to mess with him, and his home base was Montreal, where there was very little racial prejudice.

SPIDER JORGENSEN: "Hopper was tough, but Hopper treated Jackie good. We always thought maybe there would be a confrontation, but no, he treated him good. Hopper talked to him like he talked to everyone else. We never thought he was a good manager. I was just a rookie, but I used to hear the other guys say, 'We'll win it in spite of Clay Hopper.' He was always having the .300 hitters sacrifice and the .200 hitters hitting away. Things like that.

"Here's what I mean about Hopper's managing: It was our first or second meeting, and he was explaining the signs he was going to use, and someone asked him, 'Are you going to have a squeeze sign?' He said, 'No, I don't believe in the squeeze. It gets you in trouble,' and the more he talked, the more he thought about it, and finally he said, 'Yeah, we'll have a squeeze sign. Any time I pull my handkerchief out of my pocket and wipe my brow, we'll squeeze, and then you answer by tapping your bat on the plate.' But he said, 'Don't look for it too often.'

"Well, I think we squeezed every game of the season! He found out he had some ballplayers who could execute, found out about the speed in Robinson, how quick he was. Every time Jackie got on third, he'd have him edging off, getting a big lead, stealing home. Jackie must have set an International League record that year for stealing home."

RACHEL ROBINSON: "Montreal, with the exception of some early coolness, was an extraordinary experience, and we've always thought that it was absolutely either fortuitous or brilliant planning on Rickey's part for Jackie to be sent there. If he hadn't been sent there, he would not have left there with the kind of spirit and the kind of experience that allowed him to do all the other things he did. He was absolutely tremendously fortified by being there."

Away from Montreal, however, life became a good deal less idyllic. One of the worst places for Robinson to play was Syracuse. When he first played there, wrote baseball historian Robert Smith, "the fans reacted in a manner so raucous, obscene, and disgusting that it might have shamed a conclave of the KKK." The Syracuse players were particularly cruel. In the middle of a game, a player threw a black cat right at him and yelled, "Hey, Jackie, there's your cousin."

Robinson later in the game doubled and scored on a base hit. Robinson yelled over, "I guess my cousin's pretty happy now."

In Baltimore the players greeted Robinson with vile names and profanity. And on the field, players tried to spike him and hit him in the head with beanballs.

SPIDER JORGENSEN: "Baltimore was a tough town for Jackie. He had to stay at another hotel. A certain segment of the fans were hostile. But, man, we drew like hell there. Our first trip in, we went for a weekend series, Friday, Saturday, and Sunday, and we drew about 120,000 people, which isn't bad for Triple-A ball.

"Ordinarily, if Robinson wasn't playing second, Tommy Tatum would take his place and Al Campanis would play short. This day Campanis had a bad knee—it would pop out every once in a while—and so I played short. Our catcher was Herman Franks, and Herman had the notorious habit, when there was a play at the plate and he had the ball, he would swarm all over the player and dig that ball right into his ribs, and we knew that one day it was going to result in a fight.

"So we were leading Baltimore 3–2 in the bottom of the ninth, and there was two outs and a man on first, with a left-handed hitter up. Tatum and I talked it over, and we agreed that if the ball went out to right center, that I would go out and get the relay, because I had the stronger arm. And sure enough, that's what happened. The ball went out there, and I went out for the relay, and the runner was trying to score from first to tie the game, and I got the ball and wheeled and threw it to home plate. I knew when I let 'er go I had the guy by forty miles, and the ball came in to Herman on the bounce, and he got it, and there's the play, whappo, and Herman slaps it on him—hard.

"Well, Tatum and I, when we saw the umpire call him out, we started trotting out to the center-field clubhouse. The crowd started piling onto the field, and when we looked back, there was a big fight at home plate. Herman and the runner were wrestling on the ground. Tatum said to me, 'Do you think we ought to go back and help him?' I said, 'I don't think so. There's nothing we can do,' and so we continued into the clubhouse. Because Jackie had a bad leg, he was already in there. And after the rest of the players came in, a crowd started to group outside. There must have been about a hundred of them out there, and man, they were really after us. Calling us 'gutless sons a bitches,' and they were really after Jackie, taunting him, 'Where's that black bastard, that black son of a bitch, get him out here, we'll work him over.' And Jackie was concerned. Hell, we were all concerned. So we just stayed in the clubhouse. A lot of the players trickled out, because the crowd really was after Jackie, but a certain few of us stayed in there with him until about a quarter to one in the morning. Whether they really would have done anything, I don't know, but we weren't going to find out.

"See, in those days we had to get to and from the park on our own, and by a quarter to one, all the cabs had gone, and we had to take the bus back. There were four of us who waited with him: Marv Rackley, Red Durrett, Roy Partlow, who was also black, and myself. We went back on the bus, and the other people on the bus knew who we were, but they didn't do anything. It was a public bus, an old electric job. We got off by the hotel, and Jackie limped in, and that was the end of that. Everything was all right the next day.

"That was the only serious incident I can remember. There were some knockdowns here and there. Tommy Thomas was the Baltimore manager, he was from Baltimore, which was and still considers itself the South, and he was anti-Robinson, and he'd have his pitchers knock Jackie down, and there'd be a lot of stuff coming from the bench. They called him 'black son of a bitch, black bastard.'

"And despite all of this, Jackie never said a word. He never said anything about it. Somebody said that at the end of the year Jackie was on the verge of a nervous breakdown. Well, we didn't know. He never said much. On the field he was very quiet. He did his thing physically, not verbally."

RACHEL ROBINSON: "Jackie didn't have a nervous breakdown. He had a nervous stomach. He was unable to eat and unable to sleep for a few days. We went to a doctor, and the doctor said, 'Listen, it's stress. You're not coming down with anything. You're not having a nervous breakdown. You're under a lot of stress. Stay home and don't read any newspapers, and don't go to the ballpark for a week.'

"Jack stayed home one day, and we had a picnic, and he went right back, and he felt fine. The doctor made him understand that he had the right to feel under stress, and sort of sanctioned that, and he could then feel it and know what it was and deal with it.

"The trouble, the sole source of the stress that he had, came from his not being able to fight back.

"Rickey had told Jackie, 'Always, for as long as you are in baseball, you must conduct yourself as you are doing now. Always you will be on trial. That is the cross that you must bear.' "

Robinson's genius lay in that he was able to bear that cross and still perform at the very peak of his ability. In 1946 Robinson led the International League in hitting, fielded magnificently, was a darting blur on the bases, and led Montreal into the Little World Series against Louisville. In contrast pitchers

John Wright and Roy Partlow, whom Rickey had also signed from the Negro Leagues to play for Montreal, couldn't withstand the pressure.

John Wright was a twenty-seven-year-old right-handed pitcher who had played with the Newark Eagles, the Crawfords, and the Homestead Grays. He had been signed by Montreal in February after getting out of the service. John Wright couldn't take the constant pressure. He was sent down to Three Rivers, Quebec, and released at the end of the year. The next year he was back with the Homestead Grays.

JACKIE ROBINSON: "John had all the ability in the world. But John couldn't stand the pressure of going up into this new league and being one of the first. The things that went on up there were too much for him, and John was not able to perform up to his capabilities. If he had come in two or three years later when the pressure was off, John would have made the major leagues."

In May 1946, after sending Wright down, Montreal brought up Roy Partlow, a thirty-year-old pitcher. Partlow, also, was optioned to Three Rivers, and Robinson finished the year as the only Negro in the league.

SPIDER JORGENSEN: "Partlow was a big, wild left-hander, and he really should have made it, he had pretty good stuff, but the pressure got to him, too. He pitched fairly well when he first got there, but then he got awful wild. He became afraid to throw the ball over."

Robinson, however, was fearless, believed in himself totally, and was aided by his exemplary life-style and by the support system provided him by his wife and by Rickey. And toward the end of the season at Montreal, there was an added force pushing him on.

RACHEL ROBINSON: "Jackie began to understand his mission and that the mission went way beyond sports and athletics. He knew that by that time. As a result of his talks with people, traveling around, having people talk about their reactions to it, being able to see new players were starting to come in, that they were coming to the minor leagues. He could see that there was more to it than just a social experiment, that it had overtones of being something really big. And that began to supersede some of his own personal needs."

And so he endured. After Montreal won the right to play Louisville in the Little World Series, his ordeal continued. In the opening game, Louisville manager Harry Leibold and the players staged a walkout to protest Robinson's presence. When they returned to the field, Leibold and the Louisville players hurled racial slurs at him with a vengeance. From the stands Robinson could hear the taunts of "Hey, black boy, go back to Canada and stay there," followed by, "Yeah, and take all your nigger-loving friends with you."

Montreal and Louisville split the two games in Louisville, with Robinson batting but 1 for 11. Returning to Montreal, the hometown fans, who had adopted Jackie wholeheartedly, retaliated. They booed the Louisville players each time one appeared on the field to bat. They cheered for Jackie's every move, and in the final three games, all won by Montreal for the championship, Jackie positively sparkled. He singled with the bases loaded to win Game Four, doubled, tripled, and scored twice to win Game Five, and in the finale, he started two double plays to kill any chances Louisville may have had to catch up.

After the final game, thousands of fans swarmed onto the field and lifted Jackie and the other Royal players on their shoulders and marched them around the field, singing and shouting.

RACHEL ROBINSON: "The day Jackie finished the season in Montreal, Sam Malton in the *Pittsburgh Courier* wrote a story saying it was the first time a mob had chased a Negro to love him instead of to kill him. And it literally happened. He was running because he had to catch a plane, and fans were chasing him down the street."

When everyone finally got back into the clubhouse after the final game, Montreal manager Clay Hopper walked over to Robinson and said, "You're a great ballplayer and a fine gentleman. It's been wonderful having you on the team." Later he told Rickey, "You don't have to worry none about that boy. He's the greatest competitor I ever saw, and what's more, he's a gentleman."

Petitioning for Bigotry

As soon as it was announced that Robinson had signed to play for Montreal, sportswriter Joe Williams wrote, "Blacks have been kept out of big league ball because they are as a race very poor ballplayers." Williams had lived in Memphis before coming to New York, and he teamed up with Yankee owner MacPhail to snipe at Rickey whenever he could. At the end of the 1946 season, Williams asserted that Rickey had sold second baseman Billy Herman because he wanted to lose the 1946 pennant. That way, wrote Williams, if the Dodgers won in 1947 it would be a "Negro triumph." Baseball's most renowned pitcher, Bob Feller, from Van Meter, Iowa, told reporters, "He's tied up in the shoulders and can't hit an inside pitch to save his neck. If he were a white man, I doubt if they would even consider him big league material."

When Robinson proved at Montreal that he had talent, and it became clear his next step would be into the majors, the smear campaign accelerated, and the bigots among the Dodger players and the major league owners became more desperate and bold.

HAPPY CHANDLER: "In January 1947 the owners had their winter meeting at the Waldorf-Astoria in New York. While there, they made an issue out of the fact that Rickey had proposed bringing Jackie Robinson from Montreal to Brooklyn. They cited all sorts of reasons why this black boy shouldn't play, and of the fellows who spoke, not one on them except Rickey said anything in behalf of this boy. MacPhail got up and spoke, and he was violently opposed. He was from Maryland. Horace Stoneham was a good baseball man and one of my best supporters, but he got up and said that if Robinson played for the Dodgers that the Negroes in Harlem, which was where the Polo Grounds were, would riot and burn down the Polo Grounds. Clark Griffith of Washington spoke against it. He was very much against it. Topping and Webb of the Yankees were against it. Mr. Perini of the Braves too. Mr. Mack never said a word. He never did. But he voted against it. They voted fifteen to one not to let him play. Yes sir, fifteen to one, dear boy. And I announced the result of the vote. You understand, that fifteen-to-one vote was supposed to be notice to me and Rickey. But as far as I was concerned, here was a fellow with talent, and there wasn't anything wrong with him as far as anyone could see about his character. He had had a fine record at UCLA. So I had to go against fifteen fellas, and that hurt me later in 1951 when they refused to renew my contract.

"As soon as the meeting was over, Rickey came on down to Kentucky to my place here in Versailles, and we talked it out at my cabin on the backside of my place for about an hour. He wanted to know where I stood on the Robinson issue. All I had to do is say, 'I'm not going to get into it. Why should I?' and Rickey's dead. Bury him, lay him down, because he's whipped fifteen to one with his own fellows. I told Rickey, 'If Landis was still commissioner, he wouldn't let this boy play, and you wouldn't ask him.' I said, 'Mr. Rickey, I'm going to have to meet my maker some day. If He asked me why I didn't let this boy play, and I answered, "Because he's a Negro," that might not be a sufficient answer. I will approve of the transfer of Robinson's contract from Montreal to Brooklyn, and we'll make a fight with you. So you bring him on in.'

"I had a role in Robinson's breaking the color line just like Rickey, though Rickey tried to take all the credit for that, and in that I was disappointed. But I have nothing to be ashamed of. I had the respect of the respectable people in baseball, and I protected the integrity of the game, and that's just the truth, pardner."

With Chandler's blessing, Rickey had the green light to promote Robinson from Montreal to the Dodgers. But being the strategist that he was, Rickey first wanted the Dodger players to see and appreciate what an extraordinary athlete Robinson was, so he scheduled a series of seven Montreal–Brooklyn exhibition games, praying that Robinson would prove his worth to the Dodger players and incite them to beg Rickey to bring him up. Robinson batted .625 and stole seven bases in the seven games, as he literally stole the show.

SPIDER JORGENSEN: "It was spring training, '47, and Jackie and I were in Havana with Montreal, and we were playing the Dodgers, and we beat the Dodgers because we still had our same old club. They hadn't brought many of us up. In one game we had men on first and second, and Hugh Casey was pitching, and of course the bunt was in order. Robinson was up, and he squared around to bunt, and Casey broke toward third, and Robinson bunted to the other side of Casey and just walked to first base. The crowd hooted and hollered. Jackie really made the Dodgers and Casey look bad. We had heard so much about Casey being so tough, and we figured he'd stick one in Jackie's ribs, but he never did. He just pitched his game. But that was one incident we were waiting for that never happened. But I'll tell you, Jackie made them look bad."

And yet despite Robinson's heroics against them, the talk among the Dodger players was not of praise for Robinson, but rather that some of the southerners on the Dodger team were mounting a petition calling for Rickey to bar Robinson from playing on the Dodgers. Rickey had sadly underestimated how deeply the concept of segregation had been instilled into his southern players.

The rumors suggested a conspiracy, but in fact it had not been a conspiracy at all but rather a campaign instigated by one man, Brooklyn outfielder Dixie Walker, the People's Cherce, who was a Dodger third, an Alabaman second, and a southerner above all.

During spring training in Havana, Walker wrote to Rickey:

"Recently, the thought has occurred to me that a change of Ball clubs would benefit both the Brooklyn Baseball Club and myself. Therefore I would like to be traded as soon as a deal can be arranged. My association with you, the people of Brooklyn, the press and Radio has been very pleasant and one can truthfully say I am sorry it has to end. For reasons I don't care to go into I feel my decision is the best for all concerned."

Walker sought allies in his cause, and he enlisted the support of third-string catcher Bobby Bragan; Dixie Howell, another sub; and Eddie Stanky, an Alabaman playing second. Pitchers Hugh Casey and Kirby Higbe were less enthusiastic, but Walker wrote out a petition calling for Rickey not to bring up Robinson, and while the Dodgers were playing exhibitions in Panama, he carried it personally from room to room for all the other southerners to sign. He was optimistic, until the usually mild-mannered Pee Wee Reese, a southern boy from Louisville, opposed him.

PEE WEE REESE: "When I was growing up in Louisville, I lived in a poor neighborhood, but there were no blacks around there. There were a few blacks that lived in what we called the alley, not far from us, but they were not allowed in the parks. And they rode in the back of the buses and the back of the street cars. You just thought, 'That's the way of life. That's where they should be.' That's the way we were brought up. And the first experience I had with Jackie was kind of strange, really. I hadn't gone to school with blacks, no, no, no, oh lordy, no. They had their own schools. All the schools were segregated. I can't say that we really looked down on the blacks. We just thought that that was the way it was supposed to be.

"I was in the Third Marine Division when I found out the war had ended, and I was coming home from Guam on a ship when somebody came and told

Dodgers

me that the Dodgers had signed a black ballplayer. I said, 'Hey, I can't believe this.' And then the guy came back and said, 'Pee Wee, not only is he black, but he's a shortstop.' But I didn't think a helluva lot about it, not really, until I went to spring training."

Reese thought more about it than he cares to admit. It was on his mind the entire rest of the voyage home, and when the ship landed in San Francisco, he went out and got roaring drunk for the only time in his life. He had grown up in Louisville, where Negroes were invisible but second-class citizens, and here was one who might very well take away his job. After his head cleared the next day, however, Reese managed to come to terms with the situation. "If he's man enough to take my job," Reese told himself, "he deserves it." And so when the petition came around, Reese said no. And by doing so, Reese established his reputation as a man of dignity and integrity, and for the next ten years, Reese and Robinson became Dodger symbols of integration and harmony.

PEE WEE REESE: "Dixie was really one of my best friends on the ballclub. He was responsible for my wife and me getting married. I always had great respect for Dixie. Hell, I can't knock Dixie. I know how he was brought up, and that was his feelings.

"We were in Panama, and Dixie came to the room, and he asked Pete Reiser and me to sign that I wouldn't play with a black man. I looked at it, and I just flatly refused. I just said, 'Hey look, man, I just got out of the service after three years. I don't care if this man is black, blue, or what the hell color he is. I have to play baseball.' I wasn't trying to be the Great White Father. I just wanted to play ball. And Pete refused to sign it too."

PETE REISER: "I'd had an experience when I was in the army. This was in Richmond. I'd just been transferred there. My daughter got very sick. So I looked up a doctor in the phone book. He told me to bring my daughter to his office. The office was in a Negro neighborhood. The doctor was a Negro. I didn't think anything of it. What the hell was the difference? He gave her a shot, penicillin I think it was, and cured her.

"I told the story to Dixie Walker, who wanted me to sign the petition against Robinson. I said, 'What would you have done?' He said, 'I would have turned around and walked away from that neighborhood.' I told him I thought he was a Goddamned fool, and then I told him what he could do with his petition."

One man who was ambivalent was pitcher Kirby Higbe. On the one hand he believed in segregation. When asked by Branch Rickey, he said he preferred not to have to play with a "negruh." He was from Columbia, South Carolina, where as a youth he spent many hours throwing rocks at blacks. But Higbe was also a great competitor, and he believed that denying an outstanding athlete such as Robinson the right to compete was wrong. He wasn't certain which side of the fence to sit on.

* * *

KIRBY HIGBE: "I remember when I was a young boy, my grandfather used to tell me about the Civil War. That was the worst war we ever had. One grandfather fought for the South, the other fought for the North. Neither grandfather had anything to eat.

"When I was growing up, it never was no problem. Sure, we were segregated. I reckon that was the old Southern custom. I don't know. I don't suppose anyone would have objected if a colored wanted to come to our church when I was growing up as a boy. I was going to Baptist Church, and we never objected to them coming to church."

Not that a Negro would dare walk into his church, any lack of objection notwithstanding. The question was, would Kirby object to a Negro playing alongside him on the Dodgers? In the end his southern side convinced him to sign the petition.

KIRBY HIGBE: "I felt real bad about this. I told them, 'You all ought not to do it just because he's colored.' But everybody said, 'You're from down South.' I said, 'I don't care where I'm from. If he's good enough to play baseball, then he's good enough.' But we talked about it more, and I was from the South, and finally I said, 'Hell, I'll sign it.' I said to myself, 'What's the difference? It ain't gonna hurt nobody.' So I signed."

But it didn't sit right with him, and over too many beers one night Higbe spilled the details of the Southern insurgence to Dodger traveling secretary Harold Parrott.

KIRBY HIGBE: "I told Hal. I says, 'Hal, ole buddy, we're going to have a little trouble if he brings Robinson up. Definitely.' I remember it like I was sitting with him now. 'Hal, when Rickey brings Robinson up, we're going to have some problems.' He said, 'What do you mean?' I said, 'Well, there's a few ballplayers who have started to have meetings, and there's going to be some problems.' And I told him about the petition. He said, 'Who are the players?' I said, 'I ain't namin' names, 'cause it ain't none of my business. But I'm telling you you're going to have trouble.'

"And then I went and told Rickey. Hal told me to do it. When I told Rickey there was going to be trouble, he said, 'I don't think so, Kirby.' I said, 'That's good enough for me, Mr. Rickey.' And as far as I was concerned, that's all there was to it."

Higbe never got credit for his sabotage, but in his own way, he too helped pave the way for Robinson's coming.

Before Rickey arrived in Panama to interrogate the petitioners, manager Leo Durocher attacked them. During the 1946 pennant race, Leo had been pushing Rickey to bring Robinson up, and now that some of his players were causing trouble, Durocher became enraged.

* * *

HAROLD PARROTT: "He called the midnight meeting in the barracks, and I can still hear him as he challenged the mutineers. He was wrapped in a yellow bathrobe, and he looked like a fighter about to enter the ring. He stared down Walker and Bragan and started punching out the words.

" 'I don't care if the guy is yellow or black, or if he has stripes like a fuckin' zebra. I'm the manager of this team, and I say he plays. What's more, I say he can make us all rich.' After a pause, the Lip added, 'An' if any of you can't use the money, I'll see that you're traded.'

"There had been dollar signs dancing in Durocher's eyes from the very first day he saw Robinson. Leo wanted the black man right then. He thought Jack could ring the cash register for us all."

Rickey then spoke to the rebels. Two Dodgers, Dixie Walker and Bobby Bragan, still wanted out. Rickey couldn't understand why Bragan, a young kid, a third-string catcher whose position on the team was tenuous at best, would ask to be traded. Rickey told Bragan, "I've got Bruce Edwards. I've got Gil Hodges. You're the third-string catcher, and you're expendable." Bragan, who was born in Alabama, said, "Mr. Rickey, I live down in Ft. Worth, Texas. My friends there would never forgive me."

Rickey was willing to accommodate the two players, but he made it clear he would get value in return or he would not make a trade. Rickey had worked out a deal to trade Dixie Walker to the Pirates, but early in the '47 season outfielder Pete Reiser was hospitalized. At the end of the season Rickey offered Walker the manager's job at St. Paul. Walker said he wanted to continue as a player, and during the off-season Rickey traded him to Pittsburgh in a deal for Preacher Roe and Billy Cox.

Rickey also agreed to trade Bragan, but never did.

BOBBY BRAGAN: "Mr. Rickey held individual meetings, with Arthur Mann, a writer and a good friend of Mr. Rickey's, there taking notes. Mr. Rickey asked me pointedly, he said, 'You and nobody else is going to tell me who to play on this team. I don't care about a fellow's color or if he's got hair all over him. If he can do the best job, he's going to play. Now how do you feel?'

"I said, 'If I had my choice, I'd just as soon be traded as stay here.'

"He stared at me for a while, very thoughtfully, and said, 'I appreciate your honesty, Bobby.'

"A few days later Arthur Mann came to me and said, 'Bobby, Mr. Rickey really appreciated what you told him in there. You leveled with him,' and that started a wonderful relationship between me and Mr. Rickey. I'm as great a booster of Mr. Rickey as anyone who ever lived. He understood why I took the position that I took, that I had been raised that way, and within thirty days, maximum, those of us who were reluctant to sit with Jackie in the dining room car would readily sit down with him. It soon became apparent to all of us that there wasn't any way we were going to win without Jackie."

Bob Bragan

Rickey kept Bragan on the Dodgers in 1947, and early in '48 Rickey made him manager of the Ft. Worth minor league team. During a distinguished career as manager, Bragan had a reputation for helping young black players. He made Maury Wills a switch hitter, propelling him to stardom. He helped Tommy Davis, Roberto Clemente, Lee May, Mack Jones, Curt Roberts, and many others.

BOBBY BRAGAN: "I had a lot better rapport and understanding of the black players because of Jackie Robinson. If I hadn't had that experience with Jackie, I don't think I could have done it."

The one other player somehow involved in all of this was outfielder Carl Furillo, from Reading, Pennsylvania. Kirby Higbe swears that Furillo signed the petition. Furillo swears he never did. The resulting flap over Furillo's role left the moody outfielder with the rifle arm feeling betrayed by his teammates. Throughout his career as a Dodger, Furillo never again allowed himself to become close to his teammates. He wasn't going to allow himself to be burned a second time.

CARL FURILLO: "We went to Havana for spring training, and one day when I was at the ballfield, and I don't remember who it was anymore, whether it was Bragan or Dixie Howell, he said to me, 'Furillo, what would you do if he came after your job?' And I wasn't thinking. I just said, 'I'd cut his legs off.' And the remark got in the papers, and before you know it, I was the guy in the middle. By me making that stupid remark. So I see young Branch Rickey, and I said, 'What the hell's the matter here?' He said, 'What's the matter, Carl?' I says, 'I have nothing to do with this. This is the bunch that really was at it, the southern boys. I'm the guy in the middle, and these guys are standing off and looking at me, laughing.' He said, 'We know who's behind it. But you should never have made that stupid remark.' I says, 'I know that.' But I had made it, and it was too late. You couldn't retract it. But I got along good with Jackie. And I told Jackie about it. I said, 'I'm sorry, but I didn't mean it the way they put it.' Jackie said, 'Don't worry about it.'

"But if you saw *The Jackie Robinson Story*—I didn't see it, but I heard about it—that's what got me a little bit annoyed about the whole Goddamn thing is in the picture there's an Italian kid, and Old Man Rickey uses the Italian kid as the whipping post. And he says to him, 'Where's your parents from?' And the kid says, 'From Italy.' 'Well, how would you feel if they were treated that way?' I said to my wife, 'Them sons a bitches, that's me.' I never said a Goddamn word about the guy. They pushed that blame off on me, and that son of a bitch Italian in the picture, that was really a southern kid. So I passed it off, I said, 'The hell with it. I don't want to have nothing to do with none of them.' And I didn't associate with them. I lived in Flushing, and the rest of them lived over in Brooklyn. When the game was over, they went their way, and I went mine. And I didn't see them until the following day. I thought to myself, 'The hell with this. The hell with them.' "

* * *

Though much has been written about the petition against Robinson, it was a well-kept secret at the time of its circulation. The sports reporters found out about it when Rickey blew the whistle on the petitioners, and yet at the time, the sportswriters didn't write it. Dodger fans knew of Dixie Walker's stand—Walker had been vocal about it—but they didn't learn about the petition until several weeks after the incident occurred.

Meanwhile Rickey was taking his time announcing his next move. He wanted his players to come around to his way of thinking. He didn't want to force Robinson upon the Dodgers unless he had to. When the players remained unenthusiastic, Rickey decided to help step up the campaign. He scheduled an April 10 press conference at which Durocher was to announce that in order for the Dodgers to win the pennant, they needed a first baseman and that Robinson was that man. Leo, however, never got to that press conference. On that day Happy Chandler suspended him from baseball.

One day Rickey had wanted Durocher to help take the heat off Robinson. The next he needed Robinson to take the heat off Durocher. In an attempt to wrest the Durocher story from the front pages, Rickey announced on April 11 that Robinson had signed a Brooklyn contract.

The press release that announced Robinson's signing was distributed at Ebbets Field during the sixth inning of a Montreal–Brooklyn exhibition. It made news, of course, but the next day the big story still revolved around Durocher. As one writer described it, Robinson entered the big leagues "as a whisper in a whirlwind."

N.Y. *Daily News* Photo

JACKIE ROBINSON AND BRANCH RICKEY

5

Brooklyn Embraces Robinson

Between 1935 and 1945 there were around 3 million people packed into the borough of Brooklyn. Had Brooklyn not been a part of the city of New York, it would have been the second-largest municipality in the country, just behind Chicago. Immigrants or sons and daughters of immigrants made up most of Brooklyn's populace. About half were Jews, many Eastern Europeans who escaped first the czars and then Hitler. The rest were Catholics—Irish and Italian—along with a sprinkling of Swedes, Norwegians, and Germans.

Three million people, and hardly a Mayflower descendant among them. The populace had landed in boats all right, but they had steamed past the Statue of Liberty and docked at Ellis Island. Brooklyn was different from the rest of the country. Everyone came as a minority, and they discovered that when they arrived in Brooklyn, everyone was the same: Everyone was poor. Everyone was struggling. No one felt persecuted, unless they rooted for the Giants or the Yankees instead of the Dodgers.

Although different areas had different ethnic characters, there was little serious prejudice.

Bill Reddy grew up in the area of Ditmas Avenue and Avenue F in Borough Park. It was a typical Brooklyn neighborhood, predominantly Irish and Jewish, with some Italian, and he remembers the congruence that existed then.

BILL REDDY: "Where I grew up, guys were named Gangello, Ishkowitz, and McGee, but the great thing about being a kid in Brooklyn in those days was that it didn't matter what your ethnic background was. Everybody was the same. Nobody had anything.

"We grew up in each other's home. I knew what gefilte fish and cherry blintzes were at an early age, and the Italian *gabutzel,* or lamb's brains, and ravioli, and it's true, when somebody was sick, the neighbor woman would come over with a pot of chicken soup. And you also learned to talk to each other in the smattering of all these languages. When an Irish kid called an Italian a shmuck, the Italian knew what he was calling him. It was nothing for an Irish kid to tell a Jewish kid, *'a fangool,'* and the Jewish kid would know exactly what he was saying. I learned words: *'shlimazel,' 'shmegegge,' 'shmuck.'* When you grew up in a Jewish neighborhood, you learned these things.

"In my neighborhood there were't too many blacks. Hardly any. There was one black fellow who used to play ball with us. He was a superintendent of an apartment house, and all I ever knew him as was Bibby. Our team was a rather cosmopolitan group, and Bibby fitted right in. He was our catcher. In fact the only time we noticed he was black was when our pitcher couldn't see the signals, because his fingers didn't show up against his pants. You had to look for the pink fingernails.

"There was very little prejudice against blacks because we didn't come into contact with them much. The black people lived around Greene Avenue, Reid Avenue, and Fulton Street. They had their own neighborhood, a pretty good large area, it was the edge of what is now called Bedford-Stuyvesant, where the Bedford section edges into Williamsburg. That's where they lived and existed, but you never came into contact with them, except at work, or you saw black ladies coming around to work as maids in the apartment houses on Ocean Parkway. Or you saw them when you played a team in a baseball game or went to a Holy Name rally, when black churches would send representatives.

"I never knew that blacks weren't playing in the big leagues because they were black. I don't know whether I was an awfully naive kid when I was growing up, but it never occurred to me that a guy wasn't playing because he was a different color than the other guys. I thought they weren't playing because the guys who were playing were better. I always had an idea that the heavyweight champion of the world was the best fighter in the world, that nobody could beat him. I believed these things, as most kids did in those days.

"When Robinson came up, all of a sudden we saw Negroes not only as human beings, but we lionized them. You'd say, 'Oh my God, there are wonderful people in there.' "

Joe Flaherty: "The enclave of Brooklyn where Bill Reddy and I grew up was one in which a Protestant was exotic. They didn't believe in the Blessed Mother. That was enough to handle. Our minds didn't reach far enough to consider that there were blacks in the world. We weren't college-educated or -oriented. You got out of high school and went to work to put the buck on the table. And we weren't pondering social issues. We read the *News,* the *Mirror,* and the Catholic paper, *The Tablet,* which served one purpose: to tell you what were the hot movies you weren't supposed to see, though that was always a major disappointment because they were always banning movies for anticlerical remarks, not for the right reasons. We went to see tits and ass, but usually we'd go because the *Tablet* warned us not to, and one character would be yelling at a bishop, and it would be banned for that.

"I remember sitting by Prospect Park once about the time the Dodgers were bringing Robinson up. I heard my uncle say, 'What the hell does he want in the game? It's a white man's game.' I didn't really know what he was getting at. I knew there was controversy about Robinson coming up, but you have to understand that what President Reagan said was true. He said, 'I grew up at a time when we didn't have a race problem,' and everyone jumped on him for being insensitive. But we didn't know we had a race problem.

"Back when Robinson was coming up, we liked to think that Negroes didn't need anything, that they were happy in their place. Sure it was a little dangerous to walk in Prospect Park at night. There were some tough black kids. But there wasn't this myopic focus on blacks that there is today. To me the Montagues and Capulets of Brooklyn will always be the Irish and Italians. I thought the Italians were the ones you had to kick the shit out of all the time. When I speak at colleges and black kids accuse my generation of being racist, I tell them, 'Don't call my generation racist. I didn't know you people even existed.' "

GUS ENGLEMAN: "We were kids then. We never really discussed it in specific social issues, 'Is it right or is it wrong?' It was, 'Do you think there will be fights on the Dodgers? Gee, I wonder what's going to happen.' Not, 'I hate Dixie Walker to talk that way.' No rights or wrongs, just kids wondering whether it was going to destroy baseball, whether baseball is going to stay the same, whether the Dodgers will be okay. Remember, this was during a period in Brooklyn when the Dodgers were all. It was all we had, a great, great love affair for the borough and all its inhabitants with the team."

BILL REDDY: "It was strange to go out to Ebbets Field and root for a guy of another color. We had never seen this before. As Dodger fans, we'd say to ourselves, 'How good is this guy? Is he worth all the trouble?' And yet, because he was a Dodger, we had to defend him. All some wise-guy Giant fan had to say was, 'Hey, you got a nigger on first base,' and we'd reply, 'What's it your business, Mac? He's better than anybody you got on your team.' And if he was a southerner, we'd be even more protective. We'd say, 'So what if he's black? He plays for Brooklyn, don't he?' "

Rickey knew he was chancing losing some of his rooters by signing Negroes, and though few of the kids cared what color Robinson's skin was, there were blue collar adults who loathed what Robinson's presence symbolized: rivalry from the Negro worker.

TOM "DUKE" BUNDERICK: "When Jackie Robinson came up, there were a lot of adults who dropped their allegiance to the Dodgers. There was a lot of bigotry, among the working class more than anything: the Irish, the Italians, the Swedes. They said, 'I'm never gonna root from them again, Goddamn it.' It was a lot of union guys saying, 'Sure, first they get into baseball, and then they'll be taking my job.'

"The young kids didn't care, 'cause we felt, 'Here's another great ballplayer.' The anti-Dodger kids would say, 'Robinson's a Goddamn showboat, and I'd like to see him get hit in the head with the ball,' but that had nothing to do with his being black. It had to do with fierce fanaticism."

Robinson's first game as a Dodger was on April 15, 1947, against the Boston Braves. It was opening day at Ebbets Field. Johnny Sain started for the Braves, Joe Hatten for the Dodgers. Robinson played first base.

The attendance was announced at 26,623. Of those, 14,000 were black. In his first game, Robinson had earned his $5,000 salary. "They would have had a sellout today," one reporter said. "You know why they didn't?" "No," said Arthur Daley of the *Times*. The reporter replied, "They kept out all the gamblers." The ghost of Leo Durocher walked.

In his first at bat, Robinson hit the ball hard at the shortstop. The throw arrived at first about the same time as he did, but umpire Al Barlick called him out. Robinson made a face and took a step toward Barlick—if it had been the Negro League he would have been all over him, for Robinson was one of the worst crybabies when it came to complaining about getting the wrong end of close calls—but Rickey had trained him to be silent, and sullenly he went back to the dugout.

The Dodgers beat the Braves, 5 to 3. Clyde Sukeforth managed the game in Durocher's stead. Though Robinson didn't get a hit, he did score a run. Pete Reiser won the game with a double off Sain in the seventh. Much of the talk was about Robinson, but Leo Durocher's suspension also was a hot topic.

That day eighteen-year-old Joel Oppenheimer was working in his dad's leather goods store in mid-Manhattan. Joel was home from Cornell University for Easter vacation.

JOEL OPPENHEIMER: "There are two kinds of fathers in this world to work for. There's the kind who makes his kid the president of the firm, and there's the kind who is convinced that he must bend over backward not to show favoritism. Guess which type of father I had? Not that Dad was mean. He just didn't want the other employees to think his son was getting away with anything.

"On this particular day I was sweeping the floor. It was about eleven in the morning, and Dad was standing behind the cash register up front. He called me over, and I assumed he had another errand for me to do. Instead, he asked me, 'If you could do anything in the world today, what would you like to do?' I was so stunned I couldn't answer. He said, 'Isn't there something you want to do?' 'You mean like going to the moon?' I said. 'No,' he said, 'something real.' I couldn't think of anything to say. He asked me, 'Wouldn't you like to be at Ebbets Field today?' And I couldn't believe my ears. Of course I wanted to go. I knew Jackie Robinson would be playing his first game, and I was astounded that, one, my father was even aware of Robinson, and, two, aware that I would want to go.

"So off I went, and when I arrived in the grandstand it was standing room only. I remember standing behind third base in a thick crowd of people, and for the first time in my life I was in a crowd of blacks.

"For years we used to hear stories about this fantastic black pitcher who once was supposed to have struck out all the Yankees. We didn't know his name—it was Satchel Paige—but we had heard about all the great black ballplayers and how they weren't allowed to play, and so for me Jackie was all those guys rolled into one, and he was going to lead my Dodgers to glory.

"During the game Jackie made a good play in the field, at which point everyone was yelling, 'Jackie, Jackie, Jackie,' and I was yelling with them. And suddenly I realized that behind me someone was yelling, 'Yonkel, Yonkel, Yonkel,' which is Yiddish for Jackie. With great wonderment and pleasure, I realized that here was this little Jewish tailor—I always assumed he was a tailor—the only white face in a crowd of blacks aside from me, and he's yelling 'Yonkel, Yonkel, Yonkel.' It was a very moving moment."

Of the three—Jewish, Irish, and Italian—Robinson's most vocal support came from the Jewish community. Yet characteristically, when Robinson sought to move into a Jewish community, the Jews there pulled a Dixie Walker and started passing around a petition to keep the Robinsons out. But as happened on the Dodgers, it didn't take long for the neighbors to embrace the Robinsons. After the first month, Jackie had become a hero.

Ty Cobb in Technicolor

On the field integration came less easily. The abuse began with hate mail and threats. Get out of the game or be killed. Get out or your wife will die. Get out or your baby boy will be kidnapped and killed. In addition Robinson was made acutely aware that not all his teammates were for him.

AL GIONFRIDDO: "The two Dodgers who gave Jackie the most trouble were Dixie Walker and Bobby Bragan. If Jackie was sitting in one spot, they would make it a point to sit somewhere else."

There were also the small humiliations that southern blacks had routinely suffered at the hands of whites. One time Robinson was playing poker with pitcher Hugh Casey, and Hugh was losing. To everyone in the room, Hugh hollered, "You know what ah used to do down in Georgia when ah ran into bad luck. Ah used to go out and fine me the biggest, blackest nigger woman ah could find and rub her teats to change my luck." Robinson became dizzy, but did nothing. "Deal the cards," he said icily.

But that was mild compared to what Jackie faced from the opposition.

When the Dodgers played the Phillies in Philadelphia in a three-game series beginning April 22, Phils manager Ben Chapman and several of the Phils, including Dixie Walker's brother, Harry, started yelling during batting practice, "Nigger, go back to the cotton fields where you belong." "They're waiting for you in the jungles, black boy." "Hey, snowflake, which one of you white boy's wives are you dating tonight?" Chapman, a tough and ornery Tennessean who had made a reputation while a Yankee outfielder for yelling anti-Semitic slurs at Jewish fans and who once while managing Richmond was suspended for a year when he yanked off the mask from the home-plate umpire and punched him in the face, yelled to Jackie's Dodger teammates that they would get diseases and sores if they touched his combs or towels. They razzed Robinson about the death threats, and when Robinson took the field, they pointed bats at him and made machine-gunlike noises.

Robinson stood there, silent, fearing he was having a breakdown. For an instant Robinson considered breaking his promise to Rickey. He pondered pummeling Chapman, quitting the game, and returning to his home in California. But Robinson also was mindful of the chance Rickey was taking, and he held back.

Asked about it later, Chapman argued that in the past he had razzed DiMaggio, calling him "The Wop," and Whitey Kurowski, "The Polock." Chapman accused Robinson of being a "weakling who couldn't take it."

During the entire series, the abuse from the Philadelphia bench never let up. One time Robinson hit a pop up right in front of home plate with two men on. "It's a home run," shouted one Philly player.

"Yeah," cracked Puddin' Head Jones, as catcher Andy Seminick made the catch, "if you're playing in an elevator shaft."

"You can't play ball up here, you black bum," shouted another Philly from the dugout. "You're only up here to draw those nigger bucks at the gate for Rickey."

Shouted Chapman, "If you were a white boy, you'd have been shipped down to Newport News long ago."

When Robinson first reported to the Dodgers, second baseman Eddie Stanky, who had been raised in the South, told him, "I don't like you, but we'll play together and get along because you're my teammate." But by the end of the third Philadelphia game, Stanky became the first Dodger to stand up for Robinson. "Listen, you cowards," he screamed into the Phils' dugout. "Why don't you yell at someone who can answer back?" The Phillies responded with cries of "nigger lover."

Traveling secretary Harold Parrott phoned Rickey to tell him what was going on. Parrott, like everyone else, initially had been against the Robinson experiment. As traveling secretary he knew that Robinson's presence would seriously complicate his life. Now Rickey told Parrott to be patient. "On this team, on any team, there are some fair-minded men of quality who will rebel against the treatment Robinson is getting, and they'll do something about it. There will be an incident, perhaps a small one, perhaps something big. But they'll be drawn closer to him and become a protective cordon around him. You'll see."

HAROLD PARROTT: "It occurred to me right then that I hadn't even told him about Stanky taking Robinson's side against the Phillies. I had wanted to make the situation sound as bleak as possible, I guess."

It took only two more days of the abuse designed to make Jackie quit before another of Rickey's "fair-minded men of quality" made a step in Robinson's defense.

After the Philadelphia series, the Dodgers took the train to Cincinnati. Robinson had started the season in a slump. He had been pressing too hard, began 0 for 20, but broke out of it against the Phils with hard, powerful line drives.

Even when Robinson wasn't hitting, he had proved he could run; he had stolen the third game in that Philadelphia series away from Chapman and the Phils.

The Dodgers moved on from the City of Brotherly Love to the Queen City of Cincinnati, which was just across the river from Kentucky, a southern state and the home of Dodger shortstop Pee Wee Reese. The terrorist tactics continued. Three separate death threats put Robinson on notice that the rednecks didn't approve of him playing with whites. Reese and a couple of the other players were informed of the threats. What the other players didn't know was that Reese had gotten death threats as well. His fellow Kentuckians couldn't understand how their favorite son could play alongside a nigger.

In the top of the first, Jackie popped up for the third out. As the Dodgers ran onto the field, Reese stopped by first to speak to Robinson.

REX BARNEY: "I was warming up on the mound, and I could hear the Cincinnati players screaming at Jackie, 'You nigger sonofabitch, you shoeshine boy,' and all the rest, and then they started to get on Pee Wee. They were yelling at him, 'How can you play with this nigger bastard?' and all this stuff, and while Jackie was standing by first base, Pee Wee went over to him and put his arm around him as if to say, 'This is my boy. This is the guy. We're gonna win with him.' Well, it drove the Cincinnati players right through the ceiling, and you could have heard the gasp from the crowd as he did it. That's one reason Pee Wee was such an instrumental person contributing to Jackie's success, Pee Wee more than anyone else because Pee Wee was from the South. Pee Wee understood things a little better, and still does. They became very close friends, and they understood each other. Listen, a lot of us did, Branca, Erskine, Bruce Edwards, Pee Wee, myself. We did a lot for him. He hadn't realized that there were people like us around. Thank God for him there were, but it was Pee Wee most of all."

In little ways, there were others on the Dodgers who tried as best as they could to show Robinson he had their support.

AL GIONFRIDDO: "What I remember most about the 1947 season was the heroics of Jackie Robinson. He was the first colored boy to come into the major leagues, but it never bothered me because I came from a small town in Pennsylvania, and we had only one or two colored people in that whole town, and they were friends of everyone. I just figured that Jackie was there trying to make a living the same as me.

"In fact Jackie Robinson was my roommate in the clubhouse. He and I dressed right together, lockers next to each other. And I remember Jackie would sit there and wait until everyone else had showered. One day I hit him on the butt and I said, 'You're part of this team. Why are you waiting to be the last guy in the shower? Just because in some states Negroes can't shower with whites, that doesn't mean it has to apply here in our clubhouse.' And he just looked at me and laughed, and we both got up and took a shower."

* * *

CLYDE KING: "There used to be an iron fence and iron bars going from the dugout to the clubhouse to keep the fans from getting to you. There was a big iron gate there, and the wives would come inside that gate after the game to wait for their husbands, and the fans would be jammed up against it, reaching for autographs. For the first several games, Rachel Robinson stood outside that gate, and my wife, Norma, who was also from North Carolina, who went to the university, went out one day and invited her in with the other wives."

By early May Jackie Robinson was an accepted member of the Dodgers. That is to say, within the short period of but one month, not a soul doubted that Robinson would remain with the team. One month. That's how quickly it took for his teammates to recognize his value. They saw him as the difference between their winning a pennant or not, and though none of them warmed up to him that first year, they certainly appreciated what he was doing for them. In one game in June, Robinson scored from first on a sacrifice fly hit by Gene Hermanski. In another game he walked, and when he stepped on first, he noticed that the pitcher and catcher were daydreaming and kept on going into second. In a game against the Giants, Robinson singled in a run, went to second on a long fly, and after reaching third, stole home. Robinson's teammates marveled at his raw skill and at his ability to play with so much grace under pressure.

CLYDE KING: "I remember one day Jackie was on first base, and there was a base hit into left field, and he rounded second looking right at the left fielder, and when he threw the ball into second, Jackie just trotted into third, no contest. All the guys on the bench looked at that like, 'God, did you see that?' Without saying a word. He was such a good base runner. A good bunter. He was one of the best curveball hitters I've ever seen. And whether they talked about it or not, they admired the way he played."

Jackie had clearly triumphed. Fans were flooding National League ballparks to watch him, and when the Dodgers returned to Philadelphia to play the Phillies, Robinson gained his sweetest revenge. Influential Broadway columnist Walter Winchell had gone after Chapman, mounting a crusade to get Chapman fired for his racist behavior. Winchell made it so hot for Chapman that his job seemed to be on the line. Chapman approached Dodger traveling secretary Harold Parrott, whom he had known when he had tried out for the Dodgers as a pitcher in 1944.

HAROLD PARROTT: "With a sickly smile, Chapman got out something that was obviously very hard for him to say: 'For old times sake, will you do me a big favor? Ask Robinson if he'll agree to have a picture taken shaking hands with me?'

"I must have looked stunned, for Chapman added, as a humbling afterthought, 'A picture like this in the newspapers may save my job. I'll come over to your dugout this evening to have it taken, if he'll agree.'

"Robinson smiled wanly when I told him of Chapman's request and—to my surprise—quickly agreed.

"Tell Ben he doesn't have to come over to our dugout, either. I'll meet him halfway, behind the plate during batting practice.'

" 'I'll go with you,' I said, thinking to make the chore easier. I had often been Jack's ice breaker.

" 'No,' said Robinson. 'This is something I should do alone, not as if I'm being urged.'

"Dixie Walker, Chapman's pal from Alabama, and a fine man through and through, had listened to this whole conversation, from the moment I relayed the strange request to Robbie. Dixie watched wide-eyed—we both did, in fact—as Robinson and Chapman, each marching from his own dugout, met on the neutral ground behind home plate. Ben extended a hand, smiling broadly as if they had been buddy-buddy for a lifetime. Robinson reached out and grasped it. The flicker of a smile crept across his face as the photographer snapped away, getting several shots.

"Beside me Walker gasped, groping for words.

" 'I swear,' he said softly, 'I never thought I'd see Ol' Ben eat shit like that.' "

Robinson made every team in the league eat shit. The team he seemed to humiliate the most often was the world champion St. Louis Cardinals. In early May the Cardinal players, spurred on by southerners Enos Slaughter and Terry Moore, had discussed going on strike. It was just hot air. No one was going to risk his career by striking, but the talk forced National League President Ford Frick to take a stand. Frick, who had kept Bill Veeck from forming an all-black team, who had prevented "contamination" of baseball, for the first time in his presidency acted with guts: He came out strongly for Jackie, threatening to kick all the strikers out of baseball.

By August the Dodgers were leading the Cardinals for the pennant. The Cardinals had won the World Series the year before, and their southern ringleader, Enos Slaughter, had been the hero of the 1946 Series, racing home from first with the winning run on a single by Harry Walker. But here it was August of 1947, and the nigger Robinson was threatening both the southern-town Cardinals and the North Carolinean Slaughter. There is a thin line between being a hustler and a dirty player, and though Slaughter generally was thought of as a hustler, he was also known to sometimes cross that line. Whenever he slid into an infielder, he did so with spikes high. He could afford to do so. No one could spike him back from his defensive post in the outfield. In August he decided to take on Robinson. Several of Jackie's teammates recall the incident:

REX BARNEY: "Jackie was playing first that year, just so he wouldn't be playing a position like second base where the runners would get a crack at him, and Slaughter got up, and he hit a ground ball, and the throw came to Jackie, and he was out by ten feet. As Slaughter ran toward the bag, he jumped, not on Jackie's foot, but up on the thigh of his leg, and he cut him, and Jackie went down. He wasn't hurt badly, but he was very upset, and the next inning Jackie got a hit, and he's standing on first, and Stan Musial's the first baseman, and Jackie said to Stan: 'I don't care what happens, but when I get to second base, I'm gonna kill somebody. I'm gonna knock him into center field. I don't care what kind of play it is, he's going down.' Stan, being the gentleman that he is, said: 'I don't blame you. You have every right to do it.'

"Jackie told us later that it took it all out of him, that after Musial said that, he didn't have the heart to do it. Musial was such a class guy. He understood. His teammate had done that, and yet he understood how Jackie felt, and he was telling Jackie he didn't like it."

RALPH BRANCA: "I was pitching, and I had retired twenty-one batters in a row, I was pitching a no-hitter, and Slaughter grounded out to Stanky at second base who threw him out, and Jackie was playing first and was stretched out, and Enos stepped on his leg just below the calf. Fortunately he must have got him right in the middle of the spikes, cause I don't think he was cut badly.

"After Enos stepped on his leg, I went over to Jackie and said, 'Don't worry, Jackie. I'll get that son of a bitch for you,' and Jackie said, 'No, Ralph, just get them out.' "

CARL FURILLO: "I'll never forget it. Enos Slaughter went down to first base, and Jackie was reaching out for the ball, and he had his foot out, and Slaughter stepped right on his Goddamn leg and cut it. And we tried to get him. But we couldn't. In fact, when Slaughter was going into second base, Pee Wee said to Stanky, our second baseman, 'Give me the ball fast so I can get him.' 'Cause what Pee Wee wanted to do was come underneath, to nail Slaughter with the relay. They didn't give a shit about throwing out the guy at first. They were going to try to hit him square in the mouth with the ball. But they didn't get the chance. If they could of, they would have smacked him square in the mouth with it."

By June Robinson had paved the way so successfully that Rickey brought up a second Negro, pitcher Dan Bankhead.

AL GIONFRIDDO: "Dan roomed with Jackie, kept Jackie company, because when we went into certain towns, like St. Louis, they couldn't stay with us at the hotel. They had to go stay in the colored section of town. Now that was a bunch of shit. But there was nothing the ballplayers could do about it. It was the law of the city. We couldn't fight the city. What the hell are you gonna do?

"Dan was a happy-go-lucky sort of guy. Wouldn't bother anyone. A great guy who loved baseball. Could run like a deer. Could he run! Oh, could that guy run! But he never did make it as a pitcher. What I remember most about him was how he used to stamp his foot down so hard, whoom, stamp the hell out of the rubber when he pitched. And I remember in his first at bat he hit a home run against Fritz Ostermueller of the Pirates."

* * *

It was during a night game in Pittsburgh, the twenty-fourth of June. Earlier Robinson had noticed that Fritz Ostermueller had become careless and relaxed. With the score 2 to 2 and Robinson dancing off third base, the Pirate left-hander, ignoring Robinson's darting movements, went into a full windup. As he did so, Robinson took off and slid home safely.

In the fourth inning, pitcher Dan Bankhead hit Ostermueller for a home run. Said Kirby Higbe, who in May had been traded to the Pirates, "That really got Fritz mad. It also taught him that Negroes were here to stay."

On September 12 Robinson was named Rookie of the Year by the *Sporting News*. His record: forty-two successful bunts, fourteen for hits, twenty-eight sacrifices; twenty-nine stolen bases, twelve home runs, and a .297 average. In the article announcing its selection, there was a quote from Dixie Walker. Walker said:

"No other ballplayer on this club with the possible exception of Bruce Edwards has done more to put the Dodgers up in the race as Robinson has. He is everything Branch Rickey said he was when he came up from Montreal."

It was a gracious statement from a man who had told Happy Chandler he would stay home and paint his house rather than play on the same team with Robinson.

The next day the Dodgers crept closer to the pennant when Robinson made a spectacular catch of a high pop up. Jackie raced to the dugout's edge, caught the ball, then fell into the dugout, where Ralph Branca caught him before he landed. The catch was the third out, and after he made it pitcher Hal Gregg ran over and pounded Jackie on the chest in gratitude.

On September 19 the Dodgers arrived in New York at Penn Station. Greeting the Dodgers were thousands of fans led by Hilda Chester and the Dodger Symphony Band. Robinson needed a police escort to get away from his adoring supporters.

The Dodgers needed just one game to clinch the pennant, and on September 22 they got it when the Cardinals went down to defeat.

When news reached Brooklyn a little before midnight, joyous, cheering rooters poured into the streets, forming impromptu parades and celebrating into the morning.

The next day was proclaimed Jackie Robinson Day at Ebbets Field. Jackie received a sedan, a TV, radios, a gold watch, cutlery and silverware, an electric broiler, a gold pen-and-pencil set, and a check. The *Amsterdam News* presented him with a plaque for his contribution to international goodwill.

Among the speakers was Bill "Bojangles" Robinson, who said, "I'm sixty-nine years old but never thought I'd live to see the day when I'd stand face-to-face with Ty Cobb in Technicolor."

On September 26 a seventeen-car motorcade drove down Flatbush Avenue to Borough Hall where Borough President John Cashmore gave watches to each of the twenty-seven Dodgers. The ticker tape was piled high on the street. Dixie Walker and Robinson spoke. Jackie received his Rookie of the

Year award from J. G. Taylor Spink, the owner of the *Sporting News,* and as he accepted it, close observers could see his eyes filled with tears.

In one incredible year, in the face of almost unanimous opposition, Jackie Robinson had proved that the Negro could not only compete in the major leagues but that he could sparkle. Because he was so spectacular, there was a rush by other teams to sign black talent. The others were limited, however, by the fact that Branch Rickey had gotten a significant headstart on them. Coming to the Dodgers would be Roy Campanella, Don Newcombe, Joe Black, and Junior Gilliam. On other teams, Monte Irvin, Larry Doby, Hank Thompson, and Sam Jethroe would soon appear. Black stars from Willie Mays to Hank Aaron to Reggie Jackson would someday follow. All because of the courage and dignity and skill and intelligence of Jack Roosevelt Robinson.

Around the country, especially in the South, Jackie Robinson became much more than just a great ballplayer. He became a savior.

ED CHARLES: "I can recall after Jackie had gone up to the Dodgers and established himself, our family had moved from Daytona to St. Petersburg, and I used to go down to Al Lang Field to watch the Cardinals and the Yankees, and this one game the Dodgers came over to play the Yankees, a Sunday afternoon, and everybody in the black community was there. It was overflowing. You've never seen anything like it. It was a happening. People in wheelchairs came. Christ, we had people there who were in their nineties. In fact everyone was there. And in the game he just did everything. He fielded balls flawlessly. He got a couple of hits, he ran and was aggressive on the base paths. He danced and excited the crowds and excited the players, and he excited everybody. He couldn't do anything wrong. And we just stared in awe of him. We were praying that he would be good and do the job for us, but we didn't expect him to be that good. So it was a big happening. It was a big moment in our lives.

"After the game, we followed the Dodger bus to the train depot, and we found out which of the cars had the Dodger players, and we went just to look at Jackie, and we just stood and stared at him. He was like a god to us, he was our idol, and when the train started to pull away, we chased the train down the side of the platform, waving to him, and he was waving back, and we were running beside the train, as though we were trying to hold the train back, our hands were against the train along the section where Jackie was sitting, as though we were trying to stop Jackie from leaving.

"We had dreamed often of becoming major league ballplayers. But we would say, 'We'll never make it because that's for whites. We can't dream beyond being in some black league.' And a lot of times I would go home and start asking questions, 'Why God? Why is it like this? WHY?' As a kid you couldn't understand. I can recall myself talking to God, asking why things were the way they were, asking, 'When will there be a better day for our people?' And then when Jackie came, it was like, 'My dreams have come true now. We'll have that opportunity to prove to the world that given a fair chance, we can produce, we can be responsible.' "

* * *

For his part Branch Rickey will always be remembered for bringing Jackie Robinson into the major leagues, but while he was alive, he refused to accept any awards for advancing the cause of blacks in America.

BRANCH RICKEY: "To accept honors, public applause for signing a superlative ballplayer to a contract? I would be ashamed."

Boit Stands In

Leo Durocher's suspension on April 9, 1947, the day before Branch Rickey brought up Jackie Robinson, compounded Rickey's problems. Without the right man running the team, Rickey knew his experiment might fail. He needed a manager with experience whom he could trust implicitly and who would support Robinson.

Rickey's first choice was former Yankee manager Joe McCarthy. Marse Joe had quit the Yankees in midseason the year before after suffering what he felt was too much interference from Larry MacPhail. He was living peacefully on his farm in Tonawanda, New York, near Buffalo, and he told Rickey he was going to stay there. In the interim coach Clyde Sukeforth was managing the team. Sukeforth, however, wasn't interested in the job, and Clyde suggested the eventual choice, Burt Shotton.

CLYDE SUKEFORTH: "After Leo was suspended, Mr. Rickey appointed me manager. I managed a couple of exhibition games against the Yankees, and then the first two games of the season against the Braves. But I didn't enjoy it. I had all the managing I had wanted in the minors, and I told Mr. Rickey that. I had had three years in Montreal and two years in Elmira and Clinton and down in Carolina, and I just didn't like it, particularly the higher up you went, where you're dealing with older players, and they're more difficult. It's enjoyable down in the lower leagues working with kids, but the higher up you move, the more trouble you run into.

"Ray Blades and I were Leo's coaches, and I went to Mr. Rickey and told him, 'Burt Shotton's your man. I don't want to struggle along with this thing. Ray and I know Burt well. We both respect and like him.' Mr. Rickey said he'd try to get him but said that Barney [Shotton's nickname] was retired and that he didn't know whether he'd be interested or not. Barney and Mr. Rickey were bosom pals for years. He'd do anything for Mr. Rickey, and he liked Mr. Rickey, and he knew that Ray and I were on his side and that there would be no problems there, and so he took the job."

Shotton and Rickey went way back. Shotton had been Rickey's Sunday manager when Rickey was managing the St. Louis Browns between 1913 and 1925. Rickey sent Shotton a telegram: "BE IN BROOKLYN TOMORROW MORNING. SEE NOBODY. SAY NOTHING."

When Shotton walked into the Dodger clubhouse for the first time, he told

his players: "You fellas can win the pennant in spite of me. Don't be afraid of me as a manager. I cannot possibly hurt you."

Shotton watched the game in a pearl gray hat, a topcoat, and spectacles. Soft-spoken and subdued, he was the antithesis of Durocher. The players who had loved Durocher were disappointed with Shotton. Those who hated Durocher, loved Shotton.

CARL FURILLO: "Burt Shotton, that one was a prince. Oh, he was a prince. Burt Shotton was the type of man who could talk to a young ballplayer. He would walk over to you and put his arm around you or pat you on the back. He'd say, 'C'mon now, forget about that game. It's over with. Tomorrow's a new game.' Shotton was a quiet man. He did his job. He knew the game. He wasn't like Leo, and he didn't say, 'I want to be in the front all the time.' He would say, 'Here's my ballplayers. Take my ballplayers.' Durocher was, 'I'm the guy here. I'm this. I'm that.' Not Burt Shotton, God bless him."

RALPH BRANCA: "In '47 Charley Dressen went over to the Yankees, Durocher got suspended, and Rickey brought in Shotton, which was another Rickey mistake. Shotton was an old friend, and after having Durocher, who was three or four steps ahead of everybody—to have this man who was a step behind or two steps behind as far as strategy went, it was a big comedown to me. The man just wasn't competent enough to be a big league manager, except he was a friend of Rickey's. And I'm being very strong about this. I think it was a crime perpetrated on the people of Brooklyn.

"We would sit on the bench, and we'd laugh at some of the moves Shotton made. We're up and the count is 2 and 0, and you have to anticipate that it's going to be 3 and 0, and what are you going to do, have the man hit or take? And Shotton didn't give the signs, Clyde Sukeforth did, and Suke would say, 'What do you want him to do?' And he'd say, 'Let him take.' So now it's 3 and 0, and Suke says, 'What do you want him to do?' So to me, he was always behind. Shotton should have been saying, 'It's 1 and 0, if it goes to 2 and 0, I want him to take.' And the manager should have all that planned out.

"Yeah, he won in '47, but if you had a Cadillac and you were racing a Model A Ford, you're gonna win the race. Just like Secretariat winning the Belmont. You got the horse. It's what the jockey had under him. There were a lot of guys with potential and no experience. And we had Pete Reiser, Dixie Walker, Cookie Lavagetto, Pee Wee, Eddie Stanky, Arky Vaughan, good people to have on a ballclub. Stabilizing influences. We had such a super club."

The Dodgers opened the season with a pitching staff consisting of two veterans and eight rookies, but at the other positions they were a strong and talented club. Robinson played first, Stanky and Eddie Miksis at second, Reese and Stan Rojek at short, Jorgensen and Lavagetto at third, Walker and Furillo in right, Hermanski and Vaughan in left, and Furillo and Reiser in center. Bruce Edwards and Bobby Bragan caught. There were two quality players at every position, and Shotton handled his personnel adroitly. By midseason Shotton was hearing praise as the Dodgers raced far in front. Wrote *New York Times* columnist Arthur Daley, "The team is being managed more capably and rationally. Last year, Durocher's gyrations ended up confusing the team. Shotton's head is calmer and cooler, better-suited to a pennant winner." Daley hadn't liked Durocher much either.

The most solemn moment for the Dodgers during the 1947 season was the time center fielder Pete Reiser almost killed himself running into the Ebbets Field wall. On June 4 the Pirates' Culley Rikard hit a line drive over his head. Reiser raced back, farther and farther toward the looming wall, and he caught it—just before crashing head-on into concrete unconsciousness, at the same time managing to keep the ball in his glove. It was the second time—the first in 1942—that he hit the unpadded wall in Ebbets Field.

PETE REISER: "Rickey had cut the fences. He made center field about forty feet shorter than it had been. There was a long fly to center, and I'm saying to myself, 'This is an easy out.' I was going full speed, and it wasn't until just before I hit that I remembered about the forty feet that weren't there anymore. I almost died. When I woke up, I couldn't move. For ten days I was paralyzed.

"When I came back, I was standing out on the field during batting practice, and Clyde King ran into me. We bumped heads. I was knocked out, but I thought I was okay. That night I was sitting up with Pee Wee in our hotel room. He looked at me kind of funny. 'You all right?' he asked. 'Yeah. Why?' I said. He said, 'What's the big knot on your head? Maybe you better call a doctor.'

The doctor came, took one look at me, and the next thing I knew I was flown to Johns Hopkins in Baltimore to be operated on. I had a blood clot. I'd had it from the wall injury, and when Clyde ran into me, that moved it. They told me I'd never play again. But I went back. Played the last two months and hit .309."

Though Reiser could still hit, defensively he was in no shape to play. On August 6 Boston beat Brooklyn when Reiser allowed a towering fly hit by Warren Spahn to fall for a triple, and later he misplayed a high line drive by Danny Litwhiler into a double. The next day Reiser was on the bench, complaining of grogginess. He would never be a full-time performer again.

RALPH BRANCA: "I always marveled at Pete's build. He had sloping shoulders and his back muscles were like two tenderloins. His spine was about five inches deep because his back muscles were so strong. And he could run. He could do everything. He had a good arm, he charged ground balls, he could hit, he could hit with power, he could throw, run, he could do it all. He knew how to play the game.

"At bat he was always getting thrown at and hit, and because of Pete we ended up wearing batting helmets, which was a Rickey innovation. Pete kept getting hit because he was fearless. He played so hard, even in batting practice. Pitchers would be shagging flies, and Pete would come out there, and a fly would go up, and Pete would take off. You'd have to yell, 'No, no, no,' because he would run into the wall in practice to catch a ball. The guy had no fear. And it's unfortunate that he played in Brooklyn, because if he played in the Polo Grounds or in Yankee Stadium, he would have never hit the wall. But Brooklyn had a small park, and only after Pete hit the wall did they end up putting padding down."

DON HONIG: "In my estimation, Pete Reiser was the greatest natural talent who ever lived. Leo Durocher once said that the only guy with more natural talent was Willie Mays. Pete had everything. I saw Reiser on three occasions that stand out. The first was in 1941 against the Cardinals. Enos Slaughter hit a ball, and Reiser chased it until he crashed into the center-field wall, and they carried him off the field. The second time was in 1942 in a doubleheader against the Cubs, when I saw him steal home. He was a streak coming down that line. He holds the record with Rod Carew of seven steals of home in a season.

"Then in 1948 I went to a game with my brother against the Boston Braves. The Braves had already clinched the pennant. It was a nothing game. Pete was in left field, and one of the Braves batters hit a line drive at him, nothing hard, and he dropped it. Those were my images of Pete Reiser. The injury, the steal of home, and then suddenly he's gone. He was only twenty-eight when he had had it."

CARL FURILLO: "I remember when he hit that last wall. I can still see it. He hit it flush on, boom, and he slumped right down, and that was his Waterloo. Then I took over for him in center field."

Another man might have found it difficult to step into the shoes of a star such as Reiser, but Carl Furillo proved early in his career that he was not afraid of the job. In fact Furillo wasn't afraid of anything. During World War II Furillo served on the front lines in the Pacific. He was hit and lived to tell about it. They offered him the Purple Heart, but he turned it down. He told them he hadn't been valiant enough in sustaining the injury. It was typical of Furillo. He only would take what was right, fair, and just. As a player he wanted to be paid what he was worth and not a penny more, and when he played he gave everything he had. Treat him right, and he would be as faithful as a puppy. Cross him, and he would never forget.

Furillo had signed with his hometown Reading team, an independent club owned by a Baltimore bowling alley mogul. Dodger owner Larry MacPhail bought the Reading team for its two most valuable assets, the team bus, and Carl Furillo. The manager of the team was Fresco Thompson, later vice-president in charge of the Dodger minor league system.

FRESCO THOMPSON: "Back in 1940 the owner of the Reading club in the Inter-State League got fed up and offered to sell out to Larry MacPhail for $5,000. That was dirt cheap for a franchise—twenty players and two full sets of uniforms—but the thing that intrigued MacPhail was the new bus which the team used on road trips. This was a year before Pearl Harbor, and most automobile production was earmarked for the armed forces.

"MacPhail figured the bus was worth $2,500, and forty uniforms cost at least ten bucks apiece."

MacPhail also knew that one of its players, Furillo, had won the league batting title, looked like a professional hitter, and had an arm as strong as any his scouts had ever seen. They knew too he was one tough, no-nonsense cookie. When Furillo made the Dodgers, MacPhail's investment proved to be one of his best, though it was Branch Rickey who was the chief beneficiary.

Furillo became a cornerstone of Rickey's youth movement, and as Furillo's career began to take off, so did that of another of Rickey's youngsters, pitcher Ralph Branca.

Almost the entire Dodger pitching staff was new. Hugh Casey and Rube Melton were veterans. The other eight pitchers were inexperienced. Joe Hatten was 17–8, Vic Lombardi was 12–10, Harry Taylor 10–5, and the star of the staff was Branca, a twenty-one-year-old flamethrower. Without him, there would have been no pennant in '47. Branca started and relieved, usually with great strength, stamina, and speed. For a boy so young, he had a future some scouts believed would lead to the Hall of Fame. Branca pitched the Dodgers into first place on July 6 with a 4–0 shutout of Boston, and three days later he won both games of a doubleheader against the Cubs. He started the first game, and was relieved in the ninth. Then he relieved in the tenth inning of the second game and got another win.

On July 18, the day Enos Slaughter stomped on Jackie Robinson's leg, Branca pitched a one-hitter against the Cardinals. Only a single by Slaughter in the seventh prevented it from being a no-hitter. In mid-July the Dodgers began to pull away from the rest of the league. They had a three-and-a-half-game lead when they ran off thirteen wins in a row to take a ten-game lead. On August 29 Branca threw a four-hitter to raise his record to 19–9. He finished the year at 21–12 and was third in earned run average behind Warren Spahn of Boston and Ewell Blackwell of Cincinnati. He started more games that year than any other pitcher, and he was second in the league in strikeouts behind Blackwell. The Dodgers had not had a twenty-game winner since 1941, when Kirby Higbe and Whitlow Wyatt both did it. Branca was the youngest Dodger pitcher ever to accomplish the feat and only the sixth twenty-one-year-old in baseball history to win twenty games.

Ralph Branca: "In '47 I won twenty-one games. I was a good pitcher, and I had a good club. I went from not being pitched the year before to where I was able to pitch effectively. I was twenty-one, and I guess I was fully matured. I pitched every fourth day, and I was a good pitcher. I never missed a start, and sometimes I would relieve. I'd pitch on a Monday, and I didn't like to throw batting practice, because I felt it would only teach me bad habits, 'cause I had to throw three-quarter speed, and so I would go down to the bullpen and I'd say, 'If you need me for a man or two, I'd be available,' and so I'd go down in the seventh inning, and I would loosen up. And if Hugh Casey

Ralph Branca

had pitched three days in a row, if they needed me, I'd come in, and that would be my warmup for my next start. I'd pitch an inning or two. I did that seven times.

"I had thirty-six starts, relieved seven times, had the third-best era in the league, was second in strikeouts, gave up 251 hits in 280 innings, which is not bad. There were games when I could have struck out more men if I had wanted to, but I wanted to be a pitcher, so I let guys hit it. In one game I had a 5–0 lead in Boston. I didn't go for the strikeouts because I laid the ball in there, but I threw eighty-five pitches and pitched a shutout.

"I had a good curveball, I could throw the ball ninety-five miles an hour, I had control, and I was coachable, and I was elected to the all-star team, though I didn't pitch because I had pitched against Boston two days before. As a kid I would dream about playing in the big leagues, and here I was, twenty-one years old, a Dodger, and an all-star."

Cookie and Friddo

Burt Shotton picked Branca to start the first game of the 1947 World Series against the New York Yankees. Branca began perfectly, retiring the first twelve Yankee batters in a row. Then, in the fifth inning, he inexplicably blew up and allowed five runs. The Dodgers lost Game One by a score of 5–3.

RALPH BRANCA: "Joe D started the fifth inning with an infield hit to deep short, and looking back my inexperience hurt me, because I started pitching in a hurry. I was grabbing the ball and throwing it and not taking my time, pressing, and I ended up wild. I walked George McQuinn, and then Bill Johnson went to bunt and I hit him—I tried to throw the ball up and in, and the ball sailed in and hit him. Then I hung an inside curveball to Johnny Lindell, and he hit a double down the left-field line. This was after I had struck out five in the first four innings. My brother John was sitting in the upper deck, and if he had wings, he would have flown down and gotten to me on the mound, 'cause later he told me, 'You just started grabbing the ball and throwing. Nobody came out. No infielder came over to slow you down. Nobody came from the bench.' I ended up giving five runs. I didn't complete the inning. I got taken out. And I didn't start another game. I won Game Six in relief when Gionfriddo made that catch on Joe D. At least I won one game. But I would have liked to have had another start in that Series. I mean, I carried the club all year as a starter, and I just didn't get it.

"Before the game Yogi Berra said that Robinson never stole a base on him when they played against each other in the International League. In the first Jackie walked and stole second, as Yogi's throw bounced and came in late. In the third, Jackie walked with two out. Four times Spec Shea threw to first. Then he balked. After the game Jackie said that if Yogi were in the National League he'd steal sixty bases on him."

* * *

In Game Two Allie Reynolds beat Brooklyn 10–3, and then in Game Three the Dodgers scored six runs in the second inning against ole buddy Bobo Newsom and Vic Raschi and hung on to win 9–8 as Hugh Casey saved it, allowing no runs in the final two and two-thirds.

Game Four of the 1947 World Series was perhaps the most exciting single game ever played at Ebbets Field. With two outs in the ninth, Yankee pitcher Bill Bevens was pitching a no-hitter. The Yankees were winning 2–1. The Dodgers had scored one run on a base on balls, an error, and a fly ball. In the Dodger ninth, Carl Furillo led off with a walk, and Shotton sent Al Gionfriddo in to run for him.

AL GIONFRIDDO: "Bill Bevens had a no-hitter going for eight and two-thirds innings, and he had us beat 2 to 1. In the top of the ninth with two outs, my roommate that year, Carl Furillo, walked, and that year Carl missed touching the base seven times, and so with Pete Reiser going up to pinch hit, I went in to run for Carl. When the count got to 2–0, I looked over at third-base coach Ray Blades, and I see him going crazy trying to give me the steal sign. I took off for second, and I stole second headfirst. The throw came in a little high and the tag was a little late. The pitch to Reiser was ball three."

PETE REISER: "Gionfriddo steals second, and then Bucky Harris, who was managing the Yankees, told Bevens to put me on. The winning run. Pretty unorthodox move. Because I had a bad ankle. DiMaggio told me years later that Harris knew I had a broken ankle but still didn't want to pitch to me. Eddie Miksis ran for me, and Gionfriddo was on second. Lavagetto then came up to hit."

AL GIONFRIDDO: "I'm the tying run at second. Shotton sent Eddie Miksis in to run for Reiser, so he's the winning run. Eddie Stanky is the next hitter, but Shotton calls him back and sends Cookie Lavagetto up to pinch hit. This surprised me, because Eddie can get on base. I don't give a darn who's pitching, in a tight spot Eddie would get on. If anyone could break up a no-hitter, Eddie could, because he would foul off fifty pitches if he had to, shake up a pitcher, get on somehow. But Shotton brought in Cookie Lavagetto, who was not a real good pull hitter. He hit in the gaps mostly.

"The first pitch was right down the middle, and Cookie swung and missed. The second pitch he hit off the right-field wall. Two outs, and so I'm running as soon as the ball is hit, and I scored the tying run, and when I crossed home plate, I start waving like hell at Miksis because I can see Tommy Henrich in right having a hell of a time trying to pick the ball up, and I stood there at home plate whistling and hollering for Miksis to score, and all the way from first Miksis scored the winning run.

"Oh, Jesus, we just went crazy. We tied up the Series, and we busted up his no-hitter, and we're jumping all over the place, everyone's throwing their hats around, grabbing Cookie, mobbing him, and with the fans swarming onto the field, it was all we could do to get into the clubhouse."

* * *

COOKIE LAVAGETTO: "All the time people ask me whether my hit off Bevens was my most important hit, and of course it was important, but my most important hit was one I got in 1933. I graduated from Oakland Technical High School in 1931, and for one year, 1932, I was unemployed. February had rolled around, and I hadn't even gotten an offer to play ball. I wasn't going to get a chance to play. But a fella by the name of Charley Tighe, who was the head of the semi-pro organization in Oakland, dreamt up the idea of playing a game to raise money to pay for insurance for the players in case anyone got hurt. And I was picked to play for the second team. I wasn't even on the first team, mind you.

"I came up to bat late in the game, and I guess the good Lord had the setting all in place. We had the bases loaded, and on the mound was a pitcher by the name of Pudgy Gould, a spitball pitcher who had gone up to the majors but who had spent a long career in the minors. So it was bases loaded, and he pitched, and I almost hit the ball out of the ballpark in left center. And, for crying out loud, that one base hit got me some offers."

Lavagetto played for Oakland in the minors and the Pirates and then in 1937 was traded to the Dodgers.

COOKIE LAVAGETTO: "As far as I know, Leo wanted to get rid of me right from the beginning. Why? I don't know. He never said anything to me. But I know he wanted to trade me to the Cardinals for Don Gutteridge. MacPhail told me that. Then the war came, and it was too bad, but that's the way life is—I was just getting to be a good ballplayer, and then it kind of washed everything up. When I came out four years later, the only reason Leo kept me was that they were allowed to keep three extra GI veterans. Instead of having twenty-five players, you could have twenty-eight. So I was one of the extra three.

"And then, right after I returned from the war, in spring training 1946, I went to throw a baseball after a long period of inactivity, and my arm locked. I threw it straight up in the air. I had to be operated on for a bone chip.

"After the operation Leo kept pushing me to get back in there. I kept telling him, 'I'm not ready.' Every day he asked me. Finally I got tired of listening to him. I said, 'I'll try,' and I went out there, and the first batter hit a swinging bunt. I came in, picked it up bare-handed, threw the guy out, and I felt like somebody stuck a knife in my elbow. It swelled up, and I had to rest again.

"Then later in '46, I hurt my Achilles tendon, and I was down grade ever since. I don't know whether I stepped in a hole or what. You hurt your Achilles tendon running on hard ground. But one morning I woke up, and my right toe felt like it was pointing straight up. I looked down there and saw my feet laying on the ground, but it sure didn't feel that way.

"I had my share of trouble, all right. They moved me from second to third because I was always pulling a charley horse in my leg. I was like Mel Ott. Ott had those problems too, and he and I would discuss it a lot of times.

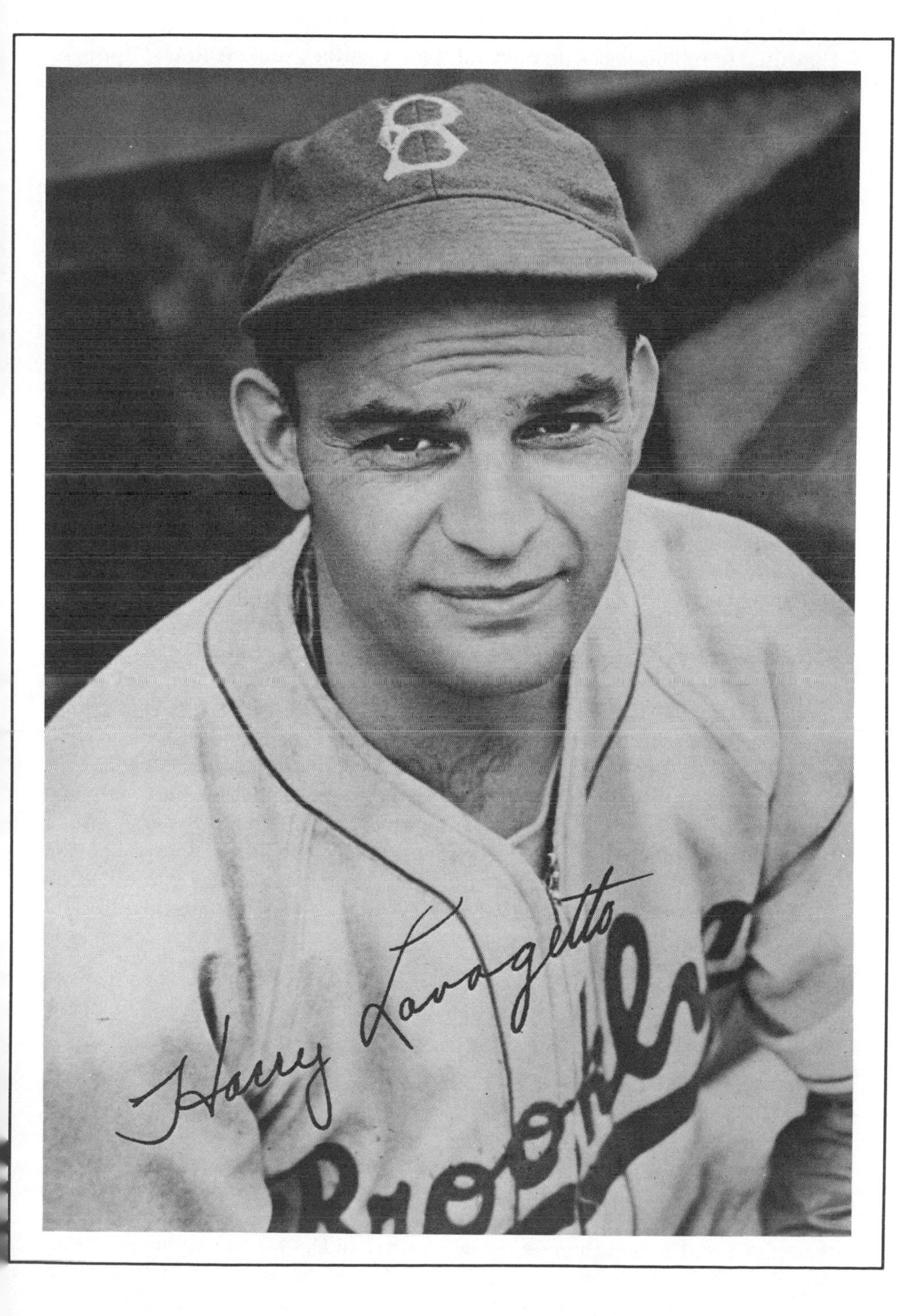
Harry Lavagetto

They used to rub his legs with olive oil. One year they sent me to Hot Springs, Arkansas, and I walked the hills, and I took the baths for about six weeks, and hell, the first exhibition game I pulled my leg. Some guys just have better legs than others. That's all. Christ sake, I had tendonitis one year. I had that elbow operation, had that Achilles tendon. Christ. Whatever, it's done past now.

"In '47 I just hung around. If Leo had been there, I would never have been there. But Burt Shotton became manager when Chandler put Leo on the sidelines for associating with gamblers, and so I stayed, and I was with the Dodgers for the World Series.

"I had never faced Bevens before, didn't know anything about him, but you can observe for nine innings. I could see he was wild. He had walked eleven or twelve men. He didn't go into the ninth with a shutout—we had one run by a base on balls, an error, and a fly ball. Bevens was simply a fastball pitcher, so you go up there looking for it. And I know fastball pitchers pitch me up and in. They try to crowd me with the ball. The first ball was in tight, and it was a good pitch, and I swung hard and missed. But the next pitch he got out over the plate a little bit more, and then I just laid the bat on it, and it took off to right center. I used to hit a lot of balls to right center. And it hit the wall, came off the wall, hit Tommy Henrich in the chest and bounced away from him, and Gionfriddo scored, and Eddie Miksis, who ran for Reiser, scored all the way from first base.

"Of course, it was an important hit, after all, we were trying to win a ballgame. But all it meant was winning. I had gotten base hits that meant just as much to me as the one I got off Bevens. See, I kind of took my job as just a job. I didn't feel like I was an extraordinary person.

"That one time against Bevens, I think it was the only time Shotton pinch hit for Stanky. Arky Vaughan, who the Dodgers got from Pittsburgh after I went into the service, had already been used as a pinch hitter. And so Shotton called on me. Was I surprised? Let me put it this way: Hell, I was called on all during the year to pinch hit. It was nothing. It was just another day out there."

In Game Five the Yankees took a three games to two lead when Yankee pitcher Spec Shea allowed five hits and struck out Lavagetto to end the game with the tying run on second.

COOKIE LAVAGETTO: "I didn't get no butterflies against Bevens, but I sure got them the next day, because now I figure, 'What the hell, I did it before. Everyone expects me to do it again.' We were facing Spec Shea, and they were leading 2–1, and I just told myself, 'Now is the time to get a base hit. You got one yesterday. Get one today.' I had Shea 2 and nothing, he threw me a slider, and even though I was looking for it, I missed it. And then I had him 3 and 1, and then he threw another slider. He was trying to get me to hit the ball down, he was pitching me down and away, and I fouled that off. And on the 3 and 2 pitch he threw a change of pace, kind of a slow curve, and I was so anxious to get a base hit that I miscalculated. I waited on the ball, but I wound up swinging and missing the damn thing. I still dream of that one."

The Dodgers won Game Six by the score of 8–6. Branca got the win in relief, but he was able to win the game only because in the bottom of the sixth, with Joe Hatten pitching for Brooklyn, pint-sized Dodger outfielder Al Gionfriddo made what sportswriter Arthur Daley called "one of the most unbelievable catches ever seen anywhere."

Though Gionfriddo rarely started, he often played outfield defense in the late innings because he had great speed—he once ran the 100-yard dash in ten seconds flat in high school. Because Gionfriddo was short, standing just over five foot five and a half, he was discriminated against despite his obvious skills. Gionfriddo could bunt, he was an excellent base runner, and he was an accomplished fielder who could sub in either left or center, but he played just four seasons in the majors, and after the 1947 Series, the Dodgers shipped him to Montreal and kept him there despite excellent statistics. As with Bevens and Lavagetto, the 1947 World Series was Gionfriddo's final appearance in the major leagues.

Game Six was played in cavernous Yankee Stadium, and as usual Dixie Walker was in right and Carl Furillo in center. In a move that none of the Dodger players understood, rarely used Eddie Miksis started in left. What made Shotton's move even more perplexing was that Miksis was a right-handed batter facing the right-handed Allie Reynolds.

Al Gionfriddo: "Miksis was an infielder, he wasn't an outfielder, and with Reiser, Hermanski, and I all lefties, we just couldn't figure out why Shotton would go with Miksis in such a crucial game.

"Anyway we jumped in front of the Yankees, 8 to 5 in the sixth inning, and I was sitting on the bench enjoying the ballgame because we were out front. I'm sitting there just like a spectator when I heard Shotton call, 'GI.' The players called me 'GI' or 'Friddo' or 'The Little Italian.' Shotton never could remember my name. He used to say, 'What's that Little Italian's name?' So like I say, I'm sitting there enjoying the game, we're leading, and he sends me in. I couldn't understand it. What the hell, we're leading, why does Shotton want to change anything? I went out to play left field.

"The Yankees got two men on, and there were two outs when Joe DiMaggio came up.

"In the old Yankee Stadium it was short down the lines, and then it went out something like 600 feet to center field. You knew it was a helluva ways out there, because for them to put monuments out there and not be afraid an outfielder would run into them, it had to be. Believe me, it was a long way out there. A good drive in a Buick.

"Anyway I was in left, and I look into the dugout, and they're waving me toward the line to play DiMaggio to pull, because ordinarily he is a pull hitter. I'm positioned between the 315-foot marker and the 415-foot marker, which is where the bullpen was. I thought I was playing DiMaggio awfully shallow.

With two on and two out and Joe Hatten pitching, they were figuring him to pull, but that much?

"So Hatten pitches, and shit, DiMaggio hits the ball up the gap. I put my head down and ran, because I knew the direction it was going. Now I'm not saying I was the greatest outfielder in the world, but when a ball was hit, I could tell where it was going, and I could run to the spot pretty well. And that's what I did. I knew the ball was headed toward the bullpen, and I started running with my back toward home plate. I looked over my shoulder once, and I could see the ball was still coming, and I put my head down again, and I kept running and running, and when I got to just about where I thought the ball would come down, I reached out with my glove like I was catching a football pass over my shoulder, and I caught the ball. I was up in the air when I got it, and as I came down, I twisted a little bit to take the shock of hitting the fence with my ass instead of my stomach, and I hit that fence with my butt. And you know, when I caught that ball, I really didn't think much about it. When you're the one involved, you really don't realize whether it's important or not. I figured it was just part of the game. And of course if that ball would have flown into the bullpen, it would have tied the score 8 to 8, and as it turned out, the Yankees did score one more run, and so they would have won 9 to 8. But as I said, when I caught the ball, I just ran back to the dugout. My hat had come off, and my roommate, Carl Furillo, he picked it up and handed it to me, and we both ran in together. And as we were running in, I noticed DiMaggio kick the dirt around second base.

"When I got to the dugout the guys were slapping me on the back, and everyone was happy I made the catch, but I didn't have much time to think about it because I was first up that inning, and I had to go up and hit. At the time I didn't think it was such a big deal."

The 1947 World Series came down to a winner-take-all seventh game, and the Dodgers, as they had done in 1916, 1920, and again in 1941, didn't win. The Yankees' relief star, Joe Page, allowed but one hit over the last five innings as the Dodgers were defeated by a score of 5 to 2.

Al Gionfriddo: "We never should have lost that last game and the Series. It might have been different if in the first inning we didn't have two guys thrown out stealing. The Yankees started Aaron Robinson instead of Yogi Berra, who was having real trouble keeping us from stealing, and Aaron threw out both Pee Wee and Jackie.

"But as things turned out, the really bad part of how they beat us goes back to Eddie Miksis. Shotton played Miksis in left again, and, oh, did he hurt us. Eddie will admit this himself. Snuffy Stirnweiss hit a pop fly, just a little pop fly to the outfield, and Miksis lost it. He ran in an almost complete circle trying to catch the ball, and he lost it. It dropped in for a triple, and two runs scored. And then Stirnweiss scored for a third run.

"We ended up losing 5 to 2, and like I said, none of us could understand Shotton's thinking. We had a lot of good people sitting on the bench who could play the outfield. If one of the regular outfielders isn't hitting, put him

George Brace Photo

AL GIONFRIDDO

farther down in the order. Let somebody else worry about driving in the runs. Here it was, the seventh game of the World Series, and he's playing a utility infielder in left field! A lot of the guys were confused. Why not play everyone where they belonged? Play an outfielder out there. It was our last chance. But Shotton didn't. And we got beat because of it."

BILL REDDY: "We expected to win. We had hopes, anyway. In 1941 the loss had a lot to do with that dropped third strike by Mickey Owen. That really took the heart out of the people. We didn't expect to win that Series after that. But in '47 I thought we would win that one. And we didn't. We were sick and sad. Sick and sad, everybody. As a matter of fact, all across the neighborhood, radios got turned off, and everybody just sat despondently drinking.

"I got very, very disgusted, very mad. I went home, sat down, and my wife tried to console me, 'It's all right,' she said. 'Maybe next year.' "

6

The Ole Redhead

With the World's Fair of 1939 came the mass popularity of the portable radio. At the beach, in homes, in stores, in cars, in baby carriages, there would be a radio. You could walk through the streets of Brooklyn and follow the play-by-play of the Dodger game going from your house down into the subway or wherever it was you were going. Everyone had a radio, and all those radios were tuned to the Dodger game as it was being described by Walter "Red" Barber. It was a prevailing sound of the street.

Many fans built their entire lives around the Dodgers. For some, a whole summer was based on the team, and wherever people gathered in Brooklyn, at game time there would be a radio. On the boardwalk, in the cars, on the trolleys. During the summer, all anyone talked about was the Dodgers, and the only station tuned in during the afternoon was the Dodger station. If the Dodgers were a religion, then Red Barber was Billy Graham.

DONALD HALL: The beginning for me was as far back as 1939, and it was in an automobile, driving with the family, who always went on rides in our Studebaker on Sunday afternoons. Everybody in America who had a car in 1939 went on rides on Sunday afternoons. Every Sunday we would drive and listen. At first my mother was totally disinterested in baseball, but more and more she began to listen, the three of us sitting in the front seat, and finally she got into it. These were the kind of dreamy afternoons that I remember with Red Barber, that sleepy voice. It was alert, but it had that gentleness, that southern tone to it, coming in off the radio.

"I don't know how my father got to be a Dodger fan, but it may have been Red Barber. We all loved Red, and I still love him in memory. That wonderful soft voice coming out with a wonderful gentleness and calm, managing to rise to the pitch. We loved his clichés, his individual expressions, 'the bases are COD,' chock full of Dodgers. If we were playing the Pirates, the bases would be 'FOB,' full of Buccaneers."

Next to Leo Durocher, Barber was Larry MacPhail's greatest coup, the strongest influence on Brooklyn and its fans. When MacPhail took over the Dodgers in 1939, he began negotiating with General Mills, the maker of

Wheaties, to sponsor Dodger radio broadcasts. In 1938, just before MacPhail arrived in Brooklyn, the three New York clubs had agreed to a five-year ban on radio broadcasting of their games under the theory that such broadcasts would hurt attendance. From his experience with broadcasting games in Cincinnati, MacPhail knew they were wrong—that radio would serve only to promote attendance, not to hurt it, and when he took over the team in '39, he arrogantly informed the Yankees and Giants that he had not been a party to the ridiculous agreement and that he would not honor it.

The Yankees and Giants threatened him, but he ignored them. When MacPhail told the Giants of his plans, Giant secretary Eddie Brannick said to MacPhail, "If you dare broadcast, if you dare break this agreement, we'll get a 50,000-watt radio station, and we'll get the best baseball broadcaster in the world, and we'll blast you into the river."

Soon thereafter MacPhail did to the Giants what Brannick had threatened to do to him. He signed a deal with WOR, which was a 50,000-watt station, and he hired Red Barber, his announcer at Cincinnati. And as the Yankees and Giants watched, Dodger attendance soared, and sponsors paid out $113,000 in one year for ads on Barber's broadcasts. It took the Yankees and Giants two years to get a single sponsor for their games. In 1938 a lousy Dodger team drew 660,000. In 1939, with Barber behind the mike for the first time, an improved Dodger team drew 955,000. The Dodgers outdrew the pennant-winning Yankees by 100,000 and the Giants by 250,000.

Walter Lanier Barber was born February 17, 1908, in Columbus, Mississippi, the son of a locomotive engineer and a schoolteacher. His father named him Lanier after Sidney Lanier, a southern poet and distant relative.

Barber's original ambition had been to go into show business by joining a blackface troupe, a popular form of entertainment in the 1920s. White actors would cover their face and hands with black grease and sing and dance like Negroes. Barber played the trombone, bought a Joe Miller joke book, and he had a job lined up with the J. A. Coburn blackface troupe when it went out of business.

Disappointed, he attended the University of Florida at Gainesville, where he took jobs waiting tables and janitoring to earn his keep. A friend of his was scheduled to read three farm reports on the air, and the friend, who felt the reading required a contrasting voice for the middle paper, asked Red to do it. Red refused, until the friend offered to buy him dinner in return. The station manager was so taken with Red's voice that he pleaded with Barber to work for the station. For several weeks Red kept turning him down. Then the station manager finally asked Red how much money it would take for him to change his mind. Barber totalled up what he was making at his waiter job and his janitor job and added on about $10 more a month and said, "Fifty dollars a month," figuring it was a sum so high the man would leave him alone. "Done," said the station manager, and that's how Red Barber began his career, screaming and kicking.

At WRUF Red did the news, read features, interviewed professors, announced singers, announced piano recitals, played records, and did play by play for the University of Florida football games. During his junior year, he was offered a full-time job as chief announcer at $150 a month. Barber's ambition had been to become a college professor. Radio changed all that. He dropped out of college and began riding the buses north for auditions. He traveled to Atlanta, Charlotte, Louisville, Cincinatti, and Chicago, and he was hired by WLW at $25 a week to broadcast Cincinnati Reds games. MacPhail loved him, nurtured him, and in 1939 lured Red to Brooklyn.

Red Barber brought baseball and the Dodgers into everybody's home. Women who had never seen a game became fans because of Red Barber. Because of his ease of delivery and his southern down-home style, the women took to him immediately. In the past fans had been almost 100 percent men. You could count the number of women in the park on one hand. But because of Barber more and more women began flocking to Ebbets Field, encouraged by a Larry MacPhail promotion called "Ladies Day." If a man brought a female companion, she got in free.

At first Barber's southern accent and funny expressions startled Brooklynites. Fans listening to the games would say, "What da hell is dat bum talking about? I can't understand him. He's speakin' a foreign language, da bum." But they soon learned that when Barber said, "The boys are tearing up the pea patch," he was informing them that there was a rally in progress. Or if he said the game was "tied up in a crocus sack," he was telling them that the Dodgers had the game for sure, that it was a cinch. The argot became a challenge. Whoever had heard of players rambling in a pea patch or taking part in a rhubarb? Certainly no one had ever seen a suckegg mule. But before you knew it, there were kids in the neighborhood strutting up and down and talking about the bases being FOB, pea patches, and suckegg mules.

Barber's two most notable expressions were "rhubarb" and the "catbird seat." Here are their origins:

In 1937 two men got into an argument in a bar. One of them, a Giant fan, ragged a Brooklyn fan so unmercifully that the Brooklyn fan left, got a gun, came back, and shot the Giant fan in the stomach.

The day after the shooting, writer Tom Meany stepped into the tavern and the bartender told him, "We had quite a rhubarb last night, Mr. Meany." Meany told the story to Gary Schumacher, another writer, and Red later heard the expression from him. Any time there was a fight or an argument, Red would say, "We have quite a rhubarb going, friends."

The "catbird seat" came from a poker game. Red was playing, and during one hand, he raised on the first bet, and he kept raising on every card. At the end the other fellow turned over his hole cards—a pair of aces—and won the pot. He said, "Thank you, Red. I had those aces from the start. I was sitting in the catbird seat." Red took it from there.

Barber, above all else, was a reporter, and he used his reportorial skills to the fullest because MacPhail and later Rickey gave him carte blanche to report. MacPhail did not care if Barber criticized him or the Dodgers. What MacPhail wanted was for the fans to be thinking and talking about the team all the time. MacPhail once told Barber straight out, "Report the games. Let me worry about the quality of the team on the field." And Brooklyn fans became the most knowledgeable fans that ever were, because of Red Barber.

LARRY KING: "Red Barber was an indelible part of my life. He was the best sports announcer I ever heard. His voice is the earliest memory of my life, him and Arthur Godfrey. I never heard anyone do a baseball game like him.

"He was a journalist. Red would go to the ballpark three hours before a game, and he'd stand around the batting cage like Arthur Daley and take notes, and he'd intersperse these tidbits throughout the broadcast. He gathered little insights. He was the only one I ever heard do this.

"One day the Dodgers were playing the Cardinals. It was a tie game, with Musial coming to bat in the eighth inning. Musial had gone one for two, and the Dodgers were changing pitchers. And Red starts talking about confidence in a situation like this. Does Musial bring confidence to the plate?

"And Red tells about an incident he witnessed in the dugout before the game:

" 'Before the game, friends,' says Red, 'Wally Westlake came over to Musial in the dugout, and he says, "Isn't it a perfect day today? The bacon was perfect in the hotel. I've been whacking the ball in batting practice. I feel super today. I feel three hits today. Do you ever feel that way, Stan?" And Musial says, "Every day." '

"Now, why didn't Red relate this story the first time Musial got up, or the second time? No, he waited for the pressure point, and as the relief pitcher was coming in, he drifted into the story.

"Red was a poet in the broadcast booth. He could make a 10 to 1 game interesting with his little insights, his little truisms about baseball players.

"A batter hits a home run, and the pitcher dusts off the next hitter. Red says, 'You ever think of why he did that, friends? 'Cause baseball players are very selfish people. And that batter, his desire is to take a living away from the pitcher. That's the only point of playing.'

"He brought poetry to a dramatic situation. It was the bottom of the ninth, and the opposition was trailing by a couple of runs with the bases loaded, and he says, 'The ducks are on the pond, the pitcher delivers, and the ball is on a line to right field. I'll be back with the totals of the game in one minute.' He never said who scored, never gave the score. Now the Yankees fan, the Mel Allen fan, would have said, 'Whoa, what happened?'

"The Yankees *were* Mel Allen, who we hated. 'Going, going, gone,' he'd say when a Yankee hit a home run. Oh, Jesus, we hated him. Like with the players, we had our argument over announcers. Who was best, Mel Allen versus Red Barber versus Russ Hodges. The big complaint Yankee fans had against Barber was that he didn't get excited enough. This was because Mel Allen openly rooted for the Yankees. I remember listening with such hatred of Mel Allen when he would talk about Joe Page coming in. It was as though Mel was himself a Yankee.

"Barber to us was a class act. He never rooted for the Dodgers. And he taught us a lot more about baseball than Mel ever taught anyone. Red was the best, because you learned the game from Red.

"Red told me once that Mel had one fatal flaw as an announcer. He followed the ball, but in following the ball, he would often give you, 'Going, going, caught.' Red knew to follow the outfielder, not the ball, because it's the outfielder who tells you where the ball is, not the flight of the ball. So a lot of times Mel would say, 'It's going, going, caught up against the wall,' and the listener didn't even know the outfielder was close to the wall.

"In describing Gionfriddo's famous World Series catch of Joe DiMaggio's long hit toward the bleachers in Yankee Stadium, Red used nine 'backs.' 'Back, back, back, back, back, back, back, back, back. Gionfriddo makes a one-handed catch.' In following Gionfriddo step by step, Red told the listener two things: the ball wasn't ten rows back into the seats, and Gionfriddo's great play was not in catching the ball but in getting to it.

"Red was raised in Tallahassee, Florida. He was a decent, church-going man who in his life had known no blacks. None. His only conversation he ever had with blacks were with the guy who shined his shoes, the clubhouse attendant, press box attendant, an occasional porter on a train. I asked him once if he ever had dinner with a black. He said, 'I never sat with a black.' It was Jackie Robinson who taught Barber racial tolerance, just his seeing what Robinson went through.

"Red said, 'I began to be ashamed of the white people I grew up with.'

"Red was an idealist, and Red could be very tough. One year he wouldn't do the World Series because Gillette only paid the announcers a measly $500. Red said, 'That's not a fair price.' Gillette was shocked. 'C'mon, it's an honor. We have selected you.' Red said, 'I won't do it.' Any other announcer would have taken that job.

"Barber hated jocks who became announcers. He liked Phil Rizzuto, because Rizzuto was smart enough to go over to him and say, 'You're a great announcer. Please teach me anything you can.' But Joe Garagiola, he had come over from St. Louis, where he had been a broadcaster a while, and he had his comic routine down, and so he never deferred to Red.

"This was when Red was with the Yankees, and they were playing the Red Sox at night, and it was drizzling, and the ground crew was taking the tarp off the field with about eight minutes to go before the game, Red and Garagiola are on the air, and Red says to Joe, 'What did you do today?' Joe says, 'I hung around the lobby with the guys, and I went to see a movie.' Barber says, 'You went to a movie. I went to see Arthur Fiedler give an afternoon concert. Do you know who he is, Joe? The Boston Pops. Ever hear of them, Joe? Some of the great museums of the world are here, Joe. Ever think of visiting a museum, Joe?' "

The Return of the Prodigal Son

At a press conference held January 7, 1948, the Dodgers announced that Branch Rickey's favorite reclamation project, Leo Durocher, would once again manage the Dodgers now that his one-year suspension was up. Durocher was asked whether he would be more subdued and contrite. He snarled, "I am going to be nobody but myself, just as I've always been."

But Leo, in choosing to return to Brooklyn, was walking into a minefield. For years, many of the players had grumbled about the way he had treated them, but they always rationalized that his abuse was worth it because he was a winner. But in 1947, under Shotton, the Dodgers won the pennant. And Durocher no longer seemed indispensable. Shotton could be distant and gruff, but he kept things quiet, praised them, and stayed out of the limelight, allowing them to be the focus. As soon as Durocher returned, he redirected the limelight back onto himself.

In 1948 Rickey, to protect Jackie Robinson from unpleasant incidents during training, made a deal with dictator Rafael Trujillo to spend the spring in the Dominican Republic. The team was based in the capital, Ciudad Trujillo, now Santo Domingo, a mecca for gamblers, and Durocher wasn't manager for a week when he took up right where he had left off before the suspension. He won $300 in a card game and went around bragging about it to anyone within earshot, including Rickey's wife, Jane, who told her unbelieving husband. Rickey was also shocked to learn that Durocher's fast friends were back sitting on the Dodger bench during exhibition games. Durocher, furthermore, refused to stay in the room assigned to him at the luxurious Hotel Jaragua, which was only slightly more impressive than the Taj Mahal. Leo cavalierly demanded more sumptuous quarters. Other reports filtered back to Rickey that Leo was critical of his training camp, his training methods, and his coaching staff. Leo was also angry that Rickey had traded Dixie Walker and Eddie Stanky, two of his favorites. For Stanky, the pepperpot second baseman, the Dodgers had received a washed-up first baseman, Ray Sanders, from the Braves. "What's Rickey doing?" Durocher demanded publicly.

The truth was that Leo had been hurt when the Dodgers had won without him, and he harbored a deep-seated fear that he might not be able to duplicate Shotton's performance.

During spring training Dick Young wrote: "Durocher is no longer the cocky, outspoken, self-assured pop-off guy who typified and instilled the reckless spirit of Brooklyn. Instead, he's afraid of losing his job, a man whose every word, or absence of them, reflects that fear." Leo later barred Young from the Dodger clubhouse, accusing Young of creating discontent among the Dodger players. In reality it was Durocher who was creating the unrest.

The one player Leo should have been smart enough not to antagonize was Jackie Robinson. But Durocher immediately put Jackie on the top of his shit list after Robinson arrived in camp twenty pounds overweight. During the off-season Robinson had hit the black banquet circuit with a vengeance. Every week from October to February, two or three black groups toasted his success with overdone roast beef, potatoes au gratin, soggy green beans, and those little stale round rolls with dimples on the top.

Durocher was expecting a sleek, explosive runner, but instead Robinson looked like a teapot. Durocher, as was his wont, took it personally. "He was skinny for Shotton but fat for me." Durocher put Robinson—and his other overweight veteran, Pete Reiser—in rubber suits and made them go out on the field and chase hundreds of ground balls. In front of the other players, Durocher would shout: 'Stick a fork in him, he's done. C'mon fatso, get moving.' It was the first time as a Dodger that Robinson was subjected to such needling, and Jackie, whose ego was as big as Durocher's, also took it personally.

When he read Durocher's blast that he was too complaisant and was loafing, the sensitive, introspective Robinson fumed. He had a sore arm and his legs, which had taken a battering in college and semipro football, throbbed night and day. Also the suet wasn't coming off as fast as he thought it would. In his heart, he also worried about his weight.

Leo should have been more politically savvy. He should have realized that by antagonizing Robinson he was hurting himself. But Leo had always contended that everyone gets the same treatment, and there was to be no exception.

Besides, a bloated Robinson was only one of Durocher's many problems. The team had gotten old. Of Leo's veterans Cookie Lavagetto, Pete Reiser, and Arky Vaughan could no longer cut it, and Rickey had traded Stanky and Walker. In 1947 rookie Spider Jorgensen had starred at third base, hitting .274 with 67 rbis and giving the Dodgers some added speed, and catcher Bruce Edwards had hit for a .295 average, driven in 80 runs, and made 592 putouts, but over the winter both players had severely injured their arms, and Leo had serious doubts about them both.

SPIDER JORGENSEN: "Bruce hurt his arm up at home during the winter after the '47 season. In Sacramento, where Bruce was from, they would play ball all winter, and they would get a bunch together from the Coast League and the majors and play up at the Folsom Prison against the cons. Bruce said he went there, and he wasn't in shape, and he started throwing the ball around, popping it, and he hurt his arm. And when he came to spring training in '48, he had a bad arm. When he had to throw to second, he was very wild. After he hurt his arm, he never played regularly again.

"I hurt my arm during the winter of 1947 quail and pheasant hunting. I shot a lot, and I used to hunt without a pad, and I bruised my right arm. Plus I didn't do anything that winter. Until that year I had always been active, playing basketball or baseball. And when I went to spring training, I couldn't break that thing loose, and when I tore it, I couldn't throw. I stayed around for a couple of months, but if I hadn't hurt my arm I would have been the third baseman."

Leo's third-base problems didn't end there. Billy Cox, whom Rickey had acquired from Pittsburgh, along with Preacher Roe, in exchange for Dixie Walker, was suffering from depression, and Tommy Brown, the other third baseman, had an erratic arm and never could hit. And then there was Pete Reiser. Rickey had begged Pete Reiser to retire, but the former Pistol Pete

Bruce Edwards

wouldn't accept Rickey's assessment of his ability and insisted upon hanging on.

PETE REISER: "Mr. Rickey didn't want me playing at all in '48. He offered to pay me if I sat down all year. Being bullheaded, I told him I wanted to play. But at the same time all those injuries had taken their toll. I wasn't the same player I had been before the war. It had always been so easy for me, but now I had to struggle. By the time I was twenty-nine, the fun and the pure joy of it were gone."

The pitching staff too was a question mark. After rushing to nineteen wins by August of 1947, Ralph Branca won just two more games. Two of the starting pitchers from 1947, Vic Lombardi and Hal Gregg, were gone from the team, and a third, Harry Taylor, was ineffective. The newly acquired Preacher Roe had had a 4–15 record with Pittsburgh the year before, and little was expected of him.

But tall, stringy Roe pitched two shutouts in a row, throwing an assortment of curves at different speeds. On the mound he would play with his hair, fidget, tug at his uniform, driving hitters—and his fielders as well—to distraction. He could take three hours to pitch a 2–1 ballgame. Roe acted like a hillbilly, but it was mostly an act. His father was a physician, and before he became a professional baseball player, he had gone to Harding College in Arkansas. He was no hick.

In college Preacher, whose real name was Elwin, pitched on the team, averaging eighteen strikeouts a game, and the scouts and bird dogs raced to his Viola, Arkansas, home to sign him. The Yankees and local St. Louis Cardinals made the best offers, but Roe, a southerner, was reluctant to sign with the Yankees—Arkansas wasn't exactly Yankee country—and he went with Branch Rickey to St. Louis, where he pitched in one game in 1938 and then spent the next five years in the minors. When Frankie Frisch moved from St. Louis to Pittsburgh, he convinced the Pirates to get Roe, and for two years Roe was one of Pittsburgh's best pitchers, winning thirteen then fourteen games, leading the league with 148 strikeouts in 1945.

That winter he was coaching high school basketball when he got in a fight with a referee during a game. The referee landed a right to the head. Roe smashed against the hardwood and fractured his skull. The next two years before going to the Dodgers, Roe won only three and then four games.

PREACHER ROE: "They said that Rickey put a gun to the Pirates, but, hell, he wasn't dealin' with dummies. What was Rickey getting? An infielder who had been shook real bad during the war and a skinny pitcher with a busted head.

"In '48 we started with three left-handers, Joe Hatten, a boy named Dwain Sloat, and me. Durocher's managing. He calls in me and Sloat and says, 'Hatten's made the club, and I'm only gonna keep two left-handers. I'm gonna

start you both in Cincinnati, and the one that looks best gets to stay.' We all shook hands. Then we flipped a coin, and I got to pitch first. I had a good game, a three-hit shutout. Next day when Sloat worked, he gave up about as many hits as I did, but Pee Wee kicked one. It beat him his game.

"Now we have another meeting. Durocher says, 'Preach, you won, but you have to admit Sloat looked as good as you did. Remember, I didn't say who won. Just who looked better. You looked the same. So we're gonna do it all over again in Chicago.' And we three shake hands again.

"Well, if you look into the records, you'll see that in Chicago in '48 I pitched my second straight shutout. Next day the Cubs got to Sloat for five. He goes. I stay. That began my Brooklyn success. Those were the only two shutouts I got all year."

The Dodger bullpen was another headache. Hugh Casey was having serious marital problems, and he was becoming even more withdrawn and drinking more than ever, and it was hard to see how the Dodgers could be successful without Casey.

With Casey not pitching well, the bullpen leadership fell to Hank Behrman, who had the equipment but not the dedication.

During spring training the year before, Burt Shotton had asked each of the regulars to stand up and talk about his faults and how each hoped to cope with them. Behrman got up and said, 'I think I need to improve my hitting.'

Shotton replied: "You don't need more hitting, Henry. You need more sleep."

HAROLD ROSENTHAL: "Hank Behrman was kind of a kook. In those days it was a big thing to give a player a day, present him usually with a car, golf clubs, and gifts, and some friends of Hank decided to give him a day. They put shakers in all the saloons around Ridgewood and Williamsburg, and they collected enough to buy a $100 savings bond that cost maybe $75.

"It's enough to know that Behrman was involved in a paternity suit, and comes this Saturday afternoon, there was to be a big presentation before the game. Hank came up to the plate, and here comes the *shlump* from the Ridgewood saloon, and the guy says, 'Hank, we want to give you this.' And Hank figures it's the registration to a car or something big, and Hank opens it and says, 'What's this?' The guy says, 'It's a bond.' Behrman says, 'You mean it's a lousy $100 savings bond?' The guy says, 'Well, geez, Hank, that's all we were able to collect.' Hank says, 'What the hell do I want with this?' and he throws it down and stalks off, leaving the saloon guy to pick up his lousy bond.

"The whole ballpark is watching this, trying to figure out what's going on, and Tom Meany, who was working for the *Star,* says, 'I don't know what the hell he was so upset about. He's lucky it wasn't a summons.' "

The one bright spot was a twenty-four-year old pitcher named Rex Barney. Barney could throw a baseball as fast as Bob Feller, but he had always suffered from a lack of control that made his right arm a lethal weapon. In the spring of 1948, he was finally showing signs of maturity.

REX BARNEY: "I had pitched in three games of the 1947 World Series, started one and got beat and relieved in two. DiMaggio had hit a home run off me and won 2–1. But I had had the bases loaded in the first inning, and then I struck out the side. Struck out DiMaggio, Henrich, and Keller, and I can remember DiMaggio saying I was the fastest thing he had ever seen, and he had hit against Feller. I thought about that all winter long, and I said to myself, 'If I'm that good, why aren't I winning? What's wrong? Where am I failing? Maybe I'm not working hard enough.' So I went to spring training a little early, and Bobby Bragan and Arky Vaughan and I would meet at the ballpark at 7:30, and I would throw for a half hour, forty-five minutes with Bobby catching and Arky standing there as a hitter, and we'd talk and talk. We never told Durocher. We never told this to anybody. But what a magnificent spring I had.

"In our first exhibition game, I beat Ft. Worth 2–0, then I pitched in Tulsa and beat that club, and I pitched the last three innings of a Friday game against the Yankees in the city series. I faced nine hitters, and I struck out all nine of them. And then I was the opening day pitcher."

Some scouts felt that Barney could be one of the best pitchers who ever lived. If only he could be consistent.

Even so, 1948 began with too many question marks. Jackie Robinson had played first in 1947 only because Rickey didn't want him getting spiked at second base. He had been Rookie of the Year, and in 1948 Rickey wanted him playing second, his natural position. He had traded away Eddie Stanky so Robinson could play there. But who was going to play first if Robinson played second? Who was going to replace Reiser in the outfield? Who was going to catch? These problems persisted as the Dodgers left the Dominican Republic to begin a series of exhibitions in the South, where to the majority Robinson's ebony presence was still a slap in the face.

REX BARNEY: "In 1948 we trained in the Dominican Republic, again because of Jackie. But when we left there, we toured the South, so that wherever we played—in places like Macon, Georgia, Columbus, Georgia, Atlanta—we were the first white team ever to play with a black player. We used to get threatening letters that they were gonna kill us or kill Jackie.

"The first place we played was in Macon, which was the worst. Mr. Rickey had brought in Sam Lacy, who was the sports editor of the *Afro-American* in Baltimore, so Jackie would have someone to room with. Wherever we went, and this included major league cities, the local black doctor or black lawyer or best businessman would meet Jackie at our train and take him to his home, and that's where he would stay, because he wasn't allowed to stay with us in the hotels. Anyway, we were playing in Macon, and the game had been sold out for months. Jackie Robinson's going to play; they had to rope off the field to allow people to watch the game from the outfield.

"Just as our bus got to the park from the hotel, Sam Lacy and Jackie pull up in a car, get out, and head for the door in front of which is a big policeman and above which is a 'Whites Only' sign. Jackie and the rest of the Dodgers start walking to the door, when the big policeman says, 'You can't come in here. Can't you read?'

"Now even though Jackie and Leo never got along, this was one thing about Leo. Leo always stuck up for his players. Leo said, 'He can't go in this ballpark? He can't go in that entrance?' The policeman said, 'No, he can't.' Leo said, 'Then we are not going in there. Do you know what that means?' Well, the policeman got scared, because it was the biggest crowd in history, so finally he let us all in. This is the first time a black man ever played with white ballplayers in the South, and Jackie and Pee Wee are standing next to each other on the field, and Bruce Edwards and I are standing opposite them playing catch back and forth, and Pee Wee said, 'Wait a minute. Jack, how about going and standing down there next to Rex?' Jackie said, 'Why?' Pee Wee said, 'Because if they shoot and miss, I don't want them to get me.' Well, that kind of took the edge off."

But there were further humiliations to break a man's spirit. Robinson may have been the major league Rookie of the Year in 1947, but he was still just the Dodger nigger to many Americans.

HAROLD PARROTT: "There was only one time when I thought Robinson was close to saying the hell with it and quitting.

"That was in the gloom of a deserted Greyhound bus outside a roadside restaurant in Florida, during spring training for the 1948 season. Jackie and another black slumped dejectedly in their seats. All the other Dodgers were inside, wolfing their steaks after a hard game against the Yankees. Jackie, and the other, who was Roy Campanella, had been refused admission to the restaurant even though the rest of the team, still in their soiled uniforms, were in a private dining room.

"Getting the players transported, bedded down, and fed was part of my job, and now I tried to bribe a waiter, or even a busboy, to carry a couple of blueplate specials to the outcasts in the bus. Not a chance! They'd have lost their jobs, they told me, and been marked as 'nigger lovers.'

"As I juggled the tray of plates onto the lonely bus in the dark, I found a Robinson who was politely grateful—but seething at the put-down. Campanella was pleading to avoid a scene: 'Let's not have no trouble, Jackie. This is the onliest thing we can do right now, 'lessen we want to go back to them crummy Negro leagues . . .'

"Robinson's eyes were aflame, and I knew what was racing through his mind: He had played a big part in winning fat World Series checks for all those guys inside the restaurant, even the third-string bullpen catcher and the humpties who hardly ever got into the game. And there they were, all of them, stuffing the food down and seeming not to care that he wasn't part of it, wasn't one of them.

"He had taken the abuse without a whimper; the dusters and beanballs they threw at him didn't stop him from getting up from the dirt and socking the big base hits to prove that he really belonged. But what was the good of all the 'big experiment' when here he was, still on the outside?

"Carefully laying aside his fat cigar with all the éclat of an orchestra leader putting down his baton, the roly-poly Campanella tore into the meal I had brought.

"Robinson didn't touch a bite."

When the exhibition season ended and the team began playing for real, it was flat. It had no chemistry. In April and May, the Dodgers struggled. On the second road trip, Durocher was down to seven pitchers, and one of them had a sore arm. Toward the end of May, the Dodgers lost eight in a row, and on May 25 fell into last place. Durocher was booed every time he appeared on the field. A number of the fans still had not forgiven him for breaking up Laraine Day's marriage. A telegram addressed to Mr. and Mrs. Durocher and the Dodger players was delivered to the Brooklyn club on May 24. It read: "YOU ARE INVITED TO ATTEND A STEAK DINNER AT JOE'S BAR AND GRILLE. THE AFFAIR WILL BE HELD IN THE CONCRETE CELLAR, WHICH IS JUST WHERE YOU BELONG."

Gallows humor was running rampant in Brooklyn. Hugh Casey fell down a flight of stairs and wrenched his back. Casey was placed on the sixty-day disabled list. When Dodger officials announced that further additions to the pitching staff would have to wait until some of the pitchers could clear waivers, sports reporter Heywood Hale Broun suggested that the solution might be to push some of the others down the stairs first.

On the outer wall of Ebbets Field there was a sign: "OCCUPANCY BY MORE THAN 33,000 UNLAWFUL." Just below it someone had boldly scrawled: "AND UNLIKELY."

Every fan was asking two questions: Whose fault was it and what can be done about it? The distress of the Dodger fans was evident. It was the hottest topic of conversation in all of Brooklyn. During the losing streak, for instance, publicist Harry Markson was having a conversation with his rabbi. The Arabs were advancing on the newly independent country of Israel, and things were looking bleak there. Asked Markson: "Rabbi, have you heard the latest reports on the radio?" "Yes," replied the rabbi, "the Dodgers lost again."

As the Dodgers sank into the cellar in May, there were grumblings that the players resented Durocher after such a serene, successful year under Shotton.

By early July there were rumors that Rickey was going to fire Durocher and that Rickey was going to resign because of ill health.

All through the spring, the two problem positions had been first base and catcher. Robinson had moved over to second, his best position, leaving first to Ray Sanders and Preston Ward. Before spring camp Durocher had hoped Pete Reiser could play there, but Durocher quickly soured on the overweight

Reiser. In desperation Durocher was forced to put Robinson back on first and play Eddie Miksis on second.

Rickey had used Roy Campanella in spring training, but he wouldn't let him play much because he didn't want anyone to see how good he was. Rickey wanted Campy to go to St. Paul, something neither Leo nor Campy could understand. Rickey told him, "My boy, you are going to be the first black player in the American Association." Campy said, "I ain't no pioneer. I'm a ballplayer." But Rickey sent him to St. Paul, where he spectacularly integrated the American Association, leading the league in most batting categories. Not that that was any help to Durocher.

In early July, nine games out of first, Durocher finally was able to pressure Rickey into promoting Campanella up to the Dodgers, and in his first game the large Negro catcher hit two home runs against the Giants. Campy was in Brooklyn to stay.

Roy Campanella had been a long-time star in the Negro Leagues. Though he was only twenty-five, he had been playing professionally for almost ten years when Rickey brought him up to Brooklyn. One of his teammates on the Baltimore Elite Giants, Othello Renfroe, remembers when Campanella first joined the Elite Giants.

OTHELLO RENFROE: "In Baltimore Roy Campanella was fifteen in 1938—great big—biggest fifteen-year-old boy I ever saw in my life. But at fifteen he could throw to second base. They talk about Bench throwing now. You should talk to Pee Wee Butts, our shortstop. When Butts would take infield practice, he'd get mad at Campanella for throwing the ball so hard."

ROY CAMPANELLA: "I was only fifteen years old when I began playing in the Negro Leagues. Biz Mackey was the manager of the Baltimore Elite Giants, and he was the first-string catcher on our team, and in those days in the old Negro National League, the players could play well up in their forties, which Biz did, until he got hurt and the second-string catcher also got hurt, which is why they gave me the opportunity. They asked my parents, and my parents said, 'We'll let him play, but he can't play on Sundays.' I always went to our Baptist Church on Sundays.

"Later, during school, they gave in, and I played on the weekends, and when school let out, I played full time. I remember I felt so lost. I had no idea in the world this would be my profession. Truthfully, I wanted to be an architect.

"The first game I played, both of the catchers, Biz Mackey and Nish Williams, got hurt in the same game with foul tips, and so Mackey told me to go in and catch, and that night a spitball pitcher was pitching—we were allowed to throw a spitball in the Negro National League—and his name was Bill Byrd. This fellow would chew sillery yellow and chewing tobacco, and he had the best control of any pitcher I've ever seen. You just did not hit him.

"Our manager, Biz Mackey, advised me, 'Roy, you warm him up before you catch so you know how the ball breaks,' and this taught me to warm up

Roy Campanella

pitchers before I caught them in a game, and I always did that in the big leagues. Even in spring training I caught every young pitcher who would pitch in exhibition games to learn how he threw the ball and the way the ball would break, and this helped me quite a bit, and it helped the young pitchers to give them confidence that the main catcher was catching them.

"And I did fine in that game. I remember Josh Gibson, he used to kid me. He used to call me a little boy, a little kid. But year by year I grew up, and one of the winters I played in Puerto Rico, I led the entire league in home runs, and that year he said, 'You're growing up to be a man now.'

"I played in the Negro National League beginning in 1937, and I even played high school ball at the same time, and when I was in the eleventh grade, the owners of the Baltimore Elite Giants went to my father and mother and said, 'Can he quit school and play with us regular?' and they offered them a pretty good bonus, and back in those days, it really meant something, and they agreed because that money helped so much at home, and they figured I could always go back and finish school. It didn't bother me at all to give that bonus money to my parents, and even on payday I never did see my paycheck. They sent it to my parents, and they just gave me meal money.

"It was in October 1946, and we were playing an exhibition game at Newark on a Friday night, late after the baseball season was over. We had this Negro League all-star team, and this was the first time I ever played with Jackie Robinson. Charley Dressen was the manager of the major league all-stars, and one inning I was going out to catch and he was going to third base to coach, and he stopped and said, 'Campy, can I talk to you after the game?' So I said sure, and he said, 'I'll meet you outside of your clubhouse.' That was the first time anyone spoke to me about coming to the Dodgers. He said, 'Could you come to the Dodger office tomorrow morning at ten o'clock in Brooklyn?'

"I went to the Dodger office and had a meeting with Mr. Rickey, and he had a scouting report on me three to four inches thick, and he read it all to me, and I was flabbergasted! They had followed me, and they knew everything about me, about my family, my parents, my schooling, everything. Mr. Rickey asked me what I was going to do this winter, and I told him I was going to Venezuela to play winter baseball, and he asked me, 'Did you sign a contract to that effect?' and I told him, 'No, just a gentleman's agreement that I'll play, and they said they'd give me so much per month for playing.' A man's word in those days was his bond and his contract. If you couldn't go by a man's word, then it didn't mean too much, 'cause contract or not, fellas could leave their team, not to play with another team in the league but to go to another country and play. Mr. Rickey told me, 'Don't sign a contract until I talk to you again,' and I gave him my word. He asked for my address in Venezuela, because, he said, he had plans for me. And that night I went back to my hotel, and I was rooming with Jackie, and Jackie told me he had signed with Montreal the night before. It hadn't been released in the press, and only then did I suspect that Mr. Rickey wanted me for the Dodger organization.

"I waited patiently, and Mr. Rickey contacted me in Venezuela. Just before spring training he said, 'It's time for you to come to the Dodger office. I want to talk to you.' And that's when I signed.

"Looking back, it meant the end of the Negro Leagues, though at the time I didn't think that would happen, because I didn't think they were going to take that many players. At first it was only the Dodgers who were interested in signing Negro League players, but then every team in the majors wound up with black players, which was probably the greatest advancement for blacks not only in baseball but in mankind throughout the country and the world.

"That first year the Dodgers sent me to Nashua, New Hampshire. Don Newcombe was there with me. And there was a reason we had to go to Nashua. Jackie was running into a problem at Daytona Beach because people didn't want him training with Montreal, and so Mr. Rickey told me about Jackie's problems and asked me to stay up north until he could find a team for me to play on. And it was very odd. The Dodgers couldn't find a team for us to play on because of the problem. Was I upset? No. It wasn't upsetting because, my goodness, as a youngster I never had this to look forward to. A young black player today can say, 'I want to be a big league ballplayer.' I never could say that, and it never fazed me or worried me about blacks not being in the big leagues. I would go to big league games, go to see the Philadelphia Athletics—gee, Lefty Grove and Mickey Cochrane, Jimmy Foxx, Max Bishop, Eric McNair at short, Jimmy Dykes at third, Doc Cramer in center field, Mule Haas in center field, Al Simmons in left field, and they had a fellow named George Puccinelli in right field, and I got the nickname Pooch from Puccinelli—but, no, I was interested in major league baseball, but I never thought about the big leagues, playing in it. Never.

"At Nashua the manager was Walter Alston and the general manager Buzzy Bavasi, and Mr. Rickey asked them, 'Would you accept Campanella and Newcombe to play on your team?' and both of them agreed, and so this is where we wound up, with the Nashua Dodgers in 1946, and we won the championship there and just continued on.

"It wasn't bad at Nashua. Going around the different towns, you would always find a few who would holler smart remarks out to you, but it made our teammates notice and realize how some people could be, and they just hoped it wouldn't bother me, and they'd come to me and say, 'Just pay them no mind.' I thought they were tremendous. Then the next year, I followed Jackie to Montreal, and my manager's name was Clay Hopper, that was 1947, and, gee, I caught all the games and hit good and won the Most Valuable Player.

"In the spring of 1948 in Santo Domingo, I was playing with the Dodger farm hands, and we were playing the Dodgers, and Leo Durocher called over, 'Campanella, come out here and take infield practice with us.' And so I did. Bruce Edwards had come up with a sore arm, and I guess Leo wanted to see how I did. After practice, he told me, 'You impress me by your throwing.' I never said a word to Leo.

"Now, Mr. Rickey had called me into his office at the team's hotel, and he said, 'Roy, I want you to do me a favor. I want to bring you up to the Dodgers, but I'm gonna call Durocher and tell him he isn't allowed to play you because I want to send you out to St. Paul to be the first black to play in the American Association.' He said, 'We have a farm club, and we want to be able to send some black players there in the future, and I want you to play out there for a while.' And I told him I would do that. And I went to St. Paul. Walter Alston was again my manager, and I was leading the league in just about everything when Walter got a telegram. I was dressing in the locker room right beside him, and he said, 'I have some special news for you. After the game Mr. Rickey wants you to fly to Brooklyn.' I said, 'Fly to Brooklyn? I thought Mr. Rickey wanted me here for the whole season.' He said, 'No, they want you to fly to Brooklyn tonight.' I said, 'I don't even get to go back to St. Paul to get my clothes?' He said, 'We'll ship everything to you.'

"When I arrived in the Dodger clubhouse, Dick Whitman, who had played center field with us in the minor leagues, greeted me with, 'Campanella's here. We're saved.' I didn't appreciate that too much, but I didn't say anything. We were implanted in seventh or eighth place, and the first series was against the Giants, and I got nine hits in my first twelve times at bat! I caught every game. Leo told me I was going to be his catcher.

"I thought Leo was a tremendous manager. I never had a bad word for Leo because he lived and died with me. He worked through the catcher for his whole team, had meetings every day to go over what he wanted done, who was pitching, how we were going to pitch hitters, where he wanted the infielders to play, where he wanted the outfielders to play. And he expected the catcher to do every bit of it. Leo said, 'I won't tell you, but I expect you to do what I'm thinking.'

"I'll tell you what Leo could do. If there was 30,000 people in the stands and Leo wanted my attention, he had a certain whistle, and I knew it was Leo. I would look at him, and he would give me the sign right there what he wanted me to do. And I was never surprised by what Leo did, because I always liked to know my managers.

"Mr. Rickey was a catcher, you know. The way he could sit behind his desk and talk to me before a ballgame was unbelievable. And one of the main things he taught me: I had to get all of the white pitching staff to respect my judgment in accepting signs. He told me, 'To do that you have to be sincere, know what to say to a pitcher when you go out there to talk to him, know what you're talking about, and give them ideas regardless how old they are and despite the fact that you haven't played in the big leagues.' "

When Durocher gave Campanella the catching job, he made another important move. He moved the third-string catcher, an unknown by the name of Gil Hodges, to first base.

Rex Barney: "When we first came up, Gil was a bullpen catcher, but he always worked out in the infield. I was pitching one day, and when you pitched, you sat on the bench before the game with Durocher. So Gil was working out at third this one day, and Preston Ward, who had opened the season at first, was off to a horrendous start, and Leo really didn't know who he was going to put at first.

"There was a left-handed pitcher that day, and Leo yelled, 'Gil, get over here. C'mere a minute.' Gil came over, and Leo said, 'Did you ever play first base?' Gil said no. Leo said, 'Why don't you go and work out at first base.' Gil said, 'Okay,' and he took a glove and worked out at first. Leo watched him and called over and said, 'Would it bother you if I put you at first base today? Gil, being the type of guy he was, said, 'No. I'll play anyplace,' and they didn't get him out of there until about 2,000 games later. He was magnificent.

"And before that he couldn't hit. Never. When he pinch hit or got into a game the few times he did get in, he couldn't hit anything. But once he started playing regularly, that's all he did.

"You know how big Gil Hodges's hands were. Pee Wee used to say, 'The only reason Gil wears a glove is because the rules make him.' His hands were unreal. When Gil shook hands with you, his two fingers would go around your wrist.

"There was an infielder by the name of Bobby Adams, and Adams was playing for Cincinnati. I was pitching, and Adams was taking his lead off first base, and I threw the ball to Gil to pick him off. Gil, like most first basemen, would grab the ball and without looking slap the glove down behind his back on top of the bag to try to tag the guy out. Well, Gil slapped Adams right on the head, and he was out for about three minutes. Gil knocked him out cold. And Gil, the saint that he was, thought it was the end of the world, he was so upset.

"Anytime we'd have a fight on the field, Gil was the peacemaker. Big and strong as he was, he wouldn't touch a flea. He might pick up one fighting player in one arm and the other one in the other. When he got into it, there was no more fight. Gil would never touch a soul."

Campanella and Hodges were improvements certainly, but under Durocher the Dodgers were still a team going nowhere in '48. As attendance fell owners Walter O'Malley and John L. Smith were putting pressure on Rickey to fire Durocher, who O'Malley categorized as "poison at the gate." Rickey fought hard to keep Leo but finally agreed with O'Malley that if the Dodgers hit last place he would ask Durocher to resign.

Rickey never thought it would happen. But on July 6, a Friday, the Dodgers lost their sixth game in a row. The next day the Dodgers were in the cellar. Leo had to go.

Leo Becomes the Enemy

Rickey was not happy with the decision. He didn't think the Dodgers' poor showing was Durocher's fault, and he didn't give a damn about what O'Malley called Leo's "negative public relations."

The day the team actually hit last place, Rickey was flat on his back at

Peck Memorial Hospital with a bladder infection. He called Harold Parrott and told Parrott to ask Durocher to resign.

It was a cat and mouse game between Rickey and O'Malley. Rickey figured Leo would refuse, and Leo obliged. Durocher told Parrott, "I'll make it so tough for him he won't be able to fire me."

When Rickey heard he bellowed: "Good. He's my manager as long as he wants to be."

And Leo didn't make it any easier for O'Malley and Smith. The next day he led the Dodgers to a sweep of a doubleheader against the Phils. After the first win, Durocher popped his head above the visiting dugout, slapped the top of the dugout, and shouted, "We'll keep this up and see who gets fired!" The Dodgers won five of the next six games, and Leo managed the National League in the all-star game. Rickey knew he would have to eventually let Leo go—what O'Malley wanted, O'Malley got—but how could he do it gracefully?

The key came from across the Harlem River, where Giant owner Horace Stoneham also had a problem. Stoneham desperately wanted to fire his manager, Mel Ott, but Ott had been the most popular Giant in the history of the team. He had come to the Giants in 1926 as a peach-fuzzed teen, and with his leg-up stance, he had had a Hall of Fame career for the Giants spanning twenty-one years. He had managed the team since 1942. Firing Mel Ott would be akin to abolishing Thanksgiving—unless, of course, Stoneham could come up with a substitute who could make the Giant fans forget Ott.

Stoneham, who was never a clever man, decided he would hire Burt Shotton, the man who had led the Dodgers to the 1947 pennant. Stoneham called Rickey to ask his permission.

Rickey had found his way to move Durocher.

Branch Rickey: "It was in St. Louis, when Frank Shaughnessy told me about Horace Stoneham's intention to change managers. I happened to know with what high esteem Horace held Durocher as a manager. Only recently I had heard him say Durocher was the greatest manager in the world. So, I returned to Brooklyn as quickly as possible and got in touch with Horace."

But it was Shotton that Stoneham wanted, not Durocher. What was Rickey up to? Leo Durocher knew exactly what Rickey was up to.

Leo Durocher: "As a trader of ballplayers Rickey was simply without peer. Over and over, he'd throw two men at the other club, 'Take your pick,' and have it set up so they'd take the wrong one. He gave Pittsburgh their choice between Enos Slaughter and Johnny Rizzo and Chicago their choice between Marty Marion and Bobby Sturgeon, and in both cases they picked the wrong one. It wasn't quite that simple, though, because it doesn't give either Rickey or the man on the other side of the table enough credit. Believe me, Rickey wasn't taking that kind of a chance of losing such great players as Slaughter and Marion.

"Slaughter had been the best minor-league prospect to come along in years.

But he was a left-handed hitter, and the Pirates were so overstocked with left-handed hitters, like the Waner brothers, Arky Vaughan, and Gus Suhr, that they had been seeing every left-handed pitcher in the league for years. The one thing they needed was a big right-handed bomb like Rizzo in the middle of their lineup. By throwing Slaughter into the pot—'take your pick'—the Old Man was able to set a much higher price, and even upgrade Rizzo in Pittsburgh's mind. He was only making it seem as if Rizzo was as valuable as Slaughter, but also that he was angling to save Rizzo for himself.

"That was always a favorite tactic with Rickey. Watch out when he threw out a string and pulled it back.

"When Mr. Stoneham asked for permission to talk to Barney Shotton about managing the New York Giants, Rickey, of course, gave it. 'And then,' Mr. Rickey said, measuring me carefully, 'I told him he could have his choice. I told him he could have either Shotton or Durocher.' I could just hear him: 'Durocher or Shotton, take your pick.' The two strings, held out as always, and knowing all the time which string was going to be plucked. How many times had I seen him do it? Only this time one of the strings had been me.

" 'You mean I have a choice?' Stoneham had asked. 'If I have a choice, Durocher is the man I want.'

"Rickey said, 'I have Mr. Stoneham's telephone number right here in my desk. If you're interested, you have only to pick up the phone and call him.' He slid his chair toward me and leaned over until we were eyeball to eyeball. Very slowly and very emphatically, he said, 'But . . . you . . . don't . . . have . . . to . . . go. You are the manager of this ballclub.'

"I had told him I was never going to desert any ship that was sinking, and he was not only putting down the gangplank he was throwing me a lifesaver. Hell, he was putting me aboard an ocean liner. How did I know I wasn't going to be fired tomorrow anyway? Right there, I made up my mind.

" 'Two questions, Mr. Rickey. One: Am I the manager of this ball club now?'

" 'Yes, sir.'

" 'Two: Will I be the manager of this ballclub tomorrow, next week, next month and until the close of the 1948 season?'

"And with that, he just looked at me and said, 'Well . . .' And then he swiveled around and looked out the window into the pitch blackness. He chewed on his cigar. He said nothing.

" 'I don't know what the hell you expect to see out there!' I said, jumping up. 'Where is that number?' "

The meeting at an end, Durocher told Rickey he would call as soon as he had worked out the arrangements with Stoneham. Later that night Durocher called to say he and Stoneham had come to terms. Rickey told Durocher he would have to first come over to write out a resignation. Durocher returned, and after it was signed, Rickey and Durocher shook hands.

"Goodbye, Branch."

"Goodbye, boy."

On July 15, 1948, Stoneham fired Ott, Rickey fired Durocher. Stoneham hired Durocher, and Rickey rehired Burt Shotton.

Under a smaller headline, there was a news story that the Phils had fired Ben Chapman and replaced him with Dusty Cooke. It was a double victory for Jackie Robinson. When Shotton arrived in Cincinnati to join the Dodgers, the most enthusiastic player to greet him was Robinson.

"I love playing for Shotton," exulted Robinson. "I can't wait to see him. It's going to be a lot different. When Shotton wants to bawl out a player he takes him aside and does it in private. That gives you a sort of lift. If Leo has something on his mind, you hear it right there—but loud, and in front of everyone who's around." Then to be politic, he added, "But they are both great managers."

LARRY KING: "Leo had been Brooklyn. He epitomized Brooklyn. And when he went to the Giants, we couldn't believe it. And then I hated him. We all hated him."

And so evolved the fiercest rivalry perhaps in all of sports, and it was a rivalry that existed not only among the rabid fans but between the ballplayers on the two teams as well. After Durocher went over to the Giants, Jackie Robinson, finally shedding the excess weight, began to hit again. And true to form, Leo took it personally: "Jackie played for Shotton, but he wouldn't play for me," and he never forgave Robinson. Whenever the Dodgers and Giants played, Leo and Jackie went at each other's throats with a vengeance.

It's interesting to speculate as to what life on the Dodgers would have been like had Durocher remained. Would Durocher and Robinson have gotten along?

ROGER KAHN: "It certainly would have been more complicated with Durocher as manager. Durocher would have had to adjust his personality to Robinson's. Obviously the way to handle Robinson was to tell him how terrific he is. I don't know if it would have worked. It would have been hard for Durocher to deal with a character that enormous. I think Durocher was great for Willie Mays, but Mays was a simple guy. There was always an Uncle Tom in Durocher's view of Mays. He was always having Mays call him Mr. Leo. But I don't believe Mays did that. Mays called him Skipper or Leo, but Durocher would always cast Mays in an Uncle Tom role. No, I don't think Durocher and Robinson would have gotten into fistfights, but I think Durocher would have been a bad manager for him. When did Durocher ever manage a superstar? Mays, but that was a carefully orchestrated role. He was the straw boss and Mays the plantation hand. I think Robinson was probably too complicated for Durocher. I think he would have had a lot of trouble with Robinson. And Robinson with him.

"After Durocher went to the Giants, Jack became the editor of the magazine, *Our Sports,* which was a spinoff of the magazine *Our World,* which was a spinoff of the magazine *Ebony.* And Jack engaged me as his pale ghost. And the first piece we wrote was called 'My Feud with Leo Is Over.' And so

I talked with Jack a while, and we talked back and forth, and I wrote the piece under Jackie's byline. Durocher had said publicly maybe fifteen times that Robinson was his kind of ballplayer, so I had the piece ending, 'He says I'm his kind of ballplayer, well he's my kind of man.' And Robinson crossed out the word 'man' and wrote 'manager.' "

With Durocher gone, a blanket of quiet settled back over the Dodgers. With the exception of Robinson, who was much more outspoken and opinionated than most ballplayers, the Dodgers fit Rickey's mold. They were solid citizens, family men, serious young men with character, such as Gil Hodges, Roy Campanella, Pee Wee Reese, Carl Furillo, Billy Cox, Duke Snider, Ralph Branca, Rex Barney. And later, under Walter O'Malley, the atmosphere became more serious and businesslike.

JOE FLAHERTY: "There's a certain thing that happens in sports after you get your popularity. All of a sudden money starts to accrue, and where in the past the team has a rough-tough image, now the owner wants respectability. So thus the O'Malleys say, 'Let me have the pristine stadium where, if blacks are going to come, they're going to be on the freeway for half an hour, and I'll get the suburbanites.' O'Malley is saying to himself, 'I want to be respectable, and I'll never get it if I keep Durocher.'

"There is a great co-option of success. The O'Malleys of the world want sterility. And they begin to believe *they* are the team, not the players. And they hire milktoasts, the corporate men. And Shotton was certainly that. Dressen didn't fit O'Malley's mold, and he was let go despite his success, and Alston was the ultimate. With his one-year contracts, he wouldn't make demands. And Tom Lasorda, who succeeded Alston, is the worst. They talk about color. Color, my ass. He's the worst ass-kisser of them all. It looks like he's throwing his résumé out on the floor. Can you imagine Durocher groveling to Rickey with that Dodger-blue nonsense?"

Boit and Oisk

Burt Shotton returned as Dodger manager July 15. In just over a month, the Dodgers were back in first place. At Ebbets Field eight pennants, one for each team in the National League, flew over the outfield in order of their standing. After winning the opening game of a doubleheader against the Braves on August 22, the Brooklyn pennant was run up the first-place pole. The Brooklyn fans broke into a roar.

Under Durocher that year, the Dodgers had been playing conservative, hesitant baseball. One thing Shotton did was return to a daring running game. In his first thirty-four games, the Dodgers stole thirty-five bases.

Under Shotton Robinson once again returned to form. In spring training he looked slow and unsure of himself. His weight had held him down. But by midseason, Jackie was as good, if not better, than in his outstanding rookie season.

* * *

REX BARNEY: "Jackie Robinson was the most exciting player I have ever seen—not the best but the most exciting. As long as he was in the game, you had a chance to win. The second he got on base, the whole ballpark, you could feel them get on the edge of their seats. They knew he was going to do something. It was just a matter of time. He played baseball with such abandon. He's the only player I've ever seen that if he was a runner at first and a sacrifice bunt was in order, I never saw him go to second and stop, he would keep right on going to third. It got to the point where there would be a bunt, and the third baseman would field it, and he'd stand there and hold it to stop him from going to third.

"He did things. He'd get on first and take such a big lead that the pitcher would throw to first, and he'd go to second. He was not fast, he was *not* fast, but he was quick. His first fifteen to twenty feet was the quickest you've ever seen. I've seen him round first base after a hit to right field, and the right fielder would bluff a throw back to first base, and he'd go right into second. And so the fans in the ballparks would go wild when he played because they knew he was going to do something. What was sad was that he didn't get to the major leagues until he was twenty-eight, but for a precious few years, Jackie could play the game."

One experimental move Shotton made was to shift Carl Furillo from center to right field, to better take advantage of his powerful arm. In center field, Shotton selected one of the hundreds of young minor league kids Rickey had signed during the war years. While other clubs stopped signing youngsters, fearing that they might be killed in combat, Rickey increased his scouting system and signed even more kids than before. With Furillo in right, Shotton began playing a twenty-two-year-old blond rookie named Edwin Donald Snider, nicknamed The Duke.

The same day young Snider came up, the Dodgers brought a twenty-year-old pitcher named Carl Erskine up from Ft. Worth. Erskine had won four letters in baseball pitching at Anderson High School in Indiana. He wasn't very big, maybe five foot ten, 150 pounds, but he had extraordinary speed and a fast-breaking rainbow curve that set scouts drooling. Rickey had given him $3,500 to sign with the Dodgers, but Commissioner Happy Chandler ruled that the Dodgers had broken the rules by signing Erskine while he was still in the service and declared the boy a free agent. Several teams, including the Braves, the Phils, and the Red Sox, had offered him $10,000 to sign, but Erskine's high school catcher had signed with Brooklyn, and Erskine had liked the way the Dodger organization had treated him, so he told Rickey that for another $5,000, he'd re-sign. The Dodgers willingly paid the money. That's how great a prospect Erskine was.

In late July of 1948, Carl came up to the Dodgers, and for the next ten years was their ace pitcher—when his arm permitted. In his very first season with the Dodgers, Carl Erskine injured himself. If manager Shotton had one failing, it was that he didn't believe in mollycoddling his ballplayers. And because he believed that the best way to heal an injury was to play with it,

George Brace Photo

CARL ERSKINE

Burt Shotton prevented Carl Erskine from becoming the Hall of Fame pitcher he should have been.

CARL ERSKINE: "I played at Danville for a full season in 1947, went to Ft. Worth, Texas, a Double-A team, the next year, in 1948, won fifteen games by July for Les Berge, and the Dodgers called me up, the middle of '48. That was two years to the day from when I joined the Danville club in Decatur. I was twenty years old.

"It was a fairly young team in 1948. Rickey was rebuilding, but I didn't know anybody. I hadn't been in the game long enough. The only guy I really knew at all was Jackie Robinson, because the Dodgers came through Ft. Worth that spring of '48, played an exhibition game, and I pitched against them three innings, and after the game was over, Jackie came over to our bench and looked me up and said, 'Young man, I just want to tell you something. You won't be here very long. You're going to be with us before you know it. You mark what I tell you.' Boy, woooo, what a boost that was to me, and when I got to Pittsburgh that day, Jackie was the first guy to my locker. He said, 'What did I tell you? It was no surprise to me that you're here. The only surprise is it wasn't sooner.' I pitched that day in relief and kind of got lucky. I relieved Hugh Casey, of all people, and we got some runs the next inning, and I got the win, so I picked up a win the first day in the big leagues.

"Burt Shotton was the manager, and he came over and said, 'That's a good way to break in. Welcome. Glad you're here.' Anyway, I won five straight before I lost one, and I thought, 'Boy, this is the easiest league I've ever been in!' I finished that half year six and three, and that was my break-in. I relieved twice, and then they started me, and I won the first three starts, all three complete games, but I hurt my shoulder severely in my first start against the Cubs. I pulled a muscle in the seventh inning pitching to Bill Nicholson. I struck him out on a high fastball, and as I released it, I felt it sharp, hot, as though someone stuck me with a knife in the back of my shoulder. I didn't know what it was. I had never had a muscle tear before. But I continued to pitch, and I finished the game, and the next day I couldn't lift it. Boy, I had done some bad damage to my shoulder.

"I was darn reluctant to tell anybody, but my second start was against the Phillies, and after I pitched about five innings, I could hardly lift my arm. It was really killing me. I went to Mr. Shotton on the bench, and I very quietly and reluctantly said, 'Mr. Shotton, I hate to tell you this, but my arm is so bad I can hardly lift it. When I go back to take my warm-ups each inning, I am really in a lot of pain.' He looked at me and said, 'Why, son, you're pitching a shutout. Now you go right ahead out there. If you get in any trouble, we'll take care of that.' I didn't say anymore. I went ahead and pitched, and I beat the Phillies 2 to 1, but I'm telling you, I couldn't lift my arm the next day. But three days later in Philly, he started me again. And I had the same tough experience, but I beat the Phillies that night, 8 to 1. But I did a lot of damage to my shoulder in those two starts, and I began then to have really, really severe arm problems, and it plagued me my whole career.

"Duke Snider, who roomed with me all those years, can tell you about the problems both physical and psychological of trying to pitch with a bad arm, and the darn thing, some days I could get good and loose, and some days I couldn't, and so I'd pitch an outstanding game, and then I'd have problems, control problems, because it was giving me a lot of trouble. I never said too much about this darn thing because I was just so thankful to be there, plus I didn't want to be known as a sore-armed pitcher. But I eventually was because I was bothered my whole career, and when I quit in L.A. years later, in '59, that was the reason.

"And it was always a mystery: The Dodgers had a lot of good, young talent, and we had a lot of arm trouble. And Burt Shotton was an outstanding man. He was a class individual. But he was from the old school, which more or less said, 'Your arm bothering you? Go on out to center field and throw at the flag. That will help you.'

"In those days you didn't go in and climb on the trainer's table. A young guy, a rookie, on the training table? Are you kidding? You didn't want to be seen near the trainer's room. If you were a veteran and you wanted to get rubbed a little, fine, but a rookie? 'On the table? Hey, you must be kidding. What are you, a fish? Tissue paper. Old fish.' Well, nobody wants that kind of needling, so you were discouraged from doing that.

"That was a frustration for me to never know when I came to the ballpark whether I was going to get my arm loose. Or sometimes I'd start a game and struggle for two or three innings and finally get it loose. And there was another problem: I could never work on any specialty pitches. I couldn't throw a lot in between. I couldn't work on a screwball or a slider—a slider would kill my arm. It really hurt, and I used it some, but it was tough, real tough. So I had to stick pretty much to fastball, curveball, change speeds on the curve, and a change of pace. Which was enough when I was healthy. And I'm not com-plaining, I'm ex-plaining. I'm very pleased and fortunate that I was not finished after I hurt my arm. But occasionally it would cross my mind, I wonder if I had not hurt my arm, how good could I have been?"

And for the next ten years, whenever the Dodgers fell short, it was because the Dodger pitching staff was short. And too often, it was short because Erskine's arm wasn't cooperating. Had he not been injured, it's quite possible the Dodgers would have won pennants in 1950 and in 1951, and its even more possible they wouldn't have had to wait as long as they did to win a world championship.

The Dodgers battled the Braves into September, and they might have won the 1948 pennant had star pitcher Ralph Branca not come down with an infection of his left ankle. Branca had begun the year spectacularly, as he had the year before. He had a 14–9 record in August, when he was hit in the leg with a line drive. An infection developed, and it settled in his arm.

He didn't win another game the entire year, and the strain on the staff was too great.

In early September Durocher returned to haunt the Dodgers, as his Giants beat Brooklyn three straight to give Boston some breathing room. During one dismal September stretch the Dodgers lost eleven of fourteen, allowing the Braves to stretch their lead and finish six and a half games ahead of the Cardinals and seven and a half ahead of Brooklyn.

Rex

The highlight of September for the Dodgers came when their enigmatic right-hander, Rex Barney, pitched a no-hitter against the Giants at the Polo Grounds. The well-dressed, handsome Barney had blazing speed, a tricky curve, and a tantalizing change-up, but his victories didn't come as often as his teammates felt they should. Some of them wondered about him.

BOBBY BRAGAN: "It was his lack of concentration. I was warming Rex up, getting ready for a game at Ebbets Field, and about five minutes into the warm-up, he threw a ball about thirty feet over my head. When I retrieved the ball, I walked it back to Rex. I said, 'You know, Rex, I can throw with you for an hour out here and never miss you by as much as you just missed me.' He took the ball. He wasn't paying any attention. He was watching the fans coming into the park. 'Look,' he said, 'isn't that Dave Snowden coming in with all those nuns?'

"Another time we were playing in the Polo Grounds. Sid Gordon was hitting for the Giants, and there was a runner at second and third. First base was open, and Burt Shotton sent Clyde Sukeforth out to the mound to tell Rex to be sure to throw nothing but smoke to Gordon and that if he walked him that would be okay too.

"Well, the first pitch Rex threw was a curveball that bounced past Bruce Edwards. Both runners scored, and we got beat. After the game was over, we were in the clubhouse, and Shotton called Barney over and said, 'What did Sukeforth tell you when he came to the mound?' Rex said, 'Sukey? I didn't even know he was at the mound.' That tells you why he was wild. His mind wandered while he was working, and the ball wandered with it."

Off the field, he also had his idiosyncrasies.

CARL FURILLO: "Rex was a hot dog. When he first came up, he figured he was going to turn baseball inside out. We were staying at the Hotel St. George, and he must have gotten a fairly good bonus, 'cause every time you looked around he was going to Abe Stark or Simmons the tailor to buy clothes. But he was really a hot dog. He would dress up real nice, and he'd go down to the lobby of the Hotel St. George—that's when the St. George was nice, a classy little place—and he'd stay down there for maybe an hour or two, and he'd go upstairs and get dressed again, change clothes, and then he'd be down in the lobby again strutting around. He was in love with himself. We often made a remark about it, that somebody ought to hit him between the eyes, change his looks a little bit. Maybe then he would play ball. And at the ballpark, Rex was what you call a lover boy. Oh, he loved to watch those broads all over the place.

"On the ballfield he would do a pretty good job, but then he would get wild. I don't know whether he was just looking in the stands at broads or what the hell he was doing.

"But every now and then he would throw you a good ballgame, about every fourth time out. Oh, could he throw the ball!"

For all his extraordinary talent, Rex Barney enjoyed just one year of success, in 1948, when he was 15–13 with a 3.10 earned run average, fifth-best. His 138 strikeouts were second in the league to Harry Brecheen's 149. But then in 1949, Barney was 9–8, the next year 2–1, and after 1950 he was gone from the Dodgers and from baseball, his control gone, his confidence shot. In writing about Barney's wildness, the *Trib*'s Bob Cooke wrote, "Barney pitched as though the plate were high and outside."

Barney tried every possible remedy to get back his control. Branch Rickey had him pitch with a patch over one eye, then a patch over the other, hoping it was a vision problem. He even went to a psychiatrist, a desperate measure in those days, and there was a joke going around that after he got finished with the psychiatrist, Rex was still wild, and the psychiatrist, while playing catch with his kid, threw the ball through a plate glass window.

But to Barney, there was nothing at all humorous about his problem. Nevertheless his speed is remembered, so that even today when a Dodger rookie shows great speed, he is informed that he has a "Rex Barney fastball." And yet the question still remains about why his control pulled a Judge Crater. Why did Barney suddenly lose his ability to find the plate after showing flashes of being almost unhittable? Not even Barney knows for certain.

REX BARNEY: "All I ever wanted to be from the time I knew what anything was all about was a major league baseball player. I can remember my mother telling me that over the years, when the other little kids were playing cops and robbers or cowboys and Indians, I was always playing a game with a ball. When I was eight, I joined a team in what they called the Midget American Legion, and I was a catcher because no one wanted to play that position, so I got to play, and as I grew older, I ended up the tallest kid, and the theory was that the tallest kid threw the hardest, so I became the pitcher. Of course I did throw harder.

"I went to a Jesuit prep school in Omaha, Nebraska, Creighton Prep, and the good priests knew I wanted to be a professional baseball player, so they tutored me Saturdays and Sundays and at night so I could graduate early. I had pitched my American Legion team to the world championship, defeating Berwyn, Illinois, 4 to 1 in the final game. I struck out seventeen, which was a record. I could have gone to college. I was offered something like thirty scholarships—Notre Dame, Indiana, Purdue, Nebraska, Creighton Univer-

Rex Barney

sity—but the war was coming on, I was eighteen years old, and if I had chosen a scholarship I would have been drafted right away. So I went to the draft board, and I said, 'If I sign a professional baseball contract, would you let me finish out the '43 season and then take me into the service?' They agreed.

"Right about that time, Mr. Rickey took over the Dodgers from Larry MacPhail, and I was to get the biggest bonus in the history of baseball, which was $5,000. Here's the way he set it up: He knew I was going into the service as soon as the season was over, and so he gave me $2,500 to sign and promised me the other $2,500 if I came back from the war in one piece and could still play. That was Mr. Rickey. But I didn't mind, because with $2,500 in my pocket, I thought I had all the money in the world. My father probably worked twenty-five years for $2,500 dollars. I was eighteen, from Omaha, and to get $2,500, well, you're a millionaire.

"The Dodgers sent me to Montreal, and in July 1943 they took me to the major leagues. I played the last three months of the season.

"I went to the ballpark, and we were playing at 1:30 in the afternoon against the Chicago Cubs. Leo Durocher, who was the manager, came up to me and said, 'Kid, when did you pitch last?' I said, 'Four days ago.' He said, 'Well, you're gonna start the second game of today's doubleheader.' Well, hell, I'd have gone back to Omaha in a flash. Here I was two months out of high school pitching in a major league ballpark! First major league game I ever saw I was pitching in. I didn't know what was going on. The first pitch that I threw in the major leagues was to Eddie Stanky of the Cubs, and I hit him right in the middle of the back. I left in the seventh inning with the score tied 2–2. Four days later I came back and won my first major league game against the Pittsburgh Pirates. Then the season ended in September, and I was in the army on Monday. That's how quick it happened.

"When I returned in 1946, Stanky was with the Dodgers, and Durocher took me around the clubhouse and introduced me to the players, 'cause I had just gotten out of the service, and he introduced me to Stanky, and Stanky said, 'I remember the son of a bitch. He hit me right in the middle of the back his first pitch in the major leagues.'

"Back then everything was different. Everything was very tough. It wasn't easy. I thought Leo was one of the best managers in all of baseball, but Leo was very, very tough. Oh, he was terrible. If Leo yelled and screamed at you that meant he liked you and was trying to help you. He got on the people who played best for him, people like myself, Jackie, Ralph Branca, Stanky, Furillo, and Hodges. Leo would throw chairs at me, shoes, everything. He couldn't have gotten away with that today, but then he could because you were so happy just to be there.

"I remember I was pitching in the Polo Grounds, and I had just won four games in a row—I finally found out what it was all about, the middle of 1948, just before he went over to the Giants. I was his best pitcher at the time, and I was pitching every fourth day. And he was such a perfectionist. I was ahead something like 4–0 late in a game, and before the game he had told me 'Make Walker Cooper hit your fastball. As hard as you throw, he'll fly out to center field.' Well, I got smart, and I threw Cooper a curve, and he hit it into the seats. I eventually won the game 4–1. And in the clubhouse after the game, Leo was so mad I threw Cooper a pitch he told me not to throw him that he threw a chair at me.

"Another time I was pitching, and there was a little slow roller to first base, and I was tardy covering first base, and the runner was safe and a run scored, and eventually it was the winning run. I got beat 2 to 1. After the game he started throwing things at me. Threw a shoe at me. He couldn't accept any mental errors. I had pitched a helluva game, but I had lost because of a mental error, which he couldn't accept. The other players had to grab him from getting at me he was so angry.

"Leo wasn't much loved, but we knew what he was trying to do, and we respected him. Leo was for his players. If you were having salary problems—and I had a couple of good years and I would ask for X amount of dollars and Mr. Rickey would say, 'No, we're not going to give that to you'—I would go to Leo, and he would say to you, 'Boy, I think you deserve this,' and he'd tell you what he thought you should get. Twice he said he thought I deserved the amount I was asking for, and he went and got it for me.

"Listen, I did some things to Leo. I started that '48 season terribly. I started out 2–5 after being the opening day pitcher, and I was supposed to do everything correct, and I was really bad. After my fifth loss, Leo said to me, 'You'll never pitch for me again as long as you live.' He said, 'I don't care if Rickey loves you, you're finished with me. I'm gonna send you so far an air mail stamp won't find you. I don't want anything to do with you. We're finished.'

"I was scared to death. I was rooming with Ralph Branca, and Ralph kept saying, 'Forget about it, you know how he is.' I said, 'I can't forget this.' I was supposed to be his best pitcher. Four days later we were playing a doubleheader in Philadelphia on July 4, and for some reason we had used up all our pitchers, and Leo came to me and said, 'All right, I'm giving you one more chance. You're gonna pitch the second game. We'll see what happens.' Well, I pitched a two- or three-hitter and won 4–0, pitched a magnificent game. Then, as I said, I reeled off four or five in a row, and then Leo left the club and went over to the Giants. But Leo had scared me, because when he said something, he meant it. Circumstances dealt that he had to use me, and luckily I got it all together.

"A lot of players didn't like Leo and liked Burt Shotton. I was anti-Shotton. I thought the game got by him, and I didn't like the cute things he did, like not wearing a uniform on the bench. I didn't think he gave his coaches enough authority, and Burt and I had special problems. Ralph Branca and I roomed together, and we were having a lot of success, and maybe it was because we were so young, but we always had a lot of fun when we were playing, and Shotton didn't kinda go for that. See, you could have fun with Leo. Leo was strict, but you could have fun with him. And Leo acknowledged the fact that you were pitching well—he certainly let you know it if you were pitching poorly. But Shotton was cold and indifferent. Maybe my personality required a manager who'd pat me on the back or kick me in the ass, but Shotton did neither, and to me, with the ballclub, with those fans at Ebbets Field, he never fit in.

"Shotton may have won in '47 and in '49, but it was Leo's club. Leo put that club together."

Despite his wildness, Rex Barney had remained an integral part of Leo's plans. Ironically it was after Durocher left that he regained his control for a while, and on September 9, 1948, pitched a no-hitter to beat Leo's Giants, 2–0.

REX BARNEY: "I had thrown a one-hitter at the tail end of 1947, and then I threw another one in 1948. The funny thing about that second one: We were playing in Philadelphia against the Phillies, and it was a night game. I was ahead 1–0 in the fifth inning, the Braves hadn't gotten any hits, and it started raining very hard. I was twenty-three years old at the time, and I kept pacing up and down in the dugout, saying, 'Let's get the damn game started.' Mr. Rickey, who had come down from the stands to sit in the dugout to get out of the rain, said, 'Son, what are you worried about? If they call the game off, we win it, and you've pitched a no-hitter. We've got five innings in.' I was too dumb to understand all that.

"Anyway the game resumed. In the second inning, I had loaded the bases with two outs, and Granny Hamner hit a line shot into center field. Duke Snider came running in, and he made the damnest catch I've ever seen in my life, sliding on his belly and coming up with the ball. Then I got through the third and fourth and fifth, and contrary to what any pitcher tells you, every pitcher knows when he's throwing a no-hitter. It's just like somebody who tells you he's not scared when he's being shot at in the war. That's baloney. You're scared as hell. We came to the seventh inning, and Ralph Caballero pinch hit. Probably the worst hitter in baseball at that time. And he hits a little looping ball into center field. I look around quick. There were two outs. And Duke starts back and then comes running in, and the ball hit his glove about a foot off the ground and dropped out. The official scorer gave him a hit. Well, I went through the rest of the night and ended up with a one-hitter.

"After the game Snider came up to me and said, 'Rex, I'm so sorry. You could have had a no-hitter. It's my fault.' I said, 'Duke, it's not your fault.' He forgot that in the second inning he had made the most spectacular catch in the world to not only save a hit but to save the game, because the Phils had had the bases loaded.

"One week later we're playing in the Polo Grounds, and Pee Wee and Duke and Carl Erskine, who Rickey had just brought up from Ft. Worth, and I met at the Gondola Restaurant in downtown Brooklyn, right across from the Brooklyn Conservatory of Music, and we car-pooled over. It was my turn to drive, and it had rained all day long. Pee Wee is saying, 'You know something, Rex, if you're ever gonna pitch a no-hitter, you're gonna do it this year.' I said, 'Pee Wee, I'm running out of time. I only have a month to go.' He said, 'Yeah, but the last seven or eight games you've gone seven, eight innings before people got hits.' My innings-to-hits ratio was unbelievable [193 hits in 246.2 innings]. I said, 'Pee Wee, we're not even gonna play.'

"We got to the Polo Grounds, and we didn't take batting practice or infield or nothing because of the rain. We were supposed to play at eight, and the park was jammed. I was sitting by that famous window in the visitor's clubhouse looking out onto the stadium, and Charley DiGiovanni, who was the batboy for the Dodgers, asked me if I wanted a hot dog. 'No,' I said, 'in case we're gonna play.' He said, 'We're not gonna play.' I said, 'I know we're not.' He said, 'Have a hot dog.' So I did. Because there was no way we were going to play that game.

"And lo and behold, the ground crew starts taking the canvas off the field. I see the Giant pitcher going to warm up, and I went up to Shotton, and I asked him if Bruce Edwards could catch the game. Bruce and I were very close. We lived together in Brooklyn, shared an apartment. I said, 'Burt, how 'bout letting Bruce catch tonight.' He said, 'Rex, Bruce can't throw.' Bruce had hurt his arm. I said, 'Please let him catch.' Burt said, 'If he does, you gotta hold the runners close. He can't throw. You know that.' I said, 'Just let him catch. Campy's got a cold,' which he did. Burt gave in.

"I found out later that Eddie Brannick, the traveling secretary for the Giants, was on his way to call the game off when he saw the ground crew taking the canvas off. Because of the big crowd, he decided to give it a try. So it had stopped raining, like it always does just before the game, and when I went out to warm up, I started throwing, and Bruce said, 'Damn, you're really throwing hard.' I said, 'I know it. There's no way I'll get beat tonight.' He said, 'I agree with you.' Then he said, 'How come I'm catching?' I said, 'I asked for you.' He said, 'I appreciate that.' And with Bruce catching, I pitched a no-hitter.

"That night in the first inning I had the bases loaded and one out. Jackie had made an error. But Willard Marshall hit into a routine double play. I made an error in the second inning, and I walked two batters. But from the second inning on I didn't allow a runner. It rained around the fifth inning, and then it started raining again in the ninth inning, but there was no way they were going to call off the game in the ninth inning. I'm ahead 2–0, I have a no-hit, no-run game, so we were going to play, and the last hitter of the game is Whitey Lockman, who just wore me out. He buried me. But I had gotten him out three times before. So Bruce came out to me and he said, 'What do you want to do?' I said, 'We'll just throw as hard as we can.' By then I didn't even know where the hell I was 'cause I was so excited. From the seventh inning on, even the Giant fans, as much as they hated the Dodgers, had been rooting for me. Lockman came up, and I thought, 'Dear God, how in the hell? Why do I have to face him?' So I just threw hard, and he popped up. Bruce caught the ball for the last out, and I remember I must have jumped twenty feet straight up in the air off of that mound. I'd never been so happy in my life. And when I came down, Jackie was the first guy to grab hold of me, to embrace me, and Pee Wee came over and said, 'See, I told ya it was a matter of time.'

"We started running toward the center-field clubhouse in the Polo Grounds, and the first Giant to meet me was Durocher. It was funny, because all the time when I would go up to the plate in the Polo Grounds, I could hear Leo razzing me. He'd be so close, and Leo would say, 'We'll get you. I can hit you, for Christ sake. You're the world's worst. You never could pitch.' But as soon as the game was over, it was a different story. He said, 'You skinny son of a bitch. Why'd you have to do it to me?' He said, 'I'm your greatest fan. Why did you do it to me?'

"I was a smart-ass kid because I had so much talent, and later that season I was pitching against the Cubs, and I had another no-hitter going into the top of the eighth. I said to Ralph Branca, 'I'm going to pitch another no-hitter.' Ralph said, 'What? Why do you talk like that?' I said, 'Ralph, I know every hitter. I have six more hitters to face and there's only one guy, Phil Cavarretta, who I have to worry about.'

"So I get the first two guys out in the eighth, and Cavarretta's the hitter. Now, when a pitcher has a reputation for being wild, the batter ordinarily takes a couple of pitches. Campanella calls for a curveball, and I shook him off, 'cause I figure Cavarretta's got to be taking. I'm gonna throw him a fastball, and I'll be ahead of him, and then I can do whatever I want. I threw a fastball down the middle, and he hit a line shot into right field for a single. Campy didn't say a word. It was one-two-three in the ninth, and I ended up pitching a one-hitter. As I was walking off the mound, Campanella said, 'Don't you ever shake me off again. You know I'm smarter than you are. And I've always been smarter than you are. And I'll always be smarter than you are. Pitchers don't know a Goddamn thing. That's why they have catchers.' "

If Barney had continued pitching as he had, he perhaps would have been compared to the Fellers, the Koufaxes, and the Nolan Ryans. But on the final day of the 1948 season, just weeks after pitching the no-hitter, Barney slid into second base and broke his leg in two places.

REX BARNEY: "I was pitching against Robin Roberts again, and I was ahead in the game, and this is a funny story: I walked off the field, and even though my ankle was bothering me, I actually pitched the next inning, but then the pain was so bad I couldn't handle it. It was just two cracks, and the next day I went to the doctor, and I was in a cast from October through January.

"In 1949 I won nine ballgames, but from then on, by my own admission, I never had the same motion, never had it again. I never got into the same flow, and in baseball everything is rhythm. And I can tell you now that there were times when I felt I was really finished. I couldn't throw a strike no matter what I did. I can admit to my problems now. I couldn't then. I thought of committing suicide. I thought the world was over. I was what, twenty-seven, twenty-eight years old, and I was finished in baseball. And looking back, I really don't know what it was that held me together. Maybe personal pride.

"I went to a psychiatrist. Mr. Rickey sent me to a psychiatrist. I went to two of them. I went to the Menninger clinic in Topeka, Kansas, which is the psychiatrist headquarters of the world. I would talk to them for an hour, and they'd say, 'Christ, you're saner than we are.' Going to a psychiatrist didn't bother me. Rickey was probably the only genius in all baseball. He went to a lot of lengths outside of baseball, and if a guy was having problems, he would do anything to try to straighten the problem out. If a player was having problems, the first thing he would ask him was, 'Are you having family problems? Are you having wife problems? Are you having children problems? Is it something off the field?' He said to me, 'You have more talent than anybody we got, but there's something wrong. There's something penned up in there. There's something causing all this. And what is it?' And he would try to get to it.

"To this day I don't know what went wrong. Was it the injury? I don't know. Physically I was all right. The only knock I ever got, and this was from Rickey, and I'd get it from psychiatrists, who'd say, 'You're overbright, you're overintelligent, you're overarticulate for what you're doing.' But then I'd come back with, 'Then explain to me why I had so much success in such a short time. Why could I put it all together at such a young age?'

"To this day people say, 'Now that you know so much about yourself and baseball, what would you do to correct that?' Hell, if I had known that, I would have pitched ten more years in the big leagues. My only regret, and I don't have many—I was a major league ballplayer, which is what I had wanted to be my whole life, and it's been good to me this very day—the only regret I have, and I know this more than anyone, is that I never lived up to my potential. I know that. I know now as we sit and talk, and I can't think of a better word, that I was awesome. I really was. I was scary. I didn't know it then. But I'd see other pitchers pitch, and I'd watch them throw, and I'd say, 'Damn, that guy throws harder than any pitcher I've ever seen,' and guys like Pee Wee or Campanella or Jackie would say, 'Rex, nothing like you threw. There's no comparison. They're nothing compared to you.'

"Sandy Koufax and I have become friends over the years. He pitched after I did, and one of the first times I met him, after he had established himself as the star he was, he said, 'I wanted to meet you for so long. I used to go see you pitch when I was a little kid. For years at Vero Beach, they'd say, 'You have a Rex Barney fastball.' He said, 'I always wanted to know what that was.' I said, 'Well, you got it, but you got control of it, and that's the difference.' That's the whole difference. During Sandy's first four or five years, he was as bad as I was, but then he got it together.

"Me, I was just getting it together, but then I broke my leg, and that was it. But I don't use that as an excuse. I don't use anything as an excuse. If I had to do it over again, I don't know what I'd do. I have no idea. I have no conception what I would do. I don't know. But I'd like to try it. I would like to try it just one more time."

The end of Rex Barney's career in professional baseball came in 1950 when he was pitching against Asheville, North Carolina. Asheville was low on the Dodger farm team totem pole, but the Dodgers were desperately trying to find a league where Barney could tame his wildness and get batters out.

* * *

JOEL OPPENHEIMER: "As the Dodgers made their swing north at the tag end of spring training 1950, Barney was scheduled to pitch against the team's Asheville farm club. Rex was told that as long as he did well, he'd stay on the roster. Screw up, and he was gone. The first few innings he was superb, but in the fourth he was wild: He hit a batter, and then he gave up a towering, massive triple. On the next pitch, Barney wound up and threw one of his classics—about twenty feet over the catcher's head. Rex dropped his glove to the mound and with his head bowed, walked off. He took himself out. He knew it was over."

REX BARNEY: "I don't remember a great deal about that because that was when I was really down on myself. All I remember about that game was that I couldn't get the ball over. Listen, it's not easy when you think you're a man, you're twenty-seven years old, and you go back to the hotel, and you just cry yourself into oblivion. I was never a drinking person. I really don't know what it means to drink. I've never smoked. But I shed many tears. Serious tears. And I'm not proud of it now. I wasn't proud of it then. But I can remember thinking of jumping off buildings, bridges, doing away with myself. I couldn't stand it anymore. I couldn't stand all that media, all the people in my business constantly asking, 'What's wrong? Why can't you throw a strike?' Laughing at you. I don't know why. I'm sitting here right now telling you I don't know why. I wish I did. It would be nice to have an answer. To this day when I go to the ballpark, the young kids will ask me, 'Could you really throw hard?' I tell them, 'Yes, I could.' And then they ask, 'Well, what happened?' I still don't know what to tell them."

7

Brooklyn Against the South

Branch Rickey had arranged in 1947 for the Dodgers to train in the Caribbean and in Central America to protect Jackie Robinson. The next year he had them train in the Dominican Republic, and on the way north tested the mood of the South by scheduling several games in some of the smaller cities, such as Macon, Georgia, and Asheville, North Carolina.

By 1949 Rickey felt bold enough to schedule a series of Dodger exhibitions in the capital of Dixie, Atlanta, Georgia. As early as February, when the Dodgers began setting up spring camp in their new Vero Beach complex, the Ku Klux Klan began sending death threats. These threats continued through the early spring.

ROY CAMPANELLA: "We were going to play the Atlanta Crackers in the Southern League a weekend series, Friday, Saturday, and Sunday, and Mr. Rickey had advised us, 'If you get any threats, please bring them right to me.' So we were in Vero Beach when we got a telegram from a wizard of the Ku Klux Klan in Atlanta that said: 'If you come to Atlanta, we'll kill you. We'll shoot you out on the field.'

"So we gave the telegram to Mr. Rickey, and he contacted Dr. Martin Luther King, and Dr. King said, 'Definitely see that Campanella and Robinson come to Atlanta and play.' "

Rickey and Robinson had been getting death threats for three years by now, and there was no question in their minds: The Dodgers were going to play the games, and Robinson would be stationed at second, and Campanella would be behind the plate.

The Ku Klux Klan didn't scare Jackie. He never showed any fear. He would walk out onto the field as brazenly as he could, his head high, defiant. If he had a cop or bodyguard next to him, he'd bark, 'Get away from me,' and he'd stand out there by himself, knowing how vulnerable he was to any cracker madman sick enough to want Robinson dead. Robinson had immense courage. Campanella never flinched either, going out knowing there might be a sniper measuring his broad back with number 39 on it through the hairs of a telescopic sight.

When *New York Post* columnist Jimmy Cannon learned of the death threats, he telephoned the head of the Klan, Dr. Samuel Green, an Atlanta dentist. His subsequent column showed Cannon at his best:

> I put the call in, person to person, for Dr. Samuel Green, a dentist, in Atlanta, Ga.
>
> "Hello, this is Dr. Green," the voice answered, small and blurry with the slowness of the region.
>
> "Is this Dr. Green, the Grand Dragon of the Ku Klux Klan in Georgia?"
>
> "Yes, I am," he replied.
>
> "Are you still trying to stop Jackie Robinson and Roy Campanella from playing with the Dodgers in Atlanta?"
>
> "Yes," he said, making it sharp and not drawling . . .
>
> "Do you go to ballgames now?"
>
> "As often as I can," Green said.
>
> "Who was your favorite baseball player?"
>
> "Ty Cobb," he said . . .
>
> "Suppose Cobb was as good as he was and was a Negro?" I asked. "Would he still be your favorite?"
>
> "I don't know," the Kleagle answered. "I'm not a Negro. In those days there were no Negroes on white teams. If people in Brooklyn want them to play, that's all right. Colored players will bring ill will or ill good in the South."
>
> I asked him if he were talking as the head of the Klan of Georgia.
>
> "As the head of the Klan and as a private citizen," he said. . . .
>
> I explained that Robinson and Campanella were big league ball players by their skills alone.
>
> "If Brooklyn wants them to play, that's all right," he said. "But when in Rome you do as the Romans do."
>
> "Isn't this an anti-American attitude?"
>
> "No, sir," he said.
>
> I asked him how the presence of Negroes on a ball field would offend the people of Georgia.
>
> "Just the simple reason they're breaking down the traditions of Georgia," he answered. "We also have laws against it. . . ."
>
> I told him that the action he was taking against Robinson and Campanella was typical of Hitler's Germany.
>
> "No sir," he said. "You Northern carpetbaggers stir up trouble . . . Northern misguided friends stir up the trouble. We get along fine otherwise.
>
> "As long as they stay in their place," Green said, "we get along fine. You don't know the South or you wouldn't have such ideas about the South. You call Negroes mister to their faces and don't feed them. We look after them. I don't care how you feel. God made people white for a purpose and black for a purpose. We're good to them, but your Yankee newspapers never say anything about that."
>
> . . . I asked him if he thought the Klan were a subversive organization.

"Subversive," Green said laughing. "My people have been in this country 400 years."

"Do you think a Negro can be a real American?"

"I know he can," he said, making it a big statement.

"But a real American can't play baseball in Atlanta," I said.

"Well, what are you going to do?" he asked. "I got a home. Do I have the right to invite people to my home?"

"We're not talking about your home," I said. "We're talking about the Atlanta ball park."

"The ball park is supported by the people of Atlanta," Green answered.

"Do Negroes go to ball games in Atlanta?"

"Sure," Green answered. "They have a section."

I explained they paid to go in. They supported baseball in Atlanta, too; but they were not being consulted about seeing Robinson and Campanella.

"They don't have to go there," was Green's amazing reply. . . .

"Can a Negro be a real man in your opinion?"

"I know some of them," Green said, "but smart Negroes tell them to keep their racial strain and keep it black."

"What has a ball game got to do with racial strains?" I asked.

"It's a question of mixing racial strains on the same baseball team," he said. "I'm brutally frank."

I hung up and took a bath. I stayed in the tub a long time.

ROY CAMPANELLA: "When we got to Atlanta we went to Dr. King's home and had dinner with him and stayed with him just about the entire trip. He told us, 'Don't worry about these threats. You carry on just as you've been doing. That's the greatest thing for our country.'

"At the ballpark we couldn't totally dismiss the threats from our minds. They wouldn't let the blacks sit in the grandstand. They made 'em all sit on the banks of the outfield with a cushion. Jackie was playing second base, and I was catching, and I told Jackie jokingly, 'You've got it made. You're playing second base. All you have to do is run into center field, and you'll be safe. I have to run all the way from home plate.' "

But Martin Luther King had been right all along. The threats turned out to be empty. On April 10, 25,221 baseball fans flooded the bleachers and grandstands of Ponce de Leon Park in Atlanta. Of that number 13,885 were Negroes. There wasn't a single episode of violence. The final two games were also played without incident.

Sam Lacy wrote in the *Baltimore Afro-American:* "The state of Georgia accepted its inter-racial baptism with grace and bearing. Immersed in the waters of liberalism, its head anointed with the oil of democracy, Georgia came up smiling. The Great Experiment is over, and none of the principals is any the worse for it."

Yet despite the pioneering of the Dodgers, some things would remain the same for many years. Tradition would not die easy.

The Real Jackie

For two years in the major leagues, Jackie Robinson in silence swallowed all the punishment one man could possibly absorb. He had been cursed, vilified, abused, slandered, and reviled. Pitchers had thrown at his head, his knees, and his heart, and opponents had tried to make a tic-tac-toe board on his legs with their spikes. Because he was a Negro. And throughout, with more self-control than one man had any right to exhibit, Robinson kept looking the other way, acting as Papini had preached and as he had promised Branch Rickey.

Toward the end of the 1948 season, for the first time, Robinson displayed the quick temper known to his Negro League teammates. One umpire, Walter "Butch" Henline, proved himself to be a bigot. Robinson knew it and so did his teammates. From the beginning Henline had called every close pitch against Robinson. In this one game in a crucial situation, the Dodger pitcher threw a perfect strike, and Henline called it a ball. Catcher Bruce Edwards and coach Clyde Sukeforth argued vehemently and were thrown out of the game, and when the criticism from the Dodger bench continued, Henline defensively yelled over, "I'm trying to do a good job out here." From the dugout in his squeaky high-pitched whine, Robinson yelled back, "Somebody ought to try." Henline kicked him out too, Robinson's first ejection.

By the spring of 1949, Robinson decided that there was no longer a need for him to play Uncle Tom. He had paid his dues, and there were enough blacks in the majors for the trend to not be reversed.

REX BARNEY: "It was spring training 1949, and there was a little get-together in the clubhouse with the guys who had been there for a while, and Jackie said, 'I realize there are some people here who don't like me. I don't like them any more than they like me. I know there are a lot of players in the league who have knocked me down, spiked me, done these things to me, and I put up with it. But I am convinced I am a major league ballplayer. That's what I'm here for, to play baseball. And from this point on, I take nothing from no one, on this team or on any other team, not from umpires or anyone else.' And from then on, he asserted himself. From 1949 on he was what he wanted to be."

RACHEL ROBINSON: "What is distorted in the legend about the relationship between Jackie and Mr. Rickey is that people didn't understand the collaborative nature of it, even though Jack was always the son, Mr. Rickey the father. People have a need to think of Rickey, and this is what racism is all about, as being the dominant person and having manipulated Jack as though he were some kind of puppet. To this business of Mr. Rickey's saying after two years, 'Okay, Jack, now the wraps are off, you can be yourself,' well, that didn't happen. Jack didn't need Rickey to signal that. Jack knew when things were settled down enough so that he could take that chance, and Rickey was never officious with Jack, never the arrogant white man, nor was he paternalistic. Mr. Rickey was always available, and he was careful about how he approached Jackie, and it became a learning experience for him as well. He would say to Jack, 'I'm learning from this.' He had made himself a partner in it. It was 'our' enterprise. It was not 'my enterprise and you're doing the acting.' "

Robinson not only told his teammates how he felt, but he was brave enough to announce it publicly. He was quoted as saying, "They better be rough on me this year, because I'm sure gonna be rough on them." For that statement, Commissioner Happy Chandler called him into his office. Proving that he intended to fight back, Robinson responded to the meeting with Chandler by asking whether Chandler would have said anything had it been Ty Cobb or another white player making the statement.

When Robinson came into St. Louis on the first road trip, he demanded that the Jim Crow arrangement at the Chase Hotel end. He wanted to stay at the Chase with the white players. Roy Campanella disagreed.

ROY CAMPANELLA: "We were playing in St. Louis, and the management of the Chase Hotel, where the Dodgers stayed, sent word to our secretary that the black players could stay at the hotel if they stayed in their rooms. They weren't allowed to eat in the dining room or stay in the lobby or go in the swimming pool. So now, between the black players, Robinson, Newcombe and myself, we had a meeting. We said, 'The majority, whatever it is, we'll go with that.' I said, 'Personally, I don't like it. If I can stay at a hotel but can't eat with my teammates or walk around in the hotel or feel free, I'd rather not stay there until they give me the privileges of my teammates.' And Newcombe felt the same way. Jackie didn't feel that way. And not that we fell out about it, but we wouldn't stay at the hotel. Jackie stayed there, and Newcombe and I went to a black hotel and stayed there."

Passionately Jackie told Campanella that it was important that they stay at the Chase, that in the future other black players could stay there, that to win, Robinson said, we have to start somewhere.

Campy told Robinson: "I'm not a crusader."

Campy may have felt the schism hadn't caused bad feelings, but when Robinson wanted something badly enough, he became resentful if he didn't get it. When Campy turned him down, he never forgave Campanella.

One time when reporters asked Robinson what he thought of churches and synagogues in the South being bombed in protest against the Supreme Court ruling on school segregation, Robinson answered that those people were "sick" and that the federal government should do everything in its power to prosecute them. The writer interviewing Robinson told him that Campanella had observed that the way to prevent such incidents was for blacks to "stop pressing to get too far too fast." Robinson said he felt sad when he heard that.

JACKIE ROBINSON: "Campy was, after all, a father, just as I was. If I had a room jammed with trophies, awards, and citations, and a child of mine came to me into that room and asked what I had done in defense of black people and decent whites fighting for freedom—and I had to tell that child I had kept quiet, that I had been timid, I would have to mark a total failure in the whole business of living."

For the rest of his career, Robinson spoke out. One time he appeared on a television show called *Youth Wants to Know,* and in answer to a question, he accused the Yankee organization of being bigots, which of course they were. The Yankees didn't bring a black to New York until 1954—a full seven years after Robinson joined the Dodgers. But the Yankees quickly denied Robinson's charges and accused Robinson of being a troublemaker.

RACHEL ROBINSON: "Jack took those risks because he always thought he was right. Even when he was wrong, he felt he was right. He used his athletics as a political forum. He never wanted to run for office, but he always wanted to influence people's thinking."

On July 18, 1949, Jackie Robinson was invited by Congress to testify before the House Un-American Activities Committee. It was during the "Red Scare," the time when Russia stole American plans for the atomic bomb, when the patriotism of citizens was being called into question. Public employees were being forced to sign loyalty oaths to keep their jobs, and anyone who had ever been a member of a left-wing organization found himself subject to intense pressure to either reveal the names of fellow travelers or be fired from his job. Egged on by Wisconsin Senator Joseph McCarthy, the House Un-American Activities Committee was out to do its patriotic duty to expunge and punish all subversives, regardless of how flimsy the evidence.

In the face of American hysteria against anything even faintly pink, American singer and actor Paul Robeson proclaimed that American Negroes would not fight in a war against Russia and stated that blacks would have more freedom in Russia than they had in America. At this time Robeson was living in Paris, where he had moved in 1931 to avoid American discrimination.

Negro FBI agent Alvin Stokes approached Robinson at the request of Georgia Congressman John Wood and asked him to come to Washington. Robinson was concerned that Robeson's statements would discredit Negroes as a race in the eyes of whites, and so he decided to go.

In his testimony before HUAC, Robinson sought to walk a fine line. He denounced Communism while at the same time condemning American racism. Robinson told the committee:

> I am a religious man. Therefore I cherish America where I am free to worship as I please, a privilege which some countries do not give. And

> I suspect that nine hundred and ninety-nine out of almost any thousand colored Americans you meet will tell you the same thing.
>
> White people must realize that the more a Negro hates Communism because it opposes democracy, the more he is going to hate the other influences that kill off democracy in this country—and that goes for racial discrimination in the Army, and segregation on trains and buses, and job discrimination because of religious beliefs or color or place of birth. . . . We can win our fight without the Communists, and we don't want their help.

But for Robinson, in retrospect, his appearance was an embarrassment, though he was roundly applauded by white America.

In 1972, writing about his HUAC appearance more than twenty years after the fact, Robinson said, "I have grown wiser and closer to painful truths about America's destructiveness. And I do have an increased respect for Paul Robeson who, over the span of that twenty years, sacrificed himself, his career, and the wealth and comfort he once enjoyed because, I believe, he was sincerely trying to help his people."

On September 2, 1949, the Westchester County war veterans arranged an anti-Communist demonstration in conjunction with Paul Robeson's concert appearance at Peekskill. Three days later Robeson appeared, and even before the concert began, protesters began stoning the buses bringing the concert-goers. The drivers fled from their vehicles, leaving their passengers stranded and stationary, and the police conveniently disappeared. Scores of men, women, and children were injured. It was a dark day in a divided America.

Five days later, before a game at Ebbets Field, the Queens County Catholic War Veterans gave Robinson an award for appearing before HUAC and answering Robeson.

The citation read: "By his voluntary appearance and by his firm stand against communism," Robinson had "assured the whole nation of the unswerving loyalty of the American Negroes and has earned the gratitude and commendation of the whole American people."

Robinson accepted the award—*under* the Ebbets Field stands.

Robinson had made the transformation from Negro ballplayer to Negro spokesman, and a lot of folks didn't like it.

JACKIE ROBINSON: "I learned that as long as I appeared to ignore insult and injury, I was a martyred hero to a lot of people who seemed to have sympathy for the underdog. But the minute I began to answer, to argue, to protest, the minute I began to sound off—I became a swellhead, a wise guy, an uppity nigger. When a white player did that, he had spirit. When a black player did it, he was 'ungrateful,' an 'upstart,' a 'sorehead.' "

One sportswriter who consistently ignored the pressures Jackie was under was Dick Young. Young had been Robinson's primary champion prior to his coming to the Dodgers, but Young could not abide the fact that Robinson preached racial politics. Young felt that ballplayers should keep politics to themselves and talk baseball. Robinson refused to accept that. He insisted on expressing his views on social issues. Friction resulted.

ROGER KAHN: "Though I didn't think so, Jackie felt that Young was bigoted. I remember we were in Philadelphia, and Robinson criticized Young for a piece he wrote, and Young threw a tantrum. In front of the whole dugout, he screamed, 'Ever since you went to Washington,' meaning the Robeson testimony, 'your head's been swollen.' Robinson screamed back at him, 'You're a bigot. I say you're a bigot, and if the shoe fits, you got to wear it.' And Young is shouting, 'Your head has been swollen since you went to Washington.' And Robinson is coming back with, 'If the shoe fits, wear it.' "

Jackie was not an easy man to get along with, even if he wasn't fighting with a person. He acted aloof toward most of the writers, except for those he though were for civil rights. Jackie had an outlook broader than most of the sports reporters or the other players. Where Carl Furillo would have some guy named Tex who owned a pizza parlor just off Eastern Parkway as his guest in the Dodger clubhouse, Robinson would have CBS broadcaster Edward R. Murrow, which in itself was a courageous political act during a period when the red-baiting Senator McCarthy and Murrow were battling each other to the death.

IRVING RUDD: "I've been with some real tough guys in my lifetime. I've been with Rocky Marciano. I've been with the boxer Bummy Davis, who was as tough a guy as you'd ever want to know, and yet I say that if I had to go down a dark alley with one guy, if I had to make a choice, that man's name was Jackie Robinson.

"I'll give you the best example. I was very friendly with Edward R. Murrow. I had helped him with a couple of *See It Now* programs, and then when *Person to Person* was formed, the very first interviews were with Gloria Vanderbilt and Roy Campanella, and I set Campanella up for Edward R. Murrow. And that afternoon I remember I said to Roy, 'Hit a home run for Ed so you'll be able to say something good tonight,' and it was a World Series game, and he hit two.

"And so, to relax, once in a while Ed would come around to Ebbets Field. And one day I said to him, 'You're a reporter. You have credentials. You want to say hello to a couple of guys in the locker room?' And he did, and he walked into the locker room, and it was before a game, and on sight the players all knew who he was, a big, towering, Lincolnesque man, and I remember Rocky Bridges off in a corner, a very funny guy with a wad of chaw in his mouth, saying, 'And good luck and good night, Mr. Murrow.'

"And the next day Mike Gavin of the *New York Journal-American,* a non-hustling sportswriter, corners me. God forgive me, the fellow is gone, and after all he was a father and a husband, but he was also a fucking jerk and a pretty good man with the grape too. So Gavin says, 'Hey, Rudd, what are you bringing Commies around to the clubhouse for?' I said, 'What's that, Mike?' He said, 'You're bringing Communists into the clubhouse.' And at that time the *Journal-American* was looking for the guys under the beds, and they were having a tremendous vendetta against Murrow, particularly Jack O'Brien, the TV critic, who was hitting Murrow off the right-field wall every fourth day. And so Gavin began to mouth this anti-Communist stuff, that Murrow was a Red and that he didn't belong in the clubhouse. Gavin said, 'He ain't a writer.' I said, 'You know that writers from *Time* and *Life* and other magazines, people not in the Baseball Writers' Association, do have right to the clubhouse, and he carries a card as a broadcaster reporter, and he certainly has a right to visit the clubhouse.'

"It began getting sticky. I'm the press agent for the club, and Gavin's a guy who writes for a pretty important, influential newspaper. And with that there's this voice in the corner that pops up and says, 'Irving, any time Edward R. Murrow wants to enter the Dodger locker room, dugout, or anyplace else, he's my guest.' It was Jackie. And it got quiet fast. And that's the end of the story. That's where it was at with Jackie."

Big Newk

In 1949, thanks to Branch Rickey's brilliance as a baseball executive, Brooklyn fielded perhaps the greatest squad in its history. Rickey was no stranger to championship teams. As a Cardinal boss, he had made the Redbirds world champs in 1926, with Jim Bottomley, Rogers Hornsby, Chick Hafey, Jesse Haines, and Grover Cleveland Alexander; in 1931 with Bottomley, Frankie Frisch, Hafey, Burleigh Grimes, Ripper Collins, and Pepper Martin; in 1934 with the Gas House Gang, and again in 1942, 1943, 1944, and 1946 with Stan Musial, Terry Moore, Enos Slaughter, the Cooper brothers, Walker and Mort, and Marty Marion. Yet in 1949, when Rickey looked at the Dodger roster, he declared, "This is the best team I have ever been associated with."

Manager Shotton called his infield "the best in the majors," and undoubtedly he was correct. As a fielder Hodges reminded old timers of the smooth-as-silk Highpockets Kelly, and in his first full year as a starter, he drove in 115 runs. At the keystone Robinson and Reese played together as flawlessly as if they had been together all their lives. Either Robinson or Reese could have been voted Most Valuable Player in 1949, though it was Robinson who finally earned the honor. Writer Bill Corum said, "Pee Wee does everything when the griddle is sizzling for the hoe-cakes, and that's my kind of ballplayer." At the beginning of the season, manager Shotton named Reese the team captain, the first since Dolph Camilli.

At third base the taciturn and moody Billy Cox had blossomed. He would stand by the bag holding his old Daviga glove in his right—throwing—hand, and as the pitcher was delivering the ball, he would then slip it onto his left hand and prepare to field. He was fast and very quick, with catlike reflexes, and he had an arm like a cannon, sometimes deliberately holding the ball as the runner ran down the baseline and then at the last moment whipping the ball sidearm to just nip the runner at first. He didn't have the finesse to always get in front of the ball, but nothing got through him. And at bat Cox came

Billy Cox

through in the clutch, and he had decent power. There wasn't a better third baseman until Brooks Robinson came along years later.

In the outfield left field was split among Luis Olmo, back after several years playing in the outlawed Mexican League, Dick Whitman, Gene Hermanski, and anyone else Shotton felt like shuttling in there. In center and right, Duke Snider and Carl Furillo were fixtures. Experts were saying that Snider would soon be a "left-handed Joe DiMaggio," and though he had had great difficulty with the high fastball in '48, in '49 Snider proved the experts correct as he averaged .292, hit twenty-three home runs and drove in ninety-two runs.

Furillo did his job efficiently, and when the dog days of summer made the others tired and listless, it was always Furillo who began to get hot. In the field, the fans were calling him the "Reading Rifle" because he was from Reading, Pennsylvania, and because he had the best arm of any outfielder in the majors. Runners learned it was a grave mistake to run if Carl Furillo had the ball.

At catcher the Dodgers had Roy Campanella. In the majors only Yogi Berra ranked with him. Campy hit for average, hit with power, and behind the plate he was sure-handed, had an excellent arm, and his most important attribute was that he had the respect of his pitchers, who trusted his judgment implicitly.

It was a team with defense and power. In 1930 the Dodgers had set a team record with 122 home runs. Babe Herman had hit thirty-five of them. In 1949 the Dodgers hit 152 home runs. Snider and Hodges each had twenty-three, Campy had twenty-two, Furillo eighteen, and infielders Robinson and Reese each hit sixteen. It was a well-balanced, classic starting lineup.

If there was a weakness, it was the pitching. Branca, Barney, Roe, and left-hander Joe Hatten were the starters. Hatten was thirty-two, Roe thirty-four, but the rest of the staff was young. Newcombe was twenty-three, Erskine twenty-two, Barney was twenty-four, Branca twenty-three, and the two top relievers, Jack Banta and Erv Palica, were twenty-four and twenty-one.

In '49 Barney unexpectedly and unexplainably became erratic. There were games when he walked too many men early and had to be yanked, and there were other games like the one-hitter he pitched against the Cubs. He finished a disappointing 9–8.

Branca, for the third year in a row, began the season like a twenty-game winner. He was 10–1 on July 1st, but he developed pain in the back of his arm. He tried wasting his fastball and getting by on his curve and his change-up, and it was working for him, but then in July the pain became too great, and he went on the disabled list. At the end of the year his record was but 13–5.

Roe, who had been 4–15 at Pittsburgh in 1947 and 12–8 for the Dodgers in '48, became a star. A country guy from Ashflat, Arkansas, Roe would entertain the other players with his hillbilly stories and southern aphorisms. "It was raining like a cow pissing on a flat rock," he would say. On the mound he was an artist to watch. For some reason the Dodgers rarely scored any runs when Roe pitched, so you knew it would be a low-scoring game with many ground balls and double plays, and you also knew that somehow Preacher would end up the winner. In '49 Roe finished the year 15–6 with a 2.79 earned run average.

With Barney inconsistent and Branca hurt the second half of the year, the Dodgers needed help, and Rickey got it from the Montreal farm club in the hulking form of six-foot-four, 235-pound Don Newcombe, the third black signed by Rickey from the Negro Leagues. Newcombe made his first start on May 22. He pitched a 3–0 shutout against Cincinnati. By July he had eight wins, and in late August and early September, Big Newk, as his teammates called him, pitched three straight shutouts, thirty-and-a-third innings of shut-out ball. In 1949 Newcombe finished the year with a 17–8 record and was named Rookie of the Year. He was also the primary reason why the opposing teams stopped throwing so much at Robinson and Campanella. There was no more race baiting so long as Newcombe was around. To the bigots he may have been just another nigger, but when this guy stood out on the mound with a baseball in his hand, he was one mean nigger. Shotton, for one, was concerned about Newcombe's volatile temperament. He once expressed his feelings that he was afraid Newcombe might "spoil it for the other two fellas," meaning Robinson and Campanella. Shotton's concern might even have kept Newcombe in the minors longer than he deserved.

DON NEWCOMBE: "I was born in Madison, New Jersey, and I lived in Madison until I was five years old. My father was a chauffeur, and for thirty years he drove for the same family, and because of the man's business, we would move from time to time. They lived in Staten Island first and then they moved to Morristown, New Jersey, and then Madison and then Union, New Jersey, and while they were moving, we were moving too. 'Cause my father had to keep that job, and it was a good job during the Depression. And I grew up in Elizabeth, which was where I spent most of my teenage life.

"I had dropped out of high school in my junior year, and I didn't know what I wanted to do, the war was on, and I had the wanderlust. I didn't know what to do with myself. I was seventeen years old, I was going from pillar to post, and I was sitting in the pool room one day, and I was playing checkers with this guy, and he says, 'How would you like to play professional baseball, or at least try out?' I said, 'Man, that would be fine.' He said, 'I know Mrs. Manley,' who owned the Newark Eagles, 'I'll call her and see if she'll give you a tryout.' I said, 'That's fine,' and so he called her, and she said, 'Bring him over and let me talk to him and see what he looks like.' So he took me over to see Mrs. Manley, and she liked me because of my size, and she said, 'Sure, I'll take you to spring training with me,' and she gave me a contract. She needed baseball players, because most of her players, like Monte Irvin and Larry Doby, were in the army. The Eagles needed players. All the teams in the Negro Leagues did.

"In the spring of 1944, she took me to Richmond, where we trained on the campus of the Virginia Union University. Mule Suttles was the manager at the time, and he gave me the chance, and I stayed with the club. I could

Don Newcombe
Dodgers

throw hard, but I was wild, and they gave me the chance, and I made the club. I won seven games that year.

"The one thing I remember about Suttles: Roy Campanella was batting, and he told me to knock Roy down. Here I am, seventeen years old, I don't know what he's talking about, to knock somebody down. So I threw the ball high, but I didn't get it in enough, and Roy hit the ball into the seats in Ruppert Stadium in Newark. Suttles came out to the mound to take me out of the ballgame. He said, 'You'll never make a big league pitcher because you're too Goddamn dumb.' I always remembered that. I had to learn to become a big league pitcher—big league, that is, as far as Negro baseball was concerned.

"The next year the manager was Willie Wells, one heck of a ballplayer, and he came up with a system that he wanted me to try. He said, 'I don't want you to throw a baseball for the first two weeks you're in spring training. All I want you to do is run, just run. I don't want you to touch a baseball. I'll tell you when to pick up a ball.' He said, 'You're so big and strong, I want you to be able to wind up and throw that ball without worrying about hurting yourself. So I want your legs in good shape first.' And for two weeks in spring training, that's all I did, and maybe that's why I developed the habit of liking to run. In fact I loved to run. In spring training, when I wasn't pitching, I would run, and I ran a lot. And that year, I had a good year with the Eagles. Wells said, 'Your legs are your most important part of your body, and the more you run, the stronger your arm will be. You never have to fear injury.' As a result, as hard as I threw, I never hurt my arm in all my baseball career.

"And in the middle of the season, I guess we weren't doing all that well, and they fired him, and they hired Biz Mackey, who was one of the most knowledgeable baseball men at that time that I ever knew, and he was also the catcher, and he was my roommate. We got along famously. He tried to counsel me like a father about taking care of myself and not cursing so much. I used to curse a lot. I guess I still do, but he used to always be on me, on the bus, in the clubhouse, on the field, and in the hotels: 'Newcombe, you gotta stop cursing so much.'

"But at age eighteen I had gone as far as I ever thought I would go. And then Jackie broke the color line in 1947. Branch Rickey and Happy Chandler made it happen. And it was time.

"Very few people know what a magnificent man Jackie Robinson was. Those black ballplayers today have no idea about the man; maybe some of them could care less. But not me. I remember that man and the things that he went through to make it possible for me to do my job, because if he had made mistakes, if he had screwed up, you'd never have seen Roy Campanella and Don Newcombe.

"In 1945 Roy Campanella and I and Monte Irvin and some of the lesser-known black baseball players—Lenny Pearson, Johnny Davis, Len Hooker, Biz Mackey was there, Terrance McDuffy, to name a few—were playing a series of three games against some of the major league all-stars returning from the service: Virgil Trucks, Ralph Branca, Frank McCormick, Goody

Rosen, Clyde Kluttz. We played Friday night in Ebbets Field, Saturday in Ruppert Stadium in Newark, and Sunday in Ebbets Field again, and that's where I pitched. And it was dreary, a rainy day, and we had 10,000 people in the stands, and Biz Mackey started me. I pitched two good innings, and then I hurt my elbow in the third. It wasn't any major injury, but it was enough for me to be taken out of the ballgame with one out in the third inning. I went into the clubhouse, and I remember sitting in the clubhouse crying like a baby because I had hurt my arm. I didn't think I was going to be able to play baseball any more, and Clyde Sukeforth came into the clubhouse and asked me, 'Did I know of Branch Rickey.' I said, 'No. Who is he?' He said, 'Well, he owns the Brooklyn Dodgers baseball club.' I said, 'Oh?' He said, 'Mr. Rickey is contemplating signing a bunch of Negro baseball players who he thinks has ability to play with a Negro team in Ebbets Field while the major league team is on the road. They will be known as the Brooklyn Brown Dodgers, and we want to know if you would like to come over to his office and talk to him tomorrow.' I said, 'You make it worth my while, and I'll come.' He said, 'We'll make it worth your while. You just come over and talk. We'll pay your expenses and make it worth your while if you agree to do what we want you to do.'

"I was making maybe $225 a month playing for Mrs. Manley, and the next day, Monday morning, I went over to Mr. Rickey's office. Clyde Sukeforth had told me how to get there. I rode the subway, went over to his office, and he sat down, and we started talking. Here was this man who I got to know as Branch Rickey sitting behind his desk with a big cigar in his mouth. He had his hat on. He never took his hat off in his office. We talked, and he signed me to a contract to play with the Brooklyn Brown Dodgers, and he gave me a $500 check as a signing bonus, and he said, 'When the team starts, we'll give you a salary. We'll pay you $375 a month, and we'll give you $1,000 in addition to the $500 as a bonus for signing.' When I left that office, that was more money than I had ever had in my life.

"In any case I signed that contract and then went back to New Jersey where I was living, and then one night my wife—my first wife—and I were coming out of a movie theater in Newark, and we stopped to get a newspaper before we caught the bus to come home. Here was a big headline, 'JACKIE ROBINSON SIGNED BY ROYALS.' We wondered who the Royals were. Who are the Royals? It was a Dodger farm team. And there was a picture of Jackie and his wife and Branch Rickey. I said to her, 'Maybe my being signed by the same man, Branch Rickey, maybe there'll be a chance for me.'

"The next day I got a call from Clyde Sukeforth. 'Mr. Rickey wants to talk to you again. Can you come over to Brooklyn?' I said, 'Yeah.' So the next day I got on the subway and went to Brooklyn to see Branch Rickey and Clyde Sukeforth, and while we were talking, he tore up the Brooklyn Brown Dodger contract and signed me to a Brooklyn Dodger organization contract, 'cause Roy had signed the day before to play with the Danville Dodgers in Danville, Illinois. I signed the contract, and he gave me $1,000 more, and I signed a Class-A ball contract, and my salary was $1,700 for the season. And

Roy and I were supposed to go to Danville. But because we were Negroes, we ended up in Nashua, which was the only place that would take us.

"Buzzy Bavasi was the general manager. Walt Alston was the field manager, and I often wonder now, after looking back in retrospect, what would have happened had Buzzy and Walt said they didn't want us. I wonder what would have happened to Roy and me. I guess maybe we wouldn't have played.

"But we went up there, and we played together in 1946. We stayed the whole season because there wasn't anyplace else for us to go, but the next year Roy jumped from Class-B ball right to Triple-A, where he should have started out in the first place. At Nashua, New Hampshire, you didn't have any fences. The stadiums were so big. The only way you could get a home run was to hit between the outfielders. You could hit a ball 400 feet, and the ball would be caught. Roy's year in Nashua he hit thirteen home runs, and that was a lot of home runs for that league. And at Nashua Roy became the first Negro manager in organized baseball. Walt Alston got put out of a game in Lawrence, Massachusetts, and without hesitation he told Roy, 'You manage the team,' and he gave Roy the lineup card. Roy put me in as a pinch hitter in the ninth inning that night, and I hit a home run and won the game for him. So he's got the record of being the first Negro manager in organized baseball. The other players all respected Roy. He was older, twenty-five or twenty-six, and he had had a lot of experience playing in Mexico, in Puerto Rico, in the Negro Leagues, where he was a star, so really it was a bringdown for him to go to Class-B, even though he was making a hell of a lot more money than he made with the Baltimore Elite Giants.

"My first year with Nashua I was 14–4, and the next year I was 19–6. I had to go back another year. I didn't know that Branch Rickey had a stair-step plan to move us up. It was Jackie, then Roy, then me. But see, I didn't know that, and I was a headstrong kid, nineteen years old. Jackie was up with the Dodgers, and he was doing well and became Rookie of the Year in 1947, and I knew that Roy was going to go up, because he had a great year at St. Paul, and he was gonna go next, and then I went back to Nashua, won 19 lost 6, and I led the league in everything. I wanted to be riding the bus, I wanted to be riding the train, and I wanted to be living like Jackie and Roy.

"They told me, 'Man, this is a great life.'

"It was spring training 1947, and Jackie was playing with the Dodgers against the Yankees in an exhibition game. It was Jackie's first game as a Dodger, and I went up to Mr. Rickey's box in Ebbets Field, and I told him that I didn't want to go back to Nashua. I was trying to tell him that I owed the club $1,000 and that I didn't want to go back there because I couldn't afford to pay him back on my Nashua salary. He misunderstood me. He thought I was telling him I just didn't want to go back to Nashua. He said, 'Now you do exactly as I tell you. If you don't want to go, you can have your outright release.'

"I left and got halfway across the ramp and something said to me, 'Go back, stupid, and tell Mr. Rickey what you're talking about. Tell him what you mean about the $1,000. That you can't afford to pay him back. Make him hear you.' I went back, and thank God for that. I said, 'Mr. Rickey, I want your attention for a minute.' And I told him. He said, 'I don't care about the $1,000, Don. Just go back to Nashua. That's all I want you to do. Do what I tell you to do.' I said, 'Okay, I'll go,' and I went back to Nashua. But had I walked out of that ballpark that day and gone back to New Jersey and then gotten my release, I don't know where I would have gone. Heck, I was only going to get $2,500 that year. If I had to pay him back $1,000, how was I going to live?

"After I won nineteen games, he said, 'Now I've got to move you. I can't send you to Ft. Worth; I can't send you to Danville, you know that. You've got to go to Montreal, and that's where you're going.' He said, 'That's what I've been planning for you all along, son. You understand?' I said, 'Well, I'm beginning to understand.'

"In 1948 I played for Montreal. Clay Hopper was the manager, and you've got to remember, he was from Greenwood, Mississippi. A plantation owner. And for him to be put into the middle of that whole morass of change, he had to be a strong man to do that and stay in that job. Clay was always a fair man. Never did he say anything racial. I don't know how he felt inside, but he never showed any of it to his black baseball players. I never heard Jackie say anything derogatory about him, never heard Roy. I don't have anything derogatory to say about him, and I played for him a year and a half. He always treated us fair. And even in Greenwood, Mississippi, when we'd go there barnstorming when the season was over, he would come up, and it wasn't fashionable, either. He put his reputation on the line with his friends in Greenwood, who were out-and-out racists. He'd come up and shake hands with us there on the field in front of all those people. He never showed any negativism about being in Mississippi and shaking hands with niggers. He was a courageous man. I know he took a lot of crap from those racists. He must have, during those years. Many times people asked him, 'Why don't you quit? Why do you stay there?' He didn't need the money. He was sure very wealthy. In cotton, with his plantation. But he loved baseball.

"In May 1949 I was called up to the Dodgers. Mr. Rickey and I got on his little Beechcraft airplane with his pilot at Roosevelt Field, and we flew from Long Island to Chicago, and on the way we picked up Billy Cox in Harrisburg, Pennsylvania. We flew into Chicago to join the Dodgers. I sat up in the cockpit with the pilot. Mr. Rickey and Cox rode in the back of the plane.

"I was in Chicago another day or so, and then we took the train to St. Louis, and in one game we were about eight runs behind, and the manager, Burt Shotton, told me to go down and warm up. He wanted to put me in the game to see what I had. Well, I went into the game, and it sure was a big thrill for me. Here I was in the big leagues, on the field now, and the first hitter that came up I had played against in Montreal. His name was Chuck Diering, and he was with Rochester, and I threw three fastballs by him and struck him out. But then, boy, did they fix me. The next four hitters got four runs, line drive base hits, Musial and Slaughter, Del Rice, and another guy, but there was four of them, and then Clyde Sukeforth came out to take me out of the ballgame. Well, I got my dobber down, and I thought I was on my way back to Montreal. And I recall sitting down at the end of the dugout by myself and feeling damn dejected, I'll tell ya. Burt Shotton came over—he was an old man who always wore civilian clothes and a damn nice man—but I didn't know him. I didn't know anything about him. He came over, and I thought, 'Uh oh. Here it comes. I'm going back to Montreal.' He said, 'How do you feel?' I said, 'I feel fine, Mr. Shotton.' He said, 'You threw pretty good tonight. You gave up some base hits, but you looked pretty good.' I said, 'I guess I'm going back to Montreal, right?' He said, 'The hell you are. You're starting the second game against Cincinnati on Sunday. That's what I'm down here to tell you. How do you feel about that?' I said, 'Fine.' He said, 'Okay, you got it.' And he went back to the other end of the dugout.

"And on Sunday I shut out the Reds 3–0. I'll never forget Jocko Conlon in that game. He must have accused Roy and me eight or ten times of throwing spitballs. Roy said to Jocko, 'What are you talking about? He's a kid, twenty-two years old. What does he know about throwing spitballs?' Jocko said, 'I don't care. It looks like a spitball to me.' He kept examining the balls and examining them and throwing them out, and I never once went to my mouth. It was a curveball, I threw it hard, and it went down, and the hitters were having a helluva time hitting it, and they were complaining.

"As much as Roy helped me, one of the reasons I was as successful as I was had to be Jackie. Because he wouldn't let me—see, I had the tendency to fool around. I had a tendency not to bear down all the time with every pitch, especially if I had a big lead. Give you an example. One day we were in Pittsburgh, and we were leading the Pirates 11 to 0 in the third inning. I had the bases loaded and no outs and Ralph Kiner at bat. And Jackie came over to me and said, 'Do you know one thing? You should go to the clubhouse and take your uniform off and go home, because you don't want to pitch. You've got no business here in the big leagues, Newk. You ought to go home, because here you are fooling around. You have an 11–0 lead, you're gonna fool around and get knocked out of the ballgame, and somebody else is gonna get the win. So why don't you just go home. You don't want to pitch.' And I struck out the side, and we beat the Pirates terribly. But that was the kind of thing he would do.

"In later years he told me, 'I knew that you could be a better pitcher when I made you mad, and I made you mad on purpose.' Many times I wanted to take a punch at him. Shit, Jackie'd kick the shit out of me. He could fight. He was an athlete. Anybody take a punch at Jackie was going to get knocked on his ass. And I knew it. So I wasn't about to try it, that's for sure.

"Now Roy is a different type of man. If you talk about Jackie and Roy, you're mixing apples and oranges. These two are different. And I put Pee Wee in the same category as Roy. Soft-spoken. Gil was in the same category. I'll tell you one thing. You find very few people in the category with Jackie. He knew what to say. A lot of times what he said got him into trouble, but he was the kind of man that if he found out he was wrong, he would apologize, and that's what I loved about him. He wasn't the kind of man who just stuck to his guns after he found out he was wrong, though sometimes it took him a helluva long time to get him to admit he was wrong. Because he always wanted to be right. That's one thing I didn't like about Jackie. He always wanted to be right, and you can't be right all the time. You have to be wrong sometimes. But he would apologize. 'Let's forget about it. Let's go on to something else.' It didn't have to be on a baseball field. In a card game. It could be playing pinochle, bridge, whatever it was, he was aggressive. He was an aggressive horse better. Everything he did was aggressive. We'd go to the racetrack together, and he'd leave me, go over somewhere in the corner by himself. He wouldn't be bothered talking to anybody. He wanted to handicap the horses, and he didn't have time to talk to people. He wanted to be by himself. I don't even know how much he bet. When the races were over, we'd get together again. He was a very complex man. Very.

"In 1949 things hadn't changed to any large degree where you could recognize it. Because they were still stepping on Jackie's foot, and they were still trying to cut Roy's chest protector off him when they slid into home plate with their spikes up in the air. Jackie knew what to do when they came into second base. Right in the mouth where you can catch them between first base in the double play. But that didn't stop pitchers from trying to hit Jackie and Roy in the head.

"And that's where I came in. See, I had a chance to protect Jackie and Roy and the rest of the team, because we have very few pitchers who would knock guys down. Ralph Branca and I, and much later Don Drysdale, when he came up. The others would say, 'I can't throw at them. I don't know how. Somebody else is going to have to do it.' All right. So I would do it. I would throw at them, because they were throwing at our guys. I don't deny it, and I never did. The way they knocked our guys down, the way they hit Roy in the head, the way they hit Carl Furillo, the way they knocked down Duke Snider, if you don't protect your men, you're just not gonna get any runs, and they're not gonna have any respect for you. We were going to be sitting ducks. Nobody's gonna protect us? Come on! Somebody's gotta help us. And it wasn't a racial thing. I knew the guys, Bob Rush of the Cubs, guys like that; Bob would throw at guys, and the way Jackie would steal on him and make a fool out of him, well, Bob would throw at guys. Sal Maglie would throw at guys, and he never denied it, just like I don't. You do whatever's necessary to help your players.

"One day, for instance, in Chicago, they knocked down one of our guys, and it wasn't a black guy, it was Rocky Nelson, because Duke Snider had hit a home run off one of their pitchers. So what do the guys say in the dugout? 'Well, there you are, Newk. What are you gonna do about it?' I said, 'I know what I'm going to do. Every son of a bitch that comes up to the plate with a bat in his hand with a Chicago Cubs uniform on is going on his ass.' And I did it. I didn't hit any of them, but they knew what I was up to. I told Roy to tell them. I said, 'Put your glove behind their head,' and Roy would stand there pounding his glove behind their ear, and he'd say, 'C'mon Roomie, right here.' If he didn't get out of the way it was too damn bad. Seven straight hitters in three innings went on their ass. Every one of them. Ernie Banks came up and said, 'What's he mad at me for?' Campy said, 'You got a bat in your hand. You got a Chicago Cubs uniform on.' Campy told them, 'You're going on your ass, so you better be ready.'

"The umpires didn't call time, not until after the seventh batter. He finally called our manager, Walt Alston, out to the mound, and he said, 'If this guy doesn't stop throwing at these guys, we're gonna suspend you and him.' Walt said, 'They can get along without me, but we can't get along without you. So I'm gonna take you out of the ballgame.' So I got mad at Walt. I said, 'You got as much fucking guts as the umpire got there, Walt,' and I walked off the fucking mound. He fined me $300 for saying that to him. I apologized the next day. I told him I was sorry. But Alston finally had to take me out of the game, 'cause I said, 'I'm going to get all of them. I'm going to get everybody until I make sure I get the right one.' That protects your players, and it breaks that crap up. Because, man, that ball hurts when it hits ya.

"I've never had a teammate tell me I was afraid. There was always that talk about me choking up and being gutless, never won the big ones, but I never had a teammate tell me that I wouldn't protect him with that baseball when it was time for somebody to go on their ass. They were going to go on their ass, and if they didn't go that pitch, they'd go on the next pitch. I'd get him sometime during the sequence of pitches. He had to go on his ass. And I wouldn't pick the eighth-place hitter or the leadoff hitter. I would get the best hitter on the ball club. Del Ennis with the Philadelphia Phillies in 1950. They had a coach named McDonald, a batting practice pitcher and a bench jockey. He'd call us all kinds of niggers, everything. That's what he was there for. In a very distinct voice, I could hear him from the dugout. And one day in Ebbets Field, I'm pitching against the Phillies, and he's calling us all these names, and Jackie comes over to the mound and says, 'Newk, did you hear that son of a bitch over there?' I said, 'Jack, I hear him. I got good ears.' Jack was playing third base. He said, 'What are you going to do about it?' I said, 'Well, when the hitter comes up who's the best hitter on the club, you'll see what happens.' Del Ennis came up, and I buzzed him, and he went down on his ass. Hat went flying, bat went one way, and he got up and picked up his bat, and I said to Jackie, 'All right now. We're ready for a fight.' Jackie said, 'I'm with you. Don't worry about it. Let him come out here.' Ennis turned around and went over to his dugout and said something to that coach in the dugout, and he came back to the plate and struck out, and so some years later I got to play with Del in Cincinnati, and I asked him what he said to the coach when he went over to the dugout. Del said, 'I told that son of a bitch, you leave that big son of a bitch alone out there on that mound, because you don't have to go up there and hit against him. I do, and he's knocking me on my ass for what you're saying to him. Now, if that's your feeling, that's fine, but if you say anything more to him while I'm at bat, I'm gonna pull your fucking tongue out of your head and lay it in your hand. Leave that man alone.'

"And the coach was released from the club. He had lost his effectiveness. What did they need him for, to be a batting practice pitcher? They had him there to call us niggers and all kinds of dirty names. That's why he was there.

But when Del took his effectiveness away from him and shut him up, they got rid of him. They didn't need him any more. I never saw him again."

A Pennant on the Final Day

Despite rookie Newcombe's heroics, the Dodgers trailed the St. Louis Cardinals by a game with four left to play. Then on one rainy but glorious Thursday afternoon in Boston, Preacher Roe beat the Braves, the defending National League champs, by 9–8 in the first game of a doubleheader, and then, as the skies darkened and the rain began to fall, Newcombe pitched a five-inning, game-called-on-account-of-rain shutout, 5–0, to beat Johnny Sain. Weather conditions were so nasty that several Braves lit a bonfire in the dugout. In the Dodger clubhouse, there was the warm glow of being in first place by a game with only two to go, after lowly Pittsburgh upset the Cardinals.

The next day both the Dodgers and Cardinals lost. It was down to the final day. The Dodgers led by one game with one to go. Playing on October 3 at the tiny Baker Bowl, their opponents were the young and talented Phillies. If the Dodgers could get by third-place Philadelphia, they would be National League champions. If they lost and the Cardinals won, it would be on to St. Louis for a repeat of the 1946 National League playoffs.

Rookie star Don Newcombe started for the Dodgers and was staked to a big lead. In the fourth, Newk, who was always vulnerable when the game wasn't close, gave up a three-run home run to Puddin' Head Jones and was relieved by Rex Barney, who pitched well until he got two outs in the sixth and then allowed two runs before manager Burt Shotton took him out.

With the score 7–6 Dodgers and men on first and third with two outs, Shotton brought in a little-publicized, twenty-four-year old rookie named Jack Banta.

Banta stood about six-foot-three, a skinny guy from Kansas who threw sidearm like Ewell Blackwell. He had been a starting pitcher and a star for Montreal in 1947 and 1948, leading the International League in strikeouts both years. In the spring Shotton had needed a reliever and chose Banta to fill that role, and Banta had pitched exceptionally, finishing the season with a 10–6 overall record, 6–2 in relief with three saves. In the end the fate of the Dodgers was in the hands of the emotionless rookie.

With the 30,834 Philly fans screaming for a hit, Banta stepped in to face the number-four hitter in the lineup, outfield star Del Ennis. Ennis was leading the Phils with 25 home runs. He was batting over .300 and had driven in 109 runs. Banta threw a ball and two strikes, then Ennis pulled a single between Reese and Cox, and the score was tied 7–7. Runners were now on first and second. The winning run was only 180 feet from home plate. The next batter was Andy Seminick, the burly Philly catcher. Seminick had homered against Banta the week before at Ebbets Field to beat the Dodgers. The day before Seminick had hit his twenty-fourth home run to help defeat them. Making things more uncomfortable, the scoreboard was announcing that the Cardinals had routed the Cubs.

Jack Banta

* * *

JACK BANTA: "The last game was the whole season, as far as I was concerned. It was a particularly big deal because the week before in Brooklyn I had the identical situation, and I got beat. Two men on base, Seminick up, and I threw him a fastball and he hit it out. So again, two men on, Seminick up, I got two strikes on him, and this time I threw him a curveball, which wasn't a strike, but he swung at it anyway. He was probably guessing fastball, and it was a rather bad pitch, a little low, and he swung at it. You don't know why he swung at it, you can't read his mind, but he swung at it, and we got out of the inning."

Banta didn't give up another hit as he shut out the Phils in the seventh, eighth, ninth, through to the tenth inning, when in the Dodger half of the inning, Pee Wee Reese led off against Ken Heintzelman, who had never lost to the Dodgers, and he looped a single to left. Eddie Miksis sacrificed him to second with a bunt. Rookie Duke Snider came up to bat. It was the same situation in which Snider would find himself for two years in a row: man on second against the Phillies and a single needed to win the game. This time Snider got the run in when he hit Heintzelman's first pitch up the middle. Snider went to second on the throw home. Robinson was then walked intentionally, and Luis Olmo singled past third to score Snider. The Dodgers now led 9–7.

All Banta needed was three outs, and the Dodgers would be National League champions. But Mike Goliat opened the inning with a single, only the second hit allowed by the rookie.

JACK BANTA: "I got the next two batters, and then the next batter was Richie Ashburn. Ashburn could hit home runs in Philly, because they had a short right field. Of course he was better known for being a speed merchant. He hit line drives, got on base a lot, and was extremely fast on the bases. But you still had to be careful with him. I threw Ashburn a fastball, and he flew out to short left field. I was so happy to get the last out and get the thing over with. That was the main thing. Jubilation broke loose. Everyone was so happy. It was a whole year's work all in one shot right there."

The Cards defeated the Cubs, 13 to 5, but it didn't matter. The Dodgers had clinched the pennant against the Phils. Jackie Robinson won the batting title with a .342 average and drove in 124 runs to finish second to Ralph Kiner's 127. In that final game, Robinson stole his thirty-sixth and thirty-seventh bases, and he was named as the Most Valuable Player in the National League. Carl Furillo hit .322, hit eighteen home runs, and drove in 106 runs, and with productive seasons from Hodges, Snider, Campanella, and Reese, the Dodgers scored 879 runs, 113 more than second place St. Louis!

For Branch Rickey and Burt Shotton, it was their second pennant in three years. Across the river Leo Durocher and his Giants finished fifth, twenty-four games back.

For Jack Banta, it was the highlight of a promising major league career that was to last exactly a third of a season more. For a pitcher with such promise, the end was sudden and cruel. Banta awoke one day to discover that the speed was gone. Luck was not to be the strong suit for the three Dodger B's on the pitching staff, Barney, Branca, and Banta.

JACK BANTA: "I had a sore arm when I started the next season. Now one time at Montreal it had been that way for a period of time, but then it came out of it. It was a similar pain, at the front of the shoulder. Then it got in pretty good shape. In fact I started off in '50 4 and 1, and then it just went bad on me again.

"When it went bad in the middle of the season, it didn't hurt. It just didn't have any life to it. I didn't have the good fastball any more. And I was throwing in the dirt, which was highly unusual. Used to be, when I'd get wild, I'd be high.

"But I ruined my record in '50 when I lost two games in two days. I started one of them and lost it, and they put me in relief the next day and I lost it. And then I lost one other one, and then they sent me back to Montreal, which really didn't do me any good, because I couldn't throw there either. But I finished the season at Montreal, and the next spring when I went to camp it was so sore I couldn't throw at all. Course in those days, they didn't have athletic doctors. They assumed it was some kind of a tendonitis type thing. And I never came back. To this day I can't throw a rock. Still hurts in the same place.

"But they sent me down to Ft. Worth to play around and see if it would come back. They were afraid to completely release me, afraid it might come back. They really didn't know what to do with me. Then I went to Class-B one year, pitched a little bit underhand relief, helped coach, then I started scouting one year, then I went to Hornell, New York, Class-D, and managed. Then I went to Shawnee, Oklahoma, and managed three years, and then I went to Great Falls, Montana, managed one year, and then I got a letter from the Dodgers saying, 'There is no place in our organization for you anymore.' That was 1958. Just out of the blue. And that's the last contact I've had with the Dodgers. The letter was from Fresco Thompson. After that I didn't want anything to do with baseball. I went to work for a grocery chain in my hometown of Hutchinson, Kansas. I was in the warehouse, the dock. Unloading trucks.

"I'm still with the same company. I'm in price coordination now. Been with them about twenty-five years. I haven't seen a ballgame since I quit."

Again

LARRY KING: "Herbie Cohen and I had a fight once. It was the only time we ever fought. The Dodgers were playing the Yankees in the Series, and we were comparing the two teams player by player, arguing over who was better. Okay, so we start. Catcher. Campanella or Berra? 'Oh, come on,' I said,

'Campy hit more home runs.' Herbie says, 'Berra's a better clutch hitter.' I said, 'Berra strikes out more.' It's a draw.

"Okay, we go to first base. The Yankees had Joe Collins. We had Hodges. I said, 'Hodges is a better fielder.' Herbie says, 'Collins has a tougher park to hit in.' Hodges would usually get the nod at first.

"Shortstop. Reese or Rizzuto. 'Who was the better team leader?' I'd say. 'How many times would Reese get a single with a man on second?' I'd give him that Rizzuto was the better bunter. I'd say, 'He's a better bunter, but who's better with the bat? Who would you rather have in a hit-and-run situation?' It was a tough choice.

"We came to second base, and I said, 'Jackie Robinson.' And Herbie says, 'George Stirnweiss.' I said, 'What did you say?' He said, 'Stirnweiss.' I said, 'Second base is over, now we go on to third.' And he says, 'Wait a minute. I think Stirnweiss is better.'

"And I went for his neck. We hit the pavement and rolled down the street, banging each other's heads.

"The crowd gathers around, and they're breaking it up, and I remember George Richland, who owned a clothing store in the neighborhood, another guy says to him, 'What are they fighting about?' and Richland says, 'Robinson–Stirnweiss.'

" 'Ah,' says the other guy, 'I understand.' "

This was the third time since 1941 that the Dodgers would be playing the Yankees. In 1941 and then in 1947, the Dodgers had not been successful. Manager Burt Shotton decided that he would begin the 1949 series with the Dodgers' hottest pitcher, rookie sensation Don Newcombe.

Don Newcombe: "I didn't know it until recently that I'm the second rookie ever in the history of baseball, behind Paul Derringer, to start the first game of a World Series. Preacher Roe was supposed to start, but he asked for another day's rest, and Shotton told me I was starting. And people ask me about the best game I ever pitched in my life, and that was the best game I pitched, even though I lost it.

"It was nothing–nothing in the ninth, and Tommy Henrich led off. I had two balls and no strikes on him. Campanella said, 'You missed the first two pitches. Let's give him your best stuff.' And I threw him a curveball. I had a good, sharp-breaking curveball. And I'd throw the same pitch to him today and dare him to hit it again. I'd like to see him hit it again. And he hit it over the right-field fence. That winter we'd go around speaking, and I asked him if he knew what it was. He said, 'No. All I knew, I hit what I saw.' They didn't call him 'Old Reliable' for nothing. And I knew when he hit it that it was gone. I never saw where it landed. I just put my glove in my pocket and walked off the Goddamn field.

"The next time I started [Game Four], I lasted three and two-thirds and lost. But the Yankees looked for everything fast and low from me, and they were a fastball-hitting and low-ball-hitting club."

HAROLD ROSENTHAL: "After the game I walked into the Dodger dressing room, and it was quiet because all the other reporters were in with the Yankees, and there was the Dodger trainer cutting an ingrown toenail out of Newk's big toe. I said, 'What the hell is he doing, Newk?' He said, 'I have an ingrown toenail, and boy, did that hurt.' I said, 'You mean you pitched the opening game of the World Series with an ingrown toenail?' He said, 'Yeah.' He said it didn't start to bother him until he started to pitch."

LARRY KING: "Dodger fans never warmed up to Newcombe. We liked him, and we didn't like him. We didn't think he was a clutch pitcher. For some strange reason, when he lost to the Yankees 1–0 in the first game of the '49 World Series, even though he pitched better than Reynolds, we said he choked."

Preacher Roe won Game Two, also by 1–0. And then the Yankees won three straight. In Game Three it was 1–1 going into the ninth, but the Yankees' Johnny Mize won it with a bases-loaded pinch single, and in Game Four the Yankees' Bobby Brown tripled with the bases loaded to beat Newcombe. Game Five, the finale, was an embarrassment for the Dodgers, as Rex Barney's wildness helped stake the Yankees to a 10–1 lead en route to a 10–6 win. As a team the Dodgers hit .210. After the last game, in the clubhouse the Dodger players expressed their disappointment. They had lost, four games to one, but not a one of them thought the Yankees were a better team than the Dodgers were.

JACK BANTA: "I think man for man we had a better club than the Yankees. They had maybe a little stronger pitching staff. They had Reynolds, Raschi, Lopat, and Page. And psychologically the Yankees were extremely hard to beat. Everyone tried too hard against them and really didn't play their best. And the Yankees go into those games with the utmost confidence because they've been there so many times. They can just relax, and when they finally get the break, they take advantage of it, and all of a sudden they've got you beat."

BILL REDDY: "It was a sad year, even though they had played good ball in '49. We had expected to win the pennat. We figured we would. We always knew we were better than anybody in the National League, but always it came to that last link in autumn, when the Yankees would come in and take all the marbles.

"You said to yourself, 'What the hell is the matter with them? Why can't we beat these guys? What do they have, the magic touch? The evil eye on us?' There was no explaining it. It just seems you played your heart out all year, and then they'd come up against the Yankees, and bam, they'd win the Series."

8

O'Malley Über Alles

Jackie Robinson had done more for Branch Rickey than the Dodger boss ever could have imagined. He had broken the color line, helped the Dodgers to two pennants, and had become an attraction of Ruthian dimensions. As the Dodgers toured the South during the preseason, the team would play an exhibition game in, for instance, Macon, Georgia, and in a stadium with a 7,000-seat capacity, the Dodgers would draw 30,000 hysterical fans, both Negro and white, who had come either to watch Robinson lace out base hits and dance off the bases or to have his legs cut out from under him.

Because of Robinson the Dodgers sold out game after game during the exhibition season, actually making money, something accomplished by not one of the other major league teams. During the season, furthermore, the Dodgers drew the highest number of fans on the road. And though Ebbets Field only sat 33,000, the Dodgers, with Robinson as the main attraction, crammed enough rooters in the seats to account for one-third of the attendance in the National League.

In 1949, moreover, Jackie Robinson had been named the National League Most Valuable Player. He had won the league batting championship. He had led the Dodgers to another pennant. In his wildest dreams, Branch Rickey could not have anticipated how enormously successful his experiment would be.

And yet despite all that, when Jackie Robinson asked Branch Rickey to hike his salary from $20,000 to $50,000, Rickey as a negotiating ploy spread rumors to the press that he was going to trade Robinson to the Boston Braves for Johnny Sain and $350,000. The *Daily News* headline read:

SALARY DEMANDS HINT DEAL FOR JACKIE

Spectacular Trade With Braves Seen

Robinson's $50,000 Salary
Goal May Cause Rickey to Dispose of Negro Star

Of course Rickey denied the rumors with vehemence. However, he added, "There are certain financial heights at which you might be tempted to trade any player."

* * *

RACHEL ROBINSON: "Everything was negotiated between Jackie and Mr. Rickey except Jack's salary. The only thing Jack never could negotiate was money. What Rickey offered you was all you were going to get.

"It was to everybody. It was not limited to Jack. Nobody had a chance. Rickey wouldn't allow them to bring their lawyers in with them either, or their agents. All the players were afraid to negotiate their salaries.

"But Rickey always in his own mind had a justification for doing that. He justified it on the proceeds from the games and how much of that had to go back into the organization. He had the best farm system of anybody. He justified it on business terms. And don't forget, he lived in a fairly frugal way himself. He wasn't into materialism. He had one or two suits. He always had his great cigars and his funny-looking hats and his old shoes, but he and his wife—he called her Ma—lived very simply.

"Not that I'm defending him on the money issue, because we all suffered as a result of that. He got Jack very cheap, even by those standards. And one time Jackie sent a letter that I wrote, asking for $5,000 more than he had been offered, and Rickey said he was outraged that we should ask and that we weren't properly grateful for what we were getting, so that part was disappointing.

"But that was the only aspect of the relationship that was disappointing."

But it did leave a bad taste. Robinson ended up signing for close to $35,000. The same year Joe DiMaggio of the Yankees was earning $100,000. During his entire career, Robinson was the cheapest bargain in baseball.

Robinson was annoyed and disappointed at Rickey, but understood why Rickey acted the way he did and remained a staunch defender. At the end of the year, he was shocked by the news that Rickey had been forced out as head of the Dodgers. It was bad enough that his mentor had been dumped. Doubling his anxiety was Robinson's knowledge of who was replacing him: Rickey's antagonist, Walter O'Malley.

For several years O'Malley had made Rickey conscious that he wanted him out. Anything Rickey wanted to do O'Malley would fight. In 1949 Rickey built the spring training complex in Vero Beach. It had the latest training facility in baseball. O'Malley grumbled that Rickey was extravagant. Rickey invested in a Brooklyn Dodger football team, and it lost $750,000. O'Malley chastised Rickey for bad judgment, saying it was consistent with the growing number of "questionable strategies." When Rickey ordered World Series rings for each of the players, O'Malley demanded that the players turn in their 1947 ring before receiving a new one. When Rickey and O'Malley fought over which beer would sponsor the Dodgers in 1950 and Rickey lost, Rickey judged his days as a Dodger to be numbered. "He's going to force me out," Rickey told his daughter, Elizabeth. "I am doomed."

The catalyst was the death of stockholder John L. Smith. Though of late Smith had been siding with O'Malley, Smith nevertheless would have allowed Rickey to continue as head of the Dodgers. The team was successful, the farm system stocked with young prospects, and the Dodgers had never made more money.

When Smith died of cancer in July of 1950, his will named his wife and the Brooklyn Trust Company as executors. O'Malley moved in on the widow. He convinced Mrs. Smith to turn over administration of her baseball stock to the bank, which O'Malley represented. When she capitulated O'Malley controlled the Dodgers.

Like a South American dictator, O'Malley's first decision was to get rid of the opposition. The question was, how could he get the stock cheaply?

Rickey's contract as president had been running from year to year after the initial five-year contract expired in 1948. His latest contract was due to expire on Saturday, October 28, 1950. After that date his pay was to stop.

Rickey was in a financial jam. He held stock on margin that was being called in, and he had borrowed up to the limit of his life insurance. And O'Malley knew it. O'Malley's plan was to squeeze Rickey hard, putting him in an untenable financial position, and then acquire his stock at a bargain price.

Rickey's future hinged entirely on his ability to sell his stock. John Galbraith had offered Rickey a job running the Pittsburgh Pirates, but the commissioner would not allow Rickey to take it until he sold his Dodger stock. No job, no pay. O'Malley knew that too.

Rickey's stock had cost him $346,667, as had O'Malley's. What was the stock worth now? Under Rickey the team had an earned surplus of $2,600,000, and there was $900,000 in the bank.

O'Malley offered Rickey $346,667—what Rickey had paid for the stock! O'Malley figured Rickey was stuck, that he needed money so badly he wouldn't have any choice but to accept.

Rickey, incensed, offered O'Malley $1 million for *his* stock. O'Malley sneeringly turned him down. At the same time, he refused to up his offer. And the Dodger board of directors, controlled by O'Malley, refused to offer Rickey a new contract.

O'Malley figured Rickey had run out of options. He was sure no one else would be foolish enough to buy Rickey's stock because O'Malley had control of the widow Smith's twenty-five percent, as well as his own. Why would anyone buy into a team knowing he would have no say in it?

All the while O'Malley was feeding information to the newspapers, helping to bury Rickey. Tommy Holmes wrote in the *Brooklyn Eagle* that any buyer of Rickey's stock would have "about as much authority in the ball club as the head usher at Ebbets Field." O'Malley also kept up a barrage of criticism aimed at Rickey. He blasted Rickey's arrangement that allowed him to keep a percentage of the profits the club made from the sale of players. He criticized his system. "We can't afford to be selling off these players," said O'Malley. He criticized his high salary. He criticized his private plane. He bitched that under Rickey the Dodgers were losing money, a lie in the face of an auditor's report showing a capital surplus of $2,600,000.

Rickey looked to be in very serious trouble. O'Malley was gleeful, the black widow waiting for its prey, but as in the old movie serials, Rickey had one means of survival, and at the last moment, he employed it. The 1943 partnership agreement had stated that if Rickey ever wanted to sell and a third party were to meet his asking price, O'Malley would have to match the offer if he still wanted the stock. O'Malley was figuring no one would be crazy enough to offer $1 million for a minority interest, but he underestimated Branch Rickey. Because he did, O'Malley ended up having to come up with the million. And for the rest of his life, he bore a grudge against Rickey and all of his friends. It was one of the very few times in his life when Walter O'Malley didn't get his way.

At the last minute, Rickey appeared with a buyer, a real estate mogul named William Zeckendorf.

Was Zeckendorf's offer for real? Or was it a bluff? Chances were Zeckendorf's bid was a sham. Or was it? Now it was O'Malley's turn to squirm.

In the end O'Malley decided he couldn't afford to take the chance. He ended up paying Rickey the million. Moreover, under the terms of the 1943 partnership agreement, the buyer who matched the offer would have to pay the disappointed buyer $50,000. O'Malley thus had to pay Zeckendorf an additional $50,000. But when O'Malley got the canceled check back, Rickey's signature appeared under Zeckendorf's endorsement. O'Malley learned to his dismay that Zeckendorf, a close friend of John Galbraith, who was a close friend of Rickey's, had not only provided Rickey the means to grab the million from O'Malley, but he had also turned over the extra $50,000 to Rickey as well!

Reporters wrote that Rickey had happily bailed out with $1 million, but that was not so. Of the million, he had to pay the bank $300,000 to retire his debt. The rest O'Malley paid out over ten years at $72,500 a year. Ultimately Rickey ended up going deep in debt to pay the capital gains taxes in advance so that the the annual payments for the estate remained free and clear.

It was a significant sum of money, but nevertheless Rickey was in tears. He didn't want to leave Brooklyn, with all his upcoming stars on the horizon. For the rest of the decade, up through the day O'Malley fled Brooklyn with the Dodgers, the teams that performed in Brooklyn would be the handiwork of baseball's most brilliant original thinker, Branch Rickey.

At the press conference announcing O'Malley's victory, both men masked their true feelings. Rickey described O'Malley as "a man of youth, courage, enterprise, and desire." Said O'Malley: "I have developed the warmest possible feelings of affection for Mr. Rickey as a person."

The next year O'Malley sought out sportswriter Red Smith on a train ride from New York to Philadelphia. O'Malley had a story for Smith. "I want to set the record straight," said O'Malley. "You know how Rickey has always said he was the one who broke the color line with Robinson? Well, Red, the true story is that it wasn't his idea. It was mine."

Abie Is Out at Home

In 1950, for the second year in a row, the pennant came down to the last day of the season in a game against the Philadelphia Phillies. It was almost a miracle the Dodgers were still in the race. As late as September 12, they had been nine full games behind the Phillies, who were led by their Whiz Kid pitchers, twenty-one-year-old Curt Simmons and twenty-three-year-old Robin Roberts. But twelve days later, Brooklyn had cut the gap to one game, and by the final day, Brooklyn was one game behind the Phils with only a head-to-head game remaining.

The Dodgers had no business being that close. The Phillies had a big lead, but in September Curt Simmons, their best pitcher, was drafted into the army, and another pitcher, Bubba Church, was hurt when Ted Kluszewski hit a line drive off his left cheek, leaving his eyeball hanging out. Another starter, Bob Miller, hurt his back picking up a piece of luggage. So it was Robin Roberts pitching almost every other day, with Ken Heintzelman, Russ Meyer, and their relief star, Jim Konstanty, backing Roberts up.

Meanwhile, the Dodgers kept winning like crazy.

On the final day of the season, the Phils had a one-game lead, and they had to play the Dodgers. If the Dodgers won the final game, there would be a three-game playoff. Roberts started against Newcombe, who in 1950 had improved to 19–10 over his 17–8 record of 1949.

Here's what most fans remember about the game: In the sixth inning, with two outs and the Phils ahead 1–0, Pee Wee Reese hit a towering fly to right field, and the ball came down at the top of the wall and lodged in the screen. Reese, thinking the ball would be in play, raced around the bases, slowing to a trot when he saw the umpire circling his arms to denote a home run.

In the ninth, with the score 1 to 1 and Robin Roberts still pitching, seldom-used rookie outfielder Cal Abrams walked on a 3–2 pitch. After twice trying to sacrifice bunt Abrams over, Reese singled him to second. The Phils were looking for Snider to bunt, but instead the young outfielder lined a rope into center field that quickly bounced into the glove of Phils outfielder Richie Ashburn.

As Dodger third-base coach Milt Stock was waving Abrams around third, Ashburn, who possessed one of the weakest throwing arms in the National League, fired home. When Abrams arrived at the plate, the Phils catcher, Stan Lopata, was waiting for him with the ball. Like Horatio at the bridge, Lopata proved unmovable, and the home plate umpire signaled Abrams out. In the tenth inning, the Dodgers lost 4 to 1 when Phils outfielder Dick Sisler hit a three-run home run off Newcombe. The talk of the day was not the home run however. It was the play in which Abrams was thrown out. If he had made it, the Dodgers would have tied for the pennant, but he didn't, and for the rest of his life the slim outfielder would be remembered for costing the Dodgers the 1950 pennant.

* * *

GUS ENGLEMAN: "I remember in 1950 when the Dodgers lost the pennant on the last day of the season. If they had won that last game against Philadelphia, they would have tied and had to have a playoff. I remember it because all of us at school had the transistors, listening to the games, because it was almost a miracle finish. The Phillies had come into Ebbets Field three games ahead with three games to go, so the Dodgers had to win all three games. But the amazing thing is that prior to coming into Ebbets Field, the Phils had to play two doubleheaders against the Giants, and we were all saying, 'The Giants are not going to win four straight games in two days. What team could win two doubleheaders in a row against the first-place team?' Because we all realized that if the Dodgers kept winning, and the Giants could beat the Phillies four games in a row, then the last three games would be against the Phillies, and the Dodgers would have that shot to tie for the pennant.

"And I'll never forget sneaking out of the classroom, because they were afternoon games, a doubleheader Wednesday and a doubleheader Thursday, and when the Giants won two on Wednesday there was such an air of excitement. 'Hey, the Dodgers won their game. Could the Giants actually do it again?' And that Thursday was a day of high excitement. Nobody had his or her mind on studies, on work, on school. Some kids stayed home to listen to the games so as not to have teachers and homework get in their way. And that night, when the Giants won another doubleheader, we decided we were going to Ebbets Field Saturday to see the Dodgers do the impossible. The Dodgers had beaten the Phils Friday. We were in school, so we couldn't attend the game, and Saturday morning, very early, my neighbor, Larry Klein, and I went to Ebbets Field. I remember when you entered, you walked into a little rotunda. It was almost like a little train station, with ticket windows like little cages. We lined up and got our tickets, and strangely enough, it wasn't a complete sellout. I guess not that many people thought the Dodgers could really do it.

"But the Dodgers won that Saturday and won convincingly, and after the game Larry and I rushed back into the rotunda to line up and buy tickets for the Sunday game. We had a long way to come because we had been in the bleachers, and it was a long walk around to get down to the rotunda. And when we got there, it was a mob scene, because everyone now figured, 'Hey, the miracle is going to happen.' The excitement was genuine, because remember, baseball was everything in Brooklyn. That's all it was, was baseball. We waited in line about an hour. People were streaming to the park from their homes, lining up to buy tickets.

"I remember getting the tickets and looking to see where we were sitting. They were directly down the left-field line, reserve seats, right where the marker ended. On the foul side.

"I wanted the Dodgers to win so badly, and I couldn't wait for that game to begin that Sunday in 1950. The Dodgers had been everything to me, and when they lost, it hurt so badly. When they lost in the World Series in 1947 it hurt, and when they lost in '49 it hurt, and it started to hurt because not everyone in Brooklyn was a Dodger fan, and they didn't let you forget when the Dodgers lost. So to me it was personal pride. The Dodgers were like my family. I wanted them to win so badly.

"I remember that the score of that final game was 1 to 0 Phillies going into the bottom of the sixth. I remember Pee Wee hit the ball down the right-field line, and the ball lodged in the screen over the scoreboard, and everyone was shouting. Reese went around first and slowed his stride, and we figured it was a ground rule double, and then I remember Larry and I and everyone standing up, wondering, 'What's happening on the field?' and then we found out that according to the ground rules of Ebbets Field, if a ball lodged in the screen and didn't roll down, it was a home run. And when they waved Reese in, we figured for sure we were going to win it. The Phillies did nothing in the ninth, and then the Dodgers came to bat.

"Cal Abrams was on second base, and it was Snider who got the hit, but I remember with the crack of the bat the ball going into center field, and before anything else, Larry and I were embracing. We were hugging each other. 'They did it. Those SOBs did it. They did it.' Crack of the bat, we saw the ball land in center field, and we figured, 'That's it,' the Dodgers had won 2 to 1, that, God, we had tied for the pennant, that nothing was going to stop us from going all the way now.'

"And then it was like being at a wake. There was that crescendo, that roar, when the 33,000-plus figured the Dodgers had won. And then this funereal atmosphere when we saw the umpire signaling out when Abrams was thrown out at the plate by Ashburn. The Impossible Throw. It had to be a perfect throw. And it was. By a guy with a weak arm.

"And then the umpire signaled with his thumb up, and everyone was shouting and screaming and yelling, and a moment later it was like turning off a record, taking the needle off: total silence when the umpire signaled out.

"Then in the tenth inning, it happened again, only the silence wasn't as deafening because the Phillies were up. Sisler's home run was down the left-field line, where I was with Larry, and we were close enough to see that it was a clean three-run shot. The final score was 4 to 1. And again, the funereal silence. And we realized that it was all over. Larry and I didn't leave. The Dodgers still had one more shot, but the older folk, the realists, silently trudged out of the ballpark. And when the Dodgers made three outs, and it was all over, we cried.

"We suffered, and we cried. And it was the way they lost. They never lost it the easy way. The Dodgers always had a way of breaking your heart."

BILL REDDY: "I could have killed Cal Abrams for making that wide turn around third base. I never forgave him. I always wished that Hodges would have taken him and thrown him over the right-field wall. Or hung him up on the top of the screen. Anything would have been too good for him. That day I could have killed him with my bare hands."

* * *

Don Honig: "Even after Abrams got thrown out, the Dodgers had a chance, because they had second and third and one out and Jackie Robinson up. Phillie manager Eddie Sawyer walked out of the dugout and told Roberts to walk Robinson to load the bases. Roberts said later, 'That made sense, didn't it?' Roberts knew that if Robinson had batted the Dodgers would have won the game. But Roberts walked Robinson intentionally, and Furillo popped out to Eddie Waitkus at first for the second out. Hodges was the next batter, and he hit a fly ball to left to end the game, and the season."

Ron Green: "I saw the last game in '50. In the ninth Snider singled, and Ashburn threw out Abrams at the plate, and then they walked Robinson, and what I remember most was screaming my head off at Furillo. He didn't wait. He swung at the first pitch and popped it up. First pitch. Pops up to first base. We went crazy. Went nuts. He was a free swinger. He started swinging the minute he got to the plate. 'What are you swinging at?' And the next batter was Hodges, and he drove one to Dick Sisler. We were sitting down the left-field line, and when it left the bat, I thought it was gone. And Sisler caught it a couple feet in front of the wall, and if Snider had been on third with one out, he would have scored, and we still would have won, and the next inning Sisler hit the homer in the left-field seats. And we were crying. We were stunned."

In the top of the tenth, Robin Roberts, the pitcher, opened the inning with a single. Waitkus failed to bunt, but then swung and dropped a pop-fly single to short center, out of everyone's reach. The Dodgers got a reprieve when Ashburn, one of the finest bunters in the game, bunted into a force-out at third, as Newcombe fielded the ball and just did throw Roberts out. The next batter was Dick Sisler, who had made three consecutive singles into right field off Newcombe. He swung for a strike, then swung and fouled off a pitch for strike two. Newk threw a ball outside. On the next pitch, Sisler swung, and as he ran to first, he watched the ball sail toward the left-field seats. In the outfield Abrams furiously raced back to the wall, but it was fruitless. Newcombe finished the inning by striking out Ennis and getting Puddin' Head Jones to ground out weakly to Reese.

Roy Campanella: "Sisler was a good hitter if you got the ball away from him, and Newcombe got the ball away from him. Keep the ball in on him, and he doesn't hurt you. Just a mistake. Newcombe had good control. He got the ball away from him, that's all. And Sisler hit it out."

In the Dodger half of the tenth, the Dodgers went down meekly against Roberts. Campy flew out easily to left, Jim Russell pinch hit for Billy Cox and struck out, and Tommy Brown, batting for Newcombe, popped out to Waitkus at first.

When the game ended, the season a sore disappointment, the burning question was who to blame for the loss. One target was the third base coach, Milt Stock.

Carl Erskine: "In '50 I was going to pitch the playoff game. Shotton had already told me, 'If we win this game against the Phillies, you're going to pitch the first playoff game tomorrow.' And Sisler hit the home run. That was it.

"Newcombe and Roberts hooked up in a classic duel, it was 1 to 1, and you normally got some runs off Robin, but he was tough, a tough pitcher, and the only run we got that day was the one that laid on the ledge at Ebbets Field and was declared a home run. The heartbreaker, of course, was the play on Abrams.

"Hindsight is great, but I would say that any experienced coach would not take any chance with nobody out. There was a man on first and second, nobody out, and the suspicion was that maybe Snider would bunt. Snider did not like to bunt, and they let him hit. Ashburn had shortened up in center because of the potential bunt, and the ball got to him so fast on one hop, that he virtually had the ball back to home plate before Abrams got around third, and Milt Stock made an error in judgment, and undoubtedly he should have held Abrams, since he was thrown out by so much, but that was one of those things that happen. And then Furillo hit a high pop to the infield, and the last hitter of the inning was Hodges, and he hit a deep fly ball that would have scored a run if it had been one out instead of two, but that was the end of the inning, and Sisler hit a wrong-way home run, and that was that. Newcombe was kind of a tough-luck pitcher in many senses, but he got the darn label, which was unfair, that he couldn't win the big one, and that was one of those quirks right there that cost him, and then he had the bad experience in the World Series, a beautifully pitched game but Tommy Henrich hit a ball that was unbelievable. But that's the way sports do ya."

The *New York Times*: Oct 2.

SHOTTON UPHOLDS STOCK.

Says Coach Made Right Move
in Sending Cal Abrams Home

> Brooklyn Dodger Manager Burt Shotton absolved third-base coach Milt Stock of any blame for sending Cal Abrams around third base in an attempt to score the winning run in the ninth inning yesterday.
>
> Stock said, "That's the way we played it all season and I'd do it again if I had to call it again."

But a few days later, Milt Stock was handed his walking papers. He never coached in the big leagues again.

Another target was manager Burt Shotton.

* * *

Milt Stock

RALPH BRANCA: "Shotton had Eddie Miksis on the bench, and Miksis could fly and was such a good runner. Cal Abrams was not a good base runner. If Miksis had been in there, he would have been across the plate, and we would have won it."

A few days later, Shotton, who had led the Dodgers to two pennants and within a whisker of a third, was let go. He never managed again in the big leagues.

But the most popular target was Abrams. Even his most fervent admirers, Brooklyn's Jewish population, were viciously critical.

LARRY KING: "We were very Jewish, and we wanted Jewish ballplayers to do well. Before he died the comedian Godfrey Cambridge told me once, 'If the blacks could only learn Jewish public relations.' He said, 'I don't know if you have an international league of P.R., but when polio was cured, a guy called me and said, "Did you hear what happened today?" I said, "What?" He said, "A Jewish doctor cured polio." Not a doctor, a Jewish doctor. Sandy Koufax was a "Jewish pitcher." '

"We rooted for Ed Levy, who changed his name from some Polish name, and we rooted for Herschel Martin, who I thought was Jewish—he wasn't—but he had the name Herschel, so we rooted for him. Hank Greenberg was our hero. To this day any Jewish person will tell you that they never let Hank Greenberg hit a homer the last two weeks after he hit fifty-eight—he never got a pitch, they walked him every time—because he was Jewish. We were convinced of it. And of course we rooted for Al Rosen, and we loved Cal Abrams. Cal was a favorite. At first there was suspicion. Was he Jewish? Then we saw the picture. We saw the nose. He was Jewish. Cal had a lot of speed, and he was a good outfielder. But we uniformly despised him for the turn he took at third base in the final game against the Phillies in 1950. I loved Cal Abrams—until he got thrown out at home."

CARL FURILLO: "Abrams goofed. It was a ground ball going through the middle, and he hesitated. He went back. He took a step back, and then he went forward. And that's what they got him by. And then when he rounded third, instead of hitting the bag and coming in straight, he made a wide sweep, which took four more steps, but otherwise he would have made it, and we would have won.

"You couldn't believe it. We said, 'Oh no.' That's all you could say. 'Oh no.' "

CAL ABRAMS: "I was leading off the top of the ninth. I got on first base. I walked. Robin Roberts was pitching. A fantastic pitcher. He had excellent control. He was a professor of the art, studied each individual ballplayer, had books on them. And he studied, did his homework.

"I didn't have to psych myself up to face Roberts. I said to myself, 'I love baseball, I'm a star, and even though Robin Roberts is pitching, I'm going to hit him.' And I was playing very nicely. The ball I walked on he was trying to throw inside. Pee Wee Reese then bunted me over to second base.

"I was on second base with one out and catcher Stan Lopata gave Robin Roberts the sign to pick me off second. This sign was flashed to the outfield, and center fielder Richie Ashburn immediately got the sign and started running in toward second base to back up the play in case there was a bobble or an error. Duke Snider was up, and instead of turning and throwing back to second, Robin Roberts missed the sign and pitched the ball home. Now, Duke hit a line drive right by me. It bounced behind second base, and I knew I was the winning run. And I started to run as hard as I could to third, watching the coach, Milt Stock, who at that precise moment suddenly saw where Ashburn was with the ball in his hand throwing it before I got to third base. And Stock with one hand was biting his nails, and with the other was giving sort of a half-go-ahead, a small circular movement, and if you're running real hard and see this—the hand in the mouth biting his nails and a small circular movement, you really don't know what the heck it is, whether to stay or to go. And so I rounded third base, and as soon as I got twenty feet past third, I saw Lopata with the ball in the glove ten feet up from home plate. And there is no way in the world I can get by him. He's 250 pounds. So the only thing I could do was run into him. But unfortunately he held onto the ball. I never reached home at all.

"That was the first out. Then Carl Furillo popped out, and Gil Hodges hit a long fly to left field, ending the inning. Had I stayed on third base, there would only have been one out, I would have tagged and scored, and that would have been the winning run, and we would have beaten the Yankees in my only World Series.

"I was in a state of shock for quite a few days after that game. There were some newspaper reporters who had written: 'Cal Abrams, at the moment of contact with the bat, leaned back toward second base rather than start at a fast run toward third base.' There were some newspapermen who said Cal Abrams rounded third in a very wide turn. There were some who said that Cal Abrams was not the fastest runner on the team. All these are things I know aren't true. It was only several months later that the story of the pickoff play came out in *Sport* magazine. I hadn't even known about it.

"I've spent years trying to explain that it wasn't my fault, that I was a victim of circumstances. But every paper came down on me. Everybody said it was Cal Abrams caught at the plate, so I looked to be the villain. Why didn't the manager have the courage to say, 'It wasn't his fault'? or even the coach? He told me to go, so I went.

"But as it turned out, all these years I go out and make speeches and meet with people, and they remember the play so vividly, and I'm very thankful that they do. Had I reached home, I don't think they would have remembered it as well, because many people get home safely and score."

If one were to analyze the play, one would see that Abrams should not even have to defend himself. For him to run home was a smart play, whether he was safe or not.

The first two men got on, it was first and second and nobody out, and Duke Snider is up. What do you ordinarily do? You bunt. That's no secret. That's good baseball. Why didn't he? Because he didn't know how. Snider was perhaps the worst bunter in baseball. Also the pitcher, Robin Roberts, was expert at foiling the bunt. So Snider swung away and hit a single up the middle, and here comes Abrams, Stock waves him home, Ashburn comes up with it, and he has the weakest arm in the National League, and he throws him out, but good.

Later Dick Sisler hits a three-run home run, the Phillies win, and Stock gets fired. He's run out of baseball, because the litany is, you don't take a chance with no outs.

But if you think of it, what chance did he take? With men on second and third and one out, the result would have been the same had Snider bunted. When he hit the ball, Stock saw that he had a chance to win it right then and there. It could have been a very smart play, and for a smart play, he was run out of baseball.

In placing blame, it is interesting that no one thought to point a finger at Don Newcombe, who threw the home-run pitch to Sisler. One year later Ralph Branca would throw another home-run pitch to lose a pennant, and the world would never let him forget it. But in 1950 Newcombe was lucky. Cal Abrams had saved him from early ignominy.

The Jewish Presence

Back in the early 1940s, the Dodgers' Larry MacPhail had the notion that because of the 1,500,000 Jews living in Brooklyn, it would be good business for the Dodgers to have a Jewish presence. There should be someone to give the day off on the holy days of Rosh Hashanah and Yom Kippur during the pennant race. The Dodgers had had Goody Rosen, and after he left in 1946, Jake Pitler, the first base coach, became the Dodgers' Jewish presence. The Jewish fan didn't necessarily root for him, but Jake's being on the field would give him a sense of comfort.

JACK NEWFIELD: "My mother would be so impressed when Jake Pitler would walk off the field in the seventh inning of a game when it got dark because it was Yom Kippur. She would say, 'That's a good Jewish man.' "

After MacPhail left the Dodgers for the Yankees, he went a little overboard, when failing to sign a real Jew, he made Ed Clarence Whitner change his name to Ed Levy to give the Waspy Yankees a Jewish player who was supposed to compete with the greatest Jewish player to ever wear spikes, Hammerin' Hank Greenberg. Levy spent two seasons with the Yankees, 1942 and 1944, and then disappeared from the majors.

MacPhail was not the first to seek a Jewish Presence. Back in the 1920s, John McGraw of the Giants had coveted a Jewish ballplayer to help him attract the Jews who packed upper Manhattan and the South Bronx.

Jake Pitler

In 1923 a Giant scout brought to the Polo Grounds a youngster named Moses Solomon. Solomon had batted .421 and hit forty-nine home runs for Hutchinson, Kansas. Reporters immediately began calling Solomon the "Rabbi of Swat."

Solomon played exactly two games.

The other Jewish hope brought to McGraw was infielder Andy Cohen, who neither fielded nor batted well.

McGraw was in the habit after the game of going to the track with his friend, comedian Georgie Jessel. On one particular day, Cohen kicked two grounders, costing the Giants the game. At the track McGraw played a hot tip for the ninth race. His horse was ridden by a Jewish jockey. The horse lost in a photo finish.

Back in the limo, McGraw and Jessel rode back to Manhattan in silence. As they drove over the Queensboro Bridge, McGraw suddenly turned to Jessel and said, "They can't ride either."

The Giants never did have much luck finding a good one. In fact, almost nobody did. Hank Greenberg and Sandy Koufax were the best of the very few Jewish ballplayers.

IRVING RUDD: "Jews were city people. Where could you play? On the concrete pavement? Stickball was the Jewish sport. And if you were good enough, you would have to go out of your way to find a place to play and a team to play on. Most of the guys on the teams were *goyim*. And maybe a Jewish kid couldn't fit in so well. And if the field was in Canarsie, maybe it was, 'What's the Jew-boy from Brownsville doing coming here to play?' Unless he was especially good, like Sid Gordon, who became a Giant, but long after McGraw had passed away.

"The power base in Brooklyn were the Brooklyn Jews who were the elite box-seat holders. In a borough of 3,000,000 people, there had to be 1,500,000 Jews. The Jews who bought the box seats were the same guys who went crazy at basketball games at the Garden. You had Abe Stark, who owned a clothing store. He owned a box. He was not a freeloading guy, even though he had paid for the sign out in right field, 'Hit Sign, Win a Free Suit.' There was a guy named Sam Abrams, who was the bossman of Esquire shoe polish. There was Judge Samuel Liebowitz, a noted judge and jurist and prior to that a very famous lawyer. And I had a friendship going with a kid named Buddy Hackett. He couldn't afford to buy. I had to smuggle him in.

"The Dodgers were looking for box office magic. When I was a kid, Eddie Cantor, Benny Leonard, these were the saints, the deities. Eddie Cantor was like the Pope. And a Jewish ballplayer or athlete was looked up to. How many were there? Al Schacht, Moe Berg, Johnny Kling, whose real name was Kline, Hank Greenberg, Sid Gordon, Goody Rosen, Al Rosen, Jimmy Reese, an old coach for the Yankees—his real name is Hymie Soloman, a Jew. And every Jew knew his name was Hymie Soloman. One thing you couldn't do was pass. It took one to know one. So obviously a Jew as a box office attraction had to be tremendous.

"What puzzles me to this day about Cal Abrams is this: How could the Dodgers have not taken full advantage of him? He was a Jew, and he was from Brooklyn, for crying out loud. He wasn't a bad player. One year he was hitting .470 something, led the league in hitting in July. But then they stopped using him.

"There was something. I'll be very blunt about it. In the Dodger organization, the *goyim* did okay. Very true. They were tolerant, but it helped if you were Irish. As James Carter once said, 'Life isn't fair.' I was hired by the Dodgers at the time O'Malley took over, and in looking back in hindsight, I wonder if being Jewish didn't hurt me. I don't know. Did it hurt Cal? I wonder about that too."

Over Abrams's eight-year major league career, he is best remembered as a Dodger, even though he appeared in exactly eight games in 1949, thirty-eight in 1950, and sixty-seven in 1951, the year he was leading the National League in hitting in July with a .477 average. That year a headline in the *Post* read, "MANTLE, SCHMANTLE, WE GOT ABIE." Shortly afterward, Abrams went into a slump, and he didn't play much the rest of the season. In 1952, after ten games, Abrams was traded to Cincinnati. His next stops were Pittsburgh and then Baltimore, and he played four games for the White Sox in 1956. Abrams had never hit lower than .300 in the minors, and Branch Rickey often said that Abrams had the tools to play regularly in the majors. He had been a hit-'em-where-they-ain't spray hitter, hit .269 lifetime, ran fast, and had a superior throwing arm. But wherever he went, he mostly sat.

CAL ABRAMS: "I was born in Philadelphia, but when I was three weeks old, my family moved to Brooklyn. I didn't start playing baseball until the middle of my junior year, and I happened to hit one of the longest home runs in the history of Madison High when Joe Labate, who was a scout for Brooklyn, was sitting in the stands. He asked me if I would like to play for Brooklyn, and I said yes, of course, and I signed in 1941 to a minor league contract for $75 a month.

"I went to Olean, New York, played three weeks in 1942, and then went into the service. I got out three years later, and I went to spring training in Sanford, Florida, before going to Danville in the Three-I League. Next I skipped Class-A and went to Mobile, Alabama, in 1947. We found a small Jewish population, and they took us in. It was quite a thing for a southern town to have a Jewish baseball player. It had never happened before in Mobile. Sometimes in the stands you would hear comments about 'that Jew.' One man asked me whether I was 'Jewish Catholic or Jewish Protestant.' But it was never a problem.

"In '48 I got my first major league contract, was making the minimum major league salary—$5,000—but there were too many left fielders trying out. I remember all the left fielders trying out. We had Dick Whitman, Marvin Rackley, George Shuba, Bill Sharman, the basketball player, Bill Antonello, Jim Russell, Ray McCormick, Gene Hermanski, and myself. There were

George Brace Photo

CAL ABRAMS

eleven or twelve or us, strictly for left field. Right field and center field were sewn up. Duke Snider and Carl Furillo were there. Rickey wouldn't even let us warm up out there.

"Then Mr. Rickey called me into his office and said, 'Look Cal, I want you to be a Dodger. You are going to be a Dodger, but I have too many left fielders. I want to trade a lot of those fellows off, so do me a favor and go back to the minor leagues for another option.' Which I did. I went back to Mobile again, where I batted .345. I came back the following year, and he said, 'Do me a favor and go to Ft. Worth.' Which I did.

"I was leading the league in hitting with about a month and a half of the season to go when Mr. Rickey said to me, 'I want you to turn your body and face right field, and I want you to pull every ball that comes over the plate, because we want you to be a home run hitter in Ebbets Field. We want you to pull the ball against the fence.' So naturally I wanted to please him, and so I did what he said, and I found it difficult to even hit the ball. My timing was off, I couldn't follow the ball, and my average dropped well below .300. I had been up over .337 with over 400 at bats, and I did not like hitting below .300 in the minor leagues, whereupon I returned to my original stance, started hitting to left field again, to center field, and by the end of the season I was back up to .327. So I knew at that point I was not going to be a pull hitter, but I also knew that I could be a heck of a leadoff hitter because I had good eyes, I could follow the ball, and I could hit."

In 1950 Abrams advanced to St. Paul, where he played for a couple of weeks, until Carl Furillo got beaned. The Dodgers needed a right fielder, and they called Abrams up.

Cal Abrams: "I was a little anxious about playing right field, because I had never played there before with that crazy scoreboard, but when I got to the ballpark that day, it turned out that Carl was not hurt as badly as they said he was, and he kept playing, and this was a very, very bad time for me because I was sitting on the bench. Even though he was one of my best friends, I was hoping Carl would hurt himself just bad enough so I would get a chance, but unfortunately he was a strong, strong guy, and he continued playing, and I was just sitting. I wasn't enjoying the life. It reminded me of being overseas during the war. On the road I hung out with Dick Williams, Tommy Brown, and Billy Loes, and we'd sit in the lobby and play cards, go to shows, eat dinner together. I liked to do crossword puzzles and write letters home. But most of the time you were really busy packing and unpacking. You'd come back to the hotel, two days later go to another city, pack and unpack again. Like a traveling salesman, you're living out of a suitcase. And that was one of the reasons I cut short my career. I wanted a home, wanted my family with me, wanted roots.

"In 1950 I shared left field with Gene Hermanski. And in the outfield next to me was Duke Snider, who was an exceptional ballplayer. Sometimes I think to myself, 'Maybe I wasn't aggressive enough out there,' because balls used to go to left center field, where I could have made an easy catch of it, and Duke would come prancing by and charge over and get them. But I wasn't going to fight with the center fielder. The center fielder is entitled to take anything he can get.

"Off the field, I didn't have too much to do with Duke. We went our separate ways. On the road I was with Tommy Brown or Billy Loes or Erv Palica or Carl Furillo, and sometimes we'd go into a local bar, and they'd order a beer, and I'd order a Coke. I didn't drink, but I wanted to be part of the team. I wanted to be one of the fellows.

"We all got along—on the bus taking us to the ballpark everyone would be friendly. But it was kind of a cliquey team. I was never close to them. They went their way, and I went mine.

"There were different levels on the Dodgers. There were the stars, and there was the rest of us. In all the time I was in Brooklyn, I only performed on *Happy Felton's Knothole Gang* show two times. Furillo would go on a dozen times, Snider would go on a dozen times, he wanted the crowd pleasers, the guys who were supposed to be the stars. One time I recall I got $50 for doing the show, and I was to pick one of three youngsters, who in turn would choose a favorite player to speak to in the dugout. So I got a hold of this one kid, and I said, 'Look, I'm going to pick you as the best fielder, and in turn I want you to say that you want to talk to me in the dugout.' That way I would get an extra $50. So he said, 'All right.' And so I was throwing the ball to the three kids, and Happy Felton says, 'Cal, who do you think is going to make it?' I said, 'Number 3.' And the kid who I had made the deal with comes over, and Happy says, 'Congratulations, here's an autographed ball, a Baby Ruth candy bar. Now who do you want to talk to in the dugout?' I'm waiting there, and the kid says, 'Carl Furillo.' I almost died.

"I always had the feeling that Charley Dressen only played me enough to give me rope to hang myself. I remember one game, I hadn't been playing, and it's the ninth inning, bases loaded, two outs. Dressen puts me in to pinch hit. I popped up. Meanwhile, there was an opportunity in the sixth and the seventh for a left-handed batter, and the fans were yelling, 'We want Abrams,' and he wouldn't put me in. He waited until the ninth. Then there was the time Pee Wee Reese had two strikes on him and Dressen sent me in to pinch hit. I don't recall in the history of baseball where any major leaguer ever had the same situation. Two strikes and to go up and pinch hit? Never in a million years. I could understand it if it was a rookie, but Pee Wee was up there. And two strikes? And I popped out.

"In 1951 I was living in Levittown. At the time I was leading both leagues by well over 160 points. We came home after I had had a beautiful road trip, and I had practically all of my friends and relatives there. Levittown was giving me Cal Abrams Day, and I come out of the clubhouse and I have my glove on, my chewing gum in my mouth, ready to show the home folks, and I looked on the wall where we kept the lineup card, and my name wasn't on it!

"Fortunately I enjoyed joking, because that took away a lot of the tension and pressure. Around the time, somebody on the Cincinnati ballclub was hiding behind another ballplayer when he yelled out, 'Why you Jew SOB, I wish I had your nose full of nickels.' I was leading off, and I yelled back, 'I wish I had it full of pennies, because I'd be a millionaire.' And then I got a base hit. I don't know who said it, but I heard it, and he thought that because I was hitting so well that it might shake me up. But by coming back with that retort, I'm laughing at myself, I get a base hit, and I'm standing on first base and I feel like God. I feel like I'm the strongest, greatest person in the world.

"There was a lot of pain involved, but there was really no one to talk to. When I first joined the Dodgers, in the clippings I have pasted in my scrapbook, it says: 'Cal Abrams comes up from the minor leagues and Leo Durocher says, "I'm going to give him every opportunity." ' And then I only played eight games. Then you get the next manager, Burt Shotton, and he says, 'Branch Rickey told me that Cal Abrams is going to be our right fielder, and I agree with him because Cal is one of the finer minor league ballplayers coming up.' And then I play thirty-eight games. Then Charley Dressen: 'He's my number-one leadoff man, because he has the best eyes in baseball.' Even Clyde Sukeforth says in the papers, 'Cal Abrams can throw as hard and as accurately as Carl Furillo.' And all these clippings, and you wonder why you never got a full season under your belt. If I went 0 for 15, they'd say, 'Cal Abrams is in a slump,' and I'd be out of the lineup. Yet other fellows, like Jackie, went 0 for 27, Hodges had 0 for 20, and they'd still play every day. So I'd say to myself, 'There has to be a reason why.' But you were so afraid to say anything that would in any way jeopardize your career. We had nothing but baseball. You had all your eggs in one basket, so you didn't dare voice your feelings or walk up to a guy like Charley Dressen and say, 'How come I'm not playing tonight?'

"And in 1952 he didn't play me at all. He said I wasn't hitting. They told me they were looking to build a young ballclub, and I was twenty-eight, and yet they went and got Andy Pafko for left field, and he was older than I was! They swapped me to Cincinnati between games of a doubleheader. I was playing right field for the Reds, and Jackie Robinson was up, and he hit a line drive to right field that I caught on one bounce, and as soon as I caught it, I knew exactly what to do, because I knew what Jackie was going to do, he was going to round first base as hard as he could and if I so much as bobbled the ball he was going to go to second base. So I decided I was going to really get him. Ted Kluszewski was playing first base, and he had never played with me, and what I did was fire the ball back into first without looking. Jackie had stopped on a dime, and suddenly saw the ball was at first base before he got back to the bag, but the ball hit Kluszewski in the chest, didn't even faze him because he's so strong, but the ball fell to the ground, and Jackie slid in safely. And then Jackie got up and turned around and looked at right field at me, and I could see a row of pearly white teeth smiling at me, and I knew he was talking to me and saying, 'Cal, you son of a gun you.' And I felt so elated, so good. I didn't get him out, but at least I showed Brooklyn that I was not going to give up just because they traded me."

9

O'Malley Takes Over

After Walter O'Malley gave Rickey the boot in 1950, he made it clear that in order to work for the Dodgers an employee had to swear personal allegiance. Anyone still loyal to Branch Rickey would have to go. When Rickey was hired to run the Pittsburgh organization, a number of his scouts and front office men left Brooklyn to join him. Three, in particular, chose to stay with O'Malley.

They were Buzzy Bavasi, Fresco Thompson, and Al Campanis. Bavasi and Thompson shared the number-two spot, with Bavasi supervising the big club and Montreal, and Thompson running the rest of the farm system. Al Campanis, who had a practiced eye for talent, scouted for the whole team and later, on Thompson's death, took over the farm teams. These men had all trained under Rickey, but their loyalties were to the Dodgers first. As soon as they saw that their link with Rickey had become a liability, they cut it quickly and signaled O'Malley that he was the new suzerain. All remained loyal O'Malley men and were key to continued O'Malley successes.

They were very aware that O'Malley didn't want to be reminded of Rickey. Rickey had bettered him in a game of high-stakes poker, and he would always be furious at the Mahatma for forcing him to fork over a million bucks for the stock. Never mind that O'Malley had intended to bilk Rickey. O'Malley didn't like to lose. Once he took over, there was a standing rule: Any employee who mentioned the name of Branch Rickey would be fined $1. It was kind of a joke—to everyone but O'Malley.

The two Rickeyphiles O'Malley detested but couldn't get rid of right away were Red Barber and Jackie Robinson. From the day he took over, O'Malley made both feel unwanted, and as soon as he had a suitable replacement for Barber and saw that Robinson no longer could cut it physically, he unceremoniously pushed radio's greatest sportscaster and the Dodger's all-time most valuable player over the side.

If O'Malley disliked Barber, the Redhead despised his new boss even more. One of the great philosophical questions surrounding the game has always been, "Is baseball a sport or a business?" Everything to O'Malley, Barber felt, was the bottom line.

What also galled Barber was that unlike Rickey, O'Malley was deeply concerned with public relations. O'Malley had been a corporate lawyer who desperately wanted the right image. Rickey had never cared about image. Truth to him was more important, as it was to Barber.

Shortly after O'Malley bought the team, Barber told his listeners that the Phils were playing at double-play depth because base runner Carl Furillo was a slow runner. O'Malley angrily called Barber on the phone and demanded to know why he was telling everyone that Furillo was a poor runner.

When O'Malley took over, Barber called him and asked whether the new owner wanted him to resign. O'Malley said no. Barber, as was his nature, was candid and direct. He said that he intended to remain close friends with Rickey. O'Malley replied, "Yes, yes, of course."

But it was always something between them.

RED BARBER: "The thing festered. It was never anything you could put a finger on, but it was there. The atmosphere was different. It was different immediately. For instance, before the meeting was over I should have realized how changed everything was. I should have quit right then."

During that meeting O'Malley asked Barber's opinion on who should be manager in 1951. Barber first suggested Shotton. O'Malley said no, he was going to make a change. Barber then suggested Eddie Dyer. O'Malley said, "Fred Saigh [owner of the Cardinals] doesn't like him. He fired him, you know." Barber suggested Dixie Walker. O'Malley said Walker didn't have experience.

"This has been very interesting and very informative," O'Malley went on. "Always interesting to know how a man's mind operates." Then he told Barber he was going to hire Charley Dressen. "We're going to announce it tomorrow."

RED BARBER: "This, after he had taken all that time to make me say who I thought would make a good manager. He played me like a cat with a mouse. For what? For why? I should have known then, when he said they were hiring Dressen. I should have said, 'Walter, tear up the contract. Good by.' "

It took Barber three years.

Robinson was around longer. O'Malley only let him go when Father Time caught up with his perennial all-star. But like Barber, Robinson from the beginning of O'Malley's reign knew that things would be much harder for him.

JACKIE ROBINSON: "The news that Branch Rickey would be leaving the Dodgers at the end of the 1950 season to take over the Pittsburgh Pirates hit me hard. As soon as O'Malley took over the presidency of the club, he made it clear that he was anti-Rickey. At the time I didn't know whether O'Malley was jealous of the man or down on him because he had brought integration into the game. All I knew was that he became furious whenever he heard the name Rickey. He knew that I felt very deeply about Mr. Rickey, and, consequently, I became the target of his insecurity. I didn't act like some sorehead who has lost his protector. I didn't need a protector at that point."

Roger Kahn: "Jack used to drive O'Malley nuts. O'Malley would say, 'He's just a publicity seeker. Whatever he says you have to discount because you know the primary motive behind anything he says is publicity. I've never met a person in my life who wanted publicity as much as Jackie Robinson.'

"Well, I did, and his name was Walter O'Malley. I honestly believe the reason Walter eventually got rid of Charley Dressen as manager was that Dressen was in the papers all the time. And Jack was bigger than Walter, the president of the club. While O'Malley was Dodger president, he would say, 'I'm the Dodger president. What's with these stories of Robinson day after day? What is it with these stories about Dressen day after day?' So what did O'Malley do? He fired Dressen, and as soon has he could possibly trade Jackie, he did."

Jackie Robinson: "One spring O'Malley called me into his office and criticized me for not being able to show up at exhibition games, owing to the fact that I had been injured. O'Malley asked Rae [Rachel] to come along.

"O'Malley sat there accusing me of being unfair to the fans by missing exhibition games. He also said that I had no right to complain about being assigned to a separate hotel. 'A separate hotel had been good enough for you in 1947, hadn't it?' O'Malley said.

"I told O'Malley that if he and other owners had more guts, that black players wouldn't have to suffer so many indignities. I told O'Malley to check out my injury with the trainer. O'Malley then accused me of being a prima donna. He said I was behaving like a crybaby over a sore leg.

"Rachel told O'Malley: 'Bringing Jack into organized baseball was not the greatest thing Mr. Rickey did for him. In my opinion it was this: Having brought Jack in, he stuck by him to the very end. He understood Jack. He never listened to the ugly little rumors like those you have mentioned today. If there was something wrong, he would go to Jack and ask him about it. He would talk to Jack and they would get to the heart of it like men with a mutual respect for the abilities and feelings for each other.'

"O'Malley saw he couldn't bully me, and he backed down. He then tried the soft sell, he said he meant no harm, and then he asked if I would 'just try to come out and play today.' "

But for the rest of his career, Robinson knew that whatever he did, whatever he said, O'Malley would be observing him, second guessing. Much of the fun baseball held for him departed with Branch Rickey.

Another man O'Malley wanted out was Rickey's manager, Burt Shotton.

O'Malley publicly said that Shotton was very much in the picture as manager and that he wanted him to come to Brooklyn to talk to him about it, but the realistic Shotton knew better. Each time O'Malley called Shotton to set up a meeting, Shotton refused to talk to him. "There was no point coming to Brooklyn to be fired," Shotton would say later.

To replace him O'Malley hired Leo Durocher's former sidekick, the effervescent Charley Dressen. Dressen had infuriated Rickey by leaving in 1947 to go back to work for Larry MacPhail and the Yankees. It's doubtful O'Malley had hired him because he had snubbed Rickey, but it isn't completely out of the question. When O'Malley hired Dressen, he told the press, "Fans like to see a manager. They like to cheer him and jeer him and suffer with him. They can't see him if he isn't in uniform. Well, our manager, Chuck Dressen, will be out there in uniform, right there on third base, and everybody can second-guess him just as much as they like."

There was one other thing O'Malley made clear when he took over. He was unhappy with having to play in undersized Ebbets Field. When the Dodgers made the World Series in 1950, he had proposed that all the games be played in Yankee Stadium, where they could pack in 75,000 fans, more than 40,000 more than at Ebbets Field. O'Malley argued that to play in Yankee Stadium would benefit Dodger fans because many more could see the game. But the Dodger fans were horrified that anyone could suggest that the games not be played at their beloved Ebbets Field. Where was O'Malley's respect for tradition? How could the man be so callous?

From the beginning O'Malley was talking about a new park for the Dodgers. He told reporters, "Sure, Brooklyn needs a new park, but a park for 52,000 would cost, right now, six million, and there's not that kind of money in baseball. We'll have to wait." He added, "A new park should have no columns." One way or another he would find a way to raise the money for a new columnless ballpark. What O'Malley wanted, O'Malley got.

Around the same time O'Malley supplanted Branch Rickey, the owners voted Happy Chandler out as baseball commissioner. Just as O'Malley had been angry, jealous, or both that Rickey had gotten the credit for bringing Robinson into baseball, so the other owners held a grudge against Chandler. He had defied their fifteen to one vote against bringing a black to the majors, and he was made to pay. The owners first changed the rules of ouster to a simple majority vote. Then they voted him out nine to seven. In March of 1951, Ford Frick was elected to replace him. The owners would never again have an independent commissioner. Led by Walter O'Malley, the defacto baseball commissioner until the day he died, the owners would make sure that subsequent commissioners would answer not to the players and not to fans—but directly to them.

Chuck and Clem

The Dodgers defeated the Giants five straight times in early April 1951. Charley Dressen, who was determined to prove to the world that he had been the brains behind Leo Durocher's success, began singing loud enough for the Giants to hear him through the wall that separated the locker rooms, "Roll out the barrel, the Giants are dead."

Jackie Robinson continued his personal feud with Durocher by lashing out nine hits. He was almost unstoppable, striking vicious liners, dropping deftly placed bunts, and stealing bases; in short, playing the game with all the ferocity and skill of Ty Cobb at his peak.

Leo retaliated as best he could. Standing in the coaching box at third base, Leo would look at Robinson, and hold his cupped hands a couple of inches from his ears to let Robinson know he had a swelled head. Across the diamond Robinson would shout back, "Hey, Leo, are you still using your wife's perfume?"

Sometimes it got vicious. Robinson and Giant pitcher Sal Maglie had a vendetta, and in one game Maglie dusted Jackie off. Robinson picked himself out of the dirt and on the next pitch bunted the ball near enough the first-base foul line that Maglie would have to come running over to field it. The ball was rolling foul, and Maglie went to touch the ball dead, and as he bent over, Robinson ran right over Maglie, leaving the fierce Giant pitcher sprawling on the ground. Durocher called it a bush stunt. Robinson replied: "If it's a bush stunt, he's a bush manager, because he taught me to do it."

In addition to Robinson, the Dodger lineup, which included Campanella, Hodges, Furillo, Snider, Reese, and Cox, indicated that this would be the most powerful Dodger team yet, hitting forty homers in their first thirty-one games. They got some unexpected help from Cal Abrams, who one week in late May went 14 for 23 to lead the National League with a .470 batting average. Robinson was second at .415, Reese third at .384. The Dodger defense was sound, and the pitching looked to be strong, with Newcombe, Roe, Branca, and Erskine.

Erskine had struggled with arm trouble during 1950 and only was able to compile a 7–6 year. The Dodgers had returned him to Montreal, where he underwent an extensive rehabilitation program for a damaged right shoulder. His arm finally did come around, and he went back to the Dodgers at the end of the season.

Erskine still had arm problems in '51, but he was learning to cope a little better, even when his arm wasn't cooperating fully.

CARL ERSKINE: "I was a year older, had a year more experience, I was healthier, and Charley Dressen used me more in a consistent role of starting than Shotton, who had used me quite a bit in relief. In fact, in '49, when I was 8 and 1, I had most of those in relief, and I mostly relieved in '50 as well. But from '51 on, Dressen used me virtually exclusively as a starter."

He won sixteen games that year, helping to lead the Dodgers to an early five-game lead.

The Giants, meanwhile, after winning the season opener, lost eleven in a row. Dodger fans gloated.

BILL REDDY: "The Dodgers had opened up in Boston, and their power was awesome, and they were hitting like crazy, and into my store came two Giant fans in the neighborhood. One of them said to me, 'How is anyone going to beat the Dodgers this year?' I smiled and said, 'No one is going to.' "

* * *

The Giants needed help, and on May 24 they brought up a young Negro outfielder from the Minneapolis Millers named Willie Mays. But the Dodgers also strengthened themselves on June 14, when they obtained veteran outfield star Andy Pafko from the Cubs in a deal for Joe Hatten, Bruce Edwards, Eddie Miksis, and Gene Hermanski. Left field had been a problem position for the Dodgers for years. Abrams and Hermanski had not done the job. With Pafko the Dodgers now had a star at every position.

Reporter Arch Murray called the trade "the most barefaced baseball swindle of recent years."

Carl Erskine: "We made one gigantic trade in '51. Swapped four for four at the field. We got to the ballpark that day. In fact I rode on the bus from the hotel to Wrigley Field with Bruce Edwards. He and I sat in the same seat and talked on the way out. When we got to the ballpark, Dressen called out. He said, 'Hey, I want Miksis, Hermanski, Edwards, and Hatten. You guys don't get dressed. Get your stuff and come up here.' They didn't know anything. Over in the Cubs clubhouse, they were telling Pafko, Walker, Terwilliger, and Johnny Schmitz the same thing. They walked across the field an hour and a half or so before game time and traded clubs. And I was pitching that day, and in the eighth inning Edwards pinch hit and hit a home run off me to beat me. And I had ridden to the ballpark with him!

"I was working on my slider. Dressen said, 'Yeah, it slid right out into whatever that avenue is.' He wasn't too keen on a slider.

"But that was an unusual trade. They made the announcement to the players at the park, they crossed the field, and that was it."

The Dodgers celebrated the July 4th holiday by beating the New York Giants twice. Preacher Roe and Ralph Branca beat two mediocre Giant pitchers, Sheldon "Available" Jones and Dave Koslo, to lead the Giants by seven and a half games. Charley Dressen again gloated. "They're through," he boasted. "Those two beatings we gave them knocked them out of it. They'll never bother us again."

On August 8 and 9, after a three-game sweep over the Giants, the Dodgers were fifteen games up in the loss column. On August 11, the Dodger lead over the Giants was thirteen and a half games. The Dodger pitching staff was holding up beautifully. Roe was 15–2, Newk 15–5, Branca 9–3, and Clyde King, back from the minors, was 12–5 in relief. With only forty-four games left in the season, the Dodgers seemed to have the pennant sewn up.

The turning point came in mid-August. The Dodgers were feeling elated, the Giants depressed. After the final game of the Dodgers' three-game sweep, both teams returned to their respective clubhouses. As the Giants showered, the Dodgers, shouting so the Giant players could hear them, began yelling about what a bad team the Giants were and what a bad manager Durocher was and how good the Dodgers were.

Don Honig: "Except for Maglie it wasn't the Giants they hated so much as it was Leo. But the Giants heard what the Dodgers were saying, and they simmered with hatred for what they felt was a very unprofessional attitude. Personal invective was coming through the wall, and the Giants' fury rose, and this added to their superhuman effort as the Giants won sixteen in a row and thirty-seven of forty-four games coming down the stretch."

Through the first half of the season, the Giants had been inconsistent because they could count on but two pitchers, Maglie and Larry Jansen. Jim Hearn had been wild high all the time, and Leo couldn't pitch him. But in July Hearn changed from pitching overhand to below three-quarters, and he started throwing strikes. And when he started throwing strikes, he began winning. Now they had three good pitchers. When the Giants brought up rookie Al Corwin, who won five of the games during the Giants' sixteen-game winning streak, they were close to unbeatable.

There was another factor too. Leo Durocher cheated. The Dodgers are convinced of that. They say that coming down the stretch in 1951, Leo illegally stationed someone out behind the center-field scoreboard to steal the opposing catcher's signals and then radio them to the dugout, where Durocher could relay them to the Giant batter.

COACH COOKIE LAVAGETTO: "I shouldn't tell you this because it's no use to stir up old bones, skeletons, but if you ever get around Leo, ask him if he ever had a message sender in center field in the Polo Grounds. That's how those guys won all those games in the last six weeks. They had a wireless. Then they had word signs from the bench. Hell, we knew they were getting them. I talked about it with Charley Dressen. I said, 'Charley, you notice when we come here, we never fool anybody? We throw a guy a change of pace, he seems to know what's coming?' And one day we took binoculars out on the bench to observe center field, then the umpire seen us, and he ran over and grabbed the damn binoculars. There was nothing I could do. We were just trying to observe center field. Whatever he had out there, he had a good system."

About this time, too, the Dodger pitching staff was decimated. The most serious injury was suffered by Dodger relief ace Clyde King. King had pitched for the Dodgers during the war years, but in 1948 a finger on his pitching hand had become infected, and it got so bad at one point that he couldn't catch or throw a ball. In '49 and '50, King played in the minors for Montreal, and during the 1950 season, while fooling around on the sidelines, he developed a slider. Using that slider along with his already outstanding curve, King was instrumental in leading the Dodgers to their huge midsummer lead in 1951. He finished the year with a 14–7 record, but because of his sore arm, during the last months of the season he was virtually useless.

CLYDE KING: "I was 13–4 in early August. I had a chance to win twenty games that year, and I came down with tendonitis, or rather I think what it was was tendonitis. If I hadn't hurt my arm, I would have been the guy who would have pitched to Bobby Thomson. [If he hadn't hurt his arm, the Dodgers wouldn't have had to pitch to Bobby Thomson.]

"I remember I was doing so well that year that between games of a doubleheader they tore up my contract and gave me a new one. Charley Dressen was our manager, and he got me the new contract.

"I never will forget, I was in the lobby of the Hotel St. George, and Charley came through and called me over and said, 'I'm going to do something for you tomorrow.' I said, 'What is it?' He said, 'You'll find out when you get to the ballpark.' And that's when I got my new contract. I got a $2,500 raise. Fantastic. Got me up to $13,000.

"Mr. O'Malley was the one who gave it to me on TV. Buzzy Bavasi was the general manager. And after that I won exactly one more game that year. Buzzy said he would never tear up a contract in the middle of the season again!"

The other problem that plagued the Dodgers in the second half of the season was that the hitters had stopped hitting.

Duke Snider: "I had a very bad September, felt very bad about it. A couple of hits here, a couple of hits there, and we wouldn't have had a playoff. You take it personally. I think everybody did. Pee Wee didn't have a good September, and he and I would talk about it and try to analyze the situation driving to and from the ballpark. It was something you had no control over; still, at the time, I was very concerned."

Ralph Branca: "The Dodgers weren't looking over their shoulders in '51. Nope. We just played lousy at the end. Everybody said, 'You're in. Just play .500 ball, and you're in.' But if you look back over the last seven weeks, you'll see that we didn't hit much. And if you want to fault anything, we had a short pitching staff. Charley Dressen was the manager, and he had five guys who he used extensively, and the pitchers ran out of gas. Plus, the hitters didn't hit.

"My record in July was 12 and 5, and I ended up 13 and 12, but in almost every game I started in September, we got one run. We just didn't hit enough.

"I remember we had a three-game series against the Giants. Erv Palica had a sore arm, and Charley pitched him in the Polo Grounds, and he gave up three runs in the first inning, and Bud Podbielan came in and shut them off the rest of the day, but we lost something like 3–2. Newcombe pitched the next day, and we lost 2–1, and I pitched the next day and lost 3–1. That's the day Willie Mays made a catch running into right center, and he made a perfect throw and got Billy Cox at the plate. So we lost three in a row to the Giants, and that's a big swing.

"I remember that the Giants kept winning, and I had to pitch with two days rest. I had pitched a shutout Friday night, and they had nobody to start, so I pitched Monday night, and I pitched another shutout, but the only thing was, I had a no-hitter, and it was a twilight game, and I knew I had the no-hitter so I was really busting it, and I strained my arm. And subsequently, I pitched effectively enough, but I didn't throw as hard. I remember losing to Maglie 3–2, and to Roberts 3–2."

From August 12 through August 27, the Giants won sixteen straight games, and at the end of the streak, the Dodger lead was cut to five. The three-game sweep by the Giants was vulgar. In the middle game, Maglie defeated Newcombe when Newk threw a wild pitch in the seventh inning that allowed Bobby Thomson to score the winning run.

To bolster their pitching, the Dodgers brought up another young rookie pitcher from one of Branch Rickey's farm teams. On August 28 rookie Clem Labine beat the Reds, pitching a complete game. He then completed three more games. In his first four starts he had two shutouts and two one-run games.

Labine had come up from Montreal, and he was one elegant pitcher. He had an overhand curveball, a hard sinker, and he was a wonderfully gutty pitcher. His four straight wins in his major league debut attested to that.

On September 21, as the Giants were edging up, he started his fifth game. He was pitching against the Phillies, and in the second inning, with Puddin' Head Jones up, he had the bases loaded and a three and two count. Dressen called time. He went out to advise Labine. Next pitch: Lower deck left field, four runs. Goodby Labine. Dressen wouldn't start him again for six weeks—in the second game of the playoffs. It cost the Dodgers the pennant.

CLEM LABINE: "The Dodgers signed me because Charley Dressen, who was the pitching coach at the time, fell in love with me for a reason I'll never know. He said I had a great slider. I never threw a slider in my life, but if he said I had one, that was okay with me. What he saw was that my ball sunk a little bit, even in those early days, and he was the one who pushed Rickey to sign me.

"I signed in 1944, and I worked my way through the minors, played for Newport News, Greenville, Asheville, Pueblo, and in 1949 went to St. Paul, Triple-A. I pitched in something like sixty-four games, led the league and finished 12–6.

"Walt Alston was my manager there. Walt was a good guy, a very good manager with youngsters. He had the ability to be fatherly, a little stern, but at the same time he was quite capable of listening, and that helps a great deal. And he knew that, hey, it's not the manager who makes the ballplayers, it's the ballplayers who make the manager, and I think any manager who ever forgets that better look at his job, because he's not doing it properly.

"I was playing winter ball in Venezuela the winter of 1950, and I was playing catch with a fellow named Ken Staplers. He was from St. Paul, and I had been throwing him spitters, just fooling around, 'cause everybody does that, and I experimented, holding the ball a little bit differently, grabbing it inside the seams, like a spitter only without the spit, and the first pitch I did that, the ball didn't sink, it rose, and it got him right in the throat. After he caught his breath, he said, 'I don't know what the hell you did, but let's try

George Brace Photo

CLEM LABINE

that thing again.' We tried it, and this time, it didn't go up, it went down, and from then on it kept going down. The ball used to drop a foot, a foot and a half, and that was unheard of on a fastball.

"He said, 'Try it when you pitch,' and in the first game, the first time I did it, I struck out fourteen. And you got some pretty good ballplayers in that league. God, I won twelve in a row down there that winter.

"So I joined the Dodgers in the spring of '51, and my biggest problem was that I was a little tired. I hadn't had a rest, came directly from playing in the Caribbean world series. Went right to spring training. They wouldn't even let me go home. I hadn't even seen my family.

"And when I got to spring training, I got wild. And that's why I started the 1951 season at St. Paul. And then the day they called me up was the day that I almost broke my ankle. So I came up to Brooklyn on a set of crutches. They didn't send me back because the club was going well. They had a thirteen-and-a-half-game lead over the Giants.

"And when the team started going poorly, I started, and I had a 4–0 record. Dressen didn't want me as a starter. He wanted me to relieve. But Preacher had a sore arm. In fact we had several sore arms.

"But then after going 4–0, I didn't pitch the last three weeks of the season. I went on Charley's list. Charley, you see, was a very vindictive type of person, and his vindictiveness cost him the pennant in 1951. Not because Clem Labine was going to pitch one game and win it, but Clem Labine could have pitched and given the other fellas, who were tired, a rest. But no, he didn't even let me go to the bullpen. He sat me on the damn bench. Now I'll tell you why.

"I had won four games in a row, and we were playing Philadelphia in Ebbets Field. We had traveled all night and all day because we had trouble with the train, and we got to the ballpark at four in the afternoon. That's a tough, tough thing, and I was pitching. I got the first two men out, and I was having a lot of trouble getting my curveball over, so I walked two men, and someone hit a pop up, but the ball was dropped. I had the bases loaded, and I went into a stretch, and Charley called time out, and he came running out. He said, 'I don't want you to go into a stretch. What are you going into a stretch for?' I said, ''Cause I can't get my curveball over. I know I can get it back much better from a stretch.' He said, 'I don't want you to take a stretch.' I said, 'I ought to know what I can do.' He said, 'You take a full windup.' I said, 'I don't see why you want me to take a full windup. There isn't any . . .' He said, 'No, you won't get enough on the ball.' 'Well, okay,' and he went back to the dugout.

"I was stubborn in those days too, and I took a stretch, and Jones hit a grand-slam home run. Charley didn't talk to me. He came out and got the ball. He never talked to me. Not one day, two days, three days, four days. Never talked to me. Never said one lousy word to me. This is the type of man he was. He bit off his nose to spite his face. Because most assuredly we had a staff that was so overworked it wasn't even funny. All he needed was for someone to spell it. That's all, and he might have gotten an extra win out of it. Hell, I was pitching well. So he might have gotten a win out of it, and it might have been different."

* * *

Looking back, there were games the Dodgers should have won that they didn't. With three games left in the season, the Dodgers lost a heartbreaker to defending National League champion Philadelphia, 4–3. Carl Erskine was leading 3–0 in the sixth, and then the Phils scored one in the sixth, two in the eighth, and in the ninth Ashburn singled, Dick Sisler made a sacrifice bunt, Bill Nicholson was walked intentionally, and Puddin' Head Jones singled in Ashburn. The Dodgers and Giants were now tied. Two games remained.

The next day the Dodgers shut out the Phils 5–0 behind a gallant Don Newcombe. It was Newcombe's twentieth victory. The Giants' Maglie won his twenty-second game when he shut out the Boston Braves 3–0. For the third year in a row, the pennant would be decided by a game between the Dodgers and the Phils on the final day of the season. But because the Dodgers had led by thirteen and a half games in August, the tie was a severe disappointment. All Brooklyn talked about was the Dodger collapse.

Don Honig: "The Dodgers didn't collapse. They played .500 ball in September, which is not a collapse. It's just the Giants never lost. Still, panic didn't really set in until very late in September. Nobody believed the Giants were going to win. There was a sense of unreality to it. We just kept waiting for the Giants to lose a couple. It's bound to happen, we said. But it never did. If the season would have ended three or four days sooner, the Dodgers would have won."

Robby Saves the Day

On September 30, 1951, a Sunday night in Philadelphia, the Dodgers played for the pennant, and Jackie Robinson singlehandedly saved the team from losing. Always a clutch performer, in the most important game of the year, Jackie Robinson gave what some experts consider the most clutch performance ever seen. Don Newcombe had also been heroic, holding the Phils in relief from the eighth through the thirteenth inning after having pitched a complete game just two days before.

Larry King: "The Dodgers were in the third inning when it was announced that the Giants had won. That game had taken one hour, fifty-two minutes. Maglie beat the Braves, 5–1. The Dodgers knew they had to win or the season would be over.

"It was 8–8 in the bottom of the twelfth. The lights are fading. The Phillies are batting, they load the bases, two are out, and Eddie Waitkus is up. He hits a line drive up the middle, and Robinson extends the full length of his body and backhands the ball, and with the umpire standing over him, he falls in a heap and hits the dirt in such a way that all the dirt came back on top of him, so that all you saw was his glove with the ball in it and dirt covering his body. The umpire raises his fist, and the inning is over, the score still tied.

"Then in the top of the fourteenth, Jackie gets up with two outs, nobody on, and hits a home run off Robin Roberts, and the Dodgers win 9–8.

"That was a pressure ballplayer."

DON HONIG: "It was the last of the twelfth, with bases loaded, two outs, when Eddie Waitkus hit the line drive through the middle. Waitkus was a left-handed hitter, and Robinson was playing over toward first, and nobody to this day can believe that he got to that ball.

"The umpire ruled it an out, but on the Philly bench Robin Roberts told a teammate, 'I bet he trapped that ball and was trying to get a force at second.' Because the way Jackie landed, you couldn't be sure.

"Later, Roberts met Jackie at a dinner and asked him if he really caught that ball. All Robinson said was, 'What did thc umpire say?' "

CLEM LABINE: "Are you good at trivia? Who won that game? I'll give you the name of a man you probably won't remember: Bud Podbeilan."

MRS. CLARENCE "BUD" PODBEILAN: "I met Pod when he was playing in the minors for Montreal. I met him on a day when he pitched here in Syracuse against the Chiefs, and he did great. It seems like such a long time ago. Pod had been a successful pitcher in the minors as a starter. But Charley Dressen put him in the bullpen when he came to the Dodgers. He had started at Montreal, and Walt Alston was there, and he won about fifteen games starting. But Dressen made him a bullpen pitcher. If he'd have left him alone, he would have been great.

"He won that final game in Philadelphia in relief. I was there. I was sitting right in back of Branch Rickey. Pod had just won the game. He pitched to six men, and he got them all out. And Rickey turned around and said, 'Your husband's a perfect pitcher.'

"But Pod never got credit for that, and it makes me mad. It didn't make him mad. He wasn't like that. He was a good man. He never said anything about himself. He would say, 'What happens, happens.' But I don't think that's true. Because you gotta get credit for what you do. And he didn't. And it made me mad."

Death to the Giants

The emotions generated by the Dodger-Giant rivalry were very much like those surrounding a Holy War. If you loved the Dodgers, you despised the Giants. You couldn't be neutral.

The rivalry began early in the century. Wilbert Robinson and John McGraw had been illustrious teammates in the 1890s on the old Baltimore Orioles, and when McGraw became manager of the New York Giants in 1902, he hired Robinson as his pitching coach. McGraw had kept Robinson on over the years because Robinson was a masterful pitching coach, but a personal feud developed between the two. They fought all through the 1913 season, and when McGraw accused Robinson of missing a sign during the World Series that the Giants lost to Connie Mack's Athletics, the breach in their friendship became permanent.

The following season Dodger owner Charley Ebbets hired Robinson to be his manager, and it proved to be an intelligent move as Robinson led the Dodgers to pennants in 1916 and 1920, much to the consternation of a jealous and headline-hungry McGraw.

In 1916, McGraw's Giants put together a 26-game winning streak, but were still only able to finish fourth, six games behind Brooklyn. The Brooklyn team was a hodgepodge of castoffs, including three former Giants, Chief Meyers, Rube Marquard, and Fred Merkle. On the final day of the season, Brooklyn was playing the Giants, and McGraw, disgusted that his team had finished behind Robinson's, stood up in the middle of the game shouting, "I won't be a party to this," and he stormed from the dugout and out of the park.

By 1934 both Robinson and McGraw had gone, but Giant manager Bill Terry did his utmost to keep the feud alive. The Giants had won the 1933 world championship, and during a press conference in the off-season, a reporter asked Terry how Brooklyn would do in '34. Terry replied with derision, "Brooklyn? Is Brooklyn still in the league?"

In 1934, when the Giants were battling the Cardinals for the pennant, they had to beat the Dodgers twice to win. Brooklyn ended up taking both games as Dodger fans taunted Bill Terry with cries of, "Hey Terry, is Brooklyn still in the league?" The Dodgers may have finished sixth, but the small victory of denying the Giants the pennant was sweet.

As the thirties progressed and the fortunes of the team sank while the Giants won several pennants, Dodger fans' hatred for the Giants grew.

Bill Reddy: "I always hated the Giants, because they were so classy. The Giants would come in, with Bill Terry, Travis Jackson, Mel Ott, JoJo Moore, and strut out onto the diamond like, 'What score shall we win by today?' The Dodgers, God help them, were so inept in those days. The Giants had had John McGraw for years, and John McGraw was always the cock of the walk. He was the greatest thing going, and his team was the greatest collection of ballplayers, and after McGraw left, Bill Terry took over. Terry was the last .400 hitter in the National League. A great, you can say. I hated him. I used to hate to see him on first base. They had Travis Jackson at shortstop, and they had Carl Hubbell, Hal Schumacher, Mickey Mouse Melton, and Fat Freddie Fitzsimmons, who I hated until he became a Dodger. They had guys who you knew could beat you, and yet on any given day, you could never make a bet against the Dodgers, because Van Lingle Mungo might just go out there at Ebbets Field and whip Hubbell's ass and tie a can to it.

"One of the greatest days I ever had in my life was a morning game at Ebbets Field against the Giants. The Dodgers must have scored ten or eleven runs, and they couldn't get us out. Every Dodger who came up got a hit, and as I sat there, I was hollering, 'More, more. Send more guys up there to hit. With bigger bats. More runs.' And I can remember another game, when Mel

Ott was the manager and Bill Voiselle was pitching for the Giants. Dixie Walker came up to bat for the Dodgers, and there were a couple men on base, and Ott came trotting in from right field, and you could see him gesticulating to Voiselle not to throw Walker a high strike. Voiselle was nodding furiously, 'Yes, yes, okay, don't worry about it,' and Ott gave him a tap on the backside and ran back to right field. Voiselle wound up, threw one in shoulder high, and Dixie Walker put it over the fence into Bedford Avenue for a home run. Ott stood there with his back to the plate watching the ball go over, and as he turned around, you could see the red coming up from his neck. His whole face turned red, and he ran back to the mound, threw his glove down and stood there looking at Voiselle. Voiselle went out of the game, another pitcher came in, and a week or two later Voiselle was traded to Boston. It was the end of him as a Giant. I'll never forget the happiness that surged through my breast when Walker pulled it out. It was gorgeous! It was beautiful!

"But it didn't happen often."

The one incident above all others that symbolized the Dodger-Giant rivalry occurred in a Brooklyn saloon on a warm July afternoon in the late 1930s.

The site was Pat Diamond's bar and grill at Ninth Street and Seventh Avenue. After the Dodgers had lost a game to the Giants, bartender William Diamond, the son of the proprietor, was teasing a customer, Robert Joyce, a post office worker. Like Joyce, Diamond was a Dodger fan, but he enjoyed teasing Joyce, who was also so serious about his team. "The Dodgers," Diamond said, "Whoever first called them bums was right. Don't you think so, Frank?"

Frank Krug, a Giant fan, chimed in, "Certainly. It takes the Giants to show them up as bums, too. Ha ha! What our guys did to them today! Why don't you get wise to yourself? Why don't you root for a real team?"

Diamond was grinning, enjoying the banter, when Joyce started screaming, "Shut up, shut up, you bastards. You lay off the Dodgers, you bastards."

Diamond smiled and said, "You don't mean to say you're mad at us, do you?"

Krug sneered at Joyce, "Don't be a jerk."

"A jerk," Joyce shouted. "I'll show you who's a jerk." He ran out of the saloon, the other bar patrons laughing at him as he fled.

"Jesus," said Diamond. "He got it bad, don't he?"

Joyce had been working at the post office for ten years, and he had the key to the revolver bin. There were six guns in the drawer. He went and got two of them. Minutes later, Joyce returned and shot Diamond in the stomach. When Krug jumped on him to take the gun away, Joyce pulled out the other one and shot Krug through the head. When the police caught him on Seventh Avenue not fifteen minutes after the shootout, he was sobbing hysterically that he hadn't meant to hurt anyone, but that he had been taunted for too long about his Dodgers.

During the 1940s the rivalry had cooled some, because the Giant teams had been so inept. The Giants had several power hitters, sluggers like John Mize, Sid Gordon, and Walker Cooper, but little else and rarely finished in contention. Then in 1948 Leo Durocher went from Dodger to Giant manager, and in 1951 his former second fiddle, Charley Dressen, took over the Dodgers. The rivalry heated up to an intensity never approached before. Venom spewed whenever the two teams played. The Dodger players hated Durocher and his Giants. Durocher—and by extension his players—hated Dressen and the Dodgers. When they played, they fought as though each game were a duel to the death. The intensity was greater than in the World Series. Games became marathons, as both Durocher and Dressen used pitcher after pitcher to win a ballgame. Rarely did they finish in under three hours.

CLEM LABINE: "The biggest rivalry with the Giants was when Leo was managing the Giants and Charley Dressen managed the Dodgers, because as you can well imagine, Charley always wanted to beat Leo, because he used to be his coach, and he always felt he was much smarter than Leo any day of the week. Charley was willing to tell that to anybody.

"We had a lot of people who never forgave Leo. Carl Furillo never forgave Leo, for one."

CARL FURILLO: "I roomed with Gil Hodges for six years, and he was a nice person, a real nice person, but anybody says he never got mad is a lot of baloney. He'd get mad when he would see that somebody was out to harm somebody. Take a guy like Durocher. Gil knew Durocher was a louse, that he was trying to harm people, and then he would get mad. Gil would say, 'He's a no good bastard.' Guys on the Giants like Rigney, they were dirty ballplayers. A guy like Alvin Dark, who was another dirty bastard, and Gil would say, 'Hi, Alvin, how are you, Alvin?' and under his breath, 'You son of a bitch.' Pee Wee used to say, 'Hello Riggy, how's everything?' and under his breath, 'You dirty bastard, you.' Rigney, he was no Goddamn good. He tried to be like Durocher, tried to copy Durocher. That Herman Franks, he was another one. They were no good bastards. They all wanted to be like Durocher. So one day we decided to get them. We decided to get that Rigney. He played with the Giants. Played second base. We said, 'We don't give a shit if we lose this game or nothing. We'll get him.' And who the hell did we get instead, poor Davey Williams.

"See, one of the Dodgers, Pee Wee or Robinson, got hit hard. They come into second base trying to get Pee Wee or Robinson, one of the two, and we said, 'Okay, we'll get somebody here, and that poor son of a bitch happened to get the ball, Rigney hesitated a little bit, and when he did, Jackie plowed into Davey Williams. And ruined him for the rest of his life. And we said to Rigney after the game, 'That was your place. You were supposed to be in that spot.' He started laughing about it. We said, 'We'll get you, don't worry.' They finally got Dark, they spiked the shit out of him.

"Listen, the Giants started it. It wasn't the Dodgers. See, they were trying to build up real friction to draw crowds. Rigney was no prize package. And Alvin Dark, if he got a shot at you, he took it. And Herman Franks, he did what Durocher said. Monte Irvin, he wasn't dirty, but we didn't give a shit who was dirty. You had that Giant uniform on, you were out to hurt us. And we were out to get you. We didn't give a shit for Monte Irvin or anybody. These guys wore spikes, and those bastards cut. And like I said, Durocher was a dirty manager. He was a dirty ballplayer. I can see knocking a man down if they knocked your man down. But to deliberately try to hit a guy in the head or spike a guy, ruin a guy for life? Look at poor Davey Williams. He got hit because of Rigney. And the dirty ballplayers all ended up being managers for look how many years.

"You know, another Giant we played against was Willie Mays. Willie was good, but he was not the ballplayer they built him up to be. He's not Superman like they claimed him to be. They tried to put him in the class with Williams, DiMaggio, and Musial. Musial, he won seven batting titles. I don't have nothing against the guy, he was a terrific ballplayer, but if I had my choice between two ballplayers at that time, him and Henry Aaron, I would of took Aaron. Every ballplayer in the league will tell you that. Hank was a steady ballplayer. If Henry would of had the publicity in Milwaukee like they had in New York with Mays, Christ, he would of been way the hell up there. But he didn't have that publicity. Leo can thank God for Mays. Right now, Leo is riding the coattails of Mays. But I never hated the ballplayers. I didn't hate Maglie, I didn't hate none of them. Gomez had to go and take orders from Durocher, Sal took his orders from Durocher. See, I knew Durocher, I knew how he talked, 'Don't let that son of a bitch beat you.' That's the way he talks. 'Don't let that son of a bitch beat you, stick it in his Goddamn ear. Don't let him take the bread and butter out of your mouth.' I knew how he talks. To me, I didn't hate the ballplayers, I hated Durocher. I hated his guts."

The Giants Get Lucky

For the second time in the history of the National League, the season had ended in a tie. The first time was 1946, when the Dodgers lost two straight to the St. Louis Cardinals. In 1951 the Dodgers were in another playoff, against the Giants.

RALPH BRANCA: "For some reason, when the Dodgers won the toss for the playoffs in 1946, they elected to go to St. Louis to play the first game and then come back and play the next two in Brooklyn. I do not know who made the decision, but because of it we had to travel by train to St. Louis, which was a twenty-six-hour trip, and we were exhausted, and of course, we lost.

"And the reason I bring that up, now it's 1951, and we're in Philadelphia, and the Giants are in Boston, and we have a playoff with the Giants, and they toss a coin, and the Dodgers win the toss again. Only this time, no one is around because they're all in Philadelphia, and they call a guy named Jack Collins, who was ticket manager. Collins remembers that the '46 decision was wrong, that we went all the way to St. Louis and then all the way back, and so he makes the decision that we'll play the first game at Ebbets Field and the next two at the Polo Grounds. I'll bet you've never heard this story, but in the first game Thomson hit a home run off me in Ebbets Field that would have been an out in the Polo Grounds, and the ball he hit in the third game in the Polo Grounds would have been an out in Ebbets Field. If the fields had been reversed, it might not have turned out the way it did.

"And as it turned out, the Dodgers won the toss twice, and they lost both playoffs because they made the wrong decision where to play the games. Twice they won the toss and lost the war.

"I pitched the first playoff game in '51, and I gave up only four hits, and I gave 'em the old line, 'I scattered four hits, two inside the park and two outside.' We were playing at Ebbets Field, and Bobby Thomson hit a home run on a high fastball, and it was hit to left center with no authority, it was just a high fly, but it drifted and drifted and drifted and went right into the first row. As I say, it would have been an easy out in the Polo Grounds. And then Monte Irvin hit a homer in the eighth inning. But I remember we had the bases loaded on Jim Hearn and one out, and Furillo popped out and Hodges swung at a bad curve, and all we got was one run, and I lost 3 to 1. I pitched effectively enough. We just didn't score enough runs."

In Game Two, rookie Clem Labine shut out the Giants 10–0 to get the Dodgers even. After the game everyone wanted to know why Dressen had refused to pitch Labine after September 21. Dressen was evasive.

Clem Labine: "I don't know why Charley decided to pitch me in Game Two. I guess I was the only thing he had left. I was the only one. I was sound. I was young. And I certainly could throw nine innings. I could throw twenty. In those days I had such a good arm. But I was the court of last resort. And it turned out well. We got ten runs.

"I remember I had the bases loaded in the second inning, and I got Bobby Thomson up at the plate. Two outs, and I got him three and two, and I had a really good curveball. It was an overhand curve, and it was breaking very large, and I threw him a bad one, it was a ball, there was no doubt he would have walked and a run would have been forced in, and it might have been, 'See you later, Clem,' but he swung at it, and he struck out. And once you get out of a situation like that, it just gives you a little bit more, and then we got a few runs to go along with it, and the more runs you get, the easier it gets to pitch because you don't have to worry about the short porch on either side of the Polo Grounds. But I was the type of pitcher, really, who the Polo Grounds was made for, because everybody tried to pull the ball all the time. I was a breaking-ball pitcher. I used a fastball as a flasher, really. It exists, but it's not what I want you to hit. I wasted the fastball most of the time. And so everyone goes, 'Here comes that soft thing,' and they go to swing at it, and it drops on you, and you get the top of the ball. So you're not gonna hit a lot of line drives off of me, just a lot of ground balls. And don't forget who we had scooping them up: Gilly, Robinson, Reese, and Cox."

* * *

Game Three of the 1951 playoffs was perhaps the most famous single game in baseball history. If you ask any baseball fan what one game in baseball annals sticks out in his mind more than any other, it doesn't matter much whether the fan is eight or eighty. If he is a true fan, the likelihood is that he will say, "The day Thomson hit the home run off Branca." And he would be right. It is a tragic day for many, like the day the stock market crashed or Franklin Roosevelt died or John Kennedy was assassinated. You can remember what you were doing at the moment you heard. People ask, "Where were you when the Japs bombed Pearl Harbor? When Lyndon Johnson announced he wasn't running again? When Martin Luther King was shot? When Bobby Thomson hit the home run?"

Most of the Dodger fans who remember October 3, 1951, can recite the detail of the game as though it had happened yesterday. And they discuss it with the same passion they felt over twenty years ago. No single game has ever been analyzed as minutely as this one. Thomson hit the shot heard round the world, and that shot found its mark in every Dodger fan's heart.

Every fan has a story about that day. Here are a few of them.

BILL REDDY: "I was in Jerry's Hardware Store watching the television set and listening to the game on the radio at the same time. God forgive me for talking like this, because I've always tried to block this whole day from my memory, but it was the bottom of the ninth, the Dodgers were leading 4 to 1, Don Newcombe was pitching, and Alvin Dark leads off the inning with a banjo single through the right side of the infield, a stinking little bouncing ball that nobody could get to.

"Don Mueller comes up, sneaky Mandrake, the German U-boat commander. He was so sneaky he would sink ships. He would put the periscope up and say, 'Where can I hit this one?' He would torpedo the Dodgers all the time.

"So Dark's on first, and Hodges is holding him on the bag. Why? I don't know. Newcombe was pitching, and he didn't have a terrific move to first. He wasn't going to pick him off. Besides, what the hell do you want to hold him on for anyway? Three more outs, and you've got the pennant. Let him run. If he steals all the way around the bases, what's he going to get, one lousy run? Later we found out that Dressen had ordered Hodges to hold him on. This had been hushed up. It was like the Pentagon Papers, only worse. It was a total bonehead play on Dressen's part. Anyway, Mueller singles. After looking through his periscope, he hits a sneaky little bouncing hopper that Hodges would have put in his back pocket ordinarily if he hadn't been holding Dark on, and as he reached for it, because he was right-handed he had to reach across his body, and when he did the ball seemed to veer another inch and a half; it saw the glove coming, and it got out of the way. Dark went to second. That was the kind of hit it was. Dark didn't even get to third.

"The next guy up is Monte Irvin, and he hits a pop fly to the right side of the infield. One out. Meanwhile, in the bullpen, Dodger pitchers are warming up. Carl Erskine was warming up. Ralph Branca was warming up. But we still had high hopes that Big Don was going to finish the game. Except that Big Don never finished any really big games in his whole life.

"Next man up was Whitey Lockman. Another sneak. For years Lockman was a sneak. He used to cheat his mother when he was a kid, steal carfare on her. Lockman, who is a left-handed batter, doubled to left. It was a line drive over short, and Dark scored to make it 4 to 2, and Mueller, who looks behind him to see where the ball is, slides funny into third and breaks his ankle. Now, I never want to see anybody get hurt. I hate the thought of it. But if somebody had to get hurt, they couldn't have picked a better guy than Don Mueller. Quite frankly, at that point, I wouldn't have cared if his head had come off and rolled all the way across the infield.

"So they took Mueller off on a stretcher, and they put in Clint Hartung, the Hondo Hurricane, who was supposed to be the greatest thing that ever lived when he came up. Only as it turned out, he wasn't much of a hurricane. He wasn't even a gale. He was just a little whistle storm. Now, there are men on second and third and first base open. What do we do? The batter is Bobby Thomson, with Willie Mays on deck. I say to myself, 'Get Newcombe out of there.' Because they're starting to get to him. They're timing his pitches, hitting these sneaky little singles. Newcombe should be blowing them out of there, and he's not.

"Okay. The Dodger coaching staff has the same thought, and out Newcombe goes, and I'm saying to myself, 'Bring Labine in.' And when I hear Russ Hodges say, 'Ralph Branca is walking in from the bullpen,' I immediately walk out of the store.

"My boss, Jerry Shiffman, says to me, 'Where are you going?' I say, 'We lost the pennant.' He says, 'Come back, you crazy bastard. What's the matter with you? They're bringing Branca in.' I tell him, 'Forget about it.'

"Outside the store there were two big barrels, one for naphthalene solution, the other for turpentine. It was against regulations to keep them in the store, so we kept them on the sidewalk. Big fifty-gallon drums. I went outside, and I climbed on one of the drums, and I sat there, my legs dangling over the side, waiting for the world to end.

"I kept hoping Branca could get Bobby Thomson out, but I knew he couldn't. Not only was Thomson the hottest hitter on the Giants—in the last seven weeks he had brought his average from .222 to .292—but he had homered off Branca in the first playoff game.

"Labine is sitting on his duster in the bullpen. Erskine, the ace of the staff, is sitting out there, and in comes Branca. I could hear Russ Hodges babbling on, and all of a sudden I hear screaming from across the street. There was Sam Harris, a diehard Dodger fan, running up from the basement of his house, and he looks at me, and he has tears in his eyes. I said to myself, 'Son of a bitch, don't tell me.'

"Jerry comes out of the store. He says, 'What do you think?' I say, 'About what?' He says, 'Thomson's home run.' I didn't say a word. I went back inside, unplugged my radio, and I dropped it into a big barrel we threw trash in. I went and got a baseball bat we had behind the counter, and I smashed that Goddamn radio into pieces so small you'd have had to be an atomic scientist to put them under a microscope to see them.

"It took years off my life. I didn't recover until the spring of '52, when the Dodgers started to play ball again. But all winter through those long, dreary months when there was no baseball, every couple of nights I'd find myself sitting at home and going over it in my mind again. How did Mueller hit that ball past Hodges? How did Lockman get that double? How, for Christ sake, could Dressen bring in Branca to pitch to a guy who had hit a homer off him two days before?"

Seated in the 56,000-seat Polo Grounds that day were some 34,000 fans who also were stunned by the sudden ending. One of those at the game was Bobby McCarthy.

Bobby McCarthy: "I had terrific seats on the third-base line for the final Dodger–Giant playoff game. I was sitting right where the third-base line hits the outfield seats in left in the old Polo Grounds.

"I was a Dodger fanatic, and I admit it—I was a terrible taunter. I was a fat, chubby little kid, and when I went to the park that day I brought with me a stuffed dummy, which looked like a corpse and which was supposed to be the corpse of the Giants. Early in the game, when the Dodgers went ahead 4 to 1, I took the dummy and hung it over the rail, and I even got my picture taken by the *Daily News.* Three or four of my buddies and I sat there chanting, 'The Dodgers won the pennant. The Dodgers won the pennant.' We were surrounded by Giant fans, but that only made it better.

"Sitting behind me was an immense, fat Sidney Greenstreet-type character, and all afternoon this horrible man kept saying, 'You're going to be sorry, 'cause the Giants are going to win the pennant. You fucking wait until Bobby Thomson gets up. He's going to hit a home run, and the Giants are going to win.' He began this litany about the third inning, and he kept it up all game long. Thomson had doubled in the first Giant run, and maybe that's what spurred the horrible fat man on, but all game long he kept telling me about Thomson.

"In the ninth, I'm cheering, screaming till I was hoarse, my hands were red from clapping, and the fat man again tells me that Thomson is going to win the game with a home run. I say, 'Bobby Thomson? He isn't even going to get up this inning.' I laughed at him, and of course, Thomson hit the homer to win it for the Giants, and when I saw Pafko going back against the wall and the ball going out, my face flooded with tears, and I turned and started running up the aisle to leave, and I ran smack into an impenetrable wall. I looked up, and there was the fat man, his arms out wide, holding me from getting past him, and he said, 'Hahaha. I told you Bobby Thomson would hit one.' I started beating on the fat man's chest, shouting, 'Let me go, you cocksucker,' as the tears were flowing down my face. But for what seemed like an eternity, the fat man wouldn't let me go.

"I walked around the streets until about ten o'clock at night, and then when I finally went home, I couldn't even go in the house, because I knew my father would rib me, and I was hungry and tired, and my aunt and uncle were over, and they took me for pizza, and I was starving, and we walked into this pizza parlor, and what do they have hanging in the pizza parlor? Toilet paper for Dodger crying towels, and a rope for a noose, with a sign, 'Dodger fans, hang yourself here.' I ran out of the pizza parlor crying. I wouldn't even eat.

"I stayed in my room for three weeks. I couldn't face anybody. I couldn't believe they had lost. And I must admit, I was a coward. I used to break people's chops and give people a hard time when the Dodgers won. But I avoided all the Giant fans for I don't know how long. I ate in my house. I wouldn't go out. I didn't want to see nobody."

DON HONIG: "I can remember that day so vividly, and I didn't even see him hit it, I was so nervous. I had gone into another room. When Lockman hit that double, I couldn't bear to watch. Then, in the other room, I could hear the screaming. Since it was being played in the Polo Grounds, Russ Hodges was announcing, and I heard the screaming, and I knew what happened.

"My best friend and I left his house, and we just walked in utter silence for miles. I was utterly desolate."

JOEL OPPENHEIMER: "Every time I hear Russ Hodges scream, 'The Giants win the pennant, the Giants win the pennant,' I go crazy inside. I remember I was over at an old high school friend's house to listen to the game with him and about eleven other Giant fans. I remember standing in the room, drinking beer, and feeling very up because we were going to win the game and then getting totally destroyed. Now, every time I hear a tape of Hodges's call, it's like I'm back there, and I'm twenty-one, and my world has been destroyed once more. Once again they did it to me. Here I was, surrounded by these jibbering idiots, screaming and yelling, these jerks who had undeservedly gotten an enormous boost in life."

JOE FLAHERTY: "I had a boyhood buddy named Noel Moran. Noel's grandfather was watching the 1951 playoff game against the Giants, and he was in his eighties. When Branca threw the pitch, and Thomson knocked it out, he bent over, called Branca a 'dago bastard,' spit at the screen, and keeled over dead."

The Fallout

CARL ERSKINE: "I had a sense of the history as Thomson's home run was going. I was a kid from Indiana, and just being in New York was history for me. Just being there! But here we were in a playoff, playing the final game in a season in which we once had had a thirteen-and-a-half-game lead.

"I had pitched a couple days before the final regular season game, and I pitched a good, strong ballgame and was winning the game 2 to 1, and it was the eighth inning. I got a fastball that was intended to be up and in, I got it down and a little bit in, and Andy Seminick of the Phillies hit it in the seats with a man on, beat us 3–2. That was a heartbreaker, because we were needing that win badly. And when Ralph threw the home run to Bobby Thomson, I thought to myself that the season could have been won if we had turned around any loss all year, and that any loss would have been just as big as that one, and particularly I thought about the home run off me by Seminick.

"Being in the bullpen that day and throwing with Branca, I was one of the first to get to the clubhouse after the home run, and as I climbed up the steps, I saw they were moving all the TV cameras from our side through the door that connected us to the Giant side, and they were carrying the champagne cases. Nobody was in there yet. And here they were, scrambling to get that stuff across.

"Outside, it was bedlam. But inside our clubhouse, it was like a tomb. And I was in there to see everybody come in off the field one at a time and go to their locker. And that's when I got the sense of history. What most people don't realize is pro athletes act more like they got beat than the amateurs do. A high school or college team gets back on the bus after a tough loss, and there might be a little horseplay, but the professional athletes, when they lose, there is no joy in losing, and it's evident in the clubhouse after the game. I remember guys coming in in great disgust and throwing their gloves in their lockers. It was quiet.

"But outside was deafening. They were chanting for Durocher and for Thomson. I saw Dressen take off his shirt without unbuttoning it. He just ripped them right down the front. Robinson just sat with a glazed look of disbelief. Branca had come in, and inside the clubhouse there were about eight wide, wooden steps going up to the trainer's room. Branca had started up those steps and turned and sat down and then pitched his body between his knees. I'm looking at Branca, and I see that big number 13, and I was never superstitious about things, but I see this.

"And then a scene came back to my mind that happened in the first series: The opening of the season that year saw Dressen with his first year with the Dodgers, and Durocher was with the Giants. Dressen had been Durocher's first lieutenant in Brooklyn. So now Dressen had inherited many of the players Durocher had had. Now you either loved Durocher and Dressen or you hated them. We had had a few players who really disliked Leo in the way they had been handled under Leo. Or they disliked the way Leo had treated them after he became a rival. At any rate Dressen had an obsession to prove to the world that he had been the brains, that it hadn't been Durocher who had called the shots, but rather that he substantially helped Leo gain his managing reputation in Brooklyn. And so Dressen wanted to make his mark, and that was an obsession with him. So the Giants came in, the season was maybe ten days old, the Giants got off to a very bad start, and we beat them three straight, just clobbered them. So that was the first encounter Dressen had had against his old boss, Leo. And he just buried him, and he was just beside himself. When he came in, he was so filled with enthusiasm, delight, that the clubhouse was just ringing. We had a door that opened between the visitors' clubhouse and the Dodger clubhouse, a wooden door, and it was never locked, but it was respected. We never went in and interrupted their meetings, or vice versa, but early, when you first get to the park, some of the guys who knew each other would open the door and shout in, a little kidding early, but the door never opened after you got into real business.

"But Dressen came in, and he was going up and down the aisles of our lockers, shouting, 'The Giants are dead. The Giants are dead.' A few of the guys liked to sing. Palica, Branca, I used to sing a little bit, kidding around on the bus. Anyway, Charley came back and he wanted Palica and Branca and me to come back and sing through the door to Leo. He wanted us to sing, 'Roll out the barrel. The Giants are dead.' He wanted something concocted quick to sing. Well, I didn't have any stomach for that. Neither did Palica. But for some reason, and I never heard Ralph say he disliked Leo, but he went back with Charley, and they sang through the door. 'The Giants are dead.'

"Well, that really bothered Leo, and he complained to the league office, and that door was bricked up, never to be used again. And that flashed in my mind when I saw Ralph sitting on those steps at the end of the season.

"Newcombe had a saying, 'What goes around, comes around.' Life has a funny way."

For years the debate raged over whether Charley Dressen might have brought in a different pitcher to face Thomson. Or should Big Newk have been able to gut it out and finish the game? Lockman's double had driven in a run to make the score 4–2, Dodgers, with men on second and third. Newcombe had pitched gallantly through September, both starting and relieving. Dressen knew he was tired. Still, critics said that Newcombe had choked because he didn't finish, and because he didn't finish, the Dodgers lost the ballgame.

Cal Abrams: "Newk came in after he got the side out in the seventh and said he was tired. Robinson got angry. He yelled at Newk, 'Don't give me that shit. Go out there and pitch.'

"In the bottom of the eighth, Newk struck out the side. He told Dressen he didn't want to pitch the ninth. 'It looks like I just don't have it anymore,' he told Dressen. 'Take me out.' "

Because he asked to be taken out, critics questioned the big pitcher's fortitude. Newcombe has never forgiven them.

Don Newcombe: "Everybody talked about my getting taken out of the final game in 1951 in the ninth inning, but nobody said one thing about what I did for the two weeks leading up to that playoff game. I gave the Dodgers everything I had. I was leading 4–1 in the ninth. And they say I choked up because I left in the ninth inning? Other pitchers get in trouble. That's what you have relief pitchers for. That's what they are supposed to come in and do, get the team out of those situations. But why is it they concentrated on me and said

I choked up in 1951? Why? I don't know, but they did. Didn't I pitch eight-and-two-thirds innings of that game? If I was gonna choke up, I would have choked up in the second or third inning. If I was afraid of the Giants, I wouldn't have pitched the game that I pitched. Nobody gave me credit for it at all, especially in the press. They tore my ass up."

One move Dressen could have pulled was to walk Thomson and pitch with the bases loaded to the next batter, Giant rookie Willie Mays. But Dressen did not walk Thomson for what most experts agree was a most compelling reason: He didn't want to put the winning run on base if he didn't have to.

One move Dressen might have considered was keeping Newcombe in the ballgame and replacing his starting catcher, Rube Walker, with his injured star, Roy Campanella. Campy had been injured in the first playoff game, and Dressen chose to play a healthy Walker rather than an injured Campanella in games two and three. In Game Two Walker had hit two home runs in the 10–0 victory against the Giants, and so Dressen started him again in Game Three. Walker remembers the two pitches Branca threw:

RUBE WALKER: "When Branca came in to the mound, we talked about how if we got ahead of Thomson, we'd waste a pitch inside and move him back. The first pitch was a fastball, right down the middle. Thomson took it. The next fastball was supposed to be inside, but it wasn't inside enough, and he hit it."

A lot of Dodger fans were convinced that if Roy Campanella had been behind the plate the Dodgers would not have lost. Branca's first pitch to Thomson was a perfect strike, waist high and right over the heart of the plate, too meaty a pitch to make in such a perilous situation. The critics say that if Campy had been back there, he would have gone out to the mound and said something like, "Ralph, what the heck are you doing?"

Bobby Thomson has said that the first pitch was a better pitch than the one he hit and that he didn't know why he didn't swing at it. Surely Campy would have gone out to the mound and told him to keep the ball down, would have told him to throw a curve and not another fastball. Campanella himself hints that he would have made a difference had he played that day.

ROY CAMPANELLA: "I had a charley horse. I pulled it in Philadelphia in the last game of the season. I hit a ball to the top of the right-center-field fence opening the inning, and I said to myself, 'Nobody out. I'm gonna try to get a triple.' I wound up with a triple, but as I was running through shortstop, I pulled my right thigh, and I dragged my leg into third.

"I played the first playoff game in Ebbets Field—the Giants beat us—and Dressen told me, 'Look, we're gonna have too much room for the catcher to run in the Polo Grounds. I'm not going to let you catch.' I told him, 'Don't worry about it. Let me catch.' He said, 'No, Rube Walker will catch,' and Rube caught, and Labine pitched a 10–0 shut out, and Walker hit two home runs. Rube was a very good catcher and thrower. The only thing was that Rube wasn't fast on his feet. He could do everything well but run.

"Rube also caught the final game, and years later they made a movie of my life at CBS, and Red Barber told a story that after Thomson hit the home run, he went to Charley Dressen and asked him, 'Charley, if you had to do it all over again, what would you have done?' And Charley Dressen told Red Barber, 'I'd have put Campanella in to catch, because he would have gotten Newcombe through.' "

The biggest question that lingers to this day concerns Dressen's choice of Branca over Erskine or Labine. Because Branca threw the home-run pitch and the Dodgers lost the pennant, coach Clyde Sukeforth was blamed for bringing in Branca, and at the end of the season, Sukeforth was let go. It was the second year in a row that the Dodgers dismissed a coach for something clearly out of his control. But if not Branca, then who should Dressen have chosen? According to Clem Labine, who had pitched a complete game the day before, he was never a candidate.

CLEM LABINE: "The record shows that I was warming up in the third game when Ralph went in and threw the home-run pitch to Bobby Thomson. But I wasn't warming up. Carl Erskine and Ralph Branca were warming up. After Ralph went in, only then did I get up to throw.

"I had pitched the day before. How could Charley Dressen have brought me in? And I still say the same thing. He could have brought Erskine in, he could have brought me in, the home run still would have been hit, because that's the way it's supposed to be in history. This man was supposed to hit the home run. So what's the difference whether he hits it off Branca or he hits it off Carl or me? It doesn't matter. But I try to tell people I was not warming up, and they say, 'No, I was at the game. I saw you warming up.' Sure you did. But *after* Branca went into the game.

"And after Thomson hit the home run, Charley blamed Clyde Sukeforth, who was in the bullpen, for picking the wrong guy to pitch to Thomson. If you ask me the question, 'Is he throwing well?' and I say, 'He's throwing well,' and you say to me, 'How is the other fella throwing?' and I say, 'He's not throwing well,' is that his decision or my decision? That's his decision. How dare anyone who is number one lay the fault on someone else? Charley certainly had the last say. It wasn't Clyde Sukeforth who put Branca in; it was Charley who said, 'Give me Ralph Branca.' "

CARL ERSKINE: "As soon as they get you up, you got to get ready. That's the order of business. So we both got ready. And we watched, pitch by pitch in between. We'd watch a pitch, throw another couple pitches, stop and watch the next pitch. The phone is on the wall. There is no dugout per se in the bullpen. There was a shelter over a bench down near where the two mounds were, which was deep left-center field. The phone was on the wall there.

"Clyde Sukeforth had been catching me, and I had thrown a curveball into the dirt—my overhand curve often was real low in the dirt—and when the phone call came, Dressen asked Sukeforth if we both were ready. 'Yeah, they are both throwing. Branca is throwing okay. Erskine is bouncing his curve some.' And Dressen said, 'Let me have Branca.' Kiddingly, I often say, 'Maybe that was my best curveball.'

"Sukeforth would have a more accurate recall of what the decision really hinged on. But I remember I was bouncing my curveball. He may have also told Dressen I wasn't throwing that well. He knew when my arm was hurting and I couldn't throw."

MRS. BUD PODBIELAN: "Pod had won that last game in Philadelphia, and yet he never got into one of the playoff games. He was in the bullpen when Branca went out, and yet Pod had always done real well against the Giants. He beat the Giants more than any of them, and they didn't put him in. I remember it so well. I was sitting in the stands, and Dressen went out to relieve Newcombe, and I saw who he was bringing in, and I said to myself, 'Pod's down in the bullpen, and they're going to bring in Branca! I don't believe it!' I said, 'My God, why are they doing that, putting that guy in there?' Branca always got preferential treatment. He had married [owner Dearie] Mulvey's daughter. Pod was better against the Giants than any of them. But they didn't give him a chance. Because of the manager. But Pod would never say anything to him. Pod was a very nice person.

"Afterwards I asked Pod why they didn't put him in, and he said, 'Well, what can you do?' At first he was mad. He thought he should have gone in. And he said, 'You can't say I would have done any better.' And maybe it would have happened the same way. But he figured he was ready. But who knows? Maybe the same thing would have happened to him. But I thought he was ready. Because he always pitched good against the Giants. And they didn't put him in."

Bullpen coach Clyde Sukeforth, whose comments from the bullpen influenced Dressen, insists that he went with Branca because he really didn't have any other choice.

CLYDE SUKEFORTH: "I'm not alibiing. Clem Labine was there, and Clem had pitched a shutout the day before. He was sitting in the bullpen sunning himself. He didn't even tape his ankles. He wasn't a candidate. Carl Erskine was a fine pitcher, but he had chronic arm trouble, and there were times when he just couldn't throw. Erskine got up and tried to throw, and he threw as best as he could, but there was no choice to be made as far as I was concerned, because Carl just couldn't throw. He didn't have anything. He was like that at times, and those times you had to bypass him. It was Branca all the way. Branca was really firing. He wanted to pitch the opening game in Yankee Stadium against the Yankees the next day, and he was really firing, and he was in good shape, looked real good. He just made a bad pitch, and they hit a 260-foot home run off a him.

"Dressen had been calling me from the seventh inning on. About a half dozen times. The last time, he said, 'You got him ready? Are you ready down there?' I said, 'Hell, yes. He's ready. He's been ready.' Now I'm talking about Branca. We had no choice.

"After the home run, we headed for the clubhouse, and when I went in there, you could have heard a pin drop. Quietest clubhouse I ever saw. Branca was lying on the steps inside the old Polo Grounds clubhouse.

"In the papers Charley told everyone that it was my fault. He never said anything to me, but you know Charley. I expected it. Charley was always critical and outspoken when things didn't go right, but it was always to his credit if something turned out good. But that's Charley. I knew him for years.

"And so I went to the World Series with Buzzy Bavasi and the bunch and came home, and that winter they called me and said they wanted me to manage a minor league club, and I told them no. I said, 'You folks apparently can't use me, so send me my release, and I'll see if I can get another job.' Then the newspapers started to make a big fuss over the oldest man in point of service in the organization being let go on one pitch, and they played it up pretty good, and well, then Mr. O'Malley called me and said he wanted me back in my old job. 'We're taking a beating in the press over here. We want you back.' I said, 'Mr. O'Malley, you don't want me back, and I don't want to come back, so you send me my release, and I'll see if I can get another job.' And that's when I went over to Pittsburgh. I didn't know for sure Branch would take me, but I figured he'd find something for me. Or somebody else would. I knew a lot of people."

For Ralph Branca, it would be a pitch that would haunt him for the rest of his life.

RALPH BRANCA: "I pitched the first playoff game at Ebbets Field, and so I sat as Labine beat the Giants in the second game, and now it's Wednesday, and we're playing the third game, in the Polo Grounds, and I'm in the bullpen, and I can't throw the ball sixty feet. So in the fifth inning I started to lob toss. Newcombe was doing all right, but I knew how stiff I was. And in those days we used a counter-irritant called Capsulin, which was hot stuff, on your arm, and I had put that on, and so I started to throw, and I kept on throwing, and finally my arm loosened up to where I could throw hard again. In the ninth, I had finally gotten loose, and the story goes that Dressen was talking to Sukey on the phone and Erskine bounced a curve, and Dressen asked, 'Who's ready?' and Sukeforth said, 'Branca.' He could have said 'Erskine' just as well. Now, I never spoke to Sukeforth about it, but Erskine says, 'If I hadn't bounced that curve, it might have been me.'

"And so Dressen called me in—I don't remember the walk to the mound—but I remember meeting Jackie and Pee Wee at shortstop, and they both said, 'Go get 'em,' and I remember Charley saying, 'Get him out.' No instructions, just 'Get him out,' and he went into the dugout, and Rube Walker and I went over the signs, and I wanted to get ahead of him on the first pitch, and I threw a fastball right through the middle, and I had mustard on it.

"And the next pitch I had wanted to waste, so I threw a fastball up and in, and I might have aimed it, which I tend to believe I probably did, and he hit it with an uppercut, it had overspin, and he hit it down the line, and it was sinking, and all I could remember saying was, 'Sink, sink, sink,' and it just did go in. It went in like six inches over the wall. Probably went over the wall at 300 feet.

"And from there to the locker room, I don't remember. I remember getting in the locker room and sitting on the steps, and I remember Barney Stein taking pictures, and I think it was Will Grimsley who gave me a hard time, wanted to talk to me, and I said, 'Just leave me alone, just leave me alone.' And that's about what I remember. I sat there a long time, and the guys drifted out, and finally I went up and took a shower and got out of there.

"Anne and I were engaged, we were going to be married in seventeen days, and when I finally got out to the car, Anne started to cry. And she had a cousin who's a priest, Father Pat Rowley, and I said to him, 'Why me?' He said, 'God chose you because he knew your faith would be strong enough to bear this cross.' And I accepted that, that it would be something I would have to bear for the rest of my life, and I would accept it. I went about my business, but it was tough on the family. Idiots would call my house and talk to my mother: 'Your son should learn how to pitch.'

"I went to dinner with Sal Maglie about three years ago, and I told him what I was trying to do with that pitch, and he said, 'If you wasted it 'cause you wanted him to hit the curveball, why didn't you just throw him the curveball? Why did you waste a fastball, especially in a situation like that?' And he was so right. But Sal had the experience. If I had gotten it way inside, if I had thought knockdown or brushback, I would have been better off. 'Cause then he wouldn't have been able to handle it.

"But all these years I've lived with it, and it really hadn't bothered me. I'll tell you, though, it has started to bother me lately. In 1976 I went to an old timers' game in Texas and an old timers' game in San Diego, and they got me out onto the field after the introduction, and each time they played Russ Hodges's record, and after two weeks in a row of this, Ralph Kiner said, 'Hey, Ralph, what are you doing? You don't need this crap.' And that kind of got to me, and since then the Mets showed a picture of me [Barney Stein's famous photo of Branca, hunched over and weeping in the Dodger clubhouse after the home run] in their ad without even consulting me. I probably would have given permission had they asked, because as I say, it doesn't really bother me, but lately it bothers me more than it had in the previous twenty-five years.

"I look back at my record. I won twenty-one in '47, I won twelve in the middle of the next year, and I had ten in the middle of the next year, and I won twelve by the middle of '51. Put 'em all together, and I got a lot of wins. I have nothing to be ashamed of. I was one of the best young pitchers in the history of the game.

"My only regret in baseball is hurting my back in spring training the next year. They had just waxed the floor in Vero Beach in the lobby of the barracks we stayed in, and I went to sit on a folding chair, and it slid out from under me, and I landed on top of a Coke bottle, and it hit me right next to the anal opening, and it really cut me, and it tilted my pelvis. I went to the trainer and I told him what happened, and he should have done a realignment on me, but he didn't, and that whole year, 1952, I was 4 and 2, but I couldn't throw. And as I said, my only regret was that because I hurt my back I couldn't prove to people that the home run didn't affect me. A writer said, 'Branca's too intelligent, and he's let it affect him.' Shit, it didn't affect me. Who had they picked to come in? I wasn't the worst pitcher on the staff, you know. They picked the best pitcher they had. I'm the guy who had the guts enough to want to pitch. As I said, any other guy who couldn't throw the ball fifty feet would have given up the ghost and said, 'I can't make it.' But I was a competitor. I relished coming in in a jam.

"Anyway, the next year, that would be 1953, I came home from spring training, and a local doctor made an adjustment on me, told me my pelvis was tilted. He asked me if I had any pain, and I didn't, but from that point on I could throw hard again, but not consistently, and I was traded to Detroit.

"I like Bobby. He's a good guy. He knows it was his moment of glory, and yet he knows he's not a Hall of Famer, and I know I'm not a Hall of Famer, and yet we both achieved notoriety. I just like Bobby. He's a good person. And yet there have been so many of these old timers' games where this has been the theme, and I've gone to them, and I shouldn't say this, but I may not go to the next one, 'cause I've had it. It's thirty years now, time to bury it. Sisler hit a home run off Newcombe and won a pennant for Philadelphia, and Mazeroski hit a home run off Ralph Terry to win the World Series, and Bench hit a home run off somebody to win the pennant in a playoff game, and you never hear about those things. Chambliss's home run off Littell. You don't hear about that. Bucky Dent's home run off Torrez. He hung him a slider inside. But you don't hear about that.

"The only reason you hear about Branca–Thomson is it was in New York, and there was a great rivalry between the Dodgers and the Giants."

10

Dick Young

Don Honig: "Every night at nine o'clock we would stand out in front of the candy store waiting for the *Daily News* truck to come up. You could see it way down the avenue—there was another candy store about a quarter of a mile down the street—and you could see the truck stop there. There were always a bunch of old guys named Eddie wearing cloth caps from the Depression, and when they spotted the *News* truck, they'd yell, 'Here it comes!' It was like the docking of a luxury liner. The *Queen Elizabeth* was coming in. The *News* truck was here.

"Why was this such an important even? Because the details of the Dodger game were in there. We already knew every pitch that was thrown. We had listened to the game on the radio. We had discussed it for three hours. Now we were going to read about it. Now it would become scripture.

"The truck would pull up, and the guy who owned the store would come out, and he would take the wired up bundles of newspapers and put them on his shoulder, and if you were lucky, you got to carry a bundle of papers and follow him in. You were holding the Holy Stuff, and you'd slam down your two cents on the table, and never mind that the Cold War was going on on the front page. The first thing you'd do was open up the back page and read about the Dodgers. That was the grip the team had. You couldn't get enough of them.

"The *Daily News* was the Dodger fans' paper, and Dick Young was the guy who covered the Dodgers. In those days he was a young, fairly liberal sportswriter, and he had a tremendous following. Young always had a great lead for every story. He got the reader right into the story, and he wrote with wit and vividness. He was controversial. You wanted to read him before anything else. I couldn't wait to read Dick Young's account of the Dodger game every night."

Larry King: "We always read a lot of newspapers. We got the *Mirror* for Walter Winchell, and *PM* and the *Post* influenced my politics because *PM* had Milton Gross and it had Barnaby, the wonderful cartoonist, and it was a marvelous paper to read. The *Post* was James Weschler and Earl Wilson. We thought the *Post* was the best paper. We didn't read the *Times*. The

Times was the Yankees. We thought the *Daily News*'s editorials were hysterical garbage, hogwash, extreme right wing, but what the *Daily News* had was Dick Young. Dick Young was our idol. Dick Young was the Dodgers to us."

DICK YOUNG: "I grew up in Washington Heights. That's uptown Manhattan, and when I was growing up, the movies were doing newspaper stories, just like they do doctor or private detective stories now on TV. They were doing Lee Tracy and *The Front Page*. Clark Gable and Spencer Tracy were newspapermen. The big guys were newspaper guys, and there was the guy with the pushed-up hat and the ribbon and the press badge in his fedora who would run in and say, 'Stop the presses.' That's who I wanted to be.

"My parents had been divorced when I was very young, so I didn't know my father too well. My mother brought me up. She worked, and she boarded me out for a while with a wonderful Italian family, and after that I lived with my grandparents for a while. My father lived in California, and when I graduated high school, my mother said that was as far as she could take me. She said I should go to California and have my father put me through college. But my father had remarried, and I wasn't too welcomed out there.

"I lied about my father having custody in order to claim California residency and go to Los Angeles Junior College and then UCLA for free, and it took them about three months to check up on me and find out my mother had custody. So they said, 'You've got to get up the $75 nonresidency fee.' In 1936 nobody had $75. That was the asshole of the Depression. And so I had to quit.

"I was working for the Civilian Conservation Corps, helping to build a beach on Upper Cayuga Lake, when my mother cut out a clipping in the *Daily News* that told about how they were going to develop their own reporters. They weren't going to do what had been accepted policy for years—go to a small-town paper and take an established writer, the way Hearst and Pulitzer and everyone else always did. They wanted to develop their own farm system, and they were going to take college graduates and give them jobs as copyboys, because in the middle of the Depression, you could get a college graduate to work as a copyboy for fifteen bucks a week. And after I read that clipping, I wrote a letter to Harvey Duell, the managing editor of the *News,* who strangely enough answered me. I told him I wasn't a college graduate and told him of my experience of trying to go to college, but he said he couldn't waive that. I asked him if I could go to college while I was working there, and he said he couldn't do that either. 'We can't waive the rule for you,' he said, but he said there were other departments at the *News* where I didn't have to be a college graduate, and he said if something opened up in that direction he would let me know.

"I wrote two or three more times to him, and he always answered, which was amazing when you think about it—here was the managing editor of a big newspaper corresponding with a kid in the CCC camp. And sure enough, one day a letter arrived saying there was an opening in the publication department as a messenger. The publication department is the mechanical advertising department, where you take the advertising copy from the department stores or agencies and you prepare it for the paper. And so I hitchhiked on Route 17 from Seneca Falls, New York, in the wintertime for an interview, and I got the job. That was the beginning. I was one step lower than copyboy.

"I worked this job maybe a year, and then I got promoted to taking photostats of advertising layouts. In the meantime Jimmy Powers was the sports editor and columnist, and I started sending little tidbits to him, and he began printing them. Commentary, wisecracks, anything out of my head. I once wrote a whole column on stickball in New York. Abbott and Costello were sponsoring a stickball league, and Powers was from the Midwest and didn't know shit about stickball, 'cause unless you were from New York you didn't know, and that's what inspired me to do it. And he printed the whole column under his byline. I didn't mind.

"Meanwhile I got married and was going to NYU taking economics and journalism courses toward a degree, but I never got very far because it was too much. Around 1939 a job opened up in the editorial department as a copyboy. I had to take a $5-a-week cut to take it. My wife went out and got a salesman's job in Woolworth's for a year or two until the guild scale got me back that $5. My mother watched the kid. When the peacetime draft came along, some of the guys were taken out of the sports department, and they needed a tabulator keeping box scores and racing scores. They needed a kid, and that kid turned out to be me, and then the war broke out, and I was deferred because I had a wife and kid, and Powers started sending me out on a couple things like the Metropolitan Trials up in the Bronx, a ballgame here and there—I made some trips with the Giants and the Yankees—and it went from there. In 1946 Rickey started a Brooklyn football team, and one of the sportswriters, Jack Smith, left the *News* to join Rickey, and I got the Dodgers, and that was the start of my life.

"I picked up the Dodgers opening day 1946. And I covered the team until they left at the end of 1957. The twelve greatest years that could ever happen to a kid. And so, because of the Brooklyn Dodgers, I got a half-assed reputation, and that's the truth, because you can write under a bushel basket, and nobody will notice.

"I was a kid. I was enthusiastic. And I had this advantage: I was their age, and I ran with the ballplayers. Sure, some of the other writers resented me. One of the guys, Joe King, was complaining that I was hanging around the Western Union office there to try to look at their copy. Ken Smith said, 'He's not doing that. He's just trying to make the Western Union girl.' Kenny Smith knew I wouldn't stoop to reading their copy.

"Charley Segar was a sour-faced guy to a lot of people, but I will always remember this: When I started out, I wrote slowly because I picked and chose each word, and the other guys would get through before I did, and Charley would say, 'I'll wait for you. We'll go back together. Don't worry about it,' which was nice. And you remember those things, and so you try to do something for the good young kids coming up. You pass it down from one generation to the other, give them a little help.

"My philosophy was always to talk to the reader as though you're talking to him in person. That's all, and I still believe in that. Guys gotta get too cute. Guys gotta get too involved. Guys get too contrived. Just write as though you're talking to a guy in the bar, wisecracking, part serious, part argumentative, part angry, and a laugh here and there. That's the whole thing. My boss, Charley Hoerter, saw this, and he moved me along fairly well. Hoerter knew very early in his career that he couldn't write, so he became an editor, and he would go to a bar, perhaps across the street from the *News* with the printers, and he'd play devil's advocate, and he'd say, 'That Young doesn't know what the hell he's talking about,' and he'd wait for a reaction. Evidently the guys in the bar said nice things about me, and so Charley would come back to me and say, 'Hey kid, I don't want you to get a swelled head, but you're the best baseball writer in New York.' "

ROGER KAHN: "Young had the idea that you don't write the game, because the game will insinuate itself. There are so many days where you have to write the game, but if you can find a way to get away from it, you write that. That was his perfectly brilliant analysis of what a morning paper does, and it still holds today. In the era of television and radio, you don't say, 'The Dodgers beat the Giants, 6 to 2.' You say, 'Yesterday, in the Dodgers' 6–2 win over the Giants, the most interesting thing that happened was . . .' That's the best definition of what a morning story of a ballgame ought to be. And he worked that out by himself, and that was the New Journalism."

The New Journalism included a frankness in reporting that had never been seen before. If a player had a weakness, Young would write about it, explain it, describe it, analyze it, and because he was a writer of influence, certain players felt that he was capable of hurting their reputation with the fans or even adversely affecting their careers, and they began to resent and distrust him. As for the managers, at one time or another Leo Durocher, Burt Shotton, and Chuck Dressen each barred Young from the dressing room because of his rapier-sharp reporting.

CARL FURILLO: "Dick was a bastard, and some guys were ready to beat the living hell out of him. I remember he used to write about Gene Hermanski. He hated Hermanski. See, Hermanski was a shufflefoot. Gene would misjudge balls. He could hit, and he could run, but he wasn't a good fielder. We were out in the outfield, and we were practicing ground balls, and Durocher said to Gene, 'Watch Furillo. He fields the ball just like an infielder.' Gene, instead of relaxing, he would be stiff-armed, and if the ball would come up, he couldn't come up, 'cause he was stiff. And we tried to show him what the hell to do, and I don't know whether he was a Polish knucklehead or what, but he just couldn't pick it up right. In other words, 'The hell with you guys, I'll do it my way. I'm a major leaguer.' And Dick Young got wind of this, and he blasted him, and Hermanski was ready to fight him. Another time Young wrote that Hermanski hit the ball 400 feet: 200 up and 200 down. Hermanski pushed Young around the clubhouse.

"And Dick would blast Durocher or Shotton or Dressen, and they would bar him from the clubhouse. I couldn't figure out why the hell they barred him, because the truth is the truth, and who the hell's afraid of the truth? But I guess a lot of people are. But Dick and I always got along. I used to say to him, 'You know the best part of you, Dick?' Dick is Jewish. 'You married an Italian.' "

CLEM LABINE: "When I first came up, I had pitched in Philadelphia, and in his column Young ended it with a postscript about me: 'Oh yes, a young reliever from St. Paul came in to relieve against Philadelphia in the eighth inning, and this young fireman's sole equipment to put out a fire seems to be gasoline.' That's writing! That's something to laugh at, not get angry at. It's a good comment. Okay, I can't get angry at that. But I got angry when Dick Young ceased to be my friend.

"It happened in Philadelphia, and I had had a pretty bad outing, lost the game, and there was a small bar next to the Warwick Hotel in Philadelphia, so I went there with someone to drown my sorrows with a couple of beers. Dick came in, and he ended up buying me a beer, and we got to talking, and he was very sympathetic. He said, 'You have to expect that you're going to lose games when you come in in the late innings.'

"When I got back to Bay Ridge after the road trip, I went to get a haircut, and my barber said, 'Hey, I saved one of Dick Young's articles for you.' And as he's cutting my hair, I'm reading this article, which Dick had written the same night as our little talk, and he wrote that I shouldn't be the late relief pitcher because I didn't seem to have the kind of fortitude that was necessary to be a late-inning reliever.

"I could hardly wait to get to the clubhouse the next day. I wanted to hit him so badly, but I wanted it to be fair, so I asked the trainer to tape one arm behind my back. He taped me, and I waited for him to come in. I said, 'Okay, Dick. I want you to do me a favor. I want you to take a swing at me first, because I want it known that I hit you after you hit me.'

"He ran out of the clubhouse. I ran out after him. But from that day on, we were never friendly again.

"I remember the last time I spoke to him. I was a Met, and I was retiring, and we were on the bus, and I said to Dick, 'You always seem to be looking for unimportant things to write about. Here's a chance: I'm leaving baseball, and yet you haven't even asked me a question about how I feel.' He said, 'How do you feel?' I said, 'I'm going to find a writer, and when I do, I'm going to tell him.'

"And that's the last time that I had anything to say to Dick Young."

When Walter O'Malley took over the Dodgers, the public relations–minded owner made certain that he would have no trouble with Young. One of the first things O'Malley did was assign Buzzy Bavasi the job of keeping Young happy.

ROGER KAHN: "O'Malley hadn't planned and schemed all his life so that Dick

Young would call him a bastard five days a week in the *Daily News,* so when he took over he put Emile J. "Buzzy" Bavasi in charge of Dick Young. I once said to Fresco Thompson in the Dodger front office, 'I guess one of the first things Walter wanted to do was get the *Daily News* and Young off their neck.' He said, '*One* of the first things? It was *the* first thing.'

"And so Bavasi captured Young, and he was in the Dodger hip pocket all the time, until it became clear that the Dodgers were going to leave. The *Daily News* was to the Dodgers what the *Osservatore Romano* was to the Vatican. It gave the Dodger line. Young gave the Dodger line. The guys he liked were the guys management liked. The *News* became a Bavasi–O'Malley house organ. He did what they wanted him to do. Young would be spicy and take little knocks, but on the large issues, he never attacked the organization until right at the end, when the Dodgers were going to move. And then he knocked the hell out of O'Malley, 'cause what was going to become of Dick?

"During the World Series in '59, I asked Dick, 'Do you see Walter? Does he say hello to you?' Dick said, 'No, he waves to me,' indicating that O'Malley was waving for him to go away.

"I remember the classic: Junior Gilliam was having a very good early spring, didn't miss a pitch at bat, at the least fouled everything off, and so Young writes a story that Gilliam is going to play second base and Robinson will play third. I'm scooped. I went to Dressen, and I said, 'What is this? Is it true?' He won't meet my eye. I said, 'Why didn't you tell me?' He said, 'Well, you didn't ask.' And I knew where it came from. From Bavasi's suite, where he made grasshopper cocktails. He had called Young and said, 'We're going to play Gilliam and make Robinson the third baseman.' I said to Young, 'How do you think you got that a day ahead of everybody else?' Young said, 'It was only logical.'

"Dick Young had 2 million circulation, he had terrific reporting ability, and he had Bavasi. How could you compete with that? Who was there? Gus Steiger of the *Mirror* didn't count. He would drive Young crazy because Dick would write a complicated game from fourteen different angles, and he would work hard to figure out how to do it, and Steiger wouldn't bother. Steiger would write: 'Normalcy returned to Ebbets Field yesterday as the Dodgers defeated the Giants 8 to 6 in a wild and woolly game.' That would be his lead, and it would drive Young crazy. Young would call Steiger with heavy sarcasm, 'Hey, coach, what's your angle gonna be on this one?' Stanley Woodward had been called 'coach,' and the word about the *Mirror* was that Dan Parker, the sports editor, didn't want any good writers around, because if he had bad writers around, his column would stand out like a jewel in a cesspool.

"At the *Journal-American* was Mike Gavin. I have a funny memory. The Dodgers beat the Reds 19–1, scoring fifteen runs in the first inning. If I was doing the story, my angle would be, how do you get fifteen runs in one inning? How do you cover the game? In a comedic way. Try to be funny. I pick up the *Journal* the next day, and here's Mike Gavin's lead: 'Overlooked in last night's 19–1 Dodger victory over Cincinnati was a fine pitching performance by Chris Van Cuyk.' Well, hell, you give me fifteen runs in the first inning, and I submit I'd win it just because the other guys just want to get out of there. But that was Gavin.

"At the *Times* was Roscoe McGowan. He was a helluva guy. I don't know how much Roscoe was limited by what the *Times* was willing to print. The *Times,* though, usually printed the score and what happened in the game.

"Who was Young really competing against? Me, that's who. Me with the *Tribune.* Mike Gavin said that the only people who read the *Tribune* were six Wall Street brokers and a lot of secretaries trying to impress their bosses. Hell, he may have been right. The *News* was selling 2 million, and the *Tribune* 350,000. So Dick Young had Bavasi. Who did I have?"

Kahn had Jackie Robinson.

DICK YOUNG: "Some of the guys felt Bavasi was giving me inside information. Living in Brooklyn I would stop off at Borough Hall, go up to see Bavasi, spend some time in the office, and then continue on to the *Daily News* to do my early editions first, before the night game. In those days, you always went to the office. And I would stop in to see Bavasi, and nobody else would. It's like anything else. If you put in the time, if you're there, you'll get things that other guys don't get. So the guys who weren't there would always look for the crutch, and they'd say I was getting special treatment. I wasn't. Buzzy himself said to the other guys, 'You come around, and I'll tell you the same thing.' He wasn't going to call them up and tell them. And that applies today. There are no shortcuts. You get stories by working. There's no substitute."

Chuck Dressen

In 1952 Charley Dressen won ninety-six games managing the Dodgers, and the ballplayers lost fifty-seven. That same year Charley Dressen won the National League pennant, and the ballplayers lost the World Series. Whenever a Dressen-led team won, after the game in the dressing room, Dressen could be heard explaining to reporters how "I did this, I did that." His three favorite words were "I," "I'm," and "I'll." (John Lardner once said that was because Dressen had spent his early playing career in the Three-I League.)

Dressen had spent many years coaching the Dodgers under Leo Durocher, and naturally there was a great deal of Durocher in Dressen, except that Dressen wasn't as abrasive as Leo. Charley would not have thrown at his mother's head in a crucial situation. The legs maybe, but not the head.

It was Dressen who once in the late innings of a losing ballgame told his players, "Wait a minute, and I'll think of something." And often he did. Though most of the men who played for him mocked his ego, they acknowledged—some grudgingly—that he had one of the brightest baseball minds they had ever seen.

ROY CAMPANELLA: "Charley was one of the best at reading pitchers' signs.

He could tell what a pitcher would throw just by watching his hands. He would then relay the information to the hitter. And I'd take advantage of that. If I knew what a pitcher was going to throw, and if it was in the zone, I'd look for it and hit it.

"I remember we were playing the Giants one day in Brooklyn, and Jim Hearn of the Giants was beating us 2 to 1 in the ninth inning, and with two outs Jackie came up and hit the ball to Alvin Dark, and Dark booted it. I was the next hitter, and Dressen called me to the sideline and said, 'Now, look, Hearn's going to throw you a curveball on the first pitch. If it's a good strike and you like it, hit it.' And that's exactly what Hearn did, he threw me a curve, and I hit it upstairs in the bleachers, and we won the game that quick. As I was rounding third base, Dressen said, 'Didn't I tell you?' He was something else. I liked his baseball charisma."

Dressen was at his best when he was leading the Dodgers of the 1950s against Durocher's Giants. For years Dressen had worked under Durocher's shadow, and when the Dodgers battled against the Giants, Dressen went out of his way to prove that he could manage as well—or better—than his former boss.

One day Durocher sent Artie Wilson up to pinch hit for the pitcher. Dressen, who had managed Wilson at Oakland, immediately signaled right fielder Carl Furillo to play on the grass in the infield between Gil Hodges at first and Junior Gilliam at second. Dressen was leaving the whole right field area open, even though Wilson batted left-handed. Five men were playing infield, and Wilson grounded out to Gilliam.

"I knew this fella just can't pull to right field," said Dressen.

A baseball and football star in high school, Dressen had been offered an athletic scholarship at Millikin University. But at the time he was making $67 a week playing quarterback for the hometown Decatur Staleys, the forerunners of the Chicago Bears, and he didn't go. Dressen once told *New York Tribune* reporter Roger Kahn that he had never read a book. "You think I should?" he asked Kahn. Kahn said, "Sure, Charley. It would help your vocabulary. You'd learn new words. You'd make better speeches." Dressen thought about it. "Aw, fuck," he said, "I got this far without reading a book. I ain't gonna start now."

ROGER KAHN: "Dressen used to say, 'I wish they wuz all Reese and Robinson.' I'd say, 'If they wuz all Reese and Robinson, they wouldn't need no manager.'

"Dressen once said, 'All ballplayers are dumb, and outfielders are the dumbest.' I said, 'What do you mean?' He said, 'That Snider, that Furiller.'

"He said the trouble with Labine as a starting pitcher was that he was an incubator baby, and no incubator baby could go nine innings.

"I remember, it was 1952, and he said to me, 'We ain't gonna win no fucking pennant this year.' I said, 'What do you mean you're not going to win the pennant this year?' He said, 'I ain't gonna win no fucking pennant. They gave me two outfielders who are minor leaguers,' meaning Dick Williams and Don Thompson. Thompson had a good glove, Williams a loud mouth.

George Brace Photo

CHARLES DRESSEN

The two pricks of summer were Williams and pitcher Jim Hughes. So I wrote what Charley told me: 'Bright, middle-aged men are messing up the team, according to manager Charley Dressen.' At that point I was rooting too much. Who cares if Montreal wins? It's the Dodgers who are important. As soon as the *Tribune* came out, one of the few people who bought the paper—all Jews in Brooklyn read the *Times,* and all the *goyim* read the *Tribune,* and there weren't many *goyim* in Brooklyn—one of the few was Buzzy Bavasi, who immediately was on the phone to Dressen. 'You want to get fired right now? What did you tell Kahn? You manage the twenty-five guys I give you. That's your job. You can be back in Oakland in ten minutes.'

"I come on the field, and Charley whistles me over. He said, 'You didn't have to write that stuff.' I said, 'What?' And he told me what Bavasi said. I said, 'Jesus, Charley, I'm sorry. I didn't know Bavasi was going to do something like that.' He said, 'Forget it. Just remember what happened. We can start again right now.' I said, 'Fine, Charley.' He said, 'And another thing, they're giving me the wrong pitchers.'

"I didn't write that."

HAROLD ROSENTHAL: "Dressen was very helpful. He'd discuss anything with a reporter. Dressen wanted to be liked. He was like a kid who, if another child expressed admiration for something he had, he'd say, 'You want it? You can have it.' Dressen especially did this with food. He had friends from all over who would send him something special like crabmeat. One guy on the coast sent him crab fingers. A guy from down South sent him pigs' knuckles, and when it arrived he'd pass the word: 'We got something special in the pressroom after the game,' and he'd stand and watch for an expression of satisfaction or enjoyment as everyone sat around eating his food.

"Dressen took the Dodgers to a playoff in '51 and to the World Series in '52 and '53, and with a little bit of luck he would have won, but each time they were a little short of pitching. They didn't have the fourth man the Yankees had. Not that Dressen didn't try to find that fourth pitcher. You never saw so many guys tried out as pitchers. They came and went, all kinds of guys."

If Dressen had one glaring fault as a manager it was that he had difficulty communicating with his players. Often he would antagonize them because he pigheadedly insisted on having his way.

CLEM LABINE: "We grumbled about Charley. You have to understand that players grumble about all managers. On a one-to-one basis, if you asked me who I'd rather play for, Charley or Walter Alston, I would say there would be a lot more excitement playing under Charley, but I'd rather play for Walter Alston. Because Walt would listen to your situation and not always be thinking of his own. When you talked to Charley, Charley wouldn't be thinking about what you were saying to him but rather what he was going to say to you. So you never really got it in.

"Charley was an old-school type of player. People might have said, 'This player you have to treat with kid gloves,' but managers in those days would have said, 'Bull. Everybody gets treated the same on my club. I got twenty-five guys, and nobody's gonna get treated any better than anybody else.' Try that today, and you're not going to have a job.

"Charley did have a lot of finesse. He knew the rules backwards and forwards. Charley was a real studier of pitchers, loved to steal signs, loved to steal signs from the catcher. Where Alston was a believer in, 'If you can get that man in scoring position, give yourself up,' Charley would say, 'Give yourself up, hell. Hit the Goddamn ball out of the ballpark, and let's go home.' And Charley was an exciting individual to play for. If he wasn't fighting one person, he was fighting another.

"Dressen had words with everybody. Dressen was not the type of person who called you into his office. He'd tell you right there. Where the smart manager would have words behind closed doors. Not Dressen. That's where he showed his lack of intelligence.

"We had a pitcher by the name of Erv Palica. Erv probably had the best stuff of any pitcher that I've ever seen. Great versatility. But Charley challenged his guts once in the clubhouse in front of everybody, and Erv never retaliated, didn't make a move toward Charley to say, 'Why, you can't do that to me.' If he had said to me, 'You don't have any guts,' well, I'm gonna crowd you, I'm gonna fight you. I don't care if you're tall or small. Especially because I was a professional athlete. But Charley made Erv lose face, and he lost confidence entirely.

"In 1952 I came up with a sore arm in spring training. When I got there, I had injured my back, I don't remember doing what, playing basketball perhaps. Finally, in the beginning of August, they sent me down to St. Paul for a couple of weeks.

"About the end of August, my arm came back, and it was in good, good shape, and I could throw! I returned to Brooklyn, but Charley refused to pitch me a single inning for the rest of the year. I remember Snider would say, 'Jeez, I can't hit you in batting practice. Why the hell doesn't he let you pitch?' Charley kept saying, 'No, you're not ready.' Christ, we went into the World Series in '52, and I had as good stuff as I was gonna have all of '53, and yet I couldn't get to pitch. I couldn't make him believe that I was better.

"He had me pitching batting practice every day. I pitched batting practice into the World Series. What a waste! I say it was a waste because it *was* a waste. I had such good stuff. I used to come home and tell my wife, 'Gee, as much as I want to get into a World Series, I can't get in and pitch, for crying out loud. He won't let me pitch, and I gotta pitch.' I used to say to him, 'Charley, Charley, for crying out loud, watch me. Why don't you come behind the batting practice cage and watch me throw?' He'd say, 'Next year. You'll play next year.'

"He wouldn't pitch me. He just wouldn't listen."

CARL ERSKINE: "Charley was a throwback to the old-school type of manager who called all the shots, made all the decisions, didn't want to be challenged.

"Ted Lyons was the first pitching coach the Dodgers ever employed, and

Ted was a little frustrated, having been an outstanding pitcher himself, because Charley made the decisions. He wasn't against Lyons. He didn't use any of his coaches. Charley even coached third base. That was the way they did it in the old days, and that's the way he wanted to do it. Leo did it that way. A lot of managers did.

"I didn't have any problem with that. Dressen, I felt, always gave me the right kind of encouragement. I guess I really could have played for anybody. I didn't fight with the manager, although I didn't agree with him all the time. A classic example: In 1952 Dressen brought Joe Black in to replace Newcombe, and Joe had one of the greatest single seasons you'd ever want to see a player have. And because it was Charley's move, he was putting his hot guy in every chance he could. If he could get five or six innings out of his starter, hey, you're gone because he wanted Joe Black in to slam the door, which he did. But one day I was in the fifth inning with a four-run lead, and had two men on and two out, and I had struggled a little bit, but I had a lead and I only needed one out to be the pitcher of record.

"Dressen had a rule. When he came to the mound, you were not to speak unless you were spoken to. So he came to the mound and took the ball away from me, made the change, Black came in, finished the game, and got the win. I was hot, angry, and I left, which was against the rules. If you were taken out of the game, you were supposed to stay until the game was over.

"The next day Dressen called me into his office, and he said, 'You don't get mad very often, do you?' I said, 'No, not unless I have a real good reason.' He said, 'Well, you didn't have a real good reason yesterday. Were you mad yesterday?' I said, 'Yeah, I was mad yesterday. But I'm all right today.' He said, 'Well, I like to see you get mad. Good for ya. You ought to get tougher once in a while.' And he said, 'I didn't call you in here to apologize. I just called you in here to tell you that I am running this team.' I said, 'Fine.' I always understood that. It was no problem. I was over it.

"Charley and I got along fine, and I think we had mutual respect for each other. Pee Wee respected Charley, and I know Jackie did. Dressen admired Jackie. Dressen had been a hardnosed player, and he admired that in Jackie. He totally admired that. He hated any hint that when you put that uniform on that you couldn't stick your chin out and be tough. And Jackie was tough.

"Still, Charley had a way of getting under your skin if you let him. Dressen was not always complimentary to pitchers, 'cause he was from the old school, and he never pitched himself, and he thought he understood pitchers, everything about pitchers. Nobody can tell a pitcher, unless you've been there, in the terms he really understands. So some of the pitchers didn't take Charley's advice all that well. He had a lot of good theories and ideas, but he had never done it, and I don't think he really did fully understand. And he couldn't understand an arm injury very well. You couldn't see any blood. A guy slides into second and tears up his knee and gets spiked, why, gosh, you can see it. You can help him out, get him out of the lineup, give him rest, but if a pitcher pulls a muscle in his arm, it doesn't bleed, no bones protrude, no discoloration, and yet the guy can't break a pane of glass. Well, Dressen and some of the other old-school guys loved to say, 'It's all in his head.' That's tough to sell to a guy who genuinely has a bad arm. So Dressen was not all that understanding with pitchers sometimes. He thought you ought to go out there and pitch a doubleheader and be ready the next day.

"With Dressen and Durocher both, you either liked playing for him or you hated it. You didn't have very much neutrality with those two guys. You either liked their style or you didn't want any part of it. Charley was a good baseball man, number one. We would be behind, and Charley would say, 'You guys hold 'em, and I'll think of something.'

"Charley knew my personality, and he helped me win twenty ball games in '53, because the first half of the season I was 5 and 4. Came the all-star break, and I had five wins and four losses. I had pitched quite a bit, and I had pitched pretty well. But I hadn't won. So Charley talked to me. We were in Milwaukee. We were on the road. He said, 'Hey, you're snakebit. You pitch well, and you're getting beat on one pitch. You make one bad pitch, and it costs you. You're having a bad stretch.' He said, 'I'm going to change your luck. I'm going to take you fishing.' He knew I liked to go fishing. So he took me fishing. We had a beautiful time. Caught some fish. And I came back, and in the second half of the year I was 15 and 2."

Loes and Black

The Dodgers in 1952 had to make up for the loss of their pitching ace, Don Newcombe, who was drafted into the service after a three-year pitching career in which he had won seventeen, nineteen, and twenty games. Among National League pitchers, only Boston's Warren Spahn had won more games during that period. Spahnie had put together three seasons of twenty-one, twenty-one, and twenty-two victories. The Phils' Robin Roberts had also won fifty-six games during that three-year stretch, winning fifteen, twenty, and twenty-one games. Spahn and Roberts were not drafted and without interrupted careers went on to post Hall of Fame numbers. Newcombe, away for what surely would have been two more twenty-game seasons, lost his niche in the Hall.

Without Newcombe, Charley Dressen appeared to have a serious case of the pitching shorts. As replacements Dressen could choose among a group of unknowns, including Ben Wade, Chris Van Cuyk, John Rutherford, bonus baby Billy Loes, and Negro League star Joe Black.

As things turned out, the pitching situation became even more desperate because Preacher Roe injured his arm. In 1951 Roe had won twenty-two games. In '52 Roe only won eleven. Dressen had thirty victories to make up between Newcombe and Roe. But Charley boasted, as usual, that if everyone stayed calm, he would come up with something, or rather somebody.

And he did. Except for Carl Erskine, who finished the year 14–6, the pitching staff was not impressive, and Dressen has to be given a lot of credit for manipulating it to bring the Dodgers a pennant. He put Joe Black in the bullpen and got a big year out of him, and he got a couple of decent performances out of Wade, who finished 11–9, and Loes, whose record was 13–8 with a 2.69 era.

Loes was almost a Brooklyn boy. He was signed out of Bryant High School, from Astoria, Long Island. Another mile or two over and he would have made it. As a teenager Loes showed great speed and remarkable maturity as a pitcher. Branch Rickey gave him as a bonus an unheard-of $21,000. But Billy Loes, the Dodgers found out later, had one minor personality quirk: He was totally lacking in ambition. There are few starting pitchers who don't dream of winning twenty games. Loes was one of them. His ambition was to *not* win twenty games!

REX BARNEY: "Billy Loes was a delightful guy. He joined us in 1950, when he was barely twenty years old, and I want to be kind, because Billy was such a neat guy, but as far as schooling was concerned, he was pretty dumb; yet he was streetwise, and on the mound he was a genius.

"I remember when he came with the club. He could sit there and tell you how to pitch to every hitter. And he had never been in a ballpark. He didn't know what was going on. But he knew how to pitch. He had baseball sense like no one I've ever known.

"Billy Loes was famous for his quotes. He was pitching in the World Series one year against the Yankees. They asked him, 'How do you think the Dodgers will do?' Usually you say, 'I think we'll win it in five or win it in six.' Billy said, 'The Yankees will win it in six.' And they did.

"He'd say things to writers. Billy hated spring training. Hated to run. Dick Young cornered him in Vero Beach and asked, 'If you got a nice job back in Brooklyn paying a hundred, a hundred and fifty a week, would you take it?' And Billy said, 'In a minute.'

"One year he had a clause in his contract that if he won fourteen games he would get a bonus. So it's August, and he's won the fourteen games, and he's on his way to twenty games, and he calls Buzzy Bavasi and says, 'I want my bonus money.' Buzzy said, 'What are you talking about?' Billy said, 'I won my fourteen games.' Buzzy said, 'Billy, the season isn't over.' He said, 'I'm not going to pitch any more. I won fourteen games. I don't want to win more than fourteen games. I get my money by winning fourteen games. That's all I want.' Billy said, 'If I win twenty, you'll want me to win twenty all my life. I don't want to win twenty. I want to win fourteen. I can win fourteen every year.' That's a true story. That's the way he was. When he was traded to Baltimore, he told them the same thing."

ROGER KAHN: "Loes was a pretty good ballplayer, talented, but he was a very strange guy. I remember I was playing Ping-Pong in Vero Beach, and my wife, Joan, had played college tennis, and she was a pretty fair Ping-Pong player, and she wore glasses, and Loes started to play with Joan, and his first words were, 'Geez, I can't lose to a goil.' Wump, wump, wump, she wins the first point, and he points to her glasses and says, 'I thought they wuz fogged up but they ain't.' That's what I remember about Billy. Not exactly a continental, debonair guy.

George Brace Photo

BILL LOES

"But Dressen seemed to have a good rapport with him. One day in spring training the pitchers were supposed to be out running, and Cookie Lavagetto comes upon Loes, who is sleeping under a palm tree. Cookie says, 'What are you doing?' Loes says, 'I'm a pitcher, not a runner.'

"And there was a funny sexual adventure where Billy and another Dodger employee both were shacking up with the same girl in New Jersey, and she got pregnant. And under the advice of a brilliant counselor, she brought an action not against the other employee but against Loes. And while the paternity suit was pending, when the Dodgers were on the train going from New York to Philadelphia and back, Loes would always spend the New Jersey part of the trip in the washroom so no process server could find him. Preacher Roe, in particular, was fascinated with Loes. He had never seen a real New York street person before. Billy would talk, and Preacher would sit and listen and listen and listen.

"Dressen would say to Billy, 'You gotta take care of yourself, Billy. You'll be a terrific pitcher. You'll go for fifteen years.' Billy would say, 'I don't have to go for fifteen years. I'm not going to get married. I'll have enough money in five.' There was very little rationality to Billy. And there he was, Robinson's buddy. I don't know what Jackie liked about him. I guess he felt he was a misfit and felt sorry for him. Billy never was a big pitcher because it wasn't important to him."

CARL ERSKINE: "Billy Loes was a very superstitious kid. Extremely superstitious. He was young, he had a terrific arm, and if you could get Loes in the right frame of mind and all the conditions right for him, he could really give you some good innings. Dressen knew that you couldn't treat Loes the way you treated Branca, Erskine, or somebody else, so he would let Loes play with his superstitions, and he would go along with him.

"When we would have our meetings in the clubhouse, it was customary, in fact it was required, that the starting pitcher take the lineup of the opposing team and discuss how he was going to pitch to each one of these hitters. In the old clubhouse in Ebbets Field, there were some huge posts down through the center of the locker room. Loes for some reason wanted to sit behind one of these big posts. The rest of the meeting was on the other side of the post in an open area of the clubhouse. So the days that Loes pitched, Dressen would let him sit back where nobody could see him, but you could hear him, and he'd go over the lineup, and he'd sit back there out of sight and talk to the rest of us at the meeting about how he was going to pitch. And that's what I mean: Charley pampered him to get him in the right frame of mind. Whatever it took, Charley would go along with it.

"One of Billy's superstitions was that he always wore the same shirt to pitch in. He never washed it. He might pick up a superstition that he never had before in a certain game. And nobody would know what was going on. For instance, he was pitching one night in Brooklyn, and apparently for the first four or five innings as he would be going to the mound, Dressen would be coming from third base, and apparently each inning as they passed, Dressen would say something to Billy. On the sixth inning, they passed, and Charley was distracted by something. Loes took about two steps past him, and Dressen hadn't said anything, so Loes turned around and grabbed him and yelled, 'Charley, say something. Say something!' He had a notion that these things helped him, and so Charley would pamper him."

Bolstered by the pitching of Loes, Joe Black, and Carl Erskine, the Dodgers remained close to the lead. On June 19 Carl Erskine made headlines when he pitched a no-hitter against Chicago and beat the Cubs, 5–0.

Carl Erskine: "It was against Chicago in Brooklyn, and up to that time I had had some good ballgames and moved into the starting rotation, but I hadn't done anything sensational. I was still trying to get my career established. That day was overcast. We scored early, but it threatened rain real badly. We were sensitive about trying to get in five innings because we had a five-run lead on the Cubs, and so I was pitching a little quicker than usual, plus I was not mixing up my pitches all that much in the third inning. I did get through it, but not before I had walked their pitcher, Willie Ramsdell, on four straight pitches. I was just trying to throw him a strike, but I was hurrying, knowing he was a very weak-hitting pitcher. So I walked him.

"It rained, and they called time, brought the canvas out. I rushed into the clubhouse like our club did often because Clyde King had introduced bridge on our team, and baseball has historically been a hearts, pinochle, or poker game, whenever the manager would let them play it. But we got introduced to bridge, and it took off like wildfire. And so at any break at any point, about half our team would rush in and say, 'Deal 'em.' And we'd play on the trunks in the clubhouse.

"And so we went inside and flopped down and began to play bridge. I was playing with Billy Cox, Snider, and Reese. We must have been playing thirty minutes or so when somebody came in just as I was finishing playing four hearts, and I had just made the hand. We had all felt the game would be a washout, and somebody rushed back in to say they were taking the canvas off. 'Erskine, you got to go back out. Start warming up again.' Sure enough, the canvas came off, and the game started. I continued to pitch, and as the game unfolded, the Cubs did not have a hit, and I was aware of it, and it got down to the last couple of innings, and I began to feel a little bit of the pressure of trying to get through the rest of the ballgame without giving up a base hit.

"And I recall that I got to the ninth and got two men out and Eddie Miksis was the last hitter. I remember I threw him a good curveball, with which he hit a routine grounder to Reese for the last out.

"What I didn't know was happening was, off the field, Willie Ramsdell was rooting for me. Willie had been a former Dodger. When I had come up from Ft. Worth, my first trip to the big leagues, I replaced Ramsdell. He was sent back to Ft. Worth. He was eventually traded to the Cubs, and here he was pitching in this ballgame. Willie knew all of us real well, and Miksis had also been a former Dodger.

"Happy Felton had the *Knothole Gang Show* at Ebbets Field, and his sidekick, Larry McDonald, would each day determine who the star of the opposing team was and the star of the Dodger team was, and they would take these two players in to a postgame show and have Star of the Game. You get fifty bucks for that.

"Larry McDonald made his way down to the Cubs dugout. A pinch hitter had been used for Ramsdell, so he was out of the game and free to go back to the clubhouse. McDonald grabbed him and said, 'Look, Willie, you're the only base runner so far. If this holds up, you will have to be the Cubs star of the game.'

"He takes Willie back to where the show is produced, and they watch the last inning on the monitor, and Larry and Happy often told the story of how Ramsdell sat there looking in the monitor and pulling for me to get the Cubs out in the last inning, and especially when Miksis was hitting, he said, 'You dirty bum. You never hit for me. If you get a hit now and cost me fifty bucks, I'll kill you!' When Miksis made out, Willie was the Cubs star of the game, and he got his $50."

By the end of June, the Dodgers were leading the pack by three games. Jackie Robinson, who led the league at .340, with Stan Musial second at .337, was never more devastating, and Gil Hodges, Roy Campanella, Andy Pafko, and Duke Snider homered often enough that around the league there was talk of a "Murderer's Row" in Brooklyn to rival the Yankees in the 1920s. If the fans had worried about the pitching, they needn't have, as Preacher Roe's record was 7–0, Erskine's 7–1, and Loes's 7–3. In relief Joe Black surprised almost everyone by coming up with fifteen wins. He was the most successful Dodger relief pitcher since Hugh Casey.

Black had come to the Dodgers in spring training as just another in a line of Negro League pitching prospects. Before him Don Newcombe had been successful, but the others, Roy Partlow, John Wright, and Dan Bankhead, had failed, and based on previous experiments, the Dodger brass was not optimistic Black would pitch well for the Dodgers.

Roger Kahn remembered Black's uncertainty during spring training. Dressen knew that Black was intelligent, that he had gone to college, and he saw that the lanky pitcher was fearless, but Black really didn't have a good curveball to go with his exceptional fastball. During most of the spring training, Dressen couldn't decide whether to put him on the Dodger roster or not. One afternoon Kahn had been asking about Black, and Dressen said he still hadn't made up his mind.

ROGER KAHN: "There was no privacy with the team and very few secrets. That night on the Pullman rolling toward Virginia Joe Black hailed me from a roomette. 'Hey, man. Sit down. Ya wanna talk a little? I used to teach in school. I'm not a dummy. Hey. How you like the South?'

"Black was six feet three and very dark, with fine features and a bull neck. 'How do you like the South?' I said.

"Black grinned. 'I can't tell you,' he said. 'They won't let me in.'

"Black looked out the window. The train was hurrying through bare Piedmont Hills. Spring had not advanced beyond Tennessee. 'Hey,' Black said, gazing with large, soft eyes, 'am I gonna make this club?'

" 'How do I know?'

" 'You talked to Number 7.'

" 'That's right.'

" 'He like that game in Mobile? Six good innings. Hey, I can give better than that. And I'll protect them. And I don't walk many. And I hum it pretty good. You know what Campy says, "Ah hums that pea." '

"I put my hand on Joe's huge arm. 'I'll see if I can find out a little more,' I said. 'You really want to make this ball club, don't you?'

"Black dropped his drawl. 'If I could express myself as well as Shakespeare,' he said, 'I still couldn't tell you how much.' "

Fortunately for the Dodgers, Dressen decided to go with Black. It was a decision that won the team the pennant.

With a starting lineup that included Gil Hodges, Roy Campanella, Duke Snider, Carl Furillo, and Jackie Robinson, all the pitchers had to do was keep the opposition under four runs, and they would win, and this they did, as the makeshift Dodger staff finished the year with the second-best earned run average in the league behind the Phils. The Dodgers, moreover, sported the stingiest defense in the league. Against the second division teams, they were almost unbeatable. On August 29 the Dodger record against the Pirates was 18 wins, 2 losses, the Reds 16–4, and the Braves 14–2 for a combined record of 48–8. Against New York, St. Louis, Philadelphia, and the Cubs, the Dodgers were 36–37.

On July 22 the Dodger record was 60–22. After that they played .500 ball. The pitching was mediocre. After July Labine, Branca, and Rutherford had bad arms, Roe a bad back, Erskine a bad elbow. The Dodgers waltzed to the pennant, though not before Dodger fans were shuttering and cringing at the possibility of a repeat of the debacle of '51.

On September 1 they led by nine and a half. In three weeks the lead was down to just three games. On that day the *Saturday Evening Post* hit the streets with an article by Charley Dressen proclaiming, "The Dodgers Won't Blow It Again." Many wondered.

But the Dodgers didn't fold. What held them together in the second half of the season despite a decimated, ragtag pitching staff was their experience and professionalism, and the heroics of Joe Black.

Black had grown up in Plainfield, New Jersey, where the schools had been integrated. As a student he owned two shirts, which he rotated to be neat. The other boys taunted him. Two fights later the ridicule stopped.

ROGER KAHN: "At Plainfield High he played varsity football, basketball, and baseball. He could play anywhere on the diamond. He could hit for power, run and field, and throw. At home, he filled a scrapbook with pictures from the *Plainfield Courier*. He liked Lou Gehrig and Mel Ott, who played up in New York, and Paul Waner, who played in Pittsburgh, and Paul Derringer, who pitched out in Cincinnati. His special team was the Detroit Tigers. They

George Brace Photo

JOE BLACK

captured him during the 1935 world series when they defeated the Cubs, four games to two.

"In April of Black's senior year, the coach asked about plans. Joe said he expected to become a ballplayer. He was team captain. The coach nodded and said something about a college scholarship, but Joe meant that he wanted to be a ballplayer in the major leagues. That May, a big league scout, who doubled as local umpire, offered contracts to three Plainfield schoolboys. Black was puzzled. 'Hey,' he said to the scout, 'how come you sign up all these guys and don't sign me?'

"The scout blinked. 'Colored guys don't play baseball.'

" 'What? You crazy? You've seen me play for three years.'

" 'I mean Organized Baseball.'

" 'This is organized. We got a coach and uniforms.'

" 'I mean there's no colored in the Big Leagues.'

"Standing on the Plainfield High School ball field, the sweat of a game running down his forehead, Black pretended that he'd been joking. 'Oh, sure,' he said to his scout. 'Just forget it.'

"That night he took his scrapbook from a drawer and studied it. Every face, Gehrig, Ott, Waner, Derringer, the others, all were white. Without tears, Joe began to shred the book in his big hands. But before he did, he carefully clipped a picture of his favorite player, Hank Greenberg, crashing out a long home run. He could not bear both, to have the dream dead and to have nothing, nothing at all to show from the scrapbook of his boyhood."

Black accepted a scholarship at Morgan State University in Baltimore. He played football and baseball, went into the army during the war, and when he got out he played for the Baltimore Elite Giants, using the pay to complete his college degree.

Soon after the end of the war, the color barrier in baseball was broken. Nevertheless, it still took Joe Black six more years to reach the big leagues, and even then he got in the back door.

The Dodgers in 1951 had coveted pitcher Leroy Farrell of the Elite Giants, which was struggling to survive in the last years of the Negro League. Every Negro League team was now losing money, and in desperation the teams were selling whatever players they could to keep from going under. The Elite Giants wanted $10,000 for Farrell, who was in the army. Fresco Thompson told the Elite Giants to throw in a couple more players, and they had a deal. Farrell never became a Dodger. When he came out of the army, he had gained too much weight. The two throw-ins were Junior Gilliam and Joe Black.

The first time Dressen used Black in relief was in Chicago. He pitched an inning, and no one touched him. After the game Dizzy Dean told Dressen, "Hey, that big colored guy throws as hard as me."

CLEM LABINE: "What I remember about Joe Black was that he would never warm up in the bullpen at the rubber. He would warm up ten feet past the rubber, and I would ask him why. He said, 'Because it made your arm stronger. You're throwing harder then when you go in.' I always tried to figure that one out. But I would say to him, 'What about your control? The most important thing about your control is to get it from sixty feet, not seventy feet.' He said, 'Nope, this is the way I do it.' Yet when he went in, he warmed up from the mound. It didn't make any sense to me, but he insisted on doing it."

Black had a gentle nature and was very easy to get along with. However, on the mound, he could be as mean as Newcombe. In one game the Cincinnati bench began singing "Old Black Joe." Black didn't say a word. But he threw his most vicious fastball at the heads of the next seven Reds batters. The chorus became silent.

In one game against the Giants, Black was involved in a beanball war. In the first, Cox homered as the Dodgers scored five runs. In the second, Dressen brought in Black in relief. He shut them out, but in the middle of the game, Giant pitcher Hoyt Wilhelm started things by throwing at and hitting Gil Hodges. Then the Giants' Monte Kennedy threw at Hodges. Then Giant pitcher Larry Jansen hit Cox. In response Hodges cut up Bill Rigney at second. To get the Dodgers back, Jansen dusted off Black. Then it was Black's turn.

DON HONIG: "Black was fast, and he was mean. He threw one pitch at a Giant I'll never forget. I was watching it on television. The batter was George Wilson, who was pinch hitting for the Giants, and this was the way you played in those days. Black threw the ball at his head, and Wilson dropped so fast his cap stayed there and the ball went between the cap and him. There were no helmets in those days. If it had hit him, it would have killed him. Boy, I'll never forget that!"

In 1952 Joe Black was named the Rookie of the Year. From May 1 to September 18, Black never was hit hard, though he did lose three games.

On September 21 a crowd of 3,000 turned out at Grand Central Station to greet the Dodgers on their return from Boston. The Dodgers had clinched a tie for the pennant as they ran away from the rest of the league. The winning pitcher: Joe Black. He also won the first game of the 1952 World Series, becoming the first Negro pitcher to win a game in the Series.

And then the next year Charley Dressen ruined him.

Dressen had demanded that Black learn a third pitch, a big-breaking curve or screwball, forkball, or a change-up. But Black was born with stretched tendons on his index and middle fingers of his pitching hand, and physically he could only throw what he threw. By April Black's confidence was shot, and so was his control. His fastball sailed high, his curveball bounced into the dirt, and the next year Clem Labine replaced Black as the top man in the bullpen. In '54 Black won no games, and in '55 he was gone from Brooklyn.

And yet Joe Black remained a gracious and grateful man. At the end of his superstar '52 season, he presented each of the nine reporters who covered the team with a bottle of champagne in gratitude for their kind words. And after he got out of baseball, he traveled the country to lecture other black athletes about his teammate, Jackie Robinson, the man whose courage and toughness allowed other blacks—including himself—to play in the major leagues.

The 1952 World Series

A cocky Joe Black started the first game. Before the game he told the press, "They aren't the same Yankees I used to pay to see. There is nothing in that lineup to be scared of." Joe DiMaggio was gone and so were Charley Keller and Tommy Henrich, but Yogi Berra was behind the plate, and Phil Rizzuto was the shortstop, and the Yankees had young stars Mickey Mantle, Gil McDougald, Billy Martin, and Hank Bauer.

Black pitched a six-hitter. Snider, Robinson, and Reese homered to win 4 to 2 at Ebbets Field.

CARL ERSKINE: "We were all surprised when Charley picked Black to start the first game, but nobody questioned it because certainly Black got us there. Not a man on the ballclub wouldn't say if you had to pick a handful of guys who were really the key people that Black had to be one of them. There was no feeling on the ballclub about Dressen being out of his mind. And Charley liked to make those kinds of moves. He liked to astound people. He wasn't a total reckless gambler. He was a good cardplayer. That's where he and Durocher were alike a lot. He would calculate a move that wasn't conventional, and this was one of them. But nobody questioned Charley on that one, and Black beat the Yankees in the opening game."

Dressen chose Erskine to start Game Two.

CARL ERSKINE: "It was a rainy day, and going clear back to Anderson, Indiana, I had been playing junior high basketball in a tournament and went after a loose ball when a guy playing for North Anderson went after the ball with me, and he piled down on me. It pulled a lot of tendons or ligaments in my knee. Periodically after that it gave me trouble.

"I went on into baseball, and it's a few years later, and I didn't wear a brace, but occasionally I'd bump that knee getting into a car, and I'd get deathly sick when I'd bump it. Anyway I was scheduled to pitch against Vic Raschi in the second game at Ebbets Field, so we were in the clubhouse ten minutes before it was time to warm up. I was in the trainer's room, dressed, ready to go out onto the field, had my jacket and glove, but we weren't sure the game was going to start on time because the canvas was on, and we were waiting to see how the rain was going. The trainer's room had a high window that you couldn't see out of unless you stepped up on something, so I stepped up on a little stepladder, looked out, saw that it had virtually stopped raining, and stepped down. As I turned around, we had a heater in the trainer's room that had a flanged back on it made of steel, and I caught the corner of that right on that real sensitive spot and hit it a good lick. I grabbed my knee and sat down on the trunk. Doc Wendler was across the room. I said, 'Oh, Doc, I hit that darn knee.' And with that, I got this very sick feeling that I always got, and I passed out cold face down on the clubhouse floor like a sack of flour.

"They picked me up quick, layed me on the trainer's table and just then Dressen walks in. Here's his starting pitcher absolutely out cold as a mackerel. He didn't know what was going on. They revived me, and then I told them what had happened. I walked around a few minutes and blinked my eyes a little bit, and I said, 'I'm all right. Hey, listen, I'm all right.' It was my first World Series start. I convinced Charley that I was all right, and he let me start the ballgame.

"The only thing that day: I was a little wild, a little bit wild, but I had good stuff. It was remarkable that Dressen went ahead and started me. I didn't remember what the score was, but when I came out of the ballgame, we were still something respectable, and the game got away after that, but Raschi didn't give us any runs. He was an outstanding pitcher, a good professional. He would bring the good ballgame when he had to. And he beat us 7–1."

Preacher Roe won Game Three in the ninth inning. Yogi Berra couldn't catch a pitch from Ed Lopat, and as Berra was chasing the ball down, Pee Wee Reese scored from third and Jackie Robinson raced in all the way from second base. In Game Four Allie Reynolds shut out the Dodgers on four hits and beat Black 2–0 to tie the Series two games each. In Game Five Erskine faced former Cincinnati Red pitcher Ewell Blackwell.

Carl Erskine: "That was another strange set of circumstances. I got to the stadium that day, and we were going through our pregame routine. I was reading mail, wires, telegrams, and one of the telegrams I received was from a friend who I had known in Texas when I was playing in the Texas League. He said, 'GOOD LUCK IN THE FIFTH GAME OF THE WORLD SERIES ON THIS FIFTH DAY OF OCTOBER AND CONGRATULATIONS ON YOUR FIFTH WEDDING ANNIVERSARY.' I smiled and said, 'Gee, that is right.' I hadn't thought about it. Fifth game, fifth day, and it is Betty and my fifth anniversary.' Red Barber was visiting with everybody, and I said, 'Red, look at this one,' and he smiled and said, 'Gee, that's interesting. Can I take it up to the booth with me? It would make a little sidelight.' 'Yeah, no problem.' So I went about my business. The game starts, and I'm pitching well. I had real good stuff, and the first four innings, I got the Yankees shut out, and we've got a four-run lead, so things are rolling along real well, until the fifth inning.

"In the fifth inning, the Yankees got five runs. It was quick. There were a couple bloops, a walk, another scratch hit, they got a couple runs in, and Mize was up with two men on, and he hits a blast. He hit a good, hard, line shot into the right-field stands. And suddenly, almost within a matter of a few minutes, the Yankees have gotten five runs off me.

"So Dressen comes out. It looks like the endgate for me. He gets to the mound, and he had heard about this wedding anniversary, and he asked me about it. Very unusual for Dressen. He should have come out there and snorted and cussed and kicked the ground. But Dressen had a rule. You never talked to him unless he asked you something. Well, he comes out to the mound, takes the ball away from me, glances around a little bit, and he says, 'Are you all right?' I said, 'I feel lousy. But I'm all right.' He said, 'There was only one ball really hit off you, Mize's home run. The rest were scratch hits here and there.' Then he says, 'Is this your wedding anniversary?' Which darn near floored me. Then he says, 'Is your wife here at the game?' I said, 'Yeah, she's here.' By now the other guys have circled around the mound. The whole stands are saying, 'I wonder what they're talking about?' I figure we must be killing time for the guy in the bullpen. Finally he asks me, 'Are you going to celebrate your anniversary tonight?' This was real strange. I said, 'Well, I suppose we will, Charley.' With that he takes my glove hand and turns it up and slams the ball back in it. And so help me, the good Lord can hear me the same as I am telling you, here's what he said: 'Well, see if you can get the side out before it gets dark.' And he left me in the game.

"I faced Yogi Berra, who hit the ball pretty well, but he hit it right at Furillo to end the inning. So I went in, and I wasn't prepared to go to the plate, because I figure he's going to pinch hit for me. But he yells down the bench at me to get my helmet. He says, 'You're my man. You're it. You're it.'

"So I hit. Stayed in the game. And I continued to pitch and continued to have good stuff, continued to get the side out. We tied it in the seventh, and got a run in the top of the eleventh, and Snider was involved in both those runs. He scored one, drove in one. Duke was my roommate, and he always played well when I was pitching. So Charley had left me in, and I kept getting the side out, and we finally tied it, and then the only controversial play was Sain's ground ball. The pictures show he was probably safe, but he was called out, and I made nineteen consecutive outs.

"And something nobody has ever written about, which to me was a traumatic thing: I'm ahead 6 to 5, pitching with two outs in the bottom of the eleventh, nobody on, and Berra is the hitter. I threw Berra a couple of pitches, and I suddenly felt something, and I looked at the second finger of my pitching hand, and I had a blister. And I never had a blister in my life. At no time in my pitching career did I ever have a blister. But I could see this blister on the little padded part of my finger, where the ball gripped. I threw another pitch to Berra, and that blister opened just a little. So now I get another pitch off, and I get the count to 2 and 2, and by now this blister has broken completely, and the skin has rolled up. It stings; I can feel it. I took a look at Dressen and thought, 'Should I say anything?' There was two outs and two strikes on Berra, so Campanella gives me a curveball sign, and I threw one of the best curveballs I ever threw for strike three. When I did, that blister tore completely off, and I couldn't have thrown another pitch. That blister was down to the red meat. With all of the excitement, that really never was made much of an issue, but that kept me from pitching the rest of the Series, although I relieved one other time. But that was an amazing thing. I never had a blister before or since."

* * *

The Dodgers now had a three to two lead in the Series. They had to win but one more game for their first world championship. The last two games were scheduled in Ebbets Field.

For six innings in Game Six, it looked like Billy Loes and the Dodgers were finally going to do it. Duke Snider hit two long home runs, and the Dodgers were leading 2–0. Then, in the seventh, Berra homered to make it 2 to 1. Woodling singled against Loes. Then Loes did something he never did before or since. While standing on the pitching rubber, he dropped the baseball. It slipped out of his hand and fell to the ground. Under the rules of baseball, that is a balk, and Woodling was waved to second base. The batter at the time was Yankee pitcher Vic Raschi, one of the league's worst pitchers. Raschi hit a bouncing ball right at Loes. Loes missed it, it ricocheted off his leg past Robinson at second and into right field as Woodling raced home with the tying run. In the eighth inning, Mickey Mantle homered, and Loes was beaten. After the game Loes would say that he had lost Raschi's grounder in the sun.

CARL ERSKINE: "You know what? That's what happened. In October the sun is right between the decks for probably no more than a couple minutes' time. And that's exactly when that happened, and when Loes said he lost it in the sun, everybody laughed, and the fact is, if you ever pitched in Ebbets Field, you know that's possible in October with a ball that's hit with a little bounce on it."

The Dodgers had opportunity after opportunity to win it in Game Seven. After the Yankees scored one in the top of the fourth, the Dodgers had the bases loaded against Reynolds and only scored one run. Both teams scored once in the fifth inning, and in the sixth Mantle hit a home run over the Ebbets Field clock on top of the right field scoreboard off Black to put the Yankees ahead by a run.

The key inning was the seventh. Vic Raschi suddenly lost his control, and he walked Carl Furillo. After Rocky Nelson popped up, Billy Cox singled, and Reese walked to load the bases. Yankee manager Casey Stengel's choice of a relief pitcher was a shock. Ordinarily, it was death to pitch a left-hander in Ebbets Field. The right-handed-hitting Dodgers (Snider was the one lefty) teed off on lefties in Brooklyn. High pops became home runs, and wins turned into losses. But Stengel went against the odds and chose as a reliever a left-hander, and a mediocre left-hander at that, Bob Kuzava. Stengel wanted a lefty to pitch to the left-handed Duke Snider.

DUKE SNIDER: "Kuzava went to 3 and 2, and I fouled off about five pitches. And then he threw me a fastball, low and away, and I tried to hit it to left center, and I popped it up to short. One of those perfect pitches. And he was a good pitcher. It was one of those things."

Now there were two outs and Jackie Robinson was the batter.

* * *

ROY CAMPANELLA: "It was the seventh inning, and we had the bases loaded and two outs, and Jackie was up. And he hit a pop-up near the pitcher's mound, and with two outs everyone's running, and I really didn't think anyone was going to get to it. In fact no one had called the play. It looked like the whole infield couldn't decide. It was 'Are you gonna take it or will I take it?' Billy Martin was playing way back at second base, and he had to come in all the way to the mound, and he just did get to it. If he hadn't caught it, everyone would have scored, and we would have won.

"We weren't really disappointed, because it was supposed to be caught from the word go. If it had fallen safe, then we would have rejoiced. But it didn't."

And because it didn't, the Dodgers did not win the game and did not win the World Series.

CARL ERSKINE: "Unbelievable. Just unbelievable. We expected to win the Series. And that was the year Kuzava beat us. Jesus. Jiminy Christmas. I want to throw up. We used to eat left-handers alive. But those were the kind of things that happened against the Yankees. Honest to God. Unexplainable. Un-ex-plain-able.

"Dressen said we were the worst club he ever managed for scoring a run from third with none or one out. We'd get a lot of runs in bunches, but when we were a run down late in the game, when we had a man on third and we needed a fly ball, it seemed we had problems doing that.

"Robinson hit a ball off his fist with the bases loaded to Martin. It was the same old thing that plagued us.

"But the thing that was a mystery, an absolute total mystery, was that a left-hander, and I won't take anything away from Kuzava at all, I don't mean that, but a left-handed pitcher statistically couldn't survive in Ebbets Field. Take Warren Spahn, who won 363 ballgames, more than any other left-hander in the history of baseball. They would not pitch him in Ebbets Field. So here's an absolute, unbelievable mystery, Kuzava, and I understand it was only a few innings, but we couldn't get any runs off of him. We had him on the ropes, and we couldn't cut it. So it was that unbelievable thing in sports where there is no explanation. I don't understand it. But it was frustrating. It was total frustration. We had been to the well, we had been to the well with one of the great clubs, we felt, that you could put on the field. In its day and probably in any day, it was one of the great clubs. And it was one of those unexplainable quirks in sports; the way it looks on paper isn't always the way it comes out."

BILL REDDY: "How those Yankees would swagger in! 'Here we are, the gentlemen from the Bronx, the Pinstripers, watch yourself, because we're going to beat your ass.' And the Yankee fans were the same way. They had that air of condescension about them when they spoke to you.

"Remember when Rizzuto and Stanky got into that controversy, when

Stanky slid in and threw sand in Rizzuto's face. Rizzuto whined about that for years. As a Brooklyn fan, I saw nothing wrong with that. The guy was playing good baseball, major league style. What the hell did Rizzuto want him to do, bend over and bow to him?

"This was the thing. You'd be watching, and our guy would be pitching a magnificent game, but there was always a Mantle coming up or a DiMaggio or a Henrich or a Berra, and you always had to say to yourself, 'Jesus, let us get past this guy.' I would find myself praying, 'Dear God, let them get past this guy. Let him get out of the inning.' But it didn't happen often enough. It just seemed as though God or the fates or whatever you believed in was frowning down on the Dodgers all those years.

"There was a great feeling of frustration, and it grew worse with every World Series loss, because you would say to yourself, 'When the hell are we ever going to beat them? They can't be invincible. Other teams beat them in the American League during the season. Why can't we beat them?' We just couldn't seem to put it together. And you knew deep down in your heart that you had a ballclub that was one of the greatest ever to be put together. And what was happening? Every year we got beat. It was such a feeling of frustration. It was getting to be galling."

Gil

He was the Dodger's Lou Gehrig. He didn't get much media recognition; Snider, Campy, and Robinson all got more ink. Gil Hodges, like Gehrig, was strong but sphinxlike, more of a presence than a personality. For seven years in a row, Hodges drove in more than 100 rbis, and eleven years in a row he hit twenty or more home runs. He holds the National League record for lifetime grand slams—fourteen—and the only player with more is Gehrig.

Physically he was as strong as Hercules. He had the biggest, strongest hands of any man. At bat he was a dead pull hitter, always looking for the inside pitch to pull into the left-field stands.

Everything Hodges did was professional. The way he knocked the dirt out of his spikes. The way he held the bat, the way he walked up to home plate, the way he stood in the on-deck circle. He was an athlete. To this day there are Brooklyn fans who will swear that in all his putouts, he never had his foot on first base. He did it in such a poetic flow of motion. Off the field Hodges was a gentleman and a gentle man, respected by all who knew him.

Irving Rudd: "Gil was a very, very kindly man. And I remember Gil had a dry, dry sense of humor. One time Hodges and Don Hoak were clowning, and Hoak started talking about boxing. Hoak said, 'Don't fuck with me, Hodges. These hands are lethal weapons.' Hodges just looked at him, picked him up, and dumped him in a garbage can.

"Nobody ever knew what it was like to mess with Gil. Nobody ever wanted to. One time Eddie Stanky slid into Spider Jorgensen and slit his pants from knee to thigh, and the two of them were fighting, rolling in the dirt, and

Gil Hodges

Hodges went to break it up. He grabbed them and deposited them separately on the infield grass like two rag dolls.

"Gil was one guy I could go to for anything. If I needed a player to visit a blind kid in the stands. A kid in a wheelchair. Gil this, Gil that, and he'd be there. One time B'nai B'rith called me and asked me if Gil would speak up in Rochester. I would be the moderator, and he would get $2,500, and I would get $1,000. I went to Gil, and he said, 'Irving, really, I don't do those things.' I said, 'Gil, there's a grand in it for me.' He said, 'I'll give you the grand. We'll stay home.' I said, 'The hell you will.' I called them back and told them no dice. But he was actually going to give me the grand! That was a lot of money. What do you say about a guy like that?

"I remember I was at the Gun Hill Lodge in the Bronx. I was the speaker, and when I talked about the Dodgers, I would go position by position talking about the men, throwing in a bad joke like 'Junior Gilliam is a great American even though he goes to his left.' I would go around the diamond and say, 'Let's go to first base. You have Gil Hodges, Jack Armstrong, the All-American boy. I never heard the man utter a curse word in his life. Ever. He's the kind of guy you'd bring home to marry your daughter.'

"And from the back of the room, a Jewish guy yells out, 'No. No!' I stopped. 'Why not?' The man yelled back, ' 'Cause he's a *goy*!' "

They called him "the big marine" and that's what he was. Gil Hodges was an outstanding person of character, and despite his stature he would never complain about the hassles that often go with stardom. He would sign autographs for hours. In St. Louis there'd be no air conditioning on the bus as the team was about to ride to the airport. Everyone had to wear white shirts and ties, and with his white shirt sticking to his back, just soaking wet, Gil would be standing outside the bus signing autographs. Pee Wee and everyone would be calling, "Come on, Gil, let's go," but Gil would ignore them and sign those autographs, because he knew the fans were getting a thrill. Only when there were no more ragged slips of paper to sign would Gil finally get on the bus.

And yet Gil Hodges was not a beloved player. Respected, certainly, but not beloved. He was a lot like Gehrig or Steve Garvey, men too strong and silent for fans to adore the way they did a laughing Roy Campanella or a fallible Duke Snider. Gil Hodges only became really popular, oddly enough, during his dreadful batting slump during the 1952 World Series.

On September 23, 1952, the day the Dodgers clinched the pennant, Hodges singled off Karl Drews. He didn't hit again that week as the season played itself out, and in the World Series against the Yankees, Hodges went to bat twenty-six times, walking five times. During the other twenty-one at bats, he got no home runs, no triples, no doubles, no singles. As the Series wore on, public support for Gil Hodges, rather than shrinking, suddenly increased. By the end of the 1952 World Series, Gil Hodges and his slump were the most talked about, argued about, analyzed topic in all of Brooklyn. Hodges was a religious man, a practicing Catholic, and from pulpits in Flatbush, Canarsie,

South Brooklyn, and Williamsburg, congregations implored the Lord to aid Gil Hodges.

BOBBY MCCARTHY: In the '52 World Series, Gil Hodges was 0 for 21. Though I went to public school, I used to get release time to get my hour of religious training. And I remember going out on a Wednesday from two to three in the afternoon and on Sunday morning Mass from nine to ten. I remember Sister Helen James. She said to us, 'Do you know that the Dodgers are playing the Yankees in the World Series?' We said, 'Yes, Sister, we all know.' She said, 'Do you know that Mr. Hodges, he hasn't a hit. He's 0 for 18.' We said, 'Yes, Sister, we all know.' She said, 'You should say a prayer for him.' And we did. Everyone in Brooklyn did, it seems."

BILL REDDY: "I made a novena for Gil Hodges. A novena is a group of prayers that you as a Catholic say over a certain number of days, usually nine. And at the conclusion of each rosary, you'd say one special prayer: 'Please, dear Lord, if it is your will, help Gil Hodges get some base hits.'

"And let me tell you, there were thousands of Irish and Italian and Polish Catholics in Brooklyn saying prayers every day, and there were priests on the altar who would conclude the Mass on Sunday and turn around and say, 'Have a nice day and pray for Gil.' And not only Catholics—Protestants and Jews, too—everybody was praying for him."

Despite the prayers, Gil's slump continued into the spring of 1953. By the middle of May, Hodges was hitting .187, and manager Dressen was forced to bench him.

The fans, meanwhile, rose to his defense. More than thirty people a day wrote to Hodges. They sent him rabbits' feet, rosary beads, mezuzahs, scapulars. One man sent him pure carrot juice to restore the batting eye.

CARL ERSKINE: "Gil was distraught during his slump, but he didn't talk about it. He never talked about it. He would come out early and try things, and guys would give him advice—you get tons of advice when things are going bad—and Dressen had him out early, working on hitting to the opposite field. But it was not something talked about on the bench.

"An interesting thing happened. The '53 season opened, and Gil had gotten off badly, and it was on a Sunday in May. Gil was still in the throes of this slump, as frustrated as he could be, and it was a very hot May day, and the priest of the Catholic church where he attended in Brooklyn said to the congregation, 'It's too hot for a sermon. So today I want you all to go home, keep the Ten Commandments, and pray for Gil Hodges.' And that afternoon Gil hit two home runs and broke out of the slump. And I always kidded Gil. I'm a good Baptist. I said, 'Gil, you just about made a believer out of me.' And he went on to have a good year in '53."

ROGER KAHN: "Dressen knew what was wrong. 'The trouble,' he said, 'is that they won't let ya teach them until they is real down.' Dressen, unknown to

Hodges, had Barney Stein take hundreds of photos of Hodges. A few days after he benched Hodges, Dressen called him into his office and showed him the films. He clearly was stepping deep into the bucket. His timing was off. He was getting neither weight nor accuracy into the swing.

" 'Now ya been stepping that way for a long time, and maybe ya ain't gonna stop, but I can fix it so a step like that don't hurt ya, if you're willing to listen.'

"Hodges was ready.

" 'Keep your front foot where it is, but move the back foot farther from the plate. Now when you step back, you'll be stepping into line. It won't hurt ya so much, stepping outta the way like ya do, cuz ya won't be really stepping out of the way, you'll really be stepping into it.'

"In 1953 Hodges hit .302. In the 1953 World Series he led all Dodger hitters with .364. His weakness persisted but his career was saved."

11

Roger Kahn

Roger Kahn grew up in Brooklyn, the son of high school teachers. His father, Gordon, was the genius behind the popular radio quiz show, *Information Please.* It was his job to devise and check the esoteric questions asked each week. Gordon's knowledge was broad, but his special love was the game of baseball, a passion he kept pretty much to himself because his wife, Olga, who fiercely loved literature and had a special interest in James Joyce and classical music, neither understood nor accepted the idea that a serious man should devote himself to a silly game.

After Roger graduated from high school, his father sent him to see an acquaintance, Joseph Herzberg, the city editor at the *New York Herald Tribune* and in 1948 Kahn landed a job as copyboy at a $24.50-a-week salary. In addition to the menial jobs copyboys perform, Kahn became a stringer for the AP, covering sports for $3 a story. He developed a clip file, and before long the *Tribune* also began assigning him stories. His first effort was about a walking race. He wrote, "The walkers slowed to a crawl." His editors saw that he had a way with words, and in 1950 he was added to the sports staff. He was twenty-one years old. Two years later Harold Rosenthal, who had been covering the Dodgers for the *Tribune,* resigned the beat to spend more time with his family. Starting in the spring of 1952, Kahn spent two years covering the Dodgers.

He saw the team in all its glory. Like Dick Young he was part of the Brooklyn fabric, a skinny, shy but aggressive boy trying to be friends with the players and at the same time report objectively about them. Unlike Young, who wrote with a rapier, Kahn rarely criticized, rarely drew their ire. It wasn't his way. It made him uncomfortable. Better, he felt, to write about the good in people. As a result he was closer to many of the players than were the other reporters, and his relationships with Jackie Robinson, Carl Erskine, Clem Labine, Pee Wee Reese, Carl Furillo, and some of the others continued, even after he left the newspapers.

After the 1953 season, Kahn left the *Trib* to go into magazine work. He wrote for *Sports Illustrated,* the *Saturday Evening Post,* and *Newsweek,* though most readers know him best for the many articles he wrote for *Sport* magazine in the late 1950s and early '60s. With Ed Linn and Arnold Hano, Kahn completed a troika that propelled *Sport* into its golden age. Then Kahn disappeared for a while to write or ghost books on various subjects, such as the Jewish people, the Columbia University riots, and Mickey Rooney. He ghosted one book in which a doctor contended that you don't have to count calories in order to lose weight, and though it was a huge best-seller, no one knew he had written it. The rest of his books didn't sell much.

In 1972 he became famous with his dazzling best-seller, *The Boys of Summer,* his autobiographical return to the Dodgers. It was about baseball, and yet it was literature. Olga Kahn was proud, and yet still she wondered what it was about the sport of baseball that caused grown men to love it so.

ROGER KAHN: "Nobody in my circle of friends believed that being a sportswriter was hard work. But you had to do a first edition story, a second edition story, a late story—three different stories in a day. It was a repetitive experience. You were always unsettled. In your suitcase. Out of your suitcase. In a sense, you're a foreign correspondent. You're on duty twenty-four hours a day. If someone falls off a curb and breaks his leg, it's your problem to report that.

"Covering the Dodgers, I saw reporting devices that were not used elsewhere. You'd go to the dressing room and ask, 'How did it feel? What did you think? What was going on in your head?' And when you had time, you got some sense of what it was like to be out on the field. I worked that out with a lot of care. And you'd mix all that into a narrative. Some of it was finding the right angle on the game, and some of it was moving your ass out of the press box and talking to people. And I thought then, and I still think, it's so far in advance of drama criticism, where a guy sits and writes, 'This is what happened in the play.' I read a Wagner opera criticism of Harold Schonberg in the *Times.* The critic wrote, '[Herbert] von Karajan changed his mind between the first and second act.' I didn't believe that. Von Karajan had been conducting it for forty years. Schonberg didn't go backstage to ask him. And nobody goes up to Reagan after a speech and asks him, 'How did it go?' When Carter spoke, no one asked him, 'Did you choke up when you brought up the hostages?' Or 'What made you stammer then?' You don't get near the President afterward. Within limits I would ask these guys anything. And they would say anything. The only thing I wouldn't touch was sex on the road.

"But over the year, you get on each other's nerves. The players get on your nerves. The other writers get on your nerves. You're cooped up together the whole time.

"I remember so well the Dodger locker room. It was rectangular. There were high windows on the far wall, and there was no air conditioning. To the right of the entrance was a corridor that led to Dressen's office. The trainer's room was also to the right, and you would make a right and a right to get to the manager's and coaches' room. The trainer's room was open. It was unthinkable to be told we couldn't go in there. We went where we pleased.

"There were never bad words between the players. Much of the complaining was done by guys like Jim Hughes. 'I should be a starter.' I didn't really know those guys. But the core of the guys, Robinson, Reese, Campanella, Roe, Erskine, Labine, they were a pretty closely knit bunch of guys. Robinson drove Robinson. Everybody knew that. Reese drove Reese.

"You had whites and blacks, and Reese was the leader of the one, and Robinson was the leader of the other. Jackie would have been the captain of the team if he had been white.

"When I was covering the team, Jackie was a terrific clutch hitter. He could hit the long ball; he could bunt. Durocher said it very well. He said, 'He beats you. He comes to beat you. He comes to shove the fucking bat up your ass.' And he could do it with a bunt, with a hit, with a home run, with a steal. The base running, it was incredible. It is not something that has been approached by Brock or by Wills or anybody I've seen. If he was on first, you were worried he'd get to second. If you look it up, the most he ever stole in a season was thirty-seven bases. But that doesn't explain the way the focus of the game had to do with the fear of his stealing. It doesn't tell you how many pitchers threw fastballs rather than curves, keeping him on, to guys who could hit a fastball. And it didn't matter what base he was on. For example, Warren Spahn had a terrific move to first and a terrible move to second. And I can remember Robinson somehow getting himself on second base with Spahn pitching, and Spahn, someone you'd never think would be bothered by base runners, the game would be delayed three minutes while Spahn would be standing there, looking back to second, looking back, looking back, and he would get rattled.

"But he'd beat you, and in addition he'd frustrate you. He made teams angry. And once in a while, he would steal home when the Dodgers were five runs ahead, and he would stick it to you. And, of course, personally he would needle very hard.

"Jackie didn't read much. He wasn't very patient. He drove like a maniac. He liked to play cards, and when the Dodgers traveled, this passion seemed to bring him near players with whom he didn't have much in common. He played a lot of cards with Billy Loes. Loes was a flawed guy, a little bit of a stranger on the club, and Jack, with his sense of the underdog, befriended Billy. Their conversations occasionally ran two sentences long, but not often.

" 'Boy, am I having lousy luck,' Loes would say.

" 'Your deal, Billy,' Robinson would answer.

"Jackie roomed with Jim Gilliam, who usually had less to say than anyone. Even when he could have roomed with Joe Black, a fairly sophisticated college man, he chose Gilliam.

"I remember we were in a plane, and it was one of the worst flights I've ever been on. We were flying a big Constellation from Pittsburgh to New York, and they're gonna shake us out of the sky, and I had my eyes closed and was holding on to the seat. Every once in a while, I'd open my eyes, and in front of me, I'd see Reese's argyle socks, and I kept saying to myself, 'As long as I can see those socks, I'm alive.' Somebody got sick, and then one ballplayer after another, and the plane began to smell. We couldn't go back to Pittsburgh, and we can't get to New York, and we're flying around in this thunderstorm, and Robinson, who is sitting about four rows away, shouts,

'It's a shame you're not gonna live to see that baby, Kahn.' Which seemed a little bit beyond bounds. My wife was pregnant then.

"And that was kinda typical of Jackie. He never knew quite when to stop needling. The storm kept getting worse and worse, and after a particularly bad bump, I summoned up all my courage, and I stood up, holding my seatbelt, and I said, 'I don't hear you now, Robinson.' And he said, 'It's not funny now.'

"I then became a hero of people like Billy Herman, who was one of the coaches, and the other redneck types, 'cause I had put down Robinson. Billy Herman said, 'Boy, you really told that guy. That's great.' So for three days, I found myself the hero of the Dodger Klan contingent. Jim Hughes. Bobby Morgan. Just a handful of them. Part one of the story.

"Part two is that our baby was born and died within twenty-four hours. I was working at *Sports Illustrated,* and I called Jackie on some business, and he said, 'How's the baby?' I said, 'The baby died.' And he said, 'What's her number?' and I gave it to him, and he called Joan, and she reported to me that he said, 'I hope my bringing this up doesn't upset you, but I just want you to know that I'm sorry.' She said, 'What a sensitive way to say a hard thing.' And that was Jack. Out of sync, but a terrific guy. That's the two sides of the guy. An extreme guy. Incredibly compassionate and warm, and the needling.

"I thought Jack was kind of shy. When I finished *The Boys of Summer,* I threw a party with my last 200 bucks. I figured if I was going broke, at least I'd have something to remember. I invited Jack to the party, and Jack came without Rachel. It was almost as if he was testing out a white party, to see if it was a party where he and his wife would be comfortable, and after a while he made a phone call, and Rachel showed up. Zero Mostel was there, and Zero, who was not shy, said, 'Jackie Robinson. I wish I was as famous as you.' And Jackie was a little embarrassed by this. Howard Fast had the bad manners to ask Jack why he testified against Paul Robeson. To which Jack said, 'If Mr. Rickey at that time had asked me to jump headfirst off the Brooklyn Bridge, I would have done it.'

"And I remember there was a couple at the party who had a diabetic child, and Robinson spent most of his time talking to those people, telling them how he had lived with diabetes and how it really wasn't such a terrible thing. There was no quality about Jackie that 'this guy's a producer, so I'll spend time with him. I'll further my career. I'll hang out with Woody Allen.' He didn't do that.

"So at the head of the hierarchy was Robinson and Reese. They were the cement of this marvelous club. And you can only interview one.

"I fault the New York press in its coverage of the Dodgers. Red Smith should have been out there a hell of a lot more. Arthur Daley should have been out there a hell of a lot more. But it was a long subway ride to Brooklyn. It was much easier to go to the Polo Grounds or Yankee Stadium.

"Whoever covered the Dodgers had to deal with Buzzy Bavasi. Bavasi had a little of the Sinatra quality, poised, good-looking, always would pick up the tab, was fun to be with, and we knew that in the middle of a dreary road trip, he would come out for a couple of days, and it would be fun to go out with him, a fresh face.

"Bavasi ran a private bar in Vero for the real inner sanctum, and his favorite concoction was the grasshopper, which looked like a green malted, and when he'd invite you in, he'd say, 'I think you've been knocking the club, and it upsets me.' I'd say, 'I don't think I've been knocking the club. I've been trying to report fairly.' He'd say, 'I didn't read it, but the people in New York seem to think you're knocking the club. You're very important to me. You're somebody I can talk to. There aren't many people I can talk to. If you keep knocking the club, how can I talk to you? So let's have a drink.' And that was his manner.

"If he was going to criticize your story, he'd begin by saying he didn't read it. 'They told me you did so and so.' I used to have a saying, 'I always could tell when Buzzy was lying. I never could tell when O'Malley was.' And after a while, I discounted Buzzy. Buzzy was always trying to plant things.

"Buzzy was an interesting man. Buzzy had a kind of Medici-Machiavellian conspiratorial nature to him. He loved planting things and throwing things out and seeing what happened. Here's his ultimate number on me: When I was finishing up with the chapter on Walter O'Malley for *The Boys of Summer,* I was interviewing Walter O'Malley, and I said, 'What are you worth, Walter?' That's a rude question. After a while Walter said, 'It's hard to say. All right, you need a figure. You can say $24 million.' I got in my car, and I drove to San Diego where Buzzy lives on a hill in La Jolla, along with Dr. Seuss.

"Buzzy and I went to his bar, and on the bar there was this Frankenstein monster, a little electrical monster, and I pushed the button, and the monster goes 'rrrrrrrrr,' the arms go out, his pants drop, revealing polka dot shorts, and the monster's face turns from green to red. Ho, ho, ho, along with the charming talk that I always enjoyed with Buzzy. I said, 'What kind of character is Dr. Seuss?' He said, 'Oh, my kids were up on his property, and he beat the hell out of them.' A 'hates kids' joke. And we're sitting there, and Buzzy says, 'What did the son of a bitch tell you he was worth?' He didn't mention O'Malley's name. I said, 'Twenty-four million.' Buzzy said, 'That's about right. All he left out was 400 acres of downtown Los Angeles.'

"I should explain that Buzzy didn't get paid a lot as general manager and was never offered a piece and felt he should have been. And when it came time to write the piece, I said to myself, 'There's this awful feud between these two people. How am I gonna write it?' and I thought, finally, 'I'll just do it as it was told to me, and try to do it nonjudgmentally, just kind of report this part of the book.'

"After the book came out, I got a blind copy of a letter from Buzzy to Walter O'Malley saying, 'I don't know where that stuff in the book came from. I never even talked to the man. Best regards, E. J. "Buzzy" Bavasi.' At first I was furious. But then I said to myself, 'Wait a minute. Let's be grown up. What is he doing? He knows I have the tape. He's saying to me, 'For Christ sake, let me off the hook with this all-powerful son of a bitch Walter O'Malley.' And I did. I never said a word to O'Malley about it. And I haven't heard from Bavasi since, not as much as a thank you.

"The other guy who made it tough on reporters was Jackie. Jack practically never praised a reporter for a story. He would say the reporter was just doing his job. But if he didn't like the story, he would come down pretty hard. Once in a while, he would come up to me and say, 'The guys didn't like your story yesterday. They thought it was a little anti.' Meaning anti-Dodger. And he'd say, 'You ought to go easy for a couple days.' I'd say, 'Jeez, Jack, the team stank. You saw the game.' He'd say, 'Just go easy, that's all.'

"But one time he called me. It was '53, we were in St. Louis, and after a night game, Robinson says, 'I just want you to know the shit has started again.' I said, 'What shit?' He said, 'The shit from the other dugout.' He said, 'I've been doing this for seven years, and I just don't want to take it anymore, Goddamnit.' And he said, 'I thought you might want to know it.' I said, 'Who?' He said, 'The bench. The Cardinals. Starting that shit again.'

"So I called Eddie Stanky, who was managing the Cardinals. Stanky is kind of Polish slick, and he said, 'I didn't hear anything out of line.' I said, 'Jackie said there was.' He said, 'Are you Jackie's little bobo? I'm telling you. I didn't hear anything out of line.'

"So I wrote the story, 'Jackie Robinson charged, Eddie Stanky denies.' And I got to the ballpark, and I see Jack around the batting cage about six, and I said, 'Stanky said there was nothing out of line.'

"Robinson made a big circular gesture with his hands, almost a Jewish hand gesture, and he said, 'Did you think I needed the publicity?' And at that moment I knew that while I had followed the journalism textbook, getting both sides, there really had been only one side to the story.

"So now I was really steamed. I went back in to see Stanky, and Stanky was a tough little bastard, and I'm really furious. There are 500,000 newspapers out there with the wrong story because this guy had misled me. I said, 'I just talked to Jack, and I don't believe you.' And he starts to get up, and there was a bat rack in his office, and I went to grab a bat, and he sat down, and he says, 'Look, I told you I didn't hear anything out of line.' He said, 'I heard "black bastard," but I don't consider that out of line. "Nigger." That's not out of line. You gotta understand this game. That is *not* out of line.'

"And so I went up to the press box, and I wrote the revised story, but the *Tribune* wouldn't run it.

"It became very uncomfortable when a player got mad. It wasn't so much a physical fear, though once I thought Campanella was gonna belt me. I wrote, 'The team doesn't have any spirit.' The Dodgers were losing, 7–2, George Shuba hit a home run, and no one even got up in the dugout. I said the team looked flat, played flat, they are flat, and Campanella said, 'I ought to punch you right in the jaw.' I went to Bob Cooke, who covered the Dodgers before Harold Rosenthal. He said, 'I'll tell you what to do. If he wants to hit you, you stick out your jaw and let him hit you, and then this paper will back you, and you'll earn a million dollars in a lawsuit.'

"I said, 'Bob, I want my jaw.'

"The next day Campanella waited in the clubhouse. 'Hey,' he said, 'I can't clap. My hand's broke.' He had chipped a bone when his throwing hand hit the batter's bat as he tried to pick a runner off third.

" 'I didn't mean just you,' I said.

" 'What do you want me to do?' Campanella said. 'Jump up when he hits one and knock my head against the top of the dugout? Is that what you want?'

" 'That's not what I want,' I said.

"Campy was shouting. 'How can you, sitting up there, see if we got spirit down here?'

" 'Roy,' I said. 'Would you do me a favor?'

" 'What's that?'

" 'Stop reading the *Tribune.* Try the *Times.*'

" 'I would,' Campy said, ' 'cept the *Tribune* is the onliest paper I can get delivered in time for me to read it in the shithouse in the morning.' "

The Mad Monk

When spring camp opened in '53, the Dodger everyday lineup seemed to be set. Gil Hodges was on first, Robinson on second, Reese at short, and Cox at third. It was a pat hand. No one had a better infield. In the outfield Dressen had Snider in center and Furillo in right, and in left he knew he'd find someone to fill in. Campy, of course, was the catcher, perhaps the best in baseball.

But Dressen, who enjoyed dazzling with his moves, announced that he was breaking up his infield. He was going to play Junior Gilliam at second, moving Robinson to third, and benching Billy Cox. Dressen told all the reporters. He neglected to tell only one person: Cox.

After they found out about the switch, Cox and his sidekick, Preacher Roe, began complaining. They were angry, and the words they used made it appear as though they were mad because Gilliam was black. In fact, it was Dressen they were mad at, not Gilliam. Newspaper accounts of the issue were making spring training a tense time.

ROGER KAHN: "During the time of the Gilliam incident, Jackie was victimized by the *Journal,* which was more interested in sensationalism than the truth. The *Post*'s Milton Gross had flown down to spring training, and he had written a piece called 'The Seeds of Bigotry,' in which he said that the Dodger players were upset because a black was taking Billy Cox's place at third base.

"The *Journal* had to get back, wanted to get its circulation back, so they ordered the Dodger writer, Mike Gavin, to do a story on Jackie Robinson, to write that there was no bigotry, there was no dissension on the Dodgers. How the hell was Gavin going to do that? What he did was get very drunk and in the middle of the night knocked on Robinson's door, and he said, 'Is it all right if I have your byline?' And Robinson said, 'What?' And Gavin closed the door and ran back and wrote a story under Robinson's byline that there was no dissension on the Dodgers. By Jackie Robinson. A big red headline.

"Jack said, 'I'm gonna sue,' and Gavin said, 'He better not, because if he sues, he's gonna get bad publicity in every Hearst newspaper in the country.'

I didn't take it upon myself to advise Jackie at that point, but someone did, told him, 'Just walk away from it.' Because there would be a statement that he had given verbal consent to the use of his byline, and there was a question whether he was damaged. Jack didn't sue. But he had never given Gavin permission to use his name, and he believed there was a lot of dissension on the club and so he had a pretty tough time."

Robinson finally defused the situation. He told reporters, "The only issue was the benching of Billy Cox, the best third baseman and the most underrated player in baseball, without telling him what it was all about. That I was taking his place had nothing to do with it."

The first game of the season, Gilliam was at second, Robinson at third, and Cox on the bench. In the sixth inning, Robinson pulled a groin muscle. Cox returned to third and played with his usual brilliance. Throughout the season, Dressen continued to platoon, judiciously using Cox at third, where the slight infielder hit .291, and juggling Robinson between third and left field to keep him in the lineup as often as possible. A reporter asked Robinson if he had a good enough arm to play left field.

Undiplomatically Robinson replied, "I can throw as good as George Shuba, if that means anything."

As in '52 the major Dodger headache was pitching. Newcombe was still in the army, and this time Joe Black wasn't doing the job. Carl Erskine was again the ace of the staff. Billy Loes, with Dressen's prodding, was still pitching well; Preacher Roe, though thirty-eight years old, was still good for a dozen or so wins; and for a fourth starter, Dressen had a lefty fastball pitcher named Johnny Podres, who had impressed everyone despite his youth. There was also Russ Meyer, who Buzzy Bavasi had acquired that winter from the Braves in a three-cornered deal.

On the mound Russ Meyer was all business, but because of his intensity, he could be very colorful. He was like Old Faithful, quiet one moment and then prone to eruption. Only you knew when Old Faithful was going to go off. You never knew about Meyer. The umpire would call a pitch, and suddenly he would go crazy. Or if a teammate made an error behind him, he would turn around, right there in the middle of the inning, and berate him. His infielders hated him because they knew that if Meyer lost somehow it was never his fault, always theirs. Meyer was a talented pitcher, but it wasn't his pitching everyone talked about, it was his temper.

One time Meyer was knocked out early in a game when he was pitching for Philadelphia. He stormed into the clubhouse, and while he was taking off his uniform piece by piece, he kept swearing at himself for his poor performance, becoming more and more furious. Finally, after sitting down on his stool and removing his cleats, he strode toward the shower room, still holding one of the shoes, still talking to himself, calling himself foul and derogatory names. As he stepped into the shower, the water hitting his body, he suddenly wound up and pitched his spiked shoe at the ceiling. The spikes stuck in the plaster, and there they remained until someone got a ladder, climbed up, and

George Brace Photo

RUSS MEYER

removed them. The spike marks remained as a lasting memorial to Meyer's violent nature.

One time he threw the resin bag up in the air, and it came down and exploded in a cloud of dust right on top of his head. Scared the hell out of him. He thought he got shot.

BILL REDDY: "Meyer had a phenomenal temper. When Meyer was in a rage, the San Francisco earthquake looked mild in comparison.

"I was out at Ebbets Field one day. Meyer was pitching for Philadelphia, and he walked Robinson. Now this annoyed Meyer no end. The next batter, Campy, got decked immediately. Right at the head. Robinson danced off first, Meyer looked at him, threw to first, and Robinson got back. He danced off first, Meyer look at him, threw to first, and Robinson went to second. Stole it clean.

"Now Meyer was really furious. He walked off the mound behind the rubber, talking to himself, his hands on his hips. He got back on the mound, peered in for a signal, and on the next pitch Robinson stole third. Now Meyer is frothing at the mouth. He's hysterical. The catcher comes out, the first baseman comes out, the manager comes out. Everyone is around him, and he's screaming, frothing, jumping up and down like a madman.

"The game resumes. Robinson starts to dance off the third-base line. Everybody in the ballpark senses that he's going to go. Meyer looks over at Robinson, and he makes a wild pitch, and Robinson trots home. Two guys had to come to the mound and physically drag Meyer into the dugout."

Russ Meyer became a Dodger in 1953 because Philadelphia owner Robert Carpenter was trying both to save a buck and make a buck.

Meyer had gone 13–14 in 1952 with a 3.14 earned run average, and only Robin Roberts had pitched more innings. Meyer had made $11,500 in '52, and during the off-season asked Carpenter for a raise to $14,000. Carpenter's gracious reply, "No way." Meyer told him, "Get rid of me."

Carpenter traded Meyer to the Braves for first baseman Earl Torgeson and $100,000. Six hours later the Braves traded Meyer to the Dodgers for promising youngsters Jim Pendleton and Rocky Bridges and $75,000. Said a chagrinned Carpenter, "If I had known Meyer would end up with the Dodgers, I never would have traded him." As is so often the case, Philly fans moaned, but they were powerless. There's no way to get rid of a dumb, cheap, or incompetent owner.

When Meyer arrived in Vero Beach for spring training, he arrived unsigned. Buzzy Bavasi asked Meyer how much he wanted to sign. Meyer told him he wanted $16,000. Said Bavasi, "You got it." In addition Bavasi gave Meyer several thousand more for moving expenses. "He didn't have to do that," said Meyer. "The season hadn't officially started." The Dodgers, who needed starting pitchers badly, wanted to make Meyer happy, and he responded by giving the Dodgers a solid fourth starter behind Erskine, Loes, and Roe. In 1953 Russ Meyer finished 15–5. Even at sixteen grand, he was a bargain.

* * *

RUSS MEYER: "My nickname from high school was Monk, and then one day when I was with the Phillies, I got into a deal with Dascoli, the umpire, right here in Brooklyn. Jackie stole home, and Dascoli called him safe, and Andy Seminick and I both thought he was out, and if you go by the pictures, Jackie slid on the first-base side of the plate and never did touch the plate. Dascoli called him safe, and I proceeded to get all over Dascoli. In fact I grabbed him, and he pulled away from me, and I popped a couple of buttons off his coat, which cost me a three-day suspension. I got fined a couple hundred bucks. And after that game, Bob Carpenter hung 'the Mad Monk' tag on me. He had another name for me, 'Russell the Redneck Reindeer.'

"I was a real competitive guy, and I don't like to lose, no, and when I walk out there to the circle, I think I'm the best son of a gun there is, and I just don't like to lose. But Jackie used to hit me pretty good, and it had gotten to be a personal vendetta between him and I. Not that I threw at him to hurt anybody. I don't think I ever did that. But you have to keep them honest up there. And on this particular night with Jackie, what he did was he doubled, stole third, and then he stole home, and I called him a 'nigger motherfucker,' and you shouldn't put that in your book, but he was laughing at me because he knew that I got thrown out of the ballgame, and he was over there laughing, and I challenged him to a fight underneath the stands. He said, 'Come on.' Well, shit, that's goofy. He would have ate me up for breakfast. You know what I mean? And there were other times when we had words.

"When I was traded over to the Dodgers, I'm thinking to myself, 'Jesus, I've been tooth and nail with Robinson for about five years, and what the hell is going to happen now?' I was walking into the clubhouse, and I'm thinking to myself, 'Well, shit, you have to go in there.' So I went ahead, and there were the guys, starting to get dressed. Jackie's locker in the clubhouse was the second stall from the door. And I mean he was the first guy I saw when I walked in there. And I'll never forget it. The old Vero Beach clubhouse was one big room, and when I walked in, Jackie got up, and he walked right up to me. He held out his hand, and he said, 'We've been fighting one another. Now let's fight them together.' I said, 'Okay, pal.' I said, 'You've made things a lot easier for me.'

"Jackie was a competitor too. He'd play the Goddamn game the way its supposed to be played. He played to fucking win.

"He hated Durocher with a Goddamn passion. He used to taunt him. He'd drive that Goddamn Durocher crazy. He'd call him, 'Hey, you, pussy,' just drive the fucking guy crazy. 'Hey, Leo, who you going to marry next?' and like 'Is Laraine taking good care of you?' Shit like that. Jackie was a son of a bitch, I tell you. Let me tell you something though. When he first came into the league, Jackie took all kinds of shit from everybody, all kinds of crap, and hey, after the guy proved himself and became a great ballplayer—shit, he was a good ballplayer when he got there, but after he made himself, I will tell you, he just played like a son of a bitch, and he didn't give a shit who he hurt. It was, 'Get out of my fucking road, pal, I'm coming.' And I'll tell you something, for a big guy—Jackie was a big Goddamn strong guy, boy, I'll tell you what—he had a fast start. And he became the *great* Jackie Robinson, and he didn't take a back seat to nobody. He didn't give or ask for anything. He'd say, 'Okay, boys, we're here to go, let's go. Let the best man win.'

"When Jackie first came up, I was with the Cubs, and I remember Bobby Sturgeon was playing short for us. Sturgeon was not a great ballplayer, he was a utility infielder really, and when Jackie first came up, Sturgeon said, 'I'll get the son of a bitch.' So Jackie got on in the third inning, and they put the hit-and-run on, and the ball was hit to the second baseman, Don Johnson, and Johnson made a quick relay, and Sturgeon didn't even try for the double play. He threw the ball right into Jackie's chest. Jackie didn't say a word. He just got up and ran off the field. About six weeks later, we came back to Brooklyn, and almost the identical situation came up. Jackie got on base, and on the first pitch, he takes off, and Sturgeon was playing short, and Jackie didn't slide. He threw a block at Sturgeon and knocked him halfway into left field. Busted two of his ribs. Jackie didn't say a word, and neither did Sturgeon. That was a ballplayer retaliating in his own way."

Meyer remembers upon his arrival to the Dodgers the turmoil over Dressen's switching Gilliam to second and Robinson to third and the benching of Billy Cox.

As Meyer remembers it, the problem wasn't racial. The one who was causing the trouble, it seems, was Jackie Robinson.

RUSS MEYER: "Number one, Jackie didn't want to play third. He wanted to stay at second. True, Cox didn't want to get bumped out of his job, but the one who was doing the undercurrenting was Jackie. You know how Jackie was. Jackie could get something in his craw, and he'd agitate, instigate until he more or less got what he wanted. You know what I mean? He more or less said, 'Hey, I paid my dues. Now you guys dance to the fiddler.'

"He finally did end up on third base, but then I think that Jackie was smart enough to admit that he didn't have as much range as he used to, that he wouldn't have to make the moves and cover the ground that he did at second base. And he saw it was gonna be good for the ballclub, so he went over there. But I don't recall any talk that, 'Hey, now we got two black guys in the infield.'

"And then, if you recall, Jackie got hurt, and Billy came back, and that was like having the greatest insurance policy in the world. When Billy got back in there, he went crazy. He played fantastic ball.

"It was tough pitching in Ebbets Field. Take a look at my earned run average through the years. I'm 15 and 5 with the Dodgers, and an earned run average of 4.57. I'm 17–8 with the Phillies, and I got an earned run average of 3.02. At Ebbets Field, the power alley is about 358, a very small power alley, and that fence in right center, hell, I don't think it's more than 320, and in dead straightaway center, what is it, 390? And that field beat me some ballgames, but it also won a lot of ballgames for us. You'd go out there, and even if you allowed four or five runs, you knew damn good and well that eventually one of the guys was gonna pop one. A lead is never safe in that ballpark. And it makes you a better pitcher, because you have to bear down all the time. You can't coast through any part of an opposition's lineup. You can't coast, period."

Meyer's stay with the Dodgers was a short one. Three productive years and then he was gone. In June of 1955, he was hurt on a play at first base. It was in Milwaukee, and Bill Bruton hit a high hopper to the right side, and Gil Hodges at first went for the ball, and when he saw that Junior Gilliam was going to field it, he raced back to first. At the same time, Meyer ran to first to cover, and Gilliam threw to Meyer. As Meyer caught the ball, he was sandwiched between Hodges and Bruton. In the collision Meyer broke his shoulder blade. He was out until the end of August.

After the '55 season, the Dodgers traded Meyer to the Cubs for relief pitcher Don Elston. In his three years at Brooklyn, Russ had as good a won–lost record as anyone. He was 15–5, 11–6, and 6–2, which is 32–13, and he had had arm trouble two of the three years. "The only thing I can say," says Meyer, "is that to me it was a joy to be on a ballclub like that, because in my mind that ballclub was as good a ballclub that ever walked onto a ballfield—in either league."

When Robinson played left field, the Dodgers fielded a starting lineup with an all-star at each of the eight positions. Hodges, who had regained his hitting form once he began following Dressen's advice, suddenly came alive. In '53 he hit .302, drove in 122 runs and hit thirty-one home runs. Gilliam at second was a deer at leadoff, getting on base frequently, stealing bases, scoring 125 runs. Reese at short anchored the infield, batted .271 and was second only to the Braves' Bill Bruton with twenty-two stolen bases. Billy Cox batted .291 and played magnificently in the field.

In the outfield Robinson hit .329 and drove in ninety-five runs, Snider hit .336, hit forty-two home runs, and drove in 126 runs, and the always overlooked and underrated Carl Furillo hit a league-leading .344, with ninety-two rbis. At catcher Roy Campanella won the Most Valuable Player Award for a second time, hitting .312, with forty-one home runs and 142 runs batted in.

It was onc of thc most powcrful lineups in baseball history, stronger even than the 1936 Yankees, which featured Lou Gehrig, Joe DiMaggio, and Bill Dickey. In one four-game series against the St. Louis Cardinals in July, the Dodgers scored forty-four runs. They hit ten home runs, three of them grand slams by Hodges, Cox, and a rookie, Wayne Belardi.

Six of the hitters, Cox, Furillo, Snider, Robinson, Campanella, and Hodges, hit over .290. Five of them, Furillo, Hodges, Robinson, Campanella, and Snider, drove in more than ninety runs. Six, Robinson, Snider, Gilliam, Reese, Hodges, Campanella, scored over 100 runs. The team hit 208 home runs, and its .285 batting average was two points higher than any other team. The Dodgers were a juggernaut. By the final day of July, the Dodgers were seven games ahead of the young and coming Braves. The season was as good as over. They won the pennant on September 13, when Carl Erskine beat the Braves 5–3 in Milwaukee. No National League team had clinched a pennant so early.

The Duke of Flatbush

The advent of television coincided with the coming of age of the Dodger center fielder, Edwin "Duke" Snider, who more than any other Dodger benefited from the small rectangular box that was invading living rooms, bedrooms, stores, and bars in Brooklyn and across America. He was young, handsome, and he had a winning smile. Almost overnight the prematurely silver-haired Duke Snider became Brooklyn's matinee idol.

Snider was a different breed of ballplayer. He was the first of the California surfer-types, the young, sun-bleached blonds with the earthy good looks and the healthy complexions. Snider had grown up in Los Angeles, played only one full season in the minors, in 1944, and after two years in the service played for St. Paul the tag end of 1947 and in 1948 for Montreal, where he drove in seventy-seven runs in seventy-seven games. Rickey was very high on Snider and would tell reporters, "The boy has steel springs in his legs." As a result reporter Bill Roeder went around calling him "Steel Springs." Snider had raw talent, had a powerful swing at the plate, but throughout that first season, Snider struggled both with pitchers who knew more than he did and with his own emotions.

SPIDER JORGENSEN: "Duke was temperamental when he first came up. He sulked a lot, both when he wasn't hitting and when he wasn't playing. Shotton would make comments once in a while in the papers that 'if he didn't quit swinging at that ball in the dirt, he'd send him back to Montreal where he'd learn how.' See, they worked on you through the newspapers. But once Duke got to playing all the time, it was just a matter of time. It's hard to come up from the minors and sit on the bench for five days and then go in to pinch hit. If he chases a couple of balls in the dirt or a couple over his head, the manager says, 'Oh Christ, he's got to have another year at Montreal.' But you could just tell he was going to get better and better, 'cause he could always field and throw, and he had power. It was just a question of his laying off that high fastball, which they threw right by the young guys."

The Duke played with intensity and abandon, and his physical skills were exceptional. When a ball stayed in the ballpark, the Duke would find a way to catch it. The parks then had different nooks and crannies and stands jutting out on the field, and in an old stadium like Philadelphia's Connie Mack Stadium, where a player could jump up and catch balls that would have been in the third or fourth row, Duke would make plays that were otherworldly, running full speed and never getting hurt and leaping and hitting the wall and amazing the fans by catching balls that would have been home runs.

And starting in 1953, the first of five consecutive years when he hit forty

Duke Snider

or more home runs, Duke Snider was regarded as the premier power hitter on what some regard as the most powerful lineup ever to grace a National League diamond. At Ebbets Field he hit towering home runs into Bedford Avenue, and every once in a while he would send the baseball clear across the street, clattering through the plate glass windows of Dodger Dodge. Any left-handed kid growing up in Brooklyn wore number 4 on the back of his t-shirt and demanded that he play center field on his team. The dream, of course, was to someday replace the Duke in center field for the Dodgers.

TOM "DUKE" BUNDERICK: "I'm afraid the only similarity Duke Snider and I had was that he played center field for the Dodgers, and I played center field on our stickball team on Vanderbilt Avenue, and we were both left-handed. I used to go to Ebbets Field all the time, and sit in the center-field bleachers. I used to wear number 4 all the time, just like Duke did. Even when I played basketball I wore number 4. And so they gave me that wonderful nickname, the Duke.

"During the summer, every morning at six A.M., there was always somebody out front with a sawed-down broom handle and a rubber ball. The whole neighborhood was involved in sports. The big game was stickball, and we had home turf rules. Like we would park cars in certain areas because we knew it would place the other team at a disadvantage. If a man had parked his car on third base or near third base, we might back it up. We would release the emergency brake and move it where we wanted. Perhaps we had right-handed power hitters on our team. We would move the car back into the area where it might make it difficult for the outfielder to get the ball. So there were little tricks like that.

"Fort Hamilton Parkway was the main drag in Brooklyn where we lived, and I would run out in the middle of pretty heavy two-way traffic. And I couldn't hesitate because of the cars, because you'd get pretty well smeared by your teammates. 'Hey, Duke, why the hell didn't you go after the Goddamn ball?' they would yell. 'What are you, chicken? We'll get someone else out there who isn't afraid.' So it was very competitive. I can't remember anyone ever getting hit by a car. There were close calls, but most motorists were attuned to the fact that there was always the chance of somebody leaping out in front of the car and scaring the hell out of you.

"The cops would chase us every once in a while for making noise. One time this gangster called the cops on us. It was about eleven in the morning, and he told them, 'Jesus, I'm trying to sleep around here, and these guys are waking me up,' and either he had an in with the police force or he was an informer or something, but a whole bunch of cops came. Eight radio cars came soaring into the neighborhood just because he complained, and nobody could figure out why the hell they were sending eight cop cars around for a bunch of kids playing stickball.

"It was an era when kids identified with the players. Guys wanted to be like Snider or Hodges or Furillo. A lot of guys tried to be like Eddie Stanky—rough, aggressive, tough, scrappy. The little guys emulated Phil Rizzuto. They'd say, 'If he can play, I sure as hell can do it too.' It was a good time to grow up. A lot of fathers were immigrants who didn't really know that much about the sport. It was the kids who engendered the fanaticism. I think most of the parents looked at it as, 'It's better than having them steal cars, so let them alone.'

"It's funny what I remember about the old Duke. One of the great things I remember is that whenever Warren Spahn pitched in Ebbets Field, Duke would have a back sprain. Remember, in those days no left-handed pitcher could pitch in Ebbets Field, because you had that fantastic left-field fence where Robinson, Cox, Furillo, Hodges, Campanella, and Reese all hit, and so no left-hander would dare start in Ebbets Field but Spahn. So Duke almost never saw left-handed pitchers because he was the only left-handed batter in the lineup. So when Warren Spahn pitched, I guess he wasn't used to it, and he would get a back sprain or have a little muscle spasm, and he wouldn't be able to play that day. Because he just wasn't used to the curveball coming in from first base.

"And yet there were so many positive things I remember about the Duke. I enjoyed his fantastic grace in the outfield. He had a beautiful swing. He was a very good base runner. He had a lot of class.

"Duke was a graceful player. Everybody used to say, 'It's so easy to play in Ebbets Field because it's so shallow,' but hell, if you're playing in Yankee Stadium or the Polo Grounds where you can turn your back on the ball and take off, that's a helluva lot easier than having to roam around Ebbets Field where you're really confined and you have to learn to play the caroms. Duke mastered that. And I remember his hitting those clutch home runs. He wasn't the flashy, spectacular type of player. Mays would make the fantastic catches and steal three bases, and Robinson would do the same, and Mantle would hit all the home runs. Thinking about it now, I can't remember a single incident where you said, 'Wow, he made some play,' or 'Duke stole home against the Yankees in the World Series,' like Robinson did. You don't have those spectacular incidents, but if you look at the Duke's statistics, you'll see a steady pattern of way-above-average ball."

BILL FARRELL, JR.: "I batted left and threw right because my father trained me to play ball in Ebbets Field. 'The Duke will be getting old by the time you're eighteen,' he'd say. I was a natural righty, but I batted left. Some people say he screwed me up by making me bat left-handed, but he wanted me to be able to hit that right-field wall in Ebbets Field.

"By extension Duke became my favorite ballplayer. The Silver Fox. He was the king. He got the big runs. I can still see him running across center field, going up against the wall, and making a catch."

BILL REDDY: "There were only two center fielders in Metropolitan New York, Duke Snider and Willie Mays. Whenever we debated about the greatest center fielder, Mantle's name was in there, you had to put it in, but Mantle was just a name you threw in as a sop to the Yankee fans that might be listening. Believe me, Mantle never figured in at all, not one iota. It was Snider and

Mays, and every day we would scan the papers to see which guy made the most spectacular catch or the most hits that day.

"Snider was such a graceful ballplayer. When Mays ran he looked like Buster Keaton. He ran with his whole body. Ran out from under his hat. Hair flying, his shirt was puffing, and off Mays went. Sometimes you didn't know how long it was going to take him to get there, but you knew he was going to get there. Because he was playing three fields. Duke only had to play two fields. At least he had Furillo in right.

"I must say Mays was good. Still, a Duke Snider he wasn't. Duke Snider was the greatest. They talk about the great catches Mays made. What about Duke Snider climbing up the wall in Philadelphia and saving the game for the Dodgers in 1951 when the Giants would have won the pennant without a playoff? What about Duke Snider hitting those towering home runs up over right-center field into Bedford Avenue? And the highest pop flies for outs that I ever saw in my life. I've seen Snider hit the ball up in the air, and before it came down, the second baseman would pull a magazine out and read two or three pages. And Snider would drive us crazy because he'd do that when you were losing 2–0 and you had two men on base. And the next time, he'd come up with no one on, and he'd hit the ball four-and-a-half blocks down Bedford Avenue.

"The Duke was unique, more so than Mantle or Mays. I daresay that Snider made just as many spectacular catches as Mays did. Mays just made the one catch in the World Series. But Snider, for day in, day out baseball, Snider was the best. He could play that exit gate, which was a tricky thing in Ebbets Field. The ball would come on a bounce and hit the exit gate and bounce back and forth, and the runners would be flying around the bases, and the fielder wouldn't be able to pick it up. But never Snider. Snider always got it on the first hop, if he didn't catch it on the fly. Snider was spectacular."

RALPH BRANCA: "Duke was something. He could fly, he could throw, he could hit, he had power, he could do it all. I'm prejudiced, but when they ask who was better, Mays, Mantle, or Snider, there's no contest. Duke was a better outfielder than the other two guys by far. He got a better jump on the ball. He had a much more accurate arm than either one of them, and he played in the toughest ballpark. At Ebbets Field you have to worry about running into the wall, where the other guys could run all day to catch the ball. Duke charged ground balls super. His last five years in Ebbets Field, Duke hit forty home runs a season. If he hadn't gone to L.A., he would have ended up with a lot more than he had."

Duke, like so many of the players, lived in Brooklyn. He was one of dem, and there were times when he would come home after a ballgame and play stickball with the kids in the street.

RON GREEN: "We would be playing stickball on 18th Street, and he would come home—he and his wife lived in a private house in an upstairs apartment—and the kids knew who he was. 'Hey, Duke, want to take a few cuts?' It was like he was one of the boys in the neighborhood. He'd take a few cuts, we'd pitch it in on a bounce. We wouldn't fluke it to him, just let him hit it. He'd take a few cuts. And the ole Duke could drive that ball pretty good! He could poke! Three sewers easy!"

The fans loved him, though they sensed he was flawed. Somehow they knew he hated to hit against left-handed pitchers, and they knew that in October Mantle's team won and his team didn't. In the back of their minds always was the disquieting sense that no matter how good Snider was, somehow he should be better. Which demonstrated the perspicacity of the Dodger fans. For during his entire career, Snider fretted and worried about the same thing. When Snider was on the field, winning was all he thought about. He was consumed with the notion of winning, for to him losing was a sign of personal weakness. An error was a sign of weakness. Striking out was a sign of weakness. For Snider to be satisfied, he would have to go four for four, make a great catch, and the Dodgers would have to win. Often he seemed surly, especially during a batting slump when he was quickest to anger. The reporters who covered Snider always had to be on their toes. He distrusted them, felt they were trying to either take advantage of him or put him down.

ROGER KAHN: "I remember it was a Sunday game, and Duke was slumping at the plate, and he didn't hustle on a fly ball. Dressen said, 'That's it, he sits down.' And Furillo went to center, and another player went to right. Mike Gavin went and wrote a piece that said, 'Whatever Snider does, sources on the Dodgers guaranteed that his pay will be cut next year. If he hits .400 the rest of the year, he will still get a pay cut.' Dick Young wrote that Snider was dogging it and lazy and said that Snider had earned the benching. I wrote a piece for the *Herald Tribune* saying the same thing.

"Well, Beverly Snider didn't get the *Herald Tribune,* so Duke didn't come after me, but when she saw what Young and Gavin wrote, she began to cry. Duke was in Cincinnati, and she called him and read him the newspapers, and the next day I was sitting in the dugout, and Snider was sitting by himself at the end of the bench, and he goes, 'Psssst. Pssst.' 'Yes?' 'You got a minute?' It was like he was a leper. Nobody was near him. He said, 'Look, it probably won't do any good, but if either Dick Young or Mike Gavin comes on the field tonight, I'm gonna punch him right in the nose.' I thought, 'I wonder if he saw my piece?' I said, 'It won't do any good, Duke.' I said, 'Anyway, they didn't bench you. Dressen did. You're not gonna punch Dressen.' We talked for a couple of minutes, and I said, 'Don't hit any writers, Duke. If you've got an argument, it's with Dressen and Bavasi. Gavin's an old man. You don't want to hit him.' And that was it. I left.

"In Cincinnati there was a little German kitchen in the back of the press room where they served some pretty good food, and I was eating, and Gavin and Young appeared. I said, 'Oh boy, have I got some good news for you guys. Step on the field and say hello to number 4, and he's gonna punch you right in the mouth.' Young gets that hard look, and Gavin starts to come apart. Gavin went nowhere near the field, and Young, who would probably tell you how he went up to Snider and said, 'Listen, Duke,' didn't go near the field either. What Young did was wait until the game was over, write his story, and in Cincinnati there was a hangout called The Barn where we would sometimes go, and he traced Snider there and said, 'Let's have a drink. Let's talk this thing over,' and he did, and after they talked Snider cooled off."

Snider was an extremely serious man, and his teammates, who found him an inviting target for the needle, went after him with a vengeance. When Snider became angry at their barbs, they enjoyed it even more. Their favorite topic of conversation was in letting him know how lucky he was not to ever have to face left-handed pitching.

CARL FURILLO: "Burt Shotton told it the way it was. He would say, 'The trouble with Snider is that he doesn't want to swing the bat. He's always up there crying, "Hey, come on Furillo, Campanella, come on Robinson, Hodges, you get that son of a bitch left-hander the hell out of there." ' Soon as he saw a left-hander he started crying. Christ, you could see him crawl into a shell right away.

"Snider was always crying whenever there were left-handers pitching, and he cried when he wasn't hitting the ball, when he was in a slump, and he would cry when the manager didn't take him out. The manager figured, 'You might be able to save me a ballgame by your fielding even if you don't get a hit.' But Snider was always crying, 'Get me out of there. Oooooh. Aaaaaah.' In other words, it would hurt his batting average, and he didn't like it. When he was in a slump he wanted to sit out until he could get straightened out, then come back in. He was a funny duck.

"He was an only child growing up, a mama's boy. They used to call him that. He admitted it himself. 'California fruit' we used to call him. But don't get me wrong. He was a good ballplayer, God bless him. Snider and I got along good. We played the outfield beautiful together. We never tried to cross each other up. I played right field, and he played center, and if the play was mine, I'd holler loud enough to keep him the hell off, or if he had a better chance, he'd holler right away, and he'd grab it. And when we went back to the wall, we'd help each other out. We played the game nice. We got along good. I mean, we never ran around together, but on the ballfield we acted like we were one. And that's the way to play the game."

REX BARNEY: "Duke was a magnificent ballplayer, a magnificent athlete. But Duke was even more of a rebel than Furillo. Duke spoke his piece, and the media didn't like him for a long time, 'cause Duke was not the nicest guy. I'll tell you what he was. He was a pain in the ass and a crybaby. We would win a game, and Duke would go 0 for 4, and he'd come to the clubhouse pouting, and Pee Wee or one of the guys would say, 'Who stole his candy? What's wrong with him?' His wife, Beverly, used to tell us that Duke would be hitting .350, have twenty home runs, and he'd go 0 for 4 and come home and say, 'Jeez, I'll probably be going to Montreal. They'll be sending me there.' He was a worrywart. He's had gray hair since he was seventeen. That has to tell you something."

CLEM LABINE: "We used to call him 'The Luckiest Player in the World' to be on our club. He ought to pay each and every one of us. After all, he never faced a left-hander. All he ever got to face were right-handers. You check the records, and you'll see that Warren Spahn wouldn't pitch against us, for crying out loud.

"Pee Wee would get on him all the time. 'Who stole his lollypop? Somebody stole Duke's candy. Who was it?' Pee Wee and Duke lived out in Bay Ridge together, and he'd be on him all the time. And he'd be so blunt with him. 'For Christ sake, stop moaning.' "

Duke Snider, who personified the Dodger power, ironically had an inferiority complex. As a batter he had expected to get a hit every single time at bat, and when he didn't he would sulk. If an opposing fielder made a great play on a long hit, he would complain to the heavens about his bad luck. For his entire career, Duke Snider carried on in this manner, always raging and decrying his luck. It had been Snider whose rope into center field should have won the pennant for the Dodgers in 1950. Except that Cal Abrams got thrown out at home. Typical Snider luck. As great as he was, no matter how well he was doing, Duke Snider always felt that his luck should have been better.

IRVING RUDD: "Reese, Snider, and Erskine lived in Bay Ridge together near the Shore Parkway, and they were driving to the Polo Grounds on the West Side Highway. Reese was driving, and Snider was a passenger, and Pee Wee was speeding, and a cop motioned him to pull over. Duke said, 'Well, Captain, lets see what you're going to do about this.' The cop walked over. Pee Wee said, 'Geez, officer, I'm awfully sorry. I'm Pee Wee Reese of the Dodgers, and this is Duke Snider and Carl Erskine.' The officer said, 'Geez, so you are. Geez, easy on the pedal, will ya, Pee Wee? Take it easy, fella.'

"The next day Snider is at the wheel, and the same thing, he's speeding, and a cop pulls him over. Pee Wee says, 'It's your turn, Duke.' Duke says, 'Say, officer, I'm Duke Snider of the Dodgers.'

"The first sentence out of the cop's mouth: 'I hate baseball.'

"That's a true story."

The teammate who knew the Duke best was Carl Erskine, his roommate for many years.

CARL ERSKINE: "I'm not a psychologist, but here are just a couple observations. Duke was one of the victims that happens in life, where everyone says how great his potential was. So every place he went, no matter how good he was, they'd say, 'His potential is so great, he can do even better.' And this was a real frustration for Duke. He saw himself as not measuring up.

"I don't know a whole lot about Duke's background, his home life, but he was thrust into the limelight early in life, like a lot of pro athletes are. It was a thing—he had difficulty taking criticism, and who doesn't? But he always had to respond.

"The other thing was that Duke had a fear he was going to die young. His dad died of a heart attack at a fairly early age, and his mother had health problems, and it was almost a Mantle story in a lesser degree. Mantle had this tremendous fear of dying young.

"And Duke had a fear of being traded. I can remember a couple of road trips where Duke was really beside himself. These were in the building years, the late '40s. It would be mentioned in the papers that he struck out a lot, and with the Duke it was all or nothing. He'd have a great day, or he'd strike out three times, and in trying to find that consistency, Duke was having frustrations.

"And he would give the wrong responses to the writers. He might be curt or cause them to treat him like a spoiled brat. Or he might blow up. The classic example was after he had a very bad night in Brooklyn, got booed substantially, and came into the clubhouse, he slammed the big iron door and yelled to all the writers who could hear him, 'You want a story. I'll give you a story. These are the lousiest fans in baseball. I hope you print it. You better print it.' They did print it. So the next night, the boo birds were out. And when Duke appeared the first time, man, they gave him a real roasting. And he singled. He then had a couple of home runs, a double, and the last time they cheered the roof off the place. But it was tough for him to just take it and go on.

"Still, Duke had a solid makeup. He took care of himself. He rested right, he got in at night. We had a good room on that basis. Duke got his rest, and Duke was very helpful to me many times, with my frustrations with arm trouble. I always had the notion that Duke played harder when I pitched. He sure hit well for me.

"I'd say there was a perception of Duke as a loner. Those of us closest to Duke were Pee Wee, Rube Walker. We lived out in Bay Ridge, and Duke had a couple of things he really liked. He liked to go out to the track. I didn't go to the track. It was just something I didn't do. I liked to go fishing. But Duke loved to go to the track, so there were guys like Don Zimmer, Johnny Podres, they'd buddy together quite a bit. They'd go to the dogs in spring training. So Duke always was with people. I didn't see him as a loner. He probably gave the impression to certain guys. He didn't drum up groups to go and have a drink. But he didn't sit in a bar by himself either. He'd have a few beers with the guys. He'd have people with him.

"One of the things Duke always said to me was, 'Carl, when we're through with baseball, we've got to still be seeing each other. We need to see each other after we're apart.' He always had the feeling. 'Let's don't let this get away from us.' He talked about reunions, we'd make cruises together, things where we'd come back together. So Duke didn't see himself as a loner. If anyone was a loner, it was Carl Furillo."

During the heart of his career, Duke Snider discovered that playing baseball was hard, serious work, and in a moment of forthrightness, he told Roger Kahn that the only reason he played was the money. It was hard for Snider, all right, in large part because Snider never gave himself any leeway, always pushed himself to the limit, never being satisfied with his accomplishments. His performance was never good enough, and so, for him, it was work.

ROGER KAHN: "A lot of the road is bitching, and one evening as Duke and I sat in a bar called Holiday House—not Inn—Duke said, 'If it weren't for the money, Rog, I'd be just as happy if I never played another ballgame.' I said, 'You're just saying that.' He said, 'I'm not just saying that. I mean it.' I said, 'If you mean it, we'll do a piece.' He said, 'As long as it doesn't sound like I'm complaining.' So we did a piece. It was mild enough. God, Jim Bouton would regard that piece as capitalist propaganda for the glories of the game.

"The story came out in *Collier's,* and everyone dumped on the piece. As one who writes books learns, newspaper commentary isn't very perceptive. Here was a piece that says baseball is a helluva hard thing to do, and Red Smith wrote, 'Snider grabbed Kahn's lapel and started to weep,' which is hardly what happened or hardly the sense of the piece. It was just a superficial, slick column. It got him a column. He didn't have to leave his house, didn't have to leave his pool.

"Stanley Woodward, whom I admire enormously in so many ways, wrote a perfectly vicious piece, saying, 'This is how a column like this gets written. A writer goes into his room, makes up a piece, and then looks around for a ballplayer to use the piece.' I saw Woodward. I said, 'Wrong, Stanley, absolutely wrong.' He said, 'Ha ha. It was entertaining and short of libel, and that's *my* definition of a good piece.'

"John Lardner, who was the best sports columnist I ever read, including Red Smith, was the only person who had any sense of the piece. He wrote, 'When you're a kid, you have dreams, and in the back of your dream is that you'll be a different person, and if you're Duke Snider, the dreams come true at age twenty-four, and you're still Duke Snider, you still have to do the checkbook, your injuries still hurt you, you don't want to be in Milwaukee and worry about the train the next day to St. Louis, or whether you're going to have to fly through another thunderstorm, that it's not a magic fairyland.' This was Duke's tragedy, the point of the piece.

"Afterwards, after everyone had dumped on Snider, I said, 'Geez, Duke. I'm sorry the reaction was so rough.' He said, 'Look. I got my ink.' "

I went to visit the Duke at the West Palm Beach training site for the Montreal Expos. Duke is one of the Expo broadcasters, an ironic turnabout considering his earlier disdain for media people. It was March, and outside it was usually chilly, and as we sat in the pressroom over a tape recorder talking baseball, Duke once again became a Brooklyn Dodger. I could see his eyes narrow and his mouth harden as he tried to make sense of his career.

DUKE SNIDER: "I was born in 1926 in Los Angeles, where I was able to play baseball year-round when I was growing up. By the time I was sixteen, I was better than most of the guys I was playing against, and some of them were professional ballplayers playing in the wintertime.

"The Dodgers were my favorite team ever since the 1941 World Series, when they lost. Pee Wee was a young man on the team then, and Pete Reiser led the league in hitting. And when I got out of high school in 1943, I was offered a contract with the Dodgers and Cincinnati and Pittsburgh and St. Louis."

"What were they offering you?" I asked.

"Nothin'," Duke said glumly. "It was World War II. It was a chance to play ball, really. I got a $750 bonus, something like that. Tom Downey, the Dodger scout for California, came to my house one day with a typewriter, and he said, 'I'm going to sign you to a Dodger contract.' My father was overseas in the war. The other scouts had told me, 'Whatever the Dodgers offer you, we'll offer more,' but nobody ever offered anything, and I was at the point where I knew I'd only be able to play one season and then I'd have to go into the service, so I told my mother, 'Might as well sign,' and I did, and I was never sorry for it.

"And I wasn't in the minors very long, a total of two and a half years, in four different cities. I only played one full season in the minors. That was in Newport News, Virginia, 1944, and we finished the season with nine players that year. Two pitchers and myself played the outfield, 'cause everyone was leaving, and we either had old guys or guys too young, a couple of 4-Fs.

"Probably the two most important things that happened to me in the minor leagues was in 1946, after coming out of the service. Branch Rickey was in the stands, and I hit a home run over the clock in right-center field in Ft. Worth, and then I had a very good playoff. It got me a spring training visit with the Dodgers in '47, and the other important thing was, after being sent to St. Paul in '47, I was sent to Montreal in '48, and I had seventy-seven rbis in seventy-seven games, and when Branch Rickey sent me down at the beginning of the year he said, 'Make me bring you back,' and so he came there this night in August, and he said, 'How are you doing?' and I said, 'Don't you think seventy-seven rbis in seventy-seven games is enough to bring me back?' and he said, 'Catch a plane tomorrow, and you'll be in center field for the Dodgers.'

"Rickey had a big influence on my early career. He taught me the strike zone, and with his lectures and guidance, he made me a Hall of Famer."

The one thing Rickey didn't have to do was teach him about hitting home runs. He had been doing that since he was fourteen. Another thing he had also been doing since he began playing ball was showing his temper, throwing bats and helmets when he struck out or made a bad play. He also hated to bunt, and his first year he got in a shouting match with Burt Shotton over it, and he was fined.

DUKE SNIDER: "There was only one time when we had a problem. He gave me a bunt sign, and I popped it up, and I was mad because I had popped the bunt up, and I threw my bat in the bat rack, and I said a few things to him, and he fined me. It was the first inning! And I was a little upset about it. But I wasn't as upset about his giving me the bunt sign as I was popping it up. Yet in the first inning? It didn't make any sense to me."

Carl Furillo had said that "Duke was a problem child," and Duke agreed, at least to a point.

"My problem was that I had excelled in athletics all my life and that I really didn't know what adversity was until I came to the Dodgers. I had to learn that every day wasn't a bed of roses, and that took some time. I would sulk. I'd have a pity party for myself. I admit it."

I mentioned that Furillo had also called Duke aloof.

"Erskine, Rube Walker, myself, and Pee Wee, we all lived in the same area of Brooklyn, and some said it was a clique, and maybe it was. To a certain extent it was. But that didn't carry into the clubhouse or when we were on a road trip. We spent a lot of time with most everybody on the team, but when we were in Brooklyn, our wives would play bridge together, and after a game we'd go to whoever's house they were playing bridge at and have a bite to eat. I've heard Furillo say that we had a clique, and like I say, we probably did, but I don't ever recall ever being invited over to Carl's house, and the gals invited Fern, his wife, to several functions. But she never came. Besides, even when it's a closely knit group, you don't have twenty-five people over."

"Some of the other players said you didn't like to hit against left-handers," I said softly. His eyes bore down on me. Here was a serious man, and this was touching a raw nerve ending.

"We didn't see many left-handed pitchers. But I know in one stretch we saw five straight left-handed pitchers, and the first game I went 0 for 4, and the next game I got a home run, and for four straight games I got home runs off left-handers, so you see, the more you see them, the more you're going to hit them. I knew that I could hit them if I saw them, but I just didn't see enough of them.

"The other guys still kidded me a lot, and one of the reasons they did is that it got me fired up for the game. Sometimes I needed a little fire lit under me, and some of the players could sense that, and they would agitate me. One day we had a big argument—a discussion I should say, not an argument—Gil and Pee Wee were needling me about the short right-field fence, and I said, 'Did you guys ever realize that you guys are shooting at a three-foot fence out in left field and that there's a jet stream out in left-center field?' We went out onto the field, and I said, 'Lay your head on home plate,' and I showed them there was a crown on the field so the water would drain off the infield toward the stands where the drains were, and actually, if you got at eye level at home plate, they were only actually shooting at a three-foot fence. But of course they refused to admit it.

"This was serious business to me. Everything about playing baseball was serious business. When I'm working, I'm very serious, and I might be too serious a person too much of the time. I would go up to my room at three o'clock in the afternoon and start getting mentally prepared for a game, start thinking about the pitcher that night, and a lot of times that didn't work, but I still did it. And I don't think baseball was work, even though the article Roger Kahn and I did that came out in *Collier's* said that I played baseball for money and not fun.

"I was ridiculed quite a bit about it, but basically when I went out on the field, I tried to think about the game for two and a half hours and nothing else. You have to do that to be a successful player. You must try to be in the ballgame all the time. Maybe I did go about it in a different manner than some of the others, and maybe I had difficulty accepting some of the adversities that come about and maybe would show my emotions a little bit more than some of the others, but that was me. No way I could change that. So, no, don't say baseball was work. Baseball was never work. It was fun at times, but to me it was something I was devoted to and wanted to excel in.

"The Dodgers were a very serious group of people. We were a dedicated bunch, and we only had one goal in mind, and that was to win, and whatever it took, that's what we would do. Charley Dressen knew how to handle me. He knew how to get the most out of me. He'd get me mad, and then I'd go out and take it out on the opposing club. Sometimes I needed a fire lit under me, and he'd get me irate, something he might say in the paper, or he might have a meeting and say something, whatever, and that's what I needed sometimes. He knew how to do that. Charley was like a banty rooster. Off the field he and I were very close, and on the field he knew when I needed a kick in the butt, and he'd give it to me."

"In 1952 you hit twenty-one home runs. In '53 you hit forty-two. What changed?" I asked.

"I don't like the word maturity. I think it was just more experience, getting more at bats, maybe being a little bit more relaxed mentally, not applying as much pressure on myself as I had in earlier years. But I think it takes a guy four or five years in professional baseball before he becomes the hitter that he's going to be."

"So prior to that year you were very hard on yourself?"

"I'm still hard on myself. I'm probably more critical of myself than anyone else."

"So the nagging doubts you had about your ability continued throughout your entire career?"

Duke nodded. "But I think I learned to handle those doubts and was able to push them aside and learn to thrive on the pressures and realize that I was going to strike out ninety or a hundred times a year and not let it bother my next at bat."

I said, "When I was a kid, we were always comparing Duke Snider, Mickey Mantle, and Willie Mays. How did you compare yourself to the other two guys?"

"I didn't," Duke said dryly. "Newspaper writers did."

"Did you ever discuss it?"

"No."

"Did you ever think about it?"

"Not really. My numbers at that particular time were just as good as theirs.

That was the media. And it didn't bother any of us. We'd see each other, and we'd kid about it, but that never bothered me one bit. All I cared about was winning."

"So when you played the Yankees in the World Series, you didn't have a personal rivalry with Mickey Mantle?"

"No. See, the thing you're overlooking here is that we were a team, and when you're a team, our train of thought was that if the team won, practically everybody would have a good year, and that's the way we looked at things. Sure you knew that you had thirty-five home runs or that you had so many rbis or stolen bases, you knew that because it was in the paper every day. But that didn't mean anything. The first thing we looked at when we picked up the paper was how many games we were ahead or how many games we were behind. And this is what a lot of people are overlooking when they talk about our team. And it was a team. We had guys on the team who didn't pal around together, but when we were out on that ballfield, Carl Furillo and I were just like this." Duke crossed his pointer and index fingers. "When a pitcher was taken out, Carl and I would stand together, talking about the game or something. On the bench he'd hit a home run, and I might be the first one to come up to him and shake his hand. Off the field we didn't hang around together. But yet we were very close. We knew each other very well. We never collided together in the outfield, never had a fly ball drop in between us because of indecision. We were very professional, and I think this is what is being overlooked as far as our team was concerned.

"The satisfaction we had came from winning. In the 1952 World Series, I hit four home runs, individually a very good Series for me. But it didn't mean a thing because in the seventh game I popped up in the seventh inning against Bob Kuzava with the bases loaded and one out, and Jackie popped out to end the inning, and we lost 4 to 2. That is what I remember about the '52 Series. That I didn't come through when they really needed me. If I had hit a double, three runs score, and we're ahead 5 to 4. That's the way I looked at it."

"In the '55 Series, you hit four home runs *and* the Dodgers won. That must have been satisfying?"

"The satisfaction was there," Snider said, "but still, it was because we won. Winning, you see, that was the only thing that mattered."

Skoonj

All the fans knew about Carl Furillo was that he was Italian (he was called Skoonj, short for scungilli) and that all season long he would play good, consistent ball, and then in August, when everyone else would begin to slump in the heat, he would build his batting average by twenty points. For some, Furillo was the glue to the team, the guy who did his best as the others began to tire.

In 1952 Furillo was having trouble with his eyes. He went to the hospital, and doctors discovered a cataract in one eye. Over the winter he was operated on, and in 1953, as he put it, he saw the ball so clearly, the ball looked like a balloon. All year he led the league in batting. Plus the fact that no one in baseball could play the right-field wall at Ebbets Field like Furillo, and no one else had Furillo's arm.

BILL REDDY: "Carl Furillo was the best at playing Ebbets Field's right-field wall, which was the craziest wall in baseball. The right-field wall was thirty feet high, with a twenty-eight-foot screen on top of it. The scoreboard was in the middle of the wall, between center and right, and on top of the scoreboard was the Bulova clock—they made a big thing about 'Baseball time is Bulova time.' There was a Schaefer beer sign, and the 'h' in Schaefer lit up for a hit, and the 'e' lit up for an error. The scoreboard took up a good portion of the wall.

"Now a ball hitting the scoreboard or the screen fell back into the field and was in play. The wall sloped at an angle starting halfway up, and then it went up straight the rest of the way. A fly ball or a ball bouncing once or twice before it hit the wall would ricochet off that wall in the weirdest directions you ever saw. It never seemed to go the same way twice, and it used to give enemy outfielders fits as Dodger runners would be flying around the bases. Furillo, though, knew the wall like the back of his hand. He was always in the right place to pick that ball up. So he nailed more runners going into second and third base, because he had a terrific arm."

CARL FURILLO: "I worked at it. I'd be out early and study it. Players would go out there and hit fungoes with me. When the ball came out, you had to imagine where it was going. Will it hit above the cement and hit the screen? Then you run like hell toward the wall, because it's gonna drop dead. Will it hit the cement? Then you gotta run like hell to the infield because it's gonna come shooting out. I can't even tell you if it's gonna hit the scoreboard. The angles were crazy. I had to work. I studied every angle of that fucking wall. I'd take that sight line and know just where it would go. I worked, that's how I learned it."

Carl Furillo was a professional in the literal sense. Duke Snider may have said he was playing for the money, but it was Furillo who *really* was. Money was what impressed Furillo more than anything else. His one worry was, "How much money do we get at the end of the year?" He shunned camaraderie. He had only an eighth-grade education, and he felt isolated. He was a loner on a gregarious team.

CARL ERSKINE: "I've written to Carl a few times, and he knows that I care about him and always did. Carl somehow excluded himself. It's a two-way street there, and Carl somehow got the feeling he was left out, and then he perpetuated it by saying, 'That's the way it is, so that's the way I'm going to make it.' And I know most of us, the guys who counted on that team, respected Carl very much. He was one of the most consistent players we had. He gave nobody a problem. Furillo played it straight, and we had a lot of respect for him."

Some players are glamorous, controversial, what writers call "good copy." Furillo was not good copy. He was reserved, serious, sometimes menacing. He was there to do a job, and he did it very, very efficiently. Coldly efficient. He was the type of guy who didn't talk much about fighting, but if somebody knocked him down, he'd come out to the mound and get him. Coldly efficient, he just went out there and did a superior job in the field and at bat, and he did it day after day.

CLEM LABINE: "Carl was a hardworking man, like an iron-hat type worker, and he may have felt some of the other players were aloof because they had a better education. He didn't think he fit in. And he wouldn't socialize. Very, very seldom did he socialize with the Sniders, the Erskines. He just wouldn't do it.

"Put that together with the fact that at the end of his career he thought he got a raw deal from Bavasi. This shows you his personality. Raw deals come a dime a dozen, and maybe he was right, but they are all things that you take with a grain of salt. You can either go out graciously or you can go out vindictively, and I would personally take the gracious way out than the vindictive way out. But that wasn't Carl's way. Carl could be stubborn about things. Carl's mood could turn dark."

HAROLD ROSENTHAL: "We were in Atlanta during spring training, and the traveling secretary, Harold Parrott, called the reporters together and said, 'Lookit, fellows, you may have noticed that one of our guys isn't with us any more. Well, we had to send him home.' I asked Parrott, 'Who's that?' Parrott said it was Tommy Brown. Naturally, I asked him what happened.

"He said, 'He got into a little scrape. He was fooling around with some dame, and they had her car, and they were parked in an alley, and when they went to leave, they found that the dame's boy friend had blocked the alley and had a couple of guys with him with bats and pipes, and they beat him up so badly we had to take him to the hospital, and then we sent him home. His eyes are shut, and you know . . .' and he asked us not to use the story. Brown wasn't a star, he was just a utility player, so the reporters didn't run the story.

"I found out about two years later that Tommy had been beaten up, all right, but it wasn't by hoods. It was by Carl Furillo. They were rooming together, and Furillo barked at Brown to turn the lights off, only to be told by Brown to 'wait till I get through with what I'm reading.' Furillo again ordered him to turn out the lights. Brown got mad and swore at Furillo, and the next thing you know, Furillo was on him like a gorilla, and he beat him up so badly he had to be taken to the hospital. And they had been friends."

In September of 1953 the Giants finally enraged Carl Furillo to the point where he was ready to do to Durocher what he had done to Brown. Ever since he had played in Brooklyn for Durocher, Furillo had disliked him, and when Leo went over to the Giants, Furillo's head became a favorite target of the Giant pitchers. In 1949 Sheldon Jones hit the side of Carl Furillo's head, sending Furillo to the hospital with a concussion. Afterward Jones apologized saying, "I just did what Durocher told me to do."

The next year Sal Maglie threw a pitch close to Furillo. Furillo yelled something out to Maglie. Maglie threw the next one even closer. Furillo took his bat and hurled it toward the mound and made Maglie skip rope.

On September 6, during the 1953 season, as Furillo went up to bat against Giant pitcher Ruben Gomez in the Polo Grounds, Durocher began cursing him. Furillo returned the curses. Even though there were 50,000 fans in the seats, Furillo could hear Leo's sweet voice yelling, 'Stick it in his ear.' Gomez let fire and hit Furillo in the side. Furillo, ignoring Gomez, turned toward the Giant dugout.

DON HONIG: "I was watching the game on TV, and they kept the camera on Furillo because he was gesturing into the dugout to Durocher. They put the camera on Leo, and Leo is signaling to Furillo to come on, and the next thing you know Furillo takes off like a shot for the Giant dugout.

"Now a lot of people will tell you that Leo was a tough guy, that he knew how to throw a punch, and he came out, and they tangled, and bingo, there were fifty guys out there, and forty-eight were peacemakers. The only fighters were the two guys at the bottom."

HAROLD ROSENTHAL: "Furillo raced into the dugout, and before anyone could get in his way, he got Durocher in a headlock. Leo's hat fell off, and you could see Durocher's bald head start to turn purple from the pressure. And Carl would have probably choked Leo to death if they hadn't fallen to the floor of the dugout as they were struggling. Monte Irvin came over to break it up, and he stepped on the back of Carl's little finger and broke it. Furillo was leading the league in hitting at the time, and he didn't hit again that year until the World Series. He won the batting title at .344."

DON HONIG: "Carl was out for the rest of the season. This was September, and that was how he won the batting crown. Carl's average was frozen at .344, and Red Schoendienst of the Cardinals was like a predator coming on. He had a carcass, and he was going after it, and every day he was 2 for 4, 1 for 3, but on the final day he just missed by two points. In 1953 Carl Furillo was the batting champion of the National League."

The Best Team Loses—Again

CARL ERSKINE: "The '53 Brooklyn team, on paper, man for man, was the greatest Dodger team I played on. We won 105 games, the most of any Dodger team, and I always had a deep sense of appreciation that somehow the skinny kid from Anderson, Indiana, had found his way onto the mound and was surrounded—and I still get chills up my back when I think of looking around me at that infield and outfield—by Campy, Gil, Gilliam, Reese, Robinson, and Snider, Furillo, Pafko. I could not in my wildest dreams have ever placed myself on a team that gave any greater advantage to a pitcher.

"Ebbets Field was a difficult park to pitch in, and I'm sure any pitcher who pitched there had earned run average problems that he might not have had in another park, but the offsetting benefit to be pitching there on a regular basis was that we had a team that could take better advantage of Ebbets Field than anybody who came in.

"Also the record book will bear this out, the team's defense was perhaps not as strong as its offense, but we made only 118 errors, and the next best team had 129, and we ranked high in double plays, and we did things that didn't necessarily show up spectacularly in the numbers.

"If you're pitching, and your team makes three miscues, and I don't necessarily mean errors, but if you do things like fail to get the other end of the double, that doesn't show up anyplace in the stats. It's a fielder's choice if the guy is safe. If he scores, it's a run. If your team does three things like that in a nine-inning ballgame and allows the opposition to get one more time at bat, you've given them an extra inning to hit. And I'm telling you that our ballclub snuffed out a lot of those extra innings that other clubs used to give us. That's how we used to win. We'd get three miscues out of the other club, and we'd get to hit one more inning.

"And on that basis, I thank the good Lord then, and now, to have been a pitcher on that team. So I was privileged. Definitely privileged.

"We sensed that we had one of the outstanding teams. We would play our season with an expectation of winning. We just felt that we were going to win, no two ways about it. And we had that same healthy feeling going into the World Series, though when we were going to play the Yankees, we knew we weren't playing Pittsburgh. There was a healthy respect there that the Yankees were not going to be pushovers. We didn't ever go into those Series other than with good professional confidence that we were going to do it. We believed we would go and win it."

The Yankees had beaten the Dodgers in 1941, 1947, 1949, and in 1952. The fans were beginning to feel that their team was jinxed when it came to playing the Yankees.

JOE FLAHERTY: "Charley Wright was a Yankee fan living on Vanderbilt Street near Bill Reddy and myself. He lived in an old wooden house, a big frame affair that had maybe ten families living inside, and to the neighborhood it was known as the Grand Hotel. Charley loved to play dice baseball, a game in which you threw two die: if you threw a four, it was a walk, a nine was a triple, a ten a double, a twelve a home run, seven was a strikeout, and so forth.

"Charley was a Yankee fan, and what he liked to do while he was playing dice baseball was to take his lineup and find a baseball card for each player, and he'd line up his Yankees on the floor while he played. When the other team was up, he'd put his pitcher on the floor. The point of all this is that the whammy the Yankees had over the Dodgers extended to Charley's dice. If the Dodgers got a couple of runners on base, Charley would call time out, and he'd remove the Allie Reynolds card from the floor, and he'd replace it with Joe Page's, and inevitably 'Page' would get the side out.

"Charley played dice baseball in a regular league, kept statistics on the games, and every year for about five years the Yankees would run away from the league. Years later the guys who had played against Charley read Robert Coover's *The Universal Baseball Association of J. Henry Waugh,* but they never believed for a second that the author was Robert Coover. They all swore it was Charley Wright."

LARRY KING: "When we played the Yankees, it was us poor Dodger fans against the rich. To us the Yankees were considered suburban, even though they were in the Bronx. Yankee Stadium was in a nice neighborhood then. The Grand Concourse Hotel was a palace.

"The Yankees and Yankee fans were different from us. You would never wear blue jeans to a Yankee game. And the Yankee fans didn't scream. They clapped, like at the opera. We used to kid Herbie Cohen. We'd say to him, 'Yankee fans are boring.' I never felt that the Yankees were part of New York City. The Yankees were corporations who bought tickets and sent people out to see the games. There was always a feeling: 'If you puh-leeze, this is the Yankees.' As if to say, 'We slide, but we don't get our uniforms dirty.' And you knew the Yankees weren't going to have a black ballplayer unless it was a white black. And you knew they weren't going to lose."

The Series opened with two games in Yankee Stadium, and the Yankees won them both as Billy Martin continued his clutch hitting. In the first game, Gilliam, Hodges, and Shuba each hit home runs, but with the bases loaded, Martin hit a ball off Erskine into the left-center-field alley for a triple, and then a Joe Collins home run put the Yankees ahead to win 9 to 5. In the second game Martin hit a home run against Preacher Roe, but Roe managed to keep the Dodgers even until the eighth when Mickey Mantle hit a two-run home run to win 4–2.

When the series moved back to Ebbets Field, Dressen started Carl Erskine in Game Three with only two days' rest.

CARL ERSKINE: "Personally, going into that Series, I had just come off my best year [20–6], my best second half ever, and Dressen talked to me and said, 'You're going to be my man. You're gonna open in the stadium, and you'll start three times if we need it.' By this time my confidence was at a peak. I finished the season with twenty wins, and I could have had two more wins real easy, but Dressen wouldn't let me pitch long enough. I had great command of myself and my pitches, and my arm wasn't giving me any trouble. I had already participated in a couple of World Series, had pitched one complete game in extra innings the year before at the stadium, and it wasn't like I was pitching for the first time.

"So I opened the Series at the stadium, had a bad first inning. I warmed up good, felt good, but starting out the first inning is always a little difficult; I don't care how many years you pitch, that opening inning of a ballgame is a new day. I was a little wild, got a couple men on, a run in, and Martin hit a ball to left center that was in between, so that was a disappointing start. Pitched one inning. Boy, that was a blow, to have taken the club the whole second half, to have been in command in every game I pitched. And I did not get the loss that day. We tied the score, and Clem lost it.

"Dressen came to me after that ballgame, and he said, 'I know something about you. You've come back with short rest in spite of the fact you've had arm trouble. Sometimes you've come back with short rest and been good. Could you pitch with two days' rest? I want to bring you back in the third game.' And I was dee-lighted. You don't often get that second shot that quick. And probably never before or since have I had as much determination as I had that day, and I told Duke and Campy, 'I may not last more than one inning today, but I'm going to go down swinging. I'm going to pitch every inning like it's my last, and these guys are not going to jump on me early.'

"And I did pitch to each hitter like it was no tomorrow. I struck McDougald out to start off the ballgame. I did not have a count of the strikeouts. The Yankees only hit one ball decent off of me, and that was Woodling's liner to center. It could well have been a shutout ballgame, but it was not. There were three or four infield hits, and the Yankees put one run together to tie us, 1–1, in the third inning, and then we scored again, and they scratched around and got another run, and so here we are tied 2–2 going into the eighth, bottom of the eighth, and Raschi, tough as always, hung a slider or curveball to Roy, and Roy hit it into the seats in left field, and that gave us a one-run lead.

"Going out in the ninth, I remember exactly who I faced and what happened, because I had faced Don Bollweg in the Texas League. He had belonged to the Cardinals, and he was the first batter, and I struck him out on all fastballs, and I did not know that tied a record, though the crowd was really frenzied by this time. That was the thirteenth strikeout, tied for the most ever in the World Series game. And up comes John Mize, who was one of the most respected hitters in baseball. John Mize had a unique quality of being a power hitter and having a very good concept of the strike zone. He swung at very few bad pitches.

"And I was not thinking about strikeouts. I was thinking about giving him my best shot. He took two well-placed curveballs on the outside part of the plate and low, overhand curves, and then I almost made a mistake. I wanted to get a fastball up and in on him, and I got it up, but I got it up over the plate, and he had a rip, really had a cut, but he fouled it back, 'cause I had good stuff that day. I could see John's expression of 'That was it, darn it.' Then we came right back with another overhand curve, probably the worst swing I ever saw Mize have at a ball, and then the crowd erupted, and I will tell you for the first time—and I didn't know why because I didn't know about the record—but I turned and faced center field to gain my composure because I had a sensation about that strikeout that moved me emotionally.

I had to collect myself. And then I turned back to face Irv Noren, who I had played with in the Texas League. He had been a property of the Dodgers. I knew he was a good hitter. I walked him on four straight pitches. And gee, that was because I had momentarily—the emotions just got to me a little bit. The crowd was so frenzied, and it was down to the last out. I had walked Noren and now had to face Joe Collins, who I had already struck out four times. And I knew that.

"I was talking to myself. I'm saying, 'Oh, man, I have seen this happen so many times that a guy is a goat or looks so bad, to come up in the crucial spot and be the hero.' And in Ebbets Field, you're looking at 296 feet down the right-field line, and we were only ahead 3 to 2, and there's a man on first. I'm saying, 'This guy is not going to hit one out on me.'

"What I didn't know, and what Joe Collins told me later: He said, 'You know, when I was on the bench, the guys kept telling me, "Joe, you want to be in the record book, you're going to get up there five times, and if you strike out again, you're going to go into the book. You're going to be struck out five times in one game in the World Series." ' They were giving him the needle because he already had four. So Joe said, 'When I went to the plate, the last thing in the world I was thinking about was hitting a home run. I was thinking about getting a piece of it some place.' It's so interesting, because there is a battle that goes on that nobody sees. There's a game that nobody sees, and when you pitch in a league where you face the same hitters year after year over a period of time, there becomes a second game which becomes more important than the physical game, and that is: You know the batter's strength, and he knows your stuff, now what are you going to do with that? You start using that psychologically, and that's really, other than just overpowering the guy—if you have that type of equipment, which most guys don't—you then are relying on your good stuff and the psychology of how you use it. You might even pitch a guy in his power sometimes, because it would virtually disarm him.

"Well, here we are. Joe knows I'm going to throw him my overhand curveball. He knows that. Because that's what I've been striking him out with. So he's guarding the plate like he has a flyswatter. So I get two strikes on him, and waste a pitch and throw him a real good overhand curve, which he barely, barely topped back to me for the last out.

"The relief came in Joe not taking good cuts, because my fear was that after all this hard work the whole game, it boiled down to one guy who can win it on one swing.

"And when he swung at the last pitch, and nubbed it back to me, and I threw to first, that was a sweet out."

Dressen started Billy Loes in Game Four, and the Dodgers tied the Series as Duke Snider drove in four runs with two doubles and a home run. For Game Five Casey Stengel decided to go with a free-spirited race car fanatic by the name of Jim McDonald. Dressen had to choose between the veteran Russ Meyer, and twenty-year-old left-hander Johnny Podres. The Yankees had excellent left-handed power. In addition to Mantle, who was a switch-hitter, the Yankees boasted Joe Collins, Yogi Berra, Gene Woodling, Johnny Mize, and Irv Noren hitting from the left side. Dressen decided that Podres would be the best choice to blunt the Yankee power.

RUSS MEYER: "There was one word Charley really loved, and that was 'I.' Make that two words. 'I' and 'me.' You ask whether Charley knew anything about pitching. In 1953 I went 15 and 5, and I beat the Braves five or six times—I was either 5–0 or 6–0 against them—and they were the ballclub we had to beat for the pennant. But we get to the World Series, and I'm not good enough to start for him. To this day I'll never understand that. I mean, you trade for a guy, and I start for him all year, and I win fifteen ballgames for the guy, and I can't start in the Series because he's a great believer in percentages. The Yankees had a lot of left-handed power, so he didn't start me.

"Pitching coach Teddy Lyons told me I was going to start the second game. So, hey, I came to the ballpark. I'm hyped up. I'm gonna pitch. I walk into the clubhouse, and I find out I'm not pitching, and shit, hey, it just . . . what are you gonna say? Sure you can get mad, but you don't do that in the World Series. You don't think about yourself when you're trying to win the World Series. And the thing was, Dressen would never come to you himself. He always had someone do it for him. His coach, Billy Herman, Bubble Eyes we called him. Bubble Eyes was his messenger boy. Hatchet man. That's really what he was. So Billy told Teddy, and Teddy told me, and he said, 'But you're going to be the long guy in the bullpen.' I said, 'Great. Swell.' So I went down to the bullpen. Dressen started Johnny Podres, and that was his first World Series, and shit, Johnny was just a baby. Hey, he was a helluva pitcher, but Johnny loaded the bases in the second inning, so Dressen brought me in. I was throwing real good.

"When I got to the mound, the bases were loaded, two men were out, and Mickey Mantle was the batter. Dressen said to me, 'Make him hit your curveball.' Erskine had struck Mantle out several times on overhand curves the day before. I said, 'Charley, I got a real good fastball, and my screwball's going good.' He said, 'I want you to make him hit your curve.' Hey, okay, and the first one I threw, I hung the sonofabitch, and he hit the shit out of it, bingo, a grand slammer. The next time up I struck him out on three straight fastballs. He took the last one. And the next time up I threw him a fastball he took for a strike, threw him a ball inside, and then struck him out on two screwballs. I never threw him another fucking curve."

Down in games three to two, the Dodgers were back at Yankee Stadium, and for Game Six Dressen came back with Erskine, against the Yankees' Whitey Ford.

CARL ERSKINE: "There wasn't anything awesome about Whitey. I remember Whitey as a young pitcher, learning to throw the curve.

"I went out, and I pitched okay, but Dressen took me out in the fourth with the score 3–0, and we were losing 3–1 in the top of the ninth, when, with a runner on first, Carl Furillo hit the ball to right field to tie the score. He hadn't played any in the end of the season, and he hit that wrong field home run. And in the bottom of the ninth, with Clem Labine in, Woodling got to second, and then Martin hit a chopper up the middle to beat us.

"See, somehow in sports, life, somehow when you get momentum, it seems you can't turn the dumb stuff around. The Yankees appeared, and I'm not saying we were snakebit, but whenever there was a fluke break, bounce, loop, anything, the darn thing always seemed to go their way in these close Series.

"Everything was tough, tough, tough, and let me tell you, even that third game that I was fortunate enough to win 3–2. That thing was by a thread that we won that, and we were already down two games. That's just the way it was with the Yankees. Those suckers were tough. I don't say they were lucky, either. It seemed that they got the breaks, but I would say in '53, that ground ball had eyes that beat us, just was another one. Now they hit a few good ones in between, I don't mean all their hits were lucky. But that was the frustration of playing those guys. Darn it, I don't know if psychologically there was a difference, or whether the Yankee tradition played a part, I don't know what it was, but there was a fine line there somehow that in five World Series against them, we only managed to win one. In '49 they wiped us out, and I think we were awestruck in that one, but in the others, we certainly brought everything we had to bring, and it certainly was toe to toe with the Yankees, but it was a frustration to go with our great team and not win.

"And with all the great hitters, to have a guy like Martin beat you! I tell you, Martin and Kuzava. Those are the two guys I think of when I think about the Yankees. How can those two guys beat us? You'd expect Mantle or Raschi and Reynolds, and it's not sour grapes, I don't mean it that way, I just mean the fortunes of sports are unusual. It's the old story. If we played them ten times, who knows? They had a great team, and they were on a roll at that time with Casey Stengel. They had a combination, and Martin fit in that team like he was designed for it. And Berra's unique personality fit in. The pitching staff dominated that team. Berra called the game, but listen, they told him what they were throwing. Berra just put the signs down. But Yogi fit in a slot there, and Martin was a brat, and he fit. Here's Mantle, and the whole lineup was a classic lineup, and Martin fit it. To Stengel's credit, he liked Martin. He liked him, and Martin fit."

Roy Campanella: "In 1953 Martin beat us again. He was a little choke hitter, and it was just that the balls were falling in. You can't do much about that. If you get Mantle and Berra out, and Martin comes up and hits a little bloop that beats you, that's tough. And that's what happened."

Clem Labine: "All I remember was that I made a really good sinker pitch to Martin, but he was having a good Series, and he hit it right up the middle. In fact every hit off me was a ground ball. Not one ball was a fly ball. Ground balls you have no jurisdiction over. If it's in a hole, it's in a hole, and you're dead.

"I always felt that our team was certainly as good as the Yankee teams we played, and I don't care if it was Mickey Mantle who was on the other side or anyone else. Yogi Berra, well, that was a different hitting animal. He hit differently than anyone else I've ever seen. But as far as the two teams were concerned, we were equal. Just the outcome was unbalanced."

ROGER KAHN: "In the clubhouse after the game, Labine had removed his baseball cap and was slumped on the locker stool, his head between his arms. His chest was moving oddly, and when I came closer, I saw he was sobbing. And Clem was a man who was so proud of his poise. Duke Snider caught my eye. 'I still say we're the better team,' he said.

" 'I know,' I said. 'That's the hell of it. That's the rottenest thing in this life, isn't it? The best team doesn't always win.' "

BILL REDDY: "Having to go out and listen to these Yankee fans jeer at you and laugh at you and rub it in, that was the thing that killed you. There were more damn fistfights. I tell you, when the frustration got to be too much, you had to strike out at something. Even me. Normally I'm a peace-loving guy, but I can remember I was in the Parkside Tavern one night, and I whapped a guy in the head.

"A group of us were talking, and he was a friend of somebody, and he started in about the Yankees, 'You Goddamn Dodgers. You lay down like dogs.' That was as far as he got. I popped him in the mouth, and, of course, everybody jumped in and held on. I went home. I figured it was no good, a married man getting mixed up in something like this. But you had to strike out at something because it was too much. The frustration was overwhelming. It gave you a feeling that God and everybody was against you. What the hell. What could you do? Wait for the next year? But next year never seemed to come."

Where's The Heart?

At the end of the 1953 season, Walter O'Malley allowed two of his employees to depart. Forever after the Dodgers would seem much less colorful and exciting.

Red Barber quit as Dodger announcer. And it didn't have to happen except for O'Malley's crassness. In 1952 Red had broadcast the World Series on TV, and they had paid him $200 a game. Gillette hadn't told the announcers what they were making until after the Series was over. Nothing was negotiated. When it was over, they just sent the check. Gillette's thinking was that the announcers would be glad to do the Series just to get the exposure. "Peanuts," Barber called the money. He then decided that he would not do the 1953 Series unless he negotiated his fee in advance of the telecast. In '53 Gillette told Barber that under no circumstances would they negotiate, telling him to take the token payment or leave it. So Barber left it.

After Barber made his decision not to work the Series cheap, as a courtesy he called O'Malley, who easily could have backed him in his fight with Gillette.

But O'Malley, who never forgave Barber for remaining friends with Branch Rickey, said tersely, "That's your problem." Barber hung up. A few days later his regular season contract expired, and when Red Barber switched to the Yankees, it became O'Malley's problem.

Sentiment meant nothing. Business was everything. By then O'Malley knew he had Vin Scully in the wings, and Scully was making $18,000 and Barber $60,000. O'Malley was fond of expounding: "It's like marbles in a pipe. You push the cheaper marble in one end, and the expensive marble falls out the other end, and that's how you make money." Vin became the new Voice of the Dodgers, and thirty years later he's still around.

The second star O'Malley allowed to depart was Charley Dressen. In three years Dressen had brought the Dodgers to a playoff in '51 and then won two straight National League pennants. Dressen thought he deserved a better contract, a contract that gave him more protection than the single-year contracts he had signed in the past.

During the 1953 season, the *Sporting News* had printed a cartoon of Dressen, Leo Durocher, Charlie Grimm, and Eddie Stanky sitting around a table playing poker. The cartoon showed the Cardinals giving Stanky a three-year contract, the Braves giving Grimm a three-year contract, the Giants giving Durocher a two-year contract, and Dressen receiving a question mark. The artist was suggesting that Dressen would do better than any of the other three. The artist, though, didn't know Walter O'Malley.

Dressen wanted security. Only Casey Stengel had been more successful. Dressen wanted three years. O'Malley told Dressen it was against his policy. Dressen refused to budge. He couldn't believe that O'Malley would allow him to go. But O'Malley did.

Dressen had been successful. He had brought controversy, humor, and excitement, and he increased attendance, but O'Malley didn't care.

The owner had resented Dressen's manner, his personal publicity, and the fact that Dressen's wife, Ruth, had written a letter demanding a three-year contract. O'Malley became angry.

CARL ERSKINE: "Again, Charley was his own worst enemy, with an absolute blind passion to be as good or better than Durocher. Durocher had gotten a two-year contract after '53, and Dressen went to the ownership and wanted at least a two-year contract, which was unheard of in those days, and O'Malley, being a tough businessman himself, would not give in to Charley's requests, desires, or demands. They came to an impasse, and O'Malley must have said, 'As good as Charley is, I run this team, he doesn't, and we're going to get a new manager.' "

ROGER KAHN: "Dressen saw himself as a heroic leader who had managed the Dodgers to successive pennants. He did not see himself as the overbearing, semigrammatical encyclopedist whose indiscriminate chatter with the press, whose innate bluntness, and whose blossoming pride made him an irritant to his employers."

* * *

O'Malley told publicity director Frank Graham, Jr., to announce a "very important" press conference for eleven in the morning.

"Dressen signing?" Graham asked.

O'Malley grinned. "A switch," he half-whispered, wagging his forefinger.

One of the reporters had anticipated the story incorrectly. The headline shouted a $50,000-a-year salary. But when O'Malley began the press conference, to the reporter's chagrin, it was announced that Dressen was not returning to Brooklyn.

FRANK GRAHAM, JR.: "Both O'Malley and Dressen were present at the press conference to announce that Dressen would not return in 1954. The writers learned that Dressen's wife, Ruth, had conceived of the idea of writing a letter demanding a new contract covering three years at $50,000 a year.

" 'The Dodgers do not believe in long-term contracts,' O'Malley told the reporters. 'Dressen is free to sign a one-year contract to manage the Dodgers. In fact, I have one here in my desk drawer, and if Charley says the word now, I'll take it out and he can sign it and manage the Dodgers next year.'

"Dressen sat hunched in his chair, looking like a man whose bluff had been called and his fate decided, manfully sticking to his decision. None of the reporters challenged O'Malley as to whether there was really a contract in that drawer. The press conference closed with Dressen insisting that he had earned a three-year contract but that he would accept one for two years, and with O'Malley telling him 'the door is still open' to sign the one-year contract.

"Charley told a reporter, 'I won't second-guess Ruth now.'

"He left Montague Street believing that he had twenty-four hours of grace in which to mull over his decision. But O'Malley had already made up his mind to hire someone else. Dressen repeatedly called the Dodger office during the next couple of days, but his calls were never answered. Two weeks later, realizing he was out, he signed a three-year contract to manage Oakland in the Pacific Coast League.

"O'Malley told the press, 'I'm sure Mrs. Dressen will be very happy in Oakland.' "

12

Walt Alston

The O'Malleyfication of the Dodgers became complete when the new manager was named in the winter of 1953. As soon as it dawned on the New York reporters that O'Malley was merely jerking Charley Dressen around, that O'Malley had no intention of taking him back under any circumstances, the guessing game began as to who was going to replace the little bantam. Pee Wee Reese was mentioned frequently, though the Dodgers never seriously considered him. Buzzy Bavasi had called him into his office and said to him, "You're not interested in the job, are you?" so that even if Pee Wee had wanted it, he was savvy enough to know the answer Bavasi was eliciting. O'Malley hadn't wanted a playing manager, and Reese was still the best shortstop in the National League, and there was no way O'Malley was going to let him retire just to become manager.

Among the prominent names mentioned in the papers as candidates were Frankie Frisch, Rogers Hornsby, Joe DiMaggio, Tommy Henrich, and even Leo Durocher. Near the bottom of the list, buried with names such as Lefty O'Doul and Bill Terry, was that of a virtual unknown, "Wally" Alston, the manager of the Dodgers' farm team in Montreal.

FRANK GRAHAM, JR: "What must have been one of baseball's best-kept secrets was Bavasi's selection of Alston. The two men had been together for a long time, as business manager and manager of Nashua and Montreal. Buzzy, supported by Fresco Thompson and other officials in the minor-league organization, convinced O'Malley that Alston could manage in Brooklyn."

In late November, six weeks after Dressen was axed, the Dodgers called a press conference. When Alston was introduced, most of the writers looked around in disbelief. Who was this guy? Why did O'Malley pick a guy with no experience to manage the National League champions? But these men did not understand the Dodger concept of organization. The notion of the company man had not yet been branded into the soul of America, though it would be shortly.

There are usually two reasons why an organization will hire an employee. The first is that he can do the job. Assuming many people can do the job, the search committee then looks for the next-most-important attribute: Will the man follow orders and take whatever guff we dump on him? Not all men will. Unless such individualists are exceptionally talented, like Leo Durocher or Billy Martin, they will be bypassed. Walt Alston believed in the O'Malley organization first, everything else second. And like every loyal employee, Alston put up with whatever Bavasi and O'Malley threw at him. Every single year—long after he had established himself—he had to keep signing one-year contracts. It was said that he would show his loyalty by signing a blank contract in the fall and then wait until spring training to meet with Bavasi to discover how much money they were paying him. And always there were the rumors. Rarely did a season begin without word from some "unnamed source" high in the Dodger organization whispering that if Alston doesn't win the pennant this year he will be fired. His employers did little to make life any easier. They kept hiring assistants for him such as Leo Durocher and Charley Dressen, and each time, it was said that one or another of his assistants was going to replace him. As a reward for his unswerving loyalty, they seemed to relish letting Alston wonder each season whether he would get the ax or not. It made for a very subservient and pliable manager. Which, of course, was exactly what Walter O'Malley wanted.

At the end of Alston's first press conference, O'Malley gave reporters a significant clue as to why he had chosen Alston. Posing for pictures O'Malley stood over Alston, beaming and holding up the index finger of his right hand. With his one finger, O'Malley was telling everyone that Alston would do what O'Malley wanted him to do, that he would always get a one-year contract, and that never again would a manager grab the headlines from the owner. Never again would a manager dare challenge the authority of Walter O'Malley.

The irony is that, like Buzzy Bavasi and Fresco Thompson, Alston originally had been a protégé of O'Malley's nemesis, Branch Rickey. Alston had gone to Miami University in Oxford, Ohio. The day after he graduated in June 1933, Frank Rickey, Branch's brother, offered him a contract to play in the Cardinal farm system for $125 a month.

In his second year, playing for Huntington, West Virginia, Alston led the league in home runs, and at the end of the season the Cards brought him up. At the time Johnny Mize and Ripper Collins were the first basemen. It was 1936, the wild era of the Gas House Gang.

In the final game of the season, Mize got thrown out for arguing with the umpire, and because Collins had already been used, Alston got to play the last few innings. He got up once against Lon Warneke, hit a long foul ball, and then struck out. It was Alston's only at bat in the majors. You can find Walter Emmons (Smokey) Alston in the 1979 edition of the *Baseball Encyclopedia* on page 697 between Thomas Edison Alston, a Cardinal first baseman from the '50s, and Jesse Howard Altenburg, who played with the Pirates in 1916 and 1917. One game. One at bat. One strikeout. Every other digit is a zero.

By the end of the 1936 season, Rickey had decided Alston would never

George Brace Photo

WALTER ALSTON

make a major leaguer, and he was returned to the minors where he played for eight years.

When Alston returned home after the 1944 season with Rochester, he received a call from Rickey, who by now was with the Dodgers. Would Alston be interested in a job managing Trenton in the Dodger organization? Thirty years later Alston was still managing in the Dodger organization.

Alston was strong and silent, patient and tolerant, but with a powerful build that was intimidating. He was a Puritanical man who believed in fairness. When questioned, his answers were always straight. The word, wherever he went, was that you shouldn't mess with him. Alston was playing-manager at Trenton in '44 and '45, and then he took over the Nashua club in '46. Roy Campanella and Don Newcombe were on the team, and it was Alston who helped pave the road to success for his two Negro stars.

Alston went from Nashua to Montreal, where he replaced Clay Hopper. When Alston took over the Dodgers in 1954, seventeen of the Dodger players had once played under him. The first day Alston arrived for spring training, Roy Campanella went into his office and told him, "Skip, don't worry about anything, we'll make it."

The others weren't so sure. Some grumbled about his rules outside the ballpark. Dressen had let the players alone, treated them like adult men, didn't impose curfews, didn't interfere with their private lives. Alston was not a drinker, didn't carouse, and he liked his ballplayers to be where they were supposed to be after hours—asleep. But the players could live with the inconvenience. Rather, it was a question of know-how. Alston was a minor league manager. He had spent exactly one day in the majors. Could he manage in the big leagues as well as Dressen, who some believed to be the smartest manager in baseball. Could he gain their respect?

CHARLEY EINSTEIN: "Alston was taking over a pennant winner. He was taking over Dressen's team. Opening day of spring training, Snider is at bat in the cage. Alston's standing there, and he says to Duke 'Do you always hold your back leg that way.' Duke turns around and says, 'I hit forty-two home runs in the big leagues last year. Where did you make your mistakes?' "

It was an untenable situation for a rookie manager. The Dodgers started poorly in '54, and never seemed to pull together. The players had difficulty getting used to Alston, and he spent the year getting to know them and the National League. He was not confident in himself, and the players realized he was depending heavily on his coaches, Billy Herman and Jake Pitler. Alston was not earning respect. All these stars, and he had to learn to handle them.

The one he had the most trouble with was Jackie Robinson. Robinson had loved Charley Dressen. Every day Charley Dressen would tell Robinson what a wonderful player he was, how much he appreciated him, how special he was, and Robinson thrived on Dressen's kind words. Alston, on the other hand, saw Robinson as a threat to his authority. In '54 the two men silently fought for control of the Dodgers. Robinson bitched that Alston lost his cool under pressure, and he would rail at what he saw as "bonehead judgments" during games. Some of the others grumbled about Alston, but Robinson, whose emotions were always close to the surface, let Alston know that he didn't think much of him as a manager.

Carl Furillo: "The only time there was real friction with Robinson was when Alston came with us as manager. Jackie resented it that he took Dressen's place, and Alston resented us because we were making the money, and we didn't need a manager. We may have needed a man to take out a pitcher or put a pitcher in or make out a lineup, but we didn't need a manager. Hell, we were always on our own. 'Cause he never, never hit and ran. We were slugging away.

"I remember more than once, Pee Wee, Jackie, Gil, and all of them were talking about Alston, and the boys were really down on him, and Pee Wee made a remark, 'If he keeps fooling around like this, I'll take his damn job.' I wish Pee Wee would have. 'Cause Alston was not a manager. I got along good with him—don't get me wrong—but he was not a manager."

Toward the end of the 1954 season, the tension between Robinson and Alston grew. Robinson didn't like O'Malley, and he didn't like O'Malley's choice for manager. It was Alston's feeling that Robinson, now thirty-five, should be a utility player, and it didn't help Robinson's disposition any when Alston began playing Don Hoak at third base. Robinson also didn't like the fact that Alston rarely argued with umpires. Robinson loved umpire baiting, loved the wordplay and the flow of adrenaline it brought. Toward the end of the year Duke Snider hit a ball into the left-field seats that bounced back onto the field. It should have been a home run. Umpire Bill Stewart called it a double.

Robinson, furious, sprinted out of the dugout and ran to protest. He was figuring that other teammates would join him, but no one moved. And manager Alston, coaching at third, just stood there, watching, with his hands on his hips.

Robinson felt humiliated. Later, in the dugout, someone said to him, "You should have heard what Walt was saying when you were out arguing on the field." Robinson replied, "If that guy hadn't stood standing out there at third base like a wooden Indian, this club might go somewhere." By the end of the 1954 season Robinson had had it with O'Malley and Alston both, and he was ready to leave baseball.

Roger Kahn: "Until Alston it was Robinson and Reese, and the manager would never challenge either of them. Alston was twenty years of bad managing.

"Witness what happened in '54. They had a real good team, and they weren't even close in '54. They never got going. Alston was managing with seventeen men as if he were still in the minor leagues. I would say to Robinson, 'Well, why don't you tell him what's bothering you?' And Jack would say, 'I can't.' He said, 'Aren't there guys at the paper you can't talk to when something's bothering you?' I'd say, 'Yeah, I guess so.' He said, 'Well, I cannot sit and tell Alston what is bothering me about the way he's managing the club. I can't do it. I just can't.' "

After the 1954 season, during which the Dodgers finished five games behind Leo Durocher's Giants, reporters were asking serious questions about Alston's capabilities, and there were rumors, as there would be for all twenty-three years of Alston's tenure, that the Dodgers would be looking for a new manager.

Before he retired Alston won seven pennants and four World Series and in 1983 was voted into the Hall of Fame. There is a theory in baseball that the best manager is the one who makes the fewest mistakes and affects his personnel the least adversely. In other words most managers screw things up by frustrating, confusing, infuriating, misusing, or destroying the egos of their players. After his first couple of years with the Dodgers, Walter Alston never did. Once he learned his personnel, he merely wrote the proper names into the proper slots, and he left his players alone. When he had the best players, he won. When he didn't, he lost. Alston won two pennants with Brooklyn and its first world championship, and after the Dodgers moved to the Coast, he finished first five times and second seven times, though by then, few in Brooklyn noticed.

CHARLEY EINSTEIN: "Alston did his managing in Los Angeles. Once they got to Chavez Ravine, he had a team that included one hard-throwing pitcher after another, some very fast men, very little power, and the worst lighting in baseball. And that was important, because the worse the lights were, the faster the pitchers looked to the batters. God knows how many games Alston's Dodgers won 1–0 with bad lighting. An official of the Cubs once said to me, "Every time we went in there, it was like playing in a cave.' Bad lighting. And how intentional that was, I don't know. But Alston knew it. He played night games with bad lights, and his team was perfect for those conditions. If he had to play a day game, he was in trouble. Like Willie Davis dropping three balls in the World Series.

"Alston was not an ingenious or inventive manager. You might say, 'Gee, the same infield played together for nine straight years—Garvey, Lopes, Russell, and Cey.' Why? Because Alston didn't take any chances, that's why. It was Alston's infield. You might say he was ingenious moving Garvey to first base. Here was a guy who couldn't throw. He put him where he would have to make the fewest throws. How inventive must you be?"

CARL FURILLO: "I'll never forget, this was after we moved to California, Dressen was a coach, along with Pee Wee and Joe Becker. Sandy Koufax was pitching, and he was wild. I don't know if you ever saw Sandy pitch, but when he was in Brooklyn, he didn't know where the plate was half the time. So anyhow, to make a long story short, I wasn't playing that night. I don't know if my leg was bothering me or what it was. I was sitting right where the water cooler was, and Alston was off to my right. And Sandy was starting to have a hard time out there, couldn't get the ball where he wanted it, right?

So I seen Alston call Dressen over, call Pee Wee over, call Mulleavy over. And Alston says, 'I think he might have had it. What do you guys think?' And they said, 'Yeah.' And he said, 'Well, just as long as you're agreeable, because most likely I'll be called on the carpet about it with Bavasi.' And from that day on, I said to myself, 'This guy is not a manager. This guy's afraid of his own shadow.' Later I had friction with him, and he didn't have the guts to talk to you right and back you up. He was afraid of his own job. Let's put it this way: He did a good job at keeping his job, because he was there for twenty years."

13

King Karl and Sandy Koufax

The previous season had been a disaster. After winning the pennant in '52 and '53, the Dodgers in '54 had blown the pennant to the Giants by five full games. At the beginning of the season, O'Malley had been so confident that he had rashly predicted another pennant. When the team only finished second, O'Malley was embarrassed and said so.

He considered replacing Alston but realized that the press would blast the management with even greater intensity if he did that, so Alston remained for another season despite his shortcomings. O'Malley also understood that it wasn't Alston's fault that Campanella had injured his hand, causing the all-star catcher to hit but .207, or that Don Newcombe, who had returned from the service, had only finished 9–8 or that Carl Erskine had won 18 but lost 15.

As for Alston's insistence that Don Hoak become the new Dodger third baseman, Alston's pet finished the year hitting .245 with seven home runs and twenty-six runs batted in, while the thirty-six-year-old Jackie Robinson made the new manager eat crow by hitting .311 with fifteen home runs and fifty-nine runs batted in.

There were other bright spots. Duke Snider established himself as one of the premier players in the league with a year of .341, with forty home runs, and 130 runs batted in, and Gil Hodges had perhaps his finest year, leading the league in most fielding categories and hitting .304, with forty-two home runs and 130 runs batted in. Carl Furillo hit .294, nineteen home runs, ninety-six runs batted in, and 36-year-old captain Pee Wee surprised everyone by hitting .309.

And there was one other ray of sunshine in '54—a twenty-three-year-old pitcher by the name of Karl Spooner. In the final week of '54, Spooner was brought up from the minors with a big reputation. In 749 innings of minor league pitching, he had struck out 844 batters. With the Dodger pennant lost in '54, Alston decided to give the youngster a taste of major league competition, and in late September in his first start, Spooner reminded old timers of Nap Rucker in his prime, as he pitched a 3–0 shutout against the Giants, striking out fifteen batters! Awed, Alston started him against the Pirates a few days later, and this time he won the game 1–0 and struck out twelve!

Two games, two shutouts, twenty-seven strikeouts! Dodger fans couldn't wait until '55. This kid couldn't miss. The question was, would he win twenty or twenty-five?

Clem Labine: "That man had a fastball that was unbelievable, not for sheer speed, but for how much the ball moved. He was one of the toughest left-handers that I've ever seen. I can remember Dusty Rhodes, who was having a tremendous season, saying to Leo, 'Give me a bat. I can hit this kid.' and he went out there and took three strikes, boom, boom, boom, never swung at one. He went back to the dugout and conceded, 'Yeah, he has good stuff.' "

Ed Roebuck: "He was very cocky. We used to call him, 'King Karl.' He thought he was the best pitcher ever to put on a uniform. And he proved his cockiness. He came out of Ft. Worth, where he was striking out fifteen, sixteen a game, and he went to the big leagues, and he was doing the same thing. What was remarkable about him was his deception. He was very long-armed, and the hitters would think they had him timed good, but they didn't."

Then, during spring training in 1955, there was an innocuous notice tacked up in the press room: "Karl Spooner has a kink in his left shoulder." It was no big deal, a minor problem. He was to be out only a few days for rest. But Karl Spooner never again could throw the way he had in those two games at the tail end of '54. Alston started him a few games in '55, and he relieved a little, but he had to get by with guile, not that overpowering fastball. He won 8 games and lost 6 in '55, and then he was gone. Over the course of Dodger history, there had been some great might-have-been players, such as Pete Reiser, who got hurt after a season and a half of Hall of Fame–caliber play; Jack Banta, who hurt his arm; and Rex Barney, who lost his control. But of the might-have-beens, none might have been greater than Karl Spooner.

Karl Spooner: "I remember when I first knew I had a good arm. I was just a young kid. We used to throw snowballs, and nobody could stand up to me in a snowball fight. I was ten or eleven, and one time I threw a snowball and hit one of my teachers square in the face, and I was really quite shaken up about that. I went right to her and apologized as best as I could, and for a while I stayed out of snowball fights.

"I grew up in Oriskany Falls. It's between Utica and Syracuse, a little, small town in New York State, pretty remote, only about ninety people. There was no newspaper in town, and by the time news got to us, it was usually a day or two old. I went to high school there, but I didn't start pitching until my senior year. Where they really saw me was American Legion for Clinton, New York. Our coach was Ken Patrick, who was a teacher at Hamilton College, which is in Clinton, he used to play for the House of David years back, and we were in a game that had gotten out of hand, and so he sent me behind the stands to warm up with one of the guys, who wasn't even wearing a catcher's glove. Anyway, I went into the ballgame and pitched extremely well from then on until the end of the game, and I hit a grand-

George Brace Photo

KARL SPOONER

slam home run, and I ended up winning the ballgame, and so for the rest of the summer, every Wednesday night and every Sunday afternoon, I was their pitcher. And I didn't lose many ballgames.

"A scout by the name of Greg Mulleavy used to sneak into the park and not tell anybody he was there. But it didn't take long to notice him, because the scouts stuck out like sore thumbs.

"He approached me in the summer of 1950, and he told me I had a chance to play professional ball, which was what was in my heart. That's all I wanted to do was play ball. I understand the Phillies were also interested in me, but they were too slow, and anyway, I don't think it would have made any difference. I signed with the Dodgers because they were my team. I always loved the Dodgers. I loved Preacher Roe.

"The Dodgers gave me a $500 bonus. I started in Hormel, New York, in the Pony League. I remember I had a lot of control trouble. Mostly I lost ballgames, and I met my lovely wife there. Ended up marrying her in 1954. During the middle of the season in '54, I was pitching for Ft. Worth, and I pulled a cartilage in my right knee, and I was on the disabled list for fifteen days. When I came back, they had a big brace on me, and I was all taped up, and I really couldn't take much of a windup, so I just sorta stepped and threw. And I lay a lot of my control from that. I ended up winning twenty-one ballgames during the regular season and three in the playoffs.

"We got into the playoffs and went all the way to the end, and the last night I pitched fifteen innings. I lost 2 to 1 when our right fielder tried to make a shoestring catch and couldn't come up with it. That was just before the Dodgers called me up. I probably could have been up earlier in the season, but Spencer Harris was general manager of Ft. Worth, and he had a lot of pull with O'Malley, and I was his only left-handed pitcher, plus their big winner, so I think Spencer Harris kinda squashed me going to the big leagues sooner.

"My manager, Al Vincent, told me I was going to the Dodgers. It was the fall of 1954, and the day I arrived Alston came to me and said, 'You're going to pitch tomorrow. Why don't you go over and sit next to Roe and go through the lineup with him.' That did my heart good, because Preacher was always one of my favorites, being left-handed and all. And when a hitter would come up, Preacher would say, 'This is the way the club pitches him, but this is the way I pitch him. And you, you just throw strikes.' And that was how it went through the whole lineup. 'Cause he knew I could throw hard and had good stuff, a curveball and a change, and he figured the best thing for me was to just throw the ball over the plate. And being a rookie and just being brought up, I think it really helped.

"I pitched against the Giants and I struck out fifteen. One of the things real weird that happened, the day before, Johnny Podres was pitching, and in the first inning he gave up a grand slam to Bobby Hofman, and we got beat. And the day I pitched, it was also the first inning, and I've got the bases loaded and two outs, and Bobby Hofman up in the identical situation, and I struck him out. And that was the closest they came to scoring that day. They got two hits. And the next time out, Pittsburgh, three hits. That was the last day of the season. I shut them out 1–0, struck out twelve, and Hodges hit a home run in the upper deck at Ebbets Field.

"And when I went home that winter, I was on Cloud Nine. All these people calling me, wanting me to go here, go there. I spent most of that winter doing banquets, some of it charity work, like the March of Dimes in Buffalo, and I talked to a couple of mental hospitals.

"I figured the next year I was going to set the world on fire.

"And I hurt my arm in spring training.

"The ballplayers had been grumbling about the long spring trainings, and so the Dodgers decided that no one would report until March 1 that year. And on March 9, after we had played a couple of exhibition games, I pitched. Podres was supposed to go the first three innings, and I was supposed to go the second three, but Podres got in trouble and only pitched two innings. I tried to warm up real fast. I don't think I was really good and loose, and I guess I just tried to throw too hard, too soon.

"I threw a real good curveball to Jim Rivera, struck him out, and I felt a kind of a pull in my shoulder, but it didn't hurt that much, and so I finished the inning and the next inning. After I took a shower and was dressing, jiminy crickets, it started hurting real bad, and I could hardly even put my damn shirt on. And that's when I told the trainer. He rubbed me down real good, put some diathermy on me. Of course back then they didn't know near what they know today about arms.

"And though I was on the team in '55, I really didn't start to throw real good until June. I had had a losing record until then, and I remember one day in New York, I was pitching against the Giants, and even though I wasn't throwing hard, I was still getting them out. Whitey Lockman hit a solo home run off me down the right-field line, it looked like a little ole pop fly, and I'll be damned if Alston didn't come and pull me out, said I wasn't throwing good. It didn't matter that I was getting them out. He didn't think I was throwing good. Hey, I was getting them out! And we were ahead in the ballgame. But what can you say?

"Then I won a few games in a row. Alston used to use me in relief every once in a while. When he needed a strikeout to get out of a troubled inning. He knew I could get a third strike by them a lot of times. And when we got to the World Series, I pitched relief in the second game, and I threw exceptionally good that day. In fact I think I struck out five in three innings.

"Then in the sixth game, I got in trouble. Moose Skowron hit a dying quail to right field for a home run. Just inside the foul pole. Two hundred and ten feet. Wasn't very far. On a waste pitch. He was fighting it away from his face, because it was high and tight. I was ahead of him, and he kind of tommyhawked it. Nine out of ten times, he'd never hit that pitch. And that was the last pitch I threw in the majors, though of course at the time I had no idea I'd never pitch again.

"Over the winter all the adhesions and everything I had from the tears just kind of drawed up and tightened. In '56 they sent me down to the minor leagues. I went to Macon, Georgia. I went to St. Paul. And you know the arm isn't the same. You know it. I just couldn't throw at all. I couldn't have busted your lip. And I was a young kid, and it kind of takes the wind out of your sails, that's what it does.

"And I was real concerned, but I was always optimistic that it wouldn't be permanent, until in '57 when I had the arm operated on. That's the point when I knew it was over. I went to Long Island College Hospital in Brooklyn, and before I went in, the doctor said the chances were less than fifty-fifty that I'd be able to pitch good again. He operated, and I didn't pitch again until 1958. Over the winter the Cardinals bought my contract off the Montreal roster, and they let me bring it along as I saw fit, real slow, which I did, and I was in real good physical shape. But any time I tried to extend myself, it just wasn't there. It was the same feeling I had before they operated. Tendonitis is what they called it. What this is, I don't know, even to this day. Even today, when I work, if I have to get into a certain position, I can feel it.

"Anyway '58 was my last year. They released me. I had no place to go, really. I had friends in Vero Beach, and so I came back here and went to work. I had no profession, no idea what I was going to do, and I didn't have no money put away, because even though I had a World Series check, you don't think of tomorrow when you're a twenty-three-year-old kid. If you want a new car, you go buy it. I didn't think it was going to be over with that quick. I thought I was set for life.

"The first thing I did was take a job refinishing floors. And for a while I tended bar, built roof trusses, then I went to work for the guy I'm working for right now. I'm a manager of a citrus-packing house.

"In two years I went from the Dodgers to floors, but I had and have a lovely wife, we had two girls and had another on the way, and you just make up your mind that you have to put food on the table, that's all.

"There was nothing for me in baseball. Minor league managers and scouts were a dime a dozen. I had thought about going to umpire school. I was talking to a guy who had a school in Daytona. He said I could be in the big leagues in four or five years. I said, 'What kind of pay can I get?' When he told me, I said, 'Hell, I can dig ditches and make more money than that.' I don't think I'd have made a good umpire anyway. I don't think I have the disposition for it.

"Regrets? I have to have regrets. To have something taken away from you that you really love, you have to miss it. And it was certainly something I loved."

There was another young left-handed pitcher on the Dodgers by the name of Sanford Koufax. Koufax, just twenty, had signed a $20,000 bonus out of the University of Cincinnati, and under a new rule passed by the major leagues, because of the large bonus, the Dodgers were forced to keep him on the team for two years. It was a stupid rule. The idea was to cut down on the number of bonus babies a team could sign. It was supposed to protect penurious team owners from big-spending owners. What would stop the rich Yankees, for instance, from signing dozens of bonus babies? Under the new rule, if a team signed six kids for big money and had to keep them all on the team, there wouldn't be enough roster spots for vets. The rule worked, all right. Clubs couldn't afford to place these green peas on their rosters. But for the one or two kids it did sign for big money, the rule was a disaster. For two years these kids languished on the major league benches. They weren't ready to play big-time ball. How could a manager put them in? They should have been in the low minors getting experience. That same year the Yankees signed Frank Leja and Tommy Carroll. Leja got up seven times in two seasons and made one hit. Carroll got up twenty-three times for the Yankees and made eight hits. During Koufax's first two years, he was 2 and 2 and then 2 and 4. The raw talent was there. In his second start, he pitched a two-hit shutout against the Reds, striking out fourteen. But he couldn't do it often enough. Unlike Spooner, who began with a bang and disappeared in a puff of smoke, Koufax began as the twenty-fifth player on the roster, a kid who would sit on the bench for days without getting into a game. As a Brooklyn Dodger, Sandy Koufax won exactly nine games.

Only after the team moved west did the young Brooklynite with the scatter arm become one of the best pitchers in the history of the game, a Hall of Famer against whom all future left-handers would be compared.

Few knew, however, how close Sandy Koufax came to quitting before he became good.

LARRY KING: "The only reason Sandy signed a baseball contract was that his stepfather needed the money. Sandy was always a much better basketball player. He was all-city at Lafayette, led Lafayette to the PSAL finals at Madison Square Garden, and broke the freshman scoring record at Cincinnati University. When he was a senior in high school, Lafayette scrimmaged the Knicks once, and Harry Gallatin came over and told Sandy, 'You're gonna be in the NBA.' He was 6 feet 2 inches, had a very good touch, and he had extraordinary spring. To this day Sandy will tell you he liked basketball better. In high school he was just a backup first baseman, and occasionally he'd pitch, but he had absolutely no control. They'd warm him up in the bullpen to scare the other team. He'd be warming up, and he'd throw it over the catcher's head or bounce it past him, and the ball would roll out onto the field, and the umpire would have to call time. We knew he had a lot of speed, he could throw the ball like a rocket, but he certainly was no star. The day Sandy signed with the Dodgers, he was pitching in the Bay Ridge–Prospect Park League, and he gave up two home runs. But Al Campanis liked his speed, and the Dodgers signed him anyway.

"In truth I do not think Sandy thought he was going to make it as a pro baseball player. When he signed, he told Campanis he had to have $20,000. He was always very smart, and he did this for two reasons. One, the money would go to his stepfather who needed it, and two, if he got over $18,000, they couldn't send him to the minor leagues. He had to be put on the Dodger twenty-five-man roster. Sandy had determined that he would never play in the minors, and he told himself, 'If I don't make it in baseball in two years, I'll continue to play basketball as much as I can, and my class will be graduating at Cincinnati, and I'll see if I can get into the NBA. The guy who got cut when Sandy signed was Tom Lasorda. If Sandy hadn't signed, Lasorda would have made the team."

ED ROEBUCK: "He was a bonus-designated player in that he couldn't be sent to the minors, and he just wasted away there. Only time he would pitch would be to mop up. Really a terrible thing to do to a kid. He never pitched in the minors, never got a chance to develop. I roomed with Sandy one year, and one day he told me he was thinking seriously of quitting. I said, 'Sandy, if you do, how about giving me your left arm?'

"He was really an intelligent person, he wanted to excel, but he couldn't. You can't just start in the majors. You have to start in the minors and work your way up to it, but he wasn't able to do that. And constant failure was getting to him. He said he was going to quit.

"I remember it was around 1961, we were at a place in Vero, and some of us were drinking beer at Lenny's, which is just beyond the batting cages. The game was over, and the group of us, Podres, Norm Sherry, Don Zimmer, myself, and Sandy, and we were talking baseball, and there with us was Kenny Meyers, the guy who signed Willie Davis, and I remember Kenny was smoking a cigar, and there was a plaster dry wall in the bar, and he took his cigar and made a spot on the wall. Kenny said, 'Sandy, stand back like you have a baseball in your hand, wind up, and throw at the spot.' So Sandy did, and Kenny saw that the way he was throwing, it was impossible for him to even see the spot. Kenny said, 'How are you going to throw to that spot when you can't even see it?' He said, 'Instead of taking your top part, your head and shoulders, all the way back on your windup, take your hands back and leave the rest of your body up front.' So Norm Sherry interpreted what Kenny was saying as saying, 'Sandy, you don't have to throw so hard,' because what Sandy would do literally was to rare back with the top part of his body, and he wouldn't release the ball far enough forward, and he couldn't throw strikes. And a couple days later, Sherry was catching Sandy in a game against Minnesota, and he kept telling him, 'Sandy, you don't have to throw that hard.' Sandy began throwing with a loose, easy delivery and throwing harder.

"Goes to show you how hard baseball is. Casey Stengel once said that Sandy was probably the best pitcher who ever lived. He said, 'Forget the other fellow,' meaning Walter Johnson. 'You can forget Waddell. The Jewish kid is probably the best of all of them.' "

LARRY KING: "What I remember most about Sandy, what the whole neighborhood knew, was that he was what we call a *hemisha* boy. He was a *mensch*. Unlike us, Sandy did not do crazy things. We'd sit in the PAL section in Ebbets Field and then sneak down into the box seats. Sandy, never.

"He was as close to being an Orthodox Jew as any of the neighborhood kids. Most of us observed the dietary laws, but Sandy wouldn't even drive a car on Saturday, and he always observed the High Holidays. To the end of his career, he wouldn't pitch on Yom Kippur.

"Once it was the day before Rosh Hashanah, and I was interviewing him, and this was right before the start of the World Series, and he said, 'Don't

George Brace Photo

SANDY KOUFAX

forget to remind everybody we taped this the day before.' He didn't want people to think that he would do an interview on Rosh Hashanah.

"We loved to tease Sandy even after he grew up. I remember it was spring training, and there was an annual Yankee–Dodger series just before the start of the season, and it was Passover, and we went to Ebbets Field, and we brought matzo sandwiches with chicken fat on it. Herbie Cohen and Hooha and I went down to the Dodger dugout, and we started calling, 'Sandy, hey, Sandy, we got matzo for you.' And Sandy's going, 'Go away. Go away.' And Russ Meyer, who was from Illinois, comes over and says to us, 'What's matzo?' So we gave him some matzo with chicken fat on it, and Meyer started giving some to one of the other Dodgers, and pretty soon all the Dodgers were eating matzo with chicken fat, and they're all saying, 'This is terrific.' Even Jackie Robinson. So the Dodgers are passing around the matzo, and Sandy is going, 'I don't know these guys.'

"Anyway, in the third inning, Meyer gives up eleven runs, I mean the Yankees bombed him, and Herbie Cohen, a Yankee fanatic, is going around saying, 'It was my plot. I planned it. I fed him matzo and chicken fat, and no man has ever pitched five innings with matzo and chicken fat in him.' "

CLEM LABINE: "Sandy was always quiet. He was quiet when he was a rookie, and he was quiet when he was one of the best pitchers around. Another very internal man. It was very hard to find out what Sandy was feeling emotionally."

Ed Roebuck

The Old Gang was beginning to break up. Bavasi sold both Preacher Roe and Billy Cox to Baltimore over the winter, and manager Alston was hinting strongly that he was going to force Jackie Robinson into a utility role. At the start of his career, Robinson had to fight for his job. Now, at age thirty-six, he once again found himself fighting for a job. With Bavasi and O'Malley looking on, Robinson became convinced that management was trying to end his career.

For most of the 1955 exhibition season, Alston kept Robinson on the bench while Don Hoak, whom Alston had managed at Montreal, played third. Alston had tried this in '54, and Robinson resented it, and even after outplaying Hoak, Robinson saw that Alston intended to do it again. During an exhibition in Montgomery, Alabama, a disgusted Robinson spent the game sitting in the bullpen with the pitchers. Dick Young, smelling a big story, joined him out there. Nervous, Robinson wanted to know if Young had heard how Alston was planning to use him. Young said he had not.

Robinson told Young, "When I'm fit, I've got as much right to be in the lineup as any man on this club, and Alston knows that." He paused. "Or maybe he doesn't know that." The discussion appeared in the *Daily News*.

The next day, before a game in Chattanooga, an angry Alston refused to give his starting lineup to reporters, most of whom were sympathetic to Robinson.

FRANK GRAHAM, JR,: "The writers found Alston uncommunicative and seemed to enjoy his discomfiture; some equated his taciturnity with mindlessness. The high point of the spring trip for the writers was when the Dodgers played the Washington Senators, whose new manager was Charley Dressen. Dick Young and the others rushed to Dressen for a story, and he played along with them, composing what they could not extract from Alston—the Dodger's opening day lineup."

The day after was a Sunday, April 3, and before this game Alston told the writers, "If Robinson has any complaints, why the hell doesn't he come to me and not tell them to a writer? Only two days ago he said he had a sore arm and wanted to go to a doctor in New York. If he was ready to play, why not tell me?"

Robinson's response: "I believe it's the manager's job to know the physical condition of his players. I've been in shape all spring. I just can't play one day and then sit on the bench four days and do a good job."

Dressen threw fuel on the fire by putting in his two cents. "Why, I make it a point to know how every one of my players feel every day." Said Dressen, "I don't only ask the players themselves, I ask the trainer."

Dressen loved to tweak the men who had let him go. Reporters asked him, Would he have won the pennant for Brooklyn in 1954? "Why, yes," said Charley. "Even with the injuries that year, the Dodgers had enough stuff on the bench to do it. I knew the fellas better, and I could've gotten more out of them."

Alston's one defender was a little-used relief pitcher named Tom Lasorda. "Dressen should mind his own business," said Lasorda. "He has enough trouble with his own club."

But Dressen's comments appeared in all the New York papers, which only served to anger Alston further. When one writer wrote that Billy Herman had been the real strategist during the 1954 season, Alston told the writer, "the only reason I don't punch you in the nose is because you're twenty pounds overweight and too old."

Alston was not dealing from a position of strength. He knew that if he didn't stand up to Robinson, he would lose face with his players. He also knew that if he did, he ran the risk of losing the veterans. His job was on the line. Alston had a trump card to play in his struggle with Robinson, his brute strength.

DON HONIG: "Alston's relationship with Robinson was a sticky one. Alston came in, took over a team of all-stars, and even though he had only one at bat in the major leagues, he wasn't gonna take any shit from anybody.

"And Walt Alston was probably the strongest guy ever to be involved in baseball, and the players were scared to death of him. Dick Williams told me that once. I said to him, 'Gee, Walter's a strong guy, isn't he?' And Dick said, 'That's how he controlled his players.' Then Dick told me this story:

"They were in L.A., and the team was riding the bus, and as the bus pulled away from the ballpark, a lot of the players were complaining that the bus wasn't air conditioned. Alston ordered the bus driver to pull over to the side of the road. Alston stood up and said, 'First of all, the way you're playing, you ought to walk back to the hotel. And furthermore, anybody who doesn't like this bus, we can step outside and discuss it one at a time.'

"I said to Dick, 'Suppose they all had decided to discuss it?'

"Williams said, 'None of them would have gotten back on the bus.' And Frank Howard, who was six foot seven, 250 pounds, was on that team. Williams reconsidered. He said, 'Frank might have been the only one to get back on the bus.' Then he added, 'Maybe.' "

In 1955, before an exhibition in Louisville, Alston finally couldn't stand the pressure from Robinson anymore and challenged him to a fight. There were words, a movement toward a confrontation, but the other players kept them apart.

Carl Furillo: "We were coming north, and this thing was building, and we got to Louisville, Kentucky, playing an exhibition game, and we were in the clubhouse, and Jackie said something, I don't recall the conversation anymore, and Alston got hot. Robinson got up, and Alston walked over to him, and they almost came to blows. And the guy who stepped in between was Campanella. 'When are you guys going to grow up? Campy said. 'We came here to play ball not fight each other.' And that sort of cooled things down."

The episode was kept secret from the press. Though Alston lost some face with the veterans, it was a turning point in his managerial career. For the first time since he took over the Dodgers, Alston had established himself as the boss.

And then when the 1955 season opened, the Dodgers won their first ten games in a row, and twenty-two of their first twenty-four. By the end of the second week in May, they had an eight-game lead over the Giants, prompting former Dodger president Branch Rickey, now running the lowly Pittsburgh Pirates, to moan and groan: "A continuance of Brooklyn's runaway could be a catastrophe competitively and economically." Walter O'Malley's reaction to Rickey's sour grapes went unrecorded. More important, the dissension on the Dodger team ceased, as it always does on a winning team.

Alston ultimately decided to platoon Robinson and Hoak, and both were productive, but it was his expert handling of the pitching staff that won the Dodgers the pennant. Alston benefitted by Don Newcombe's return to top form. Big Newk finished 20–5 with seventeen complete games. The rest of the staff, Erskine, Podres, and Loes, rarely finished, but Alston effectively shuttled in relievers Clem Labine and Ed Roebuck. Labine pitched in a league-leading sixty games, finishing the year 13–5 and saving eleven.

* * *

CLEM LABINE: "Being my former manager, Alston knew me, and I became his pitcher. One way or the other, I was his late-inning man. And he kept me as late-inning man for practically all my Dodger career. Which certainly showed that he had faith in my pitching ability. I never, for the life of me, ever had a problem with Walt. I never had Walt come and grab the ball away from me. I was his relief pitcher. He never came to me and said, 'Hey, I want you to start,' and it would have been very easy for him to say that. You know, 'Now that you're an established relief pitcher, why don't you try to go nine innings.' Because suppose you hurt your arm?

"My relationship with him was that I wanted to pitch 'cause I loved game situations—it's exciting, it's your baby—and when you look around and feel that everyone feels that you can do the job, when you look around the field and see that everyone's on their toes, not on their haunches, that helps too.

"Perhaps I'm more understanding now than I was then. But one thing I can say, as far as Walter Alston is concerned, he always was fair with me. He was to the end."

Alston's other reliever was a twenty-two-year-old rookie named Ed Roebuck, who won five, saved twelve, and who during the Dodgers' big winning streak at the start of the season more often than not came in and starred in relief.

ED ROEBUCK: "In June 1949 the Dodgers had a tryout camp in Washington, Pennsylvania, and I hitchhiked over there from my hometown, East Millsboro, which was a real small town. I wasn't an unknown kid. As a matter of fact, fifteen other scouts had talked to me. I'd pitched a couple of no-hitters in high school, and when I didn't pitch I was shortstop and center field. I must have showed up real well at the Dodger tryout, because about a month later, in August, a big black Buick pulls up to our house. We lived way far off the road, a mile and a half up a lane and back through trees, and I still don't know how the guy ever made it back there with the Buick, but he said, 'I'm taking you to Brooklyn to work out.' I said, 'Brooklyn?' I hadn't even remembered talking to a Brooklyn scout except for that tryout camp. I said, 'All right. Let's go,' so we drove ten hours to Brooklyn, and I worked out at Ebbets Field. I worked out as an outfielder, and I hit real well, and they told me to run, and I couldn't. I didn't have any speed. I was tall, gangly, and I had a good arm, so they had me throw some, and they took me up in the office, and Branch Rickey signed me. I wasn't a bonus player, but they gave me a contract that was very tough to beat. It was a $3,000 bonus, and $3,000-a-year three-year Triple-A contract, so at the end of the three years, I would realize $12,000. They did it that way to keep me from being a bonus player, but that was quite a bit of money then. The rule at the time was, anything over $4,000, and you had to be put on the major league roster."

Roebuck signed with the Dodgers in 1949, but it wasn't until 1955 that he reached Brooklyn. Along the way he toured Newport News, Virginia, Ft. Worth, Texas, Elmira, New York, and finally he spent three full years playing

ED ROEBUCK

for Montreal, where he was 12–8 with a 2.29 era in '52, 15–14 in '53, and 18–14 in '54, when he led the league in wins, losses, and innings pitched. For his yeoman work, they made a relief pitcher out of him.

ED ROEBUCK: "Because I wasn't a real power pitcher. I was a sinker-ball and breaking-ball pitcher. And the Dodgers were right again. They made the right move, because my being a sinker-ball pitcher, I got a lot of double plays.

"I had been with Walter Alston for two years at Montreal, in 1952 and 1953. In the minors he was an outstanding manager, and we were always very, very close. I was instrumental in us winning the Little World Series in 1953. And then he went up in '54, and then I came in '55, and he started using me immediately, and that's why I did so well early in the season.

"Walt was always very, very low key. He wasn't like Charley Dressen, where everything was very, very positive. Walt just sat back and waited for things to happen. And he was blessed with a club with a lot of talent, and he let the guys play their game. Unlike Charley, Walt didn't toot his horn too much.

"Alston, though, was always caught up in inane shit. One night Johnny Podres, Don Drysdale, and I were in Fazio's. It was off limits, and we had been drinking there, and after we got back to the hotel, Johnny took a girl back to his room, and because Johnny's room was next to Alston's, Alston heard them.

"So after batting practice, Alston held this meeting. Alston says, 'Podres, you had a girl in your room last night.'

"Johnny said, 'Yeah, but I didn't fuck her.'

"Duke said, 'Geez, Walt, a lot of guys get laid.'

"Alston said, 'He had a girl. I heard him. He's not pitching.'

"But the coaches talked him out of it, and Johnny pitched a shutout.

"You have to understand that Buzzy could run the club with Walt managing. If Buzzy called Walt up and said, 'We should play Shuba today,' Walt would say okay. I never did like Buzzy. When I left, it was like getting out of jail, getting away from Buzzy.

"But as a rookie in 1955, I did a tremendous job. I remember my first game. We were in Philadelphia, and Carl Erskine was pitching. Carl had a 5–1 lead, and believe it or not, he got wild in the middle of the fifth inning. He walked a couple of guys and there was a base hit, and he walked another guy. And Labine and myself were warming up in the bullpen. So I'm thinking, 'He won't bring me in. Labine is the star, the great reliever.' And Walt goes to the mound and goes back to the dugout, and Erskine goes to a 3–1 count on Del Ennis, and Alston goes out to get him. I'm still warming up, thinking 'Labine's going in,' and Walt looks to the bullpen and starts pulling his arms back and forth like he's rowing a boat, the sign for Roebuck.

"It was in Connie Mack Stadium, and I was walking to the mound thinking to myself, 'Hell, if he has enough guts to bring me in here, I got enough guts to pitch.' See, I had played two years for Walt, and he knew that I could throw a strike. That's why he brought me in. And I give Walt a lot of credit. He really inspired me. I got Ennis to hit into a double play, and I pitched four and two-thirds innings, and I got credit for the win because Erskine hadn't gone far enough. I did a real, real good job, but after I won the first game, from that point on I was unconscious. I would come in a ballgame, and if a double play was needed, I'd get a double play. And I got away with some real bad pitches too. But all in all, I kept the ball down, it was sinking well, and I did a really good job.

"I ended up with a 5 and 6 record and a 4.71 earned run average, but the stats don't tell the real story because I remember I relieved in a game against Milwaukee in Brooklyn, and the score was already out of hand, and I came in and really poured some gasoline on the fire. Bruton hit a home run off me in dead center, over the corner of that second deck, right out onto Bedford Avenue, and then Eddie Mathews hit one, and Aaron hit one. They got to me, and Walt came out to the mound and said, 'I can't take you out because you're going to be the next hitter the next inning,' and he left me in there for a terrible beating. They got ten runs off me. I think my whole year went up in smoke that day. If you look at my record that year it looks like I had a terrible year. But all in all I didn't; I had a really good year. It just doesn't show it in the stats, because of that one game.

"And you know, it was sort of a self-fulfilling prophecy, and it was the way Walt managed: 'You did pretty good today, but what about tomorrow?'

"And looking back now, the thing that strikes me—I couldn't see the forest from the trees, because there was no time to relax and enjoy being on that team, because you had to fight so hard to stay there—what I remember most about the Dodger club was how businesslike and serious it was, and how much character the club had. There was no fooling around. Kids coming up to the team had to fall into a certain mold. You had to act like a Dodger. Because guys like Pee Wee and Hodges were very, very straight and respected, and they were the leaders, and they expected all the kids who came up there to fall in line. With Robinson, Hodges, Reese, and those guys, you weren't expected to be a clown. You were expected to be a ballplayer. It was a very businesslike club. They went about and executed everybody in the National League in a very businesslike way."

A Special Night for Pee Wee

The rest of the 1955 season was a breeze, as the Dodgers won the pennant by thirteen and a half games over the youthful Milwaukee Braves. The clinching date was September 8. Don Newcombe was the pitching hero, finishing with the best won–lost percentage in the league, 20–5, .800, plus hitting seven home runs and batting .359. Duke Snider, Roy Campanella, and Gil Hodges provided most of the offense, as they drove in 136, 107, and 102 runs, Carl Furillo hit .314 and drove in ninety-five runs, and Pee Wee Reese batted .282 with ten home runs and sixty-one runs batted in, not bad figures for a shortstop, especially one celebrating his thirty-seventh birthday on July 23. Captain Pee Wee, thirty-seven years old? How was it possible?

* * *

DONALD HALL: "From baseball I learned about aging. It seems such a brief time from when Pee Wee Reese was the kid with fuzz on his face until Pee Wee Reese was the seasoned veteran, the grizzled old man. All this occurs within a space of about ten years. It's an accelerated aging that takes the whole curve to itself, the whole riddle of the Sphinx. 'What is four-footed at dawn, two-footed at noon, and three-footed at twilight?' The answer, of course, is Man. In baseball it happens within ten years. Sometimes quicker. Always too quickly."

To mark the occasion of Reese's birthday, publicity director Irving Rudd organized what was to become one of the memorable events of the season.

LARRY KING: "The Dodgers gave a party for Pee Wee at Ebbets Field, and I was there. When the fans came to the park, each of them was given a little candle and a match. They were told that there was going to be a surprise party for Reese and that when the Dodgers ran out in the bottom of the fifth inning, the lights were going to be turned off, and everyone was to light their candle and sing 'Happy Birthday' to Pee Wee. It was a beautiful sight as thousands of candles flickered in the dark and everyone sang 'Happy Birthday' to Pee Wee."

IRVING RUDD: "I was in charge of Pee Wee Reese Night. We drew 35,000 fans. We closed the subways. You couldn't walk down the streets if you didn't have a ticket in your hand. One of the great, glorious nights of Dodger history.

"We hustled merchants, not fans, for gifts. In the past fans would send in money, and sometimes you'd get situations like the night they threw for Dixie Walker in 1947. They ended up with just enough money to buy him a fishing rod.

"I went around to merchants and got about $20,000 worth of gifts: vacation trips, a lifetime pass to Grossingers, golf clubs, fishing rods, rifles, and Frank Graham, Jr., came up with the pièce de résistance, the car. We set up a meeting with the Flatbush Automobile Dealers Association. In those days a car, fully equipped, cost three grand. I sat down with five guys, one from Chevy, Buick, Cadillac, Chrysler, and Pontiac. I told them, 'Cost you $600 each, your car rolls out onto the field, we mention it, plug it in advance that night on television.' And the idea was that Pee Wee's daughter, Barbara, who was twelve, would dip into a bowl, pick a key, and the key that fits the car is the car that Pee Wee would drive off in. Dramatic.

"So that night in front of 35,000 fans, 'Here come the automobiles, ladies and gentlemen.' And the cars come rolling out from the center-field gate across the infield, and the crowd is screaming bloody murder like *Let's Make a Deal*. 'Let him get the Imperial! Let him get the Imperial! The Imperial!'

"The kid picks the Chevy.

"And I'll never forget Roy Campanella, a lovely, expressive man. His cheek is bulging with chew, and he says to me afterward, 'Irvin', how come you didn't see that Pee Wee win that Imperial yesterday?' We're in the clubhouse in front of the whole gang. I said, 'Gee, the kid picked the key to the Chevrolet.' He said, 'Sheet, man, I'm talkin' about arrangin' things.' I said, 'Arranging things? You don't arrange something like that, Campy.' He got down on his knees, and he said, 'Man, if there wuz a pile of hoss shit six feet in front of me, and that fuckin' Imperial was on the other side, I'd wade through the hoss shit to git it.' "

The Catch

Once again the Dodgers went into the World Series against the Yankees with the historical baggage weighing heavy upon their shoulders. Since 1941 they had faced the Pinstripers five times, and five times they had lost. It wasn't just the Yankees they were fighting. It was the Yankee tradition, the Yankee reputation, the Yankee complex.

Ed Roebuck: "When the Yankees got on the field, they were more businesslike than anybody. They executed you nice and easy. And what the Yankees would do in those years would be to entertain the visiting clubs at night, take them out and get them drunk, and the next day beat the hell out of them. Guys like Ford and Martin and Mantle. Mickey would go out and drink with you all night long, just like Babe Ruth used to do, and then he'd go out and hit three home runs and beat the shit out of you. And let's face it, the visiting players were in awe of Yankee Stadium. They were in awe of Mickey Mantle and Whitey Ford and Billy Martin, and you would go out and have a couple of drinks, hell, it was an honor, and then they'd beat hell out of you.

"I think man for man the Dodgers could outslug the Yankees, even with Mantle and Berra and Skowron, but damn, the Yankees had the good pitching. And pitching really wins. Over the years they had Raschi and Reynolds and Lopat and Ford and Byrne and Page and other guys in the bullpen, and they always had good pitching against the Dodgers.

"The Dodgers had power, speed, defense, and pretty good pitching. The Yankees had power, defense, and very good pitching. They always had good pitching. And if they didn't, they would go out and trade for it. In '55 they got Turley and Larsen in a trade, and they had Whitey, Byrne, Grim, good pitching."

And in the first two games of the '55 series, Yankee pitching again defeated the Dodgers. Whitey Ford beat Don Newcombe in the opener, 6–5, as Newk lost on a two-run home run by Joe Collins. Jackie Robinson provided Brooklyn its moment of glory when he stole home, sweeping across home plate, beating the tag of a bellowing Yogi Berra. In the second game, Tommy Byrne became the first lefty to pitch a complete game against the Dodgers in '55 when he beat Billy Loes, 4–2.

It looked bleak, especially after Alston learned that Newcombe had a sore arm and wouldn't be able to pitch again. But when the Dodgers returned to Ebbets Field, they won all three games.

Game Three was a turning point. Alston chose Johnny Podres as his starter, and the young lefty celebrated his twenty-third birthday with a win sparked by a gimpy and heroic Robinson. With the score 2–2 in the second, and with one out, Robinson singled. Amoros was hit by a Bob Turley fastball, Podres was safe on a bunt, and the bases were loaded.

On third Robinson began his will I, won't I routine of making a series of mad dashes as though intent on stealing home. After racing several steps down the line, he would suddenly stop, but not before distracting Turley, who walked Gilliam on four pitches as Robinson in his pigeon-toed walk shuffled across the plate.

In the seventh Robinson continued the show. He doubled, racing wide past the bag at second, and as Elston Howard was picking up the ball in left, he made a feint as though he was going to try for third. Howard hesitated, and then he threw into second, hoping to catch Robinson off his guard. When Robinson saw that Howard was throwing behind him, he continued to third and slid in safe as the relay came in high. The Yankees brought the infield in to try to cut off the run, and Amoros hit a dribbler through to the outfield for another run. Podres, baffling the Yankees with his change-up, won 8–3.

In Game Four Brooklyn trailed 3–1 when, in the fourth inning, Campanella homered, Furillo singled, and Hodges hit another home run off Don Larsen to win it, and then Duke Snider rolled up the score when he hit a three-run home run deep over the right-field fence off Johnny Kucks. In Game Five Snider hit two more home runs, and left-fielder Sandy Amoros hit a two-run home run as the Dodgers took a three games to two lead in the Series.

With the three wins at Ebbets Field, the complexion of the Series had changed, along with the emotions of the skeptical Brooklyn fans. As in 1952 the Dodgers needed to win just one more to be champions of the world. And though Brooklyn wished fervently for it to happen, few really believed it would.

In Game Six Alston started the inconsistent Karl Spooner instead of Russ Meyer, choosing to go with a lefty as he had done in '53 when he picked Podres over Meyer—and with the same result.

ED ROEBUCK: "Spooner started, and in the first inning Spooner gave up two walks and two singles, and then Skowron hit a three-run home run, and then Russ Meyer came in and pitched five or six scoreless innings, and I came in and finished up, and I remember Russ Meyer saying to me in the clubhouse after the game, 'Well, we did our job. They should have started me or you.' "

In Game Seven Alston came back with Podres, the star of the third game. Because the Yankees started Tommy Byrne, a left-hander, Alston decided to play the percentages. He played right-handed hitters Don Zimmer at second base and Junior Gilliam in left, and he kept Amoros, who was his most-regular left fielder, on the bench. Jackie Robinson, who was suffering from a pulled Achilles tendon in his right heel, also didn't play, but then, neither did Mickey Mantle, who was suffering from a torn leg muscle.

The Dodgers scored a run in the fourth on a double by Campanella and a single by Hodges. The question was whether Podres could keep the Yankees from scoring.

It was a struggle. In the second, with two outs, Moose Skowron hit a double, but Podres got the next batter. Then in the third, again with two outs, Phil Rizzuto walked and went to second when Billy Martin walked. Here was the rally all of Brooklyn feared was coming. Gil McDougald was the next batter, and he chopped a ball down the third-base line, to the right of the bag, and as Rizzuto was sliding legs and arms extended into third to load the bases, the bounding ball thwacked against his body before he reached the base, and he was declared out. No rally. No runs.

In the fourth the first batter, Berra, lifted an easy fly to left center. It was an easy catch for the Duke, but Gilliam called it, and Snider stood waiting for him to make the catch. Suddenly Gilliam called, 'You take it,' but it was too late, and the ball fell as Berra chugged into second. The next batters were Bauer, Skowron, and hulking Bob Cerv. Podres got them down on pops and grounders. An easy inning after all.

It was only 1–0 when the Dodgers batted in the sixth. Pee Wee singled to start things, and then, wonder of wonders, Duke Snider bunted, and it was a beauty, and Reese went to second as Byrne fielded the ball and threw to first to Skowron, who tagged Snider, only to see the ball fly out of his glove, allowing Snider to be safe at first. Alston again called for the sacrifice, and Campanella bunted and moved the runners up. Casey Stengel left Byrne in long enough to intentionally walk Carl Furillo to load the bases, then he removed him for Bob Grim.

Hodges drove in the second Dodger run with a long sacrifice fly to score Reese. Grim then walked third baseman Don Hoak to reload the bases.

Alston wanted more runs. He sent "Shotgun" George Shuba to pinch hit for Zimmer, the second baseman. Grim retired Shuba to end the inning. At the time nobody knew it, but Alston's substitution of Shuba for Zimmer was perhaps the most important strategic decision any Brooklyn manager ever made, for with Zimmer out of the game, Alston had to find a new left fielder. He shifted Gilliam from left to second base, and in left he substituted his fleet Cuban, Sandy Amoros. Ironically, few of the millions of fans watching on television had even noticed that Alston had made the switch, and if they had noticed, they didn't think much of it. Shifting around a Snider or a Hodges, that would have been noteworthy. Shifting utility players like Gilliam or Amoros didn't draw much attention.

It was 2 to 0, Dodgers, in the bottom of the sixth, when with one out the Yankees put two men on base: Martin walked, and then Gil McDougald bunted safely. Two on, one out. Berra up. A home run and it was over for the Dodgers.

It was getting late in the game, Podres seemed to be tiring, and Berra was a dead pull hitter, so the entire Brooklyn outfield, Amoros, Snider, and Furillo, was shifted over toward right. Amoros, the left fielder, was shaded so far over he could have been the center fielder.

Podres threw an outside pitch. Berra slapped his bat on it late as it was crossing the plate. The Yankee catcher was protecting the plate and sent a looping, climbing pop toward the left-field line, in the direction of the low barrier in left field.

Had Junior Gilliam still been in left, the Dodgers would have lost the game and the Series, for even with Gilliam's good speed, he would not have caught Berra's ball. Gilliam, moreover, was right-handed, which would have made the catch very difficult. Of all the moves Alston ever made, this one must have been blessed, because he needed a man with special attributes to make the catch. And Sandy Amoros was there.

The nimble Cuban turned and fled toward the foul pole, and as he was nearing the dirt warning track at top speed, he extended his right, gloved hand, and the descending ball neatly fell into it as he took a series of quick, mincing steps to keep from banging into the low fence before him. On the field there was confusion in the Yankee camp, while Dodger heads remained cool. Pee Wee Reese had run down the third-base line for the relay. He called for the ball, and Amoros hit him in the chest, and without hesitation Reese fired over to Gil Hodges at first, where the base umpire signaled the hasty McDougald out. McDougald, who had not figured Amoros to catch the ball, had run almost to second base and was caught stranded for the third out.

The sixth inning was over. The Yankee rally was aborted. The scoreboard indicated 2 for the Dodgers. The Yankees still had nothing.

Of all the possible Dodger heroes, Amoros was among the most unlikely. He was virtually invisible to the public, for he spoke no English and was unusually diffident for a professional athlete. Reporters didn't ask him questions, because they knew he couldn't answer. Sometimes they would wave, and he would smile and nod. Sandy lived like a gypsy while on the Dodgers. He never rented an apartment, but most of the time lived on Roy Campanella's yacht. Roy had learned to speak Spanish playing winter ball in the Caribbean.

Amoros had been one of the greatest players ever to come out of pre-Castro Cuba. If he had spoken English, he certainly would have played more, because in Cuba he was a .300 hitter in a fast league, was fleet in the field, was excellent at stealing bases, and was a good bunter. But he didn't learn the language, and it was a handicap that kept him from becoming a star. A manager just doesn't trust employing a player when he isn't sure whether the guy understands him or not.

Almost thirty years after his famous catch, Sandy Amoros is shy and self-effacing as always, and though his English has improved, the effervescent Amoros is still uncomfortable speaking the language.

SANDY AMOROS: "I start play baseball in school about 1944. I play for Matanzas, Cuba. Matanzas is what we call a provincia. So I belong to Matanzas, and they play a championship in Havana, and the one that make more games is the champion of the Cuban island."

"How did Matanzas do?"

"We made it to first place."

"How did you do?"

SANDY AMOROS

"I had champion bat, I had champion field. Everything."

"You were the batting champion. What did you hit?"

"Five something. I did the best. And then they have a championship for the *joven* [youth], and I play the best too. So they move me to the national team that is going to play in Guatemala for the championship of the Central America de Caribe. We play the Republic de Haiti, Dominican Republic, Jamaica. So I went and played, and I did all right too.

"In the summertime I come over to the United States to play in the colored league. Nineteen fifty. I play over in New York with the New York Cubans. I play against Willie Mays, Yo [Joe] Black, Hunior Jilliam, and Satchel Paige. I think him the best.

"So I play summertime in the colored league, and in the winter leagues, I play in Cuba. We have a Caribbean Series, the best players from Panama, Puerto Rico, Venezuela, and Cuba. On our teams we have a lot of guys from the United States. We had Beel Vido [Virdon]; I play with him in Cuba. He play center field. We have Ken Boya [Boyer]; he played third base. And from Cuba we had Tony Taylor. We have Camilo Pascual and Pedro Ramo [Ramos] and Mike Fornieles, a pitcher from Boton [Boston]. Also Chico Fernandez."

"Were you one of the better ballplayers?"

"I lead one time, I hit .375. They say I the best in the last fifty years. Nobody heet like that, they say. So Al Campanis, he manage in Cuba one year. Not my team. But he see me, and he say, 'You sign with me, and you can play with the Brooklyn organization.' This was 1952. So I sign with him, and they send me to St. Paul."

"Did anyone else speak Spanish?"

"Nobody." A big smile.

"Were you lonely?"

"In Spanish they say, 'Yo creo de Dios.' I pray to God. I think I can do it here. But in the spring, my hand is sore, and it is cold, so I can't play. The manager we have is Clay Bryant. Bryant say, 'I don't want Sandy over here. Sandy can't do nothing. He can't hit. He can't do nothing.' So Al Campanis say, 'Don't worry. He play in the winter, so he in good shape. Keep him, and he going to be all right for the season.' So I started with St. Paul. I didn't start the game, but in the seventh or eighth inning, they had some trouble. Clay Bryant say, 'Sandy, can you hit?' I said, 'Yip.' So they put me in to pinch hit. So I have a triple. Hit the ball to left center. So Clay Bryant say, 'Can you play?' I say, 'Yip, I can play,' so I start play. And in the American Association I hit home runs in nine ballparks. So by the time they bring me to the Brooklyn Dodgers in fall 1952, I have nineteen home runs, hit .339. I have a good year. So I stay with the Dodgers two, three months in '52, and in '53 they send me to Montreal. At Montreal in '53, I lucky. I keel this league. I champ bat. I hit forty doubles. I have twenty-three home runs. A hundred rbis. And so I was the most popular player in minor leagues in '53. The best. The best player in the minor leagues in 1953. I hit champion bat. I hit .365. Years back Jackie Robinson lead league for .353. I hit .365. I had a great year in '53 at Montreal.

"So in '54 I started with the Dodgers. They have a good team. They have Furillo and Duke Snider, and they have Don Thompson, he chew tobacco, in left field. So I come over in '54, and I hit pretty good. I hit for .290 something. We finish second. I no play the whole year. But they gave me a full share because I play good the last half."

"Did anyone else speak Spanish on the Dodgers?"

"Yeah. Yo [Joe] Black and Roy Campanyella. I roomed with Campanyella for two years. Yo Black, Campanyella, I never have a problem with these men. The old Brooklyn Dodgers, I never have trouble with any of them. They explain to you everything, help you and everything. They tell me, 'I work at the ballpark. I have my yob [job]. You have your yob. When I play with the Brooklyn Dodgers, they show me something . . . I can't explain. I can explain it in Spanish but not in English."

In Spanish Sandy said, "We were brothers. We got along together. We always had this to help us win, playing together, friendship, united."

Returning to his halting English, he said, "There may have been teams better than we, but we play together, and when you saw how they played, they played separate. They played for themselves. So I say, the Brooklyn Dodgers had something: They played together."

I asked Sandy if he still remembered that seventh game back in 1955.

"Yip," he said with a shy smile. "I no start. But in the sixth inning, when the Jankees have two men on base, man on first, man on second, Walter Alston bring Hunior Jilliam to second base, put Don Zimmer out, and put me in left field.

"Walter Alston put me all the way to center field for Jogi Berra. They didn't think Yonny Podres had much left, and they figured Jogi was going to pull the ball, so they pulled me over to center field. If I had played straightaway like I should have played, it would have been easy for me to catch the baseball. But everybody say to play all the way to center field. So Berra hits the ball to the corner down the left-field line. Well, I had to do something. I run like a hawk. I run to the wall, and I figure, 'I can get it,' and so I catch it, and Pee Wee, he tells me, 'Give me the ball, give me the ball,' and Pee Wee is standing on the line down third base, and I throw it to Pee Wee, and we caught McDougald on second base, so he throw to Gil Hodges at first, and they make a double play. We finish the inning, 2–0, we play the ninth, and they don't do nothing in the ninth, so it finish 2–0. We win the championship.

"I play in '56 and '57, the last year we play in Brooklyn. We finish second to Milwaukee. I didn't go with the Dodgers to Los Anheles. They send me to Montreal."

"Why?"

"We never know."

"You don't know?"

"Nobody know. When you see Buzzy Bavasi, you ask him. They know. And in '59 they sold me to Detroit. I play one year in Detroit, 1960. And then I played two years in the minor leagues. Then I went back to Cuba."

"Did you know Castro?"

"I can't tell you anything about Castro."

"But you aren't living in Cuba. You're living here."

"My daughter is born over here in the United States, so she wanted to come to the United States. So in '67 I came to the United States. I know beisbol, footbol, keekbol. I don't know nothing about politics. I don't have any problem with nobody."

Champs At Last

For Brooklyn fans, waiting for the final nine outs of the 1955 World Series seemed like forever. Podres was perfect in the Yankee seventh, and in the Yankee eighth, Phil Rizzuto, playing in his last World Series in a career that began in 1941, singled to left field. Billy Martin flied out, but then Gil McDougald chopped a hard grounder off third baseman Hoak's shoulder for a base hit. Perhaps this was to be the Yankee rally. Time was running out. Yogi Berra was the next batter. He flied weakly to Furillo in right. Hank Bauer then struck out. Podres had but one inning to go.

ED ROEBUCK: "I remember Johnny Podres just mowing these guys down as we went along, and I just had the feeling we were going to beat them. It seemed that Johnny could always get up for the big ballgame, and if anybody could beat the Yankees, he would be the guy. And after Amoros made that catch, nothing was going to stop us, and the Yankees never came close.

"Podres set them down easy in the ninth, and the last ball was hit to shortstop by Elston Howard. Reese threw him out, and all the people ran out to see Johnny at the mound.

"I remember that after the game, Johnny and his dad were in the clubhouse in Yankee Stadium embracing, and it seemed like both of them were crying. The two were so damn happy, the impossible had happened. And then a short time later, it seemed, Johnny's dad died. He was an iron miner, and he died from a lung disease at a very young age.

"After the final game, we went to the Bossert Hotel for the celebration, and Johnny was having a helluva good time at that party. Let's face it, he ruled Brooklyn, and he was single and he was giving all the girls the once-over, and he was enjoying it all."

CLEM LABINE: "John loved girls, and he was single, and he loved to drink. And he loved to gamble, cards, horses, anything. He and Don Zimmer were two of the greatest horse players. But John was careless, didn't save any money at all. I think I'm one of the best things that happened to John, because I was a stabilizing influence on his life. I used to make him cash his paycheck and go to Western Union and make him send money home to Mineville, New

York. And he educated his younger brother through doing it. Because I guarantee you John would not have saved a dime, 'cause he no sooner got it in his pocket than he was borrowing money.

"He was a good kid, good-hearted. Anything you wanted you could have. But nothing concerned him except having a good time."

JOHNNY PODRES: "When I was a kid in school, I wanted to be a Dodger. I was a Dodger fan, loved the Dodgers, always listened to the Dodgers on the radio, and when I had a chance to sign with them, that's what I wanted to do. I always, always wanted to be a Dodger.

"I was only twenty-one when I pitched in my first World Series. It was in '53, and I didn't find out I was pitching until I came to the park that day. I had so little experience. The first batter I faced, the first hitter in the game, Gene Woodling, hit a home run off me. I didn't last very long, didn't get through the third. The last batter I faced hit a ball back to me, and the ball knocked the glove off my hand. Instead of going for the ball, I went for the glove first, and the runner was safe. They got me out of there.

"In '55 I started the year great, started off 7 and 3, but I hurt my arm, and at the end of the year was only 9 and 10. I honestly didn't think I would get a start in the Series.

"It was a tough year for me. After my fast start, I threw a pitch, and my shoulder bothered me, and I was on the disabled list for a month. My arm never did get sound until much later on, and then in September, at Ebbets Field, I was standing on the field before infield practice, about to hit fungoes to the outfielders, and as the ground crew was wheeling the batting cage across the diamond and out through the gate in center field, they hit me right in the side with it. My ribs were banged up, and for two or three weeks I could hardly breathe.

"The front office was thinking about bringing up Kenny Lehman from Montreal and taking me off the roster. He would have been eligible for the World Series, and I wouldn't have been, but then late in the season, after we clinched the pennant, I pitched in Pittsburgh and had real good stuff, so they decided to leave me on the roster for the World Series. If I hadn't looked all right in that game I don't think I would have pitched in the Series. I would have gone on the disabled list.

"We lost the first two games of the '55 Series, and after the second game, Alston told me to be ready tomorrow, that I was opening at Ebbets Field. That game was probably the most important game of the whole Series, because if we don't win that one, we're down three games to none. And I remember that Roy hit a home run in the first inning, and we hit well that day, and that day I had a great change-up. During that game I had gotten to third base—I bunted against Bob Turley and somehow got to third—and I told Billy Herman, the third base coach, that I had a great change-up. He mentioned it to Campy, but Campy knew anyway. I beat the Yankees that third game, 8–3.

"We won the next two games, and the Series went back to Yankee Stadium.

JOHNNY PODRES

We needed to win one more, but Whitey Ford won Game Six to force us into a seventh game.

"We were all pretty blue after that game. I remember Pee Wee was sitting in front of his locker with his head down. I said to him, 'Don't worry, Pee Wee. I'll shut them out tomorrow.' What else are you going to say?

"I had known I was pitching the seventh game because Alston had told me even before the sixth game.

"I remember warming up with Dixie Howell, who was our third-string catcher. When they announced the Yankee lineup I said to him, 'Dixie, there's no way that lineup can beat me today.' I had one big plus going for me: Mickey Mantle was injured and couldn't play.

"When the game began, I had the Yankees looking for my change-up. I established early in the game that I was going to throw it, and then as the shadows in the fall in Yankee Stadium came on, I went to my fastball and hard curve. In the last four or five innings, I threw only one change, the last pitch of the game. We didn't deliberately change the pattern. Campy saw how well my hard stuff was working, and he told me to stay with it, especially when those shadows started growing longer.

"In the last of the eighth, the Yankees had men on first and third and two out and I fanned Hank Bauer on as good a fastball as I ever threw in my life. I started it around his letters and when he swung and missed the ball was up at his shoulders.

"But of course the play everybody remembers in that game was Sandy Amoros's catch. You can't talk about the '55 Series with anybody without him talking about that play.

"We were leading 2–0 in the bottom of the sixth, and the Yankees got their first two batters on first and second. Gil McDougald was on first, Billy Martin on second. Yogi Berra was the batter. He was a left-handed hitter, and we played him to pull. He was a dead pull hitter. I threw a pitch that was high out over the plate, a fastball that had something on it, and he didn't get around too good on the ball, and he sliced it to left field. In left field Amoros, who was playing Berra more over to left center, had just been brought into the game by Alston.

"At first when the ball went up I wasn't concerned. In fact, when he hit it, I bent over and picked up the resin bag and said to myself, 'Well, there's one out.' But then I looked back, and I could see the ball keep slicing toward the line, and when I saw Amoros running his butt off, I thought to myself, 'Jesus Christ, what's going on here?' The ball seemed to hang up in the air forever, and there was Amoros, still running. I wondered: Is he going to get it?

"As it turned out, he did, though just barely. I know Gilliam could not have made that catch, because he was a righty, and the only way Amoros got it was that he was left-handed and didn't have to catch it backhanded. At the last moment, still going at top speed, Amoros reached out, and the ball dropped right into his glove. I let out a sigh. Like everyone else, I had been holding my breath.

"As great a catch as Amoros made, his relay to Pee Wee was even better.

Amoros hit him with a perfect peg. It was a great throw. And Pee Wee, being the great player he was, knew just what to do with it. Just before Pee Wee got the ball from Amoros, he had taken a quick look around to see where the runners were, and as soon as Pee Wee got the ball he didn't hesitate a second—he knew where he had to send it, over to Gil at first.

"I was standing there on the mound—all this was happening in a matter of seconds—watching it the same as everybody else. Pee Wee whipped around and fired that ball to Hodges as McDougald was trying to get back. Pee Wee made a perfect throw, and we had McDougald doubled off dead.

"My juices were really flowing after that. I got the next batter out, got them out in the seventh and eighth, and then in the ninth the first batter was Moose Skowron. Moose hit a one-hopper back to me that was hit so hard the ball stuck right up into the webbing of my glove, broke through the webbing. After I fielded the ball, I ran over to first base, struggling to get the ball out of my glove, and finally I was able to get it out and throw it to Gil. If I hadn't, I would have thrown Gil the glove with the ball in it.

"The next batter was Bob Cerv, who popped the ball up to short. One more to go. I was so excited I could hardly stand still. I just knew I was going to get that last batter and couldn't wait. Elston Howard came up. I tried to finish him and the game off with a strikeout, and I threw him five or six fastballs—good, hard, riding fastballs—but he kept fouling them off. Campy called for another fastball, but I shook him off. I think it was the only time in the whole game I did that. I threw a change-up, and Howard hit an easy ground ball down to a grinning Pee Wee at short. When I saw the ball heading for Pee Wee, I couldn't help thinking how ironic it was that all those years Pee Wee had been trying to beat the Yankees, and now the final out of Brooklyn's first world championship was going to Pee Wee. Then Pee Wee almost made a bad throw. He threw it low to first, but Gil picked it up easily, and we were champions.

"I don't really remember much of what happened after that. A lot was a blur. I remember I was a guest on *The Steve Allen Show* that night, and after I came back from that, there was a hell of a party at the Hotel Bossert in Brooklyn. I can remember that the champagne was really flowing. All you had to do was hold out your glass, and somebody would be there to fill it up. The streets were filled with people, and every so often I would go out and wave to them, then go back inside again where everyone came over, shook my hand, patted me on the back, poured me champagne. I doubt if there had ever been a night like that one in Brooklyn. There was one old guy who told me over and over that he had been waiting for this since 1916. Thirty-nine years. I can't imagine waiting thirty-nine years for anything. I really don't know how late that party went, or if it ever ended at all.

"I won the car, the Corvette, after they voted me Most Valuable Player in the World Series. I was flying for days. I didn't really come down until a few weeks later. I was at a deer camp in the Adirondacks, walking in the woods by myself. It was silent. You couldn't hear a thing except the rustle of the leaves. All of a sudden I stopped and said to myself, 'Hey, Podres, you beat the Yankees in the World Series!' "

Triumphant

Carl Erskine: "You can't imagine the hunger that existed in my belly along with the rest of the guys to win a World Series. I do remember that Robinson was irritated with me for yelling so hard at Podres, sort of kiddingly, but there was a lot of tension on the bench, because it looked like we had a chance. But in the latter innings, I was very tense, and I felt, 'Boy, we can't let this one get away.'

"All I remember about the ninth inning was the last out, which was a ground ball to Reese, and Pee Wee and Gil had a thing going for years about whether he made a good or a bad throw. There was a lot of kidding, but the throw was low. I don't recall whether it bounced or not. But that was the last out. Pee Wee was making so sure that he'd make the throw good that he didn't really turn it loose.

"One time we were in Los Angeles at an old timers' game some years later, and the guys were having a few drinks, and they got to talking to Pee Wee about the bad throw he made on the last out, what a great play Hodges made. Reese is saying, 'You're nuts. That was a good throw. That throw didn't bounce.' So they had a few more beers, and they said, 'We're going to call Hodges.' It was three in the morning back in New York. He was the manager of the Mets. So they called Hodges, got him out of bed to ask him if the ball bounced! Hodges, naturally, said that it was one of the toughest chances he had ever had in his life. Gil said the ball not only bounced once, it bounced three or four times!

"I'm going to tell you something I've never told another person in my life. After the game, before the writers came in, I had an inclination to call the guys together and say, 'Fellas, this is one of the high points of our whole life. I think we ought to say a prayer of thanksgiving. In gratitude we ought to bow our heads and say a prayer.' I didn't do that, but that was my feeling having won against the Yankees in the stadium after all those many, many, many, many years.

"It had so much significance. There was personal pride. There was a whole city that now could raise its head, look across the river to the Bronx and Manhattan and say, 'We're number one.'

"Everybody said, 'The ring.' Yeah, we got a ring, but it wasn't the ring. It was bigger than the ring.

"And ironically, it turned out to be the only world's championship ever in Brooklyn. It was the first and the last and the only."

Carl Furillo: "Oh God, that was a thrill of all thrills. 'Cause they never won a World Series in Brooklyn. Everybody, no matter where in hell you went, everybody couldn't do enough for you. I never in my life ever seen a town go so wild. You went out to Eastern Parkway and Atlantic Avenue, Christ, I never seen people so Goddamn happy.

"We accomplished something. We did something for the people. You did it for yourself too, but you did it for the people."

* * *

Bobby McCarthy: "I was stationed in the marines barracks in 1955. I was a corporal of the guard, and I listened to the last game of the World Series on the radio. When Elston Howard grounded out to Pee Wee, the Dodgers were the champions of the world. And here I was in Annapolis, Maryland, 200 miles away. I called my sister on the phone, and here I was in the brig guarding prisoners, and I said, 'Ronnie, what is it like in Brooklyn?' And she said, 'Listen to this,' and she stuck the phone out the window, and I could hear the roar of the crowd, the screaming. And I wanted so badly to be there, I just started to cry, and the prisoners, a couple of sailors, they started laughing when they saw me. Here I am, a big marine, and I'm crying, tears rolling down my face. Those were great days. The greatest in the world.

"Remember the headline in the *Daily News*—'WHO'S A BUM?'—with a big picture of the bum with a cigar in his mouth. I was so proud and happy."

Bill Reddy: "I was still working in Jerry's hardware, and that year we rented a television to see the Series. And as usual very little business was being conducted. Most people in the neighborhood knew this, and they came over to watch it with us. A couple of salesmen from a paint company came in, and so did Al the butcher. Al loved the Dodgers. Joe Hatten used to live in the neighborhood, and every time Hatten would win a game, Al would give him a steak.

"Before the game, we went out and bought a couple of bottles of booze. If we were going to celebrate, this was the day. In our minds were vague rumors that the Dodgers might not be around too much longer. O'Malley was making waves, complaining about not having enough parking facilities.

"Anyway, everytime the Yankees get up and don't score, we have a drink, and every time the Dodgers do something, we have a drink. By the end of the game you'd have thought I was stoking up with bituminous coal, because the fog was coming out of my ears, and this paint salesman, a young Jewish fellow, was keeping right up with me.

"When the game was over, the salesman and I wandered out into Prospect Avenue, each of us holding a tumbler full of rotgut, Old Panther Piss, and we went out there to raise our hands up to the Sun God to give our thanksgiving. The Dodgers had finally beaten the Yankees.

"All up and down Prospect Avenue, there were screams. Stuff flew out of windows. I saw a telephone come flying out of one home. Garbage cans were being knocked over. Car horns were blaring. And all of a sudden, as I stood in the middle of Prospect Avenue, I felt this tugging at my waist. I looked around, and the salesman had pulled my pants down around my ankles. So I stepped out of my pants, and I pulled his pants down, and we threw our pants into the doorway of the store, and in our underwear we started goose-stepping up the middle of Prospect Avenue. I heard a woman say, 'GlorybetoGod, you ought to be ashamed of yourself,' but I looked down to see—nothing was hanging out—and mind you, no one else seemed to notice. All everyone was doing was running over to us and shouting over and over, 'We did it. We did it,' slapping us on the back.

"Brooklyn went crazy. Harold Strongreen climbed a light pole, and he hung an effigy of the Yankees from it while all the women knelt in prayer that he wouldn't kill himself.

"All the women were standing at the bottom of the pole, holding their rosaries, and they were screaming, 'Come down, Harold. If you die, we're not covered. The kids, Harold. What about the kids?' Harold didn't care. He was half-looped. What a sight: A paunchy forty-year-old man pulling a huge dummy up a light pole on a rope! It was like VJ Day, and come to think of it, Harold Strongreen climbed the same light pole then and hung an effigy of Hirohito.

"That night nobody ate at home. If you were walking the streets, you'd have thought it was the San Gennaro festival. People brought the food into the streets. There were dozens of block parties. They brought little electric stoves outside, cooking hamburgers in the streets. They brought out growlers of beer. And mind you, you could go to Williamsburg or to Garrison Beach or any other neighborhood in Brooklyn, and people were doing the same thing. People were marching across the Brooklyn Bridge in celebration. We had had the idea of marching up to Yankee Stadium and setting it on fire. Luckily someone talked us out of it. We did go to Ebbets Field that night, however, in our cars. We drove up McKeever Place, down Bedford Avenue, blowing our horns, throwing paper up in the air, buying drinks at local bars.

"I got so loaded that night that when I came home I didn't even notice whether my wife was home. I just collapsed onto the bed and went to sleep. Tell ya, it was a night to remember."

Don Honig: "I was living in Maspeth, Queens, near Long Island City, a big Dodger neighborhood. I was watching the game on television, and as the last out was made, I ran out of the house and down the street to a local barbershop, which was a haven for Dodger fans. In the streets cars were honking, and people were getting drunk and waving Dodger pennants and screaming with joy.

"Right in the middle of this were a couple of Yankee fans standing in the back of a big convertible, and they were holding up a sign that read: 'Let the cocksuckers win one.'

"That win was very important to the borough, to a few million fans who had been rooting for what had probably been the best team in baseball for all those years. If we had beaten Cleveland or the Red Sox, it wouldn't have meant nearly as much. It was as though we were climbing a mountain, and when we won that World Series, that was the top of the mountain.

"And it wasn't simply a fan's delight. It was almost as though you were finding your manhood at stake. You rooted for this team, and every October it would die. And when you put the win in the context of a small neighborhood, where your personal relationships were very tight, it became even more important. The Yankee fans and Giant fans were always ribbing you, saying that you choked. Dodger fans very well knew the sentiments of the mythical Man on the Street. He knew that it was said that the Dodgers choked every

October, and what the hell were you going to say? They did lose every October.

"But finally we won one, and it meant an awful lot, not just for the ten bucks you had on the Series or that my team had won the World Series, but that we had beaten the Yankees, and we were better men for it.

"I know all this sounds so superficial—your team won, so what? A nonfan could not conceive of how important it was. But baseball was an important factor in my neighborhood. For twelve months a year, it was baseball and little else. Everyone knew who you rooted for before they knew your religion or nationality. It was important to you that your team did well. Baseball was very important, and rooting for the Brooklyn Dodgers was something special."

On October 8, 1955, a few days after the Dodgers had won the Series, in a Queens bar, William Christman, an off-duty cop and a Dodger fan, got into an argument with Robert Thompson, a Yankee fan. As they argued they got hotter and hotter, and they went out into the street to continue it. Thompson, the archetypical sore-losing Yankee fan, took out his revolver and shot Christman dead. He couldn't stand the thought that the Yankees had lost even once.

JOEL OPPENHEIMER: "Yankee fans had an essential meanness, like God owed them the world championship, and that if they weren't in the Series, it ain't a Series.

"Dodger fans got beaten down so often that there was an essential humility and an understanding that Yankee fans never had. Yankee fans don't understand that the world is not a very nice place to live, that more bad things happen to you than good things. When you understand this, you appreciate the good things that do happen, and you're more apt to take it easy on the other guy who's having a tough time of it.

"Dodger fans through the years learned that there was more to the game than just winning. They learned to care about excellence, even if it's someone else's excellence. Stan Musial often got standing ovations at Ebbets Field.

"Because the Dodger fans had to fight so long to become champion after coming so close so many times, when it finally did happen, they realized it was wonderful."

14

A Gift

In the spring and summer of 1956, Brooklyn's supremacy seemed at an end. The year before, the young Braves had finished thirteen and a half games behind the Dodgers. Now it looked as if they would surpass the aging veterans. The Braves were led by twenty-two-year-old outfield star Henry Aaron and young veterans Ed Mathews at third base and Joe Adcock at first. On the mound veteran Warren Spahn, spitball ace Lew Burdette, and lanky Bob Buhl kept the Braves atop the National League as the end of September neared.

For the Dodgers, who had trailed by as many as six games, there was a fear that age had finally caught up with them.

The one bright event of the spring occurred on May 12, when Carl Erskine, who in his ninth season was suffering worse arm miseries than ever, pitched his second no-hit game, a 3–0 victory over the New York Giants.

CARL ERSKINE: "I was struggling with really serious arm trouble. I had pitched a long time with problems, and they had caused more problems. The day before we opened the series with the Giants, I was in Chicago. My arm had a large knot in the back, and psychologically I was feeling real bad. I had been to our own trainer so much that I was embarrassed to go back and say, 'Doc, it still hurts.' Al Shinneman, the trainer for the Cubs, had formerly been with the Dodgers at St. Paul, so I knew him. I called him and said, 'Al, I got a real problem with my arm. I don't know what to do.' He said, 'I'll come up,' and he came up to the hotel. This is the opposing trainer now. He came up to my room, looked at my shoulder, felt it, said, 'Oh brother, you really have a spasm in there. It's bad.' He said, 'Listen, Bob Rush has had some arm trouble, and our club doctor has worked on him and helped him. I'd like to take you to see our club doctor.' I said, 'That would be unusual.' He said, 'That's all right. That's no problem.' So he made arrangements, and I went to see this doctor, and he said, 'You have a bad spasm in there. I'd like to give you an injection and relax that.' I said, 'Oh no. No needles for me.' I was upset with the doctor a little. He said, 'Hey, you came for help. I'm telling you what you need, and now you're going to refuse it?' He got a little irritated. I didn't mean to do that, but I said, 'Well, this is something new for me. Sticking a needle in my shoulder?' He said, 'Here's what will happen . . .' and he convinced me, and I told him to go ahead. So he shot a procaine and cortisone combination in there, and he said, 'I had to force that cortisone in thick, so you're going to be pretty sore for a couple of days, in addition to the soreness you already have.' Well, I didn't tell him I was scheduled to pitch the next day. I just went on my way. Back in the room I don't know if Snider, my roommate, even knew what I had done.

"We played day games in Chicago, and we weren't leaving until later, so he and Reese, Zimmer, and Labine were going bowling, and they said, 'C'mon with us.' I said, 'I can't bowl. Are you kidding?' They said, 'Hey, that broken arm of yours. It won't affect it.' So I went with these guys and bowled a couple of games. I figured, maybe this will loosen me up or help my arm.

"The next day we're back in New York, and I'm heading for the ballpark, and I can hardly lift my arm. Plus I made a bad mistake, I bought a newspaper, and I'm reading about Tom Sheehan, the chief scout for the Giants, saying, 'The Dodgers are over the hill. Campanella's too old. Snider's old, Robinson's old, and Erskine can't win with the garbage he's been throwing up there.' Boy, I read that, and I said to myself, 'The bad part is, he's right.'

"So I go to the park, and Alston walks over and brings me a new ball, and I was tempted to hand it back to him and say, 'You ought to give me another day because the arm's a little tender,' but somehow I couldn't do that. It was near time to warm up, and I went out onto the field, sat on the bench, looked at the crowd coming in, thinking, 'I'm going to cheat these people today, because they are paying to see a major league pitcher. I don't even know if I can warm up!' That's the state of mind I was in. But I grouped myself together and said, 'Carl, you've tried to develop some inner strength in your life, and you'd better lean on that.' I said, 'Lord, if I'm here for a reason, you know it and I don't; I'll do what I can, but I don't have much to offer.'

"I was pitching against Al Worthington, who was having a pretty good day himself. Through the first six innings, there wasn't any score. And I'm amazed every time I finish an inning! Each time I go back to the bench, I'm absolutely dumbfounded that I'm still pitching. And in the seventh, we got three runs. I pitched the eighth, got the side out, and on my way to the bench, the guys are running by me, hitting me on the rump, not saying anything, and I go in on the bench, and the realization comes. The leather-lunged fans are yelling at me that the Giants don't have any hits! It was just an awesome experience for me to be through eight innings and not give any hits. And man, I didn't think I had much, but it was like the good Lord was saying, 'You've asked for it. What did you expect?'

"And a strange thing happened. My glove broke in the eighth inning. The webbing split. One of the strands broke loose, which happens occasionally. There wasn't time to fix it, and Don Bessent used the same model glove, though it's like a pair of shoes, you break them in quite different. I borrowed his glove, even though it felt strange, and I took it out to pitch the last couple innings with it.

"In the ninth I was pitching to Whitey Lockman, and he had hit a high drive that cleared the foul pole screen several feet foul. I threw Lockman a good overhand curveball, and he hit a shot back right straight back at me through the middle on the ground, a hugger. I went down to get the ball, and I was aware immediately that I didn't field it, I didn't get it in the glove. Instead I pinned the ball to the ground with the back of the glove, dead. It didn't squirt to the side or anything. And when I raised my glove, it was laying there like an Easter egg. I picked it up and threw him out easy. But that ball could have been a base hit easy. Dark was the last hitter, and he fouled off two fastballs inside, and he just topped a curveball back to me, an easy one-hopper.

"I had my no-hitter. But it was the last breath of the old guard."

Erskine finished 13–11 in '56, mediocre for him. Of the other starters, second-year pitcher Roger Craig was winning as many as he was losing. A large, six-six rookie named Don Drysdale showed promise as a strikeout pitcher, but because of inexperience, he too only won as many as he lost. Don Newcombe, who toward the end of June had a 9–5 record, was virtually alone keeping the Dodgers close to the top. The Dodgers had the pitching shorts, and it was hurting them badly.

In mid-May the general manager of the Cleveland Indians, Hank Greenberg, called Buzzy Bavasi to discuss the second of two exhibition games the Dodgers and Indians were to play. The first had been played a few days before. During the conversation Greenberg told Bavasi that he was stuck with one starting pitcher too many. The Indians had Early Wynn, Herb Score, Bob Lemon, Mike Garcia, and Art Houtteman, not to mention Bob Feller, who they wanted to drop but didn't dare because he was such a Cleveland idol, and Brooklyn nemesis, former New York Giant Sal Maglie, whom the Indians had acquired the year before and rarely used. Maglie had injured his back in '55, and when he stopped winning, the Giants quickly dumped him. But he hadn't shown the Indians much, until the Jersey City exhibition game against the Dodgers. Bavasi called Walt Alston and then Pee Wee Reese to ask them whether he should buy Maglie, who for years had been a hated enemy with the Giants, and with their enthusiastic blessing, the purchase was made.

Dodger fans had hated Maglie almost as much as Leo Durocher. He was sinister-looking, with dark, hooded eyes, and a heavy beard. And he pitched mean. His nickname was Sal the Barber because his pitches came so close to opposing batters. Durocher often would say, "I came to kill ya," and Maglie pitched as though he were carrying out Durocher's order. It was a rare game that Maglie pitched against the Dodgers when two or three Dodger batters didn't end up eating dirt. For years Maglie was a symbol of all that Brooklyn detested about the scurrilous and loathsome Giants.

RON GREEN: "I hated Maglie. I had gone as a kid to almost every game Maglie pitched. I would go all the way from Brooklyn, take the subway for an hour and a half to see them beat Maglie. I loved to go to the Polo Grounds, because all the Giant fans were there, and we would sit and razz them, but inevitably, by the fourth or fifth inning, our heads would be between our knees.

"Maglie was our archenemy. And he would constantly shut us out. He would murder our right-handed hitters, absolutely murder them, curveball them to death, brush them back off the plate. He'd make guys like Hodges and Campanella want to cry. A mean pitcher. Good, though, very talented. But Maglie always was an archenemy.

"It was different back then. Your ballclub was your life. There are no great loyalties with ballplayers. It has all changed. As kids we all had our ballplayer. I was a great lover of Clem Labine. You just sort of hooked on to somebody. It's hard to say why really. A friend of mine liked Gil Hodges. Another was a Duke Snider fan. We all had our favorites, and we lived and died with them.

"And when Maglie came to the Dodgers, I was shocked. I was stunned when he came to Brooklyn."

Through the first month, as Alston used him as a spot starter, the thirty-nine-year-old Maglie struggled to regain his form. At the end of July, the pitching situation had deteriorated so that Alston inserted Maglie into the regular rotation. In the final days of July, he beat the Cubs a complete game, and from then until the end of the season, he started fifteen games for Brooklyn, winning ten and losing only two, and the two he lost were by the scores of 3–2 and 2–1. His earned run average during that stretch was 1.88. In the three games in which he didn't get a decision, he gave up two earned runs. He finished the year 13–5 with a 2.89 earned run average.

Before Maglie began pitching regularly, it didn't seem as though the Dodgers would be able to catch Milwaukee. But with Newcombe almost unbeatable, and Clem Labine winning ten and saving nineteen, Maglie became the unlikely catalyst to the pennant.

In early September Maglie fought the Braves, leading 2–1 in the seventh. Eddie Mathews's home run had given Milwaukee its one run. Maglie had driven in the Dodgers' two runs himself with a bases-loaded single.

In the eighth, with two outs, there was a Milwaukee runner on third, with Mathews coming to the bat. Alston walked out to the mound. "What do you want to do?" Alston asked. "I've got a couple of relief pitchers ready if you're tired."

"I got to pitch to this guy," Maglie said. Alston walked back to the dugout.

Mathews grounded wide of second, Gilliam made a graceful backhand stab and threw to Hodges for the third out. The ninth was a snap, and Maglie had another win.

Two weeks later, on September 25, the Dodgers hosted the Philadelphia Phillies. The Dodgers were still a half game behind the Braves, with four to play. The Braves had three to go. Maglie pitched for the Dodgers. It was an unusual game in that the Dodgers scored some early runs for Maglie, three in the second and two more in the third. Maglie did the rest. He walked pitcher Jack Meyer in the third and Puddin' Head Jones in the eighth, and he hit Richie Ashburn in the foot in the ninth, but that was all the Phils got. They didn't get a single hit.

* * *

Sal Maglie: "I had real good control, moved the ball around, and there weren't any balls hit that were questionable. Pee Wee made one play coming across the infield, picking up and throwing to first base, the only close one. He made a beautiful play out of that. You have to do that to pitch no-hitters. You can't strike enough of them out, because I didn't throw that hard. Just in and out and low.

"And in the ninth, I got two outs, and I hit Ashburn in the foot, and he was the right man to put on base, because he was the one I thought was apt to get a base hit. He splatters that ball all over the place. And I didn't care that I hit him. The last batter was Marv Blaylock, the first baseman. In fact, the first time up, he hit the best ball, he lined out to Amoros in left field. This time I threw him an outside curveball. He tried to pull it, and he hit a slow grounder down to Gilliam. And I'll never forget the last ball hit down to second base. I didn't think it would ever get there for the second baseman to throw him out.

"The no-hitter turned out to be easy. In fact Red Smith mentioned in the paper that it was the easiest no-hitter he had ever seen. That kind of made me feel pretty good. And after I got the last out, the guys came over and picked me up. And then I went to the clubhouse, and I went home.

"Yeah, I used to beat the Dodgers. That was my job. When you play professional ball, that's your job. I've always been a competitor, and I don't like to lose. And when they were on the field playing against us, they were out to break your neck too. If you're a professional, you say, 'Well, I'm going to win some ballgames.'

"I liked to beat the Dodgers. Jackie used to try to needle me a lot. He didn't say anything to me, but he would come out in the paper with it. Every time I would beat him, he would say that I was cheating or scratching up the ball or something, which was not true. But he could say whatever he wanted. My job was to get him out. I didn't get mad. I'm not that type. I'd just bear down more, and if I saw him quiet and not making too much of a ruckus, I let him alone, let him sleep. I never woke him up, because he could beat you by himself, and I was the same way. The more they'd rip me, the more I just had that little bit extra.

"To this day I don't know why the Giants traded me. You have to ask Stoneham about that. Afterwards, we'd go to Toots Shor's and have dinner, and Toots would always rib Stoneham because he traded me, which he shouldn't have done. But I think they thought I had had it. And I'm glad it worked out the way it did. But I didn't know anything about the trade. I don't ask questions. I just went, and that was it.

"And at Cleveland I didn't get to pitch. I wanted to, but I didn't get much of a chance. Al Lopez was the manager, and I can't tell you why he didn't pitch me. He had his men there who had carried him throughout, and he gave me one or two chances, but I can't get in shape that way.

"When I first went to the Dodgers, Alston asked me if I wanted to pitch against the Giants, and I told him I wasn't ready yet, but if he wanted me

George Brace Photo

SAL MAGLIE

to, I would. So he said, 'Let me know when you are ready.' So I started throwing batting practice, and kept throwing every day till I did get in shape. Took me about a week.

"And even though the Dodgers fought me hard when I was with the Giants, I don't carry a grudge with players, because that's their job. And when I got to the Dodgers, they were pretty good. In fact Carl Furillo became one of my best friends on the club. He was the first one I met at the door when I walked in. He said, 'Glad you're here.' Later Jackie came over, and he said, 'We don't have a chance to win this.' I said, 'That's not so. We have a lot of games to go yet.' And it turned out that everything worked out.

"I remember a game in Philadelphia in early July. I went in to relieve. That was the beginning. The first man up, the pitcher, Roberts, got a base hit off me. So Jackie Robinson came over and said, 'Now you're ready to go. They broke the ice and got a hit off you.' So I calmed down and pitched the rest of the way quite well. I pitched regularly after that. And I pitched a no-hitter."

RON GREEN: "It was funny. There was reaction when Maglie pitched the no-hitter, but it was not like one of your own doing it. He was like a foreigner who won a game for the team you rooted for, but it wasn't like Carl Erskine pitching a no-hitter. I saw Erskine's no-hitter against the Cubs. I cut school that day. I was going to Erasmus Hall, and four of us cut school, walked through Prospect Park, and went to Ebbets Field.

"But you never had the sense that Maglie was a part of being Brooklyn. He came from somewhere else. It was great that he threw a no-hitter, but if one of our own had done it, it would have been better. After all, he was a Giant in a Dodger uniform.

"And on top of it, he became a Yankee, which compounded the felony."

But in '56, before Maglie was dealt away, he made the pennant possible.

The day after his no-hitter, Robin Roberts beat Newcombe 7–3. There were three final games against the lowly Pittsburgh Pirates. The Braves, meanwhile, one game ahead, had to face St. Louis, which had that great infield of Musial, Don Blasingame, Al Dark, and Ken Boyer.

The next day a September rain washed out the game in Brooklyn, while the Braves got beat 5–4. A Saturday doubleheader was scheduled to make up the Dodger game. This was another break for Brooklyn. Alston had planned to start Roger Craig, but because of the one-day layoff, he was able to go with Maglie instead, and Maglie, who had a lifetime record of 21–5 against the Pirates, won the first game 6–2.

In the second game, Alston started Clem Labine. In his entire career, Labine appeared in 513 games, and he started but 38 times. Dressen had picked Labine to start Game Two of the '51 playoffs, and Clem had pitched a 10–0 shutout, and then in '55 Alston had given Clem another start, and he had won, and so for the third time in his illustrious career, Labine was commandeered from the bullpen and given the ball at the start of a crucial game. Labine pitched a seven-hitter and won 3 to 1. In St. Louis the Cards' Herman Wehmeier beat the Braves 2 to 1.

Incredibly, with one game remaining, the Braves had folded their tepee. Brooklyn was in first place by one game.

The finale was played on a sunny Sunday in Brooklyn. Alston chose Don Newcombe, with his 26–7 record and his strong right arm, and though the game ended Dodgers 8, Pirates 6, it wasn't nearly as close as the score might suggest. Duke Snider hit two towering home runs and made a spectacular catch to snuff a rally, and Jackie Robinson also hit a home run to give the Dodgers a 7–2 lead. Newcombe, who had a perplexing habit of becoming careless with a big lead, allowed a three-run triple by Bill Virdon and a solo homer by Lee Walls.

Alston brought in young Don Bessent who struck out pinch hitter Hank Foiles for the third out in the ninth at 4:30 P.M. Once again the Dodgers of Brooklyn were champions of the National League, their sixth time in nine years.

Dale Mitchell's Day

The first four games of the '56 World Series repeated the pattern of '55—in reverse. Playing the opening two in Ebbets Field, the Dodgers won them both, behind Maglie and Don Bessent, who got the win in the second game when Don Newcombe got knocked about for six runs in only two innings, the final four on a Yogi Berra grand slam. The Dodgers won Game Two 13–8 and were led by Duke Snider, who hit a Tommy Byrne fastball into Bedford Avenue with two men on. After the game Don Newcombe was walking to get his car, and the parking lot attendant was cheeky enough to say to the big pitcher, "You never can win the big ones. You're a choke." Newcombe slugged the imprudent car jockey and drove home.

Back at the Stadium, the Yankees won Games Three and Four. Mickey Mantle, who had homered in the first game, hit a towering drive off Ed Roebuck in the fourth game to help the Yankees tie the Series.

ED ROEBUCK: "I threw a hanging sinker to Mantle in the '56 Series, and he didn't try to pull it. It went right back over my head and over Duke's head. Duke didn't even turn. It went to the right of the 467 marker, over the monuments. That guy was awesome. Nobody, not even Richie Allen, had the strength of Mantle. I know Ruth was strong, but I think this guy was stronger. And he did it from both sides."

Game Five, also scheduled for the Stadium, featured Sal Maglie against Don Larsen in a duel which would symbolize forever the frustrations of rooting for the Dodgers. Here was a pivotal game in which the Dodger pitcher pitched no-hit ball for seven of the nine innings he performed. But with two outs in the fourth inning, Maglie allowed Mantle a cheap home run into the lower right-field stands. The homer was followed by a single. In the sixth he allowed a second run on three hits.

No other Yankee reached base in any of the other seven innings. In the eighth, Maglie's last inning of work, he faced Larsen, then Bauer, then Collins, and with a flourish he struck them out one after the other. It was a special performance by a great pitcher in the twilight of his career, a performance remembered by few, because on that day the Yankee pitcher, Larsen, pitched a perfect game, twenty-seven men up, twenty-seven down, the only such performance in the history of the World Series. For the final out, umpire Babe Pinelli called Dodger pinch hitter Dale Mitchell out on a pitch that appeared to be high and outside.

Ed Roebuck: "I remember being in the bullpen with Dixie Howell, who was the third-string catcher, and it was about the seventh inning. And I remember Dixie saying, 'I hope the guy does it.' And it didn't shock me, because I felt the same way. I said, 'Yeah, Dix, I do too.' And I never thought he would, but I do remember feeling that way.

"And Billy Herman didn't give one sign during the entire game. Which is unusual. Herman was the Dodger third-base coach, and Larsen had Pee Wee 3–1 in the first inning, and he didn't give him the take sign. He let him hit, and that was the only chance he had to give a sign. The rest of the time, nobody was on base, and Larsen never got behind anybody.

"The thing built up to a tremendous climax. And when he did it, I remember thinking, a perfect game. He did something that will never be beaten. It'll be tied, maybe, but to be able to say to yourself, 'I did something no one will ever do better,' it's quite a mark to make."

Carl Furillo: "I don't think I realized he had a no-hitter till the sixth or seventh inning. I remember the last time up, I was the first batter in the ninth inning, and it seemed that every ball he threw was right down the middle, and I fouled off four balls, and I was just getting myself set, and here comes what looked to me like a quick pitch. And well, I popped the ball up to the right fielder.

"I can't say the guy pitched a terrific game. It seemed that every time we would hit the ball, it seemed like it was right at somebody. The infield, the outfield did a hell of a job for him. But you can't take it away from him. He pitched good ball."

Roy Campanella: "I was the second out. He had been pitching me away, and I said, 'I'm gonna try and get a ball away from me and hit it to right center field and get on.' I hit it that way, but it wasn't far enough out over the plate. I didn't hit it good, and I hit a ground ball to the second baseman. I didn't get the good wood on it."

Dale Mitchell: "I came to Brooklyn during the 1956 season after nine and a half seasons with Cleveland. I wasn't doing that well with Cleveland, and Brooklyn was looking for a left-handed hitter. And I was very happy to go to Brooklyn because, number one, it was a pennant contender, and number two, it was a pennant contender.

"When Alston sent me up to hit for Maglie, there were two out in the ninth, but I went up there thinking I was going to get a base hit. I knew Larsen from the American League. The twenty-six in a row, the perfect game, that didn't really sink in until the game was over, because when it was that close and the score was still only 2–0, we still felt we had a chance. We knew he had a no-hitter, but how often did it happen that one man gets a base hit and the pitcher falls apart? That happens so often. We were so close that we really felt we were going to win it.

"I took the first pitch, and then I probably had as good a ball to hit as anyone had all day. It was a hanging curveball, but I fouled it off.

"The count went to 2–2, and Larsen threw me a pitch, high and outside, and umpire Babe Pinelli called it a strike, and it was not a strike, but like the man said, 'It was close enough for him to call.' I had labored under the delusion all those years that it was either over the plate or it isn't. I guess when you get in a situation like that . . . No, I didn't think it was a strike, but I looked around, and there wasn't anybody to discuss it with. I went to the clubhouse. After all, everybody else did. No reason for me to stand out there by myself."

SAL MAGLIE: "I wished we had played in Ebbets Field the game that Larsen beat me, 'cause we hit some mighty long balls that were caught. In our ballpark I don't believe they would have beat me. Mantle's home run was 310 feet, 'cause it's only a four-foot fence there, and it wouldn't have been a home run in Ebbets Field. The ball he hit would probably have been a double off the wall, and it might have been a different game altogether. And the other one was a cheap run. Carey was on second, and the ball went out to left, and they let him go on all the way through to home, and Amoros fumbled the ball a little bit. Didn't matter anyway.

"And as Larsen was going along, I didn't think anything of it. They took me out for a pinch hitter in the ninth. In fact I hit a line drive over second base that Mantle caught. I imagine he was playing in a little bit. I think if I had gotten that one hit, it would have been a different ballgame. I didn't care about his no-hitter. All I was thinking about was winning the ballgame.

"And so in the ninth, Alston had to take me out and use a pinch hitter, Dale Mitchell. I'm a pitcher, not a hitter. And when Pinelli called strike three, I thought it was a ball, high outside. It wasn't even close. But it's something the umpire called. Dale did make an attempt to swing at it, but he didn't really. He held back, so I guess Pinelli didn't see it the way I did, 'cause I know damn well Yogi knew it was a ball. I kidded with him about its being a ball, and he just laughed. But you can't argue. He called it, and that was it."

DON HONIG: "I could have gone to the game. A friend of mine had an extra seat, but I didn't want to go. I didn't want to have to go to Yankee Stadium and face 70,000 Yankee fans. And that night he came home and said, 'Aren't

George Brace Photo

DALE MITCHELL

you just eating your heart out? Didn't you miss something?' I said, 'No, a Goddamn Yankee pitched a perfect game. Why would I want to be there? You wanted me to be there? I'm delighted I wasn't there. Fuck history.' "

JOEL OPPENHEIMER: "It was one more instance of God treating us badly. Of all people, why should Don Larsen have been the one to do it. Like Casey Stengel said, 'I got my drunk.' Why should he do it? Why shouldn't Don Newcombe have pitched a perfect game? That would have been justice. Don Larsen? Never."

Don Newcombe's Legacy

The final two games were played at Ebbets Field. Once again a manager chose Clem Labine to start a crucial game, and once again Clem Labine pitched heroically. For ten innings Labine and Yankee pitcher Bob Turley battled to a scoreless tie.

Then in the eleventh, Junior Gilliam walked to lead off. Reese made a sacrifice bunt to send Gilliam to second. One out. Snider was walked intentionally. Runners on first and second. The batter was Jackie Robinson, arguably the greatest player of the decade and arguably the greatest clutch performer who ever lived. There were rumors that this would be Robinson's final year. He had been quoted as saying, "If you think Rickey was cheap, you should see O'Malley." Fighting words to the Dodger management.

Turley wound up and threw, and Robinson lined a ball deep into left field. Enos Slaughter had been playing shallow to prevent Reese from scoring on a ground single, and before he could turn, the ball was over his head and bouncing along the grass, and Gilliam was racing for home with the winning run. Thanks to Robinson, again, the Dodgers were still in it.

The seventh game was a travesty. It was over almost before it began. The Yankees started a twenty-one-year-old kid named Johnny Kucks, and Alston went with his best, Don Newcombe. Kucks allowed three hits and no runs. Objectively it wouldn't have made a whit of difference whatever Newcombe did. Without a run the Dodgers wouldn't have won. But Newcombe opened himself up to scorn and derision, even after winning twenty-seven regular season games. In the first and third, Yogi Berra hit two-run home runs, and in the fourth Elston Howard hit a home run to make it 5–0. When Roger Craig allowed a grand slam home run to Bill Skowron in the seventh, it was Yankees 9, Dodgers 0. It was Big Don's fourth consecutive loss in the World Series, and he has gone down in history as the pitcher who "couldn't win the big ones." It became an oft-repeated epitaph that drove the gruff but sensitive Dodger right-hander to alcohol and right out of baseball. He had won twenty-seven games in 1956, but after the World Series, at age thirty, when he should have been at the top of his game, Don Newcombe never pitched successfully again.

After Newk was knocked out in the seventh game, Milton Gross rode home with him and filed the following column in the *New York Post.*

> It is only 35 miles and 70 minutes between Ebbets Field and Colonia, N.J., but for Don Newcombe it was a lifetime. This was his longest voyage home and he wept all the way.
>
> Only Newcombe knew the gnawing pain within him, the doubts, the anger, the confusion and frustration of the pitcher who was reached for two home runs by Yogi Berra and one by Elston Howard, which beat the Dodgers yesterday.
>
> But it was more than the game and the Series that went with it, more than being Ko'ed by the Yankees twice within a week and five times in a career. It was so much more than the conviction that he had good stuff and threw hard and courageously. It was a man being torn apart worse inwardly than he was on the field by forces beyond his control. It was a giant of a man, who needed the comforting of a child.
>
> "It's tough, Newk," said a guy standing in the parking lot as we came to Don's car, "but you can't win them all."
>
> Last week Newcombe hit a man who needled him as he entered his car, but this time the words didn't seem to touch him.
>
> "I'm sorry, pop," Don mumbled as we drove away.
>
> His voice was so low, his father couldn't hear.
>
> "What?" he asked.
>
> "I'm sorry," Don repeated.
>
> "What have you got to be sorry for?" James Newcombe said to his son.
>
> What indeed? What could Newcombe say or what could his father say? And what are they saying today? That he doesn't win the big ones . . . that he chokes when it's tough . . . that he showered hurriedly and left the field as quickly as he could after being replaced in the fourth and left his teammates to their despair.

After dropping off Newcombe's father, Gross asked Newcombe what he had been thinking about during the entire ride.

> "I was thinking about what I do wrong," he said, "but I can't put my finger on why I do it. It always happens to me in the first two innings or the last."
>
> For a moment Newk sat silent again. "I was running in the outfield at the Stadium the other day and a guy called me a yellow-bellied slob. How do you take things like that?
>
> "Today," Newk said, "before the game, Pee Wee said: 'I don't care what you do today. We wouldn't be here without you.'
>
> "And other people say I choke up," Newk said in a voice hoarse with emotion. "I think it's rubbed off in the clubhouse."
>
> "How did you sleep last night?" I asked.
>
> "Terrible," he said. "I was up four times. I took a pill but I couldn't sleep. I told my wife what's the use keeping you awake. She said for me

to go in the other room, but I tossed and turned. It wasn't today's game. It was this other business I wanted to beat, but dammit, I can't get away from it."

We were at East Milton and Fulton in Rahway when I got out of the car. There were five boys on the corner—four Negro and one white—and they recognized Newcombe as he drove off.

"That Newk?" one asked.

"How'd he get here so soon?" another said. "The game just ended."

"He left early," I said, and the white boy giggled.

"Don't laugh," one of the Negro boys said. "Just don't laugh."

DON NEWCOMBE: "No big deal if you get beat by the Yankees. The important thing was to play the Yankees, and that's what we did. We won pennants in 1947, '49, '52, '53, '55, '56, always playing the Yankees. Hell, the Yankees had a great ballclub. People said I choked up in the World Series, couldn't win the big games. What the hell is the big game? If you win twenty games during the season, twenty-seven one year, what in the world is a big game? I don't know. Dick Young started that business about not being able to win the big ones. He said, 'Newk, I was only trying to focus attention on important games as writers saw them. There was no way that I was going to infer anything about you choking up, about you being afraid in important games. But some of the other writers picked it up and took it all out of context.' And there in the World Series you get the shit kicked out of you by the world-famous New York Yankees, and now it's a big deal. Newk chokes up again. In 1956 I won twenty-seven games. I was 27 and 7! We win the pennant, and because in the World Series Yogi Berra hits a couple of home runs off me, they say I choke up. You know, that knocked the hell out of me that year. That's when I started drinking. That's where my whole career came to an end. Really to an end. Because there I was, twenty-seven games, I won the Most Valuable Player award, the Cy Young Award, the best pitcher in baseball, and then somebody goes and harps on the fact that I don't win the big games because they beat us in the World Series? I could never understand that. Never could figure that out. Then I began to say, 'The hell with it,' and then my career started down, and four years later I was out of the major leagues.

"First of all look at the money I could have made after winning twenty-seven games that season, just traveling around speaking in the wintertime, making endorsements. You know what I did? I went over to New Jersey and crawled into a shell and stayed there. I couldn't go stand up in front of a bunch of kids and have them ask me, 'What does it mean, Mr. Newcombe, when they say you choke up?' How can I explain that to kids? So I said to myself, 'I'm not even going to go out and speak to any of them. I'm not going to do anything.' I went out, and I played golf, and I got drunk. Gained a lot of weight. 'The hell with it.' That was where my head went. Instead of being a confident baseball player, here I was the top of the big leagues, the best pitcher in baseball, the Most Valuable Player in the National League, ready to come back the next year and be great, what did I do? Came back in '57 and had a lousy year. Lousy. Because I didn't give a Goddamn. And I think it helped destroy my baseball career. That winter after the 1956 World Series, I went to Japan, and I screwed up over there. I drank the whole time I was over there. I got in trouble with the owner, got in trouble with the manager, got in trouble with my wife—everybody. Because of the way I was treated in the press, because somebody felt I was scared in not being able to win a World Series game. Everybody talked about my getting taken out of the final game in 1951 in the ninth inning, but nobody said one thing about what I did for the two weeks leading up to that playoff game. I pitched in the ninth inning. I gave the Dodgers everything I had. I was leading 4 to 1. And they say I choked up because I left in the ninth inning? Other pitchers get in trouble. That's what you have relief pitchers for. If I was gonna choke up, I would have choked up in the second or third inning. I wouldn't have pitched the game that I pitched if I was afraid of the Giants, afraid of the game. But nobody gave me credit for it, nobody gave me credit at all for it, especially the press. They tore my ass up. And those are the things I'll always live with, that I'll always have in my life."

Carl Erskine: "Newk is a guy who has never gotten his due. I'm no psychologist, but I've lived long enough to see how things happen. What is remembered about who is sometimes almost a fluke. No one got more mileage out of their career than I have, but I did not have a Hall of Fame career. I played during an interesting time with a fantastic group of people, and I loved every minute that I was in the major leagues. Everybody was my friend—umpires, writers, clubhouse boys, bell captains, cab drivers. People were exceptionally kind to me. They always have been.

"Newcombe, on the other hand, had difficulty in trying to handle his personality traits, but was just as sensitive a guy as I was, just as appreciative. The reason I know that was something that happened in '54. He had been gone two years, pitched a little bit in the service, but hadn't done very well. He's back in the big leagues, and I opened the season that year against Pittsburgh. I beat them 6–1 opening day, which is always a big thrill. Then we go right across town and open up the Giants at the Polo Grounds, and Newcombe is the pitcher for us. Newcombe beats the Giants that day, and I go right over to Newk and congratulate him. Newk turned away from me, kind of pulled away from me, and went up the steps to the trainer's room. I said, 'I'll be darned. What the heck?' Newk had a way of turning you off sometimes. I said, 'I don't know what's in that guy,' and I went about my business. A few minutes later, Newcombe comes back to my locker and he says, 'Hey, Ersk. Thank you. I just had to get out of there.' He had been crying because of the emotion of being back, winning a ballgame, he's back on the club, all that. Now that told me that Newcombe was a very sensitive person, and it helped me understand him better. But the writers found Newk defiant, haughty, and unavailable, and not congenial.

"In '56 Newk was really awesome. He won twenty-seven games. And in my opinion, he has not gotten his due, has not achieved the stature which he deserves. Nobody thinks of Newcombe when they start talking about great games, great years. Sure, he'll get a mention, but he is not held in the esteem he should. Number one, he had to fight some of the same battles Jackie did. So he did this along with that load.

"Newk had a temper, but it was a defense, a lack of self-confidence that caused him to come on strong at the wrong times. Snider used to tell him, 'Newcombe, you're always loud and wrong.' He wasn't, but he came on that way.

"It's too bad, but Newcombe came close to brilliance and being remembered so, but he never quite got there. I'll give you an example. Newcombe had asked to pitch a doubleheader on occasion. He wanted to pitch both games. And in 1950, in Philadelphia, Shotton let him. Newcombe pitches the first game and throws a minimum number of pitches and beats the Phillies, and so he starts in the second game, and he would have won that easy, except we couldn't get him any runs. And he came out in the eighth inning tied or losing by a run, and we finally won it, but Newcombe could have won a doubleheader, and he would have been the only modern-day pitcher to pitch and win two complete games on the same day. He could have done that, but we didn't get him any runs. It wasn't his fault. But he doesn't get that credit because it didn't happen.

"If you look at his record, he was the first outstanding black pitcher in baseball and an awesome pitcher. If Newcombe had not had two years away in the service, he could very well have been a Hall of Fame pitcher. And Newk, to this day, gets left out."

The End of an Era

In the 1956 World Series, Robinson was the final Dodger batter in the final game. He struck out.

DON HONIG: "Alston and Robinson didn't get along, Bavasi and Robinson didn't get along, and O'Malley and Robinson didn't get along. And in 1956, when Jackie was showing signs of slowing down, Bavasi got Ransom Jackson from the Cubs to replace Jackie at third.

"Jackson was playing third when the season began, and the Dodgers played poorly. Finally Alston put Robinson in the lineup, and in typical fashion he hit a triple and won the game with his base running and fielding, and he was in the lineup to stay."

But for three years he had felt unwanted, and now finally, his thirty-seven-year-old battered knees were sending messages that it was time to quit.

At the end of the '56 season, when he made up his mind not to play in '57, Robinson agreed to sell the story of his retirement to *Look* magazine. It was an uncomplicated transaction. *Look* was to pay Jackie $50,000 for the exclusive.

Then Buzzy Bavasi complicated the story. Robinson had neglected to inform the Dodgers he was not coming back, and a few days before the article was to run, Bavasi traded him to the Giants for Dick Littlefield and $30,000.

N.Y. Daily News Photo

JACKIE ROBINSON, 1957

Robinson had wanted to tell Bavasi he was retiring, but he had not done so, hardly anticipating that the Dodgers might trade the man who had symbolized the team for a generation. When the Dodgers told him they were trading him, Robinson knew he was in a tricky situation. To stall for time to figure out what to do, he tried to persuade the Giant front office to hold the news of the trade for a couple of days. But they would not. A couple of days later, the *Look* article came out proclaiming his retirement from baseball. The Giants had offered him $60,000 to play in 1957. It was a lot of money, more than he had ever gotten with the Dodgers. There was now a lot of pressure on him to keep playing.

Robinson was undecided, the money certainly was attractive. But when Buzzy Bavasi cuttingly told reporters that the article was merely a scheme by Robinson to get more money out of the Giants, Robinson's mind was made up. Robinson, who had never been a money grubber, who had made far less money than many star ballplayers, whose salary was earned every spring by the third exhibition game from the throngs he drew in the South, could not bear being accused of greed by Bavasi and by implication, O'Malley, the most avaricious man of them all. Jackie, a man of principle, decided to retire as planned.

The beat writers were furious at Robinson for not giving them the story.

Roger Kahn: "I was with *Newsweek* then, and he had been traded to the Giants, and I called him and said, 'Are you going to play with the Giants?' And he said a lot of silly things he didn't usually say. 'You know me. I always do what I think is best.' He was evasive, but he was so terribly uncomfortable at it, and then the *Look* story came out.

"There was a big press conference at the *Look* building, and a lot of newspaper guys wanted to jump Robinson. 'How can you sell your retirement?' 'Didn't you mislead us?' This went on for a while, and Robinson stood up fine, and finally a *Look* editor, a guy by the name of Dan Mich, said, 'I will take responsibility for Jackie's statements, and if you have any further questions, ask me,' and the press conference was over.

"And that was when I said to Robinson, 'Did you have any regrets about quitting?' And he said, 'Yeah, my kids were crying because I wasn't a ballplayer anymore, I was just a commuter.' I said, 'How long did that last?' He said, 'Until opening day. My knee hurt so badly opening day, I couldn't get out of bed.' And that was the end of his regrets.

"I'd see him for lunch every so often. We used to go to Jansen's, which was across from Chock Full o' Nuts, where he worked. And we would talk about this and about that, and Jackie was a Rockefeller Republican, and I got tired of listening to what a good guy Nixon was. I'd say, 'Hey, Jackie, Nixon is terrible. Look at his record on race relations.' And Jackie would say, 'Nixon is not as bad as you think.' This was 1960. Nixon was running against Kennedy, and Jackie said, 'I went to see Kennedy, and Kennedy said, "Being from Boston, I haven't known many Negroes in my life," ' and Jackie said, 'Having been a congressman all those years, it should have been your business to know Negroes.'

"We had lunch from time to time, moving from Jansen's to Morgan's East. And Jackie was always in these strange businesses. After Chock Full o' Nuts, he tried fast food franchising, a Sea Host, which was going to be like Arthur Treacher's Fish and Chips, and then there was going to be a black insurance company, because apparently it was very difficult to get blacks life insurance. And that didn't work, and then there was some work with a bank. And I remember him being very hurt when Dick Young wrote that the tragedy of Jackie Robinson's life is that nothing he did after baseball matched what he did in baseball.

" 'How could it?' he said passionately. 'What could I have done? The son of a bitch knows that.' "

15

The Exodus

It began as a trickle right after the war. Before, the Jews who had come to Brooklyn had been content to settle in Brooklyn and remain. Many of them had been Eastern Europeans with simple peasant values and peasant tastes. Brooklyn had been good to them, and they saw no reason to move, except to go from apartment to apartment from year to year to save rent money. These Jews were devoted to their children, revered education, and their supreme goal in life was that their children would have better, happier, wealthier lives than they had. They wanted their children to grow up American, with American values and American goals.

When these children grew up, Brooklyn—with its concrete barrenness in winter and heat brutal enough to fry eggs in summer—was no longer acceptable. The sights of these new Americans were set on something better: the verdant, quiet suburbs of Long Island, Staten Island, and New Jersey.

Marty Glickman: "I moved out of Brooklyn because even before I got married, I aspired to have a house in the country like I had heard or read about. The house in the suburbs was the dream of every young man, a house with a two-car garage.

"After all, riding the subway to go to work every day was a chore. You were packed in like sardines, it was hot as blazes in the summer, and on a wet day it was particularly miserable. And back home, in the summer months, you sat out on the stoops. We didn't have air conditioning. So you thought about the country, you thought about the grass and the leaves and the trees. I remember as a little boy my father with his Essex automobile would drive out into the country and we'd have picnics and fresh air and sunshine. It was a big deal. It was the desire to get away from the crowds, to get away from the cement, and to get out in the open and raise a family in the country."

In the early 1950s, Marty Glickman moved to Scarsdale.

That was the first wave of Brooklyn emigrants. The second wave grew to tidal force by the end of the 1950s. As the young Jews were getting mortgages and moving into the suburbs during the post–World War II economic boom, their parents were taking smaller apartments. Moving into their old places were lower-middle-class black families. These were working people, as their Jewish predecessors had been, blacks who found they could afford to live in the solid, comfortable homes and apartments left behind by the Jewish land rush. And when these black families began to move in, a curious thing happened. Many of the Jews who remained behind, often the same people who had championed the cause of Jackie Robinson, Paul Robeson, and the civil rights movement, began to move out.

JACK NEWFIELD: "It's one of the historic contradictions. Liberals, who were all for Martin Luther King when he was in Selma or Montgomery, had an entirely different outlook when it was their kids being bussed in Chicago or New York.

"My father died when I was four years old. I was an only child. We lived in a house with a bunch of relatives. We didn't have the wealth to give us mobility, and we were stuck. And I saw friends, whose fathers were doing well, who had two parents, and one by one they began to move out of the neighborhood, some to Sheepshead Bay and Flatbush, more to Queens, some to Long Island, some to Jersey. They had upward mobility. But we were stuck there. And with the blacks moving in came a great fear. There was blockbusting. There was panic selling. There were real estate speculators, the parasites and vultures who circle any changing or transitional neighborhood."

Herb Ross was born in the Brownsville section of Brooklyn in 1938. He lived off Eastern Parkway on Howard Avenue. On the block were two small apartment houses and eight two-family private homes. Doctors owned or lived in more than half the dwellings. In 1950, when Herb was twelve, black families had begun to move in, and the Rosses decided it was time to leave.

HERB ROSS: "The first black family I remember in Brownsville was the superintendent of the building, who lived in an apartment house next door to ours. I would play with his kid, and my parents didn't like that. My parents were *very much* against that, and I remember saying, 'What's the big deal?' But I was told these were not the kinds of kids they wanted me to play with. I remember one time I was going to Hebrew school on the other side of Eastern Parkway, and I had met a black kid, and he was shining shoes to make some money, and I asked my dad if I could get a shoe box, and oh, I never heard the end of it! I was a kid. I said. 'Why not?' 'This is not for you. It's not for you.' They didn't want me to be friends with the kid either. I used to say, 'What's the problem? His skin is different from ours, that's all.' They didn't want me to be friends with him. 'Not for you. Not your kind.'

"My father was an optometrist. His office was within walking distance from the house, about two blocks. The whole area was starting to change. Meanwhile my grandmother owned a two-family house on Montgomery Street, and her tenant moved out. I don't know whether she forced the tenant out because my mother and dad intended on moving, but during the summer of '50, the place was vacant, and we did move in.

"My parents didn't tell me until the very end, because they knew I did not want to move. And when the move came, I was told I had to go, although I was very, very unhappy.

"I don't know what it was about the blacks that was so frightening. Maybe they felt that . . . you used to be able to walk Pitkin Avenue on a Sunday afternoon. Some of the best clothing stores. Abe Stark of the 'Hit sign, win suit' had a store there. I guess little by little, people were afraid of getting mugged.

"The new neighborhood was a predominantly white, Jewish neighborhood. The Crown Heights section. Quite a few two-family houses. You also had apartment houses, with a lot of doctors living on a street called President Street, three blocks from where I was. A stable area, for want of better words. Meaning no blacks. I was five blocks from Ebbets Field."

The Rosses had fled deeper into the heart of Brooklyn, but slowly, block by block, by the mid-'50s the changes caught up with them.

HERB ROSS: "The same thing as what was happening in my old neighborhood. I remember when the houses started to sell. Everyone tried to hold on in the beginning. Then one or two would go, and a couple of people would panic, and everybody was worried about real estate values, and the Jews left. We all left."

The Rosses fled again, to the Flatbush section, near Brooklyn College.

By 1957 Brooklyn was no longer the same as it had been just ten years earlier.

BILL REDDY: "There were a lot more blacks and Puerto Rican people in Brooklyn, and certain sections of neighborhoods that had been German, Irish, Jewish, were now Hispanic and Jewish. And it changed the complexion of whole neighborhoods.

"Blacks brought change. They brought a whole new language. Not a foreign language but a slanguage. Different words for different things. All of a sudden, you had 'motherfucker,' which we had never heard before, that was brought into the language and which is in common use today. And new ways of doing things: the dancing styles changes, the music changed. People began to appreciate black musicians.

"The Puerto Ricans also brought change. When before you were hanging out at the corner candy store, now everyone was at the local bodega and going for, as they called it, a bag of beer. And also the graffiti artists started to appear, which to me was really a bad day when they took over. They ruined some of the nicest buildings. Even Kennedy's statue in Prospect Park, for God sake.

"The language changed, the customs changed. Groups began to take over that hadn't been there before. There was an influx of black people from Jamaica and Aruba and Trinidad, and they all talked in that singsong dialect and were all different in their regular daily living than we were. Food stores began to display different types of vegetables and fruits. Brooklyn was changing slowly from the solid Italian, German, Irish, Jewish that it had been to a tropical flavor. Who the hell ever heard of frying green bananas?

"Many of the Jews moved away and gave in to the pressure of the block-busters and the people trying to get the neighborhood away from them. In '57 everyone who could was running to Long Island. Long Island, Staten Island, and New Jersey, but mostly Long Island, which built up very, very quickly.

"A lot of things changed. Coney Island wasn't Coney Island anymore. The Steeplechase closed. There was no more Luna Park. The midway section, the rides section, got so small it really became insignificant. And the scratching for a quarter to enjoy yourself. You give a kid a quarter in '57, what could he do with it?

"The kids began to look for big money. A kid had to have twelve or fifteen dollars in 1957 to buy a pair of slacks. Where's he going to get it if he didn't steal? And everybody had to be as well-dressed as his peers. The first time I can remember young kids sixteen and seventeen years old becoming clothes conscious, becoming experts on how to dress and what to wear. And a simple night out, such as my wife and I enjoyed before we were married, a movie and go to Horn and Hardart, this wouldn't do anymore. Now you had to have folding money in your pocket.

"Tastes were changing. And sex. In my day sex before marriage was unheard of. Girls were virgins. If a girl wasn't a virgin and anyone found out about it, immediately she got a reputation of being an easy lay. And until right after World War II, girls carried their virginity like a banner. I know many a guy never had any sexual doings at all until he was twenty-one or twenty-two years old. This was not unusual. In '57 things had changed, because young Johnny was allowed to do what he pleased when he brought his friends up, and of course, the girls had to go along with them, and they had girls' clubs too that formed up in alliance with the boys. As a matter of fact, they used to carry the weapons when the gang fights would start.

"So little by little, not only Brooklyn, but the world, changed."

Rumblings

One insidious change was the shifting of baseball franchises. As white customers began to flee the inner cities, team owners searched for new markets that they wouldn't have to share with another team. Since 1903 the two leagues had been stable. In the American League, there were the Boston Red Sox, Chicago White Sox, Cleveland Indians, Detroit Tigers, New York Yankees, Philadelphia Athletics, St. Louis Browns, and Washington Senators. In the National the lineup showed the Boston Braves, Brooklyn Dodgers, Cincinnati Redlegs, Chicago Cubs, New York Giants, Pittsburgh Pirates, Philadelphia Phillies, and St. Louis Cardinals.

In 1953 there was movement. The Boston Braves bolted to Milwaukee. The Braves had always played second fiddle to the Red Sox, and owner Lou Perini wanted his own turf. Wisconsin beckoned. The next year the lowly St.

Louis Browns moved to Baltimore, and in 1955 the Philadelphia A's moved to Kansas City. Multiteam towns were growing scarce.

The change that gave Walter O'Malley pause was the Braves. Milwaukee's new County Stadium sat 43,000, and it had parking for 10,000 cars. Said O'Malley, "How long can we continue to compete on an equal basis with a team that can outdraw us two to one and outpark us almost fifteen to one, which pays its park at a token figure, and pays no city or real estate tax? If they take in twice as many dollars, they'll eventually be able to buy better talent. Then they'll be the winners, not us."

By 1956, though the Dodgers were still the second-best draw in the league, O'Malley was stepping up the pressure to get the city of New York to subsidize him. He demanded that city hall build a new ballpark, or he would move the team out of Brooklyn. Where, he wasn't saying, but to demonstrate that he wasn't kidding, he sold Ebbets Field to a housing developer, taking only a three-year lease.

O'Malley had talked about a new park even before he took over as president in 1950. Over in the Bronx, the Yankees were able to pack in 75,000 fans, and at the Polo Grounds, there were seats for 56,000. Ebbets Field sat 33,000 tops, and since its peak in 1947, attendance had been dropping.

In a conversation with reporter Dan Daniel, O'Malley blasted the Dodger fans for not flocking to the ballpark as in days of old. He specifically refused to blame the advent of television or the cold days of spring, and he boasted of the $350,000 he was getting paid by WOR for the seventy-seven home games. He was making a specific point: Decrepit Ebbets Field was at fault. The Dodgers needed a new, 55,000-seat stadium to reverse the trend.

Give me a bigger and newer stadium, he was saying. Give me. Not build me. Give me.

Between 1950 and 1957, attendance remained constant. It was never higher than 1,280,000 (1951) and never lower than 1,020,000 (1954), but O'Malley insisted the Dodgers were not making enough money. The attendance issue was the reddest of herrings. No team in all of baseball was more profitable.

IRVING RUDD: "The Brooklyn ballclub was the richest club in baseball. It was far richer than the Yankees. It made more money than the Yankees even with only 750 parking spaces! O'Malley was making more money than anybody! He talked about a bandbox ballpark, but the bandbox didn't do too badly by him. O'Malley kept saying he needed 1,200,000 to break even, but that was just O'Malley. If he had been drawing 1,800,000, he would have said he needed 1,800,000 to break even."

There was another aspect to the Ebbets Field crowd besides its small size that disturbed O'Malley. He didn't like its racial makup. It wasn't the same going to see a game at Ebbets Field anymore. The white Brooklyn fan was not driving in from his new home in the suburbs.

JOHN BELSON: "By the time Hilda Chester had returned around 1955, Ebbets Field was no longer the same. It was very ersatz. The bloom was well off the rose by the mid-'50s. Willard Mullin may have been still drawing his cartoons, but the fandom was a whole different thing. In the '40s the crowds had been all white, but by the mid-'50s, after Jackie Robinson had been there a while, you go to a Sunday doubleheader, and the dominant smell in the ballpark was bagged fried chicken. Between games out came the brown paper bags with the fried chicken in it. You had a different crowd. It was no longer a unified crowd. It was more subdued, because you weren't as apt to jump up and scream across the aisle at someone because neither the white fans nor the black fans were comfortable with each other. The black fans certainly were not dancing to the Dodger Symphony. The spontaneity in the stands was lost. And the white fans were not responding as ardently to the Symphony or to Hilda either. Hilda Chester did not lead claques of blacks in snake dances down the aisles in Ebbets Field, as she once led the whites. It was a feeling-each-other-out situation. To recapture some of that excitement, you would have had to have two pipers, and there certainly were no black pipers. So the game moved back onto the field."

Herb Ross: "Interestingly it was the Dodgers bringing in Jackie Robinson and other blacks to the ballpark, who changed the whole element of the crowd. And when they added Newcombe and Campanella and Black and Gilliam before many teams had any blacks at all, they in turn were filling up the park with blacks.

"When the blacks started coming to the game, a lot of whites stopped coming. And the black allegiance was only to Robinson and the black ballplayers. They didn't care about the Symphony or Hilda Chester or even the white players. They didn't have the history that we had. The allegiance of the blacks was not to institutions. The allegiance was to Robinson.

"I guess O'Malley was like everyone else in Brooklyn: As long as you're not my neighbor, as long as they went home at night to wherever they lived, it was okay. But once they started to live in the neighborhood, then the neighborhood started to 'change'; it was time to move out."

Bill Reddy: "After we did the big job in '55, the talk of the Dodgers moving was rampant all over the borough. Nobody wanted to believe it, but deep in your heart you knew it was true. The white families were moving out of Brooklyn, and they were the backbone of Ebbets Field. We didn't have enough blacks to replace them. We had a lot of Jamaicans and West Indians coming in who didn't appreciate baseball as we did. They were cricket players. And until the Hispanics could find jobs and get enough money to go out to Ebbets Field, they didn't have hard-core baseball fans. They would hang out at the Parade Grounds, where they could see free baseball. Attendance did fall.

"But I think O'Malley planned it that way. He didn't push for attendance like MacPhail and Rickey, where Red Barber would be talking on the radio, 'Hey, we're close to a million.' And everybody in Brooklyn was running out to go again to make sure they made it.

"O'Malley wasn't pushing for the big attendance. He didn't want it. He wanted to justify his move to California. And I think he had that in the works long, long, before the first inkling was let out to the public."

Beginning during the 1955 season, O'Malley began dropping hints that if he didn't get his new stadium, he was going to leave Brooklyn. Despite a record 22–2 beginning in '55, the fans were remaining at their television sets, and O'Malley caused ripples of panic throughout the borough by announcing at midseason that the Dodgers would play seven of their seventy-seven home games in 1956 at Roosevelt Stadium in Jersey City. He wanted a new stadium, and soon.

JOEL OPPENHEIMER: "The press was constantly full of theories as to exactly what the Dodgers were going to do, and when they announced some of the games would be played in Jersey City, I put my best face on it. 'Okay, that's okay if they play a few games in Jersey City. Why not play a couple of games there?' I assumed that would keep O'Malley happy. It never occurred to me that the Dodgers would go away. Brooklyn leave? That was crazy."

HAROLD ROSENTHAL: "Had you been alert to it, you could have picked up all the signs that the Dodgers were going to leave. The first sign was when O'Malley started to talk to sympathetic newspaper people about the problems he was having. The people who were buying season tickets, the furniture companies in Jamaica, Queens, and the manufacturers on Long Island couldn't give their tickets away to customers because it was too difficult to get there. 'Why do we want to go to Ebbets Field?' the customers would ask. 'We gotta drive.' So it was 'No thanks, we don't want the tickets.'

"And then the talk began that the area around Ebbets Field was a 'bad neighborhood,' and that after a night game you better get the hell out of there fast.

"There was an idea of building a new stadium over the Long Island Railroad tracks in downtown Brooklyn, but again there was the problem of bad parking. Then O'Malley got into an argument with Robert Moses. Moses wanted it built in Flushing, where Shea Stadium is now. O'Malley didn't want it there. Flushing wasn't in Brooklyn."

BILL REDDY: "We had the feeling that they were going to go, but I would go to bed at night hoping that the mayor would mysteriously erect a gorgeous new ballpark somewhere in Brooklyn, and they would stay. But when I read that Hollywood was giving half of L.A. to O'Malley without charge, plus all the concessions and parking, you knew it was a foregone conclusion."

In Search of Judas O'Malley

Much as it would have pained O'Malley to hear, he in many ways strongly resembled his proclaimed nemesis, Branch Rickey. Both were jowly and smoked long cigars. Both were men of presence. Both were tightfisted when it came to spending money. Both were expert at bestowing praise on employees when a raise would have been better. And both were brilliant orators who knew how to use words to get their way. In short, con artists. Blarney masters. With deep, resonant, hypnotic voices.

One of O'Malley's most valuable employees was a slight man of boundless energy by the name of Irving Rudd. Rudd had the title of Dodger promotions director, and he used his considerable skill to help O'Malley make a great deal of money, especially during the exhibition seasons and at Jersey City, where Rudd ran that operation the two years the Dodgers played seven games a season there. Rudd worked closely with O'Malley and got to watch the man up close.

IRVING RUDD: "I came to the ballclub in February 1951. O'Malley had just taken over from Rickey. He hired me to run the Brooklyn Amateur Baseball Foundation, which provided sandlot equipment for the kids in Brooklyn, Queens, and Staten Island. The Yankees took care of the Bronx, Manhattan, and Westchester. I knew Rickey could be a tight man, that he could talk you out of your pants, but this guy was just as good a bullshitter as Rickey when he wanted to be. He could turn on that charm.

"One time two American Legionnaires came in to the Dodger offices. They were wearing their legion uniforms, and they wanted to see O'Malley about getting a bigger cut of the Brooklyn Amateur Baseball Foundation. They wanted more balls and bats, and when they finished O'Malley began telling them how tough it was to run a ballclub, explaining what he was up against. Honest to God, when they left, these guys were going to write him a check! He was marvelous. He was a very subtle, clever man, one of the most brilliant men I've ever met as far as hard business. I've often said that if he was up against Khrushchev in those crucial years, the Soviet Union would be a Dodger farm club today.

"Like Rickey he was a great storyteller. I remember a funny story O'Malley once told. There was a guy named Matt Burns, an arrogant Irish straw boss for O'Malley. Ever read *The Last Hurrah*? This guy was Knocko Monahan. Very much a Catholic, almost a professional Catholic. A lot of priests and nuns and rosaries and crosses. And evidently he had suffered trench foot during World War II, 'cause he always reminded you that if it wasn't for him, the fucking Nazis would be sitting at your desk.

"So one day at a meeting, there was a diplomatic task that had to be done, and someone said, 'Why don't we send Matt Burns to handle that?'

"O'Malley said, 'I'll tell you a story why we're not going to use Matt.' He said, 'Two guys were playing poker, and one of them, Jim Kelly, toppled over and dropped dead of a heart attack. A good pot of money on the table belonged to him, and now it was decided that one Frank O'Doud was to deliver the money and the news to this poor woman. And O'Doud came to the house and rang the bell, and when she answered he said, "Is this the widow Kelly's home?" '

"Everybody was laughing and O'Malley said, 'That's why we're not going to send Matt Burns.'

"I have to say that O'Malley was one of the brightest, shrewdest of men. I'm in the office one day, and Lou Perini of Boston is on the phone. I hear O'Malley purr, 'Looouuuuu, that is why you are so brave and brilliant. That is why you are a pioneer.' This was 1953. Perini is moving his team to Milwaukee, and O'Malley's showing his support. He's lining up a vote. Thinking ahead. Always thinking.

"I started at $5,200 a year and was being paid by the Brooklyn Amateur Baseball Foundation. It wasn't costing the Brooklyn Dodgers a nickel. I got paid from the proceeds of the annual Mayor's Trophy Game, which was my job to run. When the game was over, I had fulfilled my duties, but O'Malley soft-soaped me into pitching in and helping Frank Graham in the Dodgers public relations department. And so I became ex-officio promotions director. Even though the Dodgers didn't pay me for that aspect of the job.

"O'Malley, I found out, could snow you beautifully. He could make you feel twelve feet high, but he never backed it. The next year Graham was publicity director, Harold Parrott was business manager, Lee Scott was road secretary, and I became promotions director. I promoted the Dodger exhibition games, and I helped jump attendance from 4,200 a game to 7,600, with the help of some pretty good stats, of course.

"I was in Vero Beach having breakfast, and across from me was Bobby Bragan, the Ft. Worth Cats manager. I'm slurping my oatmeal, and suddenly two vicelike hands are holding me right down into the plate, and Bobby is laughing like hell.

"I hear this gravelly voice, 'I will never forget this glorious, wonderful job that you did. It was outstanding. You are destined to become, dum da dum da dum . . .' It was O'Malley. God himself was speaking. Visions of sugar plums are dancing in my head. I'm saying to myself, 'Gertrude,' thinking of my dear bride, 'should we get the Cadillac Seville or do we move into the home with the Bigelow on the floor?' Recovering, I said, 'Thank you, Mr. O'Malley.' Not bad hearing from this guy, right? I figured I was in for a hefty raise, right?

"And after that I didn't get a chance to speak with him for two months. I could never get the guy alone. Talk about Benny Leonard in his prime or Sugar Ray Robinson. Forget it. He was beautiful. This guy was an expert. I never laid a glove on him. Forget the raise.

"That year Frank Graham and I were preparing for the next Mayor's Trophy Game, and to kick off the publicity, between games of a doubleheader there was a little home plate ceremony. The mayor was Robert Wagner, a nice man, and Frank Graham and Irving Rudd are called to home plate and presented with Dodger service rings by the mayor of the city of New York. In front of a packed house. That took care of one year's raise. After all, it isn't every time that you get called up in front of a crowd and are thanked by the mayor of New York. This was the sort of reward you got working for the Dodgers.

"By 1956 I was asking myself, 'Where's the money?' I had one conversation with him. He said, 'Irving, you don't seem to understand. The players get it all. There's hardly anything left for anybody else.' And if you looked at the player payroll, you knew it wasn't going to the players. The players didn't get it all. O'Malley got it all.

"I had started at $5,200 in 1951, and five years later I was making $5,800. Not exactly a living wage for a man with a family. During the winter of 1956, I sent O'Malley a memo asking for a $1,500 raise, and I would have settled for $750. Had I gotten the $750, I would have been with the Dodgers today. Maybe.

"In January 1957, on a snowy winter's night, I held a free rally for the Dodgers at the armory in Jersey City. I got Phil Foster, a comic, a very, very nice guy, to come for free. I had the Dodger Symphony there. Governor Meyner of New Jersey came down. And it was a smash. A smash. Twenty thousand people on a snow-filled night, and the next morning I'm lying in bed like a lox, and I hear the phone ring.

" 'Yes, Mr. O'Malley.'

" 'Irving, I have to compliment you on one of the most marvelous shows, productions, presentations.'

"I said, 'Thank you, Mr. O'Malley. Oh, by the way, Mr. O'Malley, did you get my memo?'

" 'Memo, what memo is that?'

" 'The one where I asked for a raise, Mr. O'Malley.'

"He said, 'I don't like to be pushed, Irving.'

"And I realized the point there was that I would have to start looking for a new job. I quit the Dodgers in 1957.

"Happy Felton got off a great line. We were riding down Atlantic Avenue one afternoon in a cab, and it was a poor, rundown area, near the Williamsburg Bridge on the way to Ebbets Field, and there was a neon cross in the window that said, 'Jesus saves.' And Happy said, 'They never heard of O'Malley.' Meaning that O'Malley even outsaves Jesus.

"When we won the World Series in '55, we were all going to get World Series rings. But I got wind that to get it, you had to give them back your Dodger service ring. What were they doing with them? At the office I saw they were buffing and polishing the turned-in rings. They were to go to the scout in Pascagoula, Mississippi. 'Dear Peter, for your faithful service, please accept this Dodger ring. Buh buh buh boom.' My Dodger ring was what he was going to get! Frank Graham's Dodger ring was what they were going to get!

"O'Malley could be brutal. Frankie Graham tells the story of one Dodger employee who either quits or gets fired, and O'Malley says to him, 'Oh, by the way, on the way out take this out and mail it, will you?'

"When there was trouble in the ticket department in 1951, O'Malley asked Harold Parrott, the road secretary, to take over the job. Harold loved being road secretary. It was perks, fun, and a World Series share, which was significant money. The ticket manager didn't get any of that. O'Malley said, 'Harold, you'll never be sorry. I'll make it up to you in many ways.' A year or two goes by, and finally Harold braces him one day. 'Mr. O'Malley, gee whiz, you told me when I took this job that . . .' O'Malley cut him short. 'Harold, look out the window at Montague Street. You see that crowd going to work down there?' Harold says, 'Yes, Mr. O'Malley.' 'How old are you, Harold?' 'I'm forty-six, Mr. O'Malley.' O'Malley says, 'A lot of forty-six-year-old guys down there wouldn't mind having your job.' End of question. End of raise.

"And then there was Harry Hickey, an old-time director and a longtime pal of O'Malley's who was ailing. Hickey wanted very badly to go to Japan with the Dodgers after the '56 season, and O'Malley is giving him the stonewall and ducking him, and finally Harold Parrott, who ran the Japanese tour, went to O'Malley to ask him about Hickey. O'Malley said, 'Did you ever stop to consider what it would cost to ship a body back from Tokyo?' O'Malley wasn't joking. He had it all figured out. Four thousand eight hundred dollars for the casket. 'What if the guy dies over there? Hell, let him stay home.'

"Sentiment meant nothing. Everything was business. It was a winter's night, and I was alone with him in his office, and I don't know why, but he let his hair down with me. I was confiding in him that I was having trouble with a man who had once done me a big favor. But lately he had become a real pain, and though I didn't want to seem ungrateful, I really didn't want to have anything to do with him anymore.

" 'Irving,' O'Malley says, 'sometimes you have to cut the past.' He continued, 'I had a similar thing happen to me. There's a friend of mine, a very wealthy banker, and after a while, Irving, you do outgrow certain people.' Why he suddenly confided in me I don't know, because it was very unusual for him. He was trying to teach me a lesson in life.

"He continued, 'George McLaughlin is a great guy and a great friend of mine, and in many ways he was an advisor and patron. Yes, McLaughlin did bring me into the picture. Yes, McLaughlin was responsible,' and he as much as said that without him he wouldn't have become president of the Dodgers.

" 'But it's gotten to a stage, Irving, where I have to go on beyond that.' McLaughlin had become very bitter about the fact that O'Malley did not consult him anymore. And it was making O'Malley uncomfortable.

" 'So in the future, Irving, you'll find that it's great to have loyal friendships from the past, but sometimes you have to cut the cord to seek new horizons, and you can't be tied down by the past.'

"And he did feel badly about it, and yet, fuck it, on to Los Angeles, if you know what I mean."

The Betrayal

IRVING RUDD: "Whatever anyone wants to say, New York Mayor Robert Wagner and Parks Commissioner Robert Moses were right. If they had given O'Malley what he wanted, they should have gone to jail. If you remember, the talk was about a superdome in downtown Brooklyn, where the Long Island Railroad is, with stores, apartments. And who do you think would have owned all of this? O'Malley. He was offered the use of the Flushing

Meadow site, à la Shea, and his answer was, 'You build a ballpark and *give* it to me.' Moses said, 'Fuck you.' "

Was O'Malley boxed in? Only under the guidelines he had set up—give me a new stadium or I'm leaving. Could he have built himself a modern edifice? In owning a property as valuable as the Brooklyn Dodgers and in being incestuous with the Brooklyn Trust Company, O'Malley could have condemned land and built a new park just about anyplace he would have chosen—if he had so desired. But Brooklyn was no longer middle class. Poor people drove out rich people, were nothing but trouble, and didn't spend money. O'Malley wanted to leave.

During the World Series of 1956, one of O'Malley's guests was Kenneth Hahn, a member of the Los Angeles Board of Supervisors. Hahn was serving his first term when the County of Los Angeles sent him to the World Series with all expenses paid to bring back a major league baseball team. Any team.

The World Series was being hosted by the Yankees and by Walter O'Malley and the Dodgers. Perhaps if another National League team had been playing, O'Malley would not have made his L.A. connection. Perhaps it would have been the L.A. Senators or perhaps the L.A. White Sox. Or maybe O'Malley would have merely picked up and moved his team to another panting city, such as Dallas, Houston, Atlanta, Minneapolis, or Oakland. But at the 1956 World Series, Hahn and O'Malley met, and the fate of the Brooklyn Dodgers was sealed.

The following is testimony that Hahn delivered at a hearing during a recent lawsuit between the Los Angeles Raider football team and the NFL. The most interesting excerpt is Hahn's admission that it was O'Malley who contacted Hahn, not the other way around. Hahn makes it clear that O'Malley was actively seeking to move out of Brooklyn. Sure, O'Malley had a scale model of a new domed Brooklyn stadium sitting on his desk, but if the city of New York wasn't going to give it to him, he was going to find a city that would.

KENNETH HAHN: "To make Los Angeles great we had to have a major team. There were a lot of people that said we are not ready for it, we are not ready for a major team, but I went, and I first attempted to see Calvin Griffith, the owner of the [Washington] Senators, because they were at the bottom of the league.

"When I was attending the game at Ebbets Field, Walter O'Malley sent me a note and said he is interested in coming to Los Angeles. He won the world championship [in 1955]. I never dreamt we could get a world champion.

"Then he came here, and his team, on his way to Japan. He had some play in Tokyo. I met him at the Hilton Hotel—it was called the Statler Hilton then—on Columbus Day. I remember the date because it was a legal holiday, and I didn't have to go to work, but I came down to meet him.

"He said, 'I will come down here, but I will deny it to the press' because he had another season to play at Ebbets Field. He said the Dodger fans are rough fans. Literally would kill him, he said.

N.Y. Daily News Photo

WALTER O'MALLEY

"I took Walter O'Malley in a helicopter by the Sheriff's Department and circled Los Angeles to find the best spot, and that was an abandoned housing project, and he said this is where he wanted to go.

"If you want to know the truth, and Mr. O'Malley is dead and nobody knows about it but me, but I had more faith than Walter O'Malley that the Dodgers would be a success. When he came to the Coliseum he wanted a three-year lease with an option for the next three years, because he said to me one day, 'If the people don't support major league baseball, I want to transfer my team to Phoenix or Tucson or some other place.'

"I said, 'Walter, they are going to really love you, you will be glad you moved from New York.'

"Later on my prophecy turned out to be absolutely correct. The Dodgers are the most profitable and the most liked team in the nation."

When O'Malley told Hahn he would entertain an offer from the city of Los Angeles, the town fathers did not equivocate. They made O'Malley an offer so incredible there was no way in the world he was going to turn it down. They gave him his stadium and much, much more.

IRVING RUDD: "Norris Poulson, the mayor of Los Angeles, showed up in Vero Beach one day, and he presented O'Malley with a laundry list—here's what I'll give you if you come to Los Angeles, including, 'You can sleep with my wife once a week.'

"Forget the emotion. O'Malley is a businessman. They say, 'This is what I'm giving you. The condominium is yours for life.' You say, 'But I got this contract.' They say, 'Two dancing girls and Jacqueline Bisset on weekends.' You say, 'Fuck the contract!' How many guys would say no? So what did Poulson give him? He condemned the land for him. They gave him the oil rights in case they discovered oil. They built him a stadium. Who needs Fort Knox to print money? That's why he went. Bye Bye Brooklyn."

But before he could accept Los Angeles's offer and go, O'Malley still had to pull two swindles.

First, he had to buy the rights to the Los Angeles area, then owned by the Chicago Cubs, who had a minor league team playing there. And once he did that, he had to talk another team owner into moving out to the Coast with him. With two teams on the Coast, it would be much more economical in terms of scheduling. To fly to the Coast to play but one team would be too expensive.

As it turned out, O'Malley had no trouble either buying the rights to Los Angeles or getting another team to go with him.

HAROLD PARROTT: "Walter O'Malley had been lucky enough to run into Phil Wrigley just when the chewing gum king was very angry at a whole city: Los Angeles. His team trained on Catalina Island, and the grounds were not in shape for spring training one year. Wrigley vowed he would never bring his team back. 'A bush town,' Wrigley called it, and swore he'd never have anything to do with the place again, as soon as he could get rid of his minor league franchise, the Pacific Coast League Angels.

"O'Malley was drooling but trying hard to hide his interest.

"All O'Malley did was con Wrigley into taking, in a straight swap—lock, stock, and ballpark and the L.A. franchise for Fort Worth in the Texas League. Branch Rickey had picked up the Fort Worth package ten years before for a mere $75,000.

"What the Irishman got, in addition to the franchise, was a square city block in Los Angeles."

In searching for a partner to flee west with him, O'Malley didn't have to look any farther than across the Harlem River.

HORACE STONEHAM: "I had intended to move the Giants out of New York even before I knew Mr. O'Malley was intending to move. I was unhappy playing in the Polo Grounds. The ballpark was old, and it was darn near impossible to finance one in that area. I had intended to go to Minneapolis. We had a ballclub there, so I had the rights to the area, and it's a big city in itself. Also, Minneapolis was well within transportation range of the league. Aviation at that time had been accepted by everyone.

"And then Walter called me up and asked me if I was going to move. I said, 'I think so. I think the league will give me permission.' He said, 'Why don't we both move and go to the Far West together?' So we thought about it, and that's what we finally decided to do. When he asked me about moving west, I told him that I liked the San Francisco area, that I had worked there when I was a young fellow. I didn't even know he was intending to move. But when he saw I was, he saw we could make a rivalry on the Pacific Coast."

And so the Brooklyn Dodgers became the Los Angeles Dodgers, and the New York Giants became the San Francisco Giants. In Los Angeles O'Malley had gotten a deal better than that offered Cortez by the Aztec Indians. And like Cortez, once O'Malley moved west, he discovered other imaginative ways to cheat the natives out of their gold.

CHARLEY EINSTEIN: "This story could be apocryphal, only because it's hard to imagine anyone could be so dumb, but the story has been told that when O'Malley went out there, the L.A. politicians said, 'What do you want in the way of compensation from concessions?' He said, 'Well, we play a 154-game schedule, and back in Brooklyn we got all the concessions. I want to show you my heart's in the right place. I only want concessions for half the games.' They said, 'That's more than we expected. That's great.' So the Dodgers kept the concession money for the seventy-seven games they played in the Coliseum. The other seventy-seven were on the road. It never crossed their minds what O'Malley was telling them!

"He was devious, but he built the most beautiful ballpark in baseball. The story is that O'Malley asked the Giants to send him the plans for Candlestick

Park, because Candlestick Park was the first of the postwar baseball stadiums. O'Malley said to his architect, 'Study these and learn what not to do.'

"And O'Malley built the most magnificant ballpark with a great sense of what to do with all the cars driving into the park. What he did was put all the cars in one place, and he provided for the fans to enter the park on different levels. It was a short walk from the car, no matter where in the park you were seated. Easy in. Easy out. A superb job of design.

"O'Malley only made one mistake. If he had wanted L.A. all to himself, he should have also bought the Hollywood franchise, which the California Angels ultimately bought. But O'Malley could not possibly have been that farsighted. He wasn't thinking of competition. He didn't know for sure that he was going to succeed."

In fact, even after all O'Malley's planning and scheming, at the eleventh hour, he came within a whisker of losing it all.

IRVING RUDD: "There were a few people in L.A. who didn't have orange juice for brains. The Dodgers were in the Coliseum, and they were about to take over Chavez Ravine, and people started to scream and holler, 'Hey, wait a minute. We're being gulled. We're being had.' And so there was a referendum to vote whether or not to give O'Malley all this land. The people were catching on to what he was doing, and a campaign was growing to stop him. It was on the books for a vote, yes or no Dodgers. And if it's no, O'Malley's dead.

"On the Sunday before the vote, he ran a telethon, and ironically he ran it on Gene Autry's station—and did Walter give Autry a hosing when later he tried to get into baseball!—but he got all the great and glamorous stars saying: 'Vote yes for the Dodgers.' And not one of those stars came from Los Angeles. They all came from Beverly Hills, Hollywood, Santa Monica, Santa Barbara. And as it was, it just did pass—barely. But had O'Malley not done that, gotten a last blast on the Sunday before the election, it might not have happened. And O'Malley would have been up the creek without a paddle. A ballclub with no place to play."

In the end, of course, what O'Malley wanted, O'Malley got, and the Los Angeles franchise became the most profitable team of them all.

The Last Supper

The 1957 season was funereal. The team was old. Ebbets Field was old. And depressed by the knowledge that the Dodgers were leaving, the fans were feeling old.

Newk's career was ending in the bottle, Ersk's right arm pained him too much to pitch more than once a week, and Campy's catching skills began to erode after a careless doctor had cut a nerve in his right hand while performing an operation. The Duke needed knee surgery, Pee Wee was pushing forty and had stopped hitting, and Furillo's knees were beginning to pain him. Only the stout pitching of the six-foot-six right-hander Don Drysdale, winner of seventeen games, saved Brooklyn from the second division.

Ebbets Field, which O'Malley let go to seed, was dingy. Everything seemed so somber inside, as though a loved one were about to die. The crowds were thin, the cheering hollow, and when the dreary season came to a close, the demoralized Dodgers trailed the ebullient Milwaukee Braves by eleven games.

By the season finale, the arrangements for the Dodger funeral had been completed. The official word had been issued: The Dodgers were leaving Brooklyn for the Coast. The final game at Ebbets Field this year was really the final game.

It was scheduled for September 24, 1957, before 6,702 heartsick, nostalgic fans. At the start of the game, the Brooklyn Dodger theme song was played on the loudspeaker:

Oh, follow the Dodgers
Follow the Dodgers around
The infield, the outfield,
The catcher and that fellow on the mound

Oh, the fans will come a running
When the Dodgers go a gunning
For the pennant that we're fighting for today.

The Dodgers keep swinging
And the fans will keep singing
Follow the Dodgers, hooray.

There's a ball club in Brooklyn
The team they call "Dem Bums,"
But keep your eyes right on them
And watch for hits and runs . . .

Pee Wee Reese took his customary station at the top of the dugout, and when the record had ended, with the same motion he had employed since becoming captain, for the final time in Brooklyn he signaled the starters to run onto the field. During the playing of the national anthem, there were brave tears.

The game went two hours and three minutes, as the Dodgers beat the Pirates 3–0. When it was over, announcer Tex Rickart made the pro forma announcement, as he had done since the '30s, "Please do not go on the playing field at the end of the game. Use any exit that leads to the street." He was completely ignored.

After the final out, as the throng of souvenir hunters ravaged the infield, grabbing clumps of dirt or blades of grass, Gladys Gooding began to play "May the Good Lord Bless You and Keep You." Before she was done, the recording of the Dodger theme song once again sounded, and when it was over, she played "Auld Lang Syne." It was like when the orchestra played the hymn "Nearer My God to Thee" as the Titanic was sinking. Only this time it wasn't an ocean liner but a way of life going down.

The Mourners

BILL FARRELL, JR.: "My childhood revolved around the Dodgers. Going to Ebbets Field was a family affair. It was part of growing up. I always said I was baptized a Catholic and a Dodger fan.

"We lived in Bensonhurst. My father, my uncle, and my cousins would pile into our Hudson, stop by Prospect Park in the morning, play some ball, and then walk to Ebbets Field for a two o'clock game.

"I can remember the vendor outside Ebbets Field selling steamed peanuts. I can still hear the whistle. And Ebbets Field smelled like no other ballpark I've ever been in. The thing I remember best was the smell. An unmistakable aroma of Ebbets Field. I visited several ballparks around the country, trying to see if maybe it was an old ballpark smell, but it's not. It was unique. An oily smell? Inky? Paint? Didn't smell like paint. It was pleasant. It used to smell like the *Coloroto* magazine in the *Daily News*. I heard they painted the grass. Maybe that's what it was. But no ballpark smelled like Ebbets Field.

"The game I remember best is the last Dodger game I ever went to. It was against the Philadelphia Phillies on the last home stand, 1957. The Pirates came in next to finish out the season. My uncle, my cousin Richie, and I went, and my cousin teased me all the way out there, saying the Dodgers were leaving, that they were going to Mexico. Richie was four years older than I was, and though he was teasing me, he was really teasing himself too. No one really believed the rumors. Kids don't believe it. The Dodgers were ours. How could they leave us? Richie said, 'If they win this game, they'll stay in Brooklyn, but if they lose, they're going to Mexico.' And needless to say, the Dodgers lost that game, and I cried all the way home.

"My cousin wanted to stay after the game, to wait for the Dodger players. My uncle said, 'No, they're leaving town. Why should we wait for them?'

"And that was the last time I was at Ebbets Field. But that woke me up to the reality of life, waking up to discover there is no Santa Claus in December, no Dodgers come the spring. It all happened at once. Instant maturity. It was such a disappointment, because I so looked forward to the baseball season. They were such happy hours, happy times.

"After the Dodgers left, I used to drive past there occasionally. I hated to look. For years my father had said, 'You'll be able to ride your bicycle to Ebbets Field one day and go see the games by yourself. But by the time I got my bicycle and was old enough to ride, they were long gone."

CHARLEY STEINER: "The first time I listened to a Dodger game I was about six years old. It was listening to the play-by-play that first got me interested in radio. My childhood dream, I can tell you without equivocation, was to be the play-by-play announcer for the Brooklyn Dodgers. What I would have given to join Vin Scully, Al Helfer, and Jerry Doggett in the booth! Those were the last three broadcasters for the Dodgers, of course, before they moved out. Do you realize what it's like to have your childhood dream smashed at the age of eight? Years of therapy. My childhood dream was absolutely smashed, dashed, and folded, spindled, and mutilated. It was a devastating loss for me.

"I was eight years old in 1957. Eight years old. I loved Furillo. I loved Snider. And Gil Hodges, of course. And Campy. And Gilliam and the rest of them. I can run down the '57 Dodgers even now. I have yet to vote in a presidential election, and it was perhaps the only time I exerted a political preference. I registered my vote. I called Walter O'Malley. I picked up the telephone and got through to the secretary and said, 'You can't do this.'

"I was crying and babbling like an idiot. I said to her, 'How can you do this to me? This is my baseball team.' She said, 'Mr. O'Malley is out right now,' and she listened to me for about ten minutes. I said, 'You just can't do this to me.' And she said, 'We've had similar calls. This is something beyond my control. Let me take your phone number, and Mr. O'Malley will get back to you.'

"I'm still waiting for the call."

BOBBY MCCARTHY: "I never believed the Dodgers would ever leave Brooklyn. I don't think a lot of people did. I didn't think O'Malley would take them to L.A.

"The day it was announced, if you were in Behan's Bar and Grill, you'd have thought it was a wake. This was like seceding from the Union. It was hard to believe that one of your own kind, O'Malley, could do this. Tommy Corrigan, Timmy Murray, Willie Crane were there. Willie was a sick Dodger fan. He was almost a degenerate Dodger fan, and Willie wanted to go find Walter O'Malley and kill him. He wanted to kidnap him. He wanted to go get him and shoot him. He figured if he shot him, the Dodgers wouldn't move.

"We said, 'There will be another Brooklyn team. Whoever thought they'd go out to L.A. and keep the name Dodgers? Whoever thought California should have a baseball team. That's where all the movie actors are. Baseball didn't belong in California. It belonged in Philadelphia or Boston or New York or Brooklyn. We figured we would always have the Brooklyn Dodgers, even after they said they were moving. But it didn't happen.

"And when they tore down Ebbets Field, that was like tearing away part of your heart. It was hard to believe. What do you do without Ebbets Field? I live in Staten Island now. Maybe if Ebbets Field was still there, I never would have left Brooklyn. I don't know. But after they tore it down, everything was different."

RON GREEN: "After all those years of heartbreak, to have it end like that—I never forgave the National League. I have never gone to a National League game since. To take the Dodgers and Giants out of New York, to leave New York without a National League team, was the crime of the century. How could they do that? Take both teams out of New York? And when they gave them the Mets, I thought they were selling them a bill of goods. I've never been back. Never even went to Shea Stadium."

JOEL OPPENHEIMER: "Most Dodger fans didn't take out their hatred on the players. After all it wasn't their fault the Dodgers had deserted them, so that when Koufax and Drysdale were having great seasons or when Willie Davis was running wild, they were still our boys, and you had to root for them. But then, slowly, the Brooklyn players dropped away, retired, and instead of continuing to follow the team, the Brooklyn fans either stopped following baseball or rooted for the Mets.

"By 1963, when the Yankees were playing the Dodgers in the World Series, most Brooklyn fans had no one to root for. I went only because I had tickets, and because my kid, who desperately wanted to see the game, unfortunately is a Yankee fan."

BILL REDDY: "O'Malley did nobody, including himself, any favors when he left. He may have gained a lot of money. But if it's true that there's a hereafter, every Dodger fan knows exactly where he is right now. I'll tell you something else. As old as I am now, and as much sense as I have, I was not unhappy when he died, and I don't think there were too many Dodger fans who were. He did a terrible thing to the people of Brooklyn, because he took away part of the cohesiveness that used to hold the borough together. Even if there was racial tension, at least they had something in common, something they could talk about. And whether they were Dodger fans or Giant fans, it really didn't matter. And O'Malley took away the Polo Grounds as surely as he took away Ebbets Field, and for no good reason. Stoneham was a sucker. It was the biggest mistake of his life. He never made a nickel.

"And I know, deep in my heart, that if it hadn't been for O'Malley, the team would have never moved. They would have found a way to build a stadium. Greed was the whole thing. O'Malley feathered his nest. They gave him half of Los Angeles for nothing, and the bum, he got the money, but what did he do to us?"

JOE FLAHERTY: "I think Hemingway said it, that if you live long enough, everything you love will be sullied, and it was O'Malley who was the first one to really put the shit into the game, the one who showed everyone that loyalty means nothing. O'Malley is the one who brought home the message that baseball wasn't a game, it was a business. Besides what he did—take the team away—he put the sour in. Sure, a team had to meet expenses, but he removed any illusion that he was in it for the pastime.

"Baseball always was an extension of innocence, the innocence of childhood, the innocence of America, and here was O'Malley saying, 'We're not what we think we are.' It was a terrible psychic blow. And Ebbets Field was replaced by a housing project. How could a father tell his son where Duke Snider used to hit one? Point out apartment 5Q?

"The Dodgers at the time were the best franchise. The Dodgers accounted for something like forty percent of the revenue of the National League, and you're talking about a ballpark that only had 32,000 seats. I mean, you could make a case for Stoneham leaving. His attendance was bad, and he was having a hard time making it at the Polo Grounds. But the Dodgers? O'Malley deserted Brooklyn just so he could be making more.

"When the Dodgers left, it was not only a loss of a team, it was the disruption of a social pattern. There was no more sense of waiting up for the *Daily News.* The life went out of the street corners. What were you going to stand there and talk about? Conversations in bars stopped. Except for everyone agreeing that O'Malley was a son of a bitch.

"Maybe Brooklyn was a minor borough compared to Manhattan, but Brooklyn had the Dodgers. In *Guadalcanal Diary,* William Bendix talked about the Dodgers while he was fighting the Japs. With the Dodgers you could swagger. It was like being in an elite unit, like being part of the Lafayette Escadrille, and when the Dodgers left, the feeling died.

"It wasn't just a franchise shift. It was a total destruction of a culture."

JACK NEWFIELD: "Once Pete Hamill and I were having dinner, and we began to joke about collaborating on an article called, 'The Ten Worst Human Beings Who Ever lived.' And I said to Pete, 'Let's try an experiment. You write on your napkin the names of the three worst human beings who ever lived, and I will write the three worst, and we'll compare.

"Each of us wrote down the same three names and in the same order: Hitler, Stalin, Walter O'Malley."

BILL REDDY: "O'Malley was the man who took the heart out of us. He took the Dodgers away. O'Malley had it all schemed out from the beginning. He was after the almighty buck, and how could he lose? Look what they gave him out there. We could have given him the world, and he wouldn't have stayed here. Had they built a stadium and put it in the middle of Flatbush Avenue and Fulton Street, he wouldn't have stayed. And they could have given him parking for 50,000 cars, and he wouldn't have stayed. My wife always chided me about it, but one of the best pieces of news I ever received was when I found out he was dead. That's the way I and thousands of others felt. I've never heard an old Dodger fan bless O'Malley. Not a single one of us have ever said a prayer for him."

The Ashes

GUS ENGLEMAN: "In 1957, which was the Dodgers' last season playing in Ebbets Field, I was at the army language school in San Francisco, and after I finished I went to Berlin and didn't return to the United States until March 1960. When I came back, I spent three days at Fort Hamilton, got discharged, and went back to live with my mother in Bensonhurst. You know the first thing I wanted to do? Go to Ebbets Field.

"In Germany, whenever the guys from the New York area got together, we would say, 'What's the first thing you want to do when you finally get home?' One guy would say, 'I can't wait to see the lights of Broadway.' 'I want to see Times Square again.' 'I want to go to Coney Island.' I said, 'I want to go to see for myself whether it was true, otherwise I'll never believe the Dodgers are no longer in Ebbets Field.'

"And so, when I came home, I spent the night with my mother to get reacquainted. I took the subway the way I used to, West End to Coney Island, taking the Brighton, getting off at Prospect Park. I wanted to walk, because I wanted to relive those memories as a kid when you got off at Prospect Park Botanical Gardens Station and you walked up the block and saw that big sign, Ebbets Field, 'cause when you were a kid it was a thrilling sight. It was marvelous to see that wonderful stadium with the crowds streaming towards it.

"And when I got upstairs that last time, I saw the big sign that said simply, 'Ebbets Field Apartments.' Only then did I finally accept that it did happen. And it had a tremendous effect on me. I choked up, and maybe it was then that I realized my boyhood was gone, that my great love affair was over, and most important, that you can't go home again. Thomas Wolfe had said it, and I guess he was right. It would never be the same. The Dodgers were no longer in Brooklyn."

BILL REDDY: "After the Dodgers left, I went to Ebbets Field only once. One of my kids wanted to see this thrill circus, a demolition derby, where drivers were riding automobiles backwards into each other. They had a ramp erected behind the pitcher's mound almost all the way to home plate, and one of the drivers was going to drive a car up the ramp and hurtle into open space.

"We walked into Ebbets Field, and I looked around, and I can't describe the feeling I had when I saw left field, center field, right field, just as they always had been, except for the ramp. The drivers came out in these Dodger automobiles, and they drove all the way across the outfield, where guys like Snider, Musial, Reiser, Willie Mays, Furillo, DiMaggio, Dixie Walker, oh God, had played. And as I sat there watching, as the outfield grass was being torn up by the cars, tears were streaming down my face, and I didn't even realize it. My son turned to me and said, 'Daddy, you're crying.' I was."

After the Dodgers left and the *Brooklyn Eagle* folded, newspaperman Tommy Holmes said, "Brooklyn is the only city of two million people that doesn't have an airport, a newspaper, and a ballclub."

And that's still true today.

The heart had gone out of Brooklyn. The soul had fled. It's a place to live now, that's all. It's a place to hang one's hat. It's just across the river, a place where people sleep. You don't hear Brooklyn stories or Brooklyn jokes anymore. Brooklyn lives only in loving memory, alongside Jackie, Gil, Campy, Big Newk, Clem, Oisk, Skoonj, Pee Wee, the Duke, and every other man who ever wore the Ivory Snow–white uniform with the Dodger-blue numbers and the lettering on the front that spelled out Brooklyn.

* * *

HOMETOWN PIECE FOR MESSRS. ALSTON AND REESE

By Marianne Moore

To the tune:
"Li'l baby, don't say a word: Mama goin' to buy you a mockingbird
Bird don't sing: Mama goin' to sell it and buy a brass ring."

"Millennium," yes; "pandemonium"!
Roy Campanella leaps high. Dodgerdom

crowned, had Johnny Podres on the mound.
Buzzy Bavasi and the Press gave ground;

the team slapped, mauled, and asked the Yankees' match,
"How did you feel when Sandy Amoros made the catch?"

"I said to myself"—pitcher for all innings—
"as I walked back to the mound I said, 'Everything's

getting better and better.' " (Zest: they've zest.
" 'Hope springs eternal in the Brooklyn breast.' "

And would the Dodger Band in 8, row 1, relax
if they saw the collector of income tax?

Ready with a tune if that should occur:
"Why Not Take All of Me—All of Me, Sir?")

Another series. Round-tripper Duke at bat,
"Four hundred feet from home-plate"; more like that.

A neat bunter, please; a cloud-breaker, a drive
like Jim Gilliam's great big one. Hope's alive.

Homered, flied out, fouled? Our "stylish stout"
so nimble Campanella will have him out.

A-squat in double-headers four hundred times a day,
he says that in a measure the pleasure is the pay:

catcher to pitcher, a nice easy throw
almost as if he'd just told it to go.

Willie Mays should be a Dodger. He should—
a lad for Roger Craig and Clem Labine to elude:

but you have an omen, pennant-winning Peewee,
on which we are looking superstitiously.

Ralph Branca has Preacher Roe's number, recall?
and there's Don Bessent; he can really fire the ball.

As for Gil Hodges, in custody of first—
"He'll do it by himself." Now a specialist—versed

in an extension reach far into the box seats—
he lengthens up, leans and gloves the ball. He defeats

expectation by a whisker. The modest star,
irked by one misplay, is no hero by a hair;

in a strikeout slaughter when what could matter more,
he lines a homer to the signboard and has changed the score.

Then for his nineteenth season, a home run—
with four of six runs batted in—Carl Furillo's the big gun;

almost dehorned the foe—has fans dancing in delight.
Jake Pitler and his Playground "got a Night"—

Jake, the hearty man, made heartier by a harrier
who can bat as well as field—Don Demeter.

Shutting them out for nine innings—hitter too—
Carl Erskine leaves Cimoli nothing to do.

Take off the goat-horns, Dodgers, that egret
which two very fine base-stealers can offset.

You've got plenty: Jackie Robinson
and Campy and Big Newk, and Dodgerdom again
watching everything you do. You won last year. Come on.

A Heartfelt Acknowledgment

When you're fitting together a complicated jigsaw puzzle, it isn't easy to thank all those who helped supply the pieces, but I am going to try. The obvious beginning is with the Brooklyn Dodger players, the men whose feats, thoughts, revelations, and remembrances make up a large segment of this book. All gave their precious time to me, and it is to them that I first express my gratitude: Cal Abrams, Sandy Amoros, Jack Banta, Rex Barney, Bobby Bragan, Ralph Branca, Roy Campanella, Carl Erskine, Herman Franks, Carl Furillo, Al Gionfriddo, Billy Herman, Kirby Higbe, Spider Jorgensen, Clyde King, Clem Labine, Cookie Lavagetto, Sal Maglie, Dale Mitchell, Russ Meyer, Don Newcombe, Johnny Podres, Pee Wee Reese, the late Pete Reiser, Ed Roebuck, Howie Schultz, Clyde Sukeforth, Duke Snider, and the late Karl Spooner.

In addition, my gratitude to Burleigh Grimes, to Mrs. Bud Podbeilan, to former baseball commissioner Happy Chandler, New York Giant owner Horace Stoneham, and to Irving Rudd, a New York original, and to those who covered the team and were kind to part with their remembrances: Marty Glickman, Dick Young, Harold Rosenthal, Charley Einstein, and Gus Engleman.

For their personal recollections thanks go to the late Joe Flaherty, a brave and generous man who was such a great help in bringing me to Billy Reddy and Bobby McCarthy, men whose love of the Dodgers is recorded on these pages, and my gratitude also to them and to Mort Fleishman, Larry King, Donald Honig, Jack Newfield, Joel Oppenheimer, Donald Hall, Ron Green, Herb Ross, Johnny Belson, Tom "Duke" Bunderick, Bill Farrell, Jr., Roger Draper, Mike "Trails West" Friedman, Yoshi Hasegawa, Rachel Robinson, Mack Robinson, Ed Charles, Congressman Al Vann, Art Rust, Jr., Jerry Rizzutti, Eliot Asinov, Charley Steiner, and the irrepressible Bertram Randolph Sugar.

Also, a special thanks to my close friend and supporter, Roger Kahn, for valuable insights and anecdotes and for his enthusiasm over the course of this long project, and for permission to quote from his published material, and to Ed Linn, who similarly permitted me access to his conversations with Leo Durocher. Also to former Dodger employees Harold Parrott and Frank Graham, Jr., who were most kind in allowing me to quote from their published material.

Further, I wish to extoll the genius of my enthusiastic publisher, Phyllis Grann of G. P. Putnam's Sons, for her extraordinary editorial savvy and, just as important, for the great faith she has had in me. I hope it will be rewarded. To Deni Auclair, my gratitude for making sure all the little details of publication were taken care of. To Red Wassenich, a Hall of Fame copy editor. Also, my thanks to Sterling Lord, my resolute literary agent, for his counsel and friendship.

Because this project has taken three years, and the advance didn't quite make it, I feel it is important to thank my dearest, closest friends, and I know they are dear and close, because at various times they lent me the dough to keep going: Barry Halper, Robert Book, my cousin Susan Golenbock and her husband, Mark Weisenfreund, Richard Hershenson, Dr. Larry Miller, and, of course, my family, my parents, Jerome and Annette, my sister, Wendy, and Cheryl Stein, and my brother Robert and his wife, Jane. If you're ever in need of a pediatrician in the Danbury, Connecticut, area, call Robert. To my car mechanic and friend, Louis Tsionis, of Atlas Car Repair in Fort Lee, and to my Hungry Banker, Al Bowers, of the Midlantic Bank, Englewood, and to my private banker, Keith Sohn, who has always been there when I needed him, even if he couldn't beat Camp Cobbossee. Also to Viv Sohn, who helps out just by being there. To Nate Fink, an expert lawyer and tax advisor, and friend. If you live in New Jersey and need legal advice, call Nate. Also to my Uncle Justin and his partner Joe Mello for their valuable legal assistance and moral support.

Finally, to my Xerox 820 computer, which allowed me to complete six drafts of the one-thousand page manuscript while I continued to hold on to a vestige of sanity, to Stanley Spenders of Standard Typewriters, Washington, D.C., for keeping the thing running, and to my life's partner, Rhonda Sonnenberg, who not only transcribed hours and hours of interviews without so much as a whimper, but who edited the drafts with skill and sensitivity and who put up with my craziness at any one of a scillion points along the way. And to my two canine companions, the valiant and brave Sparky, the world's most beautiful German shepherd, and to Mickey, the very good Dane who may one day approach Greatness.

My love to you all,
Peter Golenbock
Englewood, NJ

INDEX